The
The King of Torts

John Grisham

arrow books

This edition published by Arrow Books in 2005

Copyright © John Grisham 2005

The right of John Grisham to be identified as the author
of this work has been asserted by him in accordance with
the Copyright, Designs and Patents Act, 1988

The Summons copyright © Belfry Holdings Inc 2002
The King of Torts copyright © Belfry Holdings Inc 2003

Arrow Books
The Random House Group Limited
20 Vauxhall Bridge Road, London SW1V 2SA

Random House Australia (Pty) Limited
20 Alfred Street, Milsons Point, Sydney
New South Wales 2061, Australia

Random House New Zealand Limited
18 Poland Road, Glenfield
Auckland 10, New Zealand

Random House (Pty) Limited
Isle of Houghton, Corner Boundary Road & Carse O Gowrie,
Houghton, 2198, South Africa

The Random House Group Limited Reg. No. 954009

www.randomhouse.co.uk

A CIP catalogue record for this book
is available from the British Library

Papers used by Random House are natural, recyclable
products made from wood grown in sustainable forests.
The manufacturing processes conform to the environmental
regulations of the country of origin

ISBN 0 09 191107 9

Printed and bound in Great Britain by
Cox & Wyman Ltd, Reading, Berkshire

ALSO BY JOHN GRISHAM

The Summons

Chapter 1

It came by mail, regular postage, the old-fashioned way since the Judge was almost eighty and distrusted modern devices. Forget e-mail and even faxes. He didn't use an answering machine and had never been fond of the telephone. He pecked out his letters with both index fingers, one feeble key at a time, hunched over his old Underwood manual on a rolltop desk under the portrait of Nathan Bedford Forrest. The Judge's grandfather had fought with Forrest at Shiloh and throughout the Deep South, and to him no figure in history was more revered. For thirty-two years, the Judge had quietly refused to hold court on July 13, Forrest's birthday.

It came with another letter, a magazine, and two invoices, and was routinely placed in the law school mailbox of Professor Ray Atlee. He recognized it immediately since such envelopes had been a part of his life for as long as he could remember. It was from his father, a man he too called the Judge.

Professor Atlee studied the envelope, uncertain whether he should open it right there or wait a moment. Good news or bad, he never knew with the Judge, though the old man was dying and good news had been rare. It was thin and appeared to contain only one sheet of paper; nothing unusual about that. The Judge was frugal with the written word, though he'd once been known for his windy lectures from the bench.

It was a business letter, that much was certain. The Judge was not one for small talk, hated gossip and idle chitchat, whether written or spoken. Ice tea with him on the porch would be a refighting of the Civil War, probably at Shiloh, where he would once again lay all blame for the Confederate defeat at the shiny, untouched boots of General Pierre G. T. Beauregard, a man he would hate even in heaven, if by chance they met there.

He'd be dead soon. Seventy-nine years old with cancer in his stomach. He was overweight, a diabetic, a heavy pipe smoker, had a bad heart that had survived three attacks, and a host of lesser ailments that had tormented him for twenty years and were now finally closing in for the kill. The pain was constant. During their last phone call three weeks earlier, a call initiated by Ray because the Judge thought long distance was a rip-off, the old man sounded weak and strained. They had talked for less than two minutes.

2

The return address was gold-embossed: Chancellor Reuben V. Atlee, 25th Chancery District, Ford County Courthouse, Clanton, Mississippi. Ray slid the envelope into the magazine and began walking. Judge Atlee no longer held the office of chancellor. The voters had retired him nine years earlier, a bitter defeat from which he would never recover. Thirty-two years of diligent service to his people, and they tossed him out in favor of a younger man with radio and television ads. The Judge had refused to campaign. He claimed he had too much work to do, and, more important, the people knew him well and if they wanted to reelect him then they would do so. His strategy had seemed arrogant to many. He carried Ford County but got shellacked in the other five.

It took three years to get him out of the courthouse. His office on the second floor had survived a fire and had missed two renovations. The Judge had not allowed them to touch it with paint or hammers. When the county supervisors finally convinced him that he had to leave or be evicted, he boxed up three decades' worth of useless files and notes and dusty old books and took them home and stacked them in his study. When the study was full, he lined them down the hallways into the dining room and even the foyer.

Ray nodded to a student who was seated in the hall. Outside his office, he spoke to a colleague. Inside, he locked the door behind him and placed the mail in the center of his desk. He took off his jacket, hung it on the back of the door, stepped over a stack of thick law books he'd been stepping over for half a year, and then to himself uttered his daily vow to organize the place.

The room was twelve by fifteen, with a small desk and a small sofa, both covered with enough work to make Ray seem like a very busy man. He was not. For the spring semester he was teaching one section of antitrust. And he was supposed to be writing a book, another drab, tedious volume on monopolies that would be read by no one but would add handsomely to his pedigree. He had tenure, but like all serious professors he was ruled by the 'publish or perish' dictum of academic life.

He sat at his desk and shoved papers out of the way.

The envelope was addressed to Professor N. Ray Atlee, University of Virginia School of Law, Charlottesville, Virginia. The *e*'s and *o*'s were smudged together. A new ribbon had been needed for a decade. The Judge didn't believe in zip codes either.

The N was for Nathan, after the general, but few people knew it. One of their uglier fights had been over the son's decision to drop Nathan altogether and plow through life simply as Ray.

The Judge's letters were always sent to the law school, never to his son's apartment in downtown Charlottesville. The Judge liked titles and important addresses, and he wanted folks in Clanton, even the postal workers, to know that his son was a professor of law. It was unnecessary. Ray had been teaching (and writing) for thirteen years, and those who mattered in Ford County knew it.

He opened the envelope and unfolded a single sheet of paper. It too was grandly embossed with the Judge's name and former title and address, again minus the zip code. The old man probably had an unlimited supply of the stationery.

It was addressed to both Ray and his younger brother, Forrest, the only two offspring of a bad marriage that had ended in 1969 with the death of their mother. As always, the message was brief:

> Please make arrangements to appear in my study on Sunday, May 7, at 5 P.M., to discuss the administration of my estate.
> Sincerely, Reuben V. Atlee.

The distinctive signature had shrunk and looked unsteady. For years it had been emblazoned across orders and decrees that had changed countless lives. Decrees of divorce, child custody, termination of parental rights, adoptions. Orders settling will contests, election contests, land disputes, annexation fights. The Judge's autograph had been authoritative and well known; now it was the vaguely familiar scrawl of a very sick old man.

Sick or not, though, Ray knew that he would be present in his father's study at the appointed time. He had just been summoned, and as irritating as it was, he had no doubt that he and his brother would drag themselves before His Honor for one more lecture. It was typical of the Judge to pick a day that was convenient for him without consulting anybody else.

It was the nature of the Judge, and perhaps most judges for that matter, to set dates for hearings and deadlines with little regard for the convenience of others. Such heavy-handedness was learned and even required when dealing with crowded dockets, reluctant litigants, busy lawyers, lazy lawyers. But the Judge had run his family in pretty much the same manner as he'd run his courtroom, and that was the principal reason Ray Atlee was teaching law in Virginia and not practicing it in Mississippi.

He read the summons again, then put it away, on top of the pile of current matters to deal with. He walked to the window and looked out at the courtyard where everything was in bloom. He wasn't angry or bitter, just frustrated that his father could once again dictate so much. But the old man was dying, he told himself. Give him a break. There wouldn't be many more trips home.

The Judge's estate was cloaked with mystery. The principal asset was the house – an antebellum hand-me-down from the same Atlee who'd fought with General Forrest. On a shady street

6

in old Atlanta it would be worth over a million dollars, but not in Clanton. It sat in the middle of five neglected acres three blocks off the town square. The floors sagged, the roof leaked, paint had not touched the walls in Ray's lifetime. He and his brother could sell it for perhaps a hundred thousand dollars, but the buyer would need twice that to make it livable. Neither would ever live there; in fact, Forrest had not set foot in the house in many years.

The house was called Maple Run, as if it were some grand estate with a staff and a social calendar. The last worker had been Irene the maid. She'd died four years earlier and since then no one had vacuumed the floors or touched the furniture with polish. The Judge paid a local felon twenty dollars a week to cut the grass, and he did so with great reluctance. Eighty dollars a month was robbery, in his learned opinion.

When Ray was a child, his mother referred to their home as Maple Run. They never had dinners at their home, but rather at Maple Run. Their address was not the Atlees on Fourth Street, but instead it was Maple Run on Fourth Street. Few other folks in Clanton had names for their homes.

She died from an aneurysm and they laid her on a table in the front parlor. For two days the town stopped by and paraded across the front porch, through the foyer, through the parlor for last respects, then to the dining room for punch and cookies. Ray and Forrest hid in the attic and

cursed their father for tolerating such a spectacle. That was their mother lying down there, a
pretty young woman now pale and stiff in an
open coffin.

Forrest had always called it Maple Ruin. The
red and yellow maples that once lined the street
had died of some unknown disease. Their rotted
stumps had never been cleared. Four huge oaks
shaded the front lawn. They shed leaves by the
ton, far too many for anyone to rake and gather.
And at least twice a year the oaks would lose a
branch that would fall and crash somewhere
onto the house, where it might or might not get
removed. The house stood there year after year,
decade after decade, taking punches but never
falling.

It was still a handsome house, a Georgian
with columns, once a monument to those who'd
built it, and now a sad reminder of a declining
family. Ray wanted nothing to do with it. For
him the house was filled with unpleasant memories and each trip back depressed him. He
certainly couldn't afford the financial black hole
of maintaining an estate that ought to be
bulldozed. Forrest would burn it before he
owned it.

The Judge, however, wanted Ray to take the
house and keep it in the family. This had been
discussed in vague terms over the past few years.
Ray had never mustered the courage to ask,
'What family?' He had no children. There was
an ex-wife but no prospect of a current one.

Same for Forrest, except he had a dizzying collection of ex-girlfriends and a current housing arrangement with Ellie, a three-hundred-pound painter and potter twelve years his senior.

It was a biological miracle that Forrest had produced no children, but so far none had been discovered.

The Atlee bloodline was thinning to a sad and inevitable halt, which didn't bother Ray at all. He was living life for himself, not for the benefit of his father or the family's glorious past. He returned to Clanton only for funerals.

The Judge's other assets had never been discussed. The Atlee family had once been wealthy, but long before Ray. There had been land and cotton and slaves and railroads and banks and politics, the usual Confederate portfolio of holdings that, in terms of cash, meant nothing in the late twentieth century. It did, however, bestow upon the Atlees the status of 'family money.'

By the time Ray was ten he knew his family had money. His father was a judge and his home had a name, and in rural Mississippi this meant he was indeed a rich kid. Before she died his mother did her best to convince Ray and Forrest that they were better than most folks. They lived in a mansion. They were Presbyterians. They vacationed in Florida, every third year. They occasionally went to the Peabody Hotel in Memphis for dinner. Their clothes were nicer.

Then Ray was accepted at Stanford. His

bubble burst when the Judge said bluntly, 'I can't afford it.'

'What do you mean?' Ray had asked.

'I mean what I said. I can't afford Stanford.'

'But I don't understand.'

'Then I'll make it plain. Go to any college you want. But if you go to Sewanee, then I'll pay for it.'

Ray went to Sewanee, without the baggage of family money, and was supported by his father, who provided an allowance that barely covered tuition, books, board, and fraternity dues. Law school was at Tulane, where Ray survived by waiting tables at an oyster bar in the French Quarter.

For thirty-two years, the Judge had earned a chancellor's salary, which was among the lowest in the country. While at Tulane Ray read a report on judicial compensation, and he was saddened to learn that Mississippi judges were earning fifty-two thousand dollars a year when the national average was ninety-five thousand.

The Judge lived alone, spent little on the house, had no bad habits except for his pipe, and he preferred cheap tobacco. He drove an old Lincoln, ate bad food but lots of it, and wore the same black suits he'd been wearing since the fifties. His vice was charity. He saved his money, then he gave it away.

No one knew how much money the Judge donated annually. An automatic ten percent went to the Presbyterian Church. Sewanee got

10

two thousand dollars a year, same for the Sons of Confederate Veterans. Those three gifts were carved in granite. The rest were not.

Judge Atlee gave to anyone who would ask. A crippled child in need of crutches. An all-star team traveling to a state tournament. A drive by the Rotary Club to vaccinate babies in the Congo. A shelter for stray dogs and cats in Ford County. A new roof for Clanton's only museum.

The list was endless, and all that was necessary to receive a check was to write a short letter and ask for it. Judge Atlee always sent money and had been doing so ever since Ray and Forrest left home.

Ray could see him now, lost in the clutter and dust of his rolltop, pecking out short notes on his Underwood and sticking them in his chancellor's envelopes with scarcely readable checks drawn on the First National Bank of Clanton – fifty dollars here, a hundred dollars there, a little for everyone until it was all gone.

The estate would not be complicated because there would be so little to inventory. The ancient law books, threadbare furniture, painful family photos and mementos, long forgotten files and papers – all a bunch of rubbish that would make an impressive bonfire. He and Forrest would sell the house for whatever it might bring and be quite happy to salvage anything from the last of the Atlee family money.

He should call Forrest, but those calls were

always easy to put off. Forrest was a different set of issues and problems, much more complicated than a dying, reclusive old father hell-bent on giving away his money. Forrest was a living, walking disaster, a boy of thirty-six whose mind had been deadened by every legal and illegal substance known to American culture.

What a family, Ray mumbled to himself.

He posted a cancellation for his eleven o'clock class, and went for therapy.

Chapter 2

Spring in the Piedmont, calm clear skies, the foothills growing greener by the day, the Shenandoah Valley changing as the farmers crossed and recrossed their perfect rows. Rain was forecast for tomorrow, though no forecast could be trusted in central Virginia.

With almost three hundred hours under his belt, Ray began each day with an eye on the sky as he jogged five miles. The running he could do come rain or shine, the flying he could not. He had promised himself (and his insurance company) that he would not fly at night and would not venture into clouds. Ninety-five percent of all small plane crashes happened either in weather or in darkness, and after nearly three years of flying Ray was still determined to be a coward. 'There are old pilots and bold pilots,' the adage went, 'but no old bold pilots.' He believed it, and with conviction.

Besides, central Virginia was too beautiful to buzz over in clouds. He waited for perfect weather – no wind to push him around and make landings complicated, no haze to dim the horizon and get him lost, no threat of storms or moisture. Clear skies during his jog usually determined the rest of his day. He could move lunch up or back, cancel a class, postpone his research to a rainy day, or a rainy week for that matter. The right forecast, and Ray was off to the airport.

It was north of town, a fifteen-minute drive from the law school. At Docker's Flight School he was given the normal rude welcome by Dick Docker, Charlie Yates, and Fog Newton, the three retired Marine pilots who owned the place and had trained most of the private aviators in the area. They held court each day in the Cockpit, a row of old theater chairs in the front office of the flight school, and from there they drank coffee by the gallon and told flying tales and lies that grew by the hour. Each customer and student got the same load of verbal abuse, like it or not, take it or leave it, they didn't care. They were drawing nice pensions.

The sight of Ray prompted the latest round of lawyer jokes, none of which were particularly funny, all of which drew howls at the punch lines.

'No wonder you don't have any students,' Ray said as he did the paperwork.

'Where you going?' demanded Docker.

'Just punching a few holes in the sky.'

'We'll alert air traffic control.'

14

'You're much too busy for that.'

Ten minutes of insults and rental forms, and Ray was free to go. For eighty bucks an hour he could rent a Cessna that would take him a mile above the earth, away from people, phones, traffic, students, research, and, on this day, even farther from his dying father, his crazy brother, and the inevitable mess facing him back home.

There were tie-downs for thirty light aircraft at the general aviation ramp. Most were small Cessnas with high wings and fixed landing gears, still the safest airplanes ever built. But there were some fancier rigs. Next to his rented Cessna was a Beech Bonanza, a single-engine, two-hundred-horsepower beauty that Ray could handle in a month with a little training. It flew almost seventy knots faster than the Cessna, with enough gadgets and avionics to make any pilot drool. Even worse, the Bonanza was for sale – $450,000 – off the charts, of course, but not that far off. The owner built shopping centers and wanted a King Air, according to the latest analysis from the Cockpit.

Ray stepped away from the Bonanza and concentrated on the little Cessna sitting next to it. Like all new pilots, he carefully inspected his plane with a checklist. Fog Newton, his instructor, had begun each lesson with a gruesome tale of fire and death caused by pilots too hurried or lazy to use checklists.

When he was certain all outside parts and

surfaces were perfect, he opened the door and strapped himself inside. The engine started smoothly, the radios sparked to life. He finished a pre-takeoff list and called the tower. A commuter flight was ahead of him, and ten minutes after he locked his doors he was cleared for takeoff. He lifted off smoothly and turned west, toward the Shenandoah Valley.

At four thousand feet, he crossed Afton Mountain, not far below him. A few seconds of mountain turbulence bounced the Cessna, but it was nothing out of the ordinary. When he was past the foothills and over the farmlands, the air became still and quiet. Visibility was officially twenty miles, though at this altitude he could see much farther. No ceiling, not a cloud anywhere. At five thousand feet, the peaks of West Virginia rose slowly on the horizon. Ray completed an in-flight checklist, leaned his fuel mixture for normal cruise, and relaxed for the first time since taxiing into position for takeoff.

Radio chatter disappeared, and it wouldn't pick up again until he switched to the Roanoke tower, forty miles to the south. He decided to avoid Roanoke and stay in uncontrolled airspace.

Ray knew from personal experience that psychiatrists worked for two hundred dollars an hour in the Charlottesville area. Flying was a bargain, and much more effective, though it was a very fine shrink who'd suggested he pick up a new hobby, and quickly. He was seeing the

16

fellow because he had to see someone. Exactly a month after the former Mrs. Atlee filed for divorce, quit her job, and walked out of their townhouse with only her clothes and jewelry, all done with ruthless efficiency in less than six hours, Ray left the psychiatrist for the last time, drove to the airport, stumbled into the Cockpit, and took his first insult from either Dick Docker or Fog Newton, he couldn't remember which.

The insult felt good, someone cared. More followed, and Ray, wounded and confused as he was, had found a home. For three years now he had crossed the clear, solitary skies of the Blue Ridge Mountains and the Shenandoah Valley, soothing his anger, shedding a few tears, hashing out his troubled life to an empty seat beside him. She's gone, the empty seat kept saying.

Some women leave and come back eventually. Others leave and endure a painful reconsideration. Still others leave with such boldness they never look back. Vicki's departure from his life was so well planned and her execution of it was so cold-blooded that Ray's lawyer's first comment was, 'Give it up, pal.'

She'd found a better deal, like an athlete swapping teams at the trading deadline. Here's the new uniform, smile for the cameras, forget the old arena. While Ray was at work one fine morning, she left in a limousine. Behind it was a van with her things. Twenty minutes later, she walked into her new place, a mansion on a horse farm east of town where Lew the Liquidator was waiting with open arms and a prenuptial agreement. Lew was a corporate vulture whose raids had netted him a half a billion or so, according to Ray's research, and at the age of sixty-four he'd cashed in his chips, left Wall Street, and for some reason picked Charlottesville as his new nest.

Somewhere along the way he'd bumped into Vicki, offered her a deal, gotten her pregnant with the children Ray was supposed to father, and now with a trophy wife and another family he wanted to be taken seriously as the new Big Fish.

Enough of this, Ray said aloud. He talked loudly at five thousand feet, and no one talked back.

He was assuming, and hoping, that Forrest was clean and sober, though such assumptions were usually wrong and such hopes were often misguided. After twenty years of rehab and relapse, it was doubtful if his brother would ever overcome his addictions. And Ray was certain that Forrest would be broke, a condition that went hand in hand with his habits. And being broke, he'd be looking for money, as in his father's estate.

What money the Judge had not given away to charities and sick children, he had poured down the black hole of Forrest's detoxification. So much money had been wasted there, along with so many years, that the Judge, as only he could do, had basically excommunicated Forrest from their father-son relationship. For thirty-two years he had terminated marriages, taken children away from parents, given children to foster homes, sent mentally ill people away forever, ordered delinquent fathers to jail – all manner of drastic and far-reaching decrees that were accomplished merely by signing his name. When he first went on the bench, his authority had been granted by the State of Mississippi, but late in his career he took his orders only from God.

If anyone could expel a son, it was Chancellor Reuben V. Atlee.

Forrest pretended to be unbothered by his banishment. He fancied himself as a free spirit and claimed he had not set foot inside the house at Maple Run in nine years. He had visited the Judge once in the hospital, after a heart attack when the doctors rounded up the family. Surprisingly, he'd been sober then. 'Fifty-two days, Bro,' he'd whispered proudly to Ray as they huddled in the ICU corridor. He was a walking scoreboard when rehab was working.

If the Judge had plans to include Forrest in his estate, no one would have been more surprised than Forrest. But with the chance that money or assets were about to change hands, Forrest would be there looking for crumbs and leftovers.

Over the New River Gorge near Beckley, West Virginia, Ray turned around and headed back. Though flying cost less than professional therapy, it wasn't cheap. The meter was ticking.

If he won the lottery, he would buy the Bonanza and fly everywhere. He was due a sabbatical in a couple of years, a respite from the rigors of academic life. He'd be expected to finish his eight-hundred-page brick on monopolies, and there was an even chance that that might happen. His dream, though, was to lease a Bonanza and disappear into the skies.

Twelve miles west of the airport, he called the tower and was directed to enter the traffic pattern. The wind was light and variable, the landing would be a cinch. On final approach, with the runway a mile away and fifteen hundred feet down, and Ray and his little Cessna gliding at a perfect descent, another pilot came on the radio. He checked in with the controller as 'Challenger-two-four-four-delta-mike,' and he was fifteen miles to the north. The tower cleared him to land, number two behind Cessna traffic.

Ray pushed aside thoughts of the other aircraft long enough to make a textbook landing, then turned off the runway and began taxiing to the ramp.

A Challenger is a Canadian-built private jet that seats eight to fifteen, depending on the configuration. It will fly from New York to Paris, nonstop, in splendid style, with its own flight attendant serving drinks and meals. A new one sells for somewhere around twenty-five million dollars, depending on the endless list of options.

The 244DM was owned by Lew the Liquidator, who'd pinched it out of one of the many hapless companies he'd raided and fleeced. Ray watched it land behind him, and for a second he hoped it would crash and burn right there on the runway, so he could enjoy the show. It did not, and as it sped along the taxiway toward the private terminal, Ray was suddenly in a tight spot.

He'd seen Vicki twice in the years since their divorce, and he certainly didn't want to see her now, not with him in a twenty-year-old Cessna while she bounded down the stairway of her gold-plated jet. Maybe she wasn't on board. Maybe it was just Lew Rodowski returning from yet another raid.

Ray cut the fuel mixture, the engine died, and as the Challenger moved closer to him he began to sink as low as possible in his captain's seat.

By the time it rolled to a stop, less than a hundred feet from where Ray was hiding, a shiny black Suburban had wheeled out onto the ramp, a little too fast, lights on, as if royalty had arrived in Charlottesville. Two young men in matching green shirts and khaki shorts jumped out, ready to receive the Liquidator and whoever else might be on board. The Challenger's door opened, the steps came down, and Ray, peeking above his instrument deck with a complete view, watched with fascination as one of the pilots came down first, carrying two large shopping bags.

Then Vicki, with the twins. They were two years old now, Simmons and Ripley, poor children given genderless last names as first names because their mother was an idiot and their father had already sired nine others before them and probably didn't care what they were called. They were boys, Ray knew that much for sure because he'd watched the vitals in the local paper – births, deaths, burglaries, etc. They were born at Martha Jefferson Hospital seven weeks and three days after the Atlees' no-fault divorce became final, and seven weeks and two days after a very pregnant Vicki married Lew Rodowski, his fourth trip down the aisle, or whatever they used that day at the horse farm.

Clutching the boys' hands, Vicki carefully descended the steps. A half a billion dollars was looking good on her – tight designer jeans on her long legs, legs that had become noticeably thinner since she had joined the jet set. In fact, Vicki appeared to be superbly starved – bone-thin arms, small flat ass, gaunt cheeks. He couldn't see her eyes because they were well hidden behind black wrap-arounds, the latest style from either Hollywood or Paris, take your pick.

The Liquidator had not been starving. He waited impatiently behind his current wife and current litter. He claimed he ran marathons, but then so little of what he said in print turned out to be true. He was stocky, with a thick belly. Half his hair was gone and the other half was gray with age. She was forty-one and could pass for thirty. He was sixty-four and looked seventy, or at least Ray thought so, with great satisfaction.

They finally made it into the Suburban while the two pilots and two drivers loaded and reloaded luggage and large bags from Saks and Bergdorf. Just a quick shopping jaunt up to Manhattan, forty-five minutes away on your Challenger.

The Suburban sped off, the show was over, and Ray sat up in the Cessna.

If he hadn't hated her so much, he would have sat there a long time reliving their marriage.

There had been no warnings, no fights, no change in temperature. She'd simply stumbled upon a better deal.

He opened the door so he could breathe and realized his collar was wet with sweat. He wiped his eyebrows and got out of the plane.

For the first time in memory, he wished he'd stayed away from the airport.

Chapter 3

The law school was next to the business school, and both were at the northern edge of a campus that had expanded greatly from the quaint academic village Thomas Jefferson designed and built.

To a university that so revered the architecture of its founder, the law school was just another modern campus building, square and flat, brick and glass, as bland and unimaginative as many others built in the seventies. But recent money had renovated and landscaped things nicely. It was ranked in the Top Ten, as everybody who worked and studied there knew so well. A few of the Ivys were ranked above it, but no other public school. It attracted a thousand top students and a very bright faculty.

Ray had been content teaching securities law at Northeastern in Boston. Some of his writings caught the attention of a search committee, one thing led to another, and the chance to move South to a better school became attractive. Vicki was from Florida, and though she thrived in the city life of Boston, she could never adjust to the winters. They quickly adapted to the slower pace of Charlottesville. He was awarded tenure, she earned a doctorate in romance languages. They were discussing children when the Liquidator wormed his way into the picture.

Another man gets your wife pregnant, then takes her, and you'd like to ask him some questions. And perhaps have a few for her. In the days right after her exit he couldn't sleep for all the questions, but as time passed he realized he would never confront her. The questions faded, but seeing her at the airport brought them back. Ray was cross-examining her again as he parked in the law school lot and returned to his office.

He kept office hours late in the afternoon, no appointment was necessary. His door was open and any student was welcome. It was early May, though, and the days were warm. Student visits had become rare. He reread the directive from his father, and again became irked at the usual heavy-handedness.

At five o'clock he locked his office, left the law school, and walked down the street to an intramural sports complex where the third-year students were playing the faculty in the second of a three-game softball series. The professors had lost the first game in a slaughter. Games two and three were not really necessary to determine the better team.

Smelling blood, first- and second-year students filled the small bleachers and hung on the fence along the first-base line, where the faculty team was huddled for a useless pregame pep talk. Out in left field some first-years of dubious reputation were bunched around two large coolers, the beer already flowing.

There's no better place to be in the springtime than on a college campus, Ray thought to himself as he approached the field and looked for a pleasant spot to watch the game. Girls in shorts, a cooler always close by, festive moods, impromptu parties, summer approaching. He was forty-three years old, single, and he wanted to be a student again. Teaching keeps you young, they all said, perhaps energetic and mentally sharp, but what Ray wanted was to sit on a cooler out there with the hell-raisers and hit on the girls.

A small group of his colleagues loitered behind the backstop, smiling gamely as the faculty took the field with a most unimpressive lineup. Several were limping. Half wore some manner of knee brace. He spotted Carl Mirk, an associate dean and his closest friend, leaning on a fence, tie undone, jacket slung over his shoulder.

'Sad-looking crew out there,' Ray said.

'Wait till you see them play,' Mirk said. Carl was from a small town in Ohio where his father was a local judge, a local saint, everybody's grandfather. Carl, too, had fled and vowed never to return.

'I missed the first game,' Ray said.

'It was a hoot. Seventeen to nothing after two innings.'

The leadoff hitter for the students ripped the first pitch into the left-field gap, a routine double, but by the time the left fielder and center fielder hobbled over, corralled the ball, kicked it a couple of times, fought over it, then flung it toward the infield, the runner walked home and the shutout was blown. The rowdies in left field were hysterical. The students in the bleachers yelled for more errors.

'It'll get worse,' Mirk said.

Indeed it did. After a few more fielding disasters, Ray had seen enough. 'I'll be out of town early next week,' he said between batters. 'I've been called home.'

'I can tell you're excited,' Mirk said. 'Another funeral?'

'Not yet. My father is convening a family summit to discuss his estate.'

'I'm sorry.'

'Don't be. There's not much to discuss, nothing to fight over, so it'll probably be ugly.'

'Your brother?'

'I don't know who'll cause more trouble, brother or father.'

'I'll be thinking of you.'

'Thanks. I'll notify my students and give them assignments. Everything should be covered.'

'Leaving when?'

'Saturday, should be back Tuesday or Wednesday, but who knows.'

'We'll be here,' Mirk said. 'And hopefully this series will be over.'

A soft ground ball rolled untouched between the legs of the pitcher.

'I think it's over now,' Ray said.

Nothing soured Ray's mood like thoughts of going home. He hadn't been there in over a year, and if he never went back it would still be too soon.

He bought a burrito from a Mexican takeout and ate at a sidewalk café near the ice rink where the usual gang of black-haired Goths gathered and spooked the normal folks. The old Main Street was a pedestrian mall – a very nice one with cafés and antique stores and book dealers – and if the weather was pleasant, as it usually was, the restaurants spread outdoors for long evening meals.

When he'd suddenly become single again, Ray unloaded the quaint townhouse and moved downtown, where most of the old buildings had been renovated for more urban-style housing. His six-room apartment was above a Persian rug dealer. It had a small balcony over the mall, and at least once a month Ray had his students over for wine and lasagne.

It was almost dark when he unlocked the door on the sidewalk and trudged up the noisy steps to his place. He was very much alone – no mate, no dog, no cat, no goldfish. In the past few years he'd met two women he'd found attractive and had dated neither. He was much too frightened for romance. A saucy third-year student named Kaley was making advances, but his defences were in place. His sex drive was so dormant he had considered counseling, or perhaps wonder drugs. He flipped on lights and checked the phone.

Forrest had called, a rare event indeed, but not completely unexpected. Typical of Forrest, he had simply checked in, without leaving a number. Ray fixed tea with no caffeine and put on some jazz, trying to stall as he prepped himself for the call. Odd that a phone chat with his only sibling should take so much effort, but chatting with Forrest was always depressing. They had no wives, no children, nothing in common but a name and a father.

Ray punched in the number to Ellie's house in Memphis. It rang for a long time before she answered. 'Hello, Ellie, this is Ray Atlee,' he said pleasantly.

'Oh,' she grunted, as if he'd called eight times already. 'He's not here.'

Doing swell, Ellie, and you? Fine, thanks for asking. Great to hear your voice. How's the weather down there?

'I'm returning his call,' Ray said.

'Like I said, he's not here.'

'I heard you. Is there a different number?'

29

'For what?'

'For Forrest. Is this still the best number to reach him?'

'I guess. He stays here most of the time.'

'Please tell him I called.'

They met in detox, she for booze, Forrest for an entire menu of banned substances. At the time she weighed ninety-eight pounds and claimed she'd lived on nothing but vodka for most of her adult life. She kicked it, walked away clean, tripled her body weight, and somehow got Forrest in the deal too. More mother than girlfriend, she now had him a room in the basement of her ancestral home, an eerie old Victorian in midtown Memphis.

Ray was still holding the phone when it rang. 'Hey, Bro,' Forrest called out. 'You rang?'

'Returning yours. How's it going?'

'Well, I was doing fairly well until I got a letter from the old man. You get one too?'

'It arrived today.'

'He thinks he's still a judge and we're a couple of delinquent fathers, don't you think?'

'He'll always be the Judge, Forrest. Have you talked to him?'

A snort, then a pause. 'I haven't talked to him on the phone in two years, and I haven't set foot in the house in more years than I can remember. And I'm not sure I'll be there Sunday.'

'You'll be there.'

'Have you talked to him?'

'Three weeks ago. I called, he didn't. He

sounded very sick, Forrest, I don't think he'll be around much longer. I think you should seriously consider –'

'Don't start, Ray. I'm not listening to a lecture.'

There was a gap, a heavy stillness in which both of them took a breath. Being an addict from a prominent family, Forrest had been lectured to and preached at and burdened with unsolicited advice for as long as he could remember.

'Sorry,' Ray said. 'I'll be there. What about you?'

'I suppose so.'

'Are you clean?' It was such a personal question, but one that was as routine as How's the weather? With Forrest the answer was always straight and true.

'A hundred and thirty-nine days, Bro.'

'That's great.'

It was, and it wasn't. Every sober day was a relief, but to still be counting after twenty years was disheartening.

'And I'm working too,' he said proudly.

'Wonderful. What kind of work?'

'I'm running cases for some local ambulance chasers, a bunch of sleazy bastards who advertise on cable and hang around hospitals. I sign 'em up and get a cut.'

It was difficult to appreciate such a seedy job, but with Forrest any employment was good news. He'd been a bail bondsman, process server, collection agent, security guard, investigator, and at one time or another had tried virtually every job at the lesser levels of the legal profession.

'Not bad,' Ray said.

Forrest started a tale, this one involving a shoving match in a hospital emergency room, and Ray began to drift. His brother had also worked as a bouncer in a strip bar, a calling that was short-lived when he was beaten up twice in one night. He'd spent one full year touring Mexico on a new Harley-Davidson; the trip's funding had never been clear. He had tried leg-breaking for a Memphis loan shark, but again proved deficient when it came to violence.

Honest employment had never appealed to Forrest, though, in all fairness, interviewers were generally turned off by his criminal record. Two felonies, drug-related, both before he turned twenty but permanent blotches nonetheless.

'Are you gonna talk to the old man?' he was asking.

'No, I'll see him Sunday,' Ray answered.

'What time will you get to Clanton?'

'I don't know. Sometime around five, I guess. You?'

'God said five o'clock, didn't he?'

'Yes, he did.'

'Then I'll be there sometime after five. See you, Bro.'

Ray circled the phone for the next hour, deciding yes, he would call his father and just say hello, then deciding no, that anything to be said now could be said later, and in person. The Judge detested phones, especially those that rang at night and disrupted his solitude. More often than not he would simply refuse to answer. And if he picked up he was usually so rude and gruff that the caller was sorry for the effort.

He would be wearing black trousers and a white shirt, one with tiny cinder holes from the pipe ashes, and the shirt would be heavily starched because the Judge had always worn them that way. For him a white cotton dress shirt lasted a decade, regardless of the number of stains and cinder holes, and it got laundered and starched every week at Mabe's Cleaners on the square. His tie would be as old as his shirt and the design would be some drab print with little color. Navy blue suspenders, always.

And he would be busy at his desk in his study, under the portrait of General Forrest, not sitting on the porch waiting for his sons to come home. He would want them to think he had work to do, even on a Sunday afternoon, and that their arrivals were not that important.

Chapter 4

The drive to Clanton took fifteen hours, more or less, if you went with the truckers on the busy four-lanes and fought the bottlenecks around the cities, and it could be done in one day if you were in a hurry. Ray was not.

He packed a few things in the trunk of his Audi TT roadster, a two-seat convertible he'd owned for less than a week, and said farewell to no one because no one really cared when he came or went, and left Charlottesville. He would not exceed the speed limits and he would not drive on a four-lane, if he could possibly avoid it. That was his challenge – a trip without sprawl. On the leather seat next to him he had maps, a thermos of strong coffee, three Cuban cigars, and a bottle of water.

A few minutes west of town he turned left on the Blue Ridge Parkway and began snaking his way south on the tops of the foothills. The TT was a 2000 model, just a year or two off the drawing board. Ray had read Audi's announcement of a brand-new sports car about eighteen months earlier, and he'd rushed to order the first one in town. He had yet to see another one, though the dealer assured him they would become popular.

At an overlook, he put the top down, lit a Cuban, and sipped coffee, then took off again at the maximum speed of forty-five. Even at that pace Clanton was looming

Four hours later, in search of gas, Ray found himself sitting at a stoplight on Main Street in a small town in North Carolina. Three lawyers walked in front of him, all talking at once, all carrying old briefcases that were scuffed and worn almost as badly as their shoes. He looked to his left and noticed a courthouse. He looked to his right and watched as they disappeared into a diner. He was suddenly hungry, both for food and for sounds of people.

They were in a booth near the front window, still talking as they stirred their coffee. Ray sat at a table not too far away and ordered a club sandwich from an elderly waitress who'd been serving them for decades. One glass of ice tea, one sandwich, and she wrote it all down in great detail. Chef's probably older, he thought.

The lawyers had been in court all morning haggling over a piece of land up in the mountains. The land was sold, a lawsuit followed, etc., etc., and now they were having the trial. They had called witnesses, quoted precedents to the judge, disputed everything the others had said, and in general had gotten themselves heated up to the point of needing a break.

And this is what my father wanted me to do, Ray almost said aloud. He was hiding behind the local paper, pretending to read but listening to the lawyers.

Judge Reuben Atlee's dream had been for his sons to finish law school and return to Clanton. He would retire from the bench, and together they would open an office on the square. There, they would follow an honorable calling and he would teach them how to be lawyers – gentleman lawyers, country lawyers.

Broke lawyers was the way Ray had figured things. Like all small towns in the South, Clanton was brimming with lawyers. They were packed in the office buildings opposite the courthouse square. They ran the politics and banks and civic clubs and school boards, even the churches and Little Leagues. Where, exactly, around the square was he supposed to fit in?

During summer breaks from college and law school, Ray had clerked for his father. For no salary, of course. He knew all the lawyers in Clanton. As a whole, they were not bad people. There were just too many of them.

Forrest's turn for the worse came early in life and put even more pressure on Ray to follow the old man into a life of genteel poverty. The pressure was resisted, though, and by the time

Ray had finished one year of law school he had promised himself he would not remain in Clanton. It took another year to find the courage to tell his father, who went eight months without speaking to him. When Ray graduated from law school, Forrest was in prison. Judge Atlee arrived late for the commencement, sat in the back row, left early, and said nothing to Ray. It took the first heart attack to reunite them.

But money wasn't the primary reason Ray fled Clanton. Atlee & Atlee never got off the ground because the junior partner wanted to escape the shadow of the senior.

Judge Atlee was a huge man in a small town.

Ray found gas at the edge of town, and was soon back in the hills, on the parkway, driving forty-five miles an hour. Sometimes forty. He stopped at the overlooks and admired the scenery. He avoided the cities and studied his maps. All roads led, sooner or later, to Mississippi.

Near the North Carolina state line, he found an old motel that advertised air conditioning, cable TV, and clean rooms for $29.99, though the sign was crooked and rusted around the edges. Inflation had arrived with the cable because the room was now $40. Next door was an all-night café where Ray choked down dumplings, the nightly special. After dinner he sat on a bench in front of the motel, smoked another cigar, and watched the occasional car go by.

Across the road and down a hundred yards

was an abandoned drive-in movie theater. The marquee had fallen and was covered with vines and weeds. The big screen and the fences around the perimeter had been crumbling for many years.

Clanton had once had such a drive-in, just off the main highway entering town. It was owned by a chain from up North and provided the locals with the typical lineup of beach romps, horror flicks, kung-fu action, movies that attracted the younger set and gave the preachers something to whine about. In 1970, the powers up North decided to pollute the South once again by sending down dirty movies.

Like most things good and bad, pornography arrived late in Mississippi. When the marquee listed *The Cheerleaders* it went unnoticed by the passing traffic. When *XXX* was added the next day, traffic stopped and tempers rose in the coffee shops around the square. It opened on a Monday night to a small, curious, and somewhat enthusiastic crowd. The reviews at school were favorable, and by Tuesday packs of young teenagers were hiding in the woods, many with binoculars, watching in disbelief. After Wednesday night prayer meeting, the preachers got things organized and launched a counterattack, one that relied more on bullying than on shrewd tactics.

Taking a lesson from the civil rights protectors, a group they had had absolutely no sympathy for, they led their flocks to the highway in front of the drive-in, where they carried posters and prayed and sang hymns and hurriedly scribbled down the license plate numbers of those cars trying to enter.

Business was cut off like a faucet. The corporate guys up North filed a quick lawsuit, seeking injunctive relief. The preachers put together one of their own, and it was no surprise that all of this landed in the courtroom of the Honorable Reuben V. Atlee, a lifelong member of the First Presbyterian Church, a descendant of the Atlees who'd built the original sanctuary, and for the past thirty years the teacher of a Sunday School class of old goats who met in the church's basement kitchen.

The hearings lasted for three days. Since no Clanton lawyer would defend *The Cheerleaders,* the owners were represented by a big firm from Jackson. A dozen locals argued against the movie and on behalf of the preachers.

Ten years later, when he was in law school at Tulane, Ray studied his father's opinion in the case. Following the most current federal cases, Judge Atlee's ruling protected the rights of the protestors, with certain restrictions. And, citing a recent obscenity case ruling by the U.S. Supreme Court, he allowed the show to go on.

Judicially, the opinion could not have been more perfect. Politically, it could not have been uglier. No one was pleased. The phone rang at night with anonymous threats. The preachers denounced Reuben Atlee as a traitor. Wait till the next election, they promised from their pulpits.

Letters flooded the *Clanton Chronicle* and *The Ford County Times*, all castigating Judge Atlee for allowing such filth in their unblemished community. When the Judge was finally fed up with the criticism, he decided to speak. He chose a Sunday at the First Presbyterian Church as his time and place, and word spread quickly, as it always did in Clanton. Before a packed house, Judge Atlee strode confidently down the aisle, up the carpeted steps and to the pulpit. He was over six feet tall and thick, and his black suit gave him an aura of dominance. 'A Judge who counts votes before the trial should burn his robe and run for the county line,' he began sternly.

Ray and Forrest were sitting as far away as possible, in a corner of the balcony, both near tears. They had begged their father to allow them to skip the service, but missing church was not permissible under any circumstances.

He explained to the less informed that legal precedents have to be followed, regardless of personal views or opinions, and that good judges follow the law. Weak judges follow the crowd. Weak judges play for the votes and then cry foul when their cowardly rulings are appealed to higher courts.

'Call me what you want,' he said to a silent crowd, 'but I am no coward.'

Ray could still hear the words, still see his

father down there in the distance, standing alone like a giant.

After a week or so the protestors grew weary, and the porno ran its course. Kung-fu returned with a vengeance and everybody was happy. Two years later, Judge Atlee received his usual eighty percent of the vote in Ford County.

Ray flipped the cigar into a shrub and walked to his room. The night was cool so he opened a window and listened to the cars as they left town and faded over the hills.

Chapter 5

Every street had a story, every building a memory. Those blessed with wonderful child-hoods can drive the streets of their hometowns and happily roll back the years. The rest are pulled home by duty and leave as soon as possible. After Ray had been in Clanton for fifteen minutes he was anxious to get out.

The town had changed, but then it hadn't. On the highways leading in, the cheap metal buildings and mobile homes were gathering as tightly as possible next to the roads for maximum visibility. Ford County had no zoning whatso-ever. A landowner could build anything with no permit, no inspection, no code, no notice to adjoining landowners, nothing. Only hog farms and nuclear reactors required approvals and paperwork. The result was a slash-and-build clutter that got uglier by the year.

But in the older sections, nearer the square, the town had not changed at all. The long shaded streets were as clean and neat as when

Ray had roamed them on his bike. Most of the houses were still owned by people he knew, or if those folks had passed on the new owners kept the lawns clipped and the shutters painted. Only a few were being neglected. A handful had been abandoned.

This deep in Bible country, it was still an unwritten rule that little was done on Sundays except go to church, sit on porches, visit neighbors, rest and relax the way God intended.

It was cloudy, quite cool for May, and as he toured his old turf, killing time until the appointed hour, he tried to dwell on the good memories from Clanton. There was Dizzy Dean Park where he had played Little League for the Pirates, and there was the public pool he'd swum in every summer except 1969 when the city closed it rather than admit black children. There were the churches – Baptist, Methodist, and Presbyterian – facing each other at the intersection of Second and Elm like wary sentries, their steeples competing for height. They were empty now, but in an hour or so the more faithful would gather for evening services.

The square was as lifeless as the streets leading to it. With eight thousand people, Clanton was just large enough to have attracted the discount stores that had wiped out so many small towns. But here the people had been faithful to their downtown merchants, and there wasn't a single empty or boarded-up building around the square – no small miracle. The retail shops were mixed in with the banks and law offices and cafés, all closed for the Sabbath.

He inched through the cemetery and surveyed the Atlee section in the old part, where the tombstones were grander. Some of his ancestors had built monuments for their dead. Ray had always assumed that the family money he'd never seen must have been buried in those graves. He parked and walked to his mother's grave, something he hadn't done in years. She was buried among the Atlees, at the far edge of the family plot because she had barely belonged.

Soon, in less than an hour, he would be sitting in the Judge's study, sipping bad instant tea and receiving instructions on exactly how his father would be laid to rest. Many orders were about to be given, many decrees and directions, because the Judge was a great man and cared deeply about how he was to be remembered.

Moving again, Ray passed the water tower he'd climbed twice, the second time with the police waiting below. He grimaced at his old high school, a place he'd never visited since he'd left it. Behind it was the football field where Forrest Atlee had romped over opponents and almost became famous before getting bounced off the team.

It was twenty minutes before five, Sunday, May 7. Time for the family meeting.

There was no sign of life at Maple Run. The front lawn had been cut within the past few days, and the Judge's old black Lincoln was parked in the rear, but other than those two pieces of evidence there was no sign that anyone had lived there for many years.

The front of the house was dominated by four large round columns under a portico, and when Ray had lived there these columns were painted white. Now they were green with vines and ivy. The wisteria was running wildly along the tops of the columns and onto the roof. Weeds choked everything – flower beds, shrubs, walkways.

Memories hit hard, as they always did when he pulled slowly into the drive and shook his head at the condition of a once fine home. And there was always the same wave of guilt. He should've stayed, should've gone in with the old man and founded the house of Atlee & Atlee, should've married a local girl and sired a half-dozen descendants who would live at Maple Run, where they would adore the Judge and make him happy in his old age.

He slammed his door as loudly as possible, hoping to alert anyone who might need to be alerted, but the noise fell softly on Maple Run. The house next door to the east was another relic occupied by a family of spinsters who'd been dying off for decades. It was also an antebellum but without the vines and weeds, and it was completely shadowed by five of the largest oak trees in Clanton.

The front steps and the front porch had been swept recently. A broom was leaning near the door, which was open slightly. The Judge refused to lock the house, and since he also refused to use air conditioning he left windows and doors open around the clock.

Ray took a deep breath and pushed the door open until it hit the doorstop and made noise. He stepped inside and waited for the odor to hit, whatever it might be this time. For years the Judge kept an old cat, one with bad habits, and the house bore the results. But the cat was gone now, and the smell was not unpleasant at all. The air was warm and dusty and filled with the heavy scent of pipe tobacco.

'Anybody home?' he said, but not too loudly. No answer.

The foyer, like the rest of the house, was being used to store the boxes of ancient files and papers the Judge clung to as if they were important. They had been there since the county evicted him from the courthouse. Ray glanced to his right, to the dining room where nothing had changed in forty years, and he stepped around the corner to the hallway that was also cluttered with boxes. A few soft steps and he peeked into his father's study.

The Judge was napping on the sofa.

Ray backed away quickly and walked to the kitchen, where, surprisingly, there were no dirty dishes in the sink and the counters were clean. The kitchen was usually a mess, but not today. He found a diet soda in the refrigerator and sat at the table trying to decide whether to wake his father or to postpone the inevitable. The old man was ill and needed his rest, so Ray sipped his drink and watched the clock above the stove move slowly toward 5 P.M.

Forrest would show up, he was certain. The meeting was too important to blow off. He'd never been on time in his life. He refused to wear a watch and claimed he never knew what day it was, and most folks believed him.

At exactly five, Ray decided he was tired of waiting. He had traveled a long way for this moment, and he wanted to take care of business. He walked into the study, noticed his father hadn't moved, and for a long minute or two was frozen there, not wanting to wake him, but at the same time feeling like a trespasser.

The Judge wore the same black pants and the same white starched shirt he'd worn as long as Ray could remember. Navy suspenders, no tie, black socks, and black wing tips. He'd lost weight and his clothes swallowed him. His face was gaunt and pale, his hair thin and slicked back. His hands were crossed at his waist and were almost as white as the shirt.

Next to his hands, attached to his belt on the right side, was a small white plastic container. Ray took a step closer, a silent step, for a better look. It was a morphine pack.

Ray closed his eyes, then opened them and glanced around the room. The rolltop desk under General Forrest had not changed in his lifetime. The ancient Underwood typewriter still

47

sat there, a pile of papers beside it. A few feet away was the large mahogany desk left behind by the Atlee who'd fought with Forrest.

Under the stern gaze of General Nathan Bedford Forrest, and standing there in the center of a room that was timeless, Ray began to realize that his father was not breathing. He comprehended this slowly. He coughed, and there was not the slightest response. Then he leaned down and touched the Judge's left wrist. There was no pulse.

Judge Reuben V. Atlee was dead.

Chapter 6

There was an antique wicker chair with a torn cushion and a frayed quilt over the back. No one had ever used it but the cat. Ray backed into it because it was the nearest place to sit, and for a long time he sat there across from the sofa, waiting for his father to start breathing, to wake up, sit up, take charge of matters, and say, 'Where is Forrest?'

But the Judge was motionless. The only breathing at Maple Run was Ray's rather labored efforts to get control of himself. The house was silent, the still air even heavier. He stared at the pallid hands resting peacefully, and waited for them to rise just slightly. Up and down, very slowly as the blood began pumping again and the lungs filled and emptied. But nothing happened. His father was straight as a board, with hands and feet together, chin on chest, as if he knew when he lay down that this last nap would be eternal. His lips were together with a hint of a smile. The powerful drug had stopped the pain.

As the shock began to fade, the questions took over. How long had he been dead? Did the cancer get him or did the old man just crank up the morphine? What was the difference? Was this staged for his sons? Where the hell was Forrest? Not that he would be of any help.

Alone with his father for the last time, Ray fought back tears and fought back all the usual tormenting questions of why didn't I come earlier, and more often, and why didn't I write and call and the list could go on if he allowed it.

Instead, he finally moved. He knelt quietly beside the sofa, put his head on the Judge's chest, whispered, 'I love you, Dad,' then said a short prayer. When he stood he had tears in his eyes, and that was not what he wanted. Younger brother would arrive in a moment, and Ray was determined to handle the situation with no emotion.

On the mahogany desk he found the ashtray with two pipes. One was empty. The bowl of the other was full of tobacco that had recently been smoked. It was slightly warm, at least Ray thought so, though he was not certain. He could see the Judge having a smoke while he tidied up the papers on his desk, didn't want the boys to see too much of a mess, then when the pain hit he stretched out on the sofa, a touch of morphine for a little relief, then he drifted away.

Next to the Underwood was one of the

Judge's official envelopes, and across the front he had typed, 'Last Will and Testament of Reuben V. Atlee.' Under it was yesterday's date, May 6, 2000. Ray took it and left the room. He found another diet soda in the refrigerator and walked to the front porch, where he sat on the swing and waited for Forrest.

Should he call the funeral home and have his father moved before Forrest arrived? He debated this with a fury for a while, then he read the will. It was a simple, one-page document with no surprises.

He decided he would wait until precisely 6 P.M., and if Forrest hadn't arrived he would call the funeral home.

The Judge was still dead when Ray returned to his study, and that was not a complete surprise. He replaced the envelope next to the typewriter, shuffled through some more papers, and at first felt odd doing so. But he would be executor of his father's estate, and would soon be in charge of all the paperwork. He would inventory the assets, pay the bills, help lead the last remnants of the Atlee family money through probate, and finally put it to rest. The will split everything between the two sons, so the estate would be clean and relatively simple.

As he watched the time and waited for his brother, Ray poked around the study, each step watched carefully by General Forrest. Ray was quiet, still not wanting to disturb his father. The drawers to the rolltop were filled with stationery.

51

There was a pile of current mail on the mahogany desk.

Behind the sofa was a wall of bookshelves crammed with law treatises that appeared to have been neglected for decades. The shelves were made of walnut and had been built as a gift by a murderer freed from prison by the Judge's grandfather late in the last century, according to family lore, which as a rule went unquestioned, until Forrest came along. The shelves rested on a long walnut cabinet that was no more than three feet high. The cabinet had six small doors and was used for storage. Ray had never looked inside. The sofa was in front of the cabinet, almost entirely blocking it from view.

One of the cabinet doors was open. Inside, Ray could see an orderly stack of dark green Blake & Son stationer's boxes, the same ones he'd seen as long as he could remember. Blake & Son was an ancient printing company in Memphis. Virtually every lawyer and judge in the state bought letterheads and envelopes from Blake & Son, and had been doing so forever. He crouched low and moved behind the sofa for a better look. The storage spaces were tight and dark.

A box of envelopes without a top had been left sitting in the open door, just a few inches above the floor. There were no envelopes, however. The box was filled with cash – one-hundred-dollar bills. Hundreds of them packed neatly in a box that was twelve inches across, eighteen

52

inches long, and maybe five inches deep. He lifted the box, and it was heavy. There were dozens more tucked away in the depths of the cabinet.

Ray pulled another one from the collection. It too was filled with one-hundred-dollar bills. Same for the third. In the fourth box, the bills were wrapped with yellow paper bands with '$2,000' printed on them. He quickly counted fifty-three bands.

One hundred and six thousand dollars.

Crawling on all fours along the back of the sofa, and careful not to touch it and disturb anybody, Ray opened the other five doors of the cabinet. There were at least twenty dark green Blake & Son boxes.

He stood and walked to the door of the study, then through the foyer onto the front porch for fresh air. He was dizzy, and when he sat on the top step a large drop of sweat rolled down the bridge of his nose and fell onto his pants.

Though clear thinking was not entirely possible, Ray was able to do some quick math. Assuming there were twenty boxes and that each held at least a hundred thousand dollars, then the stash greatly exceeded whatever the Judge had grossed in thirty-two years on the bench. His office of chancellor had been full time, nothing on the side, and not much since his defeat nine years earlier.

He didn't gamble, and to Ray's knowledge, had never bought a single share of stock.

A car approached from down the street. Ray froze, instantly fearful that it was Forrest. The car passed, and Ray jumped to his feet and ran to the study. He lifted one end of the sofa and moved it six inches away from the bookshelves, then the same for the other end. He dropped to his knees and began withdrawing the Blake & Son boxes. When he had a stack of five, he carried them through the kitchen to a small room behind the pantry where Irene the maid had always kept her brooms and mops. The same brooms and mops were still there, evidently untouched since Irene's death. Ray swatted away spiderwebs, then set the boxes on the floor.

The broom closet had no window and could not be seen from the kitchen.

From the dining room, he surveyed the front driveway, saw nothing, then raced back to the study where he balanced seven Blake & Son boxes in one stack and took them to the broom closet. Back to the dining room window, nobody out there, back to the study where the Judge was growing colder by the moment. Two more trips to the broom closet and the job was finished. Twenty-seven boxes in total, all safely stored where no one would find them.

It was almost 6 P.M. when Ray went to his car and removed his overnight bag. He needed a dry shirt and clean pants. The house was filled with

54

dust and dirt and everything he touched left a smudge. He washed and dried himself with a towel in the only downstairs bathroom. Then he tidied up the study, moved the sofa back in place, and went from room to room looking for more cabinets.

He was on the second floor, in the Judge's bedroom with the windows up, going through his closets, when he heard a car in the street. He ran downstairs and managed to slip into the swing on the porch just as Forrest parked behind his Audi. Ray took deep breaths and tried to calm himself.

The shock of a dead father was enough for one day. The shock of the money had left him shaking.

Forrest crept up the steps, as slowly as possible, hands stuck deep in his white painter's pants. Shiny black combat boots with bright green laces. Always different.

'Forrest,' Ray said softly, and his brother turned to see him.

'Hey, Bro.'

'He's dead.'

Forrest stopped and for a moment studied him, then he gazed at the street. He was wearing an old brown blazer over a red tee shirt, an ensemble no one but Forrest would attempt to pull off. And no one but Forrest could get by with it. As Clanton's first self-proclaimed free spirit, he had always worked to be cool, offbeat, avant-garde, hip.

He was a little heavier and was carrying the weight well. His long sandy hair was turning gray much quicker than Ray's. He wore a battered Cubs baseball cap.

'Where is he?' Forrest asked.

'In there.'

Forrest pulled open the screen and Ray followed him inside. He stopped in the door of the study and seemed uncertain as to what to do next. As Forrest stared at his father his head fell slightly to one side, and Ray thought for a second he might collapse. As tough as he tried to act, Forrest's emotions were always just under the surface. He mumbled, 'Oh my God,' then moved awkwardly to the wicker chair where he sat and looked in disbelief at the Judge.

'Is he really dead?' he managed to say with his jaws clenched.

'Yes, Forrest.'

He swallowed hard and fought back tears and finally said, 'When did you get here?'

Ray sat on a stool and turned it to face his brother. 'About five, I guess. I walked in, thought he was napping, then realized he was dead.'

'I'm sorry you had to find him,' Forrest said, wiping the corners of his eyes.

'Somebody had to.'

'What do we do now?'

'Call the funeral home.'

Forrest nodded as if he knew that was exactly what you're supposed to do. He stood slowly and unsteadily and walked to the sofa. He touched his father's hands. 'How long has he been dead?' he mumbled. His voice was hoarse and strained.

'I don't know. Couple of hours.'

'What's that?'

'A morphine pack.'

'You think he cranked it up a little too much?'

'I hope so,' Ray said.

'I guess we should've been here.'

'Let's not start that.'

Forrest looked around the room as if he'd never been there before. He walked to the rolltop and looked at the typewriter. 'I guess he won't need a new ribbon after all,' he said.

'I guess not,' Ray said, glancing at the cabinet behind the sofa. 'There's a will there if you want to read it. Signed yesterday.'

'What does it say?'

'We split everything. I'm the executor.'

'Of course you're the executor.' He walked behind the mahogany desk and gave a quick look at the piles of papers covering it. 'Nine years since I set foot in this house. Hard to believe, isn't it?'

'It is.'

'I stopped by a few days after the election, told him how sorry I was that the voters had turned him out, then I asked him for money. We had words.'

'Come on, Forrest, not now.'

Stories of the war between Forrest and the Judge could be told forever.

'Never did get that money,' he mumbled as he opened a desk drawer. 'I guess we'll need to go through everything, won't we?'

'Yes, but not now.'

'You do it, Ray. You're the executor. You handle the dirty work.'

'We need to call the funeral home.'

'I need a drink.'

'No, Forrest, please.'

'Lay off, Ray. I'll have a drink anytime I want a drink.'

'That's been proven a thousand times. Come on, I'll call the funeral home and we'll wait on the porch.'

A policeman arrived first, a young man with a shaved head who looked as though someone had interrupted his Sunday nap and called him into action. He asked questions on the front porch, then viewed the body. Paperwork had to be done, and as they went through it Ray fixed a pitcher of instant tea with heavy sugar.

'Cause of death?' the policeman asked.

'Cancer, heart disease, diabetes, old age,' Ray said. He and Forrest were rocking gently in the swing.

'Is that enough?' Forrest asked, like a true smart-ass. Any respect he might've once had for cops had long since been abandoned.

'Will you request an autopsy?'

'No,' they said in unison.

He finished the forms and took signatures from both Ray and Forrest. As he drove away, Ray said, 'Word will spread like wildfire now.'

'Not in our lovely little town.'

'Hard to believe, isn't it? Folks actually gossip around here.'

'I've kept them busy for twenty years.'

'Indeed you have.'

They were shoulder to shoulder, both holding empty glasses. 'So what's in the estate?' Forrest finally asked.

'You want to see the will?'

'No, just tell me.'

'He listed his assets – the house, furniture, car, books, six thousand dollars in the bank.'

'Is that all?'

'That's all he mentioned,' Ray said, avoiding the lie.

'Surely, there's more money than that around here,' Forrest said, ready to start looking.

'I guess he gave it all away,' Ray said calmly.

'What about his state retirement?'

'He cashed out when he lost the election, a huge blunder. Cost him tens of thousands of dollars. I'm assuming he gave everything else away.'

'You're not going to screw me, are you, Ray?'

'Come on, Forrest, there's nothing to fight over.'

'Any debts?'

'He said he had none.'

'Nothing else?'

'You can read the will if you want.'

'Not now.'

'He signed it yesterday.'

'You think he planned everything?'

'Sure looks like it.'

A black hearse from Magargel's Funeral Home rolled to a stop in front of Maple Run, then turned slowly into the drive.

Forrest leaned forward, elbows on knees, face in hand, and began crying.

Chapter 7

Behind the hearse was the county coroner, Thurber Foreman, in the same red Dodge pickup he'd been driving since Ray was in college, and behind Thurber was Reverend Silas Palmer of the First Presbyterian Church, an ageless little Scot who'd baptized both Atlee sons. Forrest slipped away and hid in the backyard while Ray met the party on the front porch. Sympathies were exchanged. Mr. B. J. Magargel from the funeral home and Reverend Palmer appeared to be near tears. Thurber had seen countless dead bodies. He had no financial interest in this one, however, and appeared to be indifferent, at least for the moment.

Ray led them to the study where they respectfully viewed Judge Atlee long enough for Thurber to officially decide he was dead. He did this without words, but simply nodded at Mr. Magargel with a somber, bureaucratic dip of the chin that said, 'He's dead. You can take him now.' Mr. Magargel nodded, too, thus completing a silent ritual they'd gone through many times together.

Thurber produced a single sheet of paper and asked the basics. The Judge's full name, date of birth, place of birth, next of kin. For the second time, Ray said no to an autopsy.

Ray and Reverend Palmer stepped away and took a seat at the dining room table. The minister was much more emotional than the son. He adored the Judge and claimed him as a close friend.

A service befitting a man of Reuben Atlee's stature would draw many friends and admirers and should be well planned. 'Reuben and I talked about it not long ago,' Palmer said, his voice low and raspy, ready to choke up at any moment.

'That's good,' Ray said.

'He picked out the hymns and scriptures, and he made a list of the pallbearers.'

Ray hadn't yet thought of such details. Perhaps they would've come to mind had he not stumbled upon a couple of million in cash. His overworked brain listened to Palmer and caught most of his words, then it would switch to the broom closet and start swirling again. He was suddenly nervous that Thurber and Magargel were alone with the Judge in the study. Relax, he kept telling himself.

'Thank you,' he said, genuinely relieved that

the details had been taken care of. Mr. Magargel's assistant rolled a gurney through the front door, through the foyer, and struggled to get it turned into the Judge's study.

'And he wanted a wake,' the reverend said. Wakes were traditional, a necessary prelude to a proper burial, especially among the older folks.

Ray nodded.

'Here in the house.'

'No,' Ray said instantly. 'Not here.'

As soon as he was alone, he wanted to inspect every inch of the house in search of more loot. And he was very concerned with the stash already in the broom closet. How much was there? How long would it take to count it? Was it real or counterfeit? Where did it come from? What to do with it? Where to take it? Who to tell? He needed time alone to think, to sort things out and develop a plan.

'Your father was very plain about this,' Palmer said.

'I'm sorry, Reverend. We will have a wake, but not here.'

'May I ask why not?'

'My mother.'

He smiled and nodded and said, 'I remember your mother.'

'They laid her on the table over there in the front parlor, and for two days the entire town paraded by. My brother and I hid upstairs and cursed my father for such a spectacle.' Ray's voice was firm, his eyes hot. 'We will not have a wake in this house, Reverend.'

Ray was utterly sincere. He was also concerned about securing the premises. A wake would require a thorough scouring of the house by a cleaning service, and the preparation of food by a caterer, and flowers hauled in by a florist. And all of this activity would begin in the morning.

'I understand,' the reverend said.

The assistant backed out first, pulling the gurney, which was being pushed gently by Mr. Magargel. The Judge was covered from head to foot by a starched white sheet that was tucked neatly under him. With Thurber following behind, they rolled him out, across the front porch and down the steps, the last Atlee to live at Maple Run.

Half an hour later, Forrest materialized from somewhere in the back of the house. He was holding a tall clear glass that was filled with a suspicious-looking brown liquid, and it wasn't ice tea. 'They gone?' he asked, looking at the driveway.

'Yes,' Ray said. He was sitting on the front steps, smoking a cigar. When Forrest sat down next to him, the aroma of sour mash followed quickly.

'Where'd you find that?' Ray asked.

'He had a hiding place in his bathroom. Want some?'

'No. How long have you known that?'

'Thirty years.'

A dozen lectures leapt forward, but Ray fought them off. They'd been delivered many times before, and evidently they had failed because here was Forrest sipping bourbon after 141 days of sobriety.

'How's Ellie?' Ray asked after a long puff.

'Crazy as hell, the same.'

'Will I see her at the funeral?'

'No, she's up to three hundred pounds. One-fifty is her limit. Under one-fifty and she'll leave the house. Over one-fifty, and she locks herself up.'

'When was she under one-fifty?'

'Three or four years ago. She found some wacko doctor who gave her pills. Got all the way down to a hundred pounds. Doctor went to jail and she gained another two hundred. Three hundred is her max, though. She weighs every day and freaks out if the big needle goes beyond three.'

'I told Reverend Palmer that we would have a wake, but not here, not in the house.'

'You're the executor.'

'You agree?'

'Sure.'

A long pull on the bourbon, another long puff on the cigar.

'What about that hosebag who ditched you? What's her name?'

'Vicki.'

'Yeah, Vicki, I hated that bitch even at your wedding.'

'I wish I had.'

'She still around?'

'Yep, saw her last week, at the airport, getting off her private jet.'

'She married that old fart, right, some crook from Wall Street?'

'That's him. Let's talk about something else.'

'You brought up women.'

'Always a big mistake.'

Forrest slugged another drink, then said, 'Let's talk about money. Where is it?'

Ray flinched slightly and his heart stopped, but Forrest was gazing at the front lawn and didn't notice. What money are you talking about, dear brother? 'He gave it away.'

'But why?'

'It was his money, not ours.'

'Why not leave some for us?'

Not too many years earlier, the Judge had confided to Ray that over a fifteen-year period he had spent more than ninety thousand dollars on legal fees, court fines, and rehab for Forrest. He could leave the money for Forrest to drink and snort, or he could give it away to charities and needy families during his lifetime. Ray had a profession and could take care of himself.

'He left us the house,' Ray said.

'What happens to it?'

'We'll sell it if you want. The money goes in a

pot with everything else. Fifty percent will go for estate taxes. Probate will take a year.'

'Gimme the bottom line.'

'We'll be lucky to split fifty thousand a year from now.'

Of course there were other assets. The loot was sitting innocently in the broom closet, but Ray needed time to evaluate it. Was it dirty money? Should it be included in the estate? If so, it would cause terrible problems. First, it would have to be explained. Second, at least half would get burned in taxes. Third, Forrest would have his pockets filled with cash and would probably kill himself with it.

'So I'll get twenty-five thousand bucks in a year?' Forrest said.

Ray couldn't tell if he was anxious or disgusted. 'Something like that.'

'Do you want the house?'

'No, do you?'

'Hell no. I'll never go back in there.'

'Come on, Forrest.'

'He kicked me out, you know, told me I'd disgraced this family long enough. Told me to never set foot on this soil again.'

'And he apologized.'

A quick sip. 'Yes, he did. But this place depresses me. You're the executor, you deal with it. Just mail me a check when probate is over.'

'We should at least go through his things together.'

'I'm not touching them,' he said and got to his

feet. 'I want a beer. It's been five months, and I want a beer.' He was walking toward his car as he talked. 'You want one?'

'No.'

'You wanna ride with me?'

Ray wanted to go so he could protect his brother, but he felt a stronger urge to sit tight and protect the Atlee family assets. The Judge never locked the house. Where were the keys? 'I'll wait here,' he said.

'Whatever.'

The next visitor was no surprise. Ray was in the kitchen digging through drawers, looking for keys, when he heard a loud voice bellowing at the front door. Though he hadn't heard it in years, there was no doubt it belonged to Harry Rex Vonner.

They embraced, a bear hug from Harry Rex, a retreating squeeze from Ray. 'I'm so sorry,' Harry Rex said several times. He was tall with a large chest and stomach, a big messy bear of a man who worshiped Judge Atlee and would do anything for his boys. He was a brilliant lawyer trapped in a small town, and it was to Harry Rex that Judge Atlee had always turned during Forrest's legal problems.

'When did you get here?' he asked.

'Around five. I found him in his study.'

'I've been in trial for two weeks, hadn't talked to him. Where's Forrest?'

'Gone to buy beer.'

They both digested the gravity of this. They sat in the rocking chairs near the swing. 'It's good to see you, Ray.'

'And you too, Harry Rex.'

'I can't believe he's dead.'

'Nor can I. I thought he'd always be here.'

Harry Rex wiped his eyes with the back of a sleeve. 'I'm so sorry,' he mumbled. 'I just can't believe it. I saw him two weeks ago, I guess it was. He was movin' around, sharp as a tack, in pain but not complainin'.'

'They gave him a year, and that was about twelve months ago. I thought he'd hang on, though.'

'Me too. Such a tough old fart.'

'You want some tea?'

'That'd be nice.'

Ray went to the kitchen and poured two glasses of instant ice tea. He took them back to the porch and said, 'This stuff isn't very good.'

Harry Rex took a drink and concurred. 'At least it's cold.'

'We need to have a wake, Harry Rex, and we're not doing it here. Any ideas?'

He pondered this only for a second, then leaned in with a big smile. 'Let's put him in the courthouse, first floor in the rotunda, lay him in state like a king or somethin'.'

'You're serious?'

'Why not. He'd love it. The whole town could parade by and pay their respects.'

'I like it.'

69

'It's brilliant, trust me. I'll talk to the sheriff and get it approved. Ever'body'll love it. When's the funeral?'

'Tuesday.'

'Then we'll have us a wake tomorrow afternoon. You want me to say a few words?'

'Of course. Why don't you just organize the whole thing?'

'Done. Y'all picked out a casket?'

'We were going in the morning'

'Do oak, forget that bronze and copper crap. We buried Momma last year in oak and it was the prettiest damned thang I'd ever seen. Magargel can get one out of Tupelo in two hours. And forget the vault, too. They're just rip-offs. Ashes to ashes, dust to dust, bury 'em and let 'em rot is the only way to go. The Episcopalians do it right.'

Ray was a little dazed by the torrent of advice, but was thankful nonetheless. The Judge's will had not mentioned the casket but had specifically requested a vault. And he wanted a nice headstone. He was, after all, an Atlee, and he was to be buried among the other great ones.

If anyone knew anything about the Judge's business, it was Harry Rex. As they watched the shadows fall across the long front lawn of Maple Run, Ray said, as nonchalantly as possible, 'Looks like he gave all his money away.'

'I'm not surprised. Are you?'

'No.'

'There'll be a thousand folks at his funeral

who were touched by his generosity. Crippled
children, sick folks with no insurance, black kids
he sent to college, every volunteer fire department, civic club, all-star team, school group
headed for Europe. Our church sent some
doctors to Haiti and the Judge gave us a
thousand bucks.'

'When did you start going to church?'

'Two years ago.'

'Why?'

'Got a new wife.'

'How many is that?'

'Four. I really like this one, though.'

'Lucky for her.'

'She's very lucky.'

'I like this courthouse wake, Harry Rex. All
those folks you just mentioned can pay their
respects in public. Plenty of parking, don't have
to worry about seating.'

'It's brilliant.'

Forrest wheeled into the drive and slammed
on his brakes, stopping inches behind Harry
Rex's Cadillac. He crawled out and lumbered
toward them in the semidarkness, carrying what
appeared to be a whole case of beer.

Chapter 8

When he was alone, Ray sat in the wicker chair across from the empty sofa, and tried to convince himself that life without his father would not be greatly different than life apart from him. This day was long in coming, and he would simply take it in stride and go on with a small measure of mourning. Just go through the motions, he told himself, wrap things up in Mississippi and race back to Virginia.

The study was lit by one weak bulb under the shade of a dust-covered lamp on the rolltop, and the shadows were long and dark. Tomorrow he would sit at the desk and plunge into the paperwork, but not tonight.

Tonight he needed to think.

Forrest was gone, hauled away by Harry Rex, both of them drunk. Forrest, typically, became sullen and wanted to drive to Memphis. Ray suggested he simply stay there. 'Sleep on the porch if you don't want to sleep in the house,' he said, without pushing. Pushing would only cause a fight. Harry Rex said he would, under normal circumstances, invite Forrest to stay with him, but the new wife was a hard-ass and two drunks were probably too much.

'Just stay here,' Harry Rex said, but Forrest wouldn't budge. Bullheaded enough when he was cold sober, he was intractable after a few drinks. Ray had seen it more times than he cared to remember and sat quietly as Harry Rex argued with his brother.

The issue was settled when Forrest decided he would rent a room at the Deep Rock Motel north of town. 'I used to go there when I was seeing the mayor's wife, fifteen years ago,' he said.

'It's full of fleas,' Harry Rex said.

'I miss it already.'

'The mayor's wife?' Ray asked.

'You don't want to know,' Harry Rex said.

They left a few minutes after eleven, and the house had been growing quieter by the minute.

The front door had a latch and the patio door had a deadbolt. The kitchen door, the only one at the rear of the house, had a flimsy knob with a lock that was not working. The Judge could not operate a screwdriver and Ray had inherited this lack of mechanical skill. Every window had been closed and latched, and he was certain that the Atlee mansion had not been this secure in decades. If necessary, he would sleep in the kitchen where he could guard the broom closet.

He tried not to think about the money. Sitting

73

in his father's sanctuary, he mentally worked on an unofficial obituary.

Judge Atlee was elected to the bench of the 25th Chancery District in 1959 and was reelected by a landslide every four years until 1991. Thirty-two years of diligent service. As a jurist, his record was impeccable. Rarely did the Appellate Court reverse one of his decisions. Often he was asked by his colleagues to hear untouchable cases in their districts. He was a guest lecturer at the Ole Miss Law School. He wrote hundreds of articles on practice, procedure, and trends. Twice he turned down appointments to the Mississippi Supreme Court; he simply didn't want to leave the trial bench.

When he wasn't wearing a robe, Judge Atlee kept his finger in all local matters – politics, civic work, schools, and churches. Few things in Ford County were approved without his endorsement, and few things he opposed were ever attempted. At various times he served on every local board, council, conference, and ad hoc committee. He quietly selected candidates for local offices and he quietly helped defeat the ones who didn't get his blessing.

In his spare time, what little of it there had been, he studied history and the Bible and wrote articles on the law. Never once had he thrown a baseball with his sons, never once had he taken them fishing.

He was preceded in death by his wife, Margaret, who died suddenly of an aneurysm in 1969. He was survived by two sons.

And somewhere along the way he managed to siphon off a fortune in cash.

Maybe the mystery of the money would be solved over there on the desk, somewhere in the stacks of papers or perhaps hidden in the drawers. Surely his father had left a clue, if not an outright explanation. There had to be a trail. Ray couldn't think of a single person in Ford County with a net worth of two million dollars, and to hold that much in cash was unthinkable.

He needed to count it. He'd checked on it twice during the evening. Just counting the twenty-seven Blake & Son's boxes had made him anxious. He would wait until early morning, when there was plenty of light and before the town began moving. He'd cover the kitchen windows and take one box at a time.

Just before midnight, Ray found a small mattress in a downstairs bedroom and dragged it into the dining room, to a spot twenty feet from the broom closet, where he could see the front drive and the house next door. Upstairs he found the Judge's .38-caliber Smith & Wesson in the drawer of his night table. With a pillow that smelled of mildew and a wool blanket that smelled of mold, he tried in vain to sleep.

The rattling noise came from the other side of the house. It was a window, though it took Ray minutes to wake up, clear his head, realize where he was and what he was hearing. A pecking sound, then a more violent shaking, then silence. A long pause as he poised himself on the mattress and gripped the .38. The house was much darker than he wanted because almost all the lightbulbs had burned out and the Judge had been too cheap to replace them.

Too cheap. Twenty-seven boxes of cash.

Put lightbulbs on the list, first thing in the morning.

There was the noise again, too firm and too rapid to be leaves or limbs brushing in the wind. Tap, tap, tap, then a hard push or shove as someone tried again to pry it open.

There were two cars in the drive – Ray's and Forrest's. Any fool could see the house had people in it, so whoever this fool was he didn't care. He probably had a gun, too, and he certainly knew how to handle it better than Ray.

Ray slid across the foyer on his stomach, wiggling like a crab and breathing like a sprinter. He stopped in the dark hallway and listened to the silence. Lovely silence. Just go away, he kept saying to himself. Please go away.

Tap, tap, tap, and he was sliding again toward the rear bedroom with the pistol aimed in front of him. Was it loaded? he asked himself, much too late. Surely the Judge kept his bedside gun loaded. The noise was louder and coming from a small bedroom they had once used for guests, but for decades now it had been collecting boxes of junk. He slowly nudged the door open with his head and saw nothing but cardboard boxes. The door swung wider and hit a floor lamp, which pitched forward and crashed near the first of three dark windows.

Ray almost began firing, but he held his ammo, and his breath. He lay still on the sagging wooden floor for what seemed like an hour, sweating, listening, swatting spiders, hearing nothing. The shadows rose and fell. A light wind was hitting every branch out there, and somewhere up near the roof a limb was gently rubbing the house.

It was the wind after all. The wind and the old ghosts of Maple Run, a place of many spirits, according to his mother, because it was an old house where dozens had died. They had buried slaves in the basement, she said, and their ghosts grew restless and roamed about.

The Judge hated ghost stories and refuted them all.

When Ray finally sat up, his elbows and knees were numb. With time he stood and leaned on the door frame, watching the three windows with his gun ready. If there had actually been an intruder, the noise evidently spooked him. But the longer Ray stood there the more he convinced himself that the racket had been nothing but the wind.

Forrest had the better idea. As grungy as the Deep Rock was, it had to be more restful than this place.

Tap, tap, tap, and he hit the floor again, stricken with fear once more, except this was worse because the noise came from the kitchen. He made the tactical decision to crawl instead of slide, and by the time he got back to the foyer his knees were screaming. He stopped at the French doors that led to the dining room and waited. The floor was dark but a faint porch light slanted feebly through the blinds and shone along the upper walls and ceiling.

Not for the first time, he asked himself what, exactly, was he, a professor of law at a prestigious university, doing hiding in the darkness of his childhood home, armed, frightened out of his mind, ready to jump out of his skin, and all because he wanted desperately to protect a mysterious hoard of cash he had stumbled upon. 'Answer that one,' he mumbled to himself.

The kitchen door opened onto a small wooden deck. Someone was shuffling around out there, just beyond the door, footsteps on boards. Then the doorknob rattled, the flimsy one with the malfunctioning lock. Whoever he was, he had made the bold decision to walk straight through the door instead of sneaking through a window.

Ray was an Atlee, and this was his soil. This was also Mississippi, where guns were expected to be used for protection. No court in the state would frown on drastic action in this situation. He crouched beside the kitchen table, took aim at a spot high in the window above the sink, and began squeezing the trigger. One loud gunshot, cracking through the darkness, coming from inside and shattering a window, would no doubt terrify any burglar.

Just as the door rattled again, he squeezed harder, the hammer clicked, and nothing happened. The gun had no bullets. The chamber spun, he squeezed again, and there was no discharge. In a panic, Ray grabbed the empty pitcher of tea on the counter and hurled it at the door. To his great relief, it made more noise than any bullet could possibly have done. Scared out of his wits, he hit a light switch and went charging to the door, brandishing the gun and yelling, 'Get the hell outta here!' When he yanked it open and saw no one, he exhaled mightily and began breathing again.

For half an hour he swept glass, making as much noise as possible.

The cop's name was Andy, nephew of a guy Ray finished high school with. That relationship was established within the first thirty seconds of his arrival, and once they were linked they talked about football while the exterior of Maple Run was inspected. No sign of entry at any of the downstairs windows. Nothing at the kitchen door but broken glass. Upstairs, Ray looked for bullets while Andy went from room to room. Both searches produced nothing. Ray brewed coffee and they drank it on the porch, chatting quietly in the early morning hours. Andy was the only cop protecting Clanton at that time, and he confessed he wasn't really needed. 'Nothin' ever happens this early Monday morning,' he said. 'Folks are asleep, gettin' ready for work.' With a little prodding, he reviewed the crime scene in Ford County – stolen pickups, fights at the honky-tonks, drug activity in Lowtown, the colored section. Hadn't had a murder in four years, he said proudly. A branch bank got robbed two years ago. He prattled on and took a second cup. Ray would keep pouring it, and brewing it if necessary, until sunrise. He was comforted by the presence of a well-marked patrol car sitting out front.

Andy left at three-thirty. For an hour Ray lay on the mattress, staring holes in the ceiling, holding a gun that was useless. He fought sleep by plotting strategies to protect the money. Not investment schemes, those could wait. More pressing was a plan to get the money out of the broom closet, out of the house, and into a safe place somewhere. Would he be forced to haul it to Virginia? He certainly couldn't leave it in Clanton, could he? And when could he count it?

At some point, fatigue and the emotional drain of the day overcame him, and he drifted away. The tapping came back, but he did not hear it. The kitchen door, now secured by a jammed chair and a piece of rope, was rattled and pushed, but Ray slept through it all.

Chapter 9

At seven-thirty, sunlight woke him. The money was still there, untouched. The doors and windows had not been opened, as far as he could tell. He fixed a pot of coffee, and as he drank the first cup at the kitchen table he made an important decision. If someone was after the money, then he could not leave it, not for a moment.

But the twenty-seven Blake & Son boxes would not fit in the small trunk of his little Audi roadster.

The phone rang at eight. It was Harry Rex, reporting that Forrest had been delivered to the Deep Rock Motel, that the county would allow a ceremony in the rotunda of the courthouse that afternoon at four-thirty, that he had already lined up a soprano and a color guard. And he was working on a eulogy for his beloved friend.

'What about the casket?' he asked.

'We're meeting with Magargel at ten,' Ray answered.

'Good. Remember, go with the oak. The Judge would like that.'

They talked about Forrest for a few minutes, the same conversation they'd had many times. When he hung up, Ray began moving quickly. He opened windows and blinds so he could see and hear any visitors. Word was spreading through the coffee shops around the square that Judge Atlee had died, and visitors were certainly possible.

The house had too many doors and windows, and he couldn't stand guard around the clock. If someone was after the money, then that someone could get it. For a few million bucks, a bullet to Ray's head would be a solid investment.

The money had to be moved.

Working in front of the broom closet, he took the first box and dumped the cash into a black plastic garbage bag. Eight more boxes followed, and when he had about a million bucks in bag number one he carried it to the kitchen door and peeked outside. The empty boxes were returned to the cabinet under the bookshelves. Two more garbage bags were filled. He backed his car close to the deck, as close to the kitchen as possible, then surveyed the landscape in search of human eyes. There were none. The only neighbors were the spinsters next door, and they couldn't see the television in their own den. Darting from the door to the car, he loaded the fortune into the trunk, shoved the bags this way and that, and when it looked as though the lid might not close he slammed it down anyway. It clicked and locked and Ray Atlee was quite relieved.

He wasn't sure how he would unload the loot in Virginia and carry it from a parking lot down the busy pedestrian mall to his apartment. He would worry about that later.

The Deep Rock had a diner, a hot cramped greasy place Ray had never visited, but it was the perfect spot to eat on the morning after Judge Atlee's death. The three coffee shops around the square would be busy with gossip and stories about the great man, and Ray preferred to stay away.

Forrest looked decent. Ray had certainly seen much him worse. He wore the same clothes and he hadn't showered, but with Forrest that was not unusual. His eyes were red but not swollen. He said he'd slept well, but needed grease. Both ordered bacon and eggs.

'You look tired,' Forrest said, gulping black coffee.

Ray indeed felt tired. 'I'm fine, couple of hours of rest and I'm ready to roll.' He glanced through the window at his Audi, which was parked as close to the diner as possible. He would sleep in the damned thing if necessary.

'It's weird,' Forrest said. 'When I'm clean, I sleep like a baby. Eight, nine hours a night, a hard sleep. But when I'm not clean, I'm lucky to get five hours. And it's not a deep sleep either.'

'Just curious – when you're clean, do you think about the next round of drinking?'

'Always. It builds up, like sex. You can do without it for a while, but the pressure's building and sooner or later you gotta have some relief. Booze, sex, drugs, they all get me eventually.'

'You were clean for a hundred and forty days.'

'A hundred and forty-one.'

'What's the record?'

'Fourteen months. I came out of rehab a few years back, this great detox center that the old man paid for, and I kicked ass for a long time. Then I crashed.'

'Why? What made you crash?'

'It's always the same. When you're an addict you can lose it any time, any place, for any reason. They haven't designed a wagon that can hold me. I'm an addict, Bro, plain and simple.'

'Still drugs?'

'Sure. Last night it was booze and beer, same tonight, same tomorrow. By the end of the week I'll be doing nastier stuff.'

'Do you want to?'

'No, but I know what happens.'

The waitress brought their food. Forrest quickly buttered a biscuit and took a large bite. When he could speak he said, 'The old man's dead, Ray, can you believe it?'

Ray was anxious to change the subject too. If they dwelt on Forrest's shortcomings they would be fighting soon enough. 'No, I thought I was ready for it, but I wasn't.'

'When was the last time you saw him?'

'November, when he had prostate surgery. You?'

Forrest sprinkled Tabasco sauce on his scrambled eggs and pondered the question. 'When was his heart attack?'

There had been so many ailments and surgeries that they were difficult to remember. 'He had three.'

'The one in Memphis.'

'That was the second one,' Ray said. 'Four years ago.'

'That's about right. I spent some time with him at the hospital. Hell, it wasn't six blocks away. I figured it was the least I could do.'

'What did you talk about?'

'Civil War. He still thought we'd won.'

They smiled at this and ate in silence for a few moments. The silence ended when Harry Rex found them. He helped himself to a biscuit while offering the latest details of the splendid ceremony he was planning for Judge Atlee.

'Everybody wants to come out to the house,' he said with a mouthful.

'It's off limits,' Ray said.

'That's what I'm tellin' them. Y'all want to receive guests tonight?'

'No,' said Forrest.

'Should we?' asked Ray.

'It's the proper thing to do, either at the house or at the funeral home. But if you don't, it's no big deal. Ain't like folks'll get pissed and refuse to speak to you.'

'We're doing the courthouse wake and a funeral, isn't that enough?' Ray asked.

'I think so.'

'I'm not sittin' around a funeral home all night huggin' old ladies who've been talkin' about me for twenty years,' Forrest said. 'You can if you want, but I will not be there.'

'Let's pass on it,' Ray said.

'Spoken like a true executor,' Forrest said with a sneer.

'Executor?' said Harry Rex.

'Yes, there was a will on his desk, dated Saturday. A simple, one-page, holographic will, leaving everything to the two of us, listing his assets, naming me as the executor. And he wants you to do the probate, Harry Rex.'

Harry Rex had stopped chewing. He rubbed the bridge of his nose with a chubby finger and gazed across the diner. 'That's odd,' he said, obviously puzzled by something.

'What?'

'I did a long will for him a month ago.'

All had stopped eating. Ray and Forrest exchanged looks that conveyed nothing because neither had a clue what the other was thinking.

'I guess he changed his mind,' Harry Rex said.

'What was in the other will?' Ray asked.

'I can't tell you. He was my client, so it's confidential.'

'I'm lost here, fellas,' Forrest said. 'Forgive me for not being a lawyer.'

'The only will that matters is the last one,' said Harry Rex. 'It revokes all prior wills, so whatever the Judge put in the will I prepared is irrelevant.'

'Why can't you tell us what's in the old will?' Forrest asked.

'Because I, as a lawyer, cannot discuss a client's will.'

'But the will you prepared is no good, right?'

'Right, but I still can't talk about it.'

'That sucks,' Forrest said, and glared at Harry Rex. All three took a deep breath, then a large bite.

Ray knew in an instant that he would have to see the other will and see it soon. If it mentioned the loot hidden in the cabinet, then Harry Rex knew about it. And if he knew, then the money would quickly be removed from the trunk of the little TT convertible and repackaged in Blake & Son boxes and put back where it came from. It would then be included in the estate, which was a public record.

'Won't there be a copy of your will in his office?' Forrest asked, in the general direction of Harry Rex.

'No.'

'Are you sure?'

'I'm reasonably sure,' Harry Rex said. 'When you make a new will you physically destroy the old one. You don't want someone finding the old one and probating it. Some folks change their wills every year, and as lawyers we know to burn the old ones. The Judge was a firm believer in destroying revoked wills because he spent thirty years refereeing will contests.'

The fact that their close friend knew something about their dead father, and that he was unwilling to share it, chilled the conversation. Ray decided to wait until he was alone with Harry Rex to grill him.

'Magargel's waiting,' he said to Forrest.

'Sounds like fun.'

They rolled the handsome oak casket down the east wing of the courthouse on a funeral gurney draped with purple velvet. Mr. Magargel led while an assistant pushed. Behind the casket were Ray and Forrest, and behind them was a Boy Scout color guard with flags and pressed khaki uniforms.

Because Reuben V. Atlee had fought for his country, his casket was covered with the Stars and Stripes. And because of this a contingent of Reservists from the local armory snapped to attention when Retired Captain Atlee was stopped in the center of the courthouse rotunda. Harry Rex was waiting there, dressed in a fine black suit, standing in front of a long row of floral arrangements.

Every other lawyer in the county was present, too, and, at Harry Rex's suggestion, they were cordoned off in a special section close to the casket. All city and county officials, courthouse clerks, cops, and deputies were present, and as Harry Rex stepped forward to begin the crowd pressed closer. Above, on the second and third levels of the courthouse, another crowd leaned on the iron railings and gawked downward.

Ray wore a brand-new navy suit he'd purchased just hours earlier at Pope's, the only men's clothier in town. At $310 it was the most expensive in the store, and slashed from that hefty price was a ten percent discount that Mr. Pope insisted on giving. Forrest's new suit was dark gray. It cost $280 before the discount, and it had also been paid for by Ray. Forrest had not worn a suit in twenty years and swore he would not wear one for the funeral. Only a tongue lashing by Harry Rex got him to Pope's.

The sons stood at one end of the casket, Harry Rex at the other, and near the center of it Billy Boone, the ageless courthouse janitor, had carefully placed a portrait of Judge Atlee. It had been painted ten years earlier by a local artist, for free, and everyone knew the Judge had not been particularly fond of it. He hung it in his chambers behind his courtroom, behind a door so no one could see it. After his defeat, the county fathers placed it in the main courtroom, high above the bench.

Programs had been printed for the 'Farewell

to Judge Reuben Atlee.' Ray studied his intently because he didn't wish to look around the gathering. All eyes were on him, and Forrest. Reverend Palmer delivered a windy prayer. Ray had insisted that the ceremony be brief. There was a funeral tomorrow.

The Boy Scouts stepped forward with the flag and led the congregation in the Pledge of Allegiance, then Sister Oleda Shumpert from the Holy Ghost Church of God in Christ stepped forward and sang a mournful rendition of 'Shall We Gather at the River,' a cappella because she certainly didn't need any support. The words and melody brought tears to the eyes of many, including Forrest, who stayed close to his brother's shoulder with his chin low.

Standing next to the casket, listening to her rich voice echo upward through the rotunda, Ray for the first time felt the burden of his father's death. He thought of all the things they could have done together, now that they were men, all the things they had not done when he and Forrest were just boys. But he had lived his life and the Judge had lived his, and this had suited them both.

It wasn't fair now to relive the past just because the old man was dead. He kept telling himself this. It was only natural at death to wish he'd done more, but the truth was that the Judge had carried a grudge for years after Ray left Clanton. And, sadly, he had become a recluse since leaving the bench.

A moment of weakness, and Ray stiffened his back. He would not beat himself up because he had chosen a path that was not the one his father wanted.

Harry Rex began what he promised would be a brief eulogy. 'Today we gather here to say good-bye to an old friend,' he began. 'We all knew this day was coming, and we all prayed it would never get here.' He hit the highlights of the Judge's career, then told of his first appearance in front of the great man, thirty years ago, when Harry Rex was fresh out of law school. He was handling an uncontested divorce, which he somehow managed to lose.

Every lawyer had heard the story a hundred times, but they still managed a good laugh at the appropriate time. Ray glanced at them, then began studying them as a group. How could one small town have so many lawyers? He knew about half of them. Many of the old ones he'd known as a child and as a student were either dead or retired. Many of the younger ones he'd never seen before.

Of course they all knew him. He was Judge Atlee's boy.

Ray was slowly realizing that his speedy exit from Clanton after the funeral would only be temporary. He would be forced to return very soon, to make a brief court appearance with Harry Rex and begin probate, to prepare an inventory and do a half-dozen other duties as executor of his father's estate. That would be easy and routine and take just a few days. But weeks and perhaps months were looming out there as he tried to solve the mystery of the money.

Did one of those lawyers over there know something? The money had to originate from a judicial setting, didn't it? The Judge had no life outside of the law. Looking at them, though, Ray could not imagine a source rich enough to generate the kind of money now hidden in the trunk of his little car. They were small-town ham-and-egg lawyers, all scrambling to pay their bills and outhustle the guy next door. There was no real money over there. The Sullivan firm had eight or nine lawyers who represented the banks and insurance companies, and they earned just enough to hang out with the doctors at the country club.

There wasn't a lawyer in the county with serious cash. Irv Chamberlain over there with the thick eyeglasses and bad hairpiece owned thousands of acres handed down through generations, but he couldn't sell it because there were no buyers. Plus, it was rumored he was spending time at the new casinos in Tunica.

As Harry Rex droned on, Ray dwelt on the lawyers. Someone shared the secret. Someone knew about the money. Could it be a distinguished member of the Ford County bar?

Harry Rex's voice began to break, and it was time to quit. He thanked them all for coming and announced that the Judge would lie in state in the courthouse until 10 P.M. He directed the procession to begin where Ray and Forrest were standing. The crowd moved obediently to the east wing and formed a line that snaked its way outside.

For an hour, Ray was forced to smile and shake hands and graciously thank everyone for coming. He listened to dozens of brief stories about his father and the lives the great man had touched. He pretended to remember the names of all those who knew him. He hugged old ladies he'd never met before. The procession moved slowly by Ray and Forrest, then to the casket, where each person would stop and gaze forlornly at the Judge's bad portrait, then to the west wing where registers were waiting. Harry Rex moved about, working the crowd like a politician.

At some point during the ordeal, Forrest disappeared. He mumbled something to Harry Rex about going home, to Memphis, and something about being tired of death.

Finally, Harry Rex whispered to Ray, 'There's a line around the courthouse. You could be here all night.'

'Get me out of here,' Ray whispered back.

'You need to go to the rest room?' Harry Rex asked, just loud enough for those next in line to hear.

'Yes,' Ray said, already stepping away. They eased back, whispering importantly, and ducked into a narrow hallway. Seconds later they emerged behind the courthouse.

They drove away, in Ray's car of course, first circling the square and taking in the scene. The flag in front of the courthouse was at half-mast. A large crowd waited patiently to pay their respects to the Judge.

Chapter 10

Twenty-four hours in Clanton, and Ray was desperate to leave. After the wake, he ate dinner with Harry Rex at Claude's, the black diner on the south side of the square where the Monday special was barbecued chicken and baked beans so spicy they served ice tea by the half-gallon. Harry Rex was reveling in the success of his grand send-off for the Judge and after dinner was anxious to return to the courthouse and monitor the rest of the wake.

Forrest had evidently left town for the evening Ray hoped he was in Memphis, at home with Ellie, behaving himself, but he knew better. How many times could he crash before he died? Harry Rex said there was a fifty-fifty chance Forrest would make it to the funeral tomorrow.

When Ray was alone he drove away, out of Clanton, headed west to no place in particular. There were new casinos along the river, seventy miles away, and with each trip back to Missis-sippi he heard more talk and gossip about the state's newest industry. Legalized gambling had arrived in the state with the lowest per capita income in the country.

An hour and a half from Clanton, he stopped for gas and as he pumped it he noticed a new motel across the highway. Everything was new in what had recently been cotton fields. New roads, new motels, fast-food restaurants, gas stations, billboards, all spillover from the casinos a mile away.

The motel had rooms on two levels, with doors that opened to face the parking lot. It appeared to be a slow night. He paid $39.99 for a double on the ground level, around back where there were no other cars or trucks. He parked the Audi as close as possible to his room, and within seconds had the three garbage bags inside.

The money covered one bed. He did not stop to admire it because he was convinced it was dirty. And it was probably marked in some way. Maybe it was counterfeit. Whatever it was, it was not his to keep.

All the bills were one-hundred-dollar notes, some brand new and never used, others passed around a little. None were worn badly, and none were dated before 1986 or after 1994. About half were banded together in two-thousand-dollar stacks, and Ray counted those first – one hundred thousand dollars in one-hundred-dollar bills was about fifteen inches high. He counted the money from one bed, then arranged it on the other in neat rows and sections. He was very deliberate, time was of no concern. As he touched the money, he rubbed it between his forefingers and thumbs and even smelled it to see if it was counterfeit. It certainly appeared to be real.

Thirty-one sections, plus a few leftovers – $3,118,000 to be exact. Retrieved like buried treasure from the crumbling home of a man who had earned less than half that during his lifetime.

It was impossible not to admire the fortune spread before him. How many times in his life would he gaze upon three million bucks? How many others ever got the chance? Ray sat in a chair with his face in his hands, staring at the tidy rows of cash, dizzy with thoughts of where it came from and where it was headed.

A slamming car door somewhere outside jolted him back. This would be an excellent place to get robbed. When you travel around with millions in cash everybody becomes a potential thief.

He rebagged it, stuffed it back into the trunk of his car, and drove to the nearest casino.

His involvement with gambling was limited to a weekend junket to Atlantic City with two other law professors, both of whom had read a book on successful crap shooting and were convinced they could beat the house. They did not. Ray had rarely played cards. He found a home at the five-dollar blackjack table, and after two miserable days in a noisy dungeon he cleared sixty dollars and vowed not to return. His colleagues' losses were never nailed down, but he learned that those who gamble quite often lie about their success.

For a Monday night, there was a respectable crowd at the Santa Fe Club, a hastily built box the size of a football field. A ten-floor tower attached to it housed the guests, mostly retirees from up North who had never dreamed of setting foot in Mississippi but were now lured by unlimited slots and free gin while they gambled.

In his pocket he had five bills taken from five different sections of the loot he'd counted in the motel room. He walked to an empty blackjack table where the dealer was half-asleep and placed the first bill on the table. 'Play it,' he said.

'Playing a hundred,' the dealer said over her shoulder, where no one was there to hear it. She picked up the bill, rubbed it with little interest, then put it in play.

It must be real, he thought, and relaxed a little. She sees them all day long. She shuffled one deck, dealt the cards, promptly hit twenty-four, then took the bill from Judge Atlee's buried treasure and put down two black chips. Ray played them both, two hundred dollars a bet, nerves of steel. She dealt the cards quickly, and with fifteen showing she hit a nine. Ray now had four black chips. In less than a minute he'd won three hundred dollars.

Rattling the four black chips in his pocket, he strolled through the casino, first through the slots where the crowd was older and subdued, almost brain-dead as they sat on their stools, pulling the arm down again and again, staring sadly at the screens. At the craps table, the dice were hot and a rowdy bunch of rednecks were hollering instructions that made no sense to him. He watched for a moment, completely bewildered by the dice and the bets and the chips changing hands.

At another empty blackjack table, he tossed down the second hundred-dollar bill, more like a seasoned gambler now. The dealer pulled it close to his face, held it up to the lights, rubbed it, and took it a few steps over to the pit boss, who was immediately distrustful of it. The pit boss produced a magnifying device that he stuck in his left eye and examined the bill like a surgeon. Just as Ray was about to break and bolt through the crowd, he heard one of them say, 'It's good.' He wasn't sure which one said it because he was looking wildly around the casino for armed guards. The dealer returned to the table and placed the suspicious money in front of Ray, who said, 'Play it.' Seconds later, the queen of hearts and the king of spades were staring at Ray, and he'd won his third hand in a row.

Since the dealer was wide awake and his supervisor had done a close inspection, Ray decided to settle the matter once and for all. He pulled the other three hundred-dollar bills from his pocket and laid them on the table. The dealer inspected each carefully, then shrugged and said, 'You want change?'

'No, play them.'

'Playing three hundred cash,' the dealer said loudly, and the pit boss loomed over his shoulder.

Ray stood on a ten and a six. The dealer hit on a ten and a four, and when he turned over the jack of diamonds, Ray won his fourth straight hand. The cash disappeared and was replaced with six black chips. Ray now had ten, a thousand dollars, and he also had the knowledge that the other thirty thousand bills stuffed into the back of his car were not counterfeit. He left one chip for the dealer and went to find a beer.

The sports bar was elevated a few feet, so that if you wanted you could have a drink and take in all the action on the floor. Or you could watch pro baseball or NASCAR reruns or bowling on any of the dozen screens. But you couldn't gamble on the games; it wasn't allowed yet.

He was aware of the risks the casino posed. Now that the money was real, the next question was whether it was marked in some way. The suspicions of the second dealer and his supervisor would probably be enough to get the bills examined by the boys upstairs. They had Ray on video, he was certain, same as everybody else. Casino surveillance was extensive; he knew that from his two bright pals who'd planned to break the bank at the craps table.

If the money set off alarms, they could easily find him. Couldn't they?

But where else could he get the money examined? Walk in the First National in Clanton and hand the teller a few of the bills? 'Mind taking a look at these, Mrs. Dempsey, see if they're real or not?' No teller in Clanton had ever seen counterfeit money, and by lunch the entire town would know Judge Atlee's boy was sneaking around with a pocketful of suspicious money.

He'd thought of waiting until he was back in Virginia. He would go to his lawyer who could find an expert to examine a sample of the money, all nice and confidential. But he couldn't wait that long. If the money was fake, he'd burn it. Otherwise, he wasn't sure what to do with it.

He drank his beer slowly, giving them time to send down a couple of goons in dark suits who would walk up and say, 'Gotta minute?' They couldn't work that fast, and Ray knew it. If the money was marked, it would take days to link it to wherever it came from.

Suppose he got caught with marked money. What was his crime? He had taken it from his deceased father's house, a place that had been willed to him and his brother. He was the executor of the estate, soon to be charged with the responsibility of protecting its assets. He had months to report it to both the probate court and the tax authorities. If the Judge had somehow accumulated the money by illegal means, then sorry, he's dead now. Ray had done nothing wrong, at least for the moment.

He took his winnings back to the first blackjack table and placed a five-hundred-dollar bet. The dealer got the attention of her supervisor, who ambled over with his knuckles to his mouth and one finger tapping an ear, smugly, as if five hundred dollars on one hand of blackjack happened all the time at the Santa Fe Club. He was dealt an ace and a king, and the dealer slid over seven hundred fifty dollars.

'Would you like something to drink?' asked the pit boss, all smiles and bad teeth.

'Beck's beer,' Ray said, and a cocktail waitress appeared from nowhere.

He bet a hundred dollars on the next hand and lost. Then quickly he slid three chips out for the next hand, which he won. He won eight of the next ten hands, alternating his bets from a hundred to five hundred dollars as if he knew precisely what he was doing. The pit boss lingered behind the dealer. They had a potential card counter on their hands, a professional blackjack player, one to be watched and filmed. The other casinos would be notified.

If they only knew.

He lost consecutive bets of two hundred dollars, then just for the hell of it pushed ten chips out for a bold and reckless wager of a thousand dollars. He had another three million in the trunk. This was chicken feed. When two queens landed next to his chips, he kept a perfect poker face as if he'd been winning like this for years.

'Would you like dinner, sir?' the pit boss asked.

'No,' Ray said.

'Can we get anything for you?'

'A room would be nice.'

'King or a suite?'

A jerk would've said, 'A suite, of course,' but Ray caught himself. 'Any room will be fine,' he said. He'd had no plans to stay there, but after two beers he thought it best not to drive. What if he got stopped by a rural deputy? And what would the deputy do if he searched the trunk?

'No problem, sir,' said the pit boss. 'I'll get you checked in.'

For the next hour he broke even. The cocktail waitress stopped by every five minutes, pushing beverages, trying to loosen him up, but Ray nursed the first beer. During a shuffle, he counted thirty-nine black chips.

At midnight he began yawning, and he remembered how little he'd slept the night before. The room key was in his pocket. The table had a thousand-dollar limit per hand; otherwise he would've played it all at one time and gone down in a blaze of glory. He placed ten black chips in the circle and with an audience hit blackjack. Another ten chips, and the dealer blew it with twenty-two. He gathered his chips, left four for the dealer, and went to the cashier. He'd been in the casino for three hours.

From his fifth-floor room he could see the parking lot, and because his sports car was within view he felt compelled to watch it. As tired as he was, he could not fall asleep. He pulled a chair to the window and tried to doze, but couldn't stop thinking.

Had the Judge discovered the casinos? Could gambling be the source of his fortune, a lucrative little vice that he'd kept to himself?

The more Ray told himself that the idea was too far-fetched, the more convinced he became that he'd found the source of the money. To his knowledge, the Judge had never played the stock market, and if he had, if he'd been another Warren Buffett, why would he take his profits in cash and hide it under the bookshelves? Plus, the paperwork would be thick.

If he'd lived the double life of a judge on the take, there wasn't three million dollars to steal on the court dockets in rural Mississippi. And taking bribes would involve too many other people.

It had to be gambling. It was a cash business. Ray had just won six thousand dollars in one night. Sure it was blind luck, but wasn't all gaming? Perhaps the old man had a knack for cards or dice. Maybe he hit one of the big jackpots in the slot machines. He lived alone and answered to no one.

He could've pulled it off.

But three million dollars over seven years?

Didn't the casinos require paperwork for substantial winnings? Tax forms and such?

And why hide it? Why not give it away like the rest of his money?

Shortly after three, Ray gave it up and left his complimentary room. He slept in his car until sunrise.

Chapter 11

The front door was slightly cracked, and at eight o'clock in the morning with no one living there it was indeed an ominous sign. Ray stared at it for a long minute, not certain if he wanted to step inside but knowing he had no choice. He shoved it wider, clenched his fists as if the thief just might still be in there, and took a very deep breath. It swung open, creaking every inch of the way, and when the light fell upon the stacks of boxes in the foyer Ray saw muddy footprints on the floor. The assailant had entered from the rear lawn where there was mud and for some reason had chosen to leave through the front door.

Ray slowly removed the pistol from his pocket.

The twenty-seven green Blake & Son boxes were scattered around the Judge's study. The sofa was overturned. The doors to the cabinet below the bookshelves were open. The rolltop appeared to be unmolested but the papers from the desk were scattered on the floor.

The intruder had removed the boxes, opened them, and finding them empty, had evidently stomped them and thrown them in a fit of rage. As still as things were, Ray felt the violence and it made him weak.

The money could get him killed.

When he was able to move he fixed the sofa and picked up the papers. He was gathering boxes when he heard something on the front porch. He peeked through the window and saw an old woman tapping on the front door.

Claudia Gates had known the Judge like no one else. She had been his court reporter, secretary, driver, and many other things, according to gossip that had been around since Ray was a small boy. For almost thirty years, she and the Judge had traveled the six counties of the 25th District together, often leaving Clanton at seven in the morning and returning long after dark. When they were not in court, they shared the Judge's office in the courthouse, where she typed the transcripts while he did his paperwork.

A lawyer named Turley had once caught them in a compromising position during lunch at the office, and he made the awful mistake of telling others about it. He lost every case in Chancery Court for a year and couldn't buy a client. It took four years for Judge Atlee to get him disbarred.

'Hello, Ray,' she said through the screen. 'May I come in?'

'Sure,' he said, and opened the door wider.

Ray and Claudia had never liked each other. He had always felt that she was getting the attention and affection that he and Forrest were not, and she viewed him as a threat as well. When it came to Judge Atlee, she viewed everyone as a threat.

She had few friends and even fewer admirers. She was rude and callous because she spent her life listening to trials. And she was arrogant because she whispered to the great man.

'I'm very sorry,' she said.

'So am I.'

As they walked by the study, Ray pulled the door closed and said, 'Don't go in there.' Claudia did not notice the intruder's footprints.

'Be nice to me, Ray,' she said.

'Why?'

They went to the kitchen, where he put up some coffee and they sat across from each other. 'Can I smoke?' she asked.

'I don't care,' he said. Smoke till you choke, old gal. His father's black suits had always carried the acrid smell of her cigarettes. He'd allowed her to smoke in the car, in chambers, in his office, probably in bed. Everywhere but the courtroom.

The raspy breath, the gravelly voice, the countless wrinkles clustered around the eyes, ah, the joys of tobacco.

She'd been crying, which was not an insignificant event in her life. When he was clerking for his father one summer, Ray had had the misfortune of sitting through a gut-wrenching child abuse case. The testimony had been so sad and pitiful that everyone, including the Judge and all the lawyers, were moved to tears. The only dry eyes in the courtroom belonged to old stone-faced Claudia.

'I can't believe he's dead,' she said, then blew a puff of smoke toward the ceiling.

'He's been dying for five years, Claudia. This is no surprise.'

'It's still sad.'

'It's very sad, but he was suffering at the end. Death was a blessing.'

'He wouldn't let me come see him.'

'We're not rehashing history, okay?'

The history, depending on which version you believed, had kept Clanton buzzing for almost two decades. A few years after Ray's mother died, Claudia divorced her husband for reasons that were never clear. One side of town believed the Judge had promised to marry her after her divorce. The other side of town believed the Judge, forever an Atlee, never intended to marry such a commoner as Claudia, and that she got a divorce because her husband caught her fooling around with yet another man. Years passed with the two enjoying the benefits of married life, except for the paperwork and actual cohabitation. She continued to press the Judge to get married, he continued to postpone things. Evidently, he was getting what he wanted.

Finally she put forth an ultimatum, which proved to be a bad strategy. Ultimatums did not impress Reuben Atlee. The year before he got booted from office, Claudia married a man nine years younger. The Judge promptly fired her, and the coffee shops and knitting clubs talked of nothing else. After a few rocky years, her younger man died. She was lonely, so was the Judge. But she had betrayed him by remarrying, and he never forgave her.

'Where's Forrest?' she asked.

'He should be here soon.'

'How is he?'

'He's Forrest.'

'Do you want me to leave?'

'It's up to you.'

'I'd rather talk to you, Ray. I need to talk to someone.'

'Don't you have friends?'

'No. Reuben was my only friend.'

He cringed when she called him Reuben. She stuck the cigarette between her gluey red lips, a pale red for mourning, not the bright red she was once known for. She was at least seventy, but wearing it well. Still straight and slim, and wearing a tight dress that no other seventy-year-old woman in Ford County would attempt. She had diamonds in her ears and one on her finger, though he couldn't tell if they were real. She was also wearing a pretty gold pendant and two gold bracelets.

She was an aging tart, but still an active volcano. He would ask Harry Rex whom she was seeing these days.

He poured more coffee and said, 'What would you like to talk about?'

'Reuben.'

'My father is dead. I don't like history.'

'Can't we be friends?'

'No. We've always despised each other. We're not going to kiss and hug now, over the casket. Why would we do that?'

'I'm an old woman, Ray.'

'And I live in Virginia. We'll get through the funeral today, then we'll never see each other again. How's that?'

She lit another one and cried some more. Ray was thinking about the mess in the study, and what he would say to Forrest if he barged in now and saw the footprints and scattered boxes. And if Forrest saw Claudia sitting at the table, he might go for her neck.

Though they had no proof, Ray and Forrest had long suspected that the Judge had paid her more than the going rate for court reporters. Something extra, in exchange for the extras she was providing. It was not difficult holding a grudge.

'I want something to remember, that's all,' she said.

111

'You want to remember me?'

'You are your father, Ray. I'm clinging here.'

'Are you looking for money?'

'No.'

'Are you broke?'

'I'm not set for life, no.'

'There's nothing here for you.'

'Do you have his will?'

'Yes, and your name is not mentioned.'

She cried again, and Ray began a slow burn. She got the money twenty years ago when he was waiting tables and living on peanut butter and trying to survive another month of law school without getting evicted from his cheap apartment. She always had a new Cadillac when he and Forrest were driving wrecks. They were expected to live like impoverished gentry while she had the wardrobe and the jewelry.

'He always promised to take care of me,' she said.

'He broke it off years ago, Claudia. Give it up.'

'I can't. I loved him too much.'

'It was sex and money, not love. I'd rather not talk about it.'

'What's in the estate?'

'Nothing. He gave it all away.'

'He what?'

'You heard me. You know how he loved to write checks. It got worse after you left the picture.'

112

'What about his retirement?' She wasn't crying now, this was business. Her green eyes were dry and glowing.

'He cashed in the year after he left office. It was a terrible financial blunder, but he did it without my knowledge. He was mad and half-crazy. He took the money, lived on some of it, and gave the rest to the Boy Scouts, Girl Scouts, Lions Club, Sons of the Confederacy, Committee to Preserve Historic Battlefields, you name it.'

If his father had been a crooked judge, something Ray was not willing to believe, then Claudia would know about the money. It was obvious she did not. Ray never suspected she knew, because if she had then the money would not have remained hidden in the study. Let her have a rip at three million bucks and everybody in the county would know about it. If she had a dollar, you were going to see it. As pitiful as she looked across the table, Ray suspected she had very few dollars.

'I thought your second husband had some money,' he said, with a little too much cruelty.

'So did I,' she said and managed a smile. Ray chuckled a bit. Then they both laughed, and the ice thawed dramatically. She had always been known for her bluntness.

'Never found it, huh?'

'Not a dime. He was this nice-looking guy, nine years younger, you know –'

'I remember it well. A regular scandal.'

'He was fifty-one years old, a smooth talker, had a line about making money in oil. We drilled like crazy for four years and I came up with nothing.'

Ray laughed louder. He could not, at that moment, ever remember having a talk about sex and money with a seventy-year-old woman. He got the impression she had plenty of stories. Claudia's greatest hits.

'You're looking good, Claudia, you have time for another one.'

'I'm tired, Ray. Old and tired. I'd have to train him and all. It's not worth it.'

'What happened to number two?'

'He croaked with a heart attack and I didn't even find a thousand dollars,' she said.

'The Judge left six.'

'Is that all?' she asked in disbelief.

'No stocks, no bonds, nothing but an old house and six thousand dollars in the bank.'

She lowered her eyes, shook her head, and believed everything Ray was saying. She had no clue about the cash.

'What will you do with the house?'

'Forrest wants to burn it and collect the insurance.'

'Not a bad idea.'

'We'll sell it.'

There was noise on the porch, then a knock. Reverend Palmer was there to discuss the funeral service, which would begin in two hours. Claudia hugged Ray as they walked to her car.

114

She hugged him again and said good-bye. 'I'm sorry I wasn't nicer to you,' she whispered as he opened her car door.

'Good-bye, Claudia. I'll see you at the church.'

'He never forgave me, Ray.'

'I forgive you.'

'Do you really?'

'Yes. You're forgiven. We're friends now.'

'Thank you so much.' She hugged him a third time and started crying. He helped her into the car, always a Cadillac. Just before she turned the ignition, she said, 'Did he ever forgive you, Ray?'

'I don't think so.'

'I don't think so either.'

'But it's not important now. Let's get him buried.'

'He could be a mean old sumbitch, couldn't he?' she said, smiling through the tears.

Ray had to laugh. His dead father's seventy-year-old former lover had just called the great man a son of a bitch.

'Yes,' he agreed. 'He certainly could be.'

Chapter 12

They rolled Judge Atlee down the center aisle in his fine oak casket and parked him at the altar in front of the pulpit where Reverend Palmer was waiting in a black robe. The casket was left unopened, much to the disappointment of the mourners, most of whom still clung to the ancient Southern ritual of viewing the deceased one last time in a strange effort to maximize the grief. 'Hell no,' Ray had said politely to Mr. Magargel when asked about opening things up. When the pieces were in place, Palmer slowly stretched out his arms, then lowered them, and the crowd sat.

In the front pew to his right was the family, the two sons. Ray wore his new suit and looked tired. Forrest wore jeans and a black suede jacket and looked remarkably sober. Behind them were Harry Rex and the other pallbearers, and behind them was a sad collection of ancient judges, not far from the casket themselves. In the front pew to his left were all sorts of dignitaries – politicians, an ex-governor, a couple of Mississippi Supreme Court justices. Clanton had never seen such power assembled at one time.

The sanctuary was packed, with folks standing along the walls under the stained-glass windows. The balcony above was full. One floor below, the auditorium had been wired for audio and more friends and admirers were down there.

Ray was impressed by the crowd. Forrest was already looking at his watch. He had arrived fifteen minutes earlier and got cursed by Harry Rex, not Ray. His new suit was dirty, he'd said, and besides Ellie had bought him the black suede jacket years ago and she thought it would do just fine for the occasion.

She, at three hundred pounds, would not leave the house, and for that Ray and Harry Rex were grateful. Somehow she'd kept him sober, but a crash was in the air. For a thousand reasons, Ray just wanted to get back to Virginia.

The reverend prayed, a short, eloquent message of thanks for the life of a great man. Then he introduced a youth choir that had won national honors at a music competition in New York. Judge Atlee had given them three thousand dollars for the trip, according to Palmer. They sang two songs Ray had never heard before, but they sang them beautifully.

The first eulogy – and there would be only two short ones per Ray's instructions – was delivered by an old man who barely made it to the pulpit, but once there startled the crowd with a rich and powerful voice. He'd been in law school with the Judge a hundred years ago. He told two humorless stories and the potent voice began to fade.

The reverend read some scripture and delivered words of comfort for the loss of a loved one, even an old one who had lived a full life.

The second eulogy was given by a young black man named Nakita Poole, something of a legend in Clanton. Poole came from a rough family south of town, and had it not been for a chemistry teacher at the high school he would have dropped out in the ninth grade and become another statistic. The Judge met him during an ugly family matter in court, and he took an interest in the kid. Poole had an amazing capacity for science and math. He finished first in his class, applied to the best colleges, and was accepted everywhere. The Judge wrote powerful letters of recommendation and pulled every string he could grab. Nakita picked Yale, and its financial package covered everything but spending money. For four years Judge Atlee wrote him every week, and in each letter there was a check for twenty-five dollars.

'I wasn't the only one getting the letters or the checks,' he said to a silent crowd. 'There were many of us.'

Nakita was now a doctor and headed for Africa for two years of volunteer work. 'I'm gonna miss those letters,' he said, and every lady in the church was in tears.

The coroner, Thurber Foreman, was next. He'd been a fixture at funerals in Ford County for many years, and the Judge specifically wanted him to play his mandolin and sing 'Just a Closer Walk with Thee.' He sang it beautifully, and somehow managed to do so while weeping.

Forrest finally began wiping his eyes. Ray just stared at the casket, wondering where the cash came from. What had the old man done? What, exactly, did he think would happen to the money after he died?

When the reverend finished a very brief message, the pallbearers rolled Judge Atlee out of the sanctuary. Mr. Magargel escorted Ray and Forrest down the aisle and down the front steps to a limo waiting behind the hearse. The crowd spilled out and went to their cars for the ride to the cemetery.

Like most small towns, Clanton loved a funeral procession. All traffic stopped. Those not driving in the procession were on the sidewalks, standing sadly and gazing at the hearse and the endless parade of cars behind it. Every part-time deputy was in uniform and blocking something, a street, an alley, parking spaces.

The hearse led them around the courthouse, where the flag was at half-mast and the county employees lined the front sidewalk and lowered their heads. The merchants around the square came out to bid farewell to Judge Atlee.

He was laid to rest in the Atlee plot, next to his long-forgotten wife and among the ancestors he so revered. He would be the last Atlee returned to the dust of Ford County, though no one knew it. And certainly no one cared. Ray would be cremated and his ashes scattered over the Blue Ridge Mountains. Forrest admitted he was closer to death than his older brother, but he had not nailed down his final details. The only thing for certain was that he would not be buried in Clanton. Ray was lobbying for cremation. Ellie liked the idea of a mausoleum. Forrest preferred not to dwell on the subject.

The mourners crowded under and around a crimson Magargel Funeral Home tent, which was much too small. It covered the grave and four rows of folding chairs. A thousand were needed.

Ray and Forrest sat with their knees almost touching the casket and listened as Reverend Palmer wrapped it all up. Sitting in a folding chair at the edge of his father's open grave, Ray found it odd the things he thought about. He wanted to go home. He missed his classroom and his students. He missed flying and the views of the Shenandoah Valley from five thousand feet. He was tired and irritable and did not want to spend the next two hours lingering in the cemetery making small talk with people who remembered when he was born.

The wife of a Pentecostal preacher had the final words. She sang 'Amazing Grace,' and for five minutes time stood still. In a beautiful soprano, her voice echoed through the gentle hills of the cemetery, comforting the dead, giving hope to the living. Even the birds stopped flying.

An Army boy with a trumpet played 'Taps,' and everybody had a good cry. They folded the flag and handed it to Forrest, who was sobbing and sweating under the damned suede jacket. As the final notes faded into the woods, Harry Rex started bawling behind them. Ray leaned forward and touched the casket. He said a silent farewell, then rested with his elbows on his knees, his face in his hands.

The burial broke up quickly. It was time for lunch. Ray figured that if he just sat there and stared at the casket, then folks would leave him alone. Forrest flung a heavy arm across his shoulders, and together they looked as though they might stay until dark. Harry Rex regained his composure and assumed the role of family spokesman. Standing outside the tent, he thanked the dignitaries for coming, complimented Palmer on a fine service, praised the preacher's wife for such a beautiful rendition, told Claudia that she could not sit with the boys, that she needed to move along, and on and on. The gravediggers waited under a nearby tree, shovels in hand.

When everybody was gone, including Mr.

Magargel and his crew, Harry Rex fell into the chair on the other side of Forrest and for a long time the three of them sat there, staring, not wanting to leave. The only sound was that of a backhoe somewhere in the distance, waiting. But Forrest and Ray didn't care. How often do you bury your father?

And how important is time to a gravedigger?

'What a great funeral,' Harry Rex finally said. He was an expert on such matters.

'He would've been proud,' said Forrest.

'He loved a good funeral,' Ray added. 'Hated weddings though.'

'I love weddings,' said Harry Rex.

'Four or five?' asked Forrest.

'Four, and counting.

A man in a city work uniform approached and quietly asked, 'Would you like for us to lower it now?'

Neither Ray nor Forrest knew how to respond. Harry Rex had no doubt. 'Yes, please,' he said. The man turned a crank under the grave apron. Very slowly, the casket began sinking. They watched it until it came to rest deep in the red soil.

The man removed the belts, the apron, and the crank, and disappeared.

'I guess it's over,' Forrest said.

Lunch was tamales and sodas at a drive-in on the edge of town, away from the crowded places where someone would undoubtedly interrupt them with a few kind words about the Judge. They sat at a wooden picnic table under a large umbrella and watched the cars go by.

'When are you heading back?' Harry Rex asked.

'First thing in the morning,' Ray answered. 'We have some work to do.'

'I know. Let's do it this afternoon.'

'What kinda work?' Forrest asked.

'Probate stuff,' Harry Rex said. 'We'll open the estate in a couple of weeks, whenever Ray can get back. We need to go through the Judge's papers now and see how much work there is.'

'Sounds like a job for the executor.'

'You can help.'

Ray was eating and thinking about his car, which was parked on a busy street near the Presbyterian church. Surely it was safe there. 'I went to a casino last night,' he announced with his mouth full.

'Which one?' asked Harry Rex.

'Santa Fe something or other, the first one I came to. You been there?'

'I've been to all of them,' he said, as if he'd never go back. With the exception of illegal narcotics, Harry Rex had explored every vice.

'Me too,' said Forrest, a man with no exceptions.

'How'd you do?' Forrest asked.

'I won a couple of thousand at blackjack. They comped me a room.'

'I paid for that damned room,' Harry Rex said. 'Probably the whole floor.'

'I love their free drinks,' said Forrest. 'Twenty bucks a pop.'

Ray swallowed hard and decided to set the bait. 'I found some matches from the Santa Fe on the old man's desk. Was he sneaking over there?'

'Sure,' said Harry Rex. 'He and I used to go once a month. He loved the dice.'

'The old man?' Forrest asked. 'Gambling?'

'Yep.'

'So there's the rest of my inheritance. What he didn't give away, he gambled away.'

'No, he was actually a pretty good player.'

Ray pretended to be as shocked as Forrest, but he was relieved to pick up his first clue, slight as it was. It seemed almost impossible that the Judge could've amassed such a fortune shooting craps once a week.

He and Harry Rex would pursue it later.

Chapter 13

As he approached the end, the Judge had been diligent in organizing his affairs. The important records were in his study and easily found.

They went through his mahogany desk first. One drawer had ten years' worth of bank statements, all arranged nearly in chronological order. His tax returns were in another. There were thick ledger books filled with entries of the donations he'd made to everybody who'd asked. The largest drawer was filled with letter-size manila files, dozens of them. Files on property taxes, medical records, old deeds and titles, bills to pay, judicial conferences, letters from his doctors, his retirement fund. Ray flipped through the row of files without opening them, except for the bills to pay. There was one – $13.80 to Wayne's Lawnmower Repair – dated a week earlier.

'It's always weird going through the papers of someone who just died,' Harry Rex said. 'I feel dirty, like a peeping Tom.'

'More like a detective looking for clues,' Ray said. He was on one side of the desk, Harry Rex the other, their ties off and sleeves rolled up, with piles of evidence between them. Forrest was his usual helpful self. He'd drained half a six-pack for dessert after lunch, and was now snoring it off in the swing on the front porch.

But he was there, instead of lost in one of his patented binges. He had disappeared so many times over the years. If he'd blown off his father's funeral, no one in Clanton would've been surprised. Just another black mark against that crazy Atlee boy, another story to tell.

In the last drawer they found personal odds and ends – pens, pipes, pictures of the Judge with his cronies at bar conventions, a few photos of Ray and Forrest from years ago, his marriage license, and their mother's death certificate. In an old, unopened envelope there was her obituary clipped from the *Clanton Chronicle*, dated October 12, 1969, complete with a photograph. Ray read it and handed it to Harry Rex.

'Do you remember her?' Ray asked.

'Yes, I went to her funeral,' he said, looking at it. 'She was a pretty lady who didn't have many friends.'

'Why not?'

'She was from the Delta, and most of those folks have a good dose of blue blood. That's what the Judge wanted in a wife, but it didn't work too well around here. She thought she was marrying money. Judges didn't make squat back then, so she had to work hard at being better than everybody else.'

'You didn't like her.'

'Not particularly. She thought I was unpolished.'

'Imagine that.'

'I loved your father, Ray, but there weren't too many tears at her funeral.'

'Let's get through one funeral at a time.'

'Sorry.'

'What was in the will you prepared for him? The last one.'

Harry Rex laid the obituary on the desk and sat back in his chair. He glanced at the window behind Ray, then spoke softly. 'The Judge wanted to set up a trust so that when this place was sold the money would go there. I'd be the trustee and as such I'd have the pleasure of doling out the money to you and him.' He nodded toward the porch. 'But his first hundred thousand would be paid back to the estate. That's how much the Judge figured Forrest owed him.'

'What a disaster.'

'I tried to talk him out of it.'

'Thank God he burned it.'

'Yes indeed. He knew it was a bad idea, but he was trying to protect Forrest from himself.'

'We've been trying for twenty years.'

'He thought of everything. He was going to leave it all to you, cut him out completely, but he knew that would only cause friction. Then he got mad because neither of you would ever live here, so he asked me to do a will that gave the house to the church. He never signed it, then Palmer pissed him off over the death penalty and he ditched that idea, said he would have it sold after his death and give the money to charity.' He stretched his arms upward until his spine popped. Harry Rex had had two back surgeries and was seldom comfortable. He continued. 'I'm guessing the reason he called you and Forrest home was so the three of you could decide what to do with the estate.'

'Then why did he do a last-minute will?'

'We'll never know, will we? Maybe he got tired of the pain. I suspect he'd grown fond of the morphine, like most folks at the end. Maybe he knew he was about to die.'

Ray looked into the eyes of General Nathan Bedford Forrest, who'd been gazing sternly on the Judge's study from the same perch for almost a century. Ray had no doubt that his father had chosen to die on the sofa so that the general could help him through it. The general knew. He knew how and when the Judge died. He knew where the cash came from. He knew who had broken in last night and trashed the office.

'Did he ever include Claudia in anything?' Ray asked.

'Never. He could hold a grudge, you know that.'

'She stopped by this morning.'

'What'd she want?'

'I think she was looking for money. She said the Judge had always promised to take care of her, and she wanted to know what was in the will.'

'Did you tell her?'

'With pleasure.'

'She'll be all right, never worry about that woman. You remember old Walter Sturgis, out from Karraway, a dirt contractor for years, tight as a tick?' Harry Rex knew everybody in the county, all thirty thousand souls – blacks, whites, and now the Mexicans.

'I don't think so.'

'He's rumored to have a half a million bucks in cash, and she's after it. Got the ole boy wearing golf shirts and eating at the country club. He told his buddies he takes Viagra every day.'

'Atta boy.'

'She'll break him.'

Forrest shifted somehow in the porch swing and the chains creaked. They waited a moment, until all was quiet out there. Harry Rex opened a file and said, 'Here's the appraisal. We had it done late last year by a guy from Tupelo, probably the best appraiser in north Mississippi.'

'How much?'

'Four hundred thousand.'

'Sold.'

'I thought he was high. Of course, the Judge thought the place was worth a million.'

'Of course.'

'I figure three hundred is more likely.'

'We won't get half that much. What's the appraisal based on?'

'It's right here. Square footage, acreage, charm, comps, the usual.'

'Give me a comp.'

Harry Rex flipped through the appraisal. 'Here's one. A house about the same age, same size, thirty acres, on the edge of Holly Springs, sold two years ago for eight hundred grand.'

'This is not Holly Springs.'

'No, it's not.'

'That's an antebellum town, with lots of old houses.'

'You want me to sue the appraiser?'

'Yeah, let's go after him. What would you give for this place?'

'Nothing. You want a beer?'

'No.'

Harry Rex lumbered into the kitchen, and returned with a tall can of Pabst Blue Ribbon. 'I don't know why he buys this stuff,' he mumbled, then gulped a fourth of it.

'Always been his brand.'

Harry Rex peeked through the blinds and saw nothing but Forrest's feet hanging off the swing. 'I don't think he's too worried about his father's estate.'

'He's like Claudia, just wants a check.'

'Money would kill him.'

It was reassuring to hear Harry Rex share this belief. Ray waited until he returned to the desk because he wanted to watch his eyes carefully. 'The Judge earned less than nine thousand dollars last year,' Ray said, looking at a tax return.

'He was sick,' Harry Rex said, stretching and twisting his substantial back, then sitting down. 'But he was hearing cases until this year.'

'What kind of cases?'

'All sorts of stuff. We had this Nazi right-wing governor a few years back –'

'I remember him.'

'Liked to pray all the time when he campaigned, family values, anti-everything but guns. Turned out he liked the ladies, his wife caught him, big stink, really juicy stuff. The local judges down in Jackson wanted no part of the case for obvious reasons, so they asked the Judge to ride in and referee things.'

'Did it go to trial?'

'Oh hell yeah, big ugly trial. The wife had the goods on the governor, who thought he could intimidate the Judge. She got the governor's house and most of the money. Last I heard he was living above his brother's garage, with bodyguards, of course.'

'Did you ever see the old man intimidated?'

'Never. Not once in thirty years.'

Harry Rex worked on his beer and Ray looked at another tax return. Things were quiet, and when he heard Forrest snore again, Ray said, 'I found some money, Harry Rex.'

His eyes conveyed nothing. No conspiracy, no surprise, no relief. They didn't blink and they didn't stare. He waited, then finally shrugged and said, 'How much?'

'A boxful.' The questions would follow, and Ray had tried to predict them.

Again Harry Rex waited, then another innocent shrug. 'Where?'

'Over there, in that cabinet behind the sofa. It was cash in a box, over ninety thousand bucks.'

So far he had not told a lie. He certainly hadn't given the entire truth, but he wasn't lying. Not yet.

'Ninety thousand bucks?' Harry Rex said, a little too loudly and Ray nodded toward the porch.

'Yes, in one-hundred-dollar bills,' he said in a lower voice. 'Any idea where it came from?'

Harry Rex gulped from the can, then squinted his eyes at the wall and finally said, 'Not really.'

'Gambling? You said he could throw the dice.'

Another sip. 'Yeah, maybe. The casinos opened six or seven years ago, and he and I would go once a week, at least in the beginning."

'You stopped?'

'I wish. Between me and you, I was going all the time. I was gambling so much I didn't want the Judge to know it, so whenever he and I went

I always played it light. Next night, I'd sneak over and lose my ass again.'

'How much did you lose?'

'Let's talk about the Judge.'

'Okay, did he win?'

'Usually. On a good night he'd win a coupla thousand.'

'On a bad night?'

'Five hundred, that was his limit. If he was losin', he knew when to quit. That's the secret to gamblin', you gotta know when to quit, and you gotta have the guts to walk away. He did. I did not.'

'Did he go without you?'

'Yeah, I saw him once. I sneaked over one night and picked a new casino, hell they got fifteen now, and while I was playin' blackjack things got hot at a craps table not too far away. In the thick of things, I saw Judge Atlee. Had on a baseball cap so folks wouldn't recognize him. His disguises didn't always work because I'd hear things around town. A lot of folks go to the casinos and there were sightings.'

'How often did he go?'

'Who knows? He answered to no one. I had a client, one of those Higginbotham boys who sell used cars, and he told me he saw old Judge Atlee at the craps table at three o'clock one mornin' at Treasure Island. So I figured the Judge sneaked over at odd hours so folks wouldn't see him.'

Ray did some quick math. If the Judge gambled three times a week for five years and won two thousand dollars every time, his winnings would have been somewhere around one and a half million.

'Could he have rat-holed ninety thousand?' Ray asked. It sounded like such a small amount.

'Anything's possible, but why hide it?'

'You tell me.'

They pondered this for a while. Harry Rex finished the beer and lit a cigar. A sluggish ceiling fan above the desk pushed the smoke around. He shot a cloud of exhaust toward the fan and said, 'You gotta pay taxes on your winnings, and since he didn't want anybody to know about his gambling, maybe he just kept it all quiet.'

'But don't the casinos require paperwork if you win a certain amount?'

'I never saw any damned paperwork.'

'But if you'd won?'

'Yeah, they do. I had a client who won eleven thousand at the five-dollar slots. They gave him a form ten-ninety-nine, a notice to the IRS.'

'What about shooting craps?'

'If you cash in more than ten thousand in chips at one time, then there's paperwork. Keep it under ten, and there's nothin'. Same as cash transactions at a bank.'

'I doubt if the Judge wanted records.'

'I'm sure he did not.'

'He never mentioned any cash when y'all were doing his wills?'

'Never. The money is a secret, Ray. I can't

134

explain it. I have no idea what he was thinkin'. Surely he knew it would be found.'

'Right. The question now is what do we do with it.'

Harry Rex nodded and stuck the cigar in his mouth. Ray leaned back and watched the fan. For a long time they contemplated what to do with the money. Neither wanted to suggest that they simply continue to hide it. Harry Rex decided to fetch another beer. Ray said he'd take one too. As the minutes passed it became obvious that the money would not be discussed again, not that day. In a few weeks, when the estate was opened and an inventory of assets was filled, they could visit the issue again. Or perhaps they would not.

For two days, Ray had debated whether or not to tell Harry Rex about the cash, not the entire fortune, but just a sample of it. After doing so, there were more questions than answers.

Little light had been shed on the money. The Judge enjoyed the dice and was good at gambling, but it seemed unlikely he could have cleared $3.1 million in seven years. And to do so without creating paperwork and leaving a trail seemed impossible.

Ray returned to the tax records while Harry Rex plowed through the ledgers of donations. 'Which CPA are you gonna use?' Ray asked after a long period of silence.

'There are several.'

'Not local.'

'No, I stay away from the guys around here. It's a small town.'

'Looks to me like the records are in good shape,' Ray said, closing a drawer.

'It'll be easy, except for the house.'

'Let's put it on the market, the sooner the better. It won't be a quick sell.'

'What's the asking price?'

'Let's start at three hundred.'

'Are we spending money to fix it up?'

'There is no money, Harry Rex.'

Just before dark, Forrest announced he was tired of Clanton, tired of death, tired of hanging around a depressing old house he had never particularly cared for, tired of Harry Rex and Ray, and that he was going home to Memphis where wild women and parties were waiting.

'When are you coming back?' he asked Ray.

'Two or three weeks.'

'For probate?'

'Yes,' Harry Rex answered. 'We'll make a brief appearance before the judge. You're welcome to be there, but it's not required.'

'I don't do court. Been there enough.'

The brothers walked down the drive to Forrest's car. 'You okay?' Ray asked, but only because he felt compelled to show concern.

'I'm fine. See you, Bro,' Forrest said, in a hurry to leave before his brother blurted something stupid. 'Call me when you come back,' he said. He started the car and drove away. Ray knew he would pull over somewhere between Clanton and Memphis, either at a joint with a bar and a pool table, or maybe just a beer store where he would buy a case and slug it as he drove. Forrest had survived his father's funeral in an impressive way, but the pressure had been building. The meltdown would not be pretty.

Harry Rex was hungry, as usual, and asked if Ray wanted fried catfish. 'Not really,' he answered.

'Good, there's a new place on the lake.'

'What's it called?'

'Jeter's Catfish Shack.'

'You're kidding.'

'No, it's delicious.'

They dined on an empty deck jutting over a swamp, on the backwaters of the lake. Harry Rex ate catfish twice a week; Ray, once every five years. The cook was heavy on the batter and peanut oil, and Ray knew it would be a long night, for several reasons.

He slept with a loaded gun in the bed of his old room, upstairs, with the windows and doors locked, and the three garbage bags packed with money at his feet. With such an arrangement, it was difficult to look around in the dark and conjure up any pleasant childhood memories that would normally be just under the surface. The house had been dark and cold back then, especially after his mother died.

Instead of reminiscing, he tried to sleep by

counting little round black chips, a hundred bucks each, hauled by the Judge from the tables to the cashiers. He counted with imagination and ambition, and he got nowhere near the fortune he was in bed with.

Chapter 14

The Clanton square had three cafés, two for the whites and one for the blacks. The Tea Shoppe crowd leaned toward banking and law and retail, more of a white-collar bunch, where the chatter was a bit heavier – the stock market, politics, golf. Claude's, the black diner, had been around for forty years and had the best food.

The Coffee Shop was favored by the farmers, cops, and factory workers who talked football and bird hunting. Harry Rex preferred it, as did a few other lawyers who liked to eat with the people they represented. It opened at five every morning but Sunday, and was usually crowded by six. Ray parked near it on the square and locked his car. The sun was inching above the hills to the east. He would drive fifteen hours or so and hopefully be home by midnight.

Harry Rex had a table in the window and a Jackson newspaper that had already been rearranged and folded to the point of being useless to anyone else. 'Anything in the news?' Ray asked. There was no television at Maple Run.

'Not a damned thang,' Harry Rex grumbled with his eyes glued to the editorials. 'I'll send you all the obituaries.' He slid across a crumpled section the size of a paperback. 'You wanna read this?'

'No, I need to go.'

'You're eating first?'

'Yes.'

'Hey, Dell!' Harry Rex yelled across the café. The counter and booths and other tables were crowded with men, only men, all eating and talking.

'Dell is still here?' Ray asked.

'She doesn't age,' Harry Rex said, waving. 'Her mother is eighty and her grandmother is a hundred. She'll be here long after we're buried.'

Dell did not appreciate being yelled at. She arrived with a coffeepot and an attitude, which vanished when she realized who Ray was. She hugged him and said, 'I haven't seen you in twenty years.' Then she sat down, clutched his arm, and began saying how sorry she was about the Judge.

'Wasn't it a great funeral?' Harry Rex said.

'I can't remember a finer one,' she said, as if Ray was supposed to be both comforted and impressed.

'Thank you,' he said, his eyes watering not from sadness but from the medley of cheap perfumes swirling about her.

Then she jumped up and said, 'What're y'all eatin'? It's on the house.'

Harry Rex decided on pancakes and sausage, for both of them, a tall stack for him, short for Ray. Dell disappeared, a thick cloud of fragrances lingering behind.

'You got a long drive. Pancakes'll stick to your ribs.'

After three days in Clanton, everything was sticking to his ribs. Ray looked forward to some long runs in the countryside around Charlottesville, and to much lighter cuisine.

To his great relief, nobody else recognized him. There were no other lawyers in the Coffee Shop at that hour, and no one else who'd known the Judge well enough to attend his funeral. The cops and mechanics were too busy with their jokes and gossip to look around. Remarkably, Dell kept her mouth shut. After the first cup of coffee, Ray relaxed and began to enjoy the waves of conversation and laughter around him.

Dell was back with enough food for eight; pancakes, a whole hog's worth of sausage, a tray of hefty biscuits with a bowl of butter, and a bowl of somebody's homemade jam. Why would anyone need biscuits to eat with pancakes? She patted his shoulder again and said, 'And he was such a sweet man.' Then she was gone.

'Your father was a lot of things,' Harry Rex said, drowning his hotcakes with at least a quart of somebody's homemade molasses. 'But he wasn't sweet.'

'No he was not,' Ray agreed. 'Did he ever come in here?'

'Not that I recall. He didn't eat breakfast, didn't like crowds, hated small talk, preferred to sleep as late as possible. I don't think this was his kind of place. For the past nine years, he hasn't been seen much around the square.'

'Where'd Dell meet him?'

'In court. One of her daughters had a baby. The daddy already had a family. A real mess.' He somehow managed to shovel into his mouth a serving of pancakes that would choke a horse. Then a bite of sausage.

'And of course you were in the middle of it.'

'Of course. Judge treated her right.' Chomp, chomp.

Ray felt compelled to take a large bite of his food. With molasses dripping everywhere, he leaned forward and lifted a heavy fork to his mouth.

'The Judge was a legend, Ray, you know that. Folks around here loved him. He never got less than eighty percent of the vote in Ford County.'

Ray nodded as he worked on the pancakes. They were hot and buttery, but not particularly tasty.

'If we spend five thousand bucks on the house,' Harry Rex said without showing food, 'then we'll get it back several times over. It's a good investment.'

'Five thousand for what?'

He wiped his mouth with one long swipe. 'Clean the damned thing first. Spray it, wash it, fumigate it, clean the floors and walls and furniture, make it smell better. Then paint the outside and the downstairs. Fix the roof so the ceilings won't spot. Cut the grass, pull the weeds, just spruce it up. I can find folks around here to do it.' He thrust another serving into his jaws and waited for Ray to respond.

'There's only six thousand in the bank,' Ray said.

Dell dashed by and somehow managed to refill both coffee cups and pat Ray on the shoulder without missing a stride.

'You got more in that box you found,' Harry Rex said, carving another wedge of pancakes.

'So we spend it?'

'I been thinking about it,' he said, gulping coffee. 'Fact, I's up all night thinking about it.'

'And?'

'Got two issues, one's important, the other's not.' A quick bite of modest proportions, then using the knife and fork to help him talk, he continued: 'First, where'd it come from? That's what we want to know, but it ain't really that important. If he robbed a bank, he's dead. If he hit the casinos and didn't pay taxes, he's dead. If he simply liked the smell of cash and saved it over the years, he's still dead. You follow?'

Ray shrugged as if he was waiting for something complicated. Harry Rex used the break in his monologue to eat sausage, then began stabbing the air again: 'Second, what are you going to do with it? That's what's important. We're assuming nobody knows about the money, right?'

Ray nodded and said, 'Right. It was hidden.' Ray could hear the windows being rattled. He could see the Blake & Son boxes scattered and crushed.

He couldn't help but glance through the window and look at his TT roadster, packed and ready to flee.

'If you include the money in the estate, half will go to the IRS.'

'I know that, Harry Rex. What would you do?'

'I'm not the right person to ask. I've been at war with the IRS for eighteen years, and guess who's winnin'? Not me. Screw 'em.'

'That's your advice as an attorney?'

'No, as a friend. If you want legal advice, then I will tell you that all assets must be collected and properly inventoried pursuant to the Mississippi Code, as annotated and amended.'

'Thank you.'

'I'd take twenty thousand or so, put it in the estate to pay the up-front bills, then wait a long time and give Forrest his half of the rest.'

'Now, that's what I call legal advice.'

'Nope, it's just common sense.'

The mystery of the biscuits was solved when Harry Rex attacked them. 'How 'bout a biscuit?' he said, though they were closer to Ray.

'No thanks.'

Harry Rex sliced two in half, buttered them, added a thick layer of jam, then, at the last moment, inserted a patty of sausage. 'You sure?'

'Yes, I'm sure. Could the money be marked in any way?'

'Only if it's ransom or drug money. Don't reckon Reuben Atlee was into those sorts of things, you?'

'Okay, spend five thousand.'

'You'll be pleased.'

A small man with matching khaki pants and shirt stopped at the table, and with a warm smile said, 'Excuse me, Ray, but I'm Loyd Darling.' He stuck out a hand as he spoke. 'I have a farm just east of town.'

Ray shook his hand and half-stood. Mr. Loyd Darling owned more land than anybody in Ford County. He had once taught Ray in Sunday School. 'So good to see you,' Ray said.

'Keep your seat,' he said, gently shoving Ray down by the shoulder. 'Just wanted to say how sorry I am about the Judge.'

'Thank you, Mr. Darling.'

'There was no finer man than Reuben Atlee. You have my sympathies.'

Ray just nodded. Harry Rex had stopped eating and appeared to be ready to cry. Then Loyd was gone and breakfast resumed. Harry Rex launched into a war story about IRS abuse. After another bite or two Ray was stuffed, and as he pretended to listen he thought of all the fine folks who so greatly admired his father, all the Loyd Darlings out there who revered the old man.

What if the cash didn't come from the casinos? What if a crime had been committed, some secret horrible sting perpetrated by the Judge? Sitting there among the crowd in the Coffee Shop, watching Harry Rex but not listening to him, Ray Atlee made a decision. He vowed to himself that if he ever discovered that the cash now crammed into the trunk of his car had been collected by his father in some manner that was less than ethical, then no one would ever know it. He would not desecrate the stellar reputation of Judge Reuben Atlee.

He signed a contract with himself, shook hands, made a blood oath, swore to God. Never would anyone know.

They said good-bye on the sidewalk in front of yet another law office. Harry Rex bear-hugged him, and Ray tried to return the embrace but his arms were pinned to his sides.

'I can't believe he's gone,' Harry Rex said, his eyes moist again.

'I know, I know.'

He walked away, shaking his head and fighting back tears. Ray jumped in his Audi and left the square without looking back. Minutes later he was on the edge of town, past the old drive-in where porno had been introduced, past the shoe factory where a strike had been mediated by the Judge. Past everything until he was in the country, away from the traffic, away from the legend. He glanced at his speedometer and realized he was driving almost ninety miles an hour.

Cops should be avoided, as well as rear-end collisions. The drive was long, but the timing of the arrival in Charlottesville was crucial. Too early and there would be foot traffic on the downtown mall. Too late and the night patrol might see him and ask questions.

Across the Tennessee line, he stopped for gas and a rest room break. He'd had too much coffee. And too much food. He tried to call Forrest on his cell phone, but there was no answer. He took it as neither good news or bad – with Forrest nothing was predictable.

Moving again, he kept his speed at fifty-five and the hours began to pass. Ford County faded into another lifetime. Everyone has to be from somewhere, and Clanton was not a bad place to call home. But if he never saw it again, he would not be unhappy.

Exams were over in a week, graduation the week after, then the summer break. Because he was supposed to be researching and writing, he'd have no classes to teach for the next three months. Which meant he had very little to do at all.

He would return to Clanton and take the oath as executor of his father's estate. He would make all the decisions that Harry Rex asked him to make. And he would try to solve the mystery of the money.

Chapter 15

With ample time to plan his movements, he was not surprised when nothing went right. His arrival time was suitable, 11:20 P.M., Wednesday, May 10. He had hoped to park illegally at the curb, just a few feet from the ground-level door to his apartment, but other drivers had the same idea. The curb had never been so completely blocked with a line of cars, and, to his anxious satisfaction, every one of them had a citation under a windshield wiper.

He could park in the street while he dashed back and forth, but that would invite trouble. The small lot behind his building had four spaces, one reserved for him, but they locked the gate at eleven.

So he was forced to use a dark and almost completely abandoned parking garage three blocks away, a large cavernous multilevel that was sold out during the day and eerily empty at night. He'd thought about this alternative off and on for many hours, as he drove north and east and plotted the offensive, and it was the least attractive of all options. It was plan D or E, somewhere way down the list of ways he wanted to transfer the money. He parked on level one, got out with his overnight bag, locked the car, and with great anxiety left it there. He hurried away, eyes darting around as if armed gangs were watching and waiting. His legs and back were stiff from the drive, but he had work to do.

The apartment looked precisely the same as when he'd left it, which was an odd relief. Thirty-four messages awaited him, no doubt colleagues and friends calling with their sympathies. He would listen later.

At the bottom of a tiny closet in the hall, under a blanket and a poncho and other things that had been tossed in, as opposed to being placed or stored, he found a red Wimbledon tennis bag that he hadn't touched in at least two years. Aside from luggage, which he thought would appear too suspicious, it was the largest bag he could think of.

If he'd had a gun he would've stuck it in his pocket. But crime was rare in Charlottesville, and he preferred to live without weapons. After the episode Sunday in Clanton, he was even more terrified of pistols and such. He'd left the Judge's guns hidden in a closet at Maple Run.

With the bag slung over a shoulder, he locked his door on the street and tried his best to walk casually along the downtown mall. It was well lit, there was a cop or two always watching, and the pedestrians at this hour were the wayward kids with green hair, an occasional wino, and a few stragglers working their way home. Charlottesville was a quiet town after midnight.

A thundershower had passed through not long before his arrival. The streets were wet and the wind was blowing. He passed a young couple walking hand in hand but saw no one else on the way to the garage.

He'd given some thought to simply hauling the garbage bags themselves, just throwing them over a shoulder like Santa, one at a time, and walking hurriedly from wherever he was parked to his apartment. He could move the money in three trips and cut his exposure on the street. Two things stopped him. First, what if one ripped, and a million bucks hit the pavement? Every thug and wino in town would come out of the alleys, drawn like sharks to blood. Second, the sight of anyone hauling bags of what appeared to be trash into an apartment, as opposed to away from it, might be suspicious enough to attract the attention of the police.

'What's in the bag, sir?' a cop might ask.

'Nothing. Garbage. A million dollars.' No answer seemed correct.

So the plan was to be patient, take all the time that was necessary, move the loot in small loads, and not worry about how many trips might be required because the least important factor was Ray's fatigue. He could rest later.

The terrifying part was the transferring of the

money from one bag to another while crouching over his trunk and trying not to look guilty. Fortunately, the garage was deserted. He crammed money into the tennis bag until it would barely zip, then slammed the trunk down, looked around as if he'd just smothered someone, and left.

Perhaps a third of a garbage bag – three hundred thousand dollars. Much more than enough to get him arrested or knifed. Nonchalance was what he desperately wanted, but there was nothing fluid about his steps and movements. Eyes straight ahead, though the eyes wanted to dart up and down, right and left, nothing could be missed. A frightening teenager with studs in his nose stumbled by, stoned out of his wasted mind. Ray walked even faster, not sure if he had the nerves for eight or nine more trips to the parking garage.

A drunk on a dark bench yelled something unintelligible at him. He lurched forward, then caught himself, and was thankful he had no gun. At that moment, he might've shot anything that moved. The cash got heavier with each block, but he made it without incident. He spilled the money onto his bed, locked every door possible, and took another route back to his car.

During the fifth trip, he was confronted by a deranged old man who jumped from the shadows and demanded, 'What the hell are you doing?' He was holding something dark in his hand. Ray assumed it was a weapon with which to slaughter him.

'Get out of the way,' he said as rudely as possible, but his mouth was dry.

'You keep going back and forth,' the old man yelled. He stank and his eyes were glowing like a demon's.

'Mind your own business.' Ray had never stopped walking, and the old man was in front of him, bouncing along. The village idiot.

'What's the problem?' came a clear crisp voice from behind them. Ray stopped and a policeman ambled over, nightstick in hand.

Ray was all smiles. 'Evening, Officer.' He was breathing hard and his face was sweaty.

'He's up to something!' the old man yelled. 'Keeps going back and forth, back and forth. Goes that way, the bag is empty. Goes that way, the bag is full.'

'Relax, Gilly,' the cop said, and Ray took a deeper breath. He was horrified that someone had been watching, but relieved because that someone was of Gilly's ilk. Of all the characters on the mall, Ray had never seen this one.

'What's in the bag?' the cop asked.

It was a dumb question, far into foul territory, and for a split second Ray, the law professor, considered a lecture on stops, searches, seizures, and permissible police questioning. He let it pass, though, and smoothly delivered the prepared line. 'I played tennis tonight at Boar's Head. Got a bad hamstring, so I'm just walking it off. I live over there.' He pointed to his apartment two blocks down.

The cop turned to Gilly and said, 'You can't be yelling at people, Gilly, I've told you that. Does Ted know you're out?'

'He's got something in that bag,' Gilly said, much softer. The cop was leading him away.

'Yes, it's cash,' said the cop. 'I'm sure the guy's a bank robber, and you caught him. Good work.'

'But it's empty, then it's full.'

'Good night, sir,' the officer said over his shoulder.

'Good night.' And Ray, the wounded tennis player, actually limped for half a block for the benefit of other characters lurking in the darkness. When he dumped the fifth load on his bed, he found a bottle of scotch in his small liquor cabinet and poured a stiff one.

He waited for two hours, ample time for Gilly to return to Ted, who hopefully could keep him medicated and confined for the rest of the night, and time perhaps for a shift change so a different cop would be walking the beat. Two very long hours, in which he imagined every possible scenario involving his car in the parking garage. Theft, vandalism, fire, towed away by some misguided wrecker, everything imaginable.

At 3 A.M., he emerged from his apartment wearing jeans, hiking boots, and a navy sweatshirt with VIRGINIA across the chest. He'd ditched the red tennis bag in favor of a battered leather briefcase, one that would not hold as much money but wouldn't catch the attention of the cop either. He was armed with a steak knife stuck in his belt, under the sweatshirt, ready to be withdrawn in a flash and used on the likes of Gilly or any other assailant. It was foolish and he knew it, but he wasn't himself either and he was quite aware of that. He was dead-tired, sleep-deprived for the third night in a row, just a little tipsy from three scotches, determined to get the money safely hidden, and scared of getting stopped again.

Even the winos had given up at three in the morning. The downtown streets were deserted. But as he entered the parking garage, he saw something that terrified him. At the far end of the mall, passing under a street lamp, was a group of five or six black teenagers. They were moving slowly in his general direction, yelling, talking loudly, looking for trouble.

It would be impossible to make a half-dozen more deliveries without running into them. The final plan was created on the spot.

Ray cranked the Audi and left the garage. He circled around and stopped in the street next to the cars parked illegally on the curb, close to the door to his apartment. He killed the engine and the lights, opened the trunk, and grabbed the money. Five minutes later, the entire fortune was upstairs, where it belonged.

*

At 9 A.M. the phone woke him. It was Harry Rex. 'Wake your ass up, boy,' he growled. 'How was the trip?'

Ray swung to the edge of his bed and tried to open his eyes. 'Wonderful,' he grunted.

'I talked to a Realtor yesterday, Baxter Redd, one of the better ones in town. We walked around the place, kicked the tires, you know, whatta mess. Anyway, he wants to stick to the appraised value, four hundred grand, and he thinks we can get at least two-fifty. He gets the usual six percent. You there?'

'Yeah.'

'Then say something, okay?'

'Keep going.'

'He agrees we need to spend some dough to fix it up, a little paint, a little floor wax, a good bonfire would help. He recommended a cleaning service. You there?'

'Yes.' Harry Rex had been up for hours, no doubt refueled with another feast of pancakes, biscuits, and sausage.

'Anyway, I've already hired a painter and a roofer. We'll need an infusion of capital pretty soon.'

'I'll be back in two weeks, Harry Rex, can't it wait?'

'Sure. You hungover?'

'No, just tired.'

'Well, get your ass in gear, it's after nine there.'

'Thanks.'

'Speaking of hangovers,' he said, his voice suddenly lower, his words softer, 'Forrest called me last night.'

Ray stood and arched his back. 'This can't be good,' he said.

'No, it's not. He's tanked, couldn't tell if it was booze or drugs, probably both. Whatever he's on, there's plenty of it. He was so mellow I thought he was falling asleep, then he'd fire up and cuss me.'

'What did he want?'

'Money. Not now, he says, claims he's not broke, but he's concerned about the house and the estate and wants to make sure you don't screw him.'

'Screw him?'

'He was bombed, Ray, so you can't hold it against him. But he said some pretty bad things.'

'I'm listening.'

'I'm tellin' you so you'll know, but please don't get upset. I doubt he'll remember it this mornin'.'

'Go ahead, Harry Rex.'

'He said the Judge always favored you and that's why he made you the executor of his estate, that you've always gotten more out of the old man, that it's my job to watch you and protect his interests in the estate because you'll try to screw him out of the money, and so on.'

'That didn't take long, did it? We've hardly got him in the ground.'

'No.'

'I'm not surprised.'

'Keep your guard up. He's on a binge and he might call you with the same crap.'

'I've heard it before, Harry Rex. His problems are not his fault. Somebody's always out to get him. Typical addict.'

'He thinks the house is worth a million bucks, and said it's my job to get that much for it. Otherwise, he might have to hire his own lawyer, blah, blah, blah. It didn't bother me. Again, he was blitzed.'

'He's pitiful.'

'He is indeed, but he'll bottom out and sober up in a week or so. Then I'll cuss him. We'll be fine.'

'Sorry, Harry Rex.'

'It's part of my job. Just one of the joys of practicin' law.'

Ray fixed a pot of coffee, a strong Italian blend he was quite attached to and had missed sorely in Clanton. The first cup was almost gone before his brain woke up.

Any trouble with Forrest would run its course. In spite of his many problems, he was basically harmless. Harry Rex would handle the estate and there would be an equal division of everything left over. In a year or so, Forrest would get a check for more money than he had ever seen.

The image of a cleaning service turned loose at Maple Run bothered him for a while. He could see a dozen women buzzing around like ants, happy with so much to clean. What if they stumbled upon another treasure trove fiendishly left behind by the Judge? Mattresses stuffed with cash? Closets filled with loot? But it wasn't possible. Ray had pored over every inch of the house. You find three million bucks tucked away and you get motivated to pry under every board. He'd even clawed his way through spiderwebs in the basement, a dungeon no cleaning lady would enter.

He poured another cup of strong coffee and walked to his bedroom, where he sat in a chair and stared at the piles of cash. Now what?

Through the blur of the last four days, he had concentrated only on getting the money to the spot where it was now located. Now he had to plan the next step, and he had very few ideas. It had to be hidden and protected, he knew that much for sure.

Chapter 16

There was a large floral arrangement in the center of his desk, with a sympathy card signed by all fourteen students in his antitrust class. Each had written a small paragraph of condolences, and he read them all. Beside the flowers was a stack of cards from his colleagues on the faculty.

Word spread fast that he was back, and throughout the morning the same colleagues dropped by with a quick hello, welcome back, sorry about your loss. For the most part the faculty was a close group. They could bicker with the best of them on the trivial issues of campus politics, but they were quick to circle the wagons in times of need. Ray was very happy to see them. Alex Duffman's wife sent a platter of her infamous chocolate brownies, each weighing a pound and proven to add three more to your waist. Naomi Kraig brought a small collection of roses she'd picked from her garden.

Late in the morning Carl Mirk stopped by

and closed the door. Ray's closest friend on the faculty, his journey to the law school had been remarkably similar. They were the same age, and both had fathers who were small-town judges who'd ruled their little counties for decades. Carl's father was still on the bench, and still holding a grudge because his son did not return to practice law in the family firm. It appeared, though, that the grudge was fading with the years, whereas Judge Atlee apparently carried his to his death.

'Tell me about it,' Carl said. Before long he would make the same trip back to his hometown in northern Ohio.

Ray began with the peaceful house, too peaceful, he recalled now. He described the scene when he found the Judge.

'You found him dead?' Carl asked. The narrative continued, then, 'You think he speeded things up a bit?'

'I hope so. He was in a lot of pain.'

'Wow.'

The story unfolded in great detail, as Ray remembered things he had not thought about since last Sunday. The words poured forth, the telling became therapeutic. Carl was an excellent listener.

Forrest and Harry Rex were colorfully described. 'We don't have characters like that in Ohio,' Carl said. When they told their small-town stories, usually to colleagues from the cities, they stretched the facts and the characters

161

became larger. Not so with Forrest and Harry Rex. The truth was sufficiently colorful.

The wake, the funeral, the burial. When Ray closed with 'Taps' and the lowering of the casket, both had moist eyes. Carl bounced to his feet and said, 'What a great way to go. I'm sorry.'

'Just glad it's over.'

'Welcome back. Let's do lunch tomorrow.'

'What's tomorrow?'

'Friday.'

'Lunch it is.'

For his noon antitrust class, Ray ordered pizzas from a carryout and ate them outside in the courtyard with his students. Thirteen of the fourteen were there. Eight would be graduating in two weeks. The students were more concerned about Ray and the death of his father than about their final exams. He knew that would change quickly.

When the pizza was gone, he dismissed them and they scattered. Kaley lingered behind, as she had been doing in the past months. There was a rigid no-fly zone between faculty and students, and Ray Atlee was not about to venture into it. He was much too content with his job to risk it fooling around with a student. In two weeks, though, Kaley would no longer be a student, but a graduate, and thus not covered by the rules. The flirting had picked up a bit – a serious question after class, a drop-in at his office to get a missed assignment, and always that smile with the eyes that lingered for just a second too long.

She was an average student with a lovely face and a rear-end that stopped traffic. She had played field hockey and lacrosse at Brown and kept a lean athletic figure. She was twenty-eight, a widow with no kids and loads of money she'd received from the company that made the glider her deceased husband had been flying when it cracked up a few miles off the coast at Cape Cod. They found him in sixty feet of water, still strapped in, both wings snapped in two. Ray had researched the accident report online. He'd also found the court file in Rhode Island where she had sued. The settlement gave her four million up front and five hundred thousand a year for the next twenty years. He had kept this information to himself.

After chasing the boys for the first two years of law school, she was now chasing the men. Ray knew of at least two other law professors who were getting the same lingering routine as he. One just happened to be married. Evidently, all were as wary as Ray.

They strolled into the front entrance of the law school, chatting aimlessly about the final exam. She was easing closer with each flirtation, warming up to the zone, the only one who knew where she might be headed with this.

'I'd like to go flying sometime,' she announced.

Anything but flying. Ray thought of her young

husband and his horrible death, and for a second could think of nothing to say. Finally, with a smile he said, 'Buy a ticket.'

'No, no, with you, in a small plane. Let's fly somewhere.'

'Anyplace in particular?'

'Just buzz around for a while. I'm thinking of taking lessons.'

'I was thinking of something more traditional, maybe lunch or dinner, after you graduate.' She had stepped closer, so that anyone who walked by at that moment would have no doubt that they, student and professor, were discussing illicit activity.

'I graduate in fourteen days,' she said, as if she might not be able to wait that long before they hopped in the sack.

'Then I'll ask you to dinner in fifteen days.'

'No, let's break the rule now, while I'm still a student. Let's have dinner before I graduate.'

He almost said yes. 'Afraid not. The law is the law. We're here because we respect it.'

'Oh yes. It's so easy to forget. But we have a date?'

'No, we will have a date.'

She flashed another smile and walked away. He tried mightily not to admire her exit, but it was impossible.

The rented van came from a moving company north of town, sixty dollars a day. He tried for a half-day rate because he would need it only for a few hours, but sixty it was. He drove it exactly four tenths of a mile and stopped at Chaney's Self-Storage, a sprawling arrangement of new cinder-block rectangles surrounded by chain link and shiny new razor wire. Video cameras on light poles watched his every move as he parked and walked into the office.

Plenty of space was available. A ten-by-ten bay was forty-eight dollars a month, no heating, no air, a roll-down door, and plenty of lighting.

'Is it fireproof?' Ray asked.

'Absolutely,' said Mrs. Chaney herself, fighting off the smoke from the cigarette stuck between her lips as she filled in forms. 'Nothing but concrete block.' Everything was safe at Chaney's. They featured electronic surveillance, she explained, as she waved at four monitors on a shelf to her left. On a shelf to her right was a small television wherein folks were yelling and fighting, a Springer-style gabfest that was now a brawl. Ray knew which shelf received the most attention.

'Twenty-four-hour guards,' she said, still doing the paperwork. 'Gate's locked at all times. Never had a break-in, and if one happens then we got all kinds of insurance. Sign right here. Fourteen B.'

Insurance on three million bucks, Ray said to himself as he scribbled his name. He paid cash for six months and took the keys to 14B.

He was back two hours later with six new storage boxes, a pile of old clothes, and a stick or two of worthless furniture he'd picked up at a flea market downtown for authenticity. He parked in the alley in front of 14B and worked quickly to unload and store his junk.

The cash was stuffed into forty-two-ounce freezer bags, zipped tight to keep air and water out, fifty-three in all. The freezer bags were arranged in the bottoms of the six storage boxes, then carefully covered with papers and files and research notes that Ray had until very recently deemed useful. Now his meticulous files served a much higher calling. A few old paperbacks were thrown in for good measure.

If, by chance, a thief penetrated 14B, he would probably abandon it after a cursory look into the boxes. The money was well hidden and as well protected as possible. Short of a safety deposit box in a bank, Ray could think of no better place to secure the money.

What would ultimately become of the money was a mystery that grew by the day. The fact that it was now safely tucked away in Virginia provided little comfort, contrary to what he had hoped.

He watched the boxes and the other junk for a while, not really anxious to leave. He vowed to himself that he would not stop by every day to check on things, but as soon as the vow was made he began to doubt it.

He secured the roll-down door with a new padlock. As he drove away, the guard was awake, the video cameras scanning, the gate locked.

Fog Newton was worrying about the weather. He had a student-pilot on a cross-country to Lynchburg and back, and thunderstorms were moving in quickly, according to radar. The clouds had not been expected, and no weather had been forecast during the student's preflight briefing.

'How many hours does he have?' Ray asked.

'Thirty-one,' Fog said gravely. Certainly not enough experience to handle thunderstorms. There were no airports between Charlottesville and Lynchburg, only mountains.

'You're not flying, are you?' Fog asked.

'I want to.'

'Forget it. This storm is coming together quickly. Let's go watch it.'

Nothing frightened an instructor more than a student up in heavy weather. Each cross-country training flight had to be carefully planned – route, time, fuel, weather, secondary airports, and emergency procedures. And each flight had to be approved in writing by the instructor. Fog had once grounded Ray because there was a slight chance of icing at five thousand feet, on a perfectly clear day.

They walked through the hangar to the ramp where a Lear was parking and shutting down its engines. To the west beyond the foothills was the first hint of clouds. The wind had picked up

167

noticeably. 'Ten to fifteen knots, gusting,' Fog said. 'A direct crosswind.' Ray would not want to attempt a landing in such conditions.

Behind the Lear was a Bonanza taxiing to the ramp, and as it got closer Ray noticed that it was the one he'd been coveting for the past two months. 'There's your plane,' Fog said.

'I wish,' Ray said.

The Bonanza parked and shut down near them, and when the ramp was quiet again Fog said, 'I hear he's cut the price.'

'How much?'

'Somewhere around four twenty-five. Four-fifty was a little steep.'

The owner, traveling alone, crawled out and pulled his bags from the rear. Fog was gazing at the sky and glancing at his watch. Ray kept his eyes on the Bonanza, where the owner was locking the door and putting it to rest.

'Let's take it for a spin,' Ray said.

'The Bonanza?'

'Sure. What's the rent?'

'It's negotiable. I know the guy pretty well.'

'Let's get it for a day, fly up to Atlantic City, then back.'

Fog forgot about the approaching clouds and the rookie student. He turned and looked at Ray. 'You're serious?'

'Why not? Sounds like fun.'

Aside from flying and poker, Fog had few other interests. 'When?'

'Saturday. Day after tomorrow. Leave early, come back late.'

Fog was suddenly deep in thought. He glanced at his watch, looked once more to the west, then to the south. Dick Docker yelled from a window, 'Yankee Tango is ten miles out.'

'Thank God,' Fog mumbled to himself and visibly relaxed. He and Ray walked to the Bonanza for a closer look. 'Saturday, huh?' Fog said.

'Yep, all day.'

'I'll catch the owner. I'm sure we can work a deal.'

The winds relented for a moment and Yankee Tango landed with little effort. Fog relaxed even more and managed a smile. 'Didn't know you liked the action,' he said as they walked across the ramp.

'Just a little blackjack, nothing serious,' Ray said.

Chapter 17

The solitude of a late Friday morning was broken by the doorbell. Ray had slept late, still trying to shake off the fatigue from the trip home. Three newspapers and four coffees later he was almost fully awake.

It was a FedEx box from Harry Rex, and it was filled with letters from admirers and newspaper clippings. Ray spread them on the dining table and began with the articles. The *Clanton Chronicle* ran a front-page piece on Wednesday that featured a dignified photo of Reuben Atlee, complete with black robe and gavel. The picture was at least twenty years old. The Judge's hair was thicker and darker, and he filled out the robe. The headline read JUDGE REUBEN ATLEE DEAD AT 79. There were three stories on the front page. One was a flowery obituary. One was a collection of comments from his friends. The third was a tribute to the Judge and his amazing gift of charity.

The *Ford County Times* likewise had a picture,

one taken just a few years earlier. In it Judge Atlee was sitting on his front porch holding his pipe, looking much older but offering a rare smile. He wore a cardigan and looked like a grandfather. The reporter had cajoled him into a feature with the ruse of chatting about the Civil War and Nathan Bedford Forrest. There was the hint of a book in the works, one about the general and the men from Ford County who'd fought with him.

The Atlee sons were barely mentioned in the stories about their father. Referring to one would require referring to the other, and most folks in Clanton wanted to avoid the subject of Forrest. It was painfully obvious that the sons were not a part of their father's life.

But we could've been, Ray said to himself. It was the father who'd chosen early on to have limited involvement with the sons, not the other way around. This wonderful old man who'd given so much to so many had had so little time for his own family.

The stories and photos made him sad, which was frustrating because he had not planned to be sad this Friday. He had held up quite well since discovering his father's body five days earlier. In moments of grief and sorrow, he had dug deep and found the strength to bite his lip and push forward without breaking down. The passage of time and the distance to Clanton had helped immensely, and now from nowhere had come the saddest reminders yet.

The letters had been collected by Harry Rex from the Judge's post office box in Clanton, from the courthouse, and from the mailbox at Maple Run. Some were addressed to Ray and Forrest and some to the family of Judge Atlee. There were lengthy letters from lawyers who'd practiced before the great man and had been inspired by his passion for the law. There were cards of sympathy from people who, for one reason or another, had appeared before Judge Atlee in a divorce, or adoption, or juvenile matter, and his fairness had changed their lives. There were notes from people all over the state – sitting judges, old law school pals, politicians Judge Atlee had helped over the years, and friends who wanted to pass along their sympathies and fond memories.

The largest batch came from those who had received the Judge's charity. The letters were long and heartfelt, and all the same. Judge Atlee had quietly sent money that was desperately needed, and in many cases it had made a dramatic change in the life of someone.

How could a man so generous die with more than three million dollars hidden below his bookshelves? He certainly buried more than he gave away. Perhaps Alzheimer's had crept into his life, or some other affliction that had gone undetected. Had he slipped toward insanity? The easy answer was that the old man had simply gone nuts, but how many crazy people could put together that kind of money?

After reading twenty or so letters and cards, Ray took a break. He walked to the small balcony overlooking the downtown mall and watched the pedestrians below. His father had never seen Charlottesville, and though Ray was certain he had asked him to visit, he could not remember a specific invitation. They had never traveled anywhere together. There were so many things they could have done.

The Judge had always talked of seeing Gettysburg, Antietam, Bull Run, Chancellorsville, and Appomatox, and he would have done so had Ray shown an interest. But Ray cared nothing for the refighting of an old war, and he had always changed the subject.

The guilt hit hard, and he couldn't shake it. What a selfish ass he'd been.

There was a lovely card from Claudia. She thanked Ray for talking to her and expressing his forgiveness. She had loved his father for years and would carry her grief to her grave. Please call me, she begged, then signed off with hugs and kisses. And she's got her current boyfriend on Viagra, according to Harry Rex.

The nostalgic journey home came to an abrupt halt with a simple anonymous card that froze his pulse and sent goose bumps down the backs of both legs.

The only pink envelope in the pile contained a card with the words 'With Sympathy' on the outside. Taped to the inside was a small square piece of paper with a typed message that read:

'It would be a mistake to spend the money. The IRS is a phone call away.' The envelope had been postmarked in Clanton on Wednesday, the day after the funeral, and was addressed to the family of Judge Atlee at Maple Run.

Ray placed it aside while he scanned the other cards and letters. They were all the same at this point, and he'd read enough. The pink one sat there like a loaded gun, waiting for him to return to it.

He repeated the threat on the balcony as he grasped the railing and tried to analyze things. He mumbled the words in the kitchen as he fixed more coffee. He'd left the note on the table so he could see it from any part of his rambling den.

Back on the balcony he watched the foot traffic pick up as noon approached, and anyone who glanced up was a person who might know about the money. Bury a fortune, then realize you're hiding it from someone, and your imagination can get crazy.

The money didn't belong to him, and it was certainly enough to get him stalked, followed, watched, reported, even hurt.

Then he laughed at his own paranoia. I will not live like this, he said, and went to take a shower.

Whoever it was knew exactly where the Judge had hidden the money. Make a list, Ray told himself as he sat on the edge of his bed, naked, with water dripping onto the floor. The felon

174

who cut the lawn once a week. Perhaps he was a smooth talker who'd befriended the Judge and spent time in the house. Entry was easy. When the Judge sneaked off to the casinos, maybe the grasscutter slinked through the house, pilfering.

Claudia would be at the top of the list. Ray could easily see her easing over to Maple Run whenever the Judge beckoned. You don't sleep with a woman for years then cut her off without a replacement. Their lives had been so connected it was easy to imagine their romance continuing. No one had been closer to Reuben Atlee than Claudia. If anyone knew where the money came from, it was her.

If she wanted a key to the house, she could've had one, though a key was not necessary. Her visit on the morning of the funeral could've been for surveillance and not sympathy, though she'd played it well. Tough, smart, savvy, calloused, and old but not too old. For fifteen minutes he dwelt on Claudia and convinced himself that she was the one tracking the money.

Two other names came to mind, but Ray could not add them to the list. The first was Harry Rex, and as soon as he mumbled the name he felt ashamed. The other was Forrest, and it too was a ridiculous idea. Forrest had not been inside the house for nine years. Assuming, just for the sake of argument, that he somehow had known about the money, he would never have left it. Give Forrest three million in cash and he would've done serious damage to himself and those around him.

The list took great effort but there was little to show for it. He wanted to go for a quick run, but instead stuffed some old clothes into two pillowcases, then drove to Chaney's, where he unloaded them into 14B. Nothing had been touched, the boxes were just as he'd left them the day before. The money was still well hidden. As he loitered there, not wanting to leave until the last second, he was hit with the thought that perhaps he was creating a trail. Obviously, someone knew he had taken it from the Judge's study. For that kind of money, private investigators could be hired to follow Ray.

They could follow him from Clanton to Charlottesville, from his apartment to Chaney's Self-Storage.

He cursed himself for being so negligent. Think, man! The money doesn't belong to you!

He locked up 14B as tightly as possible. Driving across town to meet Carl for lunch, he glanced at his mirrors and watched other drivers, and after five minutes of this he laughed at himself and vowed that he would not live like wounded prey.

Let them have the damned money! One less thing to worry about. Break into 14B and haul it away. Wouldn't affect his life in the least. No sir.

Chapter 18

The estimated flying time to Atlantic City was eighty-five minutes in the Bonanza, which was exactly thirty-five minutes faster than the Cessna Ray had been renting. Early Saturday morning he and Fog did a thorough preflight under the intrusive and often obnoxious supervision of Dick Docker and Charlie Yates, who walked around the Bonanza with their tall Styrofoam cups of bad coffee as if they were flying instead of just watching. They had no students that morning, but the gossip around the airport was that Ray was buying the Bonanza and they had to see things for themselves. Hangar gossip was as reliable as coffee shop rumors.

'How much does he want now?' Docker asked in the general direction of Fog Newton, who was crouched under a wing draining a fuel sump, checking for water and dirt in the tanks.

'He's down to four-ten,' Fog said, with an air of importance because he was in charge of this flight, not them.

'Still too high,' Yates said.

'You gonna make an offer?' Docker said to Ray.

'Mind your own business,' Ray shot back without looking. He was checking the engine oil.

'This is our business,' Yates said, and they all laughed.

In spite of the unsolicited help, the preflight was completed without a problem. Fog climbed in first and buckled himself into the left seat. Ray followed in the right, and when he pulled the door hard and latched it and put on the headset he knew he had found the perfect flying machine. The two-hundred-horsepower engine started smoothly. Fog slowly went through the gauges, instruments, and radios, and when they finished a pre-takeoff checklist he called the tower. He would get it airborne, then turn it over to Ray.

The wind was light and the clouds were high and scattered, almost a perfect day for flying. They lifted off the runway at seventy miles per hour, retracted the landing gear, and climbed eight hundred feet per minute until they reached their assigned cruising altitude of six thousand feet. By then, Ray had the controls and Fog was explaining the autopilot, the radar weather, the traffic collision avoidance system. 'She's loaded,' Fog said more than once.

Fog had flown Marine fighters for one career, but for the past ten years he'd been relegated to the little Cessnas in which he'd taught Ray and a thousand others to fly. A Bonanza was the Porsche of single engines, and Fog was delighted for the rare chance to fly one. The route assigned by air traffic control took them just south and east of Washington, away from the busy airspace around Dulles and Reagan National. Thirty miles away and more than a mile up, they could see the dome of the Capitol, then they were over the Chesapeake with the skyline of Baltimore in the distance. The bay was beautiful, but the inside of the airplane was far more interesting. Ray was flying it himself without the help of the autopilot. He maintained a course, kept the assigned altitude, talked to Washington control, and listened to Fog chat incessantly about the performance ratings and features of the Bonanza.

Both pilots wanted the flight to last for hours, but Atlantic City was soon ahead. Ray descended to four thousand feet, then to three thousand, and then switched to the approach frequency. With the runway in sight, Fog took the controls and they glided to a soft touchdown. Taxiing to the general aviation ramp, they passed two rows of small Cessnas and Ray couldn't help but think that those days were behind him. Pilots were always searching for the next plane, and Ray had found his.

Fog's favorite casino was the Rio, on the boardwalk with several others. They agreed to meet for lunch in a second-floor cafeteria, then quickly lost each other. Each wanted to keep his gambling private. Ray wandered among the slots and scoped out the tables. It was Saturday and the Rio was busy. He circled around and eased up on the poker tables. Fog was in a crowd around a table, lost in his cards with a stack of chips under his hands.

Ray had five thousand dollars in his pocket – fifty of the hundred-dollar bills picked at random from the stash he'd hauled back from Clanton. His only goal that day was to drop the money in the casinos along the boardwalk and make certain it was not counterfeit, not marked, not traceable in any way. After his visit to Tunica last Monday night, he was fairly certain the money was for real.

Now he almost hoped it was marked. If so, then maybe the FBI would track him down and tell him where the money came from. He'd done nothing wrong. The guilty party was dead. Bring on the feds.

He found an empty chair at a blackjack table and laid five bills down for chips. 'Greens,' he said like a veteran gambler.

'Changing five hundred,' the dealer said, barely looking up.

'Change it,' came the reply from a pit boss. The tables were busy. Slots were ringing in the background. A crap game was hot off in the distance, men were yelling at the dice.

The dealer picked up the bills as Ray froze for a second. The other players watched with detached admiration. All were playing five- and ten-dollar chips. Amateurs.

The dealer stuffed the Judge's bills, all perfectly valid, into the money box and counted twenty twenty-five-dollar green chips for Ray, who lost half of them in the first fifteen minutes and left to find some ice cream. Down two hundred fifty and not the least bit worried about it.

He ventured near the crap tables and watched the confusion. He could not imagine his father mastering such a complicated game. Where did one learn to shoot dice in Ford County, Mississippi?

According to a thin little gambling guide he'd picked up in a bookstore, a basic wager is a come-bet, and when he mustered the courage he wedged his way between two other gamblers and placed the remaining ten chips on the pass line. The dice rolled twelve, the money was scraped away by the dealer, and Ray left the Rio to visit the Princess next door.

Inside, the casinos were all the same. Old folks staring hopelessly at the slots. Just enough coins rattling in the trays to keep them hooked. Blackjack tables crowded with subdued players slugging free beer and whiskey. Serious gamblers packed around the crap tables hollering at the dice. A few Asians playing roulette. Cocktail waitresses in silly costumes showing skin and hauling drinks.

He picked out a blackjack table and repeated

the procedure. His next five bills passed the dealer's inspection. Ray bet a hundred dollars on the first hand, but instead of quickly losing his money, he began winning.

He had too much untested cash in his pocket to waste time accumulating chips, so when he'd doubled his money, he pulled out ten more bills and asked for hundred-dollar chips. The dealer informed the pit boss, who offered a gapped smile, and said, 'Good luck.' An hour later, he left the table with twenty-two chips.

Next on his tour was the Forum, an older-looking establishment with an odor of stale cigarette smoke partially masked by cheap disinfectant. The crowd was older too because, as he soon realized, the Forum's specialty was quarter slots and those over sixty-five got a free breakfast, lunch, or dinner, take your pick. The cocktail waitresses were on the downhill side of forty and had given up the notion of showing flesh. They hustled about in what appeared to be track suits with matching sneakers.

The limit at blackjack was ten dollars a hand. The dealer hesitated when he saw Ray's cash hit the table, and he held the first bill up to the light as if he'd finally caught a counterfeiter. The pit boss inspected it too, and Ray was rehearsing his lines about procuring that particular bill down the street at the Rio. 'Cash it,' said the pit boss, and the moment passed. He lost three hundred dollars in an hour.

Fog claimed to be breaking the casino when they met for a quick sandwich. Ray was down a hundred dollars, but like all gamblers lied and said he was up slightly. They agreed to leave at 5 P.M. and fly back to Charlottesville.

The last of Ray's cash was converted to chips at a fifty-dollar table in Canyon Casino, the newest of those on the boardwalk. He played for a while but soon grew tired of cards and went to the sports bar, where he sipped a soda and watched boxing from Vegas. The five thousand he brought to Atlantic City had been thoroughly flushed through the system. He would leave with forty-seven hundred, and a wide trail. He had been filmed and photographed in seven casinos. At two of them he had filled in paperwork when cashing in chips at the cashiers' windows. At two others he had used his credit cards to make small withdrawals, just to leave more evidence behind.

If the Judge's cash was traceable, then they would know who he was and where to find him.

Fog was quiet as they rode back to the airport. His luck had turned south during the afternoon. 'Lost a couple hundred,' he finally admitted, but his demeanor suggested he'd lost much more.

'You?' he asked.

'I had a good afternoon,' Ray said. 'Won enough to pay for the charter.'

'That's not bad.'

'Don't suppose I could pay for it in cash, could I?'

'Cash is still legal,' Fog said, perking up a bit. 'Then cash it is.'

During the preflight, Fog asked if Ray wanted to fly in the left seat. 'We'll call it a lesson,' he said. The prospect of a cash transaction had raised his spirits.

Behind two commuter flights, Ray taxied the Bonanza into position and waited for traffic to clear. Under the close eye of Fog, he began the takeoff roll, accelerated to seventy miles per hour, then lifted smoothly into the air. The turbocharged engine seemed twice as powerful as the Cessna's. They climbed with little effort to seventy-five hundred feet and were soon on top of the world.

Dick Docker was napping in the Cockpit when Ray and Fog walked in to log the trip and turn in headsets. He jumped to attention and made his way to the counter. 'Didn't expect you back so soon,' he mumbled, half-asleep, as he pulled paperwork from a drawer.

'We broke the casino,' Ray said.

Fog had disappeared down into the study room of the flight school.

'Gee, I never heard that before.'

Ray was flipping through the logbook.

'You paying now?' Dick asked, scribbling numbers.

'Yes, and I want the cash discount.'

'Didn't know we had one.'

'You do now. It's ten percent.'

'We can do that. Yep, it's the old cash discount.' He figured again, then said, 'Total's thirteen hundred and twenty bucks.'

Ray was counting money from his wad of bills. 'I don't carry twenties. Here's thirteen.' As Dick was recounting the money, he said, 'Some guy came poking around today, said he wanted to take lessons and somehow your name came up.'

'Who was he?'

'Never saw him before.'

'Why was my name used?'

'It was kinda weird. I was giving him the spiel about costs and such, and out of the blue he asked if you owned an airplane. Said he knew you from someplace.'

Ray had both hands on the counter. 'Did you get his name?'

'I asked. Dolph something or other, wasn't real clear. Started acting suspicious and finally left. I watched him. He stopped by your car in the parking lot, walked around it like he might break in or something, then left. You know a Dolph?'

'I've never known a Dolph.'

'Me neither. I've never heard of a Dolph. Like I said, it was weird.'

'What'd he look like?'

'Fiftyish, small, thin, head full of grey hair slicked back, dark eyes like a Greek or something, used-car-salesman type, pointed-toe boots.'

Ray was shaking his head. Not a clue.

'Why didn't you just shoot him?' Ray asked.

'Thought he was a customer.'

'Since when are you nice to your customers?'

'You buying the Bonanza?'

'Nope. Just dreaming.'

Fog was back and they congratulated each other on a wonderful trip, promised to do it again, the usual. Driving away, Ray watched every car and every turn.

They were following him.

Chapter 19

A week passed, a week without FBI or Treasury agents knocking on his door with badges and questions about bad money tracked down in Atlantic City, a week with no sign of Dolph or anyone else following him, a week of the normal routine of running five miles in the morning and being a law professor after that.

He flew the Bonanza three times, each a lesson with Fog at his right elbow, and each lesson paid for on the spot with cash. 'Casino money,' he said with a grin, and it wasn't a lie. Fog was anxious to return to Atlantic City to reclaim his lost assets. Ray had no interest, but it wasn't a bad idea. He could boast of another good day at the tables and keep paying cash for his flying lessons.

The money was now in 37F – 14B was still rented to Ray Atlee, and it still held the old clothes and the cheap furniture; 37F was rented to NDY Ventures, named in honor of the three flight instructors at Docker's. Ray's name was nowhere on the paperwork for 37F. He leased it for three months, in cash.

'I want this confidential,' he'd said to Mrs. Chaney.

'Everything's confidential around here. We get all types.' She gave him a conspiratorial look as if to say, 'I don't care what you're hiding. Just pay me.'

He'd moved it one box at a time, hauling it at night, under the cover of darkness, with a security guard watching from a distance. Storage space 37F was identical to 14B, and when the six boxes were safely tucked away he had vowed once again to leave it alone and not stop by every day. It had never occurred to him that hauling around three million bucks could be such a chore.

Harry Rex had not called. He'd sent another overnight package with more of the same letters of sympathy and such. Ray was compelled to read them all, or least scan them just in case there was a second cryptic note. There was not.

Exams came and went and after graduation the law school would be quiet for the summer. Ray said good-bye to his students, all but Kaley, who, after her last exam, informed Ray she had decided to stay in Charlottesville through the summer. She pressed him again for a pregraduation rendezvous of some sort. Just for the hell of it.

'We are waiting until you are no longer a student,' Ray said, holding his ground but wanting to yield. They were in his office with the door open.

'That's a few days away,' she said.

'Yes it is.'

'Then let's pick a date.'

'No, let's graduate first, then we'll pick a date.'

She left him with the same lingering smile and look, and Ray knew that she was trouble. Carl Mirk caught him gazing down the hall as she walked away in very tight jeans. 'Not bad,' Carl said.

Ray was slightly embarrassed, but kept watching anyway. 'She's after me,' he said.

'You're not alone. Be careful.'

They were standing in the hallway next to the door to Ray's office. Carl handed him an odd-looking envelope and said, 'Thought you'd get a kick out of this.'

'What is it?'

'It's an invitation to the Buzzard Ball.'

'The what?' Ray was pulling out the invitation.

'The first ever Buzzard Ball, probably the last too. It's a black-tie gala to benefit the preservation of bird life in the Piedmont. Look at the hosts.'

Ray read it slowly. 'Vicki and Lew Rodowski cordially invite you to . . . '

'The Liquidator is now saving our birds. Touching, huh?'

'Five thousand bucks a couple!'

'I think that's a record for Charlottesville. It was sent to the Dean. He's on the A list, we are not. Even his wife was shocked at the price.'

'Suzie's shockproof, isn't she?'

'Or so we thought. They want two hundred couples. They'll raise a million or so and show everybody how it's done. That's the plan anyway. Suzie says they'll be lucky to get thirty couples.'

'She's not going?'

'No, and the Dean is very relieved. He thinks it's the first black-tie shindig they'll miss in the last ten years.'

'Music by the Drifters?' Ray said as he scanned the rest of the invitation.

'That'll cost him fifty grand.'

'What a fool.'

'That's Charlottesville. Some clown bails out from Wall Street, gets a new wife, buys a big horse farm, starts throwing money around, and wants to be the big man in a small town.'

'Well, I'm not going.'

'You're not invited. Keep it.'

Carl was off, and Ray returned to his desk, invitation in hand. He put his feet on his desk, closed his eyes, and began daydreaming. He could see Kaley in a slinky black dress with no back at all, slits up past her thighs, very low V-neck, drop-dead gorgeous, thirteen years younger than Vicki, a helluva lot fitter, out there on the dance floor with Ray, who was not a bad dancer himself, bobbing and jerking to the Motown rhythms of the Drifters, while everybody watched and whispered, 'Who's that?'

And in response Vicki would be forced to drag old Lew out onto the floor, Lew in his designer tux, which could not hide his dumpy little belly; Lew with shrubs of bright grey hair above his ears; Lew the old goat trying to buy respect by saving the birds; Lew with the arthritic back and slow feet who moves like a dump truck; Lew proud of his trophy wife in her million-dollar dress, which reveals too much of her magnificently starved bones.

Ray and Kaley would look much better, dance much better, and, well, what would all that prove?

A nice scene to visit, but give it up. Now that he had the money he wouldn't waste it on nonsense like that.

The drive to Washington was only two hours, and more than half of it was fairly scenic and enjoyable. But his preferred method of travel had changed. He and Fog flew the Bonanza for thirty-eight minutes to Reagan National, where they were reluctantly allowed to land, even with a preapproved slot. Ray jumped in a taxi and fifteen minutes later was at the Treasury Department on Pennsylvania Avenue.

A colleague at the law school had a brother-in-law with some clout in Treasury. Phone calls had been made, and Mr. Oliver Talbert welcomed Professor Atlee into his rather comfortable office in the BEP, Bureau of Engraving and Printing. The professor was doing research on a vaguely defined project and needed less than an hour of someone's time. Talbert was not the brother-in-law, but he was asked to fill in.

They began with the topic of counterfeiting, and in broad strokes Talbert laid out the current problems, almost all blamed on technology – primarily inkjet printers and computer-generated counterfeit currency. He had samples of some of the best imitations. With a magnifier, he pointed out the flaws – the lack of detail in Ben Franklin's forehead, the missing thin thread lines running through the design background, the bleeding ink in the serial numbers. 'This is very good stuff,' he said. 'And counterfeiters are getting better.'

'Where'd you find this?' Ray asked, though the question was completely irrelevant. Talbert looked at the tag on the back of the display board. 'Mexico,' he said, and that was all.

To outpace the counterfeiters, Treasury was investing heavily in its own technology. Printers that gave the bills an almost holographic effect, watermarks, color-shifting inks, fine line printing patterns, enlarged off-center portraits, and scanners that could spot a fake in less than a second. The most effective method so far was one that had not yet been used. Simply change the color of the money. Go from green to blue to yellow then to pink. Gather up the old, flood the banks with the new, and the counterfeiters could not catch up, at least not in Talbert's opinion. 'But Congress won't allow it,' he said, shaking his head.

Tracing real money was Ray's primary concern, and they eventually got around to it. Money is not actually marked, Talbert explained, for obvious reasons. If the crook could look at the bills and see markings, then the sting would fall apart. Marking simply meant recording serial numbers, once a very tedious task because it was done manually. He told a kidnapping and ransom story. The cash arrived just minutes before the drop was planned. Two dozen FBI agents worked furiously to write down the serial numbers of the hundred-dollar bills. 'The ransom was a million bucks,' he was saying, 'and they simply ran out of time. Got about eighty thousand recorded, but it was enough. They caught the kidnappers a month later with some of the marked bills, and that broke the case.'

But a new scanner had made the job much easier. It photographs ten bills at a time, one hundred in forty seconds.

'Once the serial numbers are recorded, how do you find the money?' Ray asked, taking notes on a yellow legal pad. Would Talbert have expected anything else?

'Two ways. First, if you find the crook with the money, you simply put two and two together and nail him. That's how the DEA and FBI catch drug dealers. Bust a street dealer, cut him a deal, give him twenty thousand in marked bills to buy coke from his supplier, then catch the bigger fish holding the government's money.'

'What if you don't catch the crook?' Ray asked, and in doing so could not help but think of his departed father.

'That's the second way, and it's much more diffficult. Once the money is lifted out of circulation by the Federal Reserve, a sample of it is routinely scanned. If a marked bill is found, it can be traced back to the bank that submitted it. By then it's too late. Occasionally, a person with marked money will use it in one general location over a period of time, and we've caught a few crooks that way.'

'Sounds like a long shot.'

'Very much so,' Talbert admitted.

'I read a story a few years ago about some duck hunters who stumbled across a wrecked airplane, a small one,' Ray said casually. The tale had been rehearsed. 'There was some cash on board, seems like it was almost a million bucks. They figured it was drug money, so they kept it. Turns out it they were right, the money was marked, and it soon surfaced in their small town.'

'I think I remember that,' Talbert said.

I must be good, thought Ray. 'My question is this: could they, or could anyone else who finds money, simply submit it to the FBI or DEA or

Treasury and have it scanned to see if it was marked, and if so, where it came from?'

Talbert scratched his cheek with a bony finger and contemplated the question, then shrugged and said, 'I don't see why they couldn't. The problem, though, is obvious. They would run the risk of losing the money.'

'I'm sure it's not a common occurrence,' Ray said, and they both laughed.

Talbert had a story about a judge in Chicago who was skimming from the lawyers, small sums, five hundred and a thousand bucks a pop, to get cases moved up the docket, and for friendly rulings. He'd done it for years before the FBI got a tip. They busted some of the lawyers and convinced them to play along. Serial numbers were taken from the bills, and during the two-year operation three hundred fifty thousand was sneaked across the bench into the judge's sticky fingers. When the raid happened, the money had vanished. Someone tipped the judge. The FBI eventually found the money in the judge's brother's garage in Arizona, and everybody went to jail.

Ray caught himself squirming. Was it a coincidence, or was Talbert trying to tell him something? But as the narrative unfolded he relaxed and tried to enjoy it, close as it was. Talbert knew nothing about Ray's father.

Riding in a cab back to the airport, Ray did the math on his legal pad. For a judge like the one in Chicago, it would take eighteen years, stealing at the rate of a hundred seventy-five thousand a year, to accumulate three million. And that was Chicago, with a hundred courts and thousands of wealthy lawyers handling cases worth much more than the ones in north Mississippi. The judicial system there was an industry where things could slip through, heads could be turned, wheels greased. In Judge Atlee's world a handful of people did everything, and if money was offered or taken folks would know about it. Three million dollars could not be taken from the 25th Chancery District because there wasn't that much in the system to begin with.

He decided that one more trip to Atlantic City was necessary. He would take even more cash and flush it through the system. A final test. He had to be certain the Judge's money wasn't marked.

Fog would be thrilled.

Chapter 20

When Vicki fled and moved in with the Liquidator, a professor friend recommended Axel Sullivan as a divorce specialist. Axel proved to be a fine lawyer, but there wasn't much he could do on the legal front. Vicki was gone, she wasn't coming back, and she didn't want anything from Ray. Axel supervised the paperwork, recommended a good shrink, and did a commendable job of getting Ray through the ordeal. According to Axel, the best private investigator in town was Corey Crawford, a black ex-cop who'd pulled time for a beating.

Crawford's office was above a bar his brother owned near the campus. It was a nice bar, with a menu and unpainted windows, live music on the weekends, no unseemly traffic other than a bookie who worked the college crowd. But Ray parked three blocks away just the same. He did not want to be seen entering the premises. A sign that read CRAWFORD INVESTIGATIONS pointed to stairs on one side of the building.

There was no secretary, or at least none was present. He was ten minutes early but Crawford was waiting. He was in his late thirties with a shaved head and handsome face, no smile whatsoever. He was tall and lean and his expensive clothes were well fitted. A large pistol was strapped to his waist in a black leather holster.

'I think I'm being followed,' Ray began.

'This is not a divorce?' They were on opposite sides of a small table in a small office that overlooked the street.

'No.'

'Who would want to follow you?'

He had rehearsed a story about family trouble back in Mississippi, a dead father, some inheritances that may or may not happen, jealous siblings, a rather vague tale that Crawford seemed to buy none of. Before he could ask questions, Ray told him about Dolph at the airport and gave him his description.

'Sounds like Rusty Wattle,' Crawford said.

'And who's that?'

'Private eye from Richmond, not very good. Does some work around here. Based on what you've said, I don't think your family would hire someone from Charlottesville. It's a small town.'

The name of Rusty Wattle was duly recorded and locked away forever in Ray's memory.

'Is there a chance that these bad guys back in Mississippi would want you to know that you're being followed?' Crawford asked.

Ray looked completely baffled, so Crawford continued. 'Sometimes we get hired to intimidate, to frighten. Sounds like Wattle or whoever it was wanted your buddies at the airport to give you a good description. Maybe he left a trail.'

'I guess it's possible.'

'What do you want me to do?'

'Determine if someone is following me. If so, who is it, and who's paying for it.'

'The first two might be easy. The third might be impossible.'

'Let's give it a try.'

Crawford opened a thin file. 'I charge a hundred bucks an hour,' he said, his eyes staring right through Ray's, looking for indecision. 'Plus expenses. And a retainer of two thousand.'

'I prefer to deal in cash,' Ray said, staring right back. 'If that's acceptable.'

The first hint of a smile. 'In my business, cash is always preferred.'

Crawford filled in some blanks in a contract.

'Would they tap my phones, stuff like that?' Ray asked.

'We'll search everything. Get another cell phone, digital, and don't register it in your name. Most of our correspondence will be by cell phone.'

'What a surprise,' Ray mumbled, taking the contract, scanning it, then signing.

Crawford put it back in the file and returned to his notepad. 'For the first week, we'll coordinate your movements. Everything will be planned. Go about your normal routine, just give us notice so we can have people in place.'

I'll have a traffic jam behind me, Ray thought. 'It's a pretty dull life,' Ray said. 'I jog, I go to work, sometimes I go fly an airplane, I go home, alone, no family.'

'Other places?'

'Sometimes I do lunch, dinner, not a breakfast guy though.'

'You're putting me to sleep,' Crawford said and almost smiled. 'Women?'

'I wish. Maybe a prospect or two, nothing serious. If you find one, give her my name.'

'These bad guys in Mississippi, they're looking for something. What is it?'

'It's an old family with lots of stuff handed down. Jewelry, rare books, crystal, and silver.' It sounded natural and this time Crawford bought it.

'Now we're getting somewhere. And you have possession of the family heirloom?'

'That's right.'

'It's here?'

'Tucked away in Chaney's Self-Storage, on Berkshire Road.'

'What's it worth?'

'Not nearly as much as my relatives think.'

'Gimme a ballpark.'

'Half a million, on the high side.'

'And you have a legitimate claim to it?'

'Let's say the answer is yes. Otherwise, I'll be forced to give you the family history, which

200

could take the next eight hours and give us both a migraine.'

'Fair enough.'

Crawford finished a lengthy paragraph and was ready to wrap things up. 'When can you get a new cell phone?'

'I'll go now.'

'Great. And when can we check your apartment?'

'Anytime.'

Three hours later, Crawford and a sidekick he called Booty finished what was known as a sweep. Ray's phones were clear, no taps or bugs. The air vents hid no secret cameras. In the cramped attic they found no receivers or monitors hidden behind boxes.

'You're clean,' Crawford said as he left.

He didn't feel very clean as he sat on his balcony. You open up your life to complete strangers, albeit some selected and paid by you, and you feel compromised.

The phone was ringing.

Forrest sounded sober – strong voice, clear words. As soon as he said 'Hello, Bro,' Ray listened to see what kind of shape he was in. It was instinctive now, after years of phone calls at all hours, from all places, many of which he, Forrest, never remembered. He said he was fine, which meant he was sober and clean, no booze or drugs, but he did not say for how long. Ray was not about to ask.

Before either could mention the Judge or his estate or the house or Harry Rex, Forrest blurted out, 'I got a new racket.'

'Tell me about it,' Ray said, settling into his recliner. The voice on the other end was full of excitement. Ray had plenty of time to listen.

'Ever heard of Benalatofix?'

'No.'

'Me neither. The nickname is Skinny Ben. Ring a bell?'

'No, sorry.'

'It's a diet pill put out by a company called Luray Products, out of California, a big private outfit that no one's ever heard of. For the last five years doctors have been prescribing Skinny Bens like crazy because the drug works. It's not for the woman who needs to drop twenty pounds, but it does wonders for the really obese, talking linebackers, defensive ends. You there?'

'I'm listening.'

'Trouble is, after a year or two these poor women develop leaky heart valves. Tens of thousands of them have been treated, and Luray is getting sued like crazy in California and Florida. Food and Drug stepped in eight months ago, and last month Luray yanked Skinny Bens off the market.'

'Where, exactly, do you come in, Forrest?'

'I am now a medical screener.'

'And what does a medical screener do?'

'Thanks for asking. Today, for example, I was

in a hotel suite in Dyersburg, Tennessee, help-ing these hefty darlings on to a treadmill. The doctor, paid by the lawyers who pay me, checks their heart capacity, and if they're not up to snuff, guess what?'

'You have a new client.'

'Absolutely. Signed up forty today.'

'What's the average case worth?'

'About ten thousand bucks. The lawyers I'm now working with have eight hundred cases. That's eight million bucks, the lawyers get half, the women get screwed again. Welcome to the world of mass torts.'

'What's in it for you?'

'A base salary, a bonus for new clients, and a piece of the back end. There could be a half a million cases out there, so we're scrambling to round them up.'

'That's five billion dollars in claims.'

'Luray's got eight in cash. Every plaintiff's lawyer in the country is talking about Skinny Bens.'

'Aren't there some ethical problems?'

'There are no ethics anymore, Bro. You're in la-la land. Ethics are only for people like you to teach to students who'll never use them. I hate to be the one to break it to you.'

'I've heard it before.'

'Anyway, I'm mining for gold. Just thought you'd want to know.'

'That's good to hear.'

'Is anybody up there doing Skinny Bens?'

'Not to my knowledge.'

'Keep your eyes open. These lawyers are teaming up with other lawyers around the country. That's how mass tort stuff works, as I'm learning. The more cases you have in a class, the bigger the settlement.'

'I'll put out the word.'

'See you, Bro.'

'Be careful, Forrest.'

The next call came shortly after 2:30 A.M., and like every call at such an hour the phone seemed to ring forever, both during sleep and afterward. Ray finally managed to grab it and switch on a light.

'Ray, this is Harry Rex, sorry to call.'

'What is it?' he said, knowing too well that it was not good.

'Forrest. I've spent the last hour talking to him and some nurse at Baptist Hospital in Memphis. They've got him there, I think with a broken nose.'

'Back up, Harry Rex.'

'He went to a bar, got drunk, got in a fight, the usual. Looks like he picked on the wrong guy, now he's getting his face stitched up. They want to keep him overnight. I had to talk to the staff there and guarantee payment. I also asked them not to give him painkillers and drugs. They have no idea who they've got there.'

'I'm sorry you're in the middle of this, Harry Rex.'

'I've been here before, and I don't mind. But he's crazy, Ray. He started again about the estate and how he's getting screwed out of his rightful share, all that crap. I know he's drunk and all, but he just won't leave it alone.'

'I talked to him five hours ago. He was fine.'

'Well, he must've been headed for the bar. They finally had to sedate him to reset his nose, otherwise it would've been impossible. I'm just worried about all the drugs and stuff. What a mess.'

'I'm sorry, Harry Rex,' Ray said again because he could think of nothing else to say. There was a pause as Ray tried to collect his thoughts. 'He was fine, just a few hours ago, clean, sober, seemed so anyway.'

'Did he call you?' Harry Rex asked.

'Yeah, he was excited about a new job.'

'That Skinny Ben crap?'

'Yeah, is it a real job?'

'I think so. There are a bunch of lawyers down here chasing those cases. Quantity's crucial. They hire guys like Forrest to go out and round 'em up.'

'They ought to be disbarred.'

'Half of us should. I think you need to come home. The sooner we can open the estate the sooner we can get Forrest calmed down. I hate these accusations.'

'Do you have a court date?'

'We can do it Wednesday of next week. I think you ought to stay for a few days.'

'I was planning on it. Book it, I'll be there.'

'I'll notify Forrest in a day or so, try to catch him sober.'

'Sorry, Harry Rex.'

Not surprisingly, Ray couldn't sleep. He was reading a biography when his new cell phone rang. Had to be a wrong number. 'Hello,' he said suspiciously.

'Why are you awake?' asked the deep voice of Corey Crawford.

'Because my phone keeps ringing. Where are you?'

'We're watching. You okay?'

'I'm fine. It's almost four in the morning. You guys ever sleep?'

'We nap a lot. I'd keep the lights out if I were you.'

'Thank you. Anybody else watching my lights?'

'Not yet.'

'That's good.'

'Just checking in.'

Ray turned off the lights in the front of his apartment and retreated to his bedroom, where he read with aid of a small lamp. Sleep was made even more difficult with the knowledge that he was being billed a hundred dollars an hour through the night.

It's a wise investment, he kept telling himself.

At exactly 5 A.M. he sneaked down his hallway as if someone on the ground down there might see him, and he brewed coffee in the dark.

Waiting for the first cup, he called Crawford, who, not surprisingly, sounded groggy.

'I'm brewing coffee, you want some?' Ray asked.

'Not a good idea, but thanks.'

'Look, I'm flying to Atlantic City this afternoon. You got a pen?'

'Yeah, let's have it.'

'I'm leaving from general aviation in a white Beech Bonanza, tail number eight-one-five-romeo, at three P.M., with a flight instructor named Fog Newton. We'll stay tonight at the Canyon Casino, and return around noon tomorrow. I'll leave my car at the airport, locked as usual. Anything else?'

'You want us in Atlantic City?'

'No, that's not necessary. I'll move around a lot up there and try to watch my rear.'

Chapter 21

The consortium was put together by one of Dick Docker's flying buddies. It was built around two local ophthalmologists who had clinics in West Virginia. Both had just learned to fly and needed to shuttle back and forth at a faster pace. Docker's pal was a pension consultant who needed the Bonanza for about twelve hours a month. A fourth partner would get the deal off the ground. Each would put up $50,000 for a quarter interest, then sign a bank loan for the balance of the purchase price, which was currently at $390,000 and not likely to move lower. The note was spread over six years and would cost each partner $890 per month.

That was about eleven hours in a Cessna for Pilot Atlee.

On the plus side, there was depreciation and potential charter business when the partners were not using the plane. On the negative, there were hangar fees, fuel, maintenance, and a list that seemed to go on too long. Unsaid by the pal of Dick Docker, and also very much on the negative side, was the possibility of getting into business with three strangers, two of whom were doctors.

But Ray had $50,000, and he could swing $890 a month, and he wanted desperately to own the airplane that he secretly considered to be his.

Bonanzas held their value, according to a rather persuasive report that was attached to the proposal. Demand had remained high in the used-aircraft market. The Beech safety record was second only to Cessna and practically as strong. Ray carried the consortium deal around with him for two days, reading it at the office, in his apartment, at the lunch counter. The other three partners were in. Just sign his name in four places, and he would own the Bonanza.

The day before he left for Mississippi, he studied the deal for the last time, said to hell with everything else, and signed the papers.

If the bad guys were watching him, they were doing an excellent job of covering their tracks. After six days of trying to find the surveillance, Corey Crawford was of the opinion that there was nobody back there. Ray paid him thirty-eight hundred in cash and promised to call if he got suspicious again.

Under the guise of storing more junk, he went to Chaney's Self-Storage every day to check on the money. He hauled in boxes filled with anything he could find around his apartment. Both 14B and 37F were slowly taking on the appearance of an old attic.

The day before he left town, he went to the front office and asked Mrs. Chaney if someone had vacated 18R. Yes, two days ago.

'I'd like to rent it,' he said.

'That makes three,' she said.

'I'm going to need the space.'

'Why don't you just rent one of our larger units?'

'Maybe later. For now, I'll use the three small ones.'

It really didn't matter to her. He rented 18R in the name of Newton Aviation and paid cash for a six-month lease. When he was certain no one was watching, he moved the money out of 37F and into 18R, where new boxes were waiting. They were made of aluminum-coated vinyl and guaranteed to resist fire up to three hundred degrees Fahrenheit. They were also waterproof, and they locked. The money fit into five of them. For good measure, Ray threw some old quilts and blankets and clothes over the boxes so things would look a little more normal. He wasn't sure whom he was trying to impress with the randomness of his little room, but he felt better when it looked disheveled.

A lot of what he was doing these days was for the benefit of someone else. A different route from his apartment to the law school. A new jogging trail. A different coffee bar. A new downtown bookstore to browse through. And always with an eye for the unusual, an eye in the rearview mirror, a quick turnaround when he walked or jogged, a peek through shelves after he entered a shop. Someone was back there, he could feel it.

He had decided to have dinner with Kaley before he went South for a while, and before she technically became a former student. Exams were over, what was the harm? She would be around for the summer and he was determined to pursue her, with great caution. Caution because that's what every female got from him. Caution because he thought he saw potential in this one.

But the first phone call to her number was a disaster. A male voice answered, a younger voice, Ray thought, and whoever he was, he wasn't too pleased that Ray had called. When Kaley got on the phone she was abrupt. Ray asked if he could call at a better time. She said no, she'd ring him back.

He waited three days then wrote her off, something he could do as easily as flipping the calendar to the next month.

So he departed Charlottesville with nothing left undone. With Fog in the Bonanza, he flew four hours to Memphis, where he rented a car and went to look for Forrest.

His first and only visit to the home of Ellie Crum had been for the same purpose as this one.

Forrest had cracked up, disappeared, and his family was curious as to whether he might be dead or thrown in jail somewhere. The Judge was still presiding back then, and life was normal, including the hunt for Forrest. Of course the Judge had been too busy to search for his youngest son, and why should he when Ray could do it?

The house was an old Victorian in midtown Memphis, a hand-me-down from Ellie's father, who'd once been prosperous. Not much else was inherited. Forrest had been attracted to the notion of trust funds and real family money, but after fifteen years he'd given up hope. In the early days of the arrangement he had lived in the main bedroom. Now his quarters were in the basement. Others lived in the house too, all rumored to be struggling artists in need of refuge.

Ray parked by the curb in the street. The shrubs needed trimming and the roof was old, but the house was aging nicely. Forrest painted it every October, always in a dazzling color scheme he and Ellie would argue over for a year. Now it was a pale blue trimmed with reds and oranges. Forrest said he'd painted it teal one year.

A young woman with snow-white skin and black hair greeted him at the door with a rude, 'Yes?'

Ray was looking at her through a screen.

Behind her the house was dark and eerie, same as last time. 'Is Ellie in?' Ray asked, as rudely as possible.

'She's busy. Who's calling?'

'I'm Ray Atlee, Forrest's brother.'

'Who?'

'Forrest, he lives in the basement.'

'Oh, that Forrest.' She disappeared and Ray heard voices somewhere in the back of the house.

Ellie was wearing a bedsheet, white with streaks and spots of clay and water and slits for her head and arms. She was drying her hands on a dirty dish towel and looked frustrated that her work had been interrupted. 'Hello, Ray,' she said like an old friend and opened the door.

'Hello, Ellie.' He followed her through the foyer and into the living room.

'Trudy, bring us some tea, will you?' she called out. Wherever Trudy was, she didn't answer. The walls of the room were covered with a collection of the wackiest pots and vases Ray had ever seen. Forrest said she sculpted ten hours a day and couldn't give the stuff away.

'I'm sorry about your father,' she said. They sat across a small glass table from each other. The table was unevenly mounted on three phallic cylinders, each a different shade of blue. Ray was afraid to touch it.

'Thank you,' he said stiffly. No calls, no cards, no letters, no flowers, not one word of sympathy uttered until now, in this happenstance meeting. An opera could barely be heard in the background.

'I guess you're looking for Forrest,' she said.

'Yes.'

'I haven't seen him lately. He lives in the basement, you know, comes and goes like an old tomcat. I sent a girl down this morning to have a look – she said she thinks he's been gone for a week or so. The bed hasn't been made in five years.'

'That's more than I wanted to know.'

'And he hasn't called.'

Trudy arrived with the tea tray, another of Ellie's hideous creations. And the cups were mismatched little pots with large handles. 'Cream and sugar?' she asked, pouring and stirring.

'Just sugar.'

She handed him his brew and he took it with both hands. Dropping it would've crushed a foot.

'How is he?' Ray asked when Trudy was gone.

'He's drunk, he's sober, he's Forrest.'

'Drugs?'

'Don't go there. You don't want to know.'

'You're right,' Ray said and tried to sip his tea. It was peach-flavored something and one drop was enough. 'He was in a fight the other night, did you know about it? I think he broke his nose.'

'It's been broken before. Why do men get

214

drunk and beat up each other?' It was an excellent question and Ray had no answer. She gulped her tea and closed her eyes to savor it. Many years ago, Ellie Crum had been a lovely woman. But now, in her late forties, she had stopped trying.

'You don't care for him, do you?' Ray asked.

'Of course I do.'

'No, really?'

'Is it important?'

'He's my brother. No one else cares about him.'

'We had great sex in the early years, then we just lost interest. I got fat, now I'm too involved with my work.'

Ray glanced around the room.

'And besides, there's always sex,' she said, nodding to the door from which Trudy had come and gone.

'Forrest is a friend, Ray. I suppose I love him, at some level. But he's also an addict who seems determined to always be an addict. After a point, you get frustrated.'

'I know. Believe me, I know.'

'And I think he's one of the rare ones. He's strong enough to pick himself up at the last possible moment.'

'But not strong enough to kick it.'

'Exactly. I kicked it, Ray, fifteen years ago. Addicts are tough on each other. That's why he's in the basement.'

He's probably happier down there, Ray

thought. He thanked her for the tea and the time, and she walked him to the door. She was still standing there, behind the screen, when he raced away.

Chapter 22

The estate of Reuben Vincent Atlee was opened for probate in the courtroom where he had presided for thirty-two years. High on the oak-paneled wall behind the bench, a grim-faced Judge Atlee looked down upon the proceedings from between the Stars and Stripes and the state flag of Mississippi. It was the same portrait they had placed near his coffin during the courthouse wake three weeks earlier. Now it was back where it belonged, in a place where it would undoubtedly hang forever.

The man who had ended his career, and sent him into exile and seclusion at Maple Run, was Mike Farr from Holly Springs. He'd been reelected once and according to Harry Rex was doing a credible job. Chancellor Farr reviewed the petition for letters of administration, and he studied the one-page will attached to the filings.

The courtroom was busy with lawyers and clerks milling about, filing papers and chatting with clients. It was a day set aside for uncontested matters and quick motions. Ray sat in the front row while Harry Rex was at the bench, whispering back and forth with Chancellor Farr. Next to Ray was Forrest, who, other than the faded bruises under his eyes, looked as normal as possible. He had insisted that he would not be present when probate was opened, but a tongue-lashing from Harry Rex had persuaded him otherwise.

He'd finally come home to Ellie's, the usual return from the streets without a word to anyone about where he'd been or what he'd been up to. No one wanted to know. There was no mention of a job, so Ray was assuming his brief career as a medical screener for the Skinny Ben lawyers was over.

Every five minutes, a lawyer would crouch in the aisle, stick out a hand, and tell Ray what a fine man his father had been. Of course Ray was supposed to know all of them because they knew him. No one spoke to Forrest.

Harry Rex motioned for Ray to join them at the bench. Chancellor Farr greeted him warmly. 'Your father was a fine man and a great judge,' he said, leaning down.

'Thank you,' Ray replied. Then why, during the campaign, did you say he was too old and out of touch? Ray wanted to ask. It had been nine years earlier and seemed like fifty. With the passing of his father, everything in Ford County was now decades older.

'You teach law?' Chancellor Farr asked.

'Yes, at the University of Virginia.'

He nodded his approval and asked, 'All the heirs are present?'

'Yes sir,' answered Ray. 'It's just my brother, Forrest, and myself.'

'And both of you have read this one-page document that purports to be the last will and testament of Reuben Atlee?'

'Yes sir.'

'And there is no objection to this will being probated?'

'No sir.'

'Very well. Pursuant to this will, I will appoint you as the executor of your late father's estate. Notice to creditors will be filed today and published in a local paper. I'll waive the bond. Inventory and accounting will be due pursuant to the statute.'

Ray had heard his father utter those same instructions a hundred times. He glanced up at Judge Farr.

'Anything further, Mr. Vonner?'

'No, Your Honor.'

'I'm very sorry, Mr. Atlee,' he said.

'Thank you, Your Honor.'

For lunch they went to Claude's and ordered fried catfish. Ray had been back for two days and he could already feel his arteries choking. Forrest had little to say. He was not clean and his system was polluted.

Ray's plans were vague. He wanted to visit

some friends around the state, he said. There was no hurry to return to Virginia. Forrest left them after lunch, said he was going back to Memphis.

'Will you be at Ellie's?' Ray asked.

'Maybe.' was his only reply.

Ray was sitting on the porch, waiting for Claudia when she arrived promptly at 5 P.M. He met her beside her car where she stopped and looked at the Realtor's For Sale sign in the front yard, near the street.

'Do you have to sell it?' she asked.

'Either that or give it away. How are you?'

'I'm fine, Ray.' They managed to hug with just the minimum of contact. She was dressed for the occasion in slacks, loafers, a checkered blouse, and a straw hat, as if she'd just stepped from the garden. The lips were red, the mascara perfect. Ray had never seen her when she wasn't properly turned out.

'I'm so glad you called,' she said as they slowly walked up the drive to the house.

'We went to court today, opened the estate.'

'I'm sorry, must've been tough on you.'

'It wasn't too bad. I met Judge Farr.'

'Did you like him?'

'Nice enough, I guess, in spite of the history.'

He took her arm and led her up the steps, though Claudia was fit and could climb hills, in spite of the two packs a day. 'I remember when he was fresh out of law school,' she said. 'Didn't know a plaintiff from a defendant. Reuben could've won that race, you know, if I'd been around.'

'Let's sit here,' Ray said, pointing to two rockers.

'You've cleaned up the place,' she said, admiring the porch.

'It's all Harry Rex. He's hired painters, roofers, a cleaning service. They had to sandblast the dust off the furniture, but you can breathe now.'

'Mind if I smoke?' she said.

'No.' It didn't matter. She was smoking regardless.

'I'm so happy you called,' she said again, then lit a cigarette.

'I have tea and coffee,' Ray said.

'Ice tea, please, lemon and sugar,' she said, and crossed her legs. She was perched in the rocker like a queen, waiting for her tea. Ray recalled the tight dresses and long legs of many years ago as she sat just below the bench, scribbling elegantly away in her shorthand while every lawyer in the courtroom watched.

They talked about the weather, as folks do in the South when there's a gap in the conversation, or when there's nothing else to talk about. She smoked and smiled a lot, truly happy to be remembered by Ray. She was clinging. He was trying to solve a mystery.

They talked about Forrest and Harry Rex, two loaded topics, and when she'd been there for half an hour Ray finally got to the point.

221

'We've found some money, Claudia,' he said, and let the words hang in the air. She absorbed them, analyzed them, and proceeded cautiously. 'Where?'

It was an excellent question. Found where, as in the bank with records and such? Found where, as in stuffed in the mattress with no trail?

'In his study, cash. Left behind for some reason.'

'How much?' she asked, but not too quickly.

'A hundred thousand.' He watched her face and eyes closely. Surprise registered, but not shock. He had a script so he pressed on. 'His records are meticulous, checks written, deposits, ledgers with every expense, and this money seems to have no source.'

'He never kept a lot of cash,' she said slowly.

'That's what I remember too. I have no idea where it came from, do you?'

'None,' she said with no doubts whatsoever. 'The Judge didn't deal in cash. Period. Everything went through the First National Bank. He was on the board for a long time, remember?'

'Yes, very well. Did he have anything on the side?'

'Such as?'

'I'm asking you, Claudia, you knew him better than anyone. And you knew his business.'

'He was completely devoted to his work. To him, being a chancellor was a great calling, and he worked very hard at it. He had no time for anything else.'

'Including his family,' Ray said, then immediately wished he had not.

'He loved his boys, Ray, but he was from a different generation.'

'Let's stay away from that.'

'Let's.'

They took a break and each regrouped. Neither wanted to dwell on the family. The money had their attention. A car eased down the street and seemed to pause just long enough for the occupants to see the For Sale sign and take a long look at the house. One look was enough because it sped away.

'Did you know he was gambling?' Ray asked.

'The Judge? No.'

'Hard to believe, isn't it? Harry Rex took him to the casinos once a week for a while. Seems as if the Judge had a knack for it and Harry Rex did not.'

'You hear rumors, especially about the lawyers. Several of them have gotten into trouble over there.'

'But you've heard nothing about the Judge?'

'No. I still don't believe it.'

'The money came from somewhere, Claudia. And something tells me it was dirty, otherwise he would have included it with the rest of his assets.'

'And if he won at gambling he would have considered that dirty, don't you think?' Indeed, she knew the Judge better than anyone.

'Yes, and you?'

'Sounds like Reuben Atlee to me.'

They finished that round of conversation and took a break, both rocking gently in the cool shade of the front porch, as if time had stopped, neither bothered by the silence. Porch-sitting allowed great lapses while thoughts were gathered, or while there was no thinking at all.

Finally Ray, still plodding through an unwritten script, mustered the courage to ask the toughest question of the day. 'I need to know something, Claudia, and please be honest.'

'I'm always honest. It's one of my faults.'

'I have never questioned my father's integrity.'

'Nor should you now.'

'Help me out here, okay.'

'Go on.'

'Was there anything on the side – a little extra from a lawyer, a slice of the pie from a litigant, a nice backhander as the Brits like to say?'

'Absolutely not.'

'I'm throwing darts, Claudia, hoping to hit something. You don't just find a hundred thousand dollars in nice crisp bills tucked away on a shelf. When he died he had six thousand dollars in the bank. Why keep a hundred buried?'

'He was the most ethical man in the world.'

'I believe that.'

'Then stop talking about bribes and such.'

'Gladly.'

She lit another cigarette and he left to fill up the tea glasses. When he returned to the porch

Claudia was deep in thought, her gaze stretching far beyond the street. They rocked for a while.

Finally, he said, 'I think the Judge would want you to have some of it.'

'Oh you do?'

'Yes. We'll need some of it now to finish fixing up the place, probably twenty-five thousand or so. What if you, me, and Forrest split the remainder?'

'Twenty-five each?'

'Yep. What do you think?'

'You're not running it through the estate?' she asked. She knew the law better than Harry Rex.

'Why bother? It's cash, nobody knows about it, and if we report it then half will go for taxes.'

'And how would you explain it?' she asked, as always, one step ahead. They used to say that Claudia would have the case decided before the lawyers began their opening statements.

And the woman loved money. Clothes, perfume, always a late-model car, and all these things from a poorly paid court reporter. If she was drawing a state pension, it couldn't be much.

'It cannot be explained,' Ray said.

'If it's from gambling, then you'll have to go back and amend his tax returns for the past years,' she said, quickly on board. 'What a mess.'

'A real mess.'

The mess was quietly put to rest. No one would ever know about her share of the money.

'We had a case once,' she said, gazing across the front lawn. 'Over in Tippah County, thirty years ago. A man named Childers owned a scrap yard. He died with no will.' A pause, a long drag on the cigarette. 'Had a bunch of kids, and they found money hidden all over the place, in his office, in his attic, in a utility shed behind his house, in his fireplace. It was a regular Easter egg hunt. Once they'd scoured every inch of the place, they counted it up and it was about two hundred thousand dollars. This, from a man who wouldn't pay his phone bill and wore the same pair of overalls for ten years.' Another pause, another long puff. She could tell these stories forever. 'Half the kids wanted to split the money and run, the other half wanted to tell the lawyer and include the money in the probate. Word leaked out, the family got scared, and the money got added to the old man's estate. The kids fought bitterly. Five years later all the money was gone – half to the government, half to the lawyers.'

She stopped, and Ray waited for the resolution. 'What's the point?' he asked.

'The Judge said it was a shame, said the kids should've kept the money quiet and split it. After all, it was the property of their father.'

'Sounds fair to me.'

'He hated inheritance taxes. Why should the government get a large portion of your wealth just because you die? I heard him grumble about it for years.'

Ray took an envelope from behind his rocker and handed it to her. 'That's twenty-five thousand in cash.'

She stared at it, then looked at him in disbelief.

'Take it,' he said, inching it closer to her. 'No one will ever know.'

She took it and for a second was unable to speak. Her eyes watered, and for Claudia that meant serious emotions were at work. 'Thank you,' she whispered, and clutched the money even tighter.

Long after she left, Ray sat in the same chair, rocking in the darkness, quite pleased with himself for eliminating Claudia as a suspect. Her ready acceptance of twenty-five thousand dollars was convincing proof that she knew nothing of the much larger fortune.

But there was no suspect to take her place on the list.

Chapter 23

The meeting had been arranged through a Virginia law alumnus who was now a partner in a New York megafirm, which in turn was counsel to a gaming group that operated Canyon Casinos across the country. Contacts had been made, favors exchanged, arms twisted slightly and very diplomatically. It was in the delicate area of security, and no one wanted to step over the line. Professor Atlee needed just the basics.

Canyon had been on the Mississippi River, in Tunica County, since the mid-nineties, arriving in the second wave of construction and surviving the first shakeout. It had ten floors, four hundred rooms, eighty thousand square feet of gaming opportunities, and had been very successful with old Motown acts. Mr. Jason Piccolo, a vice president of some sort from the home office in Vegas, was on hand to greet Ray, and with him was Alvin Barker, head of security. Piccolo was in his early thirties and dressed like an Armani model. Barker was in his fifties and had the look of a weathered old cop in a bad suit.

They began by offering a quick tour, which Ray declined. He'd seen enough casino floors in the past month to last him forever. 'How much of the upstairs is off-limits?' he asked.

'Well, let's see,' Piccolo said politely, and they led him away from the slots and tables to a hallway behind the cashiers' booths. Up the stairs and down another hallway, and they stopped in a narrow room with a long wall of one-way mirrors. Through it, there was a large, low room filled with round tables covered with closed-circuit monitors. Dozens of men and women were glued to the screens, seemingly afraid to miss anything.

'This is the eye-in-the-sky,' Piccolo was saying. 'Those guys on the left are watching the blackjack tables. In the center, craps and roulette, to the right, slots and poker.'

'And what are they watching?'

'Everything. Absolutely everything.'

'Give me the list.'

'Every player. We watch the big hitters, the pros, the card counters, the crooks. Take blackjack. Those guys over there can watch ten hands and tell if a player is counting cards. That man in the gray jacket studies faces, looking for the serious players. They bounce around, here today, Vegas tomorrow, then they'll lay low for a week and surface in Atlantic City or the

Bahamas. If they cheat or count cards, he'll spot them when they sit down.' Piccolo was doing the talking. Barker was watching Ray as if he might be a potential cheater.

'How close is the camera view?' Ray asked.

'Close enough to read the serial number of any bill. We caught a cheater last month because we recognized a diamond ring he'd worn before.'

'Can I go in there?'

'Sorry.'

'What about the craps tables?'

'The same. It's a bigger problem because the game is faster and more complicated.'

'Are there professional cheaters at craps?'

'They're rare. Same with poker and roulette. Cheating is not a huge problem. We worry more about employee theft and mistakes at the table.'

'What kind of mistakes?'

'Last night a blackjack player won a forty-dollar hand, but our dealer made a mistake and pulled the chips. The player objected and called the pit boss over. Our guys up here saw it happen and we corrected the situation.'

'How?'

'We sent a security guy down with instructions to pay the customer his forty bucks, give him an apology, and comp a dinner.'

'What about the dealer?'

'He has a good record, but one more screwup and he's gone.'

'So everything's recorded?'

'Everything. Every hand, every throw of the dice, every slot. We have two hundred cameras rolling right now.'

Ray walked along the wall and tried to absorb the level of surveillance. There seemed to be more people watching above than gambling below.

'How can a dealer cheat with all this?' he asked, waving a hand.

Piccolo said, 'There are ways,' and gave Barker a knowing look. 'Many ways. We catch one a month.'

'Why do you watch the slots?' Ray asked, changing the subject. He would kill some time scatter-shooting since he'd been promised only one visit upstairs.

'Because we watch everything,' Piccolo said. 'And because there have been some instances where minors won jackpots. The casinos refused to pay, and they won the lawsuits because they had videos showing the minors ducking away while adults stepped in. Would you like something to drink?'

'Sure.'

'We have a secret little room with a better view.'

Ray followed them up another flight of stairs to a small enclosed balcony with views of the gaming floor and the surveillance room. A waitress materialized from thin air and took their drink orders. Ray asked for cappuccino. Waters for his hosts.

'What's your biggest security concern?' Ray asked. He was looking at a list of questions he'd pulled from his coat pocket.

'Card counters and sticky-fingered dealers,' Piccolo answered. 'Those little chips are very easy to drop into cuffs and pockets. Fifty bucks a day is a thousand dollars a month, tax free, of course.'

'How many card counters do you see in here?'

'More and more. There are casinos in forty states now, so more people are gambling. We keep extensive files on suspected counters, and when we think we have one here, then we simply ask them to leave. We have that right, you know.'

'What's your biggest one-day winner?' Ray asked.

Piccolo looked at Barker, who said, 'Excluding slots?'

'Yes.'

'We had a guy win a buck eighty in craps one night.'

'A hundred and eighty thousand?'

'Right.'

'And your biggest loser?'

Barker took his water from the waitress and scratched his face for a second. 'Same guy dropped two hundred grand three nights later.'

'Do you have consistent winners?' Ray asked, looking at his notes as if serious academic research was under way.

'I'm not sure what you mean,' Piccolo said.

'Let's say a guy comes in two or three times every week, plays cards or dice, wins more than he loses, and over time racks up some nice gains. How often do you see that?'

'It's very rare,' said Piccolo. 'Otherwise, we wouldn't be in business.'

'Extremely rare,' Barker said. 'A guy might get hot for a week or two. We'll zero in on him, watch him real close, nothing suspicious, but he is taking our money. Sooner or later he's gonna take one chance too many, do something stupid, and we'll get our money back.'

'Eighty percent lose over time,' Piccolo added.

Ray stirred his cappuccino and glanced at his notes. 'A guy walks in, complete stranger, lays down a thousand bucks on a blackjack table and wants hundred-dollar chips. What happens up here?'

Barker smiled and cracked his thick knuckles. 'We perk up. We'll watch him for a few minutes, see if he knows what he's doing. The pit boss'll ask him if he wants to be rated, or tracked, and if so then we'll get his name. If he says no, then we'll offer him a dinner. The cocktail waitress will keep the drinks coming, but if he doesn't drink then that's another sign that he might be serious.'

'The pros never drink when they gamble,' Piccolo added. 'They might order a drink for cover, but they'll just play with it.'

'What is rating?'

'Most gamblers want some extras,' explained Piccolo. 'Dinner, tickets to a show, room discounts, all kinds of goodies we can throw in. They have membership cards that we monitor to see how much they're gambling. The guy in your hypothetical has no card, so we'll ask him if he wants to be rated.'

'And he says no.'

'Then it's no big deal. Strangers come and go all the time.'

'But we sure try to keep up with them,' Barker admitted.

Ray scribbled something meaningless on his folded sheet of paper. 'Do the casinos pool their surveillance?' he asked, and for the first time Piccolo and Barker squirmed in unison.

'What do you mean by pool?' Piccolo asked with a smile, which Ray returned, Barker quickly joining in.

While all three were smiling, Ray said, 'Okay, another hypothetical about our consistent winner. Let's say the guy plays one night at the Monte Carlo, the next night at Treasure Cove, the next night at Aladdin, and so on down the strip here. He works all the casinos, and he wins a lot more than he loses. And this goes on for a year. How much will you know about this guy?'

Piccolo nodded at Barker, who was pinching his lips between a thumb and an index finger. 'We'll know a lot,' he admitted.

'How much?' Ray pressed.

'Go on,' Piccolo said to Barker, who reluctantly began talking.

'We'll know his name, his address, his occupation, phone number, automobile, bank. We'll know where he is each night, when he arrives, when he leaves, how much he wins or loses, how much he drinks, did he have dinner, did he tip the waitress, and if so then how much, how much did he tip the dealer.'

'And you keep records on these people?'

Barker looked at Piccolo, who nodded yes, very slowly, but said nothing. They were clamming up because he was getting too close. On second thought, a tour was just what he needed. They walked down to the floor where, instead of looking at the tables, Ray was looking up at the cameras. Piccolo pointed out the security people. They stood close to a blackjack table where a kid who seemed like a young teenager was playing with stacks of hundred-dollar chips.

'He's from Reno,' Piccolo whispered. 'Hit Tunica last week, took us for thirty grand. Very very good.'

'And he doesn't count cards,' Barker whispered, joining the conspiracy.

'Some people just have the talent for it, like golf or heart surgery,' Piccolo said.

'Is he working all the casinos?' Ray asked.

'Not yet, but they're all waiting for him.' The kid from Reno made both Barker and Piccolo very nervous.

The visit was finished in a lounge where they

drank sodas and wrapped things up. Ray had completed his list of questions, all of which had been leading up to the grand finale.

'I have a favor,' he asked the two of them. Sure, anything.

'My father died a few weeks ago, and we have reason to believe he was sneaking over here, shooting dice, perhaps winning a lot more than he was losing. Can this be confirmed?'

'What was his name?' asked Barker.

'Reuben Atlee, from Clanton.'

Barker shook his head no while pulling a phone from his pocket.

'How much?' asked Piccolo.

'Don't know, maybe a million over a period of years.'

Barker was still shaking his head. 'No way. Anybody who wins or loses that kinda money, we'll know him well.' And then, into the phone, Barker asked the person on the other end if he could check on a Reuben Atlee.

'You think he won a million dollars?' Piccolo asked.

'Won and lost,' Ray replied. 'Again, we're just guessing.'

Barker slammed his phone shut. 'No record of any Reuben Atlee anywhere. There's no way he gambled that much around here.'

'What if he never came to this casino?' Ray asked, certain of the answer.

'We would know,' they said together.

Chapter 24

He was the only morning jogger in Clanton, and for this he got curious stares from the ladies in their flower beds and the maids sweeping the porches and the summer help cutting grass at the cemetery when he ran past the Atlee family plot. The soil was settling around the Judge, but Ray did not stop or even slow down to inspect it. The men who'd dug the grave were digging another. There was a death and a birth every day in Clanton. Things changed little.

It was not yet eight o'clock and the sun was hot and the air heavy. The humidity didn't bother him because he'd grown up with it, but he certainly didn't miss it either.

He found the shaded streets and worked his way back to Maple Run. Forrest's Jeep was there, and his brother was slouched in the swing on the porch. 'Kinda early for you, isn't it?' Ray said.

'How far did you run? You're covered in sweat.'

'That happens when you jog in the heat. Five miles. You look good.'

And he did. Clear, unswollen eyes, a shave, a shower, clean white painter's pants.

'I'm on the wagon, Bro.'

'Wonderful.' Ray sat in a rocker, still sweating, still breathing heavily. He would not ask how long Forrest had been sober. Couldn't have been more than twenty-four hours.

Forrest bounced from the swing and pulled the other rocker near Ray. 'I need some help, Bro,' he said, sitting on the edge of the chair.

Here we go again, Ray said to himself. 'I'm listening.'

'I need some help,' he blurted again, rubbing his hands fiercely as if the words were painful.

Ray had seen it before and had no patience. 'Let's go, Forrest, what is it?' It was money, first of all. After that, there were several possibilities.

'There's a place I want to go, about an hour from here. It's way out in the woods, close to nothing, very pretty, a nice little lake in the center, comfortable rooms.' He pulled a wrinkled business card from his pocket and handed it to Ray.

Alcorn Village. Drug and Alcohol Treatment Facility. A Ministry of the Methodist Church.

'Who's Oscar Meave?' Ray asked, looking at the card.

'A guy I met a few years ago. He helped me, now he's at that place.'

'It's a detox center.'

'Detox, rehab, drug unit, dry-out tank, spa, ranch, village, jail, prison, mental ward, call it whatever you want. I don't care. I need help, Ray. Now.' He covered his face with his hands and began crying.

'Okay, okay.' Ray said. 'Give me the details.'

Forrest wiped his eyes and his nose and sucked in a heavy load of air. 'Call the guy and see if they have a room,' he said, his voice quivering.

'How long will you stay?'

'Four weeks, I think, but Oscar can tell you.'

'And what's the cost?'

'Somewhere around three hundred bucks a day. I was thinking maybe I could borrow against my share of this place, get Harry Rex to ask the judge if there's a way to get some money now.' Tears were dripping from the corners of his eyes.

Ray had seen the tears before. He'd heard the pleas and the promises, and no matter how hard and cynical he tried to be at that moment, he melted. 'We'll do something,' he said. 'I'll call this guy now.'

'Please, Ray, I want to go right now.'

'Today?'

'Yes, I, uh, well, I can't go back to Memphis.' He lowered his head and ran his fingers through his long hair.

'Somebody looking for you?'

'Yeah,' he nodded. 'Bad guys.'

'Not cops?'

'No, they're a helluva lot worse than cops.'

'Do they know you're here?' Ray asked, glancing around. He could almost see heavily armed drug dealers hiding behind the bushes.

'No, they have no idea where I am.'

Ray stood and went into the house.

Like most folks, Oscar Meave remembered Forrest well. They had worked together in a federal detox program in Memphis, and while he was sad to hear that Forrest was in need of help, he was nonetheless delighted to talk to Ray about him. Ray tried his best to explain the urgency of the matter, though he had no details and was not likely to get any. Their father had died three weeks earlier, Ray said, already making excuses.

'Bring him on,' Meave said. 'We'll find a place.'

They left town thirty minutes later, in Ray's rental car. Forrest's Jeep was parked behind the house, for good measure.

'Are you sure these guys won't be snooping around here?' Ray said.

'They have no idea where I'm from,' Forrest replied. His head was back on the headrest, his eyes hidden behind funky sunshades.

'Who are they, exactly?'

'Some really nice guys from south Memphis. You'd like them.'

'And you owe them money?'

'Yes.'

'How much?'

'Four thousand dollars.'

'And where did this four thousand bucks go?'

Forrest gently tapped his nose. Ray shook his head in frustration and anger and bit his tongue to hold back another bitter lecture. Let some miles pass, he told himself. They were in the country now, farmland on both sides.

Forrest began snoring.

This would be another Forrest tale, the third time Ray actually loaded him up and hauled him away for detox. The last time had been almost twelve years earlier – the Judge was still presiding, Claudia still at his side, Forrest doing more drugs than anyone in the state. Things had been normal. The narcs had cast a wide net around him, and through blind luck Forrest had sneaked through it. They suspected he was dealing, which was true, and had they caught him he would still be in prison. Ray had driven him to a state hospital near the coast, one the Judge had pulled strings to get him into. There, he slept for a month then walked away.

The first brotherly journey to rehab had been during Ray's law school years at Tulane. Forrest had overdosed on some vile combination of pills. They pumped his stomach and almost pronounced him dead. The Judge sent them to a compound near Knoxville with locked gates and razor wire. Forrest stayed a week before escaping.

He'd been to jail twice, once as a juvenile, once as an adult, though he was only nineteen.

241

His first arrest was just before a high school football game, Friday night, the playoffs, in Clanton with the entire town waiting for kickoff. He was sixteen, a junior, an all-conference quarterback and safety, a kamikaze who loved to hit late and spear with his helmet. The narcs plucked him from the dressing room and led him away in handcuffs. The backup was an untested freshman, and when Clanton got slaughtered the town never forgave Forrest Atlee.

Ray had been sitting in the stands with the Judge, anxious as everyone else about the game. 'Where's Forrest?' folks began asking during pregame. When the coin was tossed he was in the city jail getting fingerprinted and photographed. They found fourteen ounces of marijuana in his car.

He spent two years in a juvenile facility and was released on his eighteenth birthday.

How does the sixteen-year-old son of a prominent judge become a dope pusher in a small Southern town with no history of drugs? Ray and his father had asked each other that question a thousand times. Only Forrest knew the answer, and long ago he had made the decision to keep it to himself. Ray was thankful that he buried most of his secrets.

After a nice nap, Forrest jolted himself awake and announced he needed something to drink.

'No,' Ray said.

'A soft drink, I swear.'

They stopped at a country store and bought sodas. For breakfast Forrest had a bag of peanuts.

'Some of these places have good food,' he said when they were moving again. Forrest the tour guide for detox centers. Forrest the Michelin critic for rehab units. 'I usually lose a few pounds,' he said, chomping.

'Do they have gyms and such?' Ray asked, aiding the conversation. He really didn't want to discuss the perks of various drug tanks.

'Some do,' Forrest said smugly. 'Ellie sent me to this place in Florida near a beach, lots of sand and water, lots of sad rich folks. Three days of brainwashing, then they worked our asses off. Hikes, bikes, power walks, weights if we wanted. I got a great tan and dropped fifteen pounds. Stayed clean for eight months.'

In his sad little life, everything was measured by stints of sobriety.

'Ellie sent you?' Ray asked.

'Yeah, it was years ago. She had a little dough at one point, not much. I'd hit the bottom, and it was back when she cared. It was a nice place, though, and some of the counselors were those Florida chicks with short skirts and long legs.'

'I'll have to check it out.'

'Kiss my ass.'

'Just kidding.'

'There's this place out West where all the stars go, the Hacienda, and it's the Ritz. Plush rooms, spas, daily massages, chefs who can fix great meals at one thousand calories a day. And the counselors are the best in the world. That's what I need, Bro, six months at the Hacienda.'

'Why six months?'

'Because I need six months. I've tried two months, one month, three weeks, two weeks, it's not enough. For me, it's six months of total lockdown, total brainwashing, total therapy, plus my own masseuse.'

'What's the cost?'

Forrest whistled and rolled his eyes. 'Pick a number. I don't know. You gotta have a zillion bucks and two recommendations to get in. Imagine that, a letter of recommendation. "To the Fine Folks at the Hacienda: I hereby heartily recommend my friend Doofus Smith as a patient in your wonderful facility. Doofus drinks vodka for breakfast, snorts coke for lunch, snacks on heroin, and is usually comatose by dinner. His brain is fried, his veins are lacerated, his liver is shot to hell. Doofus is your kind of person and his old man owns Idaho." '

'Do they keep people for six months?'

'You're clueless, aren't you?'

'I guess.'

'A lot of cokeheads need a year. Even more for heroin addicts.'

And which is your current poison? Ray wanted to ask. But then he didn't want to. 'A year?' he said.

'Yep, total lockdown. And then the addict has to do it himself. I know guys who've been to prison for three years with no coke, no crack, no drugs at all, and when they were released they called a dealer before they called their wives or girlfriends.'

'What happens to them?'

'It's not pretty.' He threw the last of the peanuts into his mouth, slapped his hands together, and sent salt flying.

There were no signs directing traffic to Alcorn Village. They followed Oscar's directions until they were certain they were lost deep in the hills, then saw a gate in the distance. Down a tree-lined drive, a complex spread before them. It was peaceful and secluded, and Forrest gave it good marks for first impressions.

Oscar Meave arrived in the lobby of the administration building and guided them to an intake office, where he handled the initial paperwork himself. He was a counselor, an administrator, a psychologist, an ex-addict who'd cleaned himself up years ago and received two Ph.D.s. He wore jeans, a sweatshirt, sneakers, a goatee, and two earrings, and had the wrinkles and chipped tooth of a rough prior life. But his voice was soft and friendly. He exuded the tough compassion of one who'd been where Forrest was now.

The cost was $325 a day and Oscar was recommending a minimum of four weeks. 'After that, we'll see where he is. I'll need to ask some pretty rough questions about what Forrest has been doing.'

'I don't want to hear that conversation,' Ray said.

'You won't,' Forrest said. He was resigned to the flogging that was coming.

'And we require half the money up front,' Oscar said. 'The other half before his treatment is complete.'

Ray flinched and tried to remember the balance in his checking account back in Virginia. He had plenty of cash, but this was not the time to use it.

'The money is coming out of my father's estate,' Forrest said. 'It might take a few days.'

Oscar was shaking his head. 'No exceptions. Our policy is half now.'

'No problem,' said Ray. 'I'll write a check for it.'

'I want it to come out of the estate,' Forrest said. 'You're not paying for it.'

'The estate can reimburse me. It'll work.' Ray wasn't sure how it would work, but he'd let Harry Rex worry about that. He signed the forms as guarantor of payment. Forrest signed at the bottom of a page listing all the do's and don'ts.

'You can't leave for twenty-eight days,' Oscar said. 'If you do, you forfeit all monies paid and you're never welcome back. Understand?'

'I understand,' Forrest said. How many times had he been through this?

'You're here because you want to be here, right?'

'Right.'

'And no one is forcing you?'

'No one.'

Now that the flogging was on, it was time for Ray to leave. He thanked Oscar and hugged Forrest and sped away much faster than he'd arrived.

Chapter 25

Ray was now certain that the cash had been collected since 1991, the year the Judge was voted out of office. Claudia was around until the year before, and she knew nothing of the money. It had not come from graft and it had not come gambling.

Nor had it come from skillful investing on the sly, because Ray found not a single record of the Judge ever buying or selling a stock or a bond. The accountant hired by Harry Rex to reconstruct the records and put together the final tax return had found nothing either. He said that the Judge's trail was easy to follow because everything had been run through the First National Bank of Clanton.

That's what you think, Ray thought to himself.

There were almost forty boxes of old, useless files scattered throughout the house. The cleaning service had gathered and stacked them in the Judge's study and in the dining room. It took a few hours but he finally found what he was looking for. Two of the boxes held the notes and research – the 'trial files' as the Judge had always referred to them – of the cases he'd heard as a special chancellor since his defeat in 1991.

During a trial the Judge wrote nonstop on yellow legal pads. He noted dates, times, relevant facts, anything that would aid him in reaching a final opinion in the case. Often he would interject a question to a witness and he frequently used his notes to correct the attorneys. Ray had heard him quip more than once, in chambers of course, that the notetaking helped him stay awake. During a lengthy trial, he would fill twenty legal pads with his notes.

Because he was a lawyer before he was a judge, he had acquired the lifelong habit of filing and keeping everything. A trial file consisted of his notes, copies of cases the attorneys relied on, copies of code sections, statutes, even pleadings that were not put with the official court file. As the years passed, the trial files became even more useless, and now they filled forty boxes.

According to his tax returns, since 1993, he had picked up income trying cases as a special chancellor, cases no one else wanted to hear. It was not uncommon in the rural areas to have a dispute too hot for an elected judge. One side would file a motion asking the judge to recuse himself, and he would go through the routine of grappling with the issue while proclaiming his ability to be fair and impartial regardless of the

249

facts or litigants, then reluctantly step down and hand it off to an old pal from another part of the state. The special chancellor would ride in without the baggage of any prior knowledge and without one eye on reelection and hear the case.

In some jurisdictions, special chancellors were used to relieve crowded dockets. Occasionally, they would sit in for an ailing judge. Almost all were retired themselves. The state paid them fifty dollars an hour, plus expenses.

In 1992, the year after his defeat, Judge Atlee had earned nothing extra. In 1993, he'd been paid $5,800. The busiest year – 1996 – he'd reported $16,300. Last year, 1999, he was paid $8,760, but he'd been ill most of the time.

The grand total in earnings as a special chancellor was $56,590, over a six-year period, and all earnings had been reported on his tax returns.

Ray wanted to know what kinds of cases Judge Atlee had heard in his last years. Harry Rex had mentioned one – the sensational divorce trial of a sitting governor. That trial file was three inches thick and included clippings from the Jackson newspaper with photos of the governor, his soon to be ex-wife, and a woman thought to be his current flame. The trial lasted two weeks, and Judge Atlee, according to his notes, seemed to enjoy it tremendously.

There was an annexation case near Hattiesburg that lasted for two weeks and had irritated everyone involved. The city was growing westward and eyeing some prime industrial sites. Lawsuits got filed and two years later Judge Atlee gathered everyone together for a trial. There were also newspaper articles, but after an hour of review Ray was bored with the whole mess. He couldn't imagine presiding over it for a month.

But at least there was money involved in it.

Judge Atlee spent eight days in 1995 holding court in the small town of Kosciusko, two hours away, but from his files it looked as though nothing of consequence went to trial.

There was a horrendous tanker truck collision in Tishomingo County in 1994. Five teenagers were trapped in a car and burned to death. Since they were minors, Chancery Court had jurisdiction. One sitting chancellor was related to one of the victims. The other chancellor was dying of brain cancer. Judge Atlee got the call and presided over a trial that lasted two days before it was settled for $7,400,000. One third went to the attorneys for the teenagers, the rest to their families.

Ray set the file on the Judge's sofa, next to the annexation case. He was sitting on the floor of the study, the newly polished floor, under the vigilant gaze of General Forrest. He had a vague idea of what he was doing, but no real plan on how to proceed. Go through the files, pick out the ones that involved money, see where the trail might lead.

The cash he'd found hidden less than ten feet away had come from somewhere.

His cell phone rang. It was a Charlottesville alarm company with a recorded message that a break-in was in progress at his apartment. He jumped to his feet and talked to himself while the message finished. The same call would simultaneously go to the police and to Corey Crawford. Seconds later, Crawford called him. 'I'm on the way there,' he said, and sounded like he was running. It was almost nine-thirty, CST. Ten-thirty in Charlottesville.

Ray paced through the house, thoroughly helpless. Fifteen minutes passed before Crawford called him again. 'I'm here,' he said. 'With the police. Somebody jammed the door downstairs, then jammed the one to the den. That set off the alarm. They didn't have much time. Where do we check?'

'There's nothing particularly valuable there,' Ray said, trying to guess what a thief might want. No cash, jewelry, art, hunting rifles, gold, or silver.

'TV, stereo, microwave, everything's here,' Crawford said. 'They scattered books and magazines, knocked over the table by the kitchen phone, but they were in a hurry. Anything in particular?'

'No, nothing I can think of.' Ray could hear a police radio squawking in the background.

'How many bedrooms?' Crawford asked as he moved through the apartment.

'Two, mine is on the right.'

'All the closet doors are open. They were looking for something. Any idea what?'

'No,' Ray answered.

'No sign of entry in the other bedroom,' Crawford reported, then began talking with two cops. 'Hang on,' he told Ray, who was standing in the front door, looking through the screen, motionless and trying to think of the fastest way home.

The cops and Crawford decided it was a quick strike by a pretty good thief who got surprised by the alarm. He jammed the two doors with minimal damage, realized there was an alarm, raced through the place looking for something in particular, and when he didn't find it he kicked a few things for the hell of it and fled. He or they – could've been more than one.

'You need to be here to tell the police if anything is missing and to do a report,' Crawford said.

'I'll be there tomorrow,' Ray said. 'Can you secure the place tonight?'

'Yeah, we'll think of something.'

'Call me after the cops leave.'

He sat on the front steps and listened to the crickets while yearning to be at Chaney's Self-Storage, sitting in the dark with one of the Judge's guns, ready to blast away at anyone who came near him. Fifteen hours away by car. Three and a half by private plane. He called Fog Newton and there was no answer.

His phone startled him again. 'I'm still in the apartment,' Crawford said.

'I don't think this is random,' Ray said.

'You mentioned some valuables, some family stuff, at Chaney's Self-Storage.'

'Yeah. Any chance you could watch the place tonight?'

'They got security out there, guards and cameras, not a bad outfit.' Crawford sounded tired and not enthusiastic about napping in a car all night.

'Can you do it?'

'I can't get in the place. You have to be a customer.'

'Watch the entrance.'

Crawford grunted and breathed deeply. 'Yeah, I'll check on it, maybe call a guy in to watch it.'

'Thanks. I'll call you when I get to town tomorrow.'

He called Chaney's and there was no answer. He waited five minutes, called again, counted fourteen rings then heard a voice.

'Chancey's, security, Murray speaking.'

He very politely explained who he was and what he wanted. He was leasing three units and there was a bit of concern because someone had vandalized his downtown apartment, and could Mr. Murray please pay special attention to 14B, 37F, and 18R. No problem, said Mr. Murray, who sounded as if he was yawning into the phone.

Just a little jumpy, Ray explained.

'No problem,' mumbled Mr. Murray.

It took one hour and two drinks for the edginess to relent. He was no closer to Charlottesville. There was the urge to hop in the rental car and race through the night, but it passed. He preferred to sleep and try to find an airplane in the morning. Sleep, though, was impossible, so he returned to the trial files.

The Judge had once said he knew little about zoning law because there was so little zoning in Mississippi, and virtually none in the six counties of the 25th Chancery District. But somehow someone had cajoled him into hearing a bitterly fought zoning case in the city of Columbus. The trial lasted for six days, and when it was over an anonymous phone caller threatened to shoot the Judge, according to his notes.

Threats were not uncommon, and he'd been known to carry a pistol in his briefcase over the years. It was rumored that Claudia carried one too. You'd rather have the Judge shooting at you than his court reporter, ran the conventional wisdom.

The zoning case almost put Ray to sleep. But then he found a gap, the black hole he'd been digging for, and he forgot about sleep.

According to his tax records, the Judge was paid $8,110 in January 1999 to hear a case in the 27th Chancery District. The 27th comprised two counties on the Gulf Coast, a part of the state the Judge cared little for. The fact that he would voluntarily go there for a period of days struck Ray as quite odd.

Odder still was the absence of a trial file. He searched the two boxes and found nothing related to a case on the coast, and with his curiosity barely under control he plowed through the other thirty-eight or so. He forgot about his apartment and the self-storage and whether or not Mr. Murray was awake or even alive, and he almost forgot about the money.

A trial file was missing.

Chapter 26

The US Air flight left Memphis at six-forty in the morning, which meant Ray had to leave Clanton no later than five, which meant he slept about three hours, the usual at Maple Run. On the first flight, he dozed off en route, again in the Pittsburgh airport, and again on the commuter flight to Charlottesville. He inspected his apartment, then fell asleep on the sofa.

The money hadn't been touched. No unauthorized entries into any of his little storage units at Chaney's. Nothing was out of the ordinary. He locked himself inside 18R, opened the five fireproof and waterproof boxes, and counted fifty-three freezer bags.

Sitting on the concrete floor with three million dollars strewn around him, Ray Atlee finally admitted how important the money had become. The real horror of last night had been the chance of losing it. Now he was afraid to leave it.

In the past few weeks, he had become more

curious about how much things cost, about what the money could buy, about how it could grow if invested conservatively, or aggressively. At times he thought of himself as wealthy, and then he would dismiss those thoughts. But they were always there, just under the surface and popping up with greater frequency. The questions were slowly being answered – no it was not counterfeit, no it was not traceable, no it had not been won at the casinos, no it had not been filched from the lawyers and litigants of the 25th Chancery District.

And, no, the money should not be shared with Forrest because he would kill himself with it. No, it should not be included in the estate for several excellent reasons.

One by one the options were being eliminated. He might be forced to keep it himself.

There was a loud knock on the metal door, and he almost screamed. He scrambled to his feet and yelled, 'Who is it?'

'Security,' came the reply, and the voice was vaguely familiar. Ray stepped over the cash and reached for the door, which he cracked no more than four inches. Mr. Murray was grinning at him.

'Everything okay in there?' he asked, more of a janitor than an armed guard.

'Fine, thanks,' Ray said, his heart still frozen.

'Need anything, let me know.'

'Thanks for last night.'

'Just doing my job.'

Ray repacked the money, relocked the doors,

and drove across town with one eye on the rearview mirror.

The owner of his apartment sent a crew of Mexican carpenters around to repair the two damaged doors. They hammered and sawed throughout the late afternoon, then said yes to a cold beer when they were finished. Ray chatted with them as he tried to ease them out of his den. There was a pile of mail on the kitchen table, and, after ignoring it for most of the day, he sat down to deal with it. Bills had to be paid. Catalogs and junk mail. Three notes of sympathy.

A letter from the Internal Revenue Service, addressed to Mr. Ray Atlee, Executor of the Estate of Reuben V. Atlee, and postmarked in Atlanta two days earlier. He studied it carefully before opening it slowly. A single sheet of official stationery, from one Martin Gage, Office of Criminal Investigations, in the Atlanta office. It read:

Dear Mr. Atlee:

As executor of your father's estate, you are required by law to include all assets for valuation and taxation purposes. Conceal-ment of assets may constitute tax fraud. The unauthorized disbursement of assets is a violation of the laws of Mississippi and possi-ble federal laws as well.

Martin Gage
Criminal Investigator

His first instinct was to call Harry Rex to see what notice had been given to the IRS. As executor, he had a year from the date of death to file the final return, and, according to the accountant, extensions were liberally granted.

The letter was postmarked the day after he and Harry Rex went to court to open the estate. Why would the IRS be so quick to respond? How would they even know about the death of Reuben Atlee?

Instead, he called the office number on the letterhead. The recorded message welcomed him to the world of the IRS, Atlanta office, but he would have to call back later because it was a Saturday. He went online and in the Atlanta directory found three Martin Gages. The first one he called was out of town, but his wife said he did not work for the IRS, thank heavens. The second call went unanswered. The third found a Mr. Gage eating dinner.

'Do you work for the IRS?' Ray asked, after cordially introducing himself as a professor of law and apologizing for the intrusion.

'Yes, I do.'

'Criminal Investigations?'

'Yep, that's me. Fourteen years now.'

Ray described the letter, then read it verbatim.

'I didn't write that,' Gage said.

'Then who did?' Ray snapped, and immediately wished he had not.

'How am I supposed to know? Can you fax it to me?'

Ray stared at his fax machine, and, thinking quickly, said, 'Sure, but my machine is at the office. I can do it Monday.'

'Scan it and e-mail it,' Gage said.

'Uh, my scanner's broke right now. I'll just fax it to you Monday.'

'Okay, but somebody's pulling your leg, pal. That's not my letter.'

Ray was suddenly anxious to rid himself of the IRS, but Gage was now fully involved. 'I'll tell you something else,' he continued. 'Impersonating an IRS agent is a federal offense, and we prosecute vigorously. Any idea who it is?'

'I have no idea.'

'Probably got my name from our online directory, worst thing we ever did. Freedom of Information and all that crap.'

'Probably so.'

'When was the estate opened?'

'Three days ago.'

'Three days ago! The return's not due for a year.'

'I know.'

'What's in the estate?'

'Nothing. An old house.'

'Just some crackpot. Fax it Monday and I'll give you a call.'

'Thanks.'

Ray put the phone on the coffee table and

asked himself why, exactly, had he called the IRS?

To verify the letter.

Gage would never get a copy of it. And in a month or so he would forget about it. And in a year he wouldn't recall it if anyone mentioned it.

Perhaps not the smartest move so far.

Forrest had settled into the routine of Alcorn Village. He was allowed two calls a day and they were subject to being recorded, he explained. 'They don't want us calling our dealers.'

'Not funny,' Ray said. It was the sober Forrest, with the soft drawl and clear mind.

'Why are you in Virginia?' he asked.

'It's my home.'

'Thought you were visiting some friends around here, old buddies from law school.'

'I'll be back shortly. How's the food?'

'Like a nursing home, Jell-O three times a day but always a different color. Really lousy stuff. For three hundred bucks plus a day it's a rip-off.'

'Any cute girls?'

'One, but she's fourteen, daughter of a judge, if you can believe that. Really some sad people. We have these group bitch meetings once a day where everyone lashes out at whoever got them started on drugs. We talk through our problems. We help one another. Hell, I know more than the counselors. This is my eighth detox, Bro, can you believe it?'

'Seems like more than that,' Ray said.

'Thanks for helping me. You know what's sick?'

'What?'

'I'm happiest when I'm clean. I feel great, I feel smart, I can do anything. Then I hate myself when I'm on the streets doing all that stupid stuff like the other scumbags. I don't know why I do it.'

'You sound great, Forrest.'

'I like this place, aside from the food.'

'Good, I'm proud of you.'

'Can you come see me?'

'Of course I will. Give me a couple of days.'

He checked in with Harry Rex, who was at the office, where he usually spent the weekends. With four wives under his belt, there were good reasons he wasn't home much.

'Do you recall the Judge hearing a case on the coast, early last year?' Ray asked.

Harry Rex was eating something and smacking into the phone. 'The coast?' He hated the coast, thought they were all a bunch of redneck mafia types.

'He was paid for a trial down there, January of last year.'

'He was sick last year,' Harry Rex said, then swallowed something liquid.

'His cancer was diagnosed last July.'

'I don't remember any case on the coast,' he said, and bit into something else. 'That surprises me.'

'Me too.'

'Why are you going through his files?'

'I'm just checking his payroll records against his trial files.'

'Why?'

'Because I'm the executor.'

'Forgive me. When are you coming back?'

'Couple of days.'

'Hey, I bumped into Claudia today, hadn't seen her in months, and she gets to town early, parks a brand-new black Cadillac near the Coffee Shop so everybody can see it, then spends half the morning piddling around town. Whatta piece of work.'

Ray couldn't help but smile at the thought of Claudia racing down to the car dealership with a pocket full of cash. The Judge would be proud.

Sleep came in short naps on the sofa. The walls cracked louder, the vents and ducts seemed more active. Things moved, then they didn't. The night after the break-in, the entire apartment was poised for another one.

Chapter 27

Trying hard to be normal, Ray took a long jog on a favorite trail, along the downtown mall, down Main Street to the campus, up Observatory Hill and back, six miles in all. He had lunch with Carl Mirk at Bizou, a popular bistro three blocks from his apartment, and he drank coffee afterward at a sidewalk café. Fog had the Bonanza reserved for a 3 P.M. training session, but the mail came and everything normal went out the window.

The envelope was addressed to him by hand, nothing on the return, with a postmark in Charlottesville the day before. A stick of dynamite would not have looked more suspicious lying there on the table. Inside was a letter-size sheet of paper, trifolded, and when he spread it open all systems shut down. For a moment, he couldn't think, breathe, feel, hear.

It was a color digital photo of the front of 14B at Chaney's, printed off a computer on regular copier paper. No words, no warnings, no threats. None were needed.

When he could breathe again he also started sweating, and the numbness wore off enough for a sharp pain to knife through his stomach. He was dizzy so he closed his eyes, and when he opened them and looked at the picture again, it was shaking.

His first thought, the first he could remember, was that there was nothing in the apartment he could not do without. He could leave everything. But he filled a small bag anyway.

Three hours later he stopped for gas in Roanoke, and three hours after that he pulled into a busy truck stop just east of Knoxville. He sat in the parking lot for a long time, low in his TT roadster, watching the truckers come and go, watching the movements in and out of the crowded café. There was a table he wanted in the window, and when it was available he locked the Audi and went inside. From the table, he guarded his car, fifty feet away and stuffed with three million in cash.

Because of the aroma, he guessed that grease was the café's specialty. He ordered a burger and on a napkin began scribbling his options.

The safest place for the money was in a bank, in a large lock box behind thick walls, cameras, etc. He could divide the money, scatter it among several banks in several towns between Charlottesville and Clanton, and leave a complicated trail. The money could be discreetly hauled in by briefcase. Once locked away, it would be safe forever.

The trail, though, would be extensive. Lease forms, proper ID, home address, phones, here meet our new vice president, in business with strangers, video cameras, lock box registers, and who knew what else because Ray had never hidden stuff in a bank before.

He had passed several self-storage places along the interstate. They were everywhere these days and for some reason wedged as close to the main roads as possible. Why not pick one at random, pull over, pay cash, and keep the paperwork to a minimum? He could hang around in Podunktown for a day or two, find some more fireproof boxes at a local supply house, secure his money, then sneak away. It was a brilliant idea because his tormentor would not expect it.

And it was a stupid idea because he would leave the money.

He could take it home to Maple Run and bury it in the basement. Harry Rex could alert the sheriff and the police to watch for suspicious outsiders lurking around the town. If an agent showed up to follow him, he'd get nailed in Clanton, and Dell at the Coffee Shop would have the details by sunrise. You couldn't cough there without three people catching your cold.

The truckers came in waves, most of them talking loudly as they entered, anxious to mix it up after miles of solitary confinement. They all looked the same, jeans and pointed-toe boots. A pair of sneakers walked by and caught Ray's attention. Khakis, not jeans. The man was alone and took a seat at the counter. In the mirror Ray saw his face, and it was one he'd seen before. Wide through the eyes, narrow at the chin, long flat nose, flaxen hair, thirty-five years old give or take. Somewhere around Charlottesville but impossible to place.

Or was everyone now a suspect?

Run with your loot, like a murderer with his victim in the trunk, and plenty of faces look familiar and ominous.

The burger arrived, hot and steaming, covered with fries, but he'd lost his appetite. He started on his third napkin. The first two had taken him nowhere.

His options at the moment were limited. Since he was unwilling to let the money out of his sight, he would drive all night, stopping for coffee, perhaps pulling over for a nap, and arrive at Clanton early in the morning. Once he was on his turf again, things would become clearer.

Hiding the money in the basement was a bad idea. An electrical short, a bolt of lightning, a stray match, and the house was gone. It was hardly more than kindling anyway.

The man at the counter had yet to look at Ray, and the more Ray looked at him the more convinced he was that he was wrong. It was a generic face, the kind you see every day and seldom remember. He was eating chocolate pie and drinking coffee. Odd, at eleven o'clock at night.

He rolled into Clanton just after 7 A.M. He was red-eyed, ragged with exhaustion, in need of a shower and two days' rest. Through the night, while he wasn't watching every set of headlights behind him and slapping himself to stay awake, he'd dreamed of the solitude of Maple Run. A large, empty house, all to himself. He could sleep upstairs, downstairs, on the porch. No ringing phones, no one to bother him.

But the roofers had other plans. They were hard at work when he arrived, their trucks and ladders and tools covering the front lawn and blocking the driveway. He found Harry Rex at the Coffee Shop, eating poached eggs and reading two newspapers at once.

'What are you doing here?' he said, barely looking up. He wasn't finished with his eggs or his papers, and didn't appear too excited to see Ray.

'Maybe I'm hungry.'

'You look like hell.'

'Thanks. I couldn't sleep there, so I drove here.'

'You're cracking up.'

'Yes, I am.'

He finally lowered the newspaper and stabbed an egg that appeared to be covered with hot sauce. 'You drove all night from Charlottesville?'

'It's only fifteen hours.'

A waitress brought him coffee. 'How long are those roofers planning on working?'

'They're there?'

'Oh yes. At least a dozen of them. I wanted to sleep for the next two days.'

'It's those Atkins boys. They're fast unless they start drinking and fighting. Had one fall off a ladder last year, broke his neck. Got him thirty thousand in workers' comp.'

'Anyway, why, then, did you hire them?'

'They're cheap, same as you, Mr. Executor. Go sleep in my office. I got a hideaway on the third floor.'

'With a bed?'

Harry Rex glanced around as if the gossip-mongers of Clanton were closing in. 'Remember Rosetta Rhines?'

'No.'

'She was my fifth secretary and third wife. That was where it all started.'

'Are the sheets clean?'

'What sheets? Take it or leave it. It's very quiet, but the floor shakes. That's how we got caught.'

'Sorry I asked.' Ray took a long swig of coffee. He was hungry, but not ready for a feast. He wanted a bowl of flakes with skim milk and fruit, something sensible, but he'd be ridiculed for ordering such light fare in the Coffee Shop.

'You gonna eat?' Harry Rex growled at him.

270

'No. We need to store some stuff. All those boxes and furniture. You know a place?'

'We?'

'Okay, I need a place.'

'It's nothing but crap.' A bite of a biscuit, one loaded with sausage, Cheddar, and what appeared to be mustard. 'Burn it.'

'I can't burn it, at least not now.'

'Then do what all good executors do. Store for two years, then give it to the Salvation Army and burn what they don't want.'

'Yes or no. Is there a storage place in town?'

'Didn't you go to school with that crazy Cantrell boy?'

'There were two of them.'

'No, there were three of them. One got hit by that Greyhound out near Tobytown.' A long pull of coffee, then more eggs.

'A storage place, Harry Rex.'

'Testy, aren't we?'

'No, sleep-deprived.'

'I've offered my love nest.'

'No thanks. I'll try my luck with the roofers.'

'Their uncle is Virgil Cantrell, I handled his first wife's second divorce, and he's converted the old depot into a storage warehouse.'

'Is that the only place in town?"

'No, Lundy Staggs put in some of those mini-storage units west of town, but they got flooded. I wouldn't go there.'

'What's the name of this depot?' Ray asked, tired of the Coffee Shop.

'The Depot.' Another bite of biscuit.

'By the railroad tracks?'

'That's it.' He began shaking a bottle of Tabasco sauce over the remaining pile of eggs. 'He's usually got some space, even put in a block room for fire protection. Don't go in the basement, though.'

Ray hesitated, knowing he should ignore the bait. He glanced at his car parked in front of the courthouse and finally said, 'Why not?'

'He keeps his boy down there.'

'His boy?'

'Yeah, he's crazy too. Virgil couldn't get him in Whitfield and couldn't afford a private joint, so he figured he'd just lock him up in the basement.'

'You're serious?'

'Hell yes, I'm serious. I told him it wasn't against the law. Boy's got everythang – bedroom, bathroom, television. Helluva lot cheaper than paying rent in a nuthouse.'

'What's his name?' Ray asked, digging the hole deeper.

'Little Virgil.'

'Little Virgil?'

'Little Virgil.'

'How old is Little Virgil?'

'I don't know, forty-five, fifty.'

To Ray's great relief, no Virgil was present when he walked into the Depot. A stocky woman in overalls said Mr. Cantrell was out running errands and wouldn't be back for two hours. Ray inquired about storage space, and she offered to show him around.

Years before, a remote uncle from Texas had come to visit. Ray's mother scrubbed and polished him to the point of misery. With great anticipation they drove to the depot to fetch the uncle. Forrest was an infant and they left him at home with the nanny. Ray clearly remembered waiting on the platform, hearing the train's whistle, seeing it approach, feeling the excitement as the crowd waited. The depot back then was a busy place. When he was in high school they boarded it up, and the hoodlums used it as a hangout. It was almost razed before the town stepped in with an ill-advised renovation.

Now it was a collection of chopped-up rooms flung over two floors, with worthless junk piled to the ceiling. Lumber and wallboard were stacked throughout, evidence of endless repairs. Sawdust covered the floors. A quick walk-through convinced Ray that the place was more flammable than Maple Run.

'We got more space in the basement,' the woman said.

'No thanks.'

He stepped outside to leave, and flying by on Taylor Street was a brand-new black Cadillac, glistening in the early sun, not a speck of dirt anywhere, Claudia behind the wheel with Jackie O sunglasses.

Standing there in the early morning heat, watching the car race down the street, Ray felt the town of Clanton collapse on top of him. Claudia, the Virgils, Harry Rex and his wives and secretaries, the Atkins boys roofing and drinking and fighting.

Is everybody crazy, or is it just me?

He got in his car and left the Depot, slinging gravel behind. At the edge of town the road stopped. To the north was Forrest, to the south was the coast. Life would get no simpler by visiting his brother, but he had promised.

Chapter 28

Two days later, Ray arrived on the Gulf Coast of Mississippi. There were friends from his law school days at Tulane he wanted to see, and he gave serious thought to spending time in his old haunts. He craved an oyster po'boy from Franky & Johnny's by the levee, a muffaletta from Maspero's on Decatur in the Quarter, a Dixie Beer at the Chart Room on Bourbon Street, and chicory coffee and beignets at Café du Monde, all of his old haunts from twenty years ago.

But crime was rampant in New Orleans, and his handsome little sports car could be a target. Lucky the thief who stole it and yanked open the trunk. Thieves would not catch him, nor would state troopers because he kept precisely at the posted limits. He was a perfect driver – obeying all the laws, closely eyeing every other car.

The traffic slowed him on Highway 90, and for an hour he crept eastward through Long Beach, Gulfport, and Biloxi, hugging the beach, past the shiny new casinos sitting at the water, past new hotels and restaurants. Gambling had hit the coast as fast as it had arrived in the farmlands around Tunica.

He crossed the Bay of Biloxi and entered Jackson County. Near Pascagoula, he saw a flashing rented sign beckoning travelers to stop in for All-You-Can-Eat-Cajun, just $13.99. It was a dive but the parking lot was well lit. He cased it first and realized he could sit at a table in the window and keep an eye on his car. This had become his habit.

There were three counties along the Gulf. Jackson on the east and bordering Alabama, Harrison in the middle, and Hancock on the west next to Louisiana. A local politician had succeeded nicely in Washington and kept the pork flowing back to the shipyards in Jackson County. Gambling was paying the bills and building the schools in Harrison County. And it was Hancock, the least developed and populated, that Judge Atlee had visited in January 1999 for a case that no one back home knew about.

After a slow dinner of crawfish étoufée and shrimp rémoulade, with some raw oysters thrown in, he drifted back across the bay, back through Biloxi and Gulfport. In the town of Pass Christian he found what he was searching for – a new, flat motel with doors that opened to the outside. The surroundings looked safe, the parking lot was half-full. He paid sixty dollars cash for one night and backed the car as close to his door as possible. He'd changed his mind about being without a weapon. One strange sound during the night, and he'd be outside in a flash with the Judge's .38, loaded now. He was perfectly prepared to sleep in the car, if necessary.

Hancock county was named for John, he of the bold signature on the Declaration of Independence. Its courthouse was built in 1911 in the center of Bay St. Louis, and was practically blown away by Hurricane Camille in August 1969. The eye ran right through Pass Christian and Bay St. Louis, and no building escaped severe damage. More than a hundred people died and many were never found.

Ray stopped to read a historical marker on the courthouse lawn, then turned once more to look at his little Audi. Though court records were usually open, he was nervous anyway. The clerks in Clanton guarded their records and monitored who came and went. He wasn't sure what he was looking for or where to begin. The biggest fear, however, was what he might find.

In the Chancery Clerk's office, he loitered just long enough to catch the eye of a pretty young lady with a pencil in her hair. 'May I help you?' she drawled. He was holding a legal pad, as if that would somehow qualify him and open all the right doors.

'Do y'all keep records of trials?' he asked,

trying hard to string out the 'y'all' and overemphasizing it in the process.

She frowned and looked at him as if he had committed a misdemeanor.

'We have minutes from each term of court,' she said slowly, because he obviously was not very bright. 'And we have the actual court files.' Ray was scribbling this down.

'And,' she said after a pause, 'there are the trial transcripts taken down by the court reporter, but we don't keep those here.'

'Can I see the minutes?' he asked, grasping at the first item she'd mentioned.

'Sure. Which term?'

'January of last year.'

She took two steps to her right and began pecking on a keyboard. Ray looked around the large office where several ladies were at their desks, some typing, some filing, some on the phone. The last time he'd seen the Chancery Clerk's office in Clanton there had been only one computer. Hancock County was ten years ahead.

In a corner two lawyers sipped coffee from paper cups and whispered low about important matters. Before them were the property deed books that dated back two hundred years. Both had reading glasses perched on their noses and scuffed wing tips and ties with thick knots. They were checking land titles for a hundred bucks a pop, one of a dozen dreary chores handled by legions of small-town lawyers. One of them noticed Ray and eyed him suspiciously.

That could be me, Ray thought to himself.

The young lady ducked and pulled out a large ledger filled with computer printouts. She flipped pages, then stopped and spun it around on the counter. 'Here,' she said, pointing. 'January '99, two weeks of court. Here's the docket, which goes on for several pages. This column lists the final disposition. As you'll see, most cases were continued to the March term.'

Ray was looking and listening.

'Any case in particular?' she asked.

'Do you remember a case that was heard by Judge Atlee, from Ford County? I think he was here as a special chancellor?' he asked casually. She glared at him as if he'd asked to see her own divorce file.

'Are you a reporter?' she asked, and Ray almost took a step backward.

'Do I need to be?' he asked. Two of the other deputy clerks had stopped whatever they were doing and were frowning at him.

She forced a smile. 'No, but that case was pretty big. It's right here,' she said, pointing again. On the docket it was listed simply as *Gibson v. Miyer-Brack*. Ray nodded approvingly as if he'd found exactly what he wanted. 'And where would the file be located?' he asked.

'It's thick,' she said.

He followed her into a room filled with black metal cabinets that held thousands of files. She knew exactly where to go. 'Sign here,' she said, handing over a clipboard with a ledger on it. 'Just your name, the date. I'll do the rest.'

'What kind of case was it?' he asked as he filled in the blanks.

'Wrongful death.' She opened a long drawer and pointed from one end to the other. 'All this,' she said. 'The pleadings start here, then discovery, then the trial transcript. You can take it to that table over there, but it cannot leave the room. Judge's orders.'

'Which judge?'

'Judge Atlee.'

'He died, you know.'

Walking away, she said, 'That's not such a bad thing.'

The air in the room went with her, and it took a few seconds for Ray to think again. The file was four feet thick, but he didn't care. He had the rest of the summer.

Clete Gibson died in 1997 at the age of sixty-one. Cause of death, kidney failure. Cause of kidney failure, a drug called Ryax, manufactured by Miyer-Brack, according to the allegations of the lawsuit, and found to be true by the Honorable Reuben V. Atlee, sitting as special chancellor.

Mr. Gibson had taken Ryax for eight years to battle high cholesterol. The drug was prescribed by his doctor and sold by his pharmacist, both of whom were also sued by his widow and children. After taking the drug for about five years, he began having kidney problems, which were treated by a different set of doctors. At the time, Ryax, a relatively new drug, had no known side effects. When Gibson's kidneys quit completely, he somehow came to know a Mr. Patton French, attorney-at-law. This happened shortly before his death.

Patton French was with French & French, over in Biloxi. A firm letterhead listed six other lawyers. In addition to the manufacturer, physician, and pharmacist, the defendants also included a local drug salesman and his brokerage company out of New Orleans. Every defendant had a big firm engaged, including some heavyweights from New York. The litigation was contentious, complicated, even fierce at times, and Mr. Patton French and his little firm from Biloxi waged an impressive war against the giants on the other side.

Miyer-Brack was a Swiss pharmaceutical giant, privately owned, with interests in sixty countries, according to the deposition of its American representative. In 1998, its profits were $635 million on revenues of $9.1 billion. That one deposition took an hour to read.

For some reason, Patton French decided to file a wrongful death suit in Chancery Court, the court of equity, instead of Circuit Court, where most trials were by jury. By statute, the only jury trials in Chancery were for will contests. Ray had sat through several of those miserable affairs while clerking for the Judge.

Chancery Court had jurisdiction for two reasons. First, Gibson was dead and his estate was a Chancery matter. Second, he had a child under the age of eighteen. The legal business of minors belonged in Chancery Court.

Gibson also had three children who were not minors. The lawsuit could've been filed in either Circuit or Chancery, one of a hundred great quirks in Mississippi law. Ray had once asked the Judge to explain this enigma, and as usual the answer was simply, 'We have the greatest court system in the country.' Every old chancellor believed this.

Giving lawyers the choice of where to sue was not peculiar to any state. Forum shopping was a game played on the national map. But when a lawsuit by a widow living in rural Mississippi against a mammoth Swiss company that created a drug produced in Uruguay was filed in the Chancery Court of Hancock County, a red flag was raised. The federal courts were in place to deal with such far-flung disputes, and Miyer-Brack and its phalanx of lawyers tried gallantly to remove the case. Judge Atlee held firm, as did the federal judge. Local defendants were included, thus removal to federal court could be denied.

Reuben Atlee was in charge of the case, and as he pushed the matter to trial, his patience with the defense lawyers wore thin. Ray had to smile at some of his father's rulings. They were terse, brutally to the point, and designed to light a fire under the hordes of lawyers scrambling around the defendants. The modern-day rules about speedy trials had never been necessary in Judge Atlee's courtroom.

It became evident that Ryax was a bad product. Patton French found two experts who blasted the drug, and the experts defending it were nothing but mouthpieces for the company. Ryax lowered cholesterol to amazing levels. It had been rushed through the approvals, then dumped into the marketplace, where it became extremely popular. Tens of thousands of kidneys had now been ruined, and Mr. Patton French had Miyer-Brack pinned to the mat.

The trial lasted for eight days. Against the objections of the defense, the proceedings began each morning precisely at eight-fifteen. And they often ran until eight at night, prompting more objections, which Judge Atlee ignored. Ray had seen this many times. The Judge believed in hard work, and, with no jury to pamper, he was brutal.

His final decision was dated two days after the last witness testified, a shocking blow for judicial promptness. Evidently, he had remained in Bay St. Louis and dictated a four-page ruling to the court reporter. This, too, did not surprise Ray. The Judge loathed procrastination in deciding cases.

Plus, he had his notes to rely on. For eight

days of nonstop testimony, the Judge must have filled thirty legal pads. His ruling had enough detail to impress the experts.

The family of Clete Gibson was award $1.1 million in actual damages, the value of his life, according to an economist. And to punish Miyer-Brack for pushing such a bad product, the Judge awarded $10 million in punitive damages. The opinion was a scathing indictment of corporate recklessness and greed, and it was quite obvious that Judge Atlee had become deeply troubled by the practices of Miyer-Brack.

Even so, Ray had never known his father to resort to punitive damages.

There was the usual flurry of post-trial motions, all of which the Judge dismissed with brusque paragraphs. Miyer-Brack wanted the punitive damages taken out. Patton French wanted them increased. Both sides received a written tongue-lashing.

Oddly, there was no appeal. Ray kept waiting for one. He flipped through the post-trial section twice, then dug through the entire drawer again. It was possible the case had been settled afterward, and he made a note to ask the clerk.

A nasty little fight erupted over the fees. Patton French had a contract signed by the Gibson family that gave him fifty percent of any recovery. The Judge, as always, felt that was excessive. In Chancery, the fees were within the sole discretion of the Judge. Thirty-three percent had always been his limit. The math was easy to do, and Mr. French fought hard to collect his well-earned money. His Honor didn't budge.

The Gibson trial was Judge Atlee at his finest, and Ray felt both proud and sentimental. It was difficult to believe it had taken place almost a year and a half earlier, when the Judge was suffering from diabetes, heart disease, and probably cancer, though the latter was six months from being discovered.

He admired the old warrior.

With the exception of one lady who was eating a melon at her desk and doing something else online, the clerks were off at lunch. Ray left the place and went to find a library.

Chapter 29

From a burger joint in Biloxi, he checked his voice mail in Charlottesville and found three messages. Kaley called to say she'd like to have dinner. A quick discard took care of her, forever. Fog Newton called to say the Bonanza was clear for the next week and they needed to go fly. And Martin Gage with the IRS in Atlanta checked in, still looking for the fax of the bogus letter. Keep looking, Ray thought to himself.

He was eating a prepackaged salad at a bright orange plastic table, across the highway from the beach. He could not remember the last time he'd sat alone in a fast-food joint, and he was doing so now only because he could eat with his car close by and in plain sight. Plus the place was crawling with young mothers and their children, usually a low-crime group. He finally gave up on the salad and called Fog.

The Biloxi Public Library was on Lameuse Street. Using a new map he'd purchased at a convenience store, he found it and parked in a row of cars near the main entrance. As was his habit now, he stopped and observed his car and all the elements around it before entering the building.

The computers were on the first floor, in a room encased in glass but with no windows to the outside, to his disappointment. The leading newspaper on the coast was the *Sun Herald*, and through a news-library service its archives could be searched back to 1994. He went to January 24, 1999, the day after Judge Atlee had issued his ruling in the trial. Not surprisingly, there was a story on the front page of the metro section about the $11.1 million verdict over in Bay St. Louis. And it was certainly no surprise to see that Mr. Patton French had a lot to say. Judge Atlee refused comment. The defense lawyers claimed to be shocked and promised to appeal.

There was a photo of Patton French, a man in his mid-fifties with a round face and waves of graying hair. As the story ran on it became obvious that he had called up the paper with the breaking news and had been delighted to chat. It was a 'grueling trial.' The actions of the defendants were 'reckless and greedy.' The decision by the court was 'courageous and fair.' Any appeal would be 'just another attempt to delay justice.'

He'd won many trials, he boasted, but this was his biggest verdict. Quizzed about the recent spate of high awards, he downplayed any suggestion that the ruling was a bit outrageous. 'A jury in Hinds County handed out five hundred million dollars two years ago,' he said. And in other parts of the state, enlightened juries were hitting greedy corporate defendants for ten million here and twenty million there. 'This award is legally defensible on every front,' he declared.

His specialty, he said as the story wound down, was pharmaceutical liability. He had four hundred Ryax cases alone and was adding more each day.

Ray did a word search for Ryax within the *Sun Herald*. Five days after the story, on January 29, there was a bold, full-page ad that began with the ominous question: Have You Taken Ryax? Under it were two paragraphs of dire warnings about the dangers of the drug, then a paragraph detailing the recent victory of Patton French, expert trial attorney, specializing in Ryax and other problematic drugs. A victims' screening session would take place at a Gulfport hotel for the following ten days with qualified medical experts conducting the tests. The screening was at no cost to those who responded. No strings attached, or at least none were mentioned. In clear letters across the bottom of the page was the information that the ad was paid for by the law firm of French & French, with addresses and phone numbers of their offices in Gulfport, Biloxi, and Pascagoula.

The word search produced an almost identical ad dated March 1, 1999. The only difference was the time and place of the screening. Another ad ran in the Sunday edition of the *Sun Herald* on May 2, 1999.

For almost an hour, Ray ventured out from the coast, and found the same ads in the *Clarion-Ledger* in Jackson, the *Times-Picayune* in New Orleans, the *Hattiesburg American*, the *Mobile Register*, the *Commercial Appeal* in Memphis, and *The Advocate* in Baton Rouge. Patton French had launched a massive frontal assault on Ryax and Miyer-Brack.

Convinced that the newspaper ads could spread to all fifty states, Ray grew weary of it. On a guess, he did a Web search for Mr. French, and was welcomed to the firm's own site, a very impressive piece of propaganda.

There were now fourteen lawyers in the firm, with offices in six cities and expanding by the hour. Patton French had a flattering one-page biography that would have embarrassed those with thinner skins. His father, the elder French, looked to be eighty if a day, and had taken senior status, whatever that meant.

The firm's thrust was its rabid representation of folks injured by bad drugs and bad doctors. It had brilliantly negotiated the largest Ryax settlement to date – $900 million for 7,200 clients. Now it was hammering Shyne Medical, makers of Minitrin, the widely used and obscenely profitable hypertension drug that the FDA had pulled because of its side effects. The firm had almost two thousand Minitrin clients and was screening more each week.

Patton French had hit Clark Pharmaceuticals for an eight-million-dollar jury verdict in New Orleans. The drug at war there was Kobril, an antidepressant that had been loosely linked to hearing loss. The firm had settled its first batch of Kobril cases, fourteen hundred of them, for fifty-two million.

Little was said about the other members of the firm, giving the clear impression that it was a one-man show with a squad of minions in the backrooms grappling with thousands of clients who'd been gathered up on the street. There was a page with Mr. French's speaking engagements, one with his extensive trial calendar, and two pages of screening schedules, covering no less than eight drugs, including Skinny Bens, the fat pill Forrest had mentioned earlier.

To better serve its clients, the French firm had purchased a Gulfstream IV, and there was a large color photo of it on the ramp somewhere, with, of course, Patton French posed near the nose in a dark designer suit, with a fierce smile, ready to hop on board and go fight for justice somewhere. Ray knew that such a plane probably cost about thirty million, with two full-time pilots and a list of maintenance expenses that would terrify an accountant.

Patton French was a shameless ego pit.

The airplane was the final straw, and Ray left the library. Leaning on his car, he dialed the number for French & French and worked his way through the recorded menu – client, lawyer, judge, other, screening information, paralegals, the first four letters of your lawyer's last name. Three secretaries working diligently for Mr. French passed him along until he came to the one in charge of scheduling.

Exhausted, Ray said, 'I really would like to see Mr. French.'

'He's out of town,' she said, surprisingly polite.

Of course he was out of town. 'Okay, listen,' Ray said rudely. 'I'm only doing this one time. My name is Ray Atlee. My father was Judge Reuben Atlee. I'm here in Biloxi, and I'd like to see Patton French.'

He gave her his cell phone number and drove away. He went to the Acropolis, a tacky Vegas-style casino with a Greek theme, badly done but absolutely no one cared. The parking lot was busy and there were security guards on duty. Whether they were watching anything was uncertain. He found a bar with a view of the floor, and was sipping a soda when his cell phone beeped. 'Mr. Ray Atlee,' said the voice.

'That's me,' Ray said, pressing the phone closer.

'Patton French here. Delighted you called. Sorry I wasn't in.'

'I'm sure you're a busy man.'

'Indeed I am. You're on the coast?'

'Right now I'm sitting in the Acropolis, a wonderful place.'

'Well, I'm headed back, been down to Naples

for a plaintiff's counsel meeting with some big Florida lawyers.'

Here we go, thought Ray.

'Very sorry about your father,' French said, and the signal cracked just a little. Probably at forty thousand feet, streaking home.

'Thank you,' Ray said.

'I was at the funeral, saw you there, but didn't get a chance to speak. A lovely man, the Judge.'

'Thank you,' Ray said again.

'How's Forrest?'

'How do you know Forrest?'

'I know almost everything, Ray. My pretrial preparation is meticulous. We gather information by the truckload. That's how we win. Anyway, is he clean these days?'

'As far as I know,' Ray said, irritated that a private matter would be brought up as casually as the weather. But he knew from the Web site that the man had no finesse.

'Good, look, I'll be in sometime tomorrow. I'm on my yacht, so the pace is a bit slower. Can we do lunch or dinner?'

Didn't see a yacht on the Web page, Mr. French. Must've been an oversight. Ray preferred one hour over coffee, as opposed to a two-hour lunch or an even longer dinner, but he was the guest. 'Either one.'

'Keep them both open, if you don't mind. We're hitting some wind here in the Gulf and I'm not sure when I'll be in. Can I have my girl call you tomorrow?'

'Sure.'

'Are we discussing the Gibson trial?'

'Yes, unless there's something else.'

'No, it all started with Gibson.'

Back at the Easy Sleep Inn, Ray half-watched a muted baseball game and tried to read while waiting for the sun to disappear. He needed sleep but was unwilling to tuck in before dark. He got Forrest on the second try, and they were discussing the joys of rehab when the cell phone erupted. 'I'll call you back,' Ray said and hung up.

An intruder was in his apartment again. A burglary in progress, said the robotic voice from the alarm company. When the recording went dead, Ray opened the door and stared at his car, less than twenty feet away. He held the cell phone and waited.

The alarm company also called Corey Crawford, who called fifteen minutes later with the same report. Crowbar through the door on the street, crowbar through the door to the apartment, a table knocked over, lights on, all appliances accounted for. The same policeman filing the same report.

'There's nothing valuable there,' Ray said.

'Then why do they keep breaking in?' Corey asked.

'I don't know.'

Crawford called the landlord, who promised to find a carpenter and patch up the doors. After the cop left, Corey waited in the apartment and called Ray again. 'This is not a coincidence,' he said.

'Why not?' Ray asked.

'They're not trying to steal anything. It's intimidation, that's all. What's going on?'

'I don't know.'

'I think you do.'

'I swear.'

'I think you're not telling me everything.'

You're certainly right about that, Ray thought, but he held his ground. 'It's random, Corey, relax. Just some of those downtown kids with pink hair and spikes through their jaws. They're druggies looking for a quick buck.'

'I know the area. These aren't kids.'

'A pro wouldn't return if he knew about the alarm. It's two different people.'

'I disagree.'

They agreed to disagree, though both knew the truth.

He rolled in the darkness for two hours, unable even to close his eyes. Around eleven, he went for a drive and found himself back at the Acropolis, where he played roulette and drank bad wine until two in the morning.

He asked for a room overlooking the parking lot, not the beach, and from a third-floor window he guarded his car until he fell asleep.

Chapter 30

He slept until housekeeping got tired of waiting. Checkout was noon, no exceptions, and when the maid banged on the door at eleven forty-five he yelled something through the door and jumped in the shower.

His car looked fine, no pry marks or dents or scrapes around the rear. He unlocked the trunk and quickly peered inside: three black plastic garbage bags stuffed with money. All was normal until he got behind the wheel and saw an envelope tucked under the windshield wiper in front of him. He froze and stared at it, and it seemed to stare back at him from thirty inches away. Plain white, legal size, no visible markings, at least on the side touching the glass.

Whatever it was, it couldn't be good. It wasn't a flyer for a pizza delivery or some clown running for office. It wasn't a ticket for expired parking because parking was free at the Acropolis casino.

It was an envelope with something in it.

He slowly crawled out of the car and looked around on the chance he'd spot someone out there. He lifted the wiper, took the envelope, and examined it as if it might be crucial evidence in a murder trial. Then he got back in the car because he figured someone was watching.

Inside was another trifold, another color digital picture printed off the computer, this one of unit 37F at Chaney's Self-Storage in Charlottesville, Virginia, 930 miles and at least eighteen hours away by car. Same camera, same printer, no doubt the same photographer who no doubt knew that 37F was not the last unit Ray had used to hide the money.

Though he was too numb to move, Ray drove away in a hurry. He sped along Highway 90 watching everything behind him, then suddenly veered to the left and turned onto a street that he followed north for a mile until he abruptly pulled into the parking lot of a Laundromat. No one was following. For an hour he watched every car and saw nothing suspicious. For comfort, his pistol was next to his seat, ready for action. And even more comforting was the money sitting just inches away. He had everything he needed.

The call from Mr. French's scheduling secretary came at eleven-fifteen. Crucial matters had conspired to make lunch impossible, but an early dinner would be his pleasure. She asked if Ray would come to the great man's office around 4 P.M., and the evening would proceed from there.

The office, a flattering photo of which appeared on the Web site, was a stately Georgian home overlooking the Gulf, on a long lot shaded with oaks and Spanish moss. Its neighbors were of similar architecture and age.

The rear had recently been converted into a parking lot with tall brick walls around it and security cameras scanning back and forth. A metal gate was opened for Ray and closed behind him by a guard dressed like a Secret Service agent. He parked in a reserved place, and another guard escorted him up to the rear of the building, where a crew was busy laying tile while another planted shrubs. A major renovation of the office and premises was rapidly winding down.

'The governor's coming in three days,' the guard whispered.

'Wow,' Ray said.

French's personal office was on the second floor, but he was not in it. He was still on his yacht, out in the Gulf, explained a comely young brunette in a tight, expensive dress. She led him into Mr. French's office anyway and asked him to wait in a sitting area by the windows. The room was paneled in blond oak and held enough heavy leather sofas, chairs, and ottomans to furnish a hunting lodge. The desk was the size of a swimming pool and covered with scale models of great yachts.

'He likes boats, huh?' Ray said, looking around. He was expected to be impressed.

'Yes, he does.' With a remote she opened a cabinet and a large flat screen slid out. 'He's in a meeting,' she said, 'but he'll be on in just a moment. Would you like a drink?'

'Thanks, black coffee.'

There was a tiny camera in the top right corner of the screen, and Ray assumed he and Mr. French were about to chat via satellite. His irritation at waiting was slowly building. Normally, it would've been boiling by now, but he was captivated by the show that was unfolding around him. He was a character in it. Relax and enjoy it, he told himself. You have plenty of time.

She returned with the coffee, which, of course, was served in fine china, F&F engraved on the side of the cup.

'Can I step outside?' Ray asked.

'Certainly.' She smiled and returned to her desk.

There was a long balcony through a set of doors. Ray sipped his coffee at the railing and admired the view. The wide front lawn ended at the highway, and beyond it was the beach and the water. No casinos were visible, not much in the way of development. Below him, on the front porch, some painters were chattering back and forth as they moved their ladders. Everything about the place looked and felt new. Patton French had just won the lottery.

'Mr. Atlee,' she called, and Ray stepped inside the office. On the screen was the face of Patton French, hair slightly disheveled, reading glasses perched on his nose, eyes frowning above them. 'There you are,' he barked. 'Sorry for the delay. Have a seat there, if you will, Ray, so I can see you.'

She pointed and Ray sat.

'How are you?' French asked.

'Fine. You?'

'Great, look, sorry for the mix-up, all my fault, but I've been on one of these damned conference calls all afternoon, just couldn't get away. I was thinking it would be a lot quieter here on the boat for dinner, whatta you think? My chef's a damned sight better than anything you'll find on land. I'm only thirty minutes out. We'll have a drink, just the two of us, then a long dinner and we'll talk about your father. It'll be enjoyable, I promise.'

When he finally shut up, Ray said, 'Will my car be secure here?'

'Of course. Hell, it's in a compound. I'll tell the guards to sit on the damned thing if you want.'

'Okay. Do I swim out?'

'No, I've got boats. Dickie'll bring you.'

Dickie was the same thick young man who'd escorted Ray into the building. Now he escorted him out, where a very long silver Mercedes was waiting. Dickie drove it like a tank through the traffic to the Point Cadet Marina, where a hundred small vessels were docked. One of the larger ones just happened to be owned by Patton French. Its name was the *Lady of Justice*.

'The water's smooth, take about twenty-five minutes,' Dickie said as they climbed on board. The engines were running. A steward with a thick accent asked Ray if he'd like a drink. 'Diet soda,' he said. They cast off and puttered through the rows of slips and past the marina until they were away from the pier. Ray climbed to the upper deck and watched the shoreline fade into the distance.

Anchored ten miles from Biloxi was the *King of Torts,* a hundred-forty-foot luxury yacht with a crew of five and plush quarters for a dozen friends. The only passenger was Mr. French, and he was waiting to greet his dinner guest. 'A real pleasure, Ray,' he said as he pumped his hand and then squeezed his shoulder.

'A pleasure for me as well,' Ray said, holding his ground because French liked close contact. He was an inch or two taller, with a nicely tanned face, fierce blue eyes that squinted and did not blink.

'I'm so glad you came,' French said, squeezing Ray's hand. Fraternity brothers couldn't have pawed each other with more affection.

'Stay here, Dickie,' he barked to the deck below. 'Follow me, Ray,' he said, and they were off, up one short flight to the main deck, where a steward in a white jacket was waiting with a starched F&F towel folded perfectly over his arm. 'What'll you have?' he demanded of Ray.

Suspecting that French was not a man who toyed with light booze, Ray said, 'What's the specialty of the house?'

'Iced vodka, with a twist of lime.'

'I'll try it,' Ray said.

'It's a great new vodka from Norway. You'll love it.' The man knew his vodkas.

He was wearing a black linen shirt, buttoned at the neck, and tan linen shorts, perfectly pressed and hanging nicely on his frame. There was a slight belly, but he was thick through the chest and his forearms were twice the normal size. He liked his hair because he couldn't keep his hands out of it.

'How about the boat?' he asked, waving his hands from stern to bow. 'It was built by a Saudi prince, one of the lesser ones, a coupla years ago. Dumb-ass put a fireplace in it, can you believe that? Cost him twenty million or so, and after a year he traded it in for a two-hundred-footer.'

'It's amazing,' Ray said, trying to sound sufficiently awed. The world of yachting was one he had never been near, and he suspected that after this episode he would forever keep his distance.

'Built by the Italians,' French said, tapping a railing made of some terribly expensive wood.

'Why do you stay out here, in the Gulf?' Ray asked.

'I'm an offshore kind of guy, ha, ha. If you know what I mean. Sit.' French pointed, and they lowered themselves into two long deck chairs. When they were nestled in, French nodded to the shore. 'You can barely see Biloxi, and this is close enough. I can do more work out here in one day than in a week at the office. Plus I'm transitioning from one house to the next. A divorce is in the works. This is where I hide.'

'Sorry.'

'This is the biggest yacht in Biloxi now, and most folks can spot it. The current wife thinks I've sold it, and if I get too close to the shore then her slimy little lawyer might swim out and take a picture of it. Ten miles is close enough.'

The iced vodkas arrived, in tall narrow glasses, F&F engraved on the sides. Ray took a sip and the concoction burned all the way to his toes. French took a long pull and smacked his lips. 'Whatta you think?' he asked proudly.

'Nice vodka,' Ray said. He couldn't remember the last time he'd had one.

'Dickie brought fresh swordfish out for dinner. Sound okay?'

'Great.'

'And the oysters are good now.'

'I went to law school at Tulane. I had three years of fresh oysters.'

'I know,' French said and pulled a small radio from his shirt pocket and passed along their dinner selections to someone below. He glanced at his watch and decided they would eat in two hours.

'You went to school with Hassel Mangrum,' French said.

'Yes, he was a year ahead of me.'

'We share the same trainer. Hassel has done well here on the coast. Got in early with the asbestos boys.'

'I haven't heard from Hassel in twenty years.'

'You haven't missed much. He's a jerk now, I suspect he was a jerk in law school.'

'He was. How'd you know I went to school with Mangrum?'

'Research, Ray, extensive research.' He swigged the vodka again. Ray's third sip went straight to his brain.

'We spent a bunch of dough investigating Judge Atlee, and his family, and his background, his rulings, his finances, everything we could find. Nothing illegal or intrusive, mind you, but old-fashioned detective work. We knew about your divorce, what's his name, Lew the Liquidator?'

Ray just nodded. He wanted to say something derogatory about Lew Rodowski and he wanted to rebuke French for digging through his past, but for a second the vodka was blocking signals. So he nodded.

'We knew your salary as a law professor, it's public record in Virginia, you know.'

'Yes it is.'

303

'Not a bad salary, Ray, but then it's a great law school.'

'It is indeed.'

'Digging through your brother's past was quite an adventure.'

'I'm sure it was. It's been an adventure for the family.'

'We read every ruling your father issued in damage suits and wrongful death cases. There weren't many, but we picked up clues. He was conservative with his awards, but he also favored the little guy, the working man. We knew he would follow the law, but we also knew that old chancellors often mold the law to fit their notion of fairness. I had clerks doing the grunt work, but I read every one of his important decisions. He was a brilliant man, Ray, and always fair. I never disagreed with one of his opinions.'

'You picked my father for the Gibson case?'

'Yes. When we made the decision to file the case in Chancery Court and try it without a jury, we also decided we did not want a local chancellor to hear it. We have three. One is related to the Gibson family. One refuses to hear any matter other than divorces. One is eighty-four, senile, and hasn't left the house in three years. So we looked around the state and found three potential fill-ins. Fortunately, my father and your father go back sixty years, to Sewanee and then law school at Ole Miss. They weren't close friends over the years, but they kept in touch.'

'Your father is still active?'

'No, he's in Florida now, retired, playing golf every day. I'm the sole owner of the firm. But my old man drove to Clanton, sat on the front porch with Judge Atlee, talked about the Civil War and Nathan Bedford Forrest. They even drove to Shiloh, walked around for two days – the hornet's nest, the bloody pond. Judge Atlee got all choked up when he stood where General Johnston fell.'

'I've been there a dozen times,' Ray said with a smile.

'You don't lobby a man like Judge Atlee. Earwigging is the ancient term.'

'He put a lawyer in jail once for that,' Ray said. 'The guy came in before court began and tried to plead his case. The Judge threw him in jail for half a day.'

'That was that Chadwick fella over in Oxford, wasn't it?' French said smugly, and Ray was speechless.

'Anyway, we had to impress upon Judge Atlee the importance of the Ryax litigation. We knew he wouldn't want to come to the coast and try the case, but he'd do it if he believed in the cause.'

'He hated the coast.'

'We knew that, believe me, it was a huge concern. But he was a man of great principle. After refighting the war up there for two days, Judge Atlee reluctantly agreed to hear the case.'

'Doesn't the Supreme Court assign the special chancellors?' Ray asked. The fourth sip sort of slid down, without burning, and the vodka was tasting better.

French shrugged it off. 'Sure, but there are ways. We have friends.'

In Patton French's world, anyone could be bought.

The steward was back with fresh drinks. Not that they were needed, but they were taken anyway. French was too hyper to sit still for long. 'Lemme show you the boat,' he said, and bounced out of his chair with no effort. Ray climbed out carefully, balancing his glass.

Chapter 31

Dinner was in the captain's galley, a mahogany-paneled dining room with walls adorned with models of ancient clippers and gunboats and maps of the New World and the Far East and even a collection of antique muskets thrown in to give the impression that the *King of Torts* had been around for centuries. It was on the main deck behind the bridge, just down a narrow hallway from the kitchen, where a Vietnamese chef was hard at work. The formal dining area was around an oval marble table that seated a dozen and weighed at least a ton and made Ray ask himself how, exactly, the *King of Torts* stayed afloat.

The captain's table sat only two this evening, and above it was a small chandelier that rocked with the sea. Ray was at one end, French at the other. The first wine of the night was a white burgundy that, following the scalding by two iced vodkas, was tasteless to Ray. Not to his host. French had knocked back three of the vodkas, had in fact drained all three glasses, and his tongue was beginning to thicken slightly. But he tasted every hint of fruit in the wine, even got a whiff of the oak barrels, and, as all wine snobs do, had to pass this useful information along to Ray.

'Here's to Ryax,' French said, reaching forward with his glass in a delayed toast. Ray touched his glass but said nothing. It was not a night for him to say much, and he knew it. He would just listen. His host would get drunk and say enough.

'Ryax saved me, Ray,' French said as he swirled his wine and admired it.

'In what way?'

'In every way. It saved my soul. I worship money, and Ryax has made me rich.' A small sip, followed by the requisite smacking of the lips, a rolling of the eyes. 'I missed the asbestos wave twenty years ago. Those shipyards over in Pascagoula used asbestos for years, and tens of thousands of men became ill. And I missed it. I was too busy suing doctors and insurance companies, and I was making good money but I just didn't see the potential in mass torts. You ready for some oysters?'

'Yes.'

French pushed a button; the steward popped in with two trays of raw oysters on the half shell. Ray mixed horseradish into the cocktail sauce and prepared for the feast. Patton was swirling wine and too busy talking.

'Then came tobacco,' he said sadly. 'Many of the same lawyers, from right here. I thought they were crazy, hell, everybody did, but they sued the big tobacco companies in almost every state. I had the chance to jump into the pit with them, but I was too scared. It's hard to admit that, Ray. I was just too damned scared to roll the dice.'

'What did they want?' Ray asked, then shoved the first oyster and saltine into his mouth.

'A million bucks to help finance the litigation. And I had a million bucks at the time.'

'How much was the settlement?' Ray asked, chewing.

'More than three hundred billion. The biggest financial and legal scam in history. The tobacco companies basically bought off the lawyers, who sold out. One huge bribe, and I missed it.' He appeared to be ready to cry because he'd missed a bribe, but he rallied quickly with a long pull on the wine.

'Good oysters,' Ray said, with a mouthful.

'Twenty-four hours ago, they were fifteen feet down.' French poured more wine and settled over his platter.

'What would've been the return on your one million dollars?' Ray asked.

'Two hundred to one.'

'Two hundred million bucks?'

'Yep. I was sick for a year, lots of lawyers around here were sick. We knew the players and we had chickened out.'

'Then along came Ryax.'

'Yes indeed.'

'How'd you find it?' Ray asked, knowing the question would require another windy answer, and he'd be free to eat.

'I was at a trial lawyers' seminar in St. Louis. Missouri is a nice place and all, but miles behind us when it comes to tort litigation. I mean, hell, we've had the asbestos and tobacco boys running around here for years, burning money, showing everybody else how it's done. I had a drink with this old lawyer from a small town in the Ozarks. His son teaches medicine at the university in Columbia, and the son was on to Ryax. His research was showing some horrible results. The damned drug just eats up the kidneys, and because it was so new there was not a history of litigation. I found an expert in Chicago, and he found Clete Gibson through a doctor in New Orleans. Then we started screening, and the thing snowballed. All we needed was a big verdict.'

'Why didn't you want a jury trial?'

'I love juries. I love to pick them, talk to them, sway them, manipulate them, even buy them, but they're unpredictable. I wanted a lock, a guarantee. And I wanted a speedy trial. Ryax rumors were spreading like crazy, you can imagine a bunch of hungry tort lawyers with the gossip that a new drug had gone bad. We were signing up cases by the dozens. The guy with the first big verdict would be in the driver's seat, especially if it came from the Biloxi area. Miyer-Brack is a Swiss company –'

'I've read the file.'

'All of it?'

'Yes, yesterday in the Hancock County Courthouse.'

'Well, these Europeans are terrified of our tort system.'

'Shouldn't they be?'

'Yes, but in a good way. Keeps 'em honest. What should terrify them is the possibility that one of their damned drugs is defective and might harm people, but that's not a concern when billions are at stake. It takes people like me to keep 'em honest.'

'And they knew Ryax was bad?'

French choked down another oyster, swallowed hard, gulped a half pint of wine, and finally said, 'Early on. The drug was so effective at lowering cholesterol that Miyer-Brack, along with the FDA, rushed it to the market. It was another miracle drug, and it worked great for a few years with no side effects. Then, bam! The tissue of the nephrons – do you understand how the kidneys work?'

'For the sake of this discussion, let's say I don't.'

'Each kidney has about a million little filtering units called nephrons, and Ryax contained a synthetic chemical that basically melted them. Not everybody dies, like poor Mr. Gibson, and there are varying degrees of damage. It's all

311

permanent, though. The kidney is an amazing organ that can often heal itself, but not after a five-year bout with Ryax.'

'When did Miyer-Brack know it had a problem?'

'Hard to say exactly, but we showed Judge Atlee some internal documents from their lab people to their suits urging caution and more research. After Ryax had been on the market for about four years, with spectacular results, the company's scientists were worried. Then folks started getting real sick, even dying, and by then it was too late. From my standpoint, we had to find the perfect client, which we did, the perfect forum, which we did, and we had to do it quick before some other lawyer got a big verdict. That's where your father came in.'

The steward cleared the oyster shells and presented a crabmeat salad. Another white burgundy had been selected from the onboard cellar by Mr. French himself.

'What happened after the Gibson trial?' Ray asked.

'I could not have scripted it better. Miyer-Brack absolutely crumbled. Arrogant shitheads were reduced to tears. They had a zillion bucks in cash and couldn't wait to buy off the plaintiffs' lawyers. Before the trial I had four hundred cases and no clout. Afterward, I had five thousand cases and an eleven-million-dollar verdict. Hundreds of lawyers called me. I spent a month flying around the country, in a Learjet, signing co-rep agreements with other lawyers. A guy in Kentucky had a hundred cases. One in St. Paul had eighty. On and on. Then, about four months after the trial, we flew to New York for the big settlement conference. In less than three hours we settled six thousand cases for seven hundred million bucks. A month later we settled another twelve hundred for two hundred million.'

'What was your cut?' Ray asked. It would've been a rude question if posed to a normal person, but French couldn't wait to talk about his fees.

'Fifty percent off the top for the lawyers, then expenses, the rest went to the clients. That's the bad part of a contingency contract – you have to give half to the client. Anyway, I had other lawyers to deal with, but I walked away with three hundred million and some change. That's the beauty of mass torts, Ray. Sign 'em up by the truckload, settle 'em by the trainload, take half off the top.'

They weren't eating. There was too much money in the air.

'Three hundred million in fees?' Ray said in disbelief.

French was gargling with wine. 'Ain't it sweet? It's coming so fast I can't spend it all.'

'Looks like you're giving it a good shot.'

'This is the tip of the iceberg. Ever hear of a drug called Minitrin?'

'I checked your Web site.'

'Really? What'd you think?'

'Pretty slick. Two thousand Minitrin cases.'

'Three thousand now. It's a hypertension drug that has dangerous side effects. Made by Shyne Medical. They've offered fifty thousand a case and I said no. Fourteen hundred Kobril cases, antidepressant that causes hearing loss, we think. Ever hear of Skinny Bens?'

'Yes.'

'We have three thousand Skinny Ben cases. And fifteen hundred –'

'I saw the list. I assume the Web site is updated.'

'Of course. I'm the new King of Torts in this country, Ray. Everybody's calling me. I have thirteen other lawyers in my firm and I need forty.'

The steward was back to collect their latest leftovers. He placed the swordfish in front of them and brought the next wine, though the last bottle was half full. French went through the tasting ritual and finally, almost reluctantly, nodded his approval. To Ray it tasted very similar to the first two.

'I owe it all to Judge Atlee,' French said.

'How?'

'He had the guts to make the right call, to keep Miyer-Brack in Hancock County instead of allowing them to escape to federal court. He understood the issues, and he was unafraid to punish them. Timing is everything, Ray. Less than six months after he handed down his ruling, I had three hundred million bucks in my hands.'

'Did you keep all of it?'

French had a bite on a fork close to his mouth. He hesitated for a second, then took the fish, chewed for a while, then said, 'I don't understand the question.'

'I think you do. Did you give any of the money to Judge Atlee?'

'Yes.'

'How much?'

'One percent.'

'Three million bucks?'

'And change. This fish is delicious, don't you think?'

'It is. Why?'

French put down his knife and fork and stroked his locks again with both hands. Then he wiped them on his napkin and swirled his wine. 'I suppose there are a lot of questions. Why, when, how, who.'

'You're good at stories, let's hear it.'

Another swirl, then a satisfied sip. 'It's not what you think, though I would've bribed your father or any judge for that ruling. I've done it before, and I'll happily do it again. It's just part of the overhead. Frankly, though, I was so intimidated by him and his reputation that I just couldn't approach him with a deal. He would've thrown me in jail.'

'He would've buried you in jail.'

'Yes, I know, and my father convinced me of

this. So we played it straight. The trial was an all-out war, but truth was on my side. I won, then I won big, now I'm winning even bigger. Late last summer, after we settled and the money was wired in, I wanted to give him a gift. I take care of those who help me, Ray. A new car here, a condo there, a sack full of cash for a favor. I play the game hard and I protect my friends.'

'He wasn't your friend.'

'We weren't amigos, or fraternity brothers, but in my world I've never had a greater friend. It all started with him. Do you realize how much money I'll make in the next five years?'

'Shock me again.'

'Half a billion. And I owe it all to your old man.'

'When will you have enough?'

'There's a tobacco lawyer here who made a billion. I need to catch him first.'

Ray needed a drink. He examined the wine as if he knew what to look for, then sucked it down. French was into the fish.

'I don't think you're lying,' Ray said.

'I don't lie. I cheat and bribe, but I don't lie. About six months ago, while I was shopping for airplanes and boats and beach homes and mountain cabins and new offices, I heard that your father had been diagnosed with cancer, and that it was serious. I wanted to do something nice for him. I knew he didn't have much money, and what he did have he seemed hell-bent on giving away.'

'So you sent him three million in cash?'

'Yes.'

'Just like that?'

'Just like that. I called him and told him a package was on the way. Four packages as it turned out, four large cardboard boxes. One of my boys drove them up in a van, left them on the front porch. Judge Atlee wasn't home.'

'Unmarked bills?'

'Why would I mark them?'

'What did he say?' Ray asked.

'I never heard a word, and I didn't want to.'

'What did he do?'

'You tell me. You're his son, you know him better than me. You tell me what he did with the money.'

Ray pushed back from the table, and holding his wineglass, he crossed his legs and tried to relax. 'He found the money on the porch, and when he realized what it was, I'm sure he gave you a thorough cursing.'

'God, I hope so.'

'He moved it into the foyer, where the boxes joined dozens of others. He planned to load it up and haul it back to Biloxi, but a day or two passed. He was sick and weak, and not driving too well. He knew he was dying, and I'm sure that burden changed his outlook on a lot of things. After a few days he decided to hide the money, which he did, and all the while he planned to get it back down here and flog your corrupt ass in the process. Time passed, and he got sicker.'

'Who found the money?'

'I did.'

'Where is it?'

'In the trunk of my car, at your office.'

French laughed long and hard. 'Back where it started from,' he said between breaths.

'It's had quite a tour. I found it in his study just after I found him dead. Someone tried to break in and get it. I took it to Virginia, now it's back, and that someone is following me.'

The laughter stopped immediately. He wiped his mouth with a napkin. 'How much did you find?'

'Three million, one hundred and eighteen thousand.'

'Damn! He didn't spend a dime.'

'And he didn't mention it in his will. He just left it, hidden in stationer's boxes in a cabinet beneath his bookshelves.'

'Who tried to break in?'

'I was hoping you might know.'

'I have a pretty good idea.'

'Please tell me.'

'It's another long story.'

Chapter 32

The steward brought a selection of single malts to the top deck where French had settled them in for a nightcap and another story, with a view of Biloxi flickering in the distance. Ray did not drink whiskey and certainly knew nothing about single malts, but he went along with the ritual because he knew French would get even drunker. The truth was flowing in torrents now, and Ray wanted all of it.

They settled on Lagavulin because of its smokiness, whatever that meant. There were four others, lined like proud old sentries in distinctive regalia, and Ray vowed he'd had enough to drink. He'd sip and spit and if he got the chance he'd toss it overboard. To his relief, the steward poured tiny servings in short thick glasses heavy enough to crack floors.

It was almost ten but felt much later. The Gulf was dark, no other boats were visible. A gentle wind blew from the south and rocked the *King of Torts* just slightly.

'Who knows about the money?' French asked, smacking his lips.

'Me, you, whoever hauled it up there.'

'That's your man.'

'Who is he?'

A long sip, more smacking. Ray brought the whiskey to his lips and wished he hadn't. Numb as they were, they burned all over again.

'Gordie Priest. He worked for me for eight or so years, first as a gofer, then a runner, then a bagman. His family has been on the coast forever, always on the edges. His father and uncles ran numbers, whores, moonshine, honky-tonks, nothing legal. They were part of what was once known as the coast mafia, a bunch of thugs who disdained honest work. Twenty years ago they controlled some things around here, now they're history. Most of them went to jail. Gordie's father, a man I knew very well, got shot outside a bar near Mobile. A pretty miserable lot, really. My family has known them for years.'

He was implying that his family had been part of the same bunch of crooks, but he couldn't say it. They'd been the front guys, the lawyers who smiled for the cameras and cut the backroom deals.

'Gordie went to jail when he was about twenty, a stolen car ring that covered a dozen states. I hired him when he got out, and over time he became one of the best runners on the coast. He was particularly good at the offshore cases. He knew the guys on the rigs, and when there was a death or injury he'd get the case. I'd give him a nice percentage. Gotta take care of your runners. One year I paid him almost eighty thousand, all of it in cash. He blew it, of course, casinos and women. Loved to go to Vegas and stay drunk for a week, throw money around like a big shot. He acted like an idiot but he wasn't stupid. He was always up and down. When he was broke he'd scramble and make some money. When he had money, he'd manage to lose it.'

'I'm sure this is all headed my way,' Ray said.

'Hang on,' French said. 'After the Gibson case early last year, the money hit like a tidal wave. I had favors to repay. Lots of cash got hauled around. Cash to lawyers who were sending me their cases. Cash to doctors who were screening thousands of new clients. Not all of it was illegal, mind you, but a lot of folks didn't want records. I made the mistake of using Gordie as the delivery boy. I thought I could trust him. I thought he would be loyal. I was wrong.'

French had finished one sample and was ready for another. Ray declined and pretended to work on the Lagavulin.

'And he drove the money up to Clanton and left it on the front porch?' Ray said.

'He did, and three months after that he stole a million dollars from me, in cash, and disappeared. He has two brothers, and at any given time during the past ten years one of the three has been in prison. Except for now. Now they're all on parole, and they're trying to extort big money out of me. Extortion is a serious crime, you know, but I can't exactly go to the FBI.'

'What makes you think he's after the three million bucks?'

'Wiretaps. We picked it up a few months ago. I've hired some pretty serious characters to find Gordie.'

'What will you do if you find him?'

'Oh, there's a price on his head.'

'You mean, like a contract?'

'Yes.'

And with that, Ray reached for another single malt.

He slept on the boat, in a large room somewhere under the water, and when he found his way to the main deck the sun was high in the east and the air was already hot and sticky. The captain said good morning and pointed forward, where he found French yelling into a phone.

The faithful steward materialized out of thin air and presented a coffee. Breakfast was up on the top deck at the scene of the single malts, now under a canopy for shade.

'I love to eat outdoors,' French announced as he joined Ray. 'You slept for ten hours.'

'Did I really?' Ray asked, looking again at his watch, which was still on Eastern time. He was on a yacht in the Gulf of Mexico, unsure of the day or time, a million miles from home, and now burdened with the knowledge that some very nasty people were chasing him.

The table was spread with breads and cereals. 'Tin Lu down there can fix anything you want,' French was saying. 'Bacon, eggs, waffles, grits.'

'This is fine, thanks.'

French was fresh and hyper, already tackling another grueling day with the energy that could only come from the prospect of a half a billion or so in fees. He was wearing a white linen shirt, buttoned at the top like the black one last night, shorts, loafers. His eyes were clear and dancing around. 'Just picked up another three hundred Minitrin cases,' he said as he dumped a generous portion of flakes into a large bowl. Every dish had the obligatory F&F monogram splashed on it.

Ray had had enough of mass torts. 'Good, but I'm more interested in Gordie Priest.'

'We'll find him. I'm already making calls.'

'He's probably in town.' Ray pulled a folded sheet of paper from his rear pocket. It was the photo of 37F he'd found yesterday morning on his windshield. French looked at it and stopped eating.

'And this is up in Virginia?' he asked.

'Yep, the second of three units I rented. They've found the first two, I'm sure they know about the third. And they knew exactly where I was yesterday morning.'

'But they obviously don't know where the

money is. Otherwise, they would have simply taken it from the trunk of your car while you were asleep. Or they would've pulled you over somewhere between here and Clanton and put a bullet in your ear.'

'You don't know what they're thinking.'

'Sure I do. Think like a crook, Ray. Think like a thug.'

'It may come easy for you, but it's harder for some folks.'

'If Gordie and his brothers knew you had three million bucks in the trunk of your car, they would take it. Simple as that.' He put the photo down and attacked his flakes.

'Nothing is simple,' Ray said.

'What do you wanna do? Leave the money with me?'

'Yes.'

'Don't be stupid, Ray. Three million tax-free dollars.'

'Useless if I get the ole bullet in the ear. I have a very nice salary.'

'The money is safe. Keep it where it is. Give me some time to find these boys, and they'll be neutralized.'

The neutralization sapped any appetite Ray had.

'Eat, man!' French barked when Ray grew still.

'I don't have the stomach for this. Dirty money, bad guys breaking into my apartment, chasing me all over the Southeast, wiretaps, contract killers. What the hell am I doing here?'

French never stopped chewing. His intestines were lined with brass. 'Keep cool,' he said. 'And the money'll be yours.'

'I don't want the money.'

'Of course you do.'

'No I don't.'

'Then give it to Forrest.'

'What a disaster.'

'Give it to charity. Give it your law school. Give it to something that makes you feel good.'

'Why don't I just give it to Gordie so he won't shoot me?'

French gave his spoon a rest and looked around as if others were lurking. 'All right, we spotted Gordie last night over in Pascagoula,' he said, an octave lower. 'We're hot on his trail, okay? I think we'll have him within twenty-four hours.'

'And he'll be neutralized?'

'He'll be iced.'

'Iced?'

'Gordie'll be history. Your money'll be safe. Just hang on, okay.'

'I'd like to leave now.'

French wiped skim milk off his bottom lip, then picked up his mini radio and told Dickie to get the boat ready. Minutes later, they were ready to board.

'Take a look at these,' French said, handing over an eight-by-twelve manila envelope.

'What is it?'

'Photos of the Priest boys. Just in case you bump into them.'

Ray ignored the envelope until he stopped in Hattiesburg, ninety minutes north of the coast. He bought gas and a dreadful shrink-wrapped sandwich, then was off again, in a hurry to get to Clanton, where Harry Rex knew the sheriff and all his deputies.

Gordie had a particularly menacing sneer, one that had been captured by a police photographer in 1991. His brothers, Slatt and Alvin, were certainly no prettier. Ray couldn't tell the oldest from the youngest, not that it mattered. None of the three resembled the others. Bad breeding. Same mother, no doubt different fathers.

They could have a million each, he didn't care. Just leave me alone.

Chapter 33

The hills began between Jackson and Memphis, and the coast seemed time zones away. He had often wondered at how a state so small could be so diverse: the Delta region along the river with the wealth of its cotton and rice farms and the poverty that still astonished outsiders; the coast with its blend of immigrants and laidback, New Orleans casualness; and the hills where most counties were still dry and most folks still went to church on Sundays. A person from the hills would never understand the coast and never be accepted in the Delta. Ray was just happy he lived in Virginia.

Patton French was a dream, he kept telling himself. A cartoonish character from another world. A pompous jerk being eaten alive by his own ego. A liar, a briber, a shameless crook.

Then he would glance over at the passenger's seat and see the sinister face of Gordie Priest. One glance and there was no doubt this brute and his brothers would do anything for the money Ray was still hauling around the country.

An hour from Clanton, and again within range of a tower, his cell phone rang. It was Fog Newton and he was quite agitated. 'Where the hell have you been?' he demanded.

'You wouldn't believe me.'

'I've been calling all morning.'

'What is it, Fog?'

'We've had a little excitement around here. Last night, after general aviation closed, somebody sneaked onto the ramp and put an incendiary device on the left wing of the Bonanza. Boom. A janitor in the main terminal just happened to see the blaze, and they got the fire truck out pretty fast.'

Ray had pulled onto the shoulder of Interstate 55 and stopped. He grunted something into the phone and Fog kept going. 'Severe damage though. No doubt it was an act of arson. You there?'

'Just listening,' Ray said. 'How much damage?'

'Left wing, the engine, and most of the fuselage, probably a total loss for insurance purposes. The arson investigator is already here. Insurance guy's here too. If the tanks had been full it would've been a bomb.'

'The other owners know about it?'

'Yes, everyone's been out. Of course they're first on the suspect list. Lucky you were out of town. When are you coming back?'

'Soon.'

He made it to an exit and pulled into the gravel lot of a truck stop, where he sat in the heat for a long time and occasionally glanced down at Gordie. The Priest gang moved fast – Biloxi yesterday morning, Charlottesville last night. Where are they now?

Inside, he drank coffee and listened to the chatter of the truckers. To change the subject, he called Alcorn Village to check on Forrest. He was in his room, sleeping the sleep of the righteous, as he described it. It was always amazing, he said, how much he slept in rehab. He'd complained about the food, and things had improved slightly. Either that or he had developed a taste for pink Jell-O. He asked how long he could stay, like a kid at Disney World. Ray said he wasn't sure. The money that had once seemed endless was now very much in jeopardy.

'Don't let me out, Bro,' he pleaded. 'I want to stay in rehab for the remainder of my life.'

The Atkins boys had finished the roof at Maple Run without incident. The place was deserted when Ray arrived. He called Harry Rex and checked in. 'Let's drink some beer on the porch tonight,' Ray suggested.

Harry Rex had never said no to such an invitation.

There was a level spot of thick grass just beyond the front sidewalk, directly in front of the house, and after careful deliberation Ray decided it was the place for a washing. He parked the little Audi there, facing the street, its rear and its trunk just a step from the porch. He found an old tin bucket in the basement and a leaky water hose in the back shed. Shirtless and shoeless, he sloshed around for two hours in the hot afternoon sun, scrubbing the roadster. Then he waxed and polished it for an hour. At 5 P.M., he opened a cold bottle of beer and sat on the steps, admiring his work.

He called the private cell phone number given to him by Patton French, but of course the great man was too busy. Ray wanted to thank him for his hospitality, but what he really wanted was to see if they had made any progress down there icing the Priest gang. He would never ask that question directly, but a blowhard like French would happily deliver the news if he had it.

French had probably forgotten about him. He didn't really care if the Priest boys nailed Ray or the next guy. He needed to make a half a billion or so in mass tort schemes, and that took all his energies. Indict a guy like French, for payoffs or contract killings, and he'd hire fifty lawyers and buy every clerk, judge, prosecutor, and juror.

He called Corey Crawford and got the news that the landlord had once again repaired the doors. The police had promised to keep an eye on the place for the next few days, until he returned.

The van pulled into the driveway shortly after

6 P.M. A smiling face jumped out with a thin overnight envelope, which Ray stared at long after it had been delivered. The airbill was a preprinted form from the University of Virginia School of Law, hand-addressed to Mr. Ray Atlee, Maple Run, 816 Fourth Street, Clanton, MS, dated June 2, the day before. Everything about it was suspicious.

No one at the law school had been given the address in Clanton. Nothing from there would be so urgent as to require an overnight delivery. And he could think of no reason whatsoever that the school would be sending him anything. He opened another beer and returned to the front steps, where he grabbed the damned thing and ripped it open.

Plain white legal-size envelope, with the word 'Ray' hand-scrawled on the outside. And on the inside, another of the now familiar color photos of Chaney's Self-Storage, this time the front of unit 18R. At the bottom, in a wacky font of mismatched letters, was the message: 'You don't need an airplane. Stop spending the money.'

These guys were very, very good. It was tough enough to track down the three units at Chaney's and take pictures of them. It was gutsy and also stupid to burn up the Bonanza. Oddly, though, what was most impressive at the moment was their ability to swipe an airbill from the business office at the law school.

After a prolonged moment of shock, he

realized something that should have been immediately obvious. Since they'd found 18R, then
they knew the money wasn't there. It wasn't at
Chaney's, nor at his apartment. They'd followed
him from Virginia to Clanton, and if he'd
stopped somewhere along the way to hide the
money, they would know it. They'd probably
rummaged through Maple Run again, while he
was on the coast.

Their net was tightening by the hour. All clues
were being linked, all dots connected. The
money had to be with him, and Ray had no
place to run.

He had a very comfortable salary as a professor of law, with benefits. His lifestyle was not
expensive, and he decided right there on the
porch, still shirtless and shoeless, sipping a beer
in the early evening humidity of a long hot June
day, that he preferred to continue that lifestyle.
Leave the violence for the likes of Gordie Priest
and hit men hired by Patton French. Ray was
out of his element.

The cash was dirty anyway.

'Why'd you park in the front yard?' Harry Rex
grumbled as he lumbered up the steps.

'I washed it and left it there,' Ray said. He had
showered and was wearing shorts and a tee shirt.

'You just can't get the redneck outta some
people. Gimme a beer.'

Harry Rex had been brawling in court all day,
a nasty divorce where the weighty issues were

which spouse had smoked the most dope ten years ago and which one had slept with the most people. The custody of four children was at stake, and neither parent was fit.

'I'm too old for this,' he said, very tired. By the second beer he was nodding off.

Harry Rex controlled the divorce docket in Ford County and had for twenty-five years. Feuding couples often raced to hire him first. One farmer over at Karraway kept him on retainer so he would be available for the next split. He was very bright, but could also be vile and vicious. This had wide appeal in the heat of divorce wars.

But the work was taking its toll. Like all small-town lawyers, Harry Rex longed for the big kill. The big damage suit with a forty percent contingency fee, something to retire on.

The night before, Ray had been sipping expensive wines on a twenty-million-dollar yacht built by a Saudi prince and owned by a member of the Mississippi bar who was plotting billion-dollar schemes against multinationals. Now he was sipping Bud in a rusted swing with a member of the Mississippi bar who'd spent the day bickering over custody and alimony.

'The Realtor showed the house this morning,' Harry Rex said. 'He called me during lunch, woke me up.'

'Who's the prospect?'

'Remember those Kapshaw boys up near Rail Springs?'

'No.'

'Good boys. They started buildin' chairs in an old barn ten years ago, maybe twelve. One thang led to another, and they sold out to some big furniture outfit up in the Carolinas. Each of 'em walked away with a million bucks. Junkie and his wife are lookin' for houses.'

'Junkie Kapshaw?'

'Yeah, but he's tight as Dick's hatband and he ain't payin' four hundred thousand for this place.'

'I don't blame him.'

'His wife's crazy as hell and thinks she wants an old house. The Realtor is pretty sure they'll make an offer, but it'll be low, probably about a hundred seventy-five thousand.' Harry Rex was yawning.

They talked about Forrest for a spell, then things were silent. 'Guess I'd better go,' he said. After three beers, Harry Rex began his exit.

'When are you going back to Virginia?' he asked, struggling to his feet and stretching his back.

'Maybe tomorrow.'

'Gimme a call,' he said, yawning again, and walked down the steps.

Ray watched the lights of his car disappear down the street, and he was suddenly and completely alone again. The first noise was a rustling in the shrubbery near the property line, probably an old dog or cat on the prowl, but

334

regardless of how harmless it was it spooked Ray and he ran inside.

Chapter 34

The attack began shortly after 2 A.M., at the darkest hour of the night, when sleep is heaviest and reactions slowest. Ray was dead to the world, though the world had weighed heavily on his weary mind. He was on a mattress in the foyer, pistol by his side, the three garbage bags of cash next to his makeshift bed.

It began with a brick through the window, a blast that rattled the old house and rained glass and debris across the dining room table and the newly polished wooden floors. It was a well-placed and well-timed throw from someone who meant business and had probably done it before. Ray clawed his way upright like a wounded alley cat and was lucky not to shoot himself as he groped for his gun. He darted low across the foyer, hit a light switch, and saw the brick resting ominously next to a baseboard near the china cabinet.

Using a quilt, he swept away the debris and carefully picked up the brick, a new red one with sharp edges. Attached was a note held in place by two thick rubber bands. He removed them while looking at the remains of the window. His hands were shaking to the point of not being able to read the note. He swallowed hard, tried to breathe, tried to focus on the handwritten warning.

It read simply: 'Put the money back where you found it, then leave the house immediately.'

His hand was bleeding, a small nick from a piece of glass. It was his shooting hand, if in fact he had such a thing, and in the horror of the moment he wondered how he could protect himself. He crouched in the shadows of the dining room, telling himself to breathe, to think clearly.

Suddenly, the phone rang, and he jumped out of his skin again. A second ring, and he scrambled into the kitchen where a dim light above the stove helped him grapple for the phone. 'Hello!' he barked into the receiver.

'Put the money back, and leave the house,' said a calm but rigid voice, one he'd never heard, one he thought, in the blur of the moment, carried a slight trace of a coast accent. 'Now! Before you get hurt.'

He wanted to scream, 'No,' or 'Stop it,' or 'Who are you?' But his indecision caused him to hesitate, and the line went dead. He sat on the floor, and with his back to the refrigerator he quickly ran through his options, slim as they were.

He could call the police – hustle and hide the money, stuff the bags under a bed, move the mattress, conceal the note but not the brick, and carry on as if some delinquents were vandalizing an old house just for the hell of it. The cop would walk around with a flashlight and linger for an hour or two, but he would leave at some point.

The Priest boys were not leaving. They had stuck to him like glue. They might duck for a moment, but they were not leaving. And they were far more nimble than the Clanton night-watchman. And far more inspired.

He could call Harry Rex – wake him up, tell him it was urgent, get him back over to the house and unload the entire story. Ray yearned for someone to talk to. How many times had he wanted to come clean with Harry Rex? They could split the money, or include it in the estate, or take it to Tunica and roll dice for a year.

But why endanger him too? Three million was enough to provoke more than one killing.

Ray had a gun. Why couldn't he protect himself? He could fend off the attackers. When they came through the door, he'd light the place up. The gunfire would alert the neighbors, the whole town would be there.

It just took one bullet, though, one well-aimed, pointed little missile that he would never see and probably feel only for a moment, or two. And he was outnumbered by some fellas who'd fired a helluva lot more of them than Professor

Ray Atlee. He had already decided that he was not willing to die. Life back home was too good.

Just as his heart rate peaked and he felt his pulse start to decline, another brick came crashing through the small window above the kitchen sink. He jerked and yelled and dropped his gun, then kicked it as he scrambled toward the foyer. On hands and knees he dragged the three bags of cash into the Judge's study. He yanked the sofa away from the bookshelves and began throwing the stacks of bills back into the cabinet where he'd found the wretched loot in the first place. He was sweating and cursing and expecting another brick or maybe the first round of ammo. When all of it had been crammed back into its hiding place, he picked up the pistol and unlocked the front door. He darted to his car, cranked it, spun ruts down the front lawn, and finished his escape.

He was unharmed, and at the moment that was his only concern.

North of Clanton, the land dipped in the backwaters of Lake Chatoula, and for a two-mile stretch the road was straight and flat. Known simply as The Bottoms, it had long been the turf of late-night drag racers, boozers, ruffians, and hell-raisers in general. His nearest brush with death, prior to that moment, had been in high school when he found himself in the backseat of a packed Pontiac Firebird driven by a drunken Bobby Lee West and drag racing a Camaro driven by an even drunker Doug Terring, both cars flying at a hundred miles an hour through The Bottoms. He had walked away from it, but Bobby Lee had been killed a year later when his Firebird left the road and met a tree.

When he hit the flat stretch of The Bottoms, he pressed the accelerator of his TT and let it unwind. It was two-thirty in the morning, surely everyone else was asleep.

Elmer Conway had indeed been asleep, but a fat mosquito had taken blood from his forehead and awakened him in the process. He saw lights, a car was approaching rapidly, he turned on his radar. It took almost four miles to get the funny little foreign job pulled over, and by then Elmer was angry.

Ray made the mistake of opening his door and getting out, and that was not what Elmer had in mind.

'Freeze, asshole!' Elmer shouted, over the barrel of his service revolver, which, as Ray quickly realized, was aimed at his head.

'Relax, relax,' he said, throwing up his hands in complete surrender.

'Get away from the car,' Elmer growled, and with the gun pointed to a spot somewhere around the center line.

'No problem, sir, just relax,' Ray said, shuffling sideways.

'What's your name?'

'Ray Atlee, Judge Atlee's son. Could you put that gun down, please?'

Elmer lowered the gun a few inches, enough so that a discharge would hit Ray in the stomach, but not the head. 'You got Virginia plates,' Elmer said.

'That's because I live in Virginia.'

'Is that where you're headed?'

'Yes sir.'

'What's the big hurry?'

'I don't know, I just –'

'I clocked you doing ninety-eight.'

'I'm very sorry.'

'Sorry's ass. That's reckless driving.' Elmer took a step closer. Ray had forgotten about the cut on his hand and he was not aware of the one on his knee. Elmer removed a flashlight and did a body scan from ten feet away. 'Why are you bleedin'?'

It was a very good question, and, at that moment, standing in the middle of the dark highway with a light flashed in his face, Ray could not think of an adequate response. The truth would take an hour and fall on unbelieving ears. A lie would only make matters worse. 'I don't know,' he mumbled.

'What's in the car?' Elmer asked.

'Nothing.'

'Sure.'

He handcuffed Ray and put him in the backseat of his Ford County patrol car, a brown Impala with dust on the fenders, no hubcaps, a collection of antennae mounted on the rear bumper. Ray watched as he walked around the

TT and looked inside. When Elmer was finished he crawled into the front seat, and without turning around said, 'What's the gun for?'

Ray had tried to slide the pistol under the passenger's seat. Evidently it was visible from the outside.

'Protection.'

'You got a permit?'

'No.'

Elmer called the dispatcher and made a lengthy report of his latest stop. He concluded with, 'I'm bringin' him in,' as if he had just collared one of the ten most wanted.

'What about my car?' Ray asked, as they turned around.

'I'll send a wrecker out.'

Elmer turned on the red and blue lights and pushed the speedometer to eighty.

'Can I call my lawyer?' Ray asked.

'No.'

'Come on. It's just a traffic offense. My lawyer can meet me at the jail, post bond, and in an hour I'm back on the road.'

'Who's your lawyer?'

'Harry Rex Vonner.'

Elmer grunted and his neck grew thicker. 'Sumbitch cleaned me out in my divorce.'

And with that Ray sat back and closed his eyes.

Ray had actually seen the inside of the Ford County jail on two occasions, he recalled as

Elmer led him up the front sidewalk. Both times he had taken papers to deadbeat fathers who'd been years behind in child support, and Judge Atlee had locked them up. Haney Moak, the slightly retarded jailer in an oversized uniform, was still there at the front desk, reading detective magazines. He also served as the dispatcher for the graveyard shift, so he knew of Ray's transgressions.

'Judge Atlee's boy, huh?' Haney said with a crooked grin. His head was lopsided and his eyes were uneven, and whenever Haney spoke it was a challenge to maintain a visual.

'Yes sir,' Ray said politely, looking for friends.

'He was a fine man,' he said as he moved behind Ray and unlocked the cuffs.

Ray rubbed his wrists and looked at Deputy Conway, who was busy filling in forms and being very officious. 'Reckless, and no gun permit.'

'You ain't lockin' him up, are you?' Haney said to Elmer, quite rudely as if Haney were in charge of the case now, and not the deputy.

'Damned right,' Elmer shot back, and the situation was immediately tense.

'Can I call Harry Rex Vonner?' Ray pleaded.

Haney nodded toward a wall-mounted phone as if he could not care less. He was glaring at Elmer. The two obviously had a history that was not pretty. 'My jail's full now,' Haney said.

'That's what you always say.'

Ray quickly punched Harry Rex's home number. It was after 3 A.M., and he knew the interruption would not be appreciated. The current Mrs. Vonner answered after the third ring. Ray apologized for the call and asked for Harry Rex.

'He's not here,' she said.

He's not out of town, Ray thought. He was on the front porch six hours ago. 'May I ask where he is?'

Haney and Elmer were practically yelling at each other in the background.

'He's over at the Atlee place,' she said slowly.

'No, he left there hours ago. I was with him.'

'No, they just called. The house is burning.'

With Haney in the backseat, they flew around the square, lights and sirens fully engaged. From two blocks away, they could see the blaze. 'Lord have mercy,' Haney said from the back.

Few events excited Clanton like a good fire. The town's two pumpers were there. Dozens of volunteers were darting about, all seemed to be yelling. The neighbors were gathering on the sidewalks across the street.

Flames were already shooting through the roof. As Ray stepped over a water line and eased onto the front lawn, he breathed the unmistakable odor of gasoline.

Chapter 35

The love nest wasn't a bad place for a nap after all. It was a long narrow room with dust and spiderwebs and one light hanging in the center of the vaulted ceiling. The lone window had been painted sometime in the last century and overlooked the square. The bed was an iron antique with no sheets or blankets, and he tried not to think about Harry Rex and his misadventures on that very mattress. Instead, he thought of the old house at Maple Run and the glorious way it went into history. By the time the roof collapsed, half of Clanton was there. Ray had sat alone, on the low limb of a sycamore across the street, hidden from all, trying in vain to pull cherished memories from a wonderful childhood that simply had not happened. When the flames were shooting from every window, he had not thought of the cash or the Judge's desk or his mother's dining room table, but only of old General Forrest glaring down with those fierce eyes.

Three hours of sleep, and he was awake by eight. The temperature was rising rapidly in the den of iniquity, and heavy steps were coming his way.

Harry Rex swung the door open and turned on the light. 'Wake up, felon,' he growled. 'They want you down at the jail.'

Ray swung his feet to the floor. 'My escape was fair and square.' He had lost Elmer and Haney in the crowd and simply left with Harry Rex.

'Did you tell them they could search your car?'

'I did.'

'That was a dumb-ass thing to do. What kinda lawyer are you?' He pulled a wooden folding chair from the wall and sat down near the bed.

'There was nothing to hide.'

'You're stupid, you know that? They searched the car and found nothing.'

'That's what I expected.'

'No clothes, no overnight bag, no luggage, no toothbrush, no evidence whatsoever that you were simply leaving town and going home, per your official story.'

'I did not burn the house down, Harry Rex.'

'Well, you're an excellent suspect. You flee in the middle of the night, no clothes, no nothing, you drive away like a bat outta hell. Old lady Larrimore down the street sees you in your funny little car go flyin' by, then about ten minutes later here come the fire trucks. You're

caught by the dumbest deputy in the state doin'
ninety-eight, drivin' like hell to get away from
here. Defend yourself.'

'I didn't torch it.'

'Why did you leave at two-thirty?'

'Someone threw a rock through the dining
room window. I got scared.'

'You had a gun.'

'I didn't want to use it. I'd rather run away
than shoot somebody.'

'You've been up North too long.'

'I don't live up North.'

'How'd you get cut up like that?'

'The brick broke the window, you see, and
when I checked it out, I got cut.'

'Why didn't you call the police?'

'I panicked. I wanted to go home, so I left.'

'And ten minutes later somebody soaks the
place with gasoline and throws a match.'

'I don't know what they did.'

'I'd convict you.'

'No, you're my lawyer.'

'No, I'm the lawyer for the estate, which by
the way just lost its only asset.'

'There's fire insurance.'

'Yeah, but you can't get it.'

'Why not?'

'Because if you file a claim, then they'll
investigate you for arson. If you say you didn't
do it, then I believe you. But I'm not sure
anybody else will. If you go after the insurance,

then those boys will come after you with a vengeance.'

'I didn't torch it.'

'Great, then who did?'

'Whoever threw the brick.'

'And who might that be?'

'I have no idea. Maybe some guy who got the bad end of a divorce.'

'Brilliant. And he waits nine years to get revenge on the Judge, who, by the way, is dead. I will not be in the courtroom when you offer that to the jury.'

'I don't know, Harry Rex. I swear I didn't do it. Forget the insurance money.'

'It's not that easy. Only half is yours, the other half belongs to Forrest. He can file a claim for the insurance coverage.'

Ray breathed deeply and scratched his stubble. 'Help me here, okay?'

'The sheriff's downstairs, with one of his investigators. They'll ask some questions. Answer slowly, tell the truth, blah, blah. I'll be there, so let's go slow.'

'He's here?'

'In my conference room. I asked him to come over so we can do this now. I really think you need to get out of town.'

'I was trying.'

'The reckless driving and the gun charge will be put off for a few months. Give me some time to work the docket. You got bigger problems right now.'

'I did not torch the house, Harry Rex.'

'Of course you didn't.'

They left the room and started down the unsteady steps to the second floor. 'Who's the sheriff?' Ray asked, over his shoulder.

'Guy named Sawyer.'

'Good guy?'

'It doesn't matter.'

'You close to him?'

'I did his son's divorce.'

The conference room was a wonderful mess of thick law books thrown about on shelves and credenzas and the long table itself. The impression was given that Harry Rex spent hours in tedious research. He did not.

Sawyer was not the least bit polite, nor was his assistant, a nervous little Italian named Sandroni. Italians were rare in northeast Mississippi, and during the tense introductions Ray detected a Delta accent. The two were all business, with Sandroni taking careful notes while Sawyer sipped steaming coffee from a paper cup and watched every move Ray made.

The fire call was made by Mrs. Larrimore at two thirty-four, approximately ten to fifteen minutes after she'd seen Ray's car leave Fourth Street in a hurry. Elmer Conway radioed at two thirty-six that he was in pursuit of some idiot doing a hundred miles an hour down in The Bottoms. Since it was established that Ray was driving very fast, Sandroni spent a long time nailing down his route, his estimated speeds, traffic lights, anything to slow him down at that hour of the morning.

Once Ray's exit route was determined, Sawyer radioed a deputy, who was sitting in front of the rubble at Maple Run, and told him to drive the exact course at the same estimated speeds and to stop out in The Bottoms where Elmer was once again waiting.

Twelve minutes later, the deputy called back and said he was with Elmer.

'So in less than twelve minutes,' Sandroni said as he began his recap, 'Someone – and we're assuming this someone was not already in the house, aren't we, Mr. Atlee? – entered with what evidently was a large supply of gasoline and soaked the place thoroughly, so thoroughly that the fire captain said he'd never smelled such a strong odor of gas, then threw a match or maybe two, because the fire captain was almost certain the fire had more than one point of origin, and once the matches were thrown this unknown arsonist fled into the night. Right, Mr. Atlee?'

'I don't know what the arsonist did,' Ray said.

'But the times are accurate?'

'If you say so.'

'I say so.'

'Move along,' Harry Rex growled from the end of the table.

Motive was next. The house was insured for $380,000, including contents. According to the Realtor, who'd already been consulted, he'd been writing up an offer to purchase it for $175,000.

'That's a nice gap, isn't it, Mr. Atlee?' Sandroni inquired.

'It is.'

'Have you notified your insurance company?' Sandroni asked.

'No, I thought I'd wait until their offices open,' Ray responded. 'Believe it or not, some folks don't work on Saturday.'

'Hell, the fire truck's still there,' Harry Rex added helpfully. 'We got six months to file a claim.'

Sandroni's cheeks turned crimson but he held his tongue. Moving right along, he studied his notes and said, 'Let's talk about other suspects.'

Ray didn't like the use of the word 'other.' He told the story about the brick through the window, or at least most of the story. And the phone call, warning him to leave immediately. 'Check the phone records,' he challenged them. And for good measure, he threw in the earlier adventures with some demented soul rattling windows the night the Judge died.

'Y'all had enough,' Harry Rex said after thirty minutes. In other words, my client will answer no more questions.

'When are you leaving town?' asked Sawyer.

'I've been trying to leave for the past six hours,' Ray replied.

'Real soon,' said Harry Rex.

'We may have some more questions.'

'I'll come back whenever I'm needed,' Ray said.

Harry Rex shoved them out the front door, and when he returned to the conference room he said, 'I think you're a lyin' sonofabitch.'

Chapter 36

The old fire truck was gone, the same one Ray and his friends had followed when they were teenagers and bored on summer nights. A lone volunteer in a dirty tee shirt was folding fire hoses. The street was a mess with mud strewn everywhere.

Maple Run was deserted by midmorning. The chimney on the east end was still standing, as was a short section of charred wall beside it. Everything else had collapsed into a pile of debris. Ray and Harry Rex walked around the rubble and went to the backyard, where a row of ancient pecan trees protected the rear boundary of the property. They sat in the shade, in metal lawn chairs that Ray had once painted red, and ate tamales.

'I didn't burn this place,' Ray finally said.

'Do you know who did?' Harry Rex asked.

'I have a suspect.'

'Tell me, dammit.'

'His name is Gordie Priest.'

'Oh him!'

'It's a long story.'

Ray began with the Judge, dead on the sofa, and the accidental discovery of the money, or was it an accident after all? He gave as many facts and details as he could remember, and he raised all the questions that had been dogging him for weeks. Both stopped eating. They stared at the smoldering debris but were too mesmerized to see it. Harry Rex was stunned by the narrative. Ray was relieved to be telling it. From Clanton to Charlottesville and back. From the casinos in Tunica to Atlantic City, then back to Tunica. To the coast and Patton French and his quest for a billion dollars, all to be credited to Judge Reuben Atlee, humble servant of the law.

Ray held back nothing, and he tried to remember everything. The ransacking of his apartment in Charlottesville, for intimidation only, he thought. The ill-advised purchase of a share in a Bonanza. On and on he went, while Harry Rex said nothing.

When he finished, his appetite was gone and he was sweating. Harry Rex had a million questions, but he began with, 'Why would he burn the house?'

'Cover his tracks, maybe, I don't know.'

'This guy didn't leave tracks.'

'Maybe it was the final act of intimidation.'

They mulled this over. Harry Rex finished a tamale and said, 'You should've told me.'

'I wanted to keep the money, okay? I had

three million bucks in cash in my sticky little hands, and it felt wonderful. It was better than sex, better than anything I'd ever felt. Three million bucks, Harry Rex, all mine. I was rich. I was greedy. I was corrupt. I didn't want you or Forrest or the government or anyone in the world to know that I had the money.'

'What were you gonna do with it?'

'Ease it into banks, a dozen of them, nine thousand dollars at a time, no paperwork that would alert the government, let it pile up over eighteen months, then invest it with a pro. I'm forty-three; in two years the money would be laundered and hard at work. It would double every five years. At the age of fifty, it would be six million. Fifty-five, twelve million. At the age of sixty, I'd have twenty-four million bucks. I had it all planned, Harry Rex. I could see the future.'

'Don't beat yourself up. What you did was normal.'

'It doesn't feel normal.'

'You're a lousy crook.'

'I felt lousy, and I was already changing. I could see myself in an airplane and a fancier sports car and a nicer place to live. There's a lot of money around Charlottesville, and I was thinking about making a splash. Country clubs, fox hunting –'

'Fox hunting?'

'Yep.'

'With those little britches and the hat?'

'Flying over fences on a wild horse, chasing a pack of hounds that are in hot pursuit of a thirty-pound fox that you'll never see.'

'Why would you wanna do that?'

'Why would anyone?'

'I'll stick to huntin' birds.'

'Anyway, it was a burden, literally. I mean, I've been hauling the cash around for weeks.'

'You could've left some at my office.'

Ray finished a tamale and sipped a cola. 'You think I'm stupid?'

'No, lucky. This guy plays for keeps.'

'Every time I closed my eyes, I could see a bullet coming at my forehead.'

'Look, Ray, you've done nothing wrong. The Judge didn't want the money included in his estate. You took it because you thought you were protectin' it, and also guardin' his reputation. You had a crazy man who wanted it more than you. Lookin' back, you're lucky you didn't get hurt in the whole episode. Forget it.'

'Thanks, Harry Rex.' Ray leaned forward and watched the volunteer fireman walk away. 'What about the arson?'

'We'll work it out. I'll file a claim, and the insurance company will investigate. They'll suspect arson and thangs'll get ugly. Let a few months pass. If they don't pay, then we'll sue, in Ford County. They won't risk a jury trial against the estate of Reuben Atlee right here in his own courthouse. I think they'll settle before trial. We may have to compromise some, but we'll get a nice settlement.'

Ray was on his feet. 'I really want to go home,' he said.

The air was thick with heat and smoke as they walked around the house. 'I've had enough,' Ray said, and headed for the street.

He drove a perfect fifty-five through The Bottoms. Elmer Conway was nowhere to be seen. The Audi seemed lighter with the trunk empty. Indeed, life itself was shedding burdens. Ray longed for the normalcy of home.

He dreaded the meeting with Forrest. Their father's estate had just been wiped out, and the arson issue would be difficult to explain. Perhaps he should wait. Rehab was going so smoothly, and Ray knew from experience that the slightest complication could derail Forrest. Let a month go by. Then another.

Forrest would not be going back to Clanton, and in his murky world he might never hear of the fire. It might be best if Harry Rex broke the news to him.

The receptionist at Alcorn Village gave him a curious look when he signed in. He read magazines for a long time in the dark lounge where the visitors waited. When Oscar Meave eased in with a gloomy look, Ray knew exactly what had happened.

'He walked away late yesterday afternoon,' Meave began as he crouched on the coffee table in front of Ray. 'I've tried to reach you all morning.'

'I lost my cell phone last night,' Ray said. Of all the things he'd left behind when the rocks were falling, he couldn't believe he'd forgotten his cell phone.

'He signed in for the ridge walk, a five-mile nature trail he's been doing every day. It's around the back of the property, no fencing, but then Forrest was not a security risk. We didn't think so, anyway. I can't believe this.'

Ray certainly could. His brother had been walking away from detox units for almost twenty years.

'This is not really a lockdown facility,' Meave continued. 'Our patients want to stay here, or it doesn't work.'

'I understand,' Ray said softly.

'He was doing so well,' Meave went on, obviously more troubled than Ray. 'Completely clean and very proud of it. He had sort of adopted two teenagers, both in rehab for the first time. Forrest worked with them every morning. I just don't understand this one.'

'I thought you are an ex-addict.'

Meave was shaking his head. 'I know, I know. The addict quits when the addict wants to, and not before.'

'Have you ever seen one who just couldn't quit?' Ray asked.

'We can't admit that.'

'I know you can't. But, off the record, you

and I both know that there are addicts who will never kick it.'

Meave shrugged, with reluctance.

'Forrest is one of those, Oscar. We've lived this for twenty years.'

'I take it as a personal failure.'

'Don't.'

They walked outside and talked for a moment under a veranda. Meave could not stop apologizing. For Ray, it was nothing unexpected.

Along the winding road back to the main highway, Ray wondered how his brother could simply walk away from a facility eight miles from the nearest town. But then, he had fled more secluded places.

He would go back to Memphis, back to his room in Ellie's basement, back to the streets where pushers were waiting for him. The next phone call might be the last, but then Ray had been half-expecting it for many years. As sick as he was, Forrest had shown an amazing ability to survive.

Ray was in Tennessee now. Virginia was next, seven hours away. With a clear sky and no wind, he thought of how nice it would be at five thousand feet, buzzing around in his favorite rented Cessna.

Chapter 37

Both doors were new, unpainted, and much heavier than the old ones. Ray silently thanked his landlord for the extra expense, though he knew that there would be no more break-ins. The pursuit had ended. No more quick looks over the shoulder. No more sneaking to Chaney's to play hide-and-seek. No more hushed conversations with Corey Crawford. And no more illicit money to fret over, and dream about, and haul around, literally. The lifting of that burden made him smile and walk a bit faster.

Life would become normal again. Long runs in the heat. Long solo flights over the Piedmont. He even looked forward to his neglected research for the monopolies treatise he'd promised to deliver by either this Christmas or the one after. He had softened on the Kaley issue and was ready for one last attempt at dinner. She was legal now, a graduate, and she simply looked too fine to write off without a decent effort.

His apartment was the same, its usual condition since no one else lived there. Other than the door, there was no evidence of a forced entry. He now knew that his burglar had not really been a thief after all, just a tormentor, an intimidator. Either Gordie or one of his brothers. He wasn't sure how they had divided their labors, nor did he care.

It was almost 11 A.M. He made some strong coffee and began shuffling through the mail. No more anonymous letters. Nothing now but the usual bills and solicitations.

There were two faxes in the tray. The first was a note from a former student. The second was from Patton French. He'd been trying to call, but Ray's cell phone wasn't working. It was handwritten on the stationery from the *King of Torts,* no doubt faxed from the gray waters of the Gulf where French was still hiding his boat from his wife's divorce lawyer.

Good news on the security front! Not long after Ray had left the coast, Gordie Priest had been 'located,' along with both of his brothers. Could Ray please give him a call? His assistant would find him.

Ray worked the phone for two hours, until French called from a hotel in Fort Worth, where he was meeting with some Ryax and Kobril lawyers. 'I'll probably get a thousand cases up here,' he said, unable to control himself.

'Wonderful,' said Ray. He was determined not to listen to any more crowing about mass torts and zillion-dollar settlements.

'Is your phone secure?' French asked.

'Yes.'

'Okay, listen. Priest is no longer a threat. We found him shortly after you left, laid up drunk with an old gal he's been seeing for a long time. Found both brothers too. Your money is safe.'

'Exactly when did you find them?' Ray asked. He was hovering over the kitchen table with a large calendar spread before him. Time was crucial here. He'd made notes in the margins as he'd waited for the call.

French thought for a second. 'Uh, let's see. What's today?'

'Monday, June the fifth.'

'Monday. When did you leave the coast?'

'Ten o'clock Friday morning.'

'Then it was just after lunch on Friday.'

'You're sure?'

'Of course I'm sure. Why do you ask?'

'And once you found him, there was no way they left the coast?'

'Trust me, Ray, they'll never leave the coast again. They've, uh, found a permanent home there.'

'I don't want those details.' Ray sat at the table and stared at the calendar.

'What's the matter?' French asked. 'Something wrong?'

'Yeah, you could say that.'

'What is it?'

'Somebody burned the house down.'

'Judge Atlee's?'

'Yes.'

'When?'

'After midnight, Saturday morning.'

A pause as French absorbed this, then, 'Well, it wasn't the Priest boys, I can promise you that.'

When Ray said nothing, French asked, 'Where's the money?'

'I don't know,' he mumbled.

A five-mile run did nothing to ease his tension. Though, as always, he was able to plot things, to rearrange his thoughts. The temperature was above ninety, and he was soaked with sweat when he returned to his apartment.

Now that Harry Rex had been told everything, it was comforting to have someone with whom to share the latest. He called his office in Clanton and was informed that he was in court over in Tupelo and wouldn't be back until late. He called Ellie's house in Memphis and no one bothered to answer. He called Oscar Meave at Alcorn Village, and, expecting to hear no news of his brother's whereabouts, got exactly what he expected.

So much for the normal life.

After a tense morning of back-and-forth negotiations in the hallways of the Lee County Courthouse, bickering over such issues as who'd get

363

the ski boat and who'd get the cabin on the lake, and how much he would pay in a lump-sum cash settlement, the divorce was settled an hour after lunch. Harry Rex had the husband, an overheated cowboy on wife number three who thought he knew more divorce law than his lawyer. Wife number three was an aging bimbo in her late twenties who'd caught him with her best friend. It was the typical, sordid tale, and Harry Rex was sick of the whole mess when he walked to the bench and presented a hard-fought property settlement agreement.

The chancellor was a veteran who'd divorced thousands. 'Very sorry about Judge Atlee,' he said softly as he began to review the papers. Harry Rex just nodded. He was tired and thirsty and already contemplating a cold one as he drove the backroad to Clanton. His favorite beer store in the Tupelo area was at the county line.

'We served together for twenty-two years,' the chancellor was saying.

'A fine man,' Harry Rex said.

'Are you doing the estate?'

'Yes sir.'

'Give my regards to Judge Farr over there.'

'I will.'

The paperwork was signed, the marriage mercifully terminated, the warring spouses sent to their neutral homes. Harry Rex was out of the courthouse and halfway to his car when a lawyer chased him down and stopped him on the sidewalk. He introduced himself as Jacob Spain,

Attorney-at-Law, one of a thousand in Tupelo. He'd been in the courtroom and overheard the chancellor mention Judge Atlee.

'He has a son, right, Forrest?' Spain asked.

'Two sons, Ray and Forrest.' Harry Rex took a breath and settled in for a quick visit.

'I played high school football against Forrest; in fact he broke my collarbone with a late hit.'

'That sounds like Forrest.'

'I played at New Albany. Forrest was a junior when I was a senior. Did you see him play?'

'Yes, many times.'

'You remember the game over there against us when he threw for three hundred yards in the first half? Four or five touchdowns, I think.'

'I do,' Harry Rex said, and started to fidget. How long was this going to take?

'I was playing safety that night, and he was firing passes all over the place. I picked one off right before half-time, ran it out of bounds, and he speared me while I was on the ground.'

'That was one of his favorite plays.' Hit 'em hard and hit 'em late had been Forrest's motto, especially those defensive backs unlucky enough to intercept one of his passes.

'I think he was arrested the next week,' Spain was saying. 'What a waste. Anyway, I saw him just a few weeks ago, here in Tupelo, with Judge Atlee.'

The fidgeting stopped. Harry Rex forgot about a cold one, at least for the moment. 'When was this?' he asked.

'Right before the Judge died. It was a strange scene.'

They took a few steps and found shade under a tree. 'I'm listening,' Harry Rex said, loosening his tie. His wrinkled navy blazer was already off.

'My wife's mother is being treated for breast cancer at the Taft Clinic. One Monday afternoon back in the spring I drove her over there for another round of chemo.'

'Judge Atlee went to Taft,' Harry Rex said. 'I've seen the bills.'

'Yes, that's where I saw him. I checked her in, there was a wait, so I went to my car to make a bunch of calls. While I was sitting there, I watched as Judge Atlee pulled up in a long black Lincoln driven by someone I didn't recognize. They got the thing parked, just two cars down, and they got out. His driver then looked familiar – big guy, big frame, long hair, kind of a cocky swagger that I've seen before. It hit me that it was Forrest. I could tell by the way he walked and moved. He was wearing sunglasses and a cap pulled low. They went inside, and within seconds Forrest came back out.'

'What kinda cap?'

'Faded blue, Cubs, I think.'

'I've seen that one.'

'He was real nervous, like he didn't want anyone to see him. He disappeared into some trees next to the clinic, except I could barely see his outline. He just hid there. I thought at first he might be relieving himself, but no, he was just

366

hiding. After an hour or so, I went in, waited, finally got my mother-in-law, and left. He was still out in the trees.'

Harry Rex had pulled out his pocket planner. 'What day was this?' Spain removed his, and as all busy lawyers do, they compared their recent movements. 'Monday, May the first,' Spain decided.

'That was six days before the Judge died,' Harry Rex said.

'I'm sure that's the date. It was just a strange scene.'

'Well, he's a pretty strange guy.'

'He's not running from the law or anything, is he?'

'Not at the present,' Harry Rex said, and they both managed a nervous laugh.

Spain suddenly needed to go. 'Anyway, when you see him again, tell him I'm still mad about the late hit.'

'I'll do that,' Harry Rex said, then watched him walk away.

Chapter 38

Mr. and Mrs. Vonner left Clanton on a cloudy June morning in a new sports utility four-wheel drive that promised twelve miles to the gallon and was loaded with enough luggage for a month in Europe. The District of Columbia was the destination, however, since Mrs. Vonner had a sister there whom Harry Rex had never met. They spent the first night in Gatlinburg and the second night at White Sulphur Springs in West Virginia. They arrived in Charlottesville around noon, did the obligatory tour of Jefferson's Monticello, walked the grounds at the university, and had an unusual dinner at a college dive called the White Spot, the house specialty being a fried egg on a hamburger. It was Harry Rex's kind of food.

The next morning, while she slept, he went for a stroll on the downtown mall. He found the address and waited.

A few minutes after 8 A.M., Ray double-tied the laces of his rather expensive running shoes, stretched in the den, and walked downstairs for the daily five-miler. Outside, the air was warm. July was not far away and summer had already arrived.

He turned a corner and heard a familiar voice call, 'Hey, boy.'

Harry Rex was sitting on a bench, a cup of coffee in hand, an unread newspaper next to him. Ray froze and took a few seconds to collect himself. Things were out of place here.

When he could move, he walked over and said, 'What, exactly, are you doing here?'

'Cute outfit,' Harry Rex said, taking in the shorts, old tee shirt, red runner's cap, the latest in athletic eye glasses. 'Me and the wife are passing through, headed for D.C. She has a sister up there she thinks I want to meet. Sit down.'

'Why didn't you call?'

'Didn't want to bother you.'

'But you should've called, Harry Rex. We could do dinner, I'll show you around.'

'It's not that kind of trip. Sit down.'

Smelling trouble, Ray sat next to Harry Rex. 'I can't believe this,' he mumbled.

'Shut up and listen.'

Ray removed his running glasses and looked at Harry Rex. 'Is it bad?'

'Let's say it's curious.' He told Jacob Spain's story about Forrest hiding in the trees at the oncology clinic, six days before the Judge passed away. Ray listened in disbelief and slid lower on the bench. He finally leaned forward with his elbows on his knees, his head hung low.

'According to the medical records,' Harry Rex was saying, 'he got a morphine pack that day, May the first. Don't know if it was the first pack or a refill, the records are not that clear. Looks like Forrest took him to get the good stuff.'

A long pause as a pretty young woman walked by, obviously in a hurry, her tight skirt swaying wonderfully as she sped along. A sip of coffee, then, 'I've always been suspicious of that will you found in his study. The Judge and I talked about his will for the last six months of his life. I don't think he simply cranked out one more right before he died. I've studied the signatures at length, and it's my untrained opinion that the last one is a forgery.'

Ray cleared his voice and said, 'If Forrest drove him to Tupelo, then it's safe to assume Forrest was in the house.'

'All over the house.'

Harry Rex had hired an investigator in Memphis to find Forrest, but there was no trail, no trace. From somewhere within the newspaper, he pulled out an envelope. 'Then, this came three days ago.'

Ray pulled out a sheet of paper and unfolded it. It was from Oscar Meave at Alcorn Village, and it read: 'Dear Mr. Vonner: I have been unable to reach Ray Atlee. I know the whereabouts of Forrest, if by chance the family does not. Call if you would like to talk. Everything is confidential. Best wishes, Oscar Meave.'

'So I called him right away,' Harry Rex said, eyeing another young woman. 'He has a former patient who's now a counselor at a rehab ranch out West. Forrest checked in there a week ago, and was adamant about his privacy, said he did not want his family to know where he was. Evidently this happens from time to time, and the clinics are always caught in a bind. They have to respect the wishes of their patient, but on the other hand, the family is crucial to the overall rehabilitation. So these counselors whisper among themselves. Meave made the decision to pass along the information to you.'

'Where out West?'

'Montana. A place called Morningstar Ranch. Meave said it's what the boy needs – very nice, very remote, a lockdown facility for the hard cases, said he'll be there for a year.'

Ray sat up and began rubbing his forehead as if he'd finally been shot there.

'And of course the place is pricey,' Harry Rex added.

'Of course,' Ray mumbled.

There was no more talk, not about Forrest anyway. After a few minutes, Harry Rex said he was leaving. He had delivered his message, he had nothing more to say, not then. His wife was anxious to see her sister. Perhaps next time they could stay longer, have dinner, whatever. He patted Ray on the shoulder, and left him there. 'See you in Clanton' were his last words.

Too weak and too winded for a run, Ray sat on the bench in the middle of the downtown mall, his apartment above him, lost in a world of rapidly moving pieces. The foot traffic picked up as the merchants and bankers and lawyers hustled to work, but Ray did not see them.

Carl Mirk taught two sections of insurance law each semester, and he was a member of the Virginia bar, as was Ray. They discussed the interview over lunch, and both came to the conclusion that it was just part of a routine inquiry, nothing to worry about. Mirk would tag along and pretend to be Ray's lawyer.

The insurance investigator's name was Ratterfield. They welcomed him into the conference room at the law school. He removed his jacket as if they might be there for hours. Ray was wearing jeans and a golf shirt. Mirk was just as casual.

'I usually record these,' Ratterfield said, all business as he pulled out a tape recorder and placed it between him and Ray. 'Any objections?' he asked, once the recorder was in place.

'I guess not,' Ray said.

He punched a button, looked at his notes, then began an introduction, for the benefit of the tape. He was an independent insurance examiner, hired by Aviation Underwriters, to investigate a claim filed by Ray Atlee and three other owners for damages to a 1994 Beech Bonanza on June 2. According to the state arson examiner, the airplane was deliberately burned.

Initially, he needed Ray's flying history. Ray had his logbook and Ratterfield pored through it, finding nothing remotely interesting. 'No instrument rating,' he said at one point.

'I'm working on it,' Ray replied.

'Fourteen hours in the Bonanza?'

'Yep.'

He then moved to the consortium of owners, and asked questions about the deal that brought it together. He'd already interviewed the other owners, and they had produced the contracts and documentation. Ray acknowledged the paperwork.

Changing gears, Ratterfield asked, 'Where were you on June the first?'

'Biloxi, Mississippi,' Ray answered, certain that Ratterfield had no idea where that was.

'How long had you been there?'

'A few days.'

'May I ask why you were there?'

'Sure,' Ray said, then launched into an abbreviated version of his recent visits home. His official reason for going to the coast was to visit friends, old buddies from his days at Tulane.

'I'm sure there are people who can verify that you were there on June the first,' Ratterfield said.

'Several people. Plus I have hotel receipts.'

He seemed convinced that Ray had been in

Mississippi. 'The other owners were all at home when the plane burned,' he said, flipping a page to a list of typed notes. 'All have alibis. If we're assuming it's arson, then we have to first find a motive, then whoever torched it. Any ideas?'

'I have no idea who did this,' Ray said quickly, and with conviction.

'How about motive?'

'We had just bought the plane. Why would any of us want to destroy it?'

'To collect the insurance, maybe. Happens occasionally. Perhaps one partner decided he was in over his head. The note is not small – almost two hundred grand over six years, close to nine hundred bucks a month per partner.'

'We knew that two weeks earlier when we signed on,' Ray said.

They shadowboxed for a while around the delicate issue of Ray's personal finances – salary, expenses, obligations. When Ratterfield seemed convinced that Ray could swing his end of the deal, he changed subjects. 'This fire in Mississippi,' he said, scanning a report of some type. 'Tell me about it.'

'What do you want to know?'

'Are you under investigation for arson down there?'

'No.'

'Are you sure?'

'Yes, I'm sure. You can call my attorney if you'd like.'

'I already have. And your apartment has been burglarized twice in the past six weeks?'

'Nothing was taken. Both were just break-ins.'

'You're having an exciting summer.'

'Is that a question?'

'Sounds like someone's after you.'

'Again, is that a question?'

It was the only flare-up of the interview, and both Ray and Ratterfield took a breath.

'Any other arson investigations in your past?'

Ray smiled and said, 'No.'

When Ratterfield flipped another page, and there was nothing typed on it, he lost interest in a hurry and went through the motions of wrapping things up. 'I'm sure our attorneys will be in touch,' he said as he turned off the recorder.

'I can't wait,' Ray said.

Ratterfield collected his jacket and his briefcase and made his exit.

After he left, Carl said, 'I think you know more than you're telling.'

'Maybe,' Ray said. 'But I had nothing to do with the arson here, or the arson there.'

'I've heard enough.'

Chapter 39

For almost a week, a string of turbulent summer fronts kept the ceilings low and the winds too dangerous for small planes. When the extended forecasts showed nothing but calm dry air for everywhere but South Texas, Ray left Charlottesville in a Cessna and began the longest cross-country of his brief flying career. Avoiding busy airspace and looking for easy landmarks below, he flew west across the Shenandoah Valley into West Virginia and into Kentucky, where he picked up fuel at a four-thousand-foot strip not far from Lexington. The Cessna could stay aloft for about three and a half hours before the indicator dipped below a quarter of a tank. He landed again in Terre Haute, crossed the Mississippi River at Hannibal, and stopped for the evening in Kirksville, Missouri, where he checked into a motel.

It was his first motel since the odyssey with the cash, and it was precisely because of the cash that he was back in a motel. He was also in

Missouri, and as he flipped through muted channels in his room, he remembered Patton French's story of stumbling upon Ryax at a tort seminar in St. Louis. An old lawyer from a small town in the Ozarks had a son who taught at the university in Columbia, and the son knew the drug was bad. And because of Patton French and his insatiable greed and corruption, he, Ray Atlee, was now in another motel in a town where he knew absolutely no one.

A front was developing over Utah. Ray lifted off just after sunrise and climbed to above five thousand feet. He trimmed his controls and opened a large cup of steaming black coffee. He flew more north than west for the first leg and was soon over the cornfields of Iowa.

Alone a mile above the earth, in the cool quiet air of the early morning, and with not a single pilot chattering on the airwaves, Ray tried to focus on the task before him. It was easier though, to loaf, to enjoy the solitude and the views, and the coffee, and the solitary act of leaving the world down there. And it was quite pleasant to put off thoughts of his brother.

After a stop in Sioux Falls, he turned west again and followed Interstate 90 across the entire state of South Dakota before skirting the restricted space around Mount Rushmore. He landed in Rapid City, rented a car, and took a long drive through Badlands National Park.

Morningstar Ranch was somewhere in the hills south of Kalispell, though its Web site was purposefully vague. Oscar Meave had tried but had been unsuccessful in pinpointing its exact location. At the end of the third day of his journey, Ray landed after dark in Kalispell. He rented a car, found dinner then a motel, and spent hours with aerial and road maps.

It took another day of low-altitude flying around Kalispell and the towns of Woods Bay, Polison, Bigfork, and Elmo. He crossed Flathead Lake a half-dozen times and was ready to surrender the air war and send in the ground troops when he caught a glimpse of a compound of some sort near the town of Somers on the north side of the lake. From fifteen hundred feet, he circled the place until he saw a substantial fence of green chain link almost hidden in the woods and practically invisible from the air. There were small buildings that appeared to be housing units, a larger one for administration perhaps, a pool, tennis courts, a barn with horses grazing nearby. He circled long enough for a few folks within the complex to stop whatever they were doing and look up with shielded eyes.

Finding it on the ground was as challenging as from the air, but by noon the next day Ray was parked outside the unmarked gate, glaring at an armed guard who was glaring back at him. After a few tense questions, the guard finally admitted that, yes, he had in fact found the place he was looking for. 'We don't allow visitors,' he said smugly.

Ray created a tale of a family in crisis and stressed the urgency of finding his brother. The procedure, as the guard grudgingly laid out, was to leave a name and a phone number, and there was a slight chance someone from within would contact him. The next day, he was trout fishing on the Flathead River when his cell phone rang. An unfriendly voice belonging to an Allison with Morningstar asked for Ray Atlee.

Who was she expecting?

He confessed to being Ray Atlee, and she proceeded to ask what was it he wanted from their facility. 'I have a brother there,' he said as politely as possible. 'His name is Forrest Atlee, and I'd like to see him.'

'What makes you think he's here?' she demanded.

'He's there. You know he's there. I know he's there, so can we please stop the games?'

'I'll look into it, but don't expect a return call.' She hung up before he could say anything. The next unfriendly voice belonged to Darrel, an administrator of something or other. It came late in the afternoon while Ray was hiking a trail in the Swan Range near the Hungry Horse Reservoir. Darrel was as abrupt as Allison. 'Half an hour only. Thirty minutes,' he informed Ray. 'At ten in the morning.'

A maximum security prison would have been more agreeable. The same guard frisked him at the gate and inspected his car. 'Follow him,' the guard said. Another guard in a golf cart was waiting on the narrow drive, and Ray followed him to a small parking lot near the front building. When he got out of his car Allison was waiting, unarmed. She was tall and rather masculine, and when she offered the obligatory handshake Ray had never felt so physically overmatched. She marched him inside, where cameras monitored every move with no effort at concealment. She led him to a windowless room and passed him off to a snarling officer of an unknown variety who, with the deft touch of a baggage handler, poked and prodded every bend and crevice except the groin, where, for one awful moment, Ray thought he might just take a jab there too.

'I'm just seeing my brother,' Ray finally protested, and in doing so came close to getting backhanded.

When he was thoroughly searched and sanitized, Allison gathered him up again and led him down a short hallway to a stark square room that felt as though it should have had padded walls. The only door to it had the only window, and, pointing to it, Allison said gravely, 'We will be watching.'

'Watching what?' Ray asked.

She scowled at him and seemed ready to knock him to the floor.

There was a square table in the center of the room, with two chairs on opposite sides. 'Sit

here,' she demanded, and Ray took his desig-
nated seat. For ten minutes he looked at the
walls, his back to the door.

Finally, it opened, and Forrest entered alone,
unchained, no handcuffs, no burly guards prodding him along. Without a word he sat across
from Ray and folded his hands together on the
table as if it was time to meditate. The hair was
gone. A buzz cut had removed everything but a
thin stand of no more than an eighth of an inch,
and above the ears the shearing had gone to the
scalp. He was clean-shaven and looked twenty
pounds lighter. His baggy shirt was a dark olive
button-down with a small collar and two large
pockets, almost military-like. It prompted Ray to
offer the first words: 'This place is a boot camp.'

'It's tough,' Forrest replied very slowly and
softly.

'Do they brainwash you?'

'That's exactly what they do.'

Ray was there because of money, and he
decided to confront it head-on. 'So what do you
get for seven hundred bucks a day?' he began.

'A new life.'

Ray nodded his approval at the answer.
Forrest was staring at him, no blinking, no
expression, just gazing almost forlornly at his
brother as if he were a stranger.

'And you're here for twelve months?'

'At least.'

'That's a quarter of a million dollars.'

He gave a little shrug, as if money was not a

problem, as if he just might stay for three years, or five.

'Are you sedated?' Ray asked, trying to provoke him.

'No.'

'You act as if you're sedated.'

'I'm not. They don't use drugs here. Can't imagine why not, can you?' His voice picked up a little steam.

Ray was mindful of the ticking clock. Allison would be back at precisely the thirtieth minute to break up things and escort Ray out of the building and out of the compound forever. He needed much more time to cover their issues, but efficiency was required here. Get to the point, he told himself. See how much he's going to admit.

'I took the old man's last will,' Ray said. 'And I took the summons he sent, the one calling us home on May the seventh, and I studied his signatures on both. I think they're forgeries.'

'Good for you.'

'Don't know who did the forging, but I suspect it was you.'

'Sue me.'

'No denial?'

'What difference does it make?'

Ray repeated those words, half-aloud and in disgust as if repeating them made him angry. A long pause while the clock ticked. 'I received my summons on a Thursday. It was postmarked in Clanton on Monday, the same day you drove him to the Taft Clinic in Tupelo to get a morphine pack. Question – how did you manage to type the summons on his old Underwood manual?'

'I don't have to answer your questions.'

'Sure you do. You put together this fraud, Forrest. The least you can do is tell me how it happened. You've won. The old man's dead. The house is gone. You have the money. No one's chasing you but me, and I'll be gone soon. Tell me how it happened.'

'He already had a morphine pack.'

'Okay, so you took him to get another one, or a refill, whatever. That's not the question.'

'But it's important.'

'Why?'

'Because he was stoned.' There was a slight break in the brainwashed facade as he took his hands off the table and glanced away.

'So he was suffering,' Ray said, trying to provoke some emotions here.

'Yes,' Forrest said without a trace of emotion.

'And if you kept the morphine cranked up, then you had the house to yourself?'

'Something like that.'

'When did you first go back there?'

'I'm not too good with dates. Never have been.'

'Don't play stupid with me, Forrest. He died on a Sunday.'

'I went there on a Saturday.'

'So eight days before he died?'

'Yes, I guess.'

'And why did you go back?'

He folded his arms across his chest and lowered his chin and his eyes. And his voice. 'He called me,' he began, 'and asked me to come see him. I went the next day. I couldn't believe how old and sick he was, and how lonely.' A deep breath, a glance up at his brother. 'The pain was terrible. Even with the painkillers, he was in bad shape. We sat on the porch and talked about the war and how things would've been different if Jackson hadn't been killed at Chancellorsville, the same old battles he's been refighting forever. He shifted constantly, trying to fight off the pain. At times it took his breath away. But he just wanted to talk. We never buried the hatchet or tried to make things right. We didn't feel the need to. The fact that I was there was all he wanted. I slept on the sofa in his study, and during the night I woke up to hear him screaming. He was on the floor of his room, his knees up to his chin, shivering from the pain. I got him back in his bed, helped him hit the morphine, finally got him still. It was about three in the morning. I was wild-eyed. I started roaming.'

The narrative fizzled, but the clock didn't.

'And that's when you found the money,' Ray said.

'What money?'

'The money that's paying seven hundred dollars a day here.'

'Oh, that money.'

'That money.'

'Yeah, that's when I found it, same place as you. Twenty-seven boxes. The first one had a hundred thousand bucks in it, so I did some calculations. I had no idea what to do. I just sat there for hours, staring at the boxes all stacked innocently in the cabinets. I thought he might get out of bed, walk down the hall, and catch me looking at all his little boxes, and I was hoping he would. Then he could explain things.' He put his hands back on the table and stared at Ray again. 'By sunrise, though, I thought I had a plan. I decided I'd let you handle the money. You're the firstborn, the favorite son, the big brother, the golden boy, the honor student, the law professor, the executor, the one he trusted the most. I'll just watch Ray, I said to myself, see what he does with the money, because whatever he does must be right. So I closed the cabinets, slid the sofa over, and tried to act as though I'd never found it. I came close to asking the old man about it, but I figured that if he wanted me to know, then he would tell me.'

'When did you type my summons?'

'Later that day. He was passed out under the pecan trees in the backyard, in his hammock. He was feeling a lot better, but by then he was addicted to the morphine. He didn't remember much of that last week.'

'And Monday you took him to Tupelo?'

'Yes. He'd been driving himself, but since I was around he asked me to take him over.'

'And you hid in the trees outside the clinic so no one would see you.'

'That's pretty good. What else do you know?'

'Nothing. All I have is questions. You called me the night I got the summons in the mail, said you had received one too. You asked me if I was going to call the old man. I said no. What would've happened if I had called him?'

'Phones weren't working.'

'Why not?'

'The phone line runs into the basement. There's a loose connecting switch down there.'

Ray nodded as another little mystery was solved.

'Plus, he didn't answer it half the time,' Forrest added.

'When did you redo his will?'

'The day before he died. I found the old one, didn't like it much, so I thought I'd do the right thing and equally divide his estate between the two of us. What a ridiculous idea – an equal split. What a fool I was. I just didn't understand the law in these situations. I thought that since we are the only heirs, that we should divide everything equally. I wasn't aware that lawyers are trained to keep whatever they find, to steal from their brothers, to hide assets that they are sworn to protect, to ignore their oaths. No one told me this. I was trying to be fair. How stupid.'

'When did he die?'

'Two hours before you got there.'

'Did you kill him?'

A snort, a sneer. No response.

'Did you kill him?' Ray asked again.

'No, cancer did.'

'Let me get this straight,' Ray said, leaning forward, the cross-examiner moving in for a strike. 'You hung around for eight days, and the entire time he was stoned. Then he conveniently dies two hours before I get there.'

'That's right.'

'You're lying.'

'I assisted him with the morphine, okay? Feel better? He was crying because of the pain. He couldn't walk, eat, drink, sleep, urinate, defecate, or sit up in a chair. You were not there, okay? I was. He got all dressed up for you. I shaved his face. I helped him to the sofa. He was too weak to press the button on the morphine pack. I pressed it for him. He went to sleep. I left the house. You came home, you found him, you found the money, then you began your lying.'

'Do you know where it came from?'

'No. Somewhere on the coast, I presume. I don't really care.'

'Who burned my airplane?'

'That's a criminal act, so I know nothing.'

'Is it the same person who followed me for a month?'

'Yes, two of them, guys I know from prison, old friends. They're very good, and you were very easy. They put a bug under the fender of your cute little car. They tracked you with a GPS. Every move. Piece of cake.'

'Why did you burn the house?'

'I deny any wrongdoing.'

'For the insurance? Or perhaps to completely shut me out of the estate?'

Forrest was shaking his head, denying everything. The door opened and Allison stuck her long, angular face in. 'Everything okay in here?' she demanded.

Fine, yes, we're swell.

'Seven more minutes,' she said, then closed it. They sat there forever, both staring blankly at different spots on the floor. Not a sound from the outside.

'I only wanted half, Ray,' Forrest finally said.

'Take half now.'

'Now's too late. Now I know what I'm supposed to do with the money. You showed me.'

'I was afraid to give you the money, Forrest.'

'Afraid of what?'

'Afraid you'd kill yourself with it.'

'Well, here I am,' Forrest said, waving his right arm at the room, at the ranch, at the entire state of Montana. 'This is what I'm doing with the money. Not exactly killing myself. Not quite as crazy as everybody thought.'

'I was wrong.'

'Oh, that means so much. Wrong because you got caught? Wrong because I'm not such an idiot after all? Or wrong because you want half of the money?'

'All of the above.'

'I'm afraid to share it, Ray, same as you were.

Afraid the money will go to your head. Afraid you'll blow it all on airplanes and casinos. Afraid you'll become an even bigger asshole than you are. I have to protect you here, Ray.'

Ray kept his cool. He couldn't win a fistfight with his brother, and even if he could, what would he gain by it? He'd love to take a bat and beat him around the head, but why bother? If he shot him he wouldn't find the money.

'So what's next for you?' he asked with as much unconcern as he could show.

'Oh, I don't know. Nothing definite. When you're in rehab, you dream a lot, then when you get out all the dreams seem silly. I'll never go back to Memphis, though, too many old friends. And I'll never go back to Clanton. I'll find a new home somewhere. What about you? What will you do now that you've blown your big chance?'

'I had a life, Forrest, and I still do.'

'That's right. You make a hundred and sixty thousand bucks a year, I checked it online, and I doubt if you work real hard. No family, not much overhead, plenty of money to do whatever you want. You got it made. Greed is a strange animal, isn't it, Ray? You found three million bucks and decided you needed all of it. Not one dime for your screwed-up little brother. Not one red cent for me. You took the money, and you tried to run away with it.'

'I wasn't sure what to do with the money. Same as you.'

'But you took it, all of it. And you lied to me about it.'

'That's not true. I was holding the money.'

'And you were spending it – casinos, airplanes.'

'No, dammit! I don't gamble and I've been renting airplanes for three years. I was holding the money, Forrest, trying to figure it out. Hell, it was barely five weeks ago.'

The words were louder and bouncing off the walls. Allison took a look in, ready to break up the meeting if her patient was getting stressed.

'Give me a break here,' Ray said. 'You didn't know what to do with the money, neither did I. As soon as I found it, someone, and I guess that someone was either you or your buddies, started scaring the hell out of me. You can't blame me for running with the money.'

'You lied to me.'

'And you lied to me. You said you hadn't talked to the old man, that you hadn't set foot in the house in nine years. All lies, Forrest. All part of a hoax. Why did you do it? Why didn't you just tell me about the money?'

'Why didn't you tell me?'

'Maybe I was going to, okay? I'm not sure what I had planned. It's kinda hard to think clearly when you find your father dead, then you find three million bucks in cash, then you realize somebody else knows about the money and will gladly kill you for it. These things don't happen every day, so forgive me if I'm a little inexperienced.'

The room went silent. Forrest tapped his fingertips together and watched the ceiling. Ray had said all he planned to say. Allison rattled the doorknob, but did not enter.

Forrest leaned forward and said, 'Those two fires – the house and the airplane – you got any new suspects?'

Ray shook his head no. 'I won't tell a soul,' he said.

Another pause as time expired. Forrest slowly stood and looked down at Ray. 'Give me a year. When I get out of here, then we'll talk.'

The door opened, and as Forrest walked by, he let his hand graze Ray's shoulder, just a light touch, not an affectionate pat by any means, but a touch nonetheless. 'See you in a year, Bro,' he said, then he was gone.

The King of Torts

Chapter 1

The shots that fired the bullets that entered Pumpkin's head were heard by no less than eight people. Three instinctively closed their windows, checked their door locks, and withdrew to the safety, or at least the seclusion, of their small apartments. Two others, each with experience in such matters, ran from the vicinity as fast if not faster than the gunman himself. Another, the neighborhood recycling fanatic, was digging through some garbage in search of aluminum cans when he heard the sharp sounds of the daily skirmish, very nearby. He jumped behind a pile of cardboard boxes until the shelling stopped, then eased into the alley where he saw what was left of Pumpkin.

And two saw almost everything. They were sitting on plastic milk crates, at the corner of Georgia and Lamont in front of a liquor store, partially hidden by a parked car so that the gunman, who glanced around briefly before following Pumpkin into the alley, didn't see them. Both would tell the police that they saw the boy with the gun reach into his pocket and pull it out; they saw the gun for sure, a small black pistol. A second later they heard the shots, though they did not actually see Pumpkin take them in the head. Another second, and the boy with the gun darted from the alley and, for some reason, ran straight in their direction. He ran bent at the waist, like a scared dog, guilty as hell. He wore red-and-yellow basketball shoes that seemed five sizes too big and slapped the pavement as he made his getaway.

When he ran by them he was still holding the gun, probably a .38, and he flinched just for a instant when he saw them and realized they had seen too much. For one terrifying second, he seemed to raise the gun as if to eliminate the witnesses, both of whom managed to flip backward from their plastic milk crates and scramble off in a mad flurry of arms and legs. Then he was gone.

One of them opened the door to the liquor store and yelled for someone to call the police, there had been a shooting.

Thirty minutes later, the police received a call that a young man matching the description of the one who had wasted Pumpkin had been seen twice on Ninth Street carrying a gun in open view and acting stranger than most of the people on Ninth. He had tried to lure at least one person into an abandoned lot, but the intended victim had escaped and reported the incident.

The police found their man an hour later. His name was Tequila Watson, black male, age twenty, with the usual drug-related police record. No family to speak of. No address. The last place he'd been sleeping was a rehab unit on W Street. He'd managed to ditch the gun somewhere, and if he'd robbed Pumpkin then he'd also thrown away the cash or drugs or whatever the booty was. His pockets were clean, as were his eyes. The cops were certain Tequila was not under the influence of anything when he was arrested. A quick and rough interrogation took place on the street, then he was handcuffed and shoved into the rear seat of a D.C. police car.

They drove him back to Lamont Street, where they arranged an impromptu encounter with the two witnesses. Tequila was led into the alley where he'd left Pumpkin. 'Ever been here before?' a cop asked.

Tequila said nothing, just gawked at the puddle of fresh blood on the dirty concrete. The two witnesses were eased into the alley, then led quietly to a spot near Tequila.

'That's him,' both said at the same time.

'He's wearing the same clothes, same basketball shoes, everything but the gun.'

'That's him.'

'No doubt about it.'

Tequila was shoved into the car once again and taken to jail. He was booked for murder and locked away with no immediate chance of bail. Whether through experience or just fear, Tequila never said a word to the cops as they pried and cajoled and even threatened. Nothing incriminating, nothing helpful. No indication of why he would murder Pumpkin. No clue as to their history, if one existed at all. A veteran detective made a brief note in the file that the killing appeared a bit more random than was customary.

No phone call was requested. No mention of a lawyer or a bail bondsman. Tequila seemed dazed but content to sit in a crowded cell and stare at the floor.

Pumpkin had no traceable father but his mother worked as a security guard in the basement of a large office building on New York Avenue. It took three hours for the police to determine her son's real name – Ramón Pumphrey – to locate his address, and to find a neighbor willing to tell them if he had a mother.

Adelfa Pumphrey was sitting behind a desk just inside the basement entrance, supposedly watching a bank of monitors. She was a large thick woman in a tight khaki uniform, a gun on her waist, a look of complete disinterest on her face. The cops who approached her had done so a hundred times. They broke the news, then found her supervisor.

In a city where young people killed each other every day, the slaughter had thickened skins and hardened hearts, and every mother knew many others who'd lost their children. Each loss brought death a step closer, and every mother knew that any day could be the last. The mothers had watched the others survive the horror. As Adelfa

4

Pumphrey sat at her desk with her face in her hands, she thought of her son and his lifeless body lying somewhere in the city at that moment, being inspected by strangers.

She swore revenge on whoever killed him.

She cursed his father for abandoning the child.

She cried for her baby.

And she knew she would survive. Somehow, she would survive.

Adelfa went to court to watch the arraignment. The police told her the punk who'd killed her son was scheduled to make his first appearance, a quick and routine matter in which he would plead not guilty and ask for a lawyer. She was in the back row with her brother on one side and a neighbor on the other, her eyes leaking tears into a damp handkerchief. She wanted to see the boy. She also wanted to ask him why, but she knew she would never get the chance.

They herded the criminals through like cattle at an auction. All were black, all wore orange coveralls and handcuffs, all were young. Such waste.

In addition to his handcuffs, Tequila was adorned with wrist and ankle chains since his crime was especially violent, though he looked fairly harmless when he was shuffled into the courtroom with the next wave of offenders. He glanced around quickly at the crowd to see if he recognized anyone, to see if just maybe someone was out there for him. He was seated in a row of chairs, and for good measure one of the armed bailiffs leaned down and said, 'That boy you killed. That's his mother back there in the blue dress.'

With his head low, Tequila slowly turned and looked directly into the wet and puffy eyes of Pumpkin's mother, but only for a second. Adelfa stared at the skinny boy in the oversized coveralls and wondered where his mother was and how she'd raised him and if he had a father, and, most important, how and why his path had crossed that of her boy's. The two were about the same age as the rest of them, late teens or early twenties. The cops had told her that it appeared, at least initially, that drugs were not involved in the killing. But she knew better. Drugs were involved in every layer of street life. Adelfa knew it all too well. Pumpkin had used pot and crack and he'd been arrested once, for simple possession, but he had never been violent. The cops were saying it looked like a random killing. All street killings were random, her brother had said, but they all had a reason.

On one side of the courtroom was a table around which the authorities gathered. The cops whispered to the prosecutors, who flipped through files and reports and tried valiantly to keep the paperwork ahead of the criminals. On the other side was a table where the defense lawyers came and went as the assembly line sputtered along. Drug charges were rattled off by the Judge, an armed robbery, some vague sexual attack, more drugs, lots of parole violations. When their names were called, the defendants were led forward to the bench, where they stood in silence. Paperwork was shuffled, then they were hauled off again, back to jail.

'Tequila Watson,' a bailiff announced.

He was helped to his feet by another bailiff. He stutter-stepped forward, chains rattling.

'Mr Watson, you are charged with murder,' the Judge announced loudly. 'How old are you?'

'Twenty,' Tequila said, looking down.

The murder charge had echoed through the courtroom and brought a temporary stillness. The other criminals in orange looked on with admiration. The lawyers and cops were curious.

'Can you afford a lawyer?'

'No.'

'Didn't think so,' the Judge mumbled and glanced at the defense table. The fertile fields of the D.C. Superior Court Criminal Division, Felony Branch, were worked on a daily basis by the Office of the Public Defender, the safety net for all indigent defendants. Seventy percent of the docket was handled by court-appointed counsel, and at any time there were usually half a dozen PDs milling around in cheap suits and battered loafers with files sticking out of their briefcases. At that precise moment, however, only one PD was present, the Honorable Clay Carter II, who had stopped by to check on two much lesser felonies, and now found himself all alone and wanting to bolt from the courtroom. He glanced to his right and to his left and realized that His Honor was looking at him. Where had all the other PDs gone?

A week earlier, Mr Carter had finished a murder case, one that had lasted for almost three years and had finally been closed with his client being sent away to a prison from which he would never leave, at least not officially. Clay Carter was quite happy his client was now locked up, and he was relieved that he, at that moment, had no murder files on his desk.

That, evidently, was about to change.

'Mr Carter?' the Judge said. It was not an order, but an invitation to step forward to do what every PD was expected to do – defend the indigent, regardless of the case. Mr Carter could not show weakness, especially with the cops and prosecutors watching. He swallowed hard, refused to flinch, and walked to the bench as if he just might demand a jury trial right there and then. He took the file from the Judge, quickly skimmed its rather thin contents while ignoring the pleading look of Tequila Watson, then said, 'We'll enter a plea of not guilty, Your Honor.'

'Thank you, Mr Carter. And we'll show you as counsel of record?'

'For now, yes.' Mr Carter was already plotting excuses to unload this case on someone else at OPD.

'Very well. Thank you,' the Judge said, already reaching for the next file.

Lawyer and client huddled at the defense table

for a few minutes. Carter took as much information as Tequila was willing to give, which was very little. He promised to stop by the jail the next day for a longer interview. As they whispered, the table was suddenly crowded with young lawyers from the PD's office, colleagues of Carter's who seemed to materialize from nowhere.

Was this a setup? Carter asked himself. Had they disappeared knowing a murder defendant was in the room? In the past five years, he'd pulled such stunts himself. Ducking the nasty ones was an art form at OPD.

He grabbed his briefcase and hurried away, down the center aisle, past rows of worried relatives, past Adelfa Pumphrey and her little support group, into the hallway crammed with many more criminals and their mommas and girlfriends and lawyers. There were those in OPD who swore they lived for the chaos of the H. Carl Moultrie Courthouse – the pressure of trials, the hint of danger from people sharing the same space with so many violent men, the painful conflict between victims and their assailants, the hopelessly overcrowded dockets, the calling to protect the poor and ensure fair treatment by the cops and the system.

If Clay Carter had ever been attracted to a career in OPD, he could not now remember why. In one week the fifth anniversary of his employment there would come and go, without celebration, and, hopefully, without anyone knowing it. Clay was burned out at the age of thirty-one, stuck in an office he was ashamed to show his friends, looking for an exit with no place to go, and now saddled with another senseless murder case that was growing heavier by the minute.

In the elevator he cursed himself for getting nailed with a murder. It was a rookie's mistake; he'd been around much too long to step into the trap, especially one set on such familiar turf. I'm quitting, he promised himself; the same vow he had uttered almost every day for the past year.

There were two others in the elevator. One was a court clerk of some variety, with her arms full of files. The other was a fortyish gentleman dressed in designer black – jeans, T-shirt, jacket, alligator boots. He held a newspaper and appeared to be reading it through small glasses perched on the tip of his rather long and elegant nose; in fact, he was studying Clay, who was oblivious. Why would someone pay any attention to anyone else on this elevator in this building?

If Clay Carter had been alert instead of brooding, he would have noticed that the gentleman was too well dressed to be a defendant, but too casual to be a lawyer. He carried nothing but a newspaper, which was somewhat odd because the H. Carl Moultrie Courthouse was not known as a place for reading. He did not appear to be a judge, a clerk, a victim, or a defendant, but Clay never noticed him.

10

Chapter 2

In a city of 76,000 lawyers, many of them clustered in megafirms within rifle shot of the U.S. Capitol – rich and powerful firms where the brightest associates were given obscene signing bonuses and the dullest ex-Congressmen were given lucrative lobbying deals and the hottest litigators came with their own agents – the Office of the Public Defender was far down in the minor leagues. Low A.

Some OPD lawyers were zealously committed to defending the poor and oppressed, and for them the job was not a stepping-stone to another career. Regardless of how little they earned or how tight their budgets were, they thrived on the lonely independence of their work and the satisfaction of protecting the underdog.

Other PDs told themselves that the job was transitory, just the nitty-gritty training they needed to get launched into more promising careers. Learn the ropes the hard way, get your hands dirty, see and do things no big-firm associate

11

would ever get near, and someday some firm with real vision will reward the effort. Unlimited trial experience, a vast knowledge of the judges and the clerks and the cops, workload management, skills in handling the most difficult of clients – these were just a few of the advantages PDs had to offer after only a few years on the job.

OPD had eighty lawyers, all working in two cramped and suffocating floors of the District of Columbia Public Services Building, a pale, square, concrete structure known as The Cube, on Mass Avenue near Thomas Circle. There were about forty low paid secretaries and three dozen paralegals scattered through the maze of cubbyhole offices. The Director was a woman named Glenda who spent most of her time locked in her office because she felt safe in there.

The beginning salary for an OPD lawyer was $36,000. Raises were minuscule and slow in coming. The most senior lawyer, a frazzled old man of forty-three, earned $57,600 and had been threatening to quit for nineteen years. The workloads were staggering because the city was losing its own war on crime. The supply of indigent criminals was endless. Every year for the past eight Glenda had submitted a budget requesting ten more lawyers and a dozen more paralegals. In each of the last four budgets she had received less money than the year before. Her quandary at the moment was which paralegals to terminate and which lawyers to force into part-time work.

Like most of the other PDs, Clay Carter had

not entered law school with the plan of a career, or even a brief stint, defending indigent criminals. No way. Back when Clay was in college and then law school at Georgetown his father had a firm in D.C. Clay had worked there part-time for years, and had his own office. The dreams had been boundless back then, father and son litigating together as the money poured in.

But the firm collapsed during Clay's last year of law school, and his father left town. That was another story. Clay became a public defender because there were no other last-second jobs to grab.

It took him three years to jockey and connive his way into getting his own office, not one shared with another lawyer or paralegal. About the size of a modest suburban utility closet, it had no windows and a desk that consumed half the floor space. His office in his father's old firm had been four times larger with views of the Washington Monument, and though he tried to forget those views he couldn't erase them from his memory. Five years later, he still sat at his desk at times and stared at the walls, which seemed to get closer each month, and asked himself how, exactly, did he fall from one office to the other?

He tossed the Tequila Watson file on his very clean and very neat desk and took off his jacket. It would have been easy, in the midst of such dismal surroundings, to let the place go, to let the files and papers pile up, to clutter his office and blame it on being overworked and understaffed.

But his father had believed that an organized desk was a sign of an organized mind. If you couldn't find something in thirty seconds, you were losing money, his father always said. Return phone calls immediately was another rule Clay had been taught to obey.

So he was fastidious about his desk and office, much to the amusement of his harried colleagues. His Georgetown Law School diploma hung in a handsome frame in the center of a wall. For the first two years at OPD he had refused to display the diploma for fear that the other lawyers would wonder why someone from Georgetown was working for minimum wages. For the experience, he told himself, I'm here for the experience. A trial every month – tough trials against tough prosecutors in front of tough juries. For the down-in-the-gutter, bare-knuckle training that no big firm could provide. The money would come later, when he was a battle-hardened litigator at a very young age.

He stared at the thin Watson file in the center of his desk and wondered how he might unload it on someone else. He was tired of the tough cases and the superb training and all the other crap that he put up with as an underpaid PD.

There were six pink phone message slips on his desk; five related to business, one from Rebecca, his longtime girlfriend. He called her first.

'I'm very busy,' she informed him after the required initial pleasantries.

'You called me,' Clay said.

'Yes, I can only talk a minute or so.' Rebecca worked as an assistant to a low-ranking Congressman who was the chairman of some useless subcommittee. But because he was the chairman he had an additional office he was required to staff with people like Rebecca who was in a frenzy all day preparing for the next round of hearings that no one would attend. Her father had pulled strings to get her the job.

'I'm kinda swamped too,' Clay said. 'Just picked up another murder case.' He managed to add a measure of pride to this, as if he were honored to be the attorney for Tequila Watson.

It was a game they played: Who was the busiest? Who was the most important? Who worked the hardest? Who had the most pressure?

'Tomorrow is my mother's birthday,' she said, pausing slightly as if Clay was supposed to know this. He did not. He cared not. He didn't like her mother. 'They've invited us to dinner at the club.'

A bad day just got worse. The only response he could possibly give was, 'Sure.' And a quick one at that.

'Around seven. Coat and tie.'

'Of course.' I'd rather have dinner with Tequila Watson at the jail, he thought to himself.

'I gotta run,' she said. 'See you then. Love you.'

'Love you.'

It was a typical conversation between the two, just a few quick lines before rushing off to save the world. He looked at her photo on his desk. Their romance came with enough complications to sink ten marriages. His father had once sued her father, and who won and who lost would never be clear. Her family claimed origins in old Alexandria society; he'd been an Army brat. They were right-wing Republicans, he was not. Her father was known as Bennett the Bulldozer for his relentless slash-and-burn development in the Northern Virginia suburbs around D.C. Clay hated the sprawl of Northern Virginia and quietly paid his dues to two environmental groups fighting the developers. Her mother was an aggressive social climber who wanted her two daughters to marry serious money. Clay had not seen his mother in eleven years. He had no social ambitions whatsoever. He had no money.

For almost four years, the romance had survived a monthly brawl, the majority of them engineered by her mother. It clung to life by love and lust and a determination to succeed regardless of the odds against it. But Clay sensed a fatigue on Rebecca's part, a creeping weariness brought on by age and constant family pressure. She was twenty-eight. She did not want a career. She wanted a husband and a family and long days spent at the country club spoiling the children, playing tennis, doing lunch with her mother.

Paulette Tullos appeared from thin air and startled him. 'Got nailed, didn't you?' she said with a smirk. 'A new murder case.'

'You were there?' Clay asked.

'Saw it all. Saw it coming, saw it happen, couldn't save you, pal.'

'Thanks. I owe you one.'

He would have offered her a seat, but there were no others in his office. There was no room for chairs and besides they were not needed because all of his clients were in jail. Sitting and chatting were not part of the daily routine at OPD.

'What are my chances of getting rid of it?' he said.

'Slim to impossible. Who you gonna dump it on?'

'I was thinking of you.'

'Sorry. I got two murder cases already. Glenda won't move it for you.'

Paulette was his closest friend inside the OPD. A product of a rough section of the city, she had scratched her way through college and law school at night and had seemed destined for the middle classes until she met an older Greek gentleman with a fondness for young black women. He married her and set her up comfortably in North West Washington, then eventually returned to Europe, where he preferred to live. Paulette suspected he had a wife or two over there, but she wasn't particularly concerned about it. She was well-off and seldom alone. After ten years, the arrangement was working fine.

'I heard the prosecutors talking,' she said. 'Another street killing, but questionable motive.'

'Not exactly the first one in the history of D.C.'

'But no apparent motive.'

17

'There's always a motive – cash, drugs, sex, a new pair of Nikes.'

'But the kid was pretty tame, no history of violence?'

'First impressions are seldom true, Paulette, you know that.'

'Jermaine got one very similar two days ago. No apparent motive.'

'I hadn't heard.'

'You might try him. He's new and ambitious and, who knows, you might dump it on him.'

'I'll do it right now.'

Jermaine wasn't in but Glenda's door, for some reason, was slightly open. Clay rapped it with his knuckles while walking through it. 'Got a minute?' he said, knowing that Glenda hated sparing a minute with anyone on her staff. She did a passable job running the office, managing the caseloads, holding the budget together, and, most important, playing the politics at City Hall. But she did not like people. She preferred to do her work behind a locked door.

'Sure,' she said abruptly, with no conviction whatsoever. It was clear she did not appreciate the intrusion, which was exactly the reception Clay had expected.

'I happened to be in the Criminal Division this morning at the wrong time, got nailed with a murder case, one I'd rather pass on. I just finished the Traxel case, which, as you know, lasted for almost three years. I need a break from murder. How about one of the younger guys?'

'You beggin' off, Mr. Carter?' she said, eyebrows arched.

'Absolutely. Load up the dope and burglaries for a few months. That's all I'm asking.'

'And who do you suggest should handle the, uh, what's the case?'

'Tequila Watson.'

'Tequila Watson. Who should get him, Mr. Carter?'

'I don't really care. I just need a break.'

She leaned back in her chair, like some wise old chairman of the board, and began chewing on the end of a pen. 'Don't we all, Mr. Carter? We'd all love a break, wouldn't we?'

'Yes or no?'

'We have eighty lawyers here, Mr. Carter, about half of whom are qualified to handle murder cases. Everybody has at least two. Move it if you can, but I'm not going to reassign it.'

As he was leaving, Clay said, 'I could sure use a raise if you wanted to work on it.'

'Next year, Mr. Carter. Next year.'

'And a paralegal.'

'Next year.'

The Tequila Watson file remained in the very neat and organized office of Jarrett Clay Carter II, Attorney-at-Law.

Chapter 3

The building was, after all, a jail. Though it was of recent vintage and upon its grand opening had been the source of great pride for a handful of city leaders, it was still a jail. Designed by cutting-edge urban defense consultants and adorned with high-tech security gadgetry, it was still a jail. Efficient, safe, humane, and, though built for the next century, it was overbooked the day it opened. From the outside it resembled a large red cinder-block resting on one end, windowless, hopeless, filled with criminals and the countless people who guarded them. To make someone feel better it had been labeled a Criminal Justice Center, a modern euphemism employed widely by the architects of such projects. It was a jail.

And it was very much a part of Clay Carter's turf. He met almost all of his clients there, after they were arrested and before they were released on bond, if they were able to post it. Many were not. Many were arrested for nonviolent crimes, and whether guilty or innocent, they were kept locked away until their final court appearances. Tigger Banks had spent almost eight months in the jail for a burglary he did not commit. He lost both of his part-time jobs. He lost his apartment. He lost his dignity. Clay's last phone call from Tigger had been a gut-wrenching plea from the kid for money. He was on crack again, on the streets and headed for trouble.

Every criminal lawyer in the city had a Tigger Banks story, all with unhappy endings and nothing to be done about them. It cost $41,000 a year to house an inmate. Why was the system so anxious to burn the money?

Clay was tired of those questions, and tired of the Tiggers of his career, and tired of the jail and the same surly guards who greeted him at the basement entrance used by most lawyers. And he was tired of the smell of the place, and the idiotic little procedures put in place by pencil pushers who read manuals on how to keep jails safe. It was 9 A.M., a Wednesday, though for Clay every day was the same. He went to a sliding window under a sign for ATTORNEYS, and after the clerk was certain that he had waited long enough, she opened the window and said nothing. Nothing needed to be said, since she and Clay had been scowling at each other without greetings for almost five years now. He signed a register, handed it back, and she closed the window, no doubt a bulletproof one to protect her from rampaging lawyers.

Glenda had spent two years trying to implement

a simple call-ahead method whereby OPD lawyers, and everyone else for that matter, could telephone an hour before they arrived and their clients would be somewhere in the vicinity of the attorney conference room. It was a simple request, and its simplicity had no doubt led to its demise in bureaucratic hell.

There was a row of chairs against a wall where the lawyers were expected to wait while their requests were sent along at a snail's pace to someone upstairs. By 9 A.M. there were always a few lawyers sitting there, fidgeting with files, whispering on cell phones, ignoring one another. At one point early in his young career Clay had brought along thick law books to read and highlight in yellow and thus impress the other lawyers with his intensity. Now he pulled out the *Post* and read the sports section. As always, he glanced at his watch to see how much time would be wasted waiting for Tequila Watson.

Twenty-four minutes. Not bad.

A guard led him down the hall to a long room divided by a thick sheet of Plexiglas. The guard pointed to the fourth booth from the end, and Clay took a seat. Through the glass, he could see that the other half of the booth was empty. More waiting. He pulled papers from his briefcase and began thinking of questions for Tequila. The booth to his right was occupied by a lawyer in the midst of a tense, but muted, conversation with his client, a person Clay could not see.

The guard returned and whispered to Clay, as

if such conversations were illegal. 'Your boy had a bad night,' he said, crouching and glancing up at the security cameras.

'Okay,' Clay said.

'He jumped on a kid around two this morning, beat the hell out of him, caused a pretty good brawl. Took six of our guys to break it up. He's a mess.'

'Tequila?'

'Watson, that's him. Put the other boy in the hospital. Expect some additional charges.'

'Are you sure?' Clay asked, looking over his shoulder.

'It's all on video.' End of conversation.

They looked up as Tequila was brought to his seat by two guards, each with an elbow secured. He was handcuffed, and though the inmates were customarily set free to chat with their lawyers, Tequila's handcuffs were not coming off. He sat down. The guards moved away but remained close.

His left eye was swollen shut, with dried blood in both corners. The right one was open and the pupil was bright red. There was tape and gauze in the center of his forehead, and a butterfly Band-Aid on his chin. Both lips and both jaws were puffy and oversized to the point that Clay wasn't sure he had the right client. Someone somewhere had just beaten the hell out of the guy sitting three feet away through the Plexiglas.

Clay picked up the black phone receiver and motioned for Tequila to do likewise. He cradled it awkwardly with both hands.

'You are Tequila Watson?' Clay said with as much eye contact as possible.

He nodded yes, very slowly, as if loose bones were shifting throughout his head.

'Have you seen a doctor?'

A nod, yes.

'Did the cops do this to you?'

Without hesitation he shook his head. No.

'The other guys in the cell do it?"

A nod, yes.

'The cops tell me you started the fight, beat up some kid, put him in the hospital. Is that true?'

A nod, yes.

It was hard to imagine Tequila Watson, all 150 pounds of him, bullying people in a crowded cell in the D.C. jail.

'Did you know the kid?'

Lateral movement. No.

So far his receiver had not been needed, and Clay was tired of the sign language. 'Why, exactly, did you beat up this kid?'

With great effort the swollen lips finally parted. 'I don't know,' he managed to grunt, the words slow and painful.

'That's great, Tequila. That gives me something to work with. How about self-defense? Did the kid come after you? Throw the first punch?'

'No.'

'Was he stoned or drunk?'

'No.'

'Was he trash-talking, making threats, that kind of stuff?'

'He was asleep.'

'Asleep?'

'Yeah.'

'Was he snoring too loud? Forget it.'

Eye contact was broken by the lawyer, who suddenly needed to write something on his yellow legal pad. Clay scribbled the date, time, place, client's name, then ran out of important facts to take note of. He had a hundred questions filed away in his memory, and after that a hundred more. They rarely varied in these initial interviews; just the basics of his client's miserable life and how they came to meet. The truth was guarded like rare gems to be passed through the Plexiglas only when the client wasn't threatened. Questions about family and school and jobs and friends were usually answered with a good measure of honesty. But questions related to the crime were subject to gamesmanship. Every criminal lawyer knew not to dwell too much on the crime during the first interviews. Dig for details elsewhere. Investigate without guidance from the client. The truth might come later.

Tequila, however, seemed quite different. So far, he had no fear of the truth. Clay decided to save many, many hours of his precious time. He leaned in closer and lowered his voice. 'They say you killed a boy, shot him five times in the head.'

The swollen head nodded slightly.

'A Ramón Pumphrey, also known as Pumpkin. Did you know this guy?'

A nod, yes.

'Did you shoot him?' Clay's voice was almost a whisper. The guards were asleep but the question was still one that lawyers did not ask, not at the jail anyway.

'I did,' Tequila said softly.

'Five times?'

'Thought it was six.'

Oh well, so much for a trial. I'll have this file closed in sixty days, Clay thought to himself. A quick plea bargain. A guilty plea in return for life in prison.

'A drug deal?' he asked.

'No.'

'Did you rob him?'

'No.'

'Help me here, Tequila. You had a reason, didn't you?'

'I knew him.'

'That's it? You knew him? That's your best excuse?'

He nodded but said nothing.

'A girl, right? You caught him with your girlfriend? You have a girlfriend, don't you?'

He shook his head. No.

'Did the shooting have anything to do with sex?'

No.

'Talk to me, Tequila, I'm your lawyer. I'm the only person on the planet who's working right now to help you. Give me something to work with here.'

'I used to buy drugs from Pumpkin.'

26

'Now you're talking. How long ago?'

'Couple of years.'

'Okay. Did he owe you some money or some drugs? Did you owe him something?'

'No.'

Clay took a deep breath and for the first time noticed Tequila's hands. They were nicked with small cuts and swollen so badly that none of the knuckles could be seen. 'You fight a lot?'

Maybe a nod, maybe a shake. 'Not anymore.'

'You once did?'

'Kid stuff. I fought Pumpkin once.'

Finally. Clay took another deep breath and raised his pen. 'Thank you, sir, for your help. When, exactly, did you have a fight with Pumpkin?'

'Long time ago.'

'How old were you?'

A shrug, one in response to a stupid question. Clay knew from experience that his clients had no concept of time. They got robbed yesterday or they got arrested last month, but probe beyond thirty days and all history melted together. Street life was a struggle to survive today, with no time to reminisce and nothing in the past to get nostalgic over. There was no future so that point of reference was likewise unknown.

'Kids,' Tequila said, sticking with the one-word answer, probably a habit with or without broken jaws.

'How old were you?'

'Maybe twelve.'

'Were you in school?'

'Playing basketball.'

'Was it a nasty fight, cuts and broken bones and such?'

'No. Big dudes broke it up.'

Clay laid the receiver down for a moment and summarized his defense. Ladies and gentlemen of the jury, my client shot Mr Pumphrey (who was unarmed) five or six times at point-blank range in a dirty alley with a stolen gun for two reasons; first, he recognized him, and second, they had a playground shoving match about eight years ago. May not sound like much, ladies and gentlemen, but all of us know that in Washington, D.C., those two reasons are as good as any.

Into the receiver again, he asked, 'Did you see Pumpkin often?'

'No.'

'When was the last time you saw him before he got shot?'

A shrug. Back to the time problem.

'Did you see him once a week?'

'No.'

'Once a month?'

'No.'

'Twice a year?'

'Maybe.'

'When you saw him two days ago, did you argue with him? Help me here, Tequila, I'm working too hard for details.'

'We didn't argue.'

'Why did you go into the alley?'

Tequila laid down the receiver and began

moving his head back and forth, very slowly, to work out some kinks. He was obviously in pain. The handcuffs appeared to be cutting into his skin. When he picked up the receiver again he said, 'I'll tell you the truth. I had a gun, and I wanted to shoot somebody. Anybody, it didn't matter. I left the Camp and just started walking, going nowhere, looking for somebody to shoot. I almost got a Korean dude outside his store, but there were too many people around. I saw Pumpkin. I knew him. We talked for a minute. I said I had some rock if he wanted a hit. We went to the alley. I shot the boy. I don't know why. I just wanted to kill somebody.'

When it was clear the narrative was over, Clay asked, 'What is the Camp?'

'Rehab place. That's where I was staying.'

'How long had you been there?'

Time again. But the answer was a great surprise. 'Hundred and fifteen days.'

'You had been clean for a hundred and fifteen days?'

'Yep.'

'Were you clean when you shot Pumpkin?'

'Yep. Still am. Hundred and sixteen days.'

'You ever shot anybody before?'

'No.'

'Where'd you get the gun?'

'Stole it from my cousin's house.'

'Is the Camp a lockdown place?'

'Yes.'

'Did you escape?'

'I was getting two hours. After a hundred days, you can go out for two hours, then go back in.'

'So you walked out of the Camp, went to your cousin's house, stole a gun, then began walking the streets looking for someone to shoot, and you found Pumpkin?'

Tequila was nodding by the end of the sentence. 'That's what happened. Don't ask me why. I don't know. I just don't know.'

There was possibly some moisture in the red right eye of Tequila, perhaps brought on by guilt and remorse, but Clay could not be certain. He pulled some papers out of his briefcase and slid them through the opening. 'Sign these by the red check marks. I'll come back in a couple of days.'

Tequila ignored the papers. 'What's gonna happen to me?' he asked.

'We'll talk about it later.'

'When can I get out?'

'It might be a long time.'

Chapter 4

The people who ran Deliverance Camp saw no need to hide from the problems. They made no effort to get away from the war zone from which they took their casualties. No quiet facility in the country. No secluded clinic in a better part of town. Their campers came from the streets and they would go back to the streets.

The Camp faced W Street in N.W., within view of a row of boarded-up duplexes that were sometimes used by crack dealers. Within plain sight was the notorious empty lot of an old gas station. Here drug peddlers met their wholesalers and did their exchanges regardless of who might be looking. According to unofficial police records, the lot had produced more bullet-laden corpses than any other piece of turf in D.C.

Clay drove slowly down W Street, doors locked, hands clutching the wheel, eyes cutting in all directions, ears awaiting the inevitable sound of gunfire. A white boy in this ghetto was an irresistible target, regardless of the time of day.

D Camp was an ancient warehouse, long abandoned by whoever last used it for storage, condemned by the city, then auctioned off for a few dollars to a nonprofit that somehow saw potential. It was a hulking structure, the red brick spray-painted maroon from sidewalk to roof, with the lower levels repainted by the neighborhood graffiti specialists. It rambled down the street then back an entire city block. All the doors and windows along the sides had been cemented shut and painted, so that fencing and razor wire were not needed. Anyone wishing to escape would need a hammer, a chisel, and a hard day of uninterrupted labor.

Clay parked his Honda Accord directly in front of the building and debated whether to race away or get out. There was a small sign above a set of thick double doors: DELIVERANCE CAMP. PRIVATE. No trespassing. As if someone could wander inside, or want to. There was the usual collection of street characters loitering about: some young toughs no doubt hauling drugs and enough assault weapons to hold off the police, a couple of winos staggering in tandem, what appeared to be family members waiting to visit those inside D Camp. His job had led him to most of the undesirable places in D.C., and he had grown proficient at acting as though he had no fear. I'm a lawyer. I'm here on business. Get out of my way. Don't speak to me. In nearly five years with OPD, he had yet to be shot at.

He locked the Accord and left it at the curb.

While doing so he sadly admitted to himself that few if any of the thugs on this street would be attracted to his little car. It was twelve years old and pushing two hundred thousand miles. Take it, he said.

He held his breath and ignored the curious stares from the sidewalk gang. There's not another white face within two miles of here, he thought. He pushed a button by the doors and a voice cracked through the intercom. 'Who is it?'

'My name is Clay Carter. I'm a lawyer. I have an eleven o'clock appointment with Talmadge X.' He said the name clearly, still certain that it was a mistake. On the phone he had asked the secretary how to spell Mr. X's last name, and she said, quite rudely, that it was not a last name at all. What was it? It was an X. Take it or leave it. It wasn't about to change.

'Just a minute,' the voice said, and Clay began to wait. He stared at the doors, trying desperately to ignore everything around him. He was aware of movement off to his left side, something close.

'Say, man, you a lawyer?' came the question, a high-pitched young black male voice, loud enough for everyone to hear.

Clay turned and looked into the funky sunshades of his tormentor. 'Yep,' he said, as coolly as possible.

'You ain't no lawyer,' the young man said. A small gang was forming behind him, all gawking.

'Afraid so,' Clay said.

'Can't be no lawyer, man.'

'No way,' said one of the gang.

'You sure you're a lawyer?'

'Yep,' Clay said, playing along.

'If you a lawyer, why you drivin' a shit car like that?'

Clay wasn't sure which hurt more – the laughter from the sidewalk or the truth of the statement. He made matters worse.

'My wife drives the Mercedes,' he said, a bad attempt at humor.

'You ain't got no wife. You ain't got no wedding ring.'

What else have they noticed? Clay asked himself. They were still laughing when one of the doors clicked and opened. He managed to step casually inside instead of diving for safety. The reception area was a bunker with a concrete floor, cinderblock walls, metal doors, no windows, low ceiling, a few lights, everything but sandbags and weapons. Behind a long government-issue table was a receptionist answering two phones. Without looking up she said, 'He'll be just a minute.'

Talmadge X was a wiry, intense man of about fifty, not an ounce of fat on his narrow frame, not a hint of a smile on his wrinkled and aged face. His eyes were large and wounded, scarred by decades on the streets. He was very black and his clothes were very white – heavily starched cotton shirt and dungarees. Black combat boots shined to perfection. His head was shined too, not a trace of hair.

He pointed to the only chair in his makeshift

office, and he closed the door. 'You got paper-work?' he asked abruptly. Evidently, small talk was not one of his talents.

Clay handed over the necessary documents, all bearing the indecipherable handcuffed scrawl of Tequila Watson. Talmadge X read every word on every page. Clay noticed he did not wear a watch, nor did he like clocks. Time had been left at the front door.

'When did he sign these?'

'They're dated today. I saw him about two hours ago at the jail.'

'And you're his counsel of record?' Talmadge X asked. 'Officially?'

The man had been through the criminal justice system more than once. 'Yes. Appointed by the court, assigned by the Office of the Public Defender.'

'Glenda still there?'

'Yes.'

'We go way back.' It was as close to chitchat as they would get.

'Did you know about the shooting?' Clay asked, taking a legal pad to write on from his briefcase.

'Not until you called an hour ago. We knew he left Tuesday and didn't come back, knew something was wrong, but then we expect things to go wrong.' His words were slow and precise, his eyes blinked often but never strayed. 'Tell me what happened.'

'This is all confidential, right?' Clay said.

'I'm his counselor. I'm also his minister. You're

his lawyer. Everything said in this room stays in this room. Deal?'

'Right.'

Clay gave the details he'd collected so far, including Tequila's version of events. Technically, ethically, he was not supposed to reveal to anyone statements made to him by his client. But who would really care? Talmadge X knew far more about Tequila Watson than Clay would ever learn.

As the narrative went on and the events unfolded in front of Talmadge X, his stare finally broke and he closed his eyes. He tilted his head upward, to the ceiling, as if he wanted to ask God why this happened. He drifted away, deep in thought and deeply troubled.

When Clay finished, Talmadge X said, 'What can I do?'

'I'd like to see his file. He's given me authorization.'

The file was lying squarely on the desk in front of Talmadge X. 'Later,' he said. 'But let's talk first. What do you want to know?'

'Let's start with Tequila. Where'd he come from?'

The stare was back, Talmadge was ready to help. 'The streets, same place they all come from. He was referred by Social Services, because he was a hopeless case. No family to speak of. Never knew his father. Mother died of AIDS when he was three. Raised by an aunt or two, passed around the family, foster homes here and there, in and out of court and juvenile homes. Dropped out of school. Typical case for us. Are you familiar with D Camp?'

'No.'

'We get the hard cases, the permanent junkies. We lock 'em down for months, give 'em a boot camp environment. There are eight of us here, eight counselors, and we're all addicts, once an addict always an addict, but you must know that. Four of us are now ministers. I served thirteen years for drugs and robbery, then I found Jesus. Anyway, we specialize in the young crack addicts nobody else can help.'

'Only crack?'

'Crack's the drug, man. Cheap, plentiful, takes your mind off life for a few minutes. Once you start it you can't quit.'

'He couldn't tell me much about his criminal record.'

Talmadge X opened the file and flipped pages. 'That's probably because he doesn't remember much. Tequila was stoned for years. Here it is; bunch of petty stuff when he was a juvenile, robbery, stolen cars, the usual stuff we all did so we could buy drugs. At eighteen he did four months for shoplifting. Got him for possession last year, three months there. Not a bad record for one of us. Nothing violent.'

'How many felonies?'

'I don't see one.'

'I guess that'll help,' Clay said. 'In some way.'

'Sounds like nothing will help.'

'I'm told there were at least two eyewitnesses. I'm not optimistic.'

'Has he confessed to the cops?'

'No. They've told me that he clammed up when they caught him and has said nothing.'

'That's rare.'

'It is,' Clay said.

'Sounds like life with no parole,' said Talmadge X, the voice of experience.

'You got it.'

'That's not the end of the world for us, you know, Mr. Carter. In many ways, life in prison is better than life on these streets. I got lots of pals who prefer it. Sad thing is, Tequila was one of the few who could've made it.'

'Why is that?'

'Kid's got a brain. Once we got him cleaned up and healthy, he felt so good about himself. For the first time in his adult life, he was sober. He couldn't read so we taught him. He liked to draw so we encouraged art. We never get excited around here, but Tequila made us proud. He was even thinking about changing his name, for obvious reasons.'

'You never get excited?'

'We lose sixty-six percent, Mr Carter. Two thirds. We get 'em in here, sick as dogs, stoned, their bodies and brains cooked on crack, malnourished, even starving, skin rashes, hair falling out, the sickest junkies D.C. can produce, and we fatten 'em up, dry 'em out, lock 'em down in basic training where they're up at six A.M. scrubbing their rooms and waiting on inspection, breakfast at six-thirty, then nonstop brainwashing from a tough group of counselors who've all been exactly where they've been, no bullshit, pardon my language, don't even try to con us because we're all cons ourselves. After a month they're clean and they're very proud. They don't miss the outside world because there's nothing good waiting for them – no jobs, no families, nobody loves them. They're easy to brainwash, and we are relentless. After three months we might, depending on the patient, start easing them back onto the street for an hour or two a day. Nine out of ten return, anxious to get back into their little rooms. We keep them for a year, Mr. Carter. Twelve months, not a day less. We try to educate them some, maybe a little job training with computers. We work hard at finding them jobs. They graduate, we all have a good cry. They leave, and within a year two thirds of them are doing crack again and headed for the gutter.'

'Do you take them back?'

'Rarely. If they know they can come back, then they're more likely to screw up.'

'What happens to the other third?'

'That's why we're here, Mr Carter. That's why I'm a counselor. Those folks, like me, survive in the world, and they do it with a toughness no one else understands. We've been to hell and back and it's an ugly road. Many of our survivors work with other addicts.'

'How many people can you house at one time?'

'We have eighty beds, all full. We have room for twice that many, but there's never enough money.'

'Who funds you?'

'Eighty percent federal grants, and there's no guarantee from year to year. The rest we beg from private foundations. We're too busy to raise a lot of money.'

Clay turned a page and made a note. 'There's not a single family member I can talk to?'

Talmadge X shuffled through the file, shaking his head. 'Maybe an aunt somewhere, but don't expect much. Even if you found one, how could she help you?'

'She can't. But it's nice to have a family member to contact.'

Talmadge X kept flipping through the file as if he had something in mind. Clay suspected he was looking for notes or entries to be removed before it was handed over.

'When can I see that?' Clay asked.

'How about tomorrow? I'd like to review it first.'

Clay shrugged. If Talmadge X said tomorrow, then it would be tomorrow. 'All right, Mr. Carter, I don't get his motive. Tell me why.'

'I can't. You tell me. You've known him for almost four months. No history of violence or guns. No propensity for fighting. Sounds like he was the model patient. You've seen it all. You tell me why.'

'I've seen everything,' Talmadge X said, his eyes

40

even sadder than before. 'But I've never seen this. The boy was afraid of violence. We don't tolerate fighting in here, but boys will be boys, and there are always the little rituals of intimidation. Tequila was one of the weak ones. There's no way he would leave here, steal a gun, pick a random victim, and kill him. And there's no way he would jump on a guy in jail and send him to the hospital. I just don't believe it.'

'So what do I tell the jury?'

'What jury? This is a guilty plea and you know it. He's gone, off to prison for the rest of his life. I'm sure he knows plenty of folk there.'

There was a long gap in the conversation, a break that seemed not to bother Talmadge X in the least. He closed the file and shoved it away. The meeting was about to be over. But Clay was the visitor. It was time to leave.

'I'll be back tomorrow,' he said. 'What time?'

'After ten o'clock,' Talmadge X said. 'I'll walk you out.'

'It's not necessary,' Clay said, delighted with the escort.

The gang had grown and appeared to be waiting for the lawyer to exit D Camp. They were sitting and leaning on the Accord, which was still there and still in one piece. Whatever fun they'd planned was quickly forgotten at the sight of Talmadge X. With a quick jerk of his head he scattered the gang, and Clay sped away, untouched and dreading his return the next day.

He drove eight blocks and found Lamont

Street, then the corner of Georgia Avenue, where he stopped for a moment for a quick look around. There was no shortage of alleys in which one might shoot someone, and he was not about to go looking for blood. The neighborhood was as desolate as the one he'd just left. He'd come back later with Rodney, a black paralegal who knew the streets, and they'd poke around and ask questions.

Chapter 5

The Potomac Country Club in McLean, Virginia, was established a hundred years earlier by some wealthy people who'd been snubbed by the other country clubs. Rich folks can tolerate almost anything, but not rejection. The outcasts pumped their considerable resources into Potomac and built the finest club in the D.C. area. They picked off a few Senators from rival clubs and enticed other trophy members, and before long Potomac had bought respectability. Once it had enough members to sustain itself, it began the obligatory practice of excluding others. Though it was still known as a new country club, it looked and felt and acted like all the rest.

It did, however, differ in one significant way. Potomac had never denied the fact that its memberships could be bought outright if a person had enough money. Forget waiting lists and screening committees and secret votes by the admissions board. If you were new to D.C., or if you suddenly struck it rich, then status and prestige could be obtained overnight if your check was large enough. As a result, Potomac had the nicest golf course, tennis facilities, pools, clubhouses, dining room, everything an ambitious country club could want.

As far as Clay could tell, Bennett Van Horn had written the big check. Regardless of which cloud of smoke he was blowing at the moment, Clay's parents did not have money and certainly would not have been accepted at Potomac. His father had sued Bennett eighteen years earlier over a bad real estate deal in Alexandria. At the time, Bennett was a big-talking realtor with lots of debts and very few unencumbered assets. He was not a member of the Potomac Country Club then, though he now acted as if he'd been born there.

Bennett the Bulldozer struck gold in the late eighties when he invaded the rolling hills of the Virginia countryside. Deals fell into place. Partners were found. He didn't invent the slash-and-burn style of suburban development, but he certainly perfected it. On pristine hills he built malls. Near a hallowed battleground, he built a subdivision. He leveled an entire village for one of his planned developments – apartments, condos, big houses, small houses, a park in the center with a shallow muddy pond and two tennis courts, a quaint little shopping district that looked nice in the architect's office but never got built. Ironically, though irony was lost on Bennett, he named his cookie-cutter projects after the landscape he was destroying – Rolling Meadows,

44

Whispering Oaks, Forest Hills, etcetera. He joined other sprawl artists and lobbied the state legislature in Richmond for more money for more roads so more subdivisions could be thrown up and more traffic created. In doing so, he became a figure in the political game, and his ego swelled.

In the early nineties, his BVH Group grew rapidly, with revenues increasing at a slightly faster rate than loan payments. He and his wife, Barb, bought a home in a prestigious section of McLean. They joined the Potomac Country Club and became fixtures. They worked hard at creating the illusion that they had always had money.

In 1994, according to the SEC filings that Clay had studied diligently and kept copies of, Bennett decided to take his company public and raise $200 million. He planned to use the money to retire some debt, but, more important, to '. . . invest in the unlimited future of Northern Virginia.' In other words, more bulldozers, more slash-and-burn developments. The thought of Bennett Van Horn with that kind of cash no doubt thrilled the local Caterpillar dealers. And it should have horrified the local governments, but they were asleep.

With a blue-chip investment banker leading the way, BVHG stock roared out of the blocks at $10 a share and peaked at $16.50, not a bad run but far short of what its founder and CEO had predicted. A week before the public offering he had boasted in the *Daily Profit*, a local business tabloid, that '. . . the boys on Wall Street are sure it'll hit forty bucks a share.' In the Over the

Counter market, the stock floated back to earth and landed with a thud in the $6.00 range. Bennett had unwisely refused to dump some stock like all good entrepreneurs do. He held on to all of his four million shares and watched as his market value went from sixty-six million to almost nothing.

Every weekday morning, just for the sheer fun of it, Clay checked the price of one stock and one stock only. BVHG was currently trading at $0.87 per share.

'How's your stock doing?' was the great slap-in-the-face Clay'd never had the nerve to use.

'Maybe tonight,' he mumbled to himself as he drove into the entrance of the Potomac Country Club. Since there was a potential marriage in the near future, Clay's shortcomings were fair game around the dinner table. But not Mr Van Horn's. 'Hey, congratulations, Bennett, the stock has moved up twelve cents in the past two months,' he said out loud. 'Kicking ass, aren't you, old boy! Time for another Mercedes?' All the things he wanted to say.

To avoid the tip associated with valet parking, Clay hid his Accord in a distant lot behind some tennis courts. As he hiked to the clubhouse he straightened his tie and continued his mumbling. He hated the place – hated it for all the assholes who were members, hated it because he could not join, hated it because it was the Van Horns' turf and they wanted him to feel like a trespasser. For the hundredth time that day, as every day, he asked himself why he'd fallen in love with a girl whose parents were so insufferable. If he had a plan, it was to elope with Rebecca and move to New Zealand, far from the Office of the Public Defender, and as far away as possible from her family.

The gaze from the frosty hostess told him, I know you are not a member, but I'll take you to your table anyway. 'Follow me,' she said with the slight makings of a fake smile. Clay said nothing. He swallowed hard, looked straight ahead, and tried to ignore the heavy knot in his stomach. How was he supposed to enjoy a meal in such surroundings? He and Rebecca had eaten there twice – once with Mr. and Mrs. Van Horn, once without. The food was expensive and quite good, but then Clay lived on processed turkey so his standards were low and he knew it.

Bennett was absent. Clay gently hugged Mrs. Van Horn, a ritual both of them disliked, then offered a rather pathetic, 'Happy Birthday.' He pecked Rebecca on the cheek. It was a good table, one with a sweeping view of the eighteenth green, a very prestigious spot to eat because one could watch the geezers wallow in the sand traps and miss their two-foot putts.

'Where's Mr. Van Horn?' Clay asked, hoping he was stuck out of town, or better yet, hospital-ized with some grave ailment.

'He's on his way,' Rebecca said.

'He spent the day in Richmond, meeting with the Governor,' added Mrs. Van Horn, for good measure. They were relentless. Clay wanted to say, 'You win! You win! You're more important than I am!'

'What's he working on?' he asked politely, once again astounded at his ability to sound sincere. Clay knew exactly why the Bulldozer was in Richmond. The state was broke and could not afford to build new roads in Northern Virginia, where Bennett and his ilk demanded that they be built. The votes were in Northern Virginia. The legislature was considering a local referendum on sales taxes so the cities and counties around D.C. could build their own highways. More roads, more condos, more malls, more traffic, more money for an ailing BVHG.

'Political stuff,' Barb said. In truth, she probably didn't know what her husband and the Governor were discussing. Clay doubted if she knew the current price of BVHG stock. She knew the days her bridge club met and she knew how little money Clay earned, but most other details were left to Bennett.

'How was your day?' Rebecca asked, gently but quickly steering the conversation away from politics. Clay had used the word *sprawl* two or three times when debating issues with her parents and things had become tense.

'The usual,' he said. 'And you?'

'We have hearings tomorrow, so the office was hopping today.'

'Rebecca tells me you have another murder case,' Barb said.

'Yes, that's true,' Clay said, wondering what other aspects of his job as a public defender they had been talking about. Each had a glass of white wine sitting before her. Each glass was at least half-empty. He had walked in on a discussion, probably about him. Or was he being unduly sensitive? Perhaps.

'Who's your client?' Barb asked.

'A kid from the streets.'

'Who did he kill?'

'The victim was another kid from the streets.'

This relieved her somewhat. Blacks killing blacks. Who cared if they all killed each other?

'Did he do it?' she asked.

'As of now he is presumed to be innocent. That's the way it works.'

'In other words, he did it.'

'It sort of looks that way.'

'How can you defend people like that? If you know they're guilty, how can you work so hard trying to get them off?'

Rebecca took a large gulp of wine and decided to sit this one out. She had been coming to his rescue less and less in recent months. A nagging thought was that, while life would be magical with her, it would be a nightmare with them. The nightmares were winning.

'Our Constitution guarantees everyone a lawyer and a fair trial,' he said condescendingly, as if every fool should know this. 'I'm just doing my job.'

Barb rolled her new eyes and looked at the

eighteenth green. Many of the ladies at Potomac had been using a plastic surgeon whose specialty, evidently, was the Asian look. After the second session the eyes strained backward at the corners, and, while wrinkle-free, were grossly artificial. Ol' Barb had been nipped and tucked and Botoxed without a long-range plan, and the transition simply was not working.

Rebecca took another long pull on the wine. The first time they had eaten there with her parents she had kicked off a shoe under the table and run her toes up and down his leg, as if to say, 'Let's blow this joint and hop in the sack.' But not tonight. She was icy and seemed preoccupied. Clay knew she wasn't worrying about whatever meaningless hearings she would suffer through tomorrow. There were issues here, just under the surface, and he wondered if this dinner might be a showdown, a powwow with the future on the line.

Bennett arrived in a rush, full of bogus apologies for being late. He slapped Clay on the back as if they were fraternity brothers, and kissed his girls on the cheeks.

'How's the Governor?' Barb asked, loud enough for the diners across the room to hear.

'Great. He sends his best. The President of Korea is in town next week. The Guv has invited us to a black-tie gala at the mansion.' This too was offered at full volume.

'Oh really!' Barb gushed, her redone face erupting into a contortion of delight.

Should feel right at home with the Koreans, Clay thought.

'Should be a blast,' Bennett said as he pulled a collection of cell phones from his pocket and lined them up on the table. A few seconds behind him came a waiter with a double Scotch, Chivas with a little ice, the usual.

Clay ordered an iced tea.

'How's my Congressman?' Bennett yelled across the table to Rebecca, then cut his eyes to the right to make sure the couple at the next table had heard him. I have my very own Congressman!

'He's fine, Daddy. He sends his regards. He's very busy.'

'You look tired, honey, a tough day?'

'Not bad.'

The three Van Horns took a sip. Rebecca's fatigue was a favorite topic between her parents. They felt she worked too hard. They felt she shouldn't work at all. She was pushing thirty and it was time to marry a fine young man with a well-paying job and a bright future so she could bear their grandchildren and spend the rest of her life at the Potomac Country Club.

Clay would not have been too concerned with whatever the hell they wanted, except that Rebecca had the same dreams. She had once talked of a career in public service, but after four years on the Hill she was fed up with bureaucracies. She wanted a husband and babies and a large home in the suburbs.

Menus were passed around. Bennett got a call

and rudely handled it at the table. Some deal was falling through. The future of America's financial freedom hung in the balance.

'What should I wear?' Barb asked Rebecca as Clay hid behind his menu.

'Something new,' Rebecca said.

'You're right,' Barb readily agreed. 'Let's go shopping Saturday.'

'Good idea.'

Bennett saved the deal, and they ordered. He graced them with the details of the phone call – a bank was not moving fast enough, he had to light a fire, blah, blah. This went on until the salads arrived.

After a few bites, Bennett said, with his mouth full, as usual, 'While I was down in Richmond, I had lunch with my close friend Ian Ludkin, Speaker of the House. You'd really like this guy, Clay, a real prince of a man. A perfect Virginia gentleman.'

Clay chewed and nodded as if he couldn't wait to meet all of Bennett's good friends.

'Anyway, Ian owes me some favors, most of them do down there, and so I just popped the question.'

It took Clay a second to realize that the women had stopped eating. Their forks were at rest as they watched and listened with anticipation.

'What question?' Clay asked because it seemed that they were expecting him to say something.

'Well, I told him about you, Clay. Bright young lawyer, sharp as a tack, hard worker, Georgetown

Law School, handsome young man with real character, and he said he was always looking for new talent. God knows it's hard to find. Said he has an opening for a staff attorney. I said I had no idea if you'd be interested, but I'd be happy to run it by you. Whatta you think?'

I think I'm being ambushed, Clay almost blurted. Rebecca was staring at him, watching closely for the first reaction.

According to the script, Barb said, 'That sounds wonderful.'

Talented, bright, hardworking, well educated, even handsome. Clay was amazed at how fast his stock had risen. 'That's interesting,' he said, somewhat truthfully. Every aspect of it was interesting.

Bennett was ready to pounce. He, of course, held the advantage of surprise. 'It's a great position. Fascinating work. You'll meet the real movers and shakers down there. Never a dull moment. Lots of long hours, though, at least when the legislature is in session, but I told Ian that you had broad shoulders. Pile on the responsibilities.'

'What, exactly, would I be doing?' Clay managed to get out.

'Oh, I don't know all that lawyer stuff. But, if you're interested, Ian said he'd be happy to arrange an interview. It's a hot ticket, though. He said the résumés were flooding in. Gotta move quick.'

'Richmond's not that far away,' Barb said.

It's a helluva lot closer than New Zealand, Clay

thought. Barb was already planning the wedding. He couldn't read Rebecca. At times she felt strangled by her parents, but rarely showed any desire to get away from them. Bennett used his money, if indeed he had any left, as a carrot to keep both daughters close to home.

'Well, uh, thanks, I guess,' Clay said, collapsing under the weight of his newly bestowed broad shoulders.

'Starting salary is ninety-four thousand a year,' Bennett said, an octave or two lower so the other diners couldn't hear.

Ninety-four thousand dollars was more than twice as much as Clay was currently earning, and he assumed that everyone at the table knew it. The Van Horns worshiped money and were obsessed with salaries and net worths.

'Wow,' Barb said, on cue.

'That's a nice salary,' Clay admitted.

'Not a bad start,' Bennett said. 'Ian says you'll meet the big lawyers in town. Contacts are everything. Do it a few years, and you'll be able to write your own ticket in corporate law. That's where the big money is, you know.'

It was not comforting to know that Bennett Van Horn had suddenly taken an interest in planning the rest of Clay's life. The planning, of course, had nothing to do with Clay, and everything to do with Rebecca.

'How can you say no?' Barb said, prodding with two left feet.

'Don't push, Mother,' Rebecca said.

'It's just such a wonderful opportunity,' Barb said, as if Clay couldn't see the obvious.

'Kick it around, sleep on it,' Bennett said. The gift had been delivered. Let's see if the boy is smart enough to take it.

Clay was devouring his salad with a new purpose. He nodded as if he couldn't speak. The second Scotch arrived and broke up the moment. Bennett then shared the latest gossip from Richmond about the possibility of a new professional baseball franchise for the D.C. area, one of his favorite topics. He was on the fringes of one of three investment groups jockeying for the franchise, if and when one was ever approved, and he thrived on knowing the latest developments. According to a recent article in the *Post*, Bennett's group was in third place and losing ground by the month. Their finances were unclear, downright shaky, according to one unnamed source, and throughout the article the name of Bennett Van Horn was never mentioned. Clay knew he had enormous debts. Several of his developments had been stalled by environmental groups trying to preserve whatever land was left in Northern Virginia. He had lawsuits raging against former partners. His stock was practically worthless. Yet there he sat slugging down Scotch and yapping away about a new stadium for $400 million and a franchise fee of $200 million and a payroll of at least $100 million.

Their steaks arrived just when the salads were finished, thus sparing Clay another tortured moment of conversation with nothing to stuff in his mouth. Rebecca was ignoring him and he was certainly ignoring her. The fight would come very soon.

There were stories about the Guv, a close personal friend who was putting his machine in place to run for the Senate and of course he wanted Bennett in the middle of things. A couple of his hottest deals were revealed. There was talk of a new airplane, but this had been going on for some time and Bennett just couldn't find the one he wanted. The meal seemed to last for two hours, but only ninety minutes had passed when they declined dessert and started wrapping things up.

Clay thanked Bennett and Barb for the food and promised again to move quickly on the job down in Richmond. 'The chance of a lifetime,' Bennett said gravely. 'Don't screw it up.'

When Clay was certain they were gone, he asked Rebecca to step into the bar for a minute. They waited for their drinks to arrive before either spoke. When things were tense both had the tendency to wait for the other to fire first.

'I didn't know about the job in Richmond,' she began.

'I find that hard to believe. Seems like the entire family was in on the deal. Your mother certainly knew about it.'

'My father is just concerned about you, that's all.'

Your father is an idiot, he wanted to say. 'No, he's concerned about *you*. Can't have you marrying a guy with no future, so he'll just manage the future for us. Don't you think it's presumptuous to decide he doesn't like my job so he'll find me another one?'

'Maybe he's just trying to help. He loves the favors game.'

'But why does he assume I need help?'

'Maybe you do.'

'I see. Finally the truth.'

'You can't work there forever, Clay. You're good at what you do and you care about your clients, but maybe it's time to move on. Five years at OPD is a long time. You've said so yourself.'

'Maybe I don't want to live in Richmond. Perhaps I've never thought about leaving D.C. What if I don't want to work under one of your father's cronies? Suppose the idea of being surrounded by a bunch of local politicians does not appeal to me? I'm a lawyer, Rebecca, not a paper pusher.'

'Fine. Whatever.'

'Is this job an ultimatum?'

'In what way?'

'In every way. What if I say no?'

'I think you've already said no, which, by the way, is pretty typical. A snap decision.'

'Snap decisions are easy when the choice is obvious. I'll find my own jobs, and I certainly didn't ask your father to call in a favor. But what happens if I say no?'

'Oh, I'm sure the sun will come up.'

'And your parents?'

'I'm sure they'll be disappointed.'

'And you?'

She shrugged and sipped her drink. Marriage had been discussed on several occasions but no agreement had been reached. There was no engagement, certainly no timetable. If one wanted out, there was sufficient wiggle room, though it would be a tight squeeze. But after four years of (1) dating no one else, and (2) continually re-affirming their love for each other, and (3) having sex at least five times a week, the relationship was headed toward permanent status.

However, she was not willing to admit the truth that she wanted a break from her career, and a husband and a family and then maybe no career at all. They were still competing, still playing the game of who was more important. She could not admit that she wanted a husband to support her.

'I don't care, Clay,' she said. 'It's just a job offer, not a Cabinet appointment. Say no if you want to.'

'Thank you.' And suddenly he felt like a jerk. What if Bennett had simply been trying to help? He disliked her parents so much that everything they did irked him. That was his problem, wasn't it? They had the right to be worried about their daughter's future mate, the father of their grand-children.

And, Clay grudgingly admitted, who wouldn't be worried about him as a son-in-law?

'I'd like to go,' she said.

'Sure.'

He followed her out of the club and watched her from the rear, almost suggesting that he had time to run by her apartment for a quick session. But her mood said no, and, given the tone of the evening, she would thoroughly enjoy a flat rejection. Then he would feel like a fool who couldn't control himself, which was exactly what he was at these times. So he dug deep, clenched his jaws together, and let the moment pass.

As he helped her into her BMW, she whispered, 'Why don't you stop by for a few minutes?'

Clay sprinted to his car.

Chapter 6

He felt somewhat safer with Rodney, plus 9 A.M.
was too early for the dangerous types on Lamont
Street. They were still sleeping off whatever poison
they had consumed the night before. The merchants were slowly coming to life. Clay parked
near the alley.

Rodney was a career paralegal with OPD. He'd
been enrolled in night law school off and on for
a decade and still talked of one day getting his
degree and passing the bar. But with four teenagers at home both money and time were scarce.
Because he came from the streets of D.C. he knew
them well. Part of his daily routine was a request
from an OPD lawyer, usually one who was white
and frightened and not very experienced, to
accompany him or her into the war zones to investigate some heinous crime. He was a paralegal,
not an investigator, and he declined as often as
he said yes.

But he never said no to Clay. The two had
worked closely together on many cases. They

found the spot in the alley where Ramón had fallen and inspected the surrounding area carefully, with full knowledge that the police had already combed the place several times. They shot a roll of film, then went looking for witnesses.

There were none, and this was not surprising. By the time Clay and Rodney had been on the scene for fifteen minutes, word had spread. Strangers were on-site, prying into the latest killing, so lock the doors and say nothing. The liquor store–milk crate witnesses, both men who spent many hours every day in the same spot sipping cheap wine and missing nothing, were long gone and no one had ever known them. The merchants seemed surprised that there had been a shooting at all. 'Around here?' one asked, as if crime had yet to reach his ghetto.

After an hour, they left and headed for D Camp. As Clay drove, Rodney sipped cold coffee from a tall paper cup. Bad coffee, from the look on his face. 'Jermaine got a similar case a few days ago,' he said. 'Kid in rehab, locked down for a few months, got out somehow, don't know if he escaped or was released, but within twenty-four hours he'd picked up a gun and shot two people, one died.'

'At random?'

'What's random around here? Two guys in cars with no insurance have a fender bender and they start shooting at each other. Is that random, or is it justified?'

'Was it drugs, robbery, self-defense?'

'Random, I think.'

'Where was the rehab place?' Clay asked.

'It wasn't D Camp. Some joint near Howard, I think. I haven't seen the file. You know how slow Jermaine is.'

'So you're not working the file?'

'No. Heard it through the grapevine.'

Rodney controlled the grapevine rumors and gossip and knew more about OPD lawyers and their caseloads than Glenda, the Director. As they turned on W Street, Clay said, 'You been to D Camp before?'

'Once or twice. It's for the hard cases, the last stop before the cemetery. Tough place, run by tough guys.'

'You know a gentleman by the name of Talmadge X?'

'No.'

There was no sidewalk circus to wade through. Clay parked in front of the building and they hurried inside. Talmadge X was not in, some emergency had taken him to a hospital. A colleague named Noland introduced himself pleasantly and said he was the head counselor. In his office, at a small table, he showed them Tequila Watson's file and invited them to look through it. Clay thanked him, certain that it had been purged and cleaned up for his benefit.

'Our policy is that I stay in the room while you look through the file,' Noland explained. 'If you want copies, they're twenty-five cents each.'

'Well, sure,' Clay said. The policy was not going

to be negotiated. And if he wanted the entire file he could snatch it at any time with a subpoena. Noland took his place behind his desk, where an impressive stack of paperwork was waiting. Clay began leafing through the file. Rodney took notes.

Tequila's background was sad and predictable. He had been admitted in January, referred from Social Services after being rescued from an over-dose of something. He weighed 121 pounds and was five feet ten inches tall. His medical exam had been conducted at D Camp. He had a slight fever, chills, headaches, not unusual for a junkie. Other than malnourishment, a slight case of the flu, and a body ravaged by drugs, there was nothing else remarkable, according to the doctor. Like all patients, he had been locked down for the first thirty days and fed continually.

According to entries made by TX, Tequila began his slide at the age of eight when he and his brother stole a case of beer off a delivery truck. They drank half and sold half, and with the proceeds bought a gallon of cheap wine. He'd been kicked out of various schools and somewhere around the age of twelve, about the time he discovered crack, he'd dropped out altogether. Stealing became a way of survival.

His memory worked until the crack use began, so the last few years were a blur. TX had followed up on the details and there were letters and e-mails confirming some of the official stops along the miserable trail. When he was fourteen, Tequila had spent a month in a substance abuse unit of the D.C. Youth Detention Center. Upon his release, he went straight to a dealer and bargained for crack. Two months in Orchard House, a notorious lockdown facility for teens on crack, did little good. Tequila admitted to TX that he consumed as many drugs inside 'OH' as he had on the outside. At sixteen, he was admitted to Clean Streets, a no-nonsense abuse facility very similar to D Camp. A stellar performance there lasted for fifty-three days, then he walked away without a word. TX's note said '. . . was high on crack within 2 hrs. of leaving.' The juvenile court ordered him to a summer boot camp for troubled teens when he was seventeen, but security was leaky and he actually made money selling drugs to his fellow campers. The final effort at sobriety, before D Camp, had been a program at Grayson Church, under the direction of Reverend Jolley, a well-known drug counselor. Jolley sent a letter to Talmadge X in which he expressed the opinion that Tequila was one of those tragic cases that was 'probably hopeless.'

As depressing as the history was, there was a remarkable absence of violence in it. Tequila had been arrested and convicted five times for burglary, once for shoplifting, and twice for misdemeanor possession. Tequila had never used a weapon to commit a crime, at least not one that he had been nabbed for. This had not gone unnoticed by TX, who, in one entry on Day 39 said, '. . . has a tendency to avoid even the slightest threat of physical conflict. Seems truly afraid of the bigger ones, and most of the small ones too.'

On Day 45, he was examined by a physician. His weight was a healthy 138. His skin was clear of '. . . abrasions and lesions.' There were notes about his progress in learning to read, and his interest in art. As the days passed, the notes became much shorter. Life inside D Camp was simple and grew to be mundane. Some days passed with no entries at all.

The entry on Day 80 was different: 'He realizes he needs spiritual guidance from above to stay clean. He can't do it alone. Says he wants to stay in D Camp forever.'

Day 100: 'We celebrated the hundredth day with brownies and ice cream. Tequila made a short speech. He cried. He was awarded a two-hour pass.'

Day 104: 'Two-hour pass. He left, returned in twenty minutes with a popsicle.'

Day 107: 'Sent to the post office, gone almost an hour, returned.'

Day 110: 'Two-hour pass, returned, no problem.'

The final entry was Day 115: 'Two-hour pass, no return.'

Noland was watching as they neared the end of the file. 'Any questions?' he asked, as if they had consumed enough of his time.

'It's pretty sad,' Clay said, closing the file with a deep breath. He had lots of questions but none that Noland could, or would, answer.

'In a world of misery, Mr Carter, this indeed is one of the saddest. I am rarely moved to tears, but Tequila has made me cry." Noland was rising to his feet. 'Would you like to copy anything?' The meeting was over.

'Maybe later,' Clay said. They thanked him for his time and followed him to the reception area.

In the car, Rodney fastened his seat belt and glanced around the neighborhood. Very calmly he said, 'Okay, pal, we got us a new friend.'

Clay was watching the fuel gauge and hoping there was enough gas to get back to the office. 'What kinda friend?'

'See that burgundy Jeep down there, half a block, other side of the street?'

Clay looked and said, 'So what?'

'There's a black dude behind the wheel, big guy, wearing a Redskins cap, I think. He's watching us.'

Clay strained and could barely see the shape of a driver, race and cap indistinguishable to him. 'How do you know he's watching us?'

'He was on Lamont Street when we were there, I saw him twice, both times easing by, looking at us but not looking. When we parked here to go in, I saw the Jeep three blocks back that way. Now he's over there.'

'How do you know it's the same Jeep?'

'Burgundy's an odd color. See that dent in the front fender, right side?'

'Yeah, maybe.'

'Same Jeep, no doubt about it. Let's go that way, get a closer look.'

Clay pulled onto the street and drove past the burgundy Jeep. A newspaper flew up in front of the driver. Rodney scribbled down the license plate number.

'Why would anyone follow us?' Clay asked.

'Drugs. Always drugs. Maybe Tequila was dealing. Maybe the kid he killed had some nasty friends. Who knows?'

'I'd like to find out.'

'Let's not dig too deep right now. You drive, and I'll watch our rear.'

They headed south along Puerto Rico Avenue for thirty minutes and stopped at a gas station near the Anacostia River. Rodney watched every car as Clay pumped fuel. 'The tail's off,' Rodney said when they were moving again. 'Let's go to the office.'

'Why would they stop following us?' Clay asked. He would have believed any explanation.

'I'm not sure,' Rodney said, still checking his side mirror. 'Could be that they were only curious as to whether we went to D Camp. Or maybe they know that we saw them. Just watch your tail for a while.'

'This is great. I've never been followed before.'

'Just pray they don't decide to catch you.'

Jermaine Vance shared an office with another unseasoned lawyer who happened to be out at the moment, so Clay was offered his vacant chair.

They compared notes on their most recent murder defendants.

Jermaine's client was a twenty-four-year-old career criminal named Washad Porter, who, unlike Tequila, had a long and frightening history of violence. As a member of D.C.'s largest gang, Washad had been severely wounded twice in gun battles and had been convicted once of attempted murder. Seven of his twenty-four years had been spent behind bars. He had shown little interest in getting cleaned up; the only attempt at rehab had been in prison and had been clearly unsuccessful. He was accused of shooting two people four days before the Ramón Pumphrey killing. One of the two was killed instantly, the other was barely clinging to life.

Washad had spent six months at Clean Streets, locked down and evidently surviving the rigorous program there. Jermaine had talked to the counselor, and the conversation was very similar to the one Clay had had with Talmadge X. Washad had cleaned up, was a model patient, was in good health, and gathering self-esteem every day. The only bump in the road had been an episode early on when he sneaked out, got stoned, but came back and begged for forgiveness. Then he went almost four months with virtually no problems.

He was released from Clean Streets in April, and the next day he shot two men with a stolen gun. His victims appeared to have been selected at random. The first was a produce deliveryman going about his business near Walter Reed

Hospital. There were words, then some pushing and shoving, then four shots to the head, and Washad was seen running away. The deliveryman was still in a coma. An hour later, six blocks away, Washad used his last two bullets on a petty drug dealer with whom he had a history. He was tackled by friends of the dealer who, instead of killing him themselves, held him for the police.

Jermaine had talked to Washad once, very briefly, in the courtroom during his initial appearance. 'He was in denial,' Jermaine said. 'Had this blank look on his face and kept telling me that he couldn't believe he'd shot anybody. He said that was the old Washad, not the new one.'

Chapter 7

Clay could think of only one other occasion in the past four years on which he called, or tried to call, Bennett the Bulldozer. That effort had ended dismally when he'd been unable to penetrate the layers of importance surrounding the great man. Mr. BVH wanted folks to think he spent his time 'on the job,' which for him meant out among the earth-moving machinery where he could direct matters and smell up close the unlimited potential of Northern Virginia. In the family's home there were large photos of him 'on the job,' wearing his own custom-made and monogrammed hard hat, pointing here and there as land got leveled and more malls and shopping centers got built. He said he was too busy for idle chatter and claimed to hate telephones, yet always had a supply nearby to take care of business.

Truth was, Bennett played a lot of golf, and played it badly, according to the father of one of Clay's law school classmates. Rebecca had let it slip more than once that her father played at least four rounds a week at Potomac, and his secret dream was to win the club championship.

Mr. Van Horn was a man of action with no patience for life behind a desk. He spent little time there, he claimed. The pit bull who answered 'BVH Group' reluctantly agreed to forward Clay on to another secretary deeper inside the company. 'Development' the second girl said rudely, as if the company had unlimited divisions. It took at least five minutes to get Bennett's personal secretary on the phone. 'He's out of the office,' she said.

'How can I reach him?' Clay asked.

'He's on the job.'

'Yes, I figured that. How can I reach him?'

'Leave a number and I'll put it with the rest of his messages,' she said.

'Oh thank you,' Clay said, and left his office number.

Thirty minutes later Bennett returned the call. He sounded indoors, perhaps in the Men's Lounge at the Potomac Country Club, double Scotch in hand, big cigar, a game of gin rummy in progress with the boys. 'Clay, how in the world are you?' he asked, as if they hadn't seen each other in months.

'Fine, Mr. Van Horn, and you?'

'Great. Enjoyed dinner last night.' Clay heard no roaring diesel engines in the background, no blasting.

'Oh yes, it was really nice. Always a pleasure,' Clay lied.

'What can I do for you, son?'

'Well, I want you to understand that I really appreciate your efforts to get me that job down in Richmond. I didn't expect it, and you were very kind to intervene like that.' A pause as Clay swallowed hard. 'But truthfully, Mr. Van Horn, I don't see a move to Richmond in the near future. I've always lived in D.C. and this is home.'

Clay had many reasons to reject the offer. Staying in D.C. was mid-list. The overwhelming motive was to avoid having his life planned by Bennett Van Horn and getting locked into his debt.

'You can't be serious,' Van Horn said.

'Yes, I'm very serious. Thanks, but no thanks.' The last thing Clay planned to do was to take any crap off this jerk. He loved the telephone at these moments; such a wonderful equalizer.

'A big mistake, son,' Van Horn said. 'You just don't see the big picture, do you?'

'Maybe I don't. But I'm not so sure you do either.'

'You have a lot of pride, Clay, I like that. But you're also very wet behind the ears. You gotta learn that life is a game of favors, and when someone tries to help you, then you take the favor. One day maybe you'll get the chance to repay it. You're making a mistake, here, Clay, one that I'm afraid could have serious consequences.'

'What kinds of consequences?'

'This could really affect your future.'

'Well, it's my future, not yours. I'll pick the

next job, and the one after that. Right now I'm happy where I am.'

'How can you be happy defending criminals all day long? I just don't get it.'

This was not a new conversation, and, if it followed the usual course, things would deteriorate quickly. 'I believe you've asked that question before. Let's not go there.'

'We're talking about a huge increase in salary, Clay. More money, better work, you'll be spending your time with solid folks, not a bunch of street punks. Wake up, boy!' There were voices in the background. Wherever Bennett was, he was playing for an audience.

Clay gritted his teeth and let the 'boy' pass. 'I'm not going to argue, Mr. Van Horn. I called to say no.'

'You'd better reconsider.'

'I've already reconsidered. No thanks.'

'You're a loser, Clay, you know that. I've known it for some time. This just reaffirms it. You're turning down a promising job so you can stay in a rut and work for minimum wage. You have no ambition, no guts, no vision.'

'Last night I was a hard worker – had broad shoulders, lots of talent, and I was as sharp as a tack.'

'I take it back. You're a loser.'

'And I was well educated and even handsome.'

'I was lying. You're a loser.'

Clay hung up first. He slammed the phone down with a smile, quite proud that he had so

73

irritated the great Bennett Van Horn. He'd held his ground and sent a clear message that he would not be shoved around by those people.

He would deal with Rebecca later, and it would not be pleasant.

Clay's third and final visit to D Camp was more dramatic than the first two. With Jermaine in the front seat and Rodney in the back, Clay followed a D.C. police car and parked again directly in front of the building. Two cops, both young and black and bored with subpoena work, negotiated their entrance. Within minutes they were in the midst of a tense confrontation with Talmadge X, Noland, and another counselor, a hothead named Samuel.

Partially because he had the only white face in the crowd, but primarily because he was the lawyer who'd obtained the subpoena, the three counselors focused their wrath on Clay. He could not have cared less. He would never see these people again.

'You saw the file, man!' Noland yelled at Clay.

'I saw the file that you wanted me to see,' Clay shot back. 'Now I get the rest of it.'

'What're you talking about?' Talmadge X asked.

'I want everything here with Tequila's name written on it.'

'You can't do that.'

Clay turned to the cop holding the papers and said, 'Would you please read the subpoena?'

The cop held it high for all to see, and read:

'All files pertaining to the admission, medical evaluation, medical treatment, substance abatement, substance abuse counseling, rehabilitation, and discharge of Tequila Watson. As ordered by the Honorable F. Floyd Sackman, D.C. Superior Court Criminal Division.'

'When did he sign it?' Samuel asked.

' 'Bout three hours ago.'

'We showed you everything,' Noland said to Clay.

'I doubt that. I can tell when a file has been rearranged.'

'Much too neat,' Jermaine added helpfully, finally.

'We ain't fighting,' said the larger of the two cops, leaving little doubt that a good fight would be welcome. 'Where do we start?'

'His medical evaluations are confidential,' Samuel said. 'The doctor-patient privilege, I believe.'

It was an excellent point, but slightly off the mark. 'The doctor's files are confidential,' Clay explained. 'But not the patient's. I have a release and waiver signed by Tequila Watson allowing me to see all of his files, including the medicals.'

They began in a windowless room with mismatched filing cabinets lining the walls. After a few minutes, Talmadge X and Samuel disappeared and the tension began to ease. The cops pulled up chairs and accepted the coffee offered by the receptionist. She did not offer any to the gentlemen from the Office of the Public Defender.

After an hour of digging, nothing useful had been found. Clay and Jermaine left Rodney to continue the search. They had more cops to meet.

The raid on Clean Streets was very similar. The two lawyers marched into the front office with two policemen behind them. The Director was dragged out of a meeting. As she read the subpoena she mumbled something about knowing Judge Sackman and dealing with him later. She was very irritated, but the document spoke for itself. The same language – all files and papers relating to Washad Porter.

'This was not necessary,' she said to Clay. 'We always cooperate with attorneys.'

'That's not what I hear,' Jermaine said. Indeed, Clean Streets had a reputation for contesting even the most benign requests from OPD.

When she finished reading the subpoena for the second time, one of the cops said, 'We're not going to wait all day.'

She led them to a large office and fetched an assistant who began hauling in files. 'When do we get these back?' she asked.

'When we're finished with them,' Jermaine said.

'And who keeps them?'

'The Office of the Public Defender, under lock and key.'

The romance had begun at Abe's Place. Rebecca had been in a booth with two girlfriends when Clay walked by en route to the men's room. Their eyes met, and he actually paused for a second, unsure of exactly what to do next. The girlfriends soon got lost. Clay ditched his drinking pals. They sat together at the bar for two hours and talked nonstop. The first date was the next night. Sex within a week. She kept him away from her parents for two months.

Now, four years later, things were stale and she was under pressure to move on. It seemed fitting that they would end things at Abe's Place.

Clay arrived first and stood at the bar in a crowd of Hill Rats draining their glasses, talking loud and fast and all at once about the crucial issues they had just spent long hours dealing with. He loved D.C., and he hated D.C. He loved its history and energy and importance. And he despised the countless minions who chased themselves in a frenetic game of who was more important. The nearest discussion was a passionate argument about wastewater treatment laws in the Central Plains.

Abe's Place was nothing but a watering hole, strategically placed near Capitol Hill to catch the thirsty crowd headed for the suburbs. Great-looking women. Well dressed. Many of them on the prowl. Clay caught a few looks.

Rebecca was subdued, determined, and cold. They sneaked into a booth and both ordered strong drinks for the ride ahead. He asked some pointless questions about the subcommittee hearings that had begun, amid no fanfare, at least according to the *Post*. The drinks arrived and they dived in.

'I talked to my father,' she began.

'So did I.'

'Why didn't you tell me you were not taking the job in Richmond?'

'Why didn't you tell me your father was pulling strings to get me a job in Richmond?'

'You should've told me.'

'I made it clear.'

'Nothing is clear with you.'

Both took a drink.

'Your father called me a loser. Is that the prevailing mood in your family?'

'At the moment, yes.'

'Shared by you?'

'I have my doubts. Someone has to be realistic here.'

There had been one serious intermission in the romance, a miserable failure at best. About a year earlier they had decided to let things cool off, to remain close friends, but to have a look around, perhaps play the field, make sure there was no one else out there. Barb had engineered the separation because, as Clay found out later, a very rich young man at the Potomac Country Club had just lost his wife to ovarian cancer. Bennett was a close personal friend of the family, etcetera, etcetera. He and Barb laid the trap, but the widower smelled the bait. One month on the fringes of the Van Horn family and the guy bought a place in Wyoming.

This, however, was a much more severe breakup. This was almost certainly the end. Clay took another drink and promised himself that whatever else was said, he would not, under any circumstances, say something that would hurt her. She could hit below the belt if she wanted. He would not.

'What do you want, Rebecca?'

'I don't know.'

'Yes you do. Do you want out?'

'I think so,' she said, and her eyes were instantly wet.

'Is there someone else?'

'No.'

Not yet anyway. Just give Barb and Bennett a few days.

'It's just that you're going nowhere, Clay,' she said. 'You're smart and talented, but you have no ambition.'

'Gee, it's nice to know I'm smart and talented again. A few hours ago I was a loser.'

'Are you trying to be funny?'

'Why not, Rebecca? Why not have a laugh? It's over, let's face it. We love each other, but I'm a loser who's going nowhere. That's your problem. My problem is your parents. They'll chew up the poor guy you marry.'

'The poor guy?'

'That's right. I pity the poor guy you marry because your parents are insufferable. And you know it.'

'The poor guy I marry?' Her eyes were no longer wet. They were flashing now.

'Take it easy.'

'The poor guy I marry?'

'Look, I'll make you an offer. Let's get married right now. We quit our jobs, do a quickie wedding with no one present, sell everything we own, and fly to, say, Seattle or Portland, somewhere far away from here, and live on love for a while.'

'You won't go to Richmond but you'll go to Seattle?'

'Richmond is too damned close to your parents, okay?'

'Then what?'

'Then we'll find jobs.'

'What kinds of jobs? Is there a shortage of lawyers out West?'

'You're forgetting something. Remember, from last night, that I'm smart, talented, well educated, sharp as a tack, and even handsome. Big law firms will chase me all over the place. I'll make partner in eighteen months. We'll have babies.'

'Then my parents will come.'

'No, because we won't tell them where we are. And if they find us, we'll change our names and move to Canada.'

Two more drinks arrived and they wasted no time shoving the old ones aside.

The light moment passed, and quickly. But it reminded both of why they loved each other and of how much they enjoyed their time together. There had been much more laughter than sadness, though things were changing. Fewer laughs. More senseless spats. More influence from her family.

'I don't like the West Coast,' she said, finally.

'Then pick a spot,' Clay said, finishing the adventure. Her spot had been chosen for her, and she wasn't getting too far from Mommy and Daddy.

Whatever she had brought to the meeting finally had to be said. A long pull on the drink, then she leaned forward and stared him directly in the eyes. 'Clay, I really need a break.'

'Make it easy on yourself, Rebecca. We'll do whatever you want.'

'Thank you.'

'How long a break?'

'I'm not negotiating, Clay.'

'A month?'

'Longer than that.'

'No, I won't agree to it. Let's go thirty days without a phone call, okay? Today is the seventh of May. Let's meet here on June the sixth, right here at this very table, and we'll talk about an extension.'

'An extension?'

'Call it whatever you want.'

'Thank you. I'm calling it a breakup, Clay. The big bang. Splitsville. You go your way, I go mine. We'll chat in a month, but I don't expect a change. Things haven't changed much in the past year.'

'If I'd said yes to that awful job in Richmond, would we be doing this split thing?'

'Probably not.'

'Does that mean something other than no?'

'No.'

'So, it was all a setup, wasn't it? The job, the ultimatum? Last night was just what I thought it was, an ambush. Take this job, boy, or else.'

She would not deny it. Instead, she said, 'Clay, I'm tired of fighting, okay? Don't call me for thirty days.'

She grabbed her purse and jumped to her feet. On the way out of the booth, she somehow managed to plant a dry and meaningless kiss near his right temple, but he did not acknowledge it. He did not watch her leave.

She did not look back.

Chapter 8

Clay's apartment was in an aging complex in Arlington. When he'd leased it four years earlier he had never heard of BVH Group. Later, he would learn that the company had built the place in the early eighties in one of Bennett's first ventures. The venture went bankrupt, the complex got bought and sold several times, and none of Clay's rent went to Mr. Van Horn. In fact, no member of that family knew Clay was living in something they'd built. Not even Rebecca.

He shared a two-bedroom unit with Jonah, an old pal from law school who'd flunked the bar exam four times before passing it and now sold computers. He sold them part-time and still earned more money than Clay, a fact that was always just under the surface.

The morning after the breakup, Clay fetched the *Post* from outside his door and settled down at the kitchen table with the first cup of coffee. As always, he went straight to the financial page for a quick and rewarding perusal of the dismal performance of BVHG. The stock barely traded and the few misguided investors who owned it were now willing to unload it for a mere $0.75 a share.

Who was the loser here?

There was not a single word about Rebecca's crucial subcommittee hearings.

When he was finished with his little witch hunts, he went to the sports section and told himself it was time to forget the Van Horns. All of them.

At twenty minutes after seven, a time when he was usually eating a bowl of cereal, the phone rang. He smiled and thought, It's her. Back already.

No one else would call so early. No one except the boyfriend or husband of whatever lady might be upstairs sleeping off a hangover with Jonah. Clay had taken several such calls over the years. Jonah adored women, especially those already committed to someone else. They were more challenging, he said.

But it wasn't Rebecca and it wasn't a boyfriend or a husband.

'Mr. Clay Carter,' a strange male voice said.

'Speaking.'

'Mr. Carter, my name is Max Pace. I'm a recruiter for law firms in Washington and New York. Your name has caught our attention, and I have two very attractive positions that might interest you. Could we have lunch today?'

Completely speechless, Clay would remember

later, in the shower, that the thought of a nice lunch was, oddly, the first thing that crossed his mind.

'Uh, sure,' he managed to get out. Headhunters were part of the legal business, same as every other profession. But they rarely spent their time bottom-feeding in the Office of the Public Defender.

'Good. Let's meet in the lobby of the Willard Hotel, say, noon?'

'Noon's fine,' Clay said, his eyes focusing on a pile of dirty dishes in the sink. Yes, this was real. It was not a dream.

'Thanks, I'll see you then. Mr. Carter, I promise it will be worth your time.'

'Uh, sure.'

Max Pace hung up quickly, and for a moment Clay held the receiver, looked at the dirty dishes, and wondered who from his law school class was behind this practical joke. Or could it be Bennett the Bulldozer getting one last bit of revenge?

He had no phone number for Max Pace. He did not even have the presence of mind to get the name of his company.

Nor did he have a clean suit. He owned two, both gray, one thick and one thin, both very old and well used. His trial wardrobe. Fortunately, OPD had no office dress code, so Clay usually wore khakis and a navy blazer. If he was going to court, he would put on a tie and take it off as soon as he returned to the office.

In the shower, he decided that his attire did not matter. Max Pace knew where he worked and had a rough idea of how little he earned. If Clay showed up for the interview in frayed khakis, then he could demand more money.

Sitting in traffic on the Arlington Memorial Bridge, he decided it was his father. The old guy had been banished from D.C. but still had contacts. He'd finally hit the right button, called in one last favor, found his son a decent job. When Jarrett Carter's high-profile legal career ended in a long and colorful flameout, he pushed his son toward the Office of the Public Defender. Now that apprenticeship was over. Five years in the trenches, and it was time for a real job.

What kinds of firms would be looking for him? He was intrigued by the mystery. His father hated the large corporate and lobbying outfits that were packed along Connecticut and Massachusetts Avenues. And he had no use for the small-timers who advertised on buses and billboards and clogged up the system with frivolous cases. Jarrett's old firm had ten lawyers, ten courtroom brawlers who won verdicts and were in demand.

'That's where I'm headed,' Clay mumbled to himself as he glanced at the Potomac River beneath him.

After suffering through the most unproductive morning of his career, Clay left at eleven-thirty and took his time driving to the Willard, now officially known as the Willard Inter-Continental Hotel. He was immediately met in the lobby by a muscled young man who looked vaguely familiar. 'Mr Pace is upstairs,' he explained. 'He'd like to meet with you up there, if that's all right.' They were walking toward the elevators.

'Sure,' Clay said. How he'd been recognized so easily he was not certain.

They ignored each other on the ride up. They stepped onto the ninth floor and Clay's escort knocked on the door of the Theodore Roosevelt Suite. It opened quickly and Max Pace said hello with a businesslike smile. He was in his mid-forties, dark wavy hair, dark mustache, dark everything. Black denim jeans, black T-shirt, black pointed-toe boots. Hollywood at the Willard. Not exactly the corporate look Clay had been expecting. As they shook hands he had the first hint that things were not what they seemed.

With a quick glance, the bodyguard was sent away.

'Thanks for coming,' Max said as they walked into an oval-shaped room laden with marble.

'Sure.' Clay was absorbing the suite; luxurious leathers and fabrics, rooms branching off in all directions. 'Nice place.'

'It's mine for a few more days. I thought we could eat up here, order some room service, that way we can talk with complete privacy.'

'Fine with me.' A question came to mind, the first of many. What was a Washington headhunter doing renting a horribly expensive hotel suite? Why didn't he have an office nearby? Did he really need a bodyguard?

'Anything in particular to eat?'

'I'm easy.'

'They do a great capellini and salmon dish. I had it yesterday. Superb.'

'I'll try it.' At that moment Clay would have tried anything; he was starving.

Max went to the phone while Clay admired the view of Pennsylvania Avenue below. When lunch was ordered, they sat near the window and quickly got past the weather, the Orioles' latest losing streak, and the lousy state of the economy. Pace was glib and seemed at ease talking about anything for as long as Clay wanted. He was a serious weight lifter who wanted folks to know it. His shirt stuck to his chest and arms and he liked to pick at his mustache. Whenever he did so, his biceps flexed and bulged.

A stuntman maybe, but not a headhunter in the big leagues.

Ten minutes into the chatter, and Clay said, 'These two firms, why don't you tell me a little about them?'

'They don't exist,' Max said. 'I admit I lied to you. And I promise it's the only time I will ever lie to you.'

'You're not a headhunter, are you?'

'No.'

'Then what?'

'I'm a fireman.'

'Thanks, that really clears things up.'

'Let me talk for a moment. I have some explaining to do, and when I'm finished I promise you'll be pleased.'

'I suggest you talk real fast, Max, or I'm outta here.'

'Relax, Mr. Carter. Can I call you Clay?'

'Not yet.'

'Very well. I'm an agent, a contractor, a freelancer with a specialty. I get hired by big companies to put out fires. They screw up, they realize their mistakes before the lawyers do, so they hire me to quietly enter the picture, tidy up their mess, and, hopefully, save them a bunch of money. My services are in great demand. My name may be Max Pace and it may be something else. It doesn't matter. Who I am and where I come from are irrelevant. What's important here is that I have been hired by a large company to put out a fire. Questions?'

'Too numerous to ask right now.'

'Hang on. I cannot tell you the name of my client now, perhaps never. If we reach an agreement, then I can tell you much more. Here's the story: My client is a multinational that manufactures pharmaceuticals. You'll recognize the name. It makes a wide range of products, from common household remedies that are in your medicine cabinet right now to complex drugs that will fight cancer and obesity. An old, established blue-chip company with a stellar reputation. About two years ago, it came up with a drug that might cure addiction to opium- and cocaine-based narcotics. Much more advanced than methadone, which, though it helps many addicts, is addictive itself and is widely abused. Let's call this wonder drug

Tarvan – that was its nickname for a while. It was discovered by mistake and was quickly used on every laboratory animal available. The results were outstanding, but then it's hard to duplicate crack addiction in a bunch of rats.'

'They needed humans,' Clay said.

Pace picked his mustache as his biceps rippled. 'Yes. The potential for Tarvan was enough to keep the big suits awake at night. Imagine, take one pill a day for ninety days and you're clean. Your craving for the drugs is gone. You've kicked cocaine, heroin, crack – just like that. After you're clean, take a Tarvan every other day and you're free for life. Almost an instant cure, for millions of addicts. Think of the profits – charge whatever you want for the drug because somebody somewhere will gladly pay for it. Think of the lives to be saved, the crimes that would not be committed, the families held together, the billions not spent trying to rehab addicts. The more the suits thought about how great Tarvan could be, the faster they wanted it on the market. But, as you say, they still needed humans.'

A pause, a sip of coffee. The T-shirt trembled with fitness. He continued.

'So they began making mistakes. They picked three places – Mexico City, Singapore, and Belgrade – places far outside the jurisdiction of the FDA. Under the guise of some vague international relief outfit, they built rehab clinics, really nice lockdown facilities where the addicts could be completely controlled. They picked the worst junkies they could find, got 'em in, cleaned 'em up, began using Tarvan, though the addicts had no idea. They really didn't care – everything was free.'

'Human laboratories,' Clay said. The tale so far was fascinating, and Max the fireman had a flair for the narrative.

'Nothing but human laboratories. Far away from the American tort system. And the American press. And the American regulators. It was a brilliant plan. And the drug performed beautifully. After thirty days, Tarvan blunted the cravings for drugs. After sixty days, the addicts seemed quite happy to be clean, and after ninety days they had no fear of returning to the streets. Everything was monitored – diet, exercise, therapy, even conversations. My client had at least one employee per patient, and these clinics had a hundred beds each. After three months, the patients were turned loose, with the agreement that they would return to the clinic every other day for their Tarvan. Ninety percent stayed on the drug, and stayed clean. Ninety percent! Only two percent relapsed into addiction.'

'And the other eight percent?'

'They would become the problem, but my client didn't know how serious it would be. Anyway, they kept the beds full, and over eighteen months about a thousand addicts were treated with Tarvan. The results were off the charts. My client could smell billions in profits. And there was no competition. No other company was in serious R&D for an anti-addiction drug. Most pharmaceuticals gave up years ago.'

'And the next mistake?'

Max paused for a second, then said, 'There were so many.' A buzzer sounded, lunch had arrived. A waiter rolled it in on a cart and spent five minutes fussing with the setup. Clay stood in front of the window, staring at the top of the Washington Monument, but too deep in thought to see anything. Max tipped the guy and finally got him out of the room.

'You hungry?' he asked.

'No. Keep talking,' Clay took off his jacket and sat in the chair. 'I think you're getting to the good part.'

'Good, bad, depends on how you look at it. The next mistake was to bring the show here. This is where it starts to get real ugly. My client had deliberately looked at the globe and picked one spot for Caucasians, one spot for Hispanics, and one spot for Asians. Some Africans were needed.'

'We have plenty in D.C.'

'So thought my client.'

'You're lying, aren't you? Tell me you're lying.'

'I've lied to you once, Mr. Carter. And I've promised not to do it again.'

Clay slowly got to his feet and walked around his chair to the window again. Max watched him closely. The lunch was getting cold, but neither seemed to care. Time had been suspended.

Clay turned around and said, 'Tequila?'

Max nodded and said, 'Yes.'

'And Washad Porter?'

'Yes.'

A minute passed. Clay crossed his arms and leaned against the wall, facing Max, who was straightening his mustache. 'Go ahead,' Clay said.

'In about eight percent of the patients, something goes wrong,' Max said. 'My client has no idea what or how or even who might be at risk. But Tarvan makes them kill. Plain and simple. After about a hundred days, something turns somewhere in the brain, and they feel an irresistible impulse to draw blood. It makes no difference if they have a violent history. Age, race, sex, nothing distinguishes the killers.'

'That's eighty dead people?'

'At least. But information is difficult to obtain in the slums of Mexico City.'

'How many here, in D.C.?'

It was the first question that made Max squirm, and he dodged it. 'I'll answer that in a few minutes. Let me finish my story. Would you sit down, please? I don't like to look up when I talk.'

Clay took his seat, as directed.

'The next mistake was to circumvent the FDA.'

'Of course.'

'My client has many big friends in this town. It's an old pro at buying the politicians through PAC money, and hiring their wives and girlfriends and former assistants, the usual crap that big money does here. A dirty deal was cut. It included big shots from the White House, the State

Department, the DEA, the FBI, and a couple of other agencies, none of whom put anything in writing. No money changed hands; there were no bribes. My client did a nice job of convincing enough people that Tarvan might just save the world if it could perform in one more laboratory. Since the FDA would take two to three years for approval, and since it has few friends in the White House anyway, the deal was cut. These big people, names now forever lost, found a way to smuggle Tarvan into a few, selected, federally funded rehab clinics in D.C. If it worked here, then the White House and the big folks would put relentless pressure on the FDA for quick approval.'

'When this deal was being cut, did your client know about the eight percent?'

'I don't know. My client has not told me everything and never will. Nor do I ask a lot of questions. My job lies elsewhere. However, I suspect that my client did not know about the eight percent. Otherwise, the risks would have been too great to experiment here. This has all happened very fast, Mr. Carter.'

'You can call me Clay now.'

'Thanks, Clay.'

'Don't mention it.'

'I said there were no bribes. Again, this is what my client has told me. But let's be realistic. The initial estimate of profits over the next ten years from Tarvan was thirty billion dollars. Profits, not sales. The initial estimate of tax dollars saved by Tarvan was about a hundred billion over the same period of time. Obviously, some money was going to change hands along the line.'

'But all that's history?'

'Oh yes. The drug was pulled six days ago. Those wonderful clinics in Mexico City, Singapore, and Belgrade closed up in the middle of the night and all those nice counselors disappeared like ghosts. All experiments have been forgotten. All papers have been shredded. My client has never heard of Tarvan. We'd like to keep it that way.'

'I get the feeling that I'm entering the picture at this point.'

'Only if you want to. If you decline, then I am prepared to meet with another lawyer.'

'Decline what?'

'The deal, Clay, the deal. As of now, there have been five people in D.C. killed by addicts on Tarvan. One poor guy is in a coma, probably not going to make it. Washad Porter's first victim. That's a total of six. We know who they are, how they died, who killed them, everything. We want you to represent their families. You sign them up, we pay the money, everything is wrapped up quickly, quietly, with no lawsuits, no publicity, not the slightest fingerprint anywhere.'

'Why would they hire me?'

'Because they don't have a clue that they have a case. As far as they know, their loved ones were victims of random street violence. It's a way of life here. Your kid gets shot by a street punk, you bury him, the punk gets arrested, you go to the trial, and you hope he goes to prison for the rest of his life. But you never think about a lawsuit. You gonna sue the street punk? Not even the hungriest lawyer would take that case. They'll hire you because you will go to them, tell them that they have a case, and say you can get four million bucks in a very quick, very confidential settlement.'

'Four million bucks,' Clay repeated, uncertain if it was too much or too little.

'Here's our risk, Clay. If Tarvan is discovered by some lawyer, and, frankly, you're the first one who picked up even a whiff of a scent, then there could be a trial. Let's say the lawyer is a trial stud who picks him an all-black jury here in D.C.'

'Easy enough.'

'Of course it's easy. And let's say this lawyer somehow gets the right evidence. Maybe some documents that didn't get shredded. More likely someone working for my client, a whistle-blower. Anyway, the trial plays beautifully for the family of the deceased. There could be a huge verdict. Worse yet, at least for my client, the negative publicity would be horrendous. The stock price could collapse. Imagine the worst, Clay, paint your own nightmare, and believe me, these guys see it too. They did something bad. They know it, and they want to correct it. But they're also trying to limit their damages here.'

'Four million is a bargain.'

'It is, and it isn't. Take Ramón Pumphrey. Age twenty-two, working part-time, earning six thousand dollars a year. With a normal life expectancy of fifty-three more years, and assuming annual earnings of twice the minimum wage, the economic value of his life, discounted in today's dollars, is about half a million dollars. That's what he's worth.'

'Punitive damages would be easy.'

'Depends. This case would be very hard to prove, Clay, because there's no paperwork. Those files you snatched yesterday will reveal nothing. The counselors at D Camp and Clean Streets had no idea what kind of drugs they were dispensing. The FDA never heard of Tarvan. My client would spend a billion on lawyers and experts and whoever else they need to protect them. Litigation would be a war because my client is so guilty!'

'Six times four is twenty-four million.'

'Add ten for the lawyer.'

'Ten million?'

'Yes, that's the deal, Clay. Ten million for you.'

'You must be kidding.'

'Dead serious. Thirty-four total. And I can write the checks right now.'

'I need to go for a walk.'

'How about lunch?'

'No, thanks.'

Chapter 9

Drifting now, on foot in front of the White House. Lost for a moment in a pack of Dutch tourists taking pictures and waiting for the President to give them a wave, then a stroll through Lafayette Park where the homeless vanished during the day, then to a bench in Farragut Square where he ate a cold sandwich without tasting anything. All senses were dull, all thoughts were slow and confused. It was May but the air was not clear. The humidity did little to help him think.

He saw twelve black faces sitting in the box, angry folks who'd spent a week hearing the shocking history of Tarvan. He addressed them in his final summation: 'They needed black lab rats, ladies and gentlemen, preferably Americans because this is where the money is. So they brought their miraculous Tarvan to our city.' The twelve faces hung on every word and nodded in agreement, anxious to retire and dispense justice.

What was the largest verdict in the history of the world? Did the *Guinness Book* keep tabs on such? Whatever it was, it would be his for the asking. 'Just fill in the blank, ladies and gentlemen of the jury.'

The case would never go to trial; no jury would hear it. Whoever made Tarvan would spend a helluva lot more than thirty-four million to bury the truth. And they would hire all manner of thugs to break legs and steal documents and wire phones and burn offices, whatever it took to keep their secret away from those twelve angry faces.

He thought of Rebecca. What a different girl she would be wrapped in the luxury of his money. How quickly she would leave the worries of Capitol Hill and retire to a life of motherhood. She would marry him in three months, or as soon as Barb could get things planned.

He thought of the Van Horns, but, oddly, not as people he still knew. They were out of his life; he was trying to forget about them. He was free of those people, after four years of bondage. They would never again torment him.

He was about to be free of a lot of things.

An hour passed. He found himself at DuPont Circle, staring in the windows of the small shops facing Massachusetts Avenue; rare books, rare dishes, rare costumes; rare people everywhere. There was a mirror in one storefront, and he looked himself squarely in the eyes and wondered aloud if Max the fireman was real or a fraud or a ghost. He walked along the sidewalk, sick with the thought that a respected company could prey on the weakest people it could find, then seconds later thrilled with the prospect of more money than he ever dreamed of. He needed his father. Jarrett Carter would know exactly what to do.

Another hour passed. He was expected at the office, a weekly staff meeting of some variety. 'Fire me,' he mumbled with a smile.

He browsed for a while in Kramerbooks, his favorite bookstore in D.C. Perhaps soon he could move from the paperback section to the hardbacks. He could fill his new walls with rows of books.

At exactly 3 P.M., on schedule, he walked into the rear of Kramer's, into the café, and there was Max Pace, sitting alone, drinking lemonade, waiting. He was obviously pleased to see Clay again.

'Did you follow me?' Clay asked, sitting down and stuffing his hands in his pants pockets.

'Of course. Would you like something to drink?'

'No. What if I filed suit tomorrow, on behalf of the family of Ramón Pumphrey? That one case could be worth more than what you're offering for all six.'

The question seemed to have been anticipated. Max had an answer ready. 'You'd have a long list of problems. Let me give you the top three. First, you don't know who to sue. You don't know who made Tarvan, and there's a chance no one will ever know. Second, you don't have the money to fight with my client. It would take at least ten million dollars to mount a sustainable attack.

100

Third, you'd lose the opportunity to represent all known plaintiffs. If you don't say yes quickly, I'm prepared to go to the next lawyer on my list with the same offer. My goal is to have this wrapped up in thirty days.'

'I could go to a big tort firm.'

'Yes, and that would present more problems. First, you'd give away at least half of your fee. Second, it would take five years to reach an outcome, maybe longer. Third, the biggest tort firm in the country could easily lose this case. The truth here, Clay, may never be known.'

'It should be known.'

'Maybe, but I don't care one way or the other. My job is to silence this thing; to adequately compensate the victims, then to bury it forever. Don't be foolish, my friend.'

'We're hardly friends.'

'True, but we're making progress.'

'You have a list of lawyers?'

'Yes, I have two more names, both very similar to you.'

'In other words, hungry.'

'Yes, you're hungry. But you're also bright.'

'So I've been told. And I have broad shoulders. The other two are here in the city?'

'Yes, but let's not worry about them. Today is Thursday. I need an answer by Monday, at noon. Otherwise, I'll go to the next guy.'

'Was Tarvan used in any other U.S. city?'

'No, just D.C.'

'And how many people were treated with it?'

'A hundred, give or take.'

Clay took a drink of the ice water a waiter had placed near him. 'So there are a few more killers out there?'

'Quite possibly. Needless to say, we're waiting and watching with great anxiety.'

'Can't you stop them?'

'Stop street killings in D.C.? No one could predict Tequila Watson would walk away from D Camp and within two hours kill a person. Nor Washad Porter. Tarvan gives no clue as to who might snap, nor when they might do so. There is some evidence that after ten days without the drug a person becomes harmless again. But it's all speculative.'

'So the killings should stop in just a few days?'

'We're counting on it. I'm hoping we can survive the weekend.'

'Your client should go to jail.'

'My client is a corporation.'

'Corporations can be held criminally responsible.'

'Let's not argue that, okay? It gets us nowhere. We need to focus on you and whether or not you are up to the challenge.'

'I'm sure you have a plan.'

'Yes, a very detailed one.'

'I quit my present job, then what?'

Pace pushed the lemonade aside and leaned lower, as if the good stuff was about to be delivered. 'You establish your own law firm. Rent space, furnish it nicely, and so on. You've got to sell this thing, Clay, and the only way to do so is to look and act like a very successful trial lawyer. Your potential clients will be brought into your office. They need to be impressed. You'll need a staff and other lawyers working for you. Perception is everything here. Trust me. I was a lawyer once. Clients want nice offices. They want to see success. You will be telling these people that you can obtain settlements of four million dollars.'

'Four is much too cheap.'

'Later, okay? You have to look successful; that's my point.'

'I get the point. I grew up in a very successful law firm.'

'We know. That's one of the things we like about you.'

'How tight is office space right now?"

'We've leased some footage on Connecticut Avenue. Would you like to see it?'

They left Kramer's through the rear entrance and ambled along the sidewalk as if they were two old friends out for a stroll. 'Am I still being followed?' Clay asked.

'Why?'

'Oh, I don't know. Just curious. Doesn't happen every day. I'd just like to know whether I'd get shot if I broke and ran.'

Pace actually chuckled at this. 'It is rather absurd, isn't it?'

'Damned silly.'

'My client is very nervous, Clay.'

'With good reason.'

'They have dozens of people in the city right now, watching, waiting, praying there are no more killings. And they're hoping you'll be the man to deliver the deal.'

'What about the ethical problems?'

'Which ones?'

'I can think of two – conflict of interest and solicitation of litigation?'

'Solicitation is a joke. Just look at the billboards.'

They stopped at an intersection. 'Right now I represent the defendant,' Clay said as they waited. 'How do I cross the street and represent his victim?'

'You just do it. We've researched the canons of ethics. It's sticky, but there are no violations. Once you resign from OPD, you are free to open your own office and start accepting cases.'

'That's the easy part. What about Tequila Watson? I know why he committed murder. I can't hide that knowledge from him, or his next lawyer.'

'Being drunk or under the influence of drugs is not a defense to a crime. He's guilty. Ramón Pumphrey is dead. You have to forget about Tequila.' They were walking again.

'I don't like that answer,' Clay said.

'It's the best I have. If you say no to me and continue to represent your client, it will be virtually impossible for you to prove he ever took a drug called Tarvan. You'll know it, but you won't be able to prove it. You'll look foolish using that as a defense.'

'It may not be a defense, but it could be a mitigating circumstance.'

'Only if you can prove it, Clay. Here.' They were on Connecticut Avenue, in front of a long modern building with a three-story glass-and-bronze entrance.

Clay looked up and said, 'The high-rent district.'

'Come on. You're on the fourth floor, a corner office with a fantastic view.'

In the vast marble foyer, a directory listed a who's who of D.C. law. 'This is not exactly my turf,' Clay said as he read the names of the firms.

'It can be,' Max said.

'What if I don't want to be here?'

'It's up to you. We just happen to have some space. We'll sublease it to you at a very favorable rent.'

'When did you lease it?'

'Don't ask too many questions, Clay. We're on the same team.'

'Not yet.'

Carpet was being laid and walls painted in Clay's section of the fourth floor. Expensive carpet. They stood at the window of a large empty office and watched the traffic on Connecticut Avenue below. There were a thousand things to do to open a new firm, and he could only think of a hundred. He had a hunch that Max had all the answers.

'What do you think?' Max said.

'I'm not thinking too well right now. Everything's a blur.'

'Don't blow this opportunity, Clay. It will never come again. And the clock is ticking.'

'It's surreal.'

'You can do your firm's charter online, takes about an hour. Pick a bank, open the accounts. Letterhead and such can be done overnight. The office can be complete and furnished in a matter of days. By next Wednesday you can be sitting here behind a fancy desk running your own show.'

'How do I sign up the other cases?'

'Your friends Rodney and Paulette. They know the city and its people. Hire them, triple their salaries, give them nice offices down the hall. They can talk to the families. We'll help.'

'You've thought of everything.'

'Yes. Absolutely everything. I'm running a very efficient machine, one that's in a near-panic mode. We're working around the clock, Clay. We just need a point man.'

On the way down, the elevator stopped at the third floor. Three men and a woman stepped in, all nicely tailored and manicured and carrying thick expensive leather briefcases, along with the incurable air of importance inbred in big-firm lawyers. Max was so engrossed in his details that he did not see them. But Clay absorbed them – their manners, their guarded speech, their seriousness, their arrogance. These were big lawyers, important lawyers, and they did not acknowledge his existence. Of course, in old khakis and scuffed loafers he did not exactly project the image of a fellow member of the D.C. Bar.

That could change overnight, couldn't it?

He said good-bye to Max and went for another long walk, this one in the general direction of his office. When he finally arrived, there were no urgent notes on his desk. The meeting he'd missed had evidently been missed by many others. No one asked where he had been. No one seemed to notice that he had been absent during the afternoon.

His office was suddenly much smaller, and dingier, and the furnishings were unbearably bleak. There was a stack of files on his desk, cases he could not now bring himself to think about. All of his clients were criminals anyway.

OPD policy required thirty days' notice before quitting. The rule, however, was not enforced because it could not be enforced. People quit all the time with short notice or none whatsoever. Glenda would write a threatening letter. He would write a pleasant one back, and the matter would end.

The best secretary in the office was Miss Glick, a seasoned warrior who might just jump at the chance to double her salary and leave behind the dreariness of OPD. His office would be a fun place to work, he had already decided. Salaries and benefits and long vacations and maybe even profit-sharing.

He spent the last hour of the workday behind a locked door, plotting, stealing employees, debating which lawyers and which paralegals might fit.

★　　★　　★

He met Max Pace for the third time that day, for dinner, at the Old Ebbitt Grille, on Fifteenth Street, two blocks behind the Willard. To his surprise, Max began with a martini, and this loosened him up considerably. The pressure of the situation began melting under the assault of the gin, and Max became a real person. He had once been a trial lawyer in California, before something unfortunate ended his career out there. Through contacts he found his niche in the litigation marketplace as a fireman. A fixer. A highly paid agent who sneaked in, cleaned up the mess, and sneaked out without a trace. During the steaks and after the first bottle of Bordeaux, Max said there was something else waiting for Clay after Tarvan. 'Something much bigger,' Max said, and he actually glanced around the restaurant to see if spies were listening.

'What?' Clay said after a long wait.

Another quick search for eavesdroppers, then, 'My client has a competitor who's put a bad drug on the market. No one knows it yet. Their drug is outperforming our drug. But my client now has reliable proof that the bad drug causes tumors. My client has been waiting for the perfect moment to attack.'

'Attack?'

'Yes, as in a class-action suit brought by a young aggressive attorney who possesses the right evidence.'

'You're offering me another case?'

'Yes. You take the Tarvan deal, wrap things up

108

in thirty days, then we'll hand you a file that will be worth millions.'

'More than Tarvan?'

'Much more.'

Clay had thus far managed to choke down half his filet mignon without tasting anything. The other half would remain untouched. He was starving but had no appetite. 'Why me?' he asked, more to himself than to his new friend.

'That's the same question lottery winners ask. You've won the lottery, Clay. The lawyer's lottery. You were smart enough to pick up the scent of Tarvan, and at the same time we were searching desperately for a young lawyer we could trust. We found each other, Clay, and we have this one brief moment in time in which you make a decision that will alter the course of your life. Say yes, and you will become a very big lawyer. Say no, and you lose the lottery.'

'I get the message. I need some time to think, to clear my head.'

'You have the weekend.'

'Thanks. Look, I'm taking a quick trip, leaving in the morning, coming back Sunday night. I really don't think you guys need to follow me.'

'May I ask where?'

'Abaco, in the Bahamas.'

'To see your father?'

Clay was surprised, but then he should not have been. 'Yes,' he said.

'For what purpose?'

'None of your business. Fishing.'

'Sorry, but we're very nervous. I hope you understand.'

'Not really. I'll give you my flights, just don't follow me, okay?'

'You have my word.'

Chapter 10

Great Abaco Island is a long narrow strip of land at the northern edge of the Bahamas, about a hundred miles east of Florida. Clay had been there once before, four years earlier when he'd scraped together enough money for the airfare. That trip had been a long weekend, one in which Clay had planned to discuss serious issues with his father and discard some baggage. It didn't happen. Jarrett Carter was still too close to his disgrace and concerned primarily with drinking rum punch from noon on. He was willing to talk about anything but the law and lawyers.

This visit would be different.

Clay arrived late in the afternoon on a very warm and very crowded Coconut Air turboprop. The gentleman at Customs glanced at his passport and waved him through. The taxi ride into Marsh Harbor took five minutes, on the wrong side of the road. The driver liked loud gospel music and Clay was not in the mood to argue. Nor was he in the mood to tip. He got out of the car at the harbor and went looking for his father.

Jarrett Carter had once filed suit against the President of the United States, and though he lost the case, the experience taught him that every subsequent defendant was an easier target. He feared no one, in court or out. His reputation had been secured with one great victory – a large malpractice verdict against the President of the American Medical Association, a fine doctor who'd made a mistake in surgery. A pitiless jury in a conservative county had returned the verdict, and Jarrett Carter was suddenly a trial lawyer in demand. He picked the toughest cases, won most of them, and by the age of forty was a litigator with a wide reputation. He built a firm known for its bare-knuckle ways in the courtroom. Clay never doubted he would follow his father and spend his career in trials.

The wheels came off when Clay was in college. There was an ugly divorce that cost Jarrett dearly. His firm began to split with, typically, all partners suing each other. Distracted, Jarrett went two years without winning a trial, and his reputation suffered greatly. He made his biggest mistake when he and his accountant began cooking the books – hiding income, overstating expenses. When they got caught, the accountant killed himself but Jarrett did not. He was devastated though, and prison looked likely. Luckily, an old pal from law school was the U.S. Attorney in charge of the prosecution.

The details of their agreement would forever remain a dark secret. There was never an indictment, just an unofficial deal whereby Jarrett quietly closed his office, surrendered his license to practice law, and left the country. He fled with nothing, though those close to the affair felt he'd stashed something off-shore. Clay had seen no indication of any such loot.

So the great Jarrett Carter became a fishing boat captain in the Bahamas, which to some would sound like a wonderful life. Clay found him on the boat, a sixty-foot Wavedancer wedged into a slip in the crowded marina. Other charters were returning from a long day at sea. Sunburned fishermen were admiring their catches. Cameras were flashing. Bahamian deckhands scurried about unloading coolers of iced-down grouper and tuna. They hauled away bags of empty bottles and beer cans.

Jarrett was on the bow with a water hose in one hand and a sponge in the other. Clay watched him for a moment, not wanting to interrupt a man at work. His father certainly looked the part of the expatriate on the run – barefoot with dark leathery skin, a gray Hemingway beard, silver chains around his neck, long-billed fishing cap, ancient white cotton shirt with the sleeves rolled up to his biceps. If not for a slight beer belly, Jarrett would have looked quite fit.

'Well, I'll be damned!' he yelled when he saw his son.

'Nice boat,' Clay said, stepping aboard. There

was a firm handshake, but nothing more. Jarrett was not the affectionate type, at least not with his son. Several former secretaries had told different stories. He smelled of dried perspiration, salt water, stale beer – a long day at sea. His shorts and white shirt were dirty.

'Yeah, owned by a doctor in Boca. You're looking good.'

'You too.'

'I'm healthy, that's all that matters. Grab a beer.' Jarrett pointed to a cooler on the deck.

They popped tops and sat in the canvas chairs while a group of fishermen staggered along the pier. The boat rocked gently. 'Busy day, huh?' Clay said.

'We left at sunrise, had a father and his two sons, big strong boys, all of them serious weight lifters. From someplace in New Jersey. I've never seen so many muscles on one boat. They were yanking hundred-pound sailfish out of the ocean like they were trout.'

Two women in their forties walked by, carrying small backpacks and fishing supplies. They had the same weary, sunburned look as all other fishermen. One was a little heavy, the other was not, but Jarrett observed them equally until they were out of sight. His gawking was almost embarrassing.

'Do you still have your condo?' Clay asked. The condo he'd seen four years earlier had been a run-down two-room apartment on the back side of Marsh Harbor.

'Yeah, but I live on the boat now. The owner doesn't come over much, so I just stay here. There's a sofa in the cabin for you.'

'You live on this boat?'

'Sure, it's air-conditioned, plenty of room. It's just me, you know, most of the time.'

They sipped beer and watched another group of fishermen stumble by.

'I've got a charter tomorrow,' Jarrett said. 'You along for the ride?'

'What else would I do around here?'

'Got some clowns from Wall Street who want to leave at seven in the morning.'

'Sounds like fun.'

'I'm hungry,' Jarrett said, jumping to his feet and tossing the beer can in the trash. 'Let's go.'

They walked along the pier, past dozens of boats of all varieties. Small dinners were underway on the sailboats. The fishing captains were drinking beer and relaxing. All of them yelled something to Jarrett, who had a quick retort for each one. He was still barefoot. Clay walked a step behind him and thought to himself, That's my father, the great Jarrett Carter, now a barefoot beach bum in faded shorts and an unbuttoned shirt, the king of Marsh Harbor. And a very unhappy man.

The Blue Fin bar was crowded and loud. Jarrett seemed to know everyone. Before they could find two stools together the bartender had tall glasses of rum punch waiting for them. 'Cheers,' Jarrett said, touching his glass to Clay's, then draining half of it. Serious fishing talk then followed with another captain and for a while Clay was ignored, which was fine with him. Jarrett finished the first rum punch and yelled for another. Then another.

A feast was getting organized at a large round table in one corner. Platters of lobster, crab, and shrimp were laid in the center of it. Jarrett motioned for Clay to follow, and they took seats at the table with a half-dozen others. The music was loud, the conversation louder. Everyone around the table was working hard to get drunk, with Jarrett leading the charge.

The sailor to Clay's right was an aging hippie who claimed to have dodged Vietnam and burned his draft card. He'd rejected all democratic ideas, including employment and income taxes. 'Been bouncing around the Caribbean for thirty years,' he boasted with a mouthful of shrimp. 'Feds don't even know I exist.'

Clay suspected the Feds had little interest in whether the man existed, and the same was true of the rest of the misfits he was now dining with. Sailors, boat captains, full-time fishermen, all running from something – alimony, taxes, indictments, bad business deals. They fancied themselves as rebels, nonconformists, free spirits – modern-day pirates, much too independent to be constricted by the normal rules of society.

A hurricane had hit Abaco hard the summer before, and Captain Floyd, the loudest mouth at the table, was at war with an insurance company. This prompted a round of hurricane stories, which, of course, required another round of rum punch. Clay stopped drinking; his father did not. Jarrett became louder and drunker, as did everyone else at the table.

After two hours the food was gone but the rum punch kept coming. The waiter was hauling it over by the pitcher now, and Clay decided to make a quick exit. He left the table without being noticed and sneaked out of the Blue Fin.

So much for a quiet dinner with Dad.

He awoke in the dark to the sounds of his father stomping around the cabin below, whistling loudly, even singing a tune that remotely sounded like something from Bob Marley. 'Wake up!' Jarrett yelled. The boat was rocking, but not so much from the water as from Jarrett's noisy attack on the day.

Clay stayed on the short and narrow sofa for a moment, trying to get his bearings, and he recalled the legend of Jarrett Carter. He was always in the office before 6 A.M., often by five and sometimes by four. Six days a week, often seven. He missed most of Clay's baseball and football games because he was simply too busy. He was never home before dark, and many times he didn't come home at all. When Clay was older and worked in the law firm, Jarrett was famous for crushing young associates with piles of work. As his marriage deteriorated, he slept in his office, sometimes alone. Regardless of his bad habits, Jarrett always answered the bell, and always before anyone else. He had flirted with alcoholism, but managed to stop when the booze interfered with the work.

He didn't need sleep in the glory days, and evidently some habits refused to die. He roared past the sofa singing loudly and smelling of a fresh shower and cheap aftershave. 'Let's go!' he shouted.

Breakfast was never discussed. Clay managed a quick, cold birdbath in the tiny space called the shower. He was not claustrophobic, but the notion of living in the cramped confines of the boat made him dizzy. Outside the clouds were thick and the air was already warm. Jarrett was on the bridge, listening to the radio, frowning at the sky. 'Bad news,' he said.

'What is it?'

'A big storm is moving in. They're calling for heavy rain all day.'

'What time is it?'

'Six-thirty.'

'What time did you come in last night?'

'You sound like your mother. Coffee's over there.' Clay poured strong coffee into a cup and sat by the wheel.

Jarrett's face was covered by thick sunglasses, his beard, and the bill of his cap. Clay suspected the eyes would betray a nasty hangover, but no one would ever know it. The radio was alive with weather alerts and storm warnings from larger boats at sea. Jarrett and the other charter captains yelled back and forth to each other, relaying reports, making predictions, shaking their heads at the clouds. A half-hour passed. No one was leaving the harbor.

'Dammit,' Jarrett said at one point. 'A wasted day.'

Four young Wall Street honchos arrived, all in white tennis shorts, new running shoes, and new fishing hats. Jarrett saw them coming and met them at the stern. Before they could hop into the boat, he said, 'Sorry, guys, no fishing today. Storm warnings.'

All four heads jerked upward to inspect the sky. A quick scan of the clouds led all four to the conclusion that weather forecasters were wrong. 'You're kidding,' one said.

'Just a little rain,' said another.

'Let's give it a try,' said another.

'The answer is no,' Jarrett said. 'Ain't nobody fishing today.'

'But we've paid for the charter.'

'You'll get your money back.'

They reexamined the clouds, which were getting darker by the minute. Then thunder erupted, like distant cannons. 'Sorry, fellas,' Jarrett said.

'How about tomorrow?' one asked.

'I'm booked. Sorry.'

They shuffled away, certain that they'd been cheated out of their trophy marlins.

Now that the issue of labor had been resolved, Jarrett went to the cooler and grabbed a beer. 'Want one?' he asked Clay.

'What time is it?'

119

'Time for a beer, I guess.'

'I haven't finished my coffee yet.'

They sat in the fishing chairs on the deck and listened as the thunder grew louder. The marina was bustling as captains and deckhands secured their boats and unhappy fishermen hurried back down the piers, hauling coolers and bags filled with suntan oil and cameras. The wind was slowly picking up.

'Have you talked to your mother?' Jarrett asked.

'No.'

The Carter family history was a nightmare, and both knew better than to explore it. 'You still with OPD?' Jarrett asked.

'Yes, and I want to talk to you about that.'

'How's Rebecca?'

'History, I think.'

'Is that good or bad?'

'Right now it's just painful.'

'How old are you now?'

'Twenty-four years younger than you. Thirty-one.'

'Right. You're too young to get married.'

'Thanks, Dad.'

Captain Floyd came rushing along the pier and stopped at their boat. 'Gunter's here. Poker in ten minutes. Let's go!'

Jarrett jumped to his feet, suddenly a kid on Christmas morning. 'Are you in?' he said to Clay.

'In for what?'

'Poker.'

'I don't play poker. Who's Gunter?'

Jarrett stretched and pointed. 'See that yacht over there, a hundred-footer. It's Gunter's. He's an old German fart with a billion bucks and a boatload of girls. Believe me, it's a better place to ride out the storm.'

'Let's go!' Captain Floyd yelled, walking away.

Jarrett was climbing out of the boat, onto the pier. 'Are you coming?' he snapped at Clay.

'I'll pass.'

'Don't be silly. It'll be much more fun than sitting around here all day.' Jarrett was walking away, following Captain Floyd.

Clay waved him off. 'I'll read a book.'

'Whatever.'

They hopped in a dinghy with another rogue and splashed through the harbor until they disappeared behind the yachts.

It was the last time Clay would see his father for several months. So much for advice.

He was on his own.

Chapter 11

The suite was in a different hotel. Pace was moving around D.C. as if spies were trailing him. After a quick hello and the offer of coffee, they sat down for business. Clay could tell that the pressure of burying the secret was working on Pace. He looked tired. His movements were anxious. His words came faster. The smile was gone. No questions about the weekend or the fishing down there in the Bahamas. Pace was about to cut a deal, either with Clay Carter or the next lawyer on his list. They sat at a table, each with a legal pad, pens ready to attack.

'I think five million per death is a better figure,' Clay began. 'Sure they're street kids whose lives have little economic value, but what your client has done is worth millions in punitive damages. So we blend the actual with the punitive and we arrive at five million.'

'The guy in the coma died last night,' Pace said.

'So we have six victims.'

'Seven. We lost another one Saturday morning.'

Clay had multiplied five million times six so many times he had trouble accepting the new figure. 'Who? Where?'

'I'll give you the dirty details later, okay? Let's say it's been a very long weekend. While you were fishing, we were monitoring nine-one-one calls, which on a busy weekend in this city takes a small army.'

'You're sure it's a Tarvan case?'

'We're certain.'

Clay scribbled something meaningless and tried to adjust his strategy. 'Let's agree on five million per death,' he said.

'Agreed.'

Clay had convinced himself flying home from Abaco that it was a game of zeroes. Don't think of it as real money, just a string of 0's after some numbers. For the time being, forget what the money can buy. Forget the dramatic changes about to come. Forget what a jury might do years down the road. Just play the zeroes. Ignore the sharp knife twisting in your stomach. Pretend your guts are lined with steel. Your opponent is weak and scared, and very rich and very wrong.

Clay swallowed hard and tried to speak in a normal tone. 'The attorneys' fees are too low,' he said.

'Oh really?' Pace said and actually smiled. 'Ten million won't cut it?'

'Not for this case. Your exposure would be much greater if a big tort firm were involved.'

'You catch on quick, don't you?'

'Half will go for taxes. The overhead you have planned for me will be very expensive. I'm expected to put together a real law firm in a matter of days, and do so in the high-rent district. Plus, I want to do something for Tequila and the other defendants who are getting shafted in all this.'

'Just give me a figure.' Pace was already scribbling something down.

'Fifteen million will make the transition smoother.'

'Are you throwing darts?'

'No, just negotiating.'

'So you want fifty million – thirty-five for the families, fifteen for you. Is that it?'

'That should do it.'

'Agreed.' Pace thrust a hand over and said, 'Congratulations.'

Clay shook it. He could think of nothing to say but 'Thanks.'

'There is a contract, with some details and stipulations.' Max was reaching into a briefcase.

'What kinds of stipulations?'

'For one, you can never mention Tarvan to Tequila Watson, his new lawyer, or to any of the other criminal defendants involved in this matter. To do so would be to severely compromise everything. As we discussed earlier, drug addiction is not a legal defense to a crime. It could be a mitigating circumstance during sentencing, but Mr. Watson committed murder and whatever he was taking at the time is not relevant to his defense.'

'I understand this better than you.'

'Then forget about the murderers. You now represent the families of their victims. You're on the other side of the street, Clay, so accept it. Our deal will pay you five million up front, another five in ten days, and the remaining five upon final completion of all settlements. You mention Tarvan to anyone and the deal is off. You breach our trust with the defendants, and you'll lose one helluva lot of money.'

Clay nodded and stared at the thick contract now on the table.

'This is basically a confidentiality agreement,' Max continued, tapping the paperwork. 'It's filled with dark secrets, most of which you'll have to hide from your own secretary. For example, my client's name is never mentioned. There's a shell corporation now set up in Bermuda with a new division in the Dutch Antilles that answers to a Swiss outfit headquartered in Luxembourg. The paper trail begins and ends over there and no one, not even me, can follow it without getting lost. Your new clients are getting the money; they're not supposed to ask questions. We don't think this will be a problem. For you, you're making a fortune. We don't expect sermons from a higher moral ground. Just take your money, finish the job, everybody will be happier.'

'Just sell my soul?'

'As I said, skip the sermons. You're doing nothing unethical. You're getting huge settlements for clients who have no clue that they are due anything. That's not exactly selling your soul. And what if you get rich? You won't be the first lawyer to get a windfall.'

Clay was thinking about the first five million. Due immediately.

Max filled in some blanks deep in the contract, then slid it across the table. 'This is our preliminary deal. Sign it, and I can then tell you more about my client. I'll get us some coffee.'

Clay took the document, held it as it grew heavier, then tried to read the opening paragraph. Max was on the phone to room service.

He would resign immediately, on that day, from the Office of the Public Defender and withdraw as counsel of record for Tequila Watson. The paperwork had already been done and was attached to the contract. He would charter his own law firm directly; hire sufficient staff, open bank accounts, etcetera. A proposed charter for the Law Offices of J. Clay Carter II was also attached, all boilerplate. He would, as soon as practicable, contact the seven families and begin the process of soliciting their cases.

Coffee arrived and Clay kept reading. Max was on a cell phone across the suite, whispering in a hushed, serious voice, no doubt relaying the latest events to his superior. Or perhaps he was monitoring his network to see if another Tarvan murder had occurred. For his signature on page eleven, Clay would receive, by immediate wire, the sum of $5 million, a figure that had just been neatly written in by Max. His hands shook when he signed his name, not from fear or moral uncertainty, but from zero shock.

When the first round of paperwork was complete, they left the hotel, and climbed into an SUV driven by the same bodyguard who'd met Clay in the lobby of the Willard. 'I suggest we get the bank account opened first,' Max said softly but firmly. Clay was Cinderella going to the ball, just along for the ride because it was all a dream now.

'Sure, a good idea,' he managed to say.

'Any bank in particular?' Pace asked.

Clay's current bank would be shocked to see the type of activity that was coming. His checking account there had barely managed to remain above the minimum for so long that any significant deposit would set off alarms. A lowly bank manager had once called to break the news that a small loan was past due. He could almost hear a big shot upstairs gasping in disbelief as he gawked at a printout.

'I'm sure you have one in mind,' Clay said.

'We have a close relationship with Chase. The wires will run smoother there.'

Then Chase it would be, Clay thought with a smile. Anything to speed along the wires.

'Chase Bank, on Fifteenth,' Max said to the driver, who was already headed in that direction. Max pulled out more papers. 'Here's the lease and sublease on your office. It's prime space, as you know, and certainly not cheap. My client used a straw company to lease it for two years at eighteen thousand a month. We can sublease it to you for the same rent.'

'That's four hundred thousand bucks, give or take.'

Max smiled and said, 'You can afford it, sir. Start thinking like a trial lawyer with money to burn.'

A vice president of some strain had been reserved. Max asked for the right person and red carpets were rolled down every hallway. Clay took charge of his affairs and signed all the proper documents.

The wire would be received by five that afternoon, according to the veep.

Back in the SUV, Max was all business. 'We took the liberty of preparing a corporate charter for your law firm,' he said, handing over more documents.

'I've already seen this,' Clay said, still thinking about the wire transfer.

'It's pretty basic stuff – nothing sensitive. Do it online. Pay two hundred dollars by credit card, and you're in business. Takes less than an hour. You can do it from your desk at OPD.'

Clay held the papers and looked out a window. A sleek burgundy Jaguar XJ was sitting next to them at a red light, and his mind began to wander. He tried to concentrate on business, but he simply couldn't.

'Speaking of OPD,' Max was saying, 'how do you want to handle those folks?'

'Let's do it now.'

'M at Eighteenth,' Max said to the driver, who appeared to miss nothing. Back to Clay he said, 'Have you thought about Rodney and Paulette?'

'Yes. I'll talk to them today.'

'Good.'

'Glad you approve.'

'We also have some people who know the city well. They can help. They'll work for us, but your clients won't know it.' He nodded at the driver as he said this. 'We can't relax, Clay, until all seven families have become your clients.'

'Seems as though I'll need to tell Rodney and Paulette everything.'

'Almost everything. They will be the only people in your firm who'll know what's happened. But you can never mention Tarvan or the company, and they'll never see the settlement agreements. We'll prepare those for you.'

'But they have to know what we're offering.'

'Obviously. They have to convince the families to take the money. But they can never know where the money is coming from.'

'That'll be a challenge.'

'Let's get them hired first.'

If anyone at OPD missed Clay it wasn't obvious. Even the reliable Miss Glick was preoccupied with the phones and had no time for her usual expression of 'Where have you been?' There were a dozen messages on his desk, all irrelevant now because nothing mattered anymore. Glenda was at a conference in New York, and, as usual, her absence meant longer lunches and more sick days around OPD. He quickly typed a letter of resignation and e-mailed it to her. With the door shut, he filled two briefcases with his personal office junk and left behind old books and other things he owned and once thought had sentimental value. He could always come back, though he knew he would not.

Rodney's desk was in a tiny workspace he shared with two other paralegals. 'Got a minute?' Clay said.

'Not really,' Rodney said, barely looking up from a pile of reports.

'There's a breakthrough in the Tequila Watson case. It'll just take a minute.'

Rodney reluctantly stuck a pen behind an ear and followed Clay back to his office, where the shelves had been cleared, and the door was locked behind them. 'I'm leaving,' Clay began, almost in a whisper.

They talked for almost an hour, while Max Pace waited impatiently in the SUV, parked illegally at the curb. When Clay emerged with two bulky briefcases, Rodney was with him, also laden with a briefcase and a stuffed paper shopping bag. He went to his car and disappeared. Clay jumped in the SUV.

'He's in,' Clay said.

'What a surprise.'

At the office on Connecticut Avenue, they met a design consultant who'd been retained by Max. Clay was given his choice of rather expensive furniture that happened to be in the warehouse and thus deliverable within twenty-four hours. He pointed at various designs and samples, all on the higher end of the price scale. He signed a purchase order.

A phone system was being installed. A computer consultant arrived after the decorator left. At one point, Clay was spending money so fast he began to ask himself if he'd squeezed Max for enough.

Shortly before 5 P.M., Max emerged from a freshly painted office and stuck his cell phone in his pocket. 'The wire is in,' he said to Clay.

'Five million?'

'That's it. You're now a multimillionaire.'

'I'm outta here,' Clay said. 'See you tomorrow.'

'Where are you going?'

'Don't ever ask that question again, okay? You are not my boss. And stop following me. We have our deal.'

He walked along Connecticut for a few blocks, jostling with the rush-hour crowd, smiling goofily to himself, his feet never touching the concrete. Down Seventeenth until he saw the Reflecting Pool and the Washington Monument, where hordes of high school groups clustered for photos. He turned right and walked through Constitution Gardens and past the Vietnam Memorial. Beyond it, he stopped at a kiosk, bought two cheap cigars, lit one, and continued to the steps of the Lincoln Memorial, where he sat for a long time and gazed down The Mall to the Capitol far away.

Clear thinking was impossible. One good

thought was immediately overwhelmed and pushed out by another. He thought of his father living on a borrowed fishing boat, pretending it was the good life but struggling to scrape out a living; fifty-five years old with no future whatsoever; drinking heavily to escape his misery. He puffed on the cigar and mentally shopped for a while, and just for the fun of it made a tally of how much he would spend if he bought everything he wanted – a new wardrobe, a really nice car, a stereo system, some travel. The total was but a small subtraction from his fortune. What kind of car was the big question. Successful but not pretentious.

And of course he would need a new address. He'd look around Georgetown for a quaint old town house. He'd heard tales of some of them selling for six million, but he didn't need that much. He was confident he could find something in the million-dollar range.

A million here. A million there.

He thought of Rebecca, though he tried not to dwell on her. For the past four years she had been the only friend with whom he'd shared everything. Now there was no one to talk to. Their breakup was five days old, and counting, but so much had happened that he'd had little time to think about her.

'Forget the Van Horns,' he said aloud, blowing a thick cloud of smoke.

He'd make a large gift to the Piedmont Fund, designating it for the fight to preserve the natural beauty of Northern Virginia. He'd hire a paralegal to do nothing but track the latest land grabs and proposed developments of BVH Group, and wherever possible he'd sneak around and hire lawyers for small landowners unaware that they were about to become neighbors of Bennett the Bulldozer. Oh, what fun he would have on the environmental front!

Forget those people.

He lit the second cigar and called Jonah, who was at the computer store putting in a few hours. 'I have a table at Citronelle, eight o'clock,' Clay said. It was, at that moment, everybody's favorite French restaurant in D.C.

'Right,' Jonah said.

'I'm serious. We're celebrating. I'm changing jobs. I'll explain later. Just be there.'

'Can I bring a friend?'

'Absolutely not.'

Jonah went nowhere without the girl-of-the-week. When Clay moved out he would move out alone, and he would not miss Jonah's bedroom heroics. He called two other law school pals, but both had kids and obligations, and it was pretty short notice.

Dinner with Jonah. Always an adventure.

Chapter 12

In his shirt pocket he had brand-new business cards, the ink barely dry, delivered fresh that morning from an overnight printing firm, declaring him to be the Chief Paralegal of the Law Offices of J. Clay Carter II. Rodney Albritton, Chief Paralegal, as if the firm had an entire division of paralegals under his control. It did not, but it was growing at an impressive rate.

If he'd had the time to purchase a new suit, he probably wouldn't have worn it on his first mission. The old uniform would work better – navy blazer, loosened tie, faded jeans, scuffed black Army boots. He was still working on the streets and he needed to look like it. He found Adelfa Pumphrey at her station, staring at a wall of closed-circuit monitors but seeing nothing.

Her son had been dead for ten days.

She looked at him and pointed to a clipboard where all guests were expected to sign in. He pulled out one of his cards and introduced himself. 'I work for a lawyer downtown,' he said.

'That's nice,' she said softly, without so much as glancing at the card.

'I'd like to talk to you for a couple of minutes.'

'About what?'

'About your son, Ramón.'

'What about him?'

'I know some things about his death that you don't.'

'Not one of my favorite subjects right now.'

'I understand that, and I'm sorry to be talking about it. But you'll like what I got to say, and I'll be quick.'

She glanced around. Way down the hall was another uniformed guard, standing by a door, half-asleep. 'I can take a break in twenty minutes,' she said. 'Meet me in the canteen, one floor up.'

As Rodney walked away he told himself that, yes, he was in fact worth every penny of his fat new salary. A white guy who had approached Adelfa Pumphrey with such a delicate matter would still be standing before her, nervous, shaking, grasping for words because she wouldn't budge. She wouldn't trust him, wouldn't believe anything he said, would have no interest in anything he had to say, at least not within the first fifteen minutes of conversation.

But Rodney was smooth and smart and black and she wanted to talk to someone.

Max Pace's file on Ramón Pumphrey was brief but thorough; there wasn't much to cover. His alleged father had never married his mother. The

135

man's name was Leon Tease, and he was currently serving a thirty-year sentence in Pennsylvania for armed robbery and attempted murder. Evidently, he and Adelfa had lived together just long enough to produce two children – Ramón and a slightly younger brother named Michael. Another brother had been sired later by a man Adelfa married and then divorced. She was currently unmarried and trying to raise, in addition to her two remaining sons, two young nieces who belonged to a sister who'd been sent to prison for selling crack.

Adelfa earned $21,000 working for a private company hired to guard low-risk office buildings in D.C. From her apartment in a project in the North East, she commuted downtown each day by subway. She did not own a car and had never learned to drive. She had a checking account with a very low balance and two credit cards that kept her in trouble and ruined any chance of a good credit rating. She had no criminal record. Other than work and family, her only outside interest appeared to be the Old Salem Gospel Center not far from where she lived.

Since they had both grown up in the city, they played 'Who-do-you-know?' for a few minutes. Where did you go to school? Where were your parents from? They found a couple of tenuous connections. Adelfa worked on a diet cola. Rodney had black coffee. The canteen was half-filled with low-level bureaucrats prattling about everything but the monotonous work they were supposed to be doing.

'You wanted to talk about my son,' she said after a few minutes of awkward chitchat. Her voice was soft and low, strained, still suffering.

Rodney fidgeted slightly and leaned in lower. 'Yes, and, again, I'm sorry to talk about him. I got kids. I can't imagine what you're going through.'

'You're right about that.'

'I work for a lawyer here in town, young guy, very smart, and he's on to something that can get you some big money.'

The idea of big money didn't seem to faze her.

Rodney kept going. 'The boy that killed Ramón had just walked out of a drug treatment facility where he'd been locked down for almost four months. He was a junkie, a street kid, not much of a chance in life. They'd been giving him some drugs as part of his treatment. We think one of the drugs made him crazy enough to pick a random victim and start shooting.'

'It wasn't a drug deal that went bad?'

'No, not at all.'

Her eyes drifted away, then became moist, and for a moment Rodney could see a breakdown coming. But then she looked at him and said, 'Big money? How much?'

'More than a million bucks,' he said with a straight poker face, one he'd rehearsed a dozen times because he doubted seriously if he could deliver that punch line without going wild-eyed.

No visible reaction from Adelfa, at least not at first. Another wayward gaze around the room. 'You jivin' me?' she said.

'Why would I do that? I don't know you. Why would I walk in here and feed you a line? There's money on the table, big money. Big corporate drug money that somebody wants you to take and keep quiet.'

'What big company?'

'Look, I've told you everything I know. My job is to meet you, tell you what's goin' on, and to invite you to come see Mr. Carter, the lawyer I work for. He'll explain everything.'

'White dude?'

'Yep. Good dude. I've worked with him for five years. You'll like him, and you'll like what he has to say.'

The moist eyes had cleared. She shrugged and said, 'Okay.'

'What time you get off?' he asked.

'Four-thirty.'

'Our office is on Connecticut, fifteen minutes from here. Mr. Carter will be waiting on you. You got my card.'

She looked at the card again.

'And one very important thing,' Rodney said, almost in a whisper. 'This'll work only if you keep quiet. It's a deep secret. You do what Mr. Carter advises you to do, and you'll get more money than you ever dreamed of. But if word gets out, then you'll get nothing.'

Adelfa was nodding.

'And you need to start thinking about moving.'

'Moving?'

'As in a new house in a new town where nobody knows you and nobody knows you got lots of money. Pretty house on a safe street where kids can ride their bikes on the sidewalks, no drug dealers, no gangs, no metal detectors at school. No kinfolk wanting your money. Take some advice from somebody who grew up like you. Move. Leave this place. You take this money back to Lincoln Towers and they'll eat you alive.'

Clay's raid on OPD had so far netted Miss Glick, the very efficient secretary who hesitated only slightly at the prospect of having her salary doubled, and his old pal Paulette Tullos who, though she was well maintained by her absent Greek husband, nonetheless jumped at the chance to earn $200,000 a year as opposed to a mere $40,000; and, of course, Rodney. The raid had provoked two urgent and as of yet unanswered phone calls from Glenda, and a whole series of pointed e-mails, also being ignored, at least for now. Clay vowed to himself to meet with Glenda in the very near future and offer some lame reason for stealing her good people.

To counterbalance the good people, he had hired his roommate, Jonah, who, though he had never practiced law – he'd passed the bar exam on his fifth attempt – was a friend and confidant who Clay hoped might develop some legal skills. Jonah had a big mouth and liked to drink and so Clay had been very sketchy with the details of his new firm. He planned to gradually tell Jonah more and more, but he started slow. Smelling money from somewhere, Jonah had negotiated a starting salary of $90,000, which was less than that of the Chief Paralegal, though no one at the firm knew what the others were earning. The new CPA firm down on the third floor was handling the books and payroll.

Clay had given Paulette and Jonah the same careful explanation he had given to Rodney. To wit: He had stumbled upon a conspiracy involving a bad drug – the name of the drug and the name of the company would never be disclosed to them or to anyone else. He had made contact with the company. A quick deal was struck. Serious money was changing hands. Secrecy was crucial. Just do your jobs and don't ask a lot of questions. We're going to build a nice little law firm where we make lots of money and have some fun along the way.

Who could say no to such an offer?

Miss Glick greeted Adelfa Pumphrey as if she were the very first client to ever enter the shiny new law firm, which in fact she was. Everything smelled new – the paint, the carpet, the wallpaper, the Italian leather furniture in the reception area. Miss Glick brought Adelfa water in crystal that had never been used before, then returned to her task of arranging her new glass-and-chrome desk. Paulette was next. She took Adelfa into her office for the preliminary workup, which was more than semiserious girl talk. Paulette took a bunch of notes about family and background, the same info Max Pace had already prepared. She said the right words to a grieving mother.

So far everyone had been black, and Adelfa was reassured by this.

'You may have seen Mr. Carter before,' Paulette said, working her way through the rough script she and Clay had put together. 'He was in court when you were there. He was appointed by the Judge to represent Tequila Watson, but he got rid of the case. That's how he got involved with this settlement.'

Adelfa looked as confused as they'd expected her to be.

Paulette pressed on. 'He and I worked together for five years in the Office of the Public Defender. We quit a few days ago and opened this firm. You'll like him. He's a very nice guy and a good lawyer. Honest, and loyal to his clients.'

'Y'all just opened up?'

'Yes. Clay has been wanting to have his own firm for a long time. He asked me to join him. You're in very good hands, Adelfa.'

The confusion had turned to bewilderment.

'Any questions?' Paulette asked.

'I got so many questions I don't know where to start.'

'I understand. Here's my advice to you. Don't ask a lot of questions. There's a big company out there that's willing to pay you a lot of money to settle a potential lawsuit you might have arising from the death of your son. If you hesitate and ask questions, you could easily end up with nothing.

Just take the money, Adelfa. Take it and run.'

When it was finally time to meet Mr. Carter, Paulette led her down the hall to a large office in the corner. Clay had been pacing nervously for an hour, but he greeted her calmly and welcomed her to the firm. His tie was loose, his sleeves rolled up, his desk covered with files and papers as if he were litigating on many fronts. Paulette hung around until the ice was completely broken, then, according to the plan, excused herself.

'I recognize you,' Adelfa said.

'Yes, I was in court for the arraignment of your son's murderer. The Judge dumped that case on me, but I got rid of it. Now I'm working the other side of the street.'

'I'm listening.'

'You're probably confused by all this.'

'That's right.'

'It's actually quite simple.' Clay straddled the edge of his desk and looked down at her hopelessly perplexed face. He locked his arms across his chest and tried to give the appearance that he'd done this before. He launched into his version of the big bad drug company narrative, and while it was more drawn out than Rodney's and more animated, it told the same story without revealing much in the way of new facts. Adelfa sat in a sunken leather chair, hands folded across the lap of her uniform pants, eyes watching, never blinking, not sure what to believe.

As he wrapped up his story he said, 'They want to pay you a bunch of money, right now.'

'Who, exactly, is they?'

'The drug company.'

'Does it have a name?'

'It has several, and several addresses, and you'll never know its true identity. That's part of the deal. We, you and I, lawyer and client, must agree to keep everything a secret.'

She finally blinked, then recrossed her hands and shifted her weight. Her eyes glazed over as she stared at the fine new Persian rug that consumed half the office. 'How much money?' she asked softly.

'Five million dollars.'

'Good Lord,' she managed to say before she broke down. She covered her eyes and sobbed and for a long time made no effort to stop. Clay handed her a tissue from a box.

The settlement money was sitting in Chase Bank, next to Clay's, just waiting to be distributed. Max's paperwork was on the desk, a pile of it. Clay walked her through it, explaining that the money would be transferred first thing the next morning, as soon as the bank opened. He flipped pages and pages of documents, hitting the high points of the legalities, collecting her signatures where necessary. Adelfa was too stunned to say much. 'Trust me,' he said more than once. 'If you want the money, sign right there.'

'I feel like I'm doing something wrong,' she said at one point.

'No, the wrong has been done by someone else.

You're the victim here, Adelfa, the victim and now the client.'

'I need to talk to someone,' she said once as she signed again.

But there was no one to talk to. A boyfriend came and went, according to Max's intelligence, and he was not the type to seek advice from. She had brothers and sisters scattered from D.C. to Philadelphia, but they were certainly no more sophisticated than Adelfa. Both parents were dead.

'That would be a mistake,' Clay said delicately. 'This money will improve your life if you keep it quiet. If you talk about it, then it will destroy you.'

'I'm not good at handling money.'

'We can help. If you'd like, Paulette can monitor things for you and give advice.'

'I'd like that.'

'That's what we're here for.'

Paulette drove her home, a slow ride through rush-hour traffic. She told Clay later that Adelfa said very little, and when they arrived at the housing project she did not want to get out. So they sat there for thirty minutes, talking quietly about her new life. No more welfare, no more gunshots in the night. No more prayers to God to protect her children. Never again would she worry about keeping her kids safe the way she had worried about Ramón.

No more gangs. No more bad schools.

She was crying when she finally said good-bye.

Chapter 13

The black Porsche Carrera rolled to a stop under a shade tree on Dumbarton Street. Clay got out and for a few seconds was able to ignore his newest toy, but after a quick glance in all directions he turned and admired it once again. His for three days now, and he still couldn't believe he owned it. Get used to it, he kept telling himself, and he could manage to act as though it were just another car, nothing special, but the sight of it after even a brief absence still made his pulse quicken. 'I'm driving a Porsche,' he would say to himself, out loud, as he buzzed through traffic like a Formula One driver.

He was eight blocks from the main campus of Georgetown University, the place he'd spent four years as a student before moving on to its law school near Capitol Hill. The town houses were historic and picturesque; the small lawns manicured; the streets covered by ancient oaks and maples. The busy shops and bars and restaurants on M Street were just two blocks to the south, easy walking distance. He had jogged these streets for four years, and he'd spent many long nights with his pals prowling the hangouts and pubs along Wisconsin Avenue and M Street.

Now he was about to live here.

The town house that held his attention was on the market for $1.3 million. He'd found it cruising through Georgetown two days earlier. There was another on N Street and another on Volta, all within a stone's throw of each other. He was determined to buy one before the end of the week.

The one on Dumbarton, his first choice, had been built in the 1850s and carefully preserved ever since. Its brick facade had been painted many times and was now a faded bluish color. Four levels, including a basement. The real estate agent said it had been immaculately maintained by a retired couple who had once entertained the Kennedys and the Kissingers and just fill in the blanks with all the other names one might want. Washington Realtors could drop names faster than those in Beverly Hills, especially when peddling property in Georgetown.

Clay was fifteen minutes early. The house was empty; its owners were now doing time in assisted living, according to the agent. He walked through a gate beside the house and admired the small garden in the back. There was no pool and no room for one; real estate was precious in Georgetown. There was a patio with wrought-iron furniture and weeds creeping in from the flower beds. Clay would have a few hours to spare for the gardening, but not much.

Perhaps he would just hire a lawn maintenance company.

He loved the house and the ones next to it. He loved the street, the coziness of the neighborhood, everybody living near each other but respecting each other's privacy. Sitting on the front steps, he decided he would offer one million even, then negotiate hard, bluff and walk away, and in general have a great time watching the Realtor run back and forth, but in the end he would be perfectly willing to pay the asking price.

Staring at the Porsche, he drifted away again to his fantasy world where money was growing on trees and he could buy anything he wanted. Italian suits, German sports cars, Georgetown real estate, downtown office space, and what was next? He'd been thinking about a boat for his father, a larger one of course, to generate more revenue. He could incorporate a small charter business in the Bahamas, depreciate the boat, write off most of its costs, thus allowing his father to make a decent living. Jarrett was dying down there, drinking too much, sleeping with anything he could find, living on a borrowed boat, scrambling for tips. Clay was determined to make his life easier.

A door slammed and interrupted his spending, if only for a moment. The Realtor had arrived.

Pace's list of victims stopped at seven. Seven that he knew of. Seven that he and his operatives had been able to monitor. Tarvan had now been pulled for eighteen days, and from the company's experience they knew that whatever the drug did to make people start killing usually stopped working after ten days. His list was chronological, with Ramón Pumphrey being number six.

Number one had been a college kid, a student at George Washington who had walked out of a Starbucks coffee shop on Wisconsin Avenue in Bethesda just in time to be spotted by a man with a gun. The student was from Bluefield, West Virginia. Clay made the five-hour drive there in record time, not hurried at all but rather as a race car driver speeding through the Shenandoah Valley. Following Pace's precise instructions, he found the home of the parents, a rather sad-looking little bungalow near downtown. He sat in the driveway and actually said out loud, 'I can't believe I'm doing this.'

Two things motivated him to get out of the car. First, he had no choice. Second, the prospect of the entire $15 million, not just one third or two thirds. All of it.

He was dressed casually and he left his briefcase in the car. The mother was home but the father was still at work. She reluctantly let him in, but then offered some tea and cookies. Clay waited on a sofa in the den, pictures of the dead son everywhere. The curtains were drawn. The house was a mess.

What am I doing here?

She talked about her son for a long time, and Clay hung on every word.

The father sold insurance a few blocks away, and he was home before the ice melted in the tea glass. Clay presented his case to them, as much of it as possible. At first there were some tentative questions – How many others died because of this? Why can't we go to the authorities? Shouldn't this be exposed? Clay fielded them like a veteran. Pace had prepped him well.

Like all victims, they had a choice. They could get angry, ask questions, make demands, want justice, or they could quietly take the money. The sum of $5 million didn't register at first, or if it did they did a wonderful job of deflecting it. They wanted to be angry and uninterested in money, at least initially. But as the afternoon dragged by they began to see the light.

'If you can't tell me the real name of the company, then I won't accept the money,' the father said at one point.

'I don't know the real name,' Clay said.

There were tears and threats, love and hatred, forgiveness and retribution, almost every emotion came and went during the afternoon and into the evening. They'd just buried their youngest son and the pain was numbing and immeasurable. They disliked Clay for being there, but they thanked him profusely for his concern. They distrusted him as a big-city lawyer who was obviously lying about such an outrageous settlement, but they asked him to stay for dinner, whatever dinner might be.

It arrived promptly at six. Four ladies from their church hauled in enough food for a week. Clay was introduced as a friend from Washington, and was immediately subjected to an all-out cross-examination by the four. A hard-nosed trial lawyer couldn't have been more curious.

The ladies finally left. After dinner, as the night wore on, Clay began to press them. He was offering the only deal they would get. Shortly after 10 P.M., they began signing the paperwork.

Number three was clearly the most difficult. She was a seventeen-year-old prostitute who'd worked the streets most of her life. The police thought she and her killer had once had a business relationship, but there was no clue as to why he would shoot her. He did so outside a lounge, in front of three witnesses.

She went by the name of Bandy, without the need of a last name. Pace's research had revealed no husband, mother, father, siblings, children, home address, schools, churches, or, most amazing, police record. There had been no funeral. Like two dozen others each year in D.C., Bandy had received a pauper's burial. When one of Pace's agents had inquired at the city coroner's office, he had been told, 'She's buried in the tomb of the unknown prostitute.'

Her killer had provided the only clue. He had told the police that Bandy had an aunt who lived in Little Beirut, the most dangerous housing ghetto in South East D.C. But after two weeks of relentless digging, the aunt had not been found.

With no known heirs, a settlement would be impossible.

Chapter 14

The final Tarvan clients to sign the documents were the parents of a twenty-year-old Howard University coed who'd dropped out of school one week and been murdered the next. They lived in Warrenton, Virginia, forty miles west of D.C. For an hour they had sat in Clay's office and held hands tightly, as if neither of them could function alone. They cried at times, pouring out their unspeakable grief. They were stoic at other times, so rigid and strong and seemingly unmoved by the money that Clay doubted they would accept the settlement.

But they did, though of all the clients he'd processed Clay was certain that the money would affect them the least. With time they might appreciate it; for now, they just wanted their daughter back.

Paulette and Miss Glick helped escort them out of the office and to the elevators, where everybody hugged everybody again. As the doors closed, the parents were fighting tears.

Clay's little team met in the conference room where they let the moment pass and were thankful that no more widows and grieving parents would visit them, at least not in the near future. Some very expensive champagne had been iced for the occasion, and Clay began pouring. Miss Glick declined because she drank nothing, but she was the only teetotaler in the firm. Paulette and Jonah seemed especially thirsty. Rodney preferred Budweiser, but he sipped along with the rest.

During the second bottle, Clay rose to speak. 'I have some firm announcements,' he said, tapping his glass. 'First, the Tylenol cases are now complete. Congratulations and thanks to all of you.' He'd used Tylenol as a code for Tarvan, a name they would never hear. Nor would they ever know the amount of his fees. Obviously, Clay was being paid a fortune, but they had no idea how much.

They applauded themselves. 'Second, we begin the celebration tonight with dinner at Citronelle. Eight o'clock sharp. Could be a long evening because there is no work tomorrow. The office is closed.'

More applause, more champagne. 'Third, in two weeks we leave for Paris. All of us, plus one friend each, preferably a spouse if you have one. All expenses paid. First-class air, luxury hotel, the works. We'll be gone for a week. No exceptions. I'm the boss and I'm ordering all of you to Paris.'

Miss Glick covered her mouth with both hands. They were all stunned, and Paulette spoke first, 'Not Paris, Tennessee.'

'No, dear, the real Paris.'

'What if I bump into my husband over there?' she said with a half-smile, and laughter erupted around the table.

'You can go to Tennessee if you'd like,' Clay said.

'No way, baby.'

When she could finally speak, Miss Glick said, 'I'll need a passport.'

'The forms are on my desk. I'll see to it. It'll take less than a week. Anything else?'

There was talk about weather and food and what to wear. Jonah immediately began debating which girl to take. Paulette was the only one who'd been to Paris, on her honeymoon, a brief tryst that ended badly when the Greek was called away on emergency business. She flew home alone, in coach though she'd gone over in first class. 'Honey, they bring you champagne in first class,' she explained to the rest. 'And the seats are as big as sofas.'

'I can bring anyone?' Jonah asked, obviously struggling with the decision.

'Let's limit it to anyone who doesn't have a spouse, okay?' Clay said.

'That narrows the field.'

'Who will you take?' Paulette asked.

'Maybe no one,' Clay said, and the room went quiet for a moment. They had whispered about Rebecca and the separation, with Jonah supplying most of the gossip. They wanted their boss happy, though they were not close enough to meddle.

'What's that tower over there?' Rodney asked.

'The Eiffel Tower,' Paulette said. 'You can go all the way to the top.'

'Not me. It don't look safe.'

'You're going to be a real traveler, I can tell.'

'How long are we there?' asked Miss Glick.

'Seven nights,' Clay said. 'Seven nights in Paris.' And they all drifted away, swept along by the champagne. A month earlier they had been locked in the drudgery of the OPD. All but Jonah, who'd been selling computers part-time.

Max Pace wanted to talk, and since the firm was closed Clay suggested they meet there, at noon, after the cobwebs had cleared.

Only a headache remained. 'You look like hell,' Pace began pleasantly.

'We celebrated.'

'What I have to discuss is very important. Are you up to it?'

'I can keep up with you. Fire away.'

Pace had a tall paper cup of coffee that he carried around the room as he moved about. 'The Tarvan mess is over,' he said, for finality. It was over when he said it was over, and not before. 'We settled the six cases. If anyone claiming to be related to our girl Bandy ever surfaces, then we'll expect you to deal with it. But I'm convinced she has no family.'

'So am I.'

'You did good work, Clay.'

'I'm getting paid handsomely for it.'

155

'I'll transfer in the last installment today. All fifteen million will be in your account. What's left of it.'

'What do you expect me to do? Drive an old car, sleep in a rundown apartment, keep wearing cheap clothes? You said yourself that I had to spend some money to create the right impression.'

'I'm kidding. And you're doing a great job of looking rich.'

'Thank you.'

'You're making the adjustment from poverty to wealth with remarkable ease.'

'It's a talent.'

'Just be careful. Don't create too much attention.'

'Let's talk about the next case.'

With that Pace took a seat and slid a file across. 'The drug is Dyloft, manufactured by Ackerman Labs. It's a potent anti-inflammatory drug used by sufferers of acute arthritis. Dyloft is new and the doctors have gone crazy over it. It works wonders, patients love it. But it has two problems: First, it's made by a competitor of my client's; second, it's been linked to the creation of small tumors in the bladder. My client, same client as Tarvan, makes a similar drug that was popular until twelve months ago when Dyloft hit the market. The market is worth about three billion a year, give or take. Dyloft is already number two and will probably hit a billion this year. It's hard to tell because it's growing so fast. My client's drug is doing a billion and a half and losing ground fast. Dyloft is the rage and will quickly crush all competition. It's that good. A few months ago my client bought a small pharmaceutical company in Belgium. This outfit once had a division that was later swallowed by Ackerman Labs. A few researchers got shoved out and shafted along the way. Some lab studies disappeared then surfaced where they didn't belong. My client has the witnesses and the documents to prove that Ackerman Labs has known of the potential problems for at least the past six months. You with me?'

'Yes. How many people have taken Dyloft?'

'It's really hard to tell because the number is growing so fast. Probably a million.'

'What percentage get the tumors?'

'The research indicates about five percent, enough to kill the drug.'

'How do you know whether a patient has the tumors?'

'A urinalysis.'

'You want me to sue Ackerman Labs?'

'Hang on. The truth about Dyloft will be out very shortly. As of today, there has been no litigation, no claims, no damaging studies published in the journals. Our spies tell us Ackerman is busy counting its money and stashing it away to pay off the lawyers when the storm hits. Ackerman may also be trying to fix the drug, but that takes time and FDA approvals. They're in a real quandary because they need cash. They borrowed heavily to acquire other companies, most of which have not paid off. Their stock is selling for around forty-two bucks. A year ago it was at eighty.'

'What will the news about Dyloft do to the company?'

'Hammer the stock, which is exactly what my client wants. If the litigation is handled right, and I'm assuming you and I can do it properly, the news will murder Ackerman Labs. And since we have the inside proof that Dyloft is bad, the company will have no choice but to settle. They can't risk a trial, not with such a dangerous product.'

'What's the downside?'

'Ninety-five percent of the tumors are benign, and very small. There's no real damage to the bladder.'

'So the litigation is used to shock the market?'

'Yes, and, of course, to compensate the victims. I don't want tumors in my bladder, benign or malignant. Most jurors would feel the same way. Here's the scenario: You put together a group of fifty or so plaintiffs, and file a big lawsuit on behalf of all Dyloft patients. At precisely the same time, you launch a series of television ads soliciting more cases. You hit fast and hard, and you'll get thousands of cases. The ads run coast to coast – quickie ads that'll scare folks and make them dial your toll-free number right here in D.C., where you have a warehouse full of paralegals answering the phones and doing the grunt work. It's gonna cost you some money, but if you get, say, five thousand cases, and you settle them for twenty thousand bucks each, that's one hundred million dollars. Your cut is one third.'

'That's outrageous!'

'No, Clay, that's mass tort litigation at its finest. That's how the system works these days. And if you don't do it, I guarantee you someone else will. And very soon. There is so much money involved that the mass tort lawyers wait like vultures for any hint of a bad drug. And believe me, there are plenty of bad drugs.'

'Why am I the lucky guy?'

'Timing, my friend. If my client knows exactly when you file the lawsuit, then they can react to the market.'

'Where do I find fifty clients?' Clay asked.

Max thumped another file. 'We know of at least a thousand. Names, addresses, all right here.'

'You mentioned a warehouse full of paralegals?'

'Half a dozen. It'll take that many to answer the phones and keep the files organized. You could end up with five thousand individual clients.'

'Television ads?'

'Yep, I've got the name of a company that can put the ad together in less than three days. Nothing fancy – a voice-over, images of pills dropping onto a table, the potential evils of Dyloft, fifteen seconds of terror designed to make people call the Law Offices of Clay Carter II. These ads work, believe me. Run them in all major markets for a week and you'll have more clients than you can count.'

'How much will it cost?'

'Couple of million, but you can afford it.'

It was Clay's turn to pace around the room and let the blood circulate. He'd seen some ads for diet pills that had gone bad, ads in which unseen lawyers were trying to frighten folks into dialing a toll-free number. Surely, he wasn't about to sink that low.

But thirty-three million dollars in fees! He was still numb from the first fortune.

'What's the timetable?'

Pace had a list of the first things to do. 'You'll have to sign up the clients, which will take two weeks max. Three days to finish the ad. A few days to buy the television time. You'll need to hire paralegals and put them in some rented space out in the suburbs; it's too expensive here. The lawsuit has to be prepared. You have a good staff. You should be able to get it done in less than thirty days.'

'I'm taking the firm to Paris for a week, but we'll get it done.'

'My client wants the lawsuit filed in less than a month. July the second, to be exact.'

Clay returned to the table and stared at Pace. 'I've never handled a lawsuit like this,' he said.

Pace pulled something out of his file. 'Are you busy this weekend?' he asked, looking at a brochure.

'Not really.'

'Been to New Orleans lately?'

'About ten years ago.'

'Ever heard of the Circle of Barristers?'

'Maybe.'

'It's an old group with a new life – a bunch of trial lawyers who specialize in mass torts. They get together twice a year and talk about the latest trends in litigation. It would be a productive weekend.' He slid the brochure across to Clay who picked it up. On the cover was a color photo of the Royal Sonesta Hotel in the French Quarter.

New Orleans was warm and humid as always, especially in the Quarter.

He was alone, and that was fine. Even if he and Rebecca were still together she would not have made the trip. She would've been too busy at work, with shopping to do on the weekend with her mother. The usual routine. He had thought about inviting Jonah, but that relationship was strained at the moment. Clay had moved out of their cramped apartment and into the comfort of Georgetown without offering to take Jonah with him, an affront, but one that Clay had anticipated and was prepared to deal with. The last thing he wanted in his new town house was a wild roommate coming and going at all hours with whatever stray cat he could pick up.

The money was beginning to isolate him. Old friends he once called were now being ignored because he didn't want all the questions. Old places were no longer frequented because he could afford something better. In less than a month, he had changed jobs, homes, cars, banks, wardrobes, eating places, gyms, and he was most definitely in the process of changing girlfriends, though no substitute was on the horizon. They had not spoken in twenty-eight days. He'd been under the assumption that he would call her on the thirtieth day, as promised, but so much had changed since then.

By the time Clay entered the lobby of the Royal Sonesta his shirt was wet and clinging to his back. The registration fee was $5,000, an outrageous amount for a few days of fraternizing with a bunch of lawyers. The fee said to the legal world that not everyone was invited, only the rich who were serious about their mass torts. His room was another $450 a night, and he paid for it with an unused platinum credit card.

Various seminars were under way. He drifted through a discussion on toxic torts, led by two lawyers who'd sued a chemical company for polluting drinking water that might or might not have caused cancer, but the company paid half a billion anyway and the two lawyers got rich. Next door a lawyer Clay had seen on television was in full throttle on how to handle the media, but he had few listeners. In fact, most of the seminars were lightly attended. But it was Friday afternoon and the heavyweights arrived on Saturday.

Clay eventually found the crowd in the small exhibition hall where an aircraft company was showing a video on its upcoming luxury jet, the fanciest of its generation. The show was on a wide screen in one corner of the hall, and lawyers were packed together, all silent, all gawking at this latest miracle of aviation. Range of four thousand miles – 'Coast to coast, or New York to Paris, nonstop of course.' It burned less fuel than the other four jets Clay had never heard of, and went faster too. The interior was roomy with seats and sofas everywhere, even a very comely flight attendant in a short skirt, holding a bottle of champagne and a bowl of cherries. The leather was a rich tan color. For pleasure or for work, because the Galaxy 9000 came with a cutting-edge phone system and a satellite receiver that allowed the busy lawyer to call anywhere in the world; and faxes and a copier, and, of course, instant Internet access. The video actually showed a group of harsh-looking lawyer types huddled around a small table, with their sleeves rolled up as if they were laboring over some settlement, while the comely blonde in the short skirt got ignored along with her champagne.

Clay inched closer into the crowd, feeling very much like a trespasser. Wisely, the video never gave the selling price of the Galaxy 9000. There were better deals, involving time-shares and trade-ins, and leasebacks, all of which could be explained by the sales reps who were standing nearby ready to do business. When the screen went blank, the lawyers all began talking at once, not about bad drugs and class-action suits, but about jets and how much pilots cost. The sales reps were surrounded by eager buyers. At one point, Clay overheard someone say, 'A new one is in the thirty-five range.'

Surely it wasn't thirty-five million.

Other exhibitors were offering all sorts of luxury items. A boatbuilder had a group of serious lawyers interested in yachts. There was a specialist on Caribbean real estate. Another was peddling cattle ranches in Montana. An electronics booth with the latest absurdly expensive gadgets was particularly busy.

And the automobiles. One entire wall was lined with elaborate displays of expensive cars – a Mercedes-Benz convertible coupé, a limited edition Corvette, a maroon Bentley, which every respectable mass tort lawyer had to have. Porsche was unveiling its own SUV and a salesman was taking orders. The biggest gathering was gawking over a shiny royal blue Lamborghini. Its price tag was almost hidden, as if the manufacturer was afraid of it. Only $290,000, and a very limited supply. Several lawyers appeared ready to wrestle for the car.

In a quieter section of the hall, a tailor and his assistants were measuring a rather large lawyer for an Italian suit. A sign said they were from Milan, but Clay heard some very American English.

In law school, he had once attended a panel discussion on large settlements, and what lawyers should do to protect their unsophisticated clients from the temptations of instant riches. Several trial lawyers told horror stories of working families who had ruined their lives with their settlements, and the stories were fascinating studies in human behavior. At one point, a lawyer on the panel quipped, 'Our clients spend their money almost as fast as we do.'

As Clay gazed around the exhibition hall, he saw lawyers spending money as fast as they could make it. Was he guilty of this?

Of course not. He'd stuck to the basics, at least so far. Who wouldn't want a new car and a better home? He wasn't buying yachts and planes and cattle ranches. Didn't want them. And if Dyloft earned him another fortune, he would not, under any circumstances, waste his money on jets and second homes. He would bury it in the bank, or in the backyard.

The frenzied orgy of consumption sickened him, and Clay left the hotel. He wanted some oysters and Dixie Beer.

Chapter 15

The only nine o'clock session on Saturday morning was an update on class-action legislation currently being debated in Congress. The topic drew a small crowd. For $5,000, Clay was determined to soak up as much as he could. Of the few present, he appeared to be the only one without a hangover. Tall cups of steaming coffee were being drained around the ballroom.

The speaker was a lawyer/lobbyist from Washington who got off to a bad start by telling two dirty jokes, both of which bombed. The crowd was all-white, all-male, a regular fraternity, but not in the mood for tasteless jokes. The presentation quickly went from bad humor to boredom. However, at least for Clay, the materials were somewhat interesting and mildly informative; he knew very little about class actions so everything was new.

At ten, he had to choose between a panel discussion on the latest in Skinny Ben developments and a presentation by a lawyer whose speciality was lead paint, a topic that sounded rather dull to Clay, so he went with the former. The room was full.

Skinny Ben was the nickname of an infamous obesity pill that had been prescribed for millions of patients. Its maker had pocketed billions and had been poised to own the world when problems began developing in a significant number of users. Heart problems, easily traceable to the drug. Litigation exploded overnight and the company had no desire to go to trial. Its pockets were deep and it began buying off the plaintiffs with huge settlements. For the past three years, mass tort lawyers from all fifty states had been scrambling to sign up Skinny Ben cases.

Four lawyers sat at a table with a moderator and faced the crowd. The seat next to Clay was empty until a feisty little lawyer rushed in at the last moment and wedged himself between the rows. He unpacked his briefcase – legal pads, seminar materials, two cell phones, and a pager. When his command post was properly arranged and Clay had inched as far away as possible, he whispered, 'Good morning.'

'Morning,' Clay whispered back, not at all anxious to chat. He looked at the cell phones and wondered who, exactly, might he want to call at 10 A.M. on a Saturday.

'How many cases you got?' the lawyer whispered again.

An interesting question, and one Clay was certainly not prepared to answer. He had just finished

167

the Tarvan cases and was plotting his Dyloft assault, but, at the moment, he had no cases whatsover. But such an answer was quite insufficient in the current environment where all numbers were huge and exaggerated.

'Couple of dozen,' he lied.

The guy frowned, as if this was completely unacceptable, and the conversation was iced, at least for a few minutes. One of the panelists began talking and the entire room became still. His topic was the financial report on Healthy Living, manufacturer of Skinny Bens. The company had several divisions, most of which were profitable. The stock price had not suffered. In fact, after each major settlement the stock held its own, proof that investors knew the company had plenty of cash.

'That's Patton French,' the lawyer next to him whispered.

'Who's he?' Clay asked.

'Hottest mass tort lawyer in the country. Three hundred million in fees last year.'

'He's the luncheon speaker, isn't he?'

'Right, don't miss it.'

Mr French explained, in excruciating detail, that approximately three hundred thousand Skinny Ben cases had been settled for about $7.5 billion. He, along with other experts, estimated that there were maybe another hundred thousand cases out there worth somewhere between $2 billion and $3 billion. The company and its insurers had plenty of cash to cover these lawsuits, and so it was up to those in the room to hustle on out there and find the rest of the cases. This fired up the crowd.

Clay had no desire to jump into the pit. He couldn't get past the fact that the short, pudgy, pompous little jerk with the microphone made $300 million in fees last year and was still so motivated to earn even more. The discussion drifted into creative ways to attract new clients. One panelist had made so much money that he had two doctors on his payroll full-time to do nothing but go from town to town screening those who'd taken Skinny Bens. Another had relied solely on television advertising, a topic that interested Clay for a moment but soon dissolved into a sad debate as to whether the lawyer should appear on television himself or hire some washed-up actor.

Oddly missing was any discussion about trial strategies – expert witnesses, whistle-blowers, jury selections, medical proof – the usual information lawyers exchanged at seminars. Clay was learning that these cases seldom went to trial. Courtroom skills were not important. It was all about hustling cases. And making huge fees. At various points during the discussion, all four panelists and several of those tossing up softball questions couldn't help but reveal that they had made millions in recent settlements.

Clay wanted to take another shower.

At eleven, the local Porsche dealer held a Bloody Mary reception that was wildly popular. Raw oysters and Bloody Marys and nonstop chatter about how many cases one had. And how to get more. A thousand here, two thousand there. Evidently, the popular tactic was to round up as many cases as possible, then tag team with Patton French who'd be happy to include them in his own personal class action in his backyard over in Mississippi, where the judges and juries and verdicts always went his way and the manufacturer was terrified to set foot. French worked the crowd like a Chicago ward boss.

He spoke again at one, after a buffet lunch featuring Cajun food and Dixie Beer. His cheeks were red, his tongue loose and colorful. Without notes he launched into a brief history of the American tort system and how crucial it was in protecting the masses from the greed and corruption of big corporations that make dangerous products. And, while he was at it, he didn't like insurance companies and banks and multinationals and Republicans, either. Unbridled capitalism created the need for people like those hardy souls in the Circle of Barristers, those down in the trenches who were unafraid to attack big business on behalf of the working people, the little people.

At $300 million a year in fees, it was hard to picture Patton French as an underdog. But he was playing to the crowd. Clay glanced around and wondered, not for the first time, if he was the only sane one there. Were these people so blinded by the money that they honestly believed themselves to be defenders of the poor and the sick?

Most of them owned jets!

French's war stories poured forth effortlessly. A $400 million class-action settlement for a bad cholesterol drug. A billion for a diabetes drug that killed at least a hundred patients. For faulty electrical wiring put in two hundred thousand homes that caused fifteen hundred fires killing seventeen people and burning another forty, $150 million. The lawyers hung on every word. Sprinkled throughout were indications of where his money had gone. 'That cost 'em a new Gulfstream,' he cracked at one point and the crowd actually applauded. Clay knew, after hanging around the Royal Sonesta for less than twenty-four hours, that a Gulfstream was the finest of all personal jets and a new one sold for about $45 million.

French's rival was a tobacco lawyer somewhere in Mississippi who had made a billion or so and bought a yacht that was 180 feet long. French's old yacht measured only 140 feet, so he traded it in for a 200-footer. The crowd found this funny as well. His firm now had thirty lawyers and he needed thirty more. He was on his fourth wife. The last one got the apartment in London.

And so on. A fortune earned, a fortune spent. Small wonder he worked seven days a week.

A normal crowd would have been embarrassed by such a vulgar discussion of wealth, but French knew his audience. If anything, he energized them to make more, spend more, sue more, hustle for more clients. For an hour he was crass and shameless, but seldom boring.

Five years in OPD had certainly sheltered Clay from many aspects of modern-day lawyering. He had read about mass torts but had no idea its practitioners were such an organized and specialized group. They didn't seem to be exceptionally bright. Their strategies centered around gathering the cases and settling them, not real trial work.

French could've gone on forever, but after an hour he retired to a standing ovation, albeit an awkward one. He'd be back at three for a seminar on forum shopping – how to find the best jurisdiction for your case. The afternoon promised to be a repeat of the morning, and Clay had had enough.

He roamed the Quarter, taking in not the bars and strip clubs but the antique shops and galleries, though he bought nothing because he was overcome with the urge to hoard his money. Late in the day, he sat alone at a sidewalk café in Jackson Square and watched the street characters come and go. He sipped and tried to enjoy the hot chicory, but it wasn't working. Although he had not put the figures on paper, he had mentally done the math. The Tarvan fees less 45 percent for taxes and business expenses, minus what he'd already spent, left him with around $6.5 million. He could bury that in a bank and earn $300,000 a year in interest, which was about eight times what he'd been earning in salary at OPD. Three hundred thousand a year was $25,000 a month, and he could not, sitting there in the shade on a warm New Orleans afternoon, imagine how he could ever spend that much money.

This was not a dream. This was reality. The money was already in his account. He would be rich for the rest of his life and he would not become one of those clowns back at the Royal Sonesta griping about the cost of pilots or yacht captains.

The only problem was a significant one. He had hired people and made promises. Rodney, Paulette, Jonah, and Miss Glick had all left long-time jobs and put their blind faith in him. He couldn't just pull the plug now, take his money and run.

He switched to beer and made a profound decision. He would work hard for a short period of time on the Dyloft cases, which, frankly, he would be stupid to turn down since Max Pace was handing him a gold mine. When Dyloft was over, he'd give huge bonuses to his staff and close the office. He'd live the quiet life in Georgetown, traveling the world when he wanted, fishing with his father, watching his money grow, and never, under any circumstances, ever getting near another meeting of the Circle of Barristers.

He had just ordered breakfast from room service when the phone rang. It was Paulette, the only person who knew exactly where he was. 'Are you in a nice room?' she asked.

'Indeed I am.'

'Does it have a fax?'

'Of course.'

'Gimme the number, I'm sending something down there.'

It was a copy of a clipping from the Sunday edition of the *Post*. A wedding announcement. Rebecca Allison Van Horn and Jason Shubert Myers IV. 'Mr. and Mrs. Bennett Van Horn of McLean, Virginia, announce the engagement of their daughter, Rebecca, to Mr. Jason Shubert Myers IV, son of Mr. and Mrs. D. Stephens Myers of Falls Church. . . .' The photo, though copied and faxed more than a thousand miles was quite clear – a very pretty girl was marrying someone else.

D. Stephens Myers was the son of Dallas Myers, counsel to Presidents beginning with Woodrow Wilson and ending with Dwight Eisenhower. According to the announcement, Jason Myers had attended Brown and Harvard Law School and was already a partner in Myers & O'Malley, perhaps the oldest law firm in D.C., and certainly the stuffiest. He had created the intellectual property division and had become the youngest partner in the history of Myers & O'Malley. Other than his round eyeglasses, there appeared to be nothing intellectual about him, though Clay knew he couldn't be fair even if he wanted to. He was not unattractive but clearly no match for Rebecca.

A December wedding was planned at an Episcopal church in McLean, with a reception at the Potomac Country Club.

In less than a month she had found someone she loved enough to marry. Someone willing to stomach a life with Bennett and Barb. Someone with enough money to impress all the Van Horns.

The phone rang again and it was Paulette. 'You okay?' she asked.

'I'm fine,' he said, trying hard.

'I'm real sorry, Clay.'

'It was over, Paulette. It had been unraveling for a year. This is a good thing. Now I can forget her completely.'

'If you say so.'

'I'm okay. Thanks for calling.'

'When you coming home?'

'Today. I'll be in the office in the morning.'

The breakfast arrived but he'd forgotten that he'd ordered it. He drank some juice but ignored everything else. Maybe this little romance had been brewing for some time. All she needed was to get rid of Clay, which she'd been able to do rather easily. Her betrayal grew as the minutes passed. He could see and hear her mother pulling strings in the background, manipulating their breakup, laying the trap for Myers, now planning every detail of the wedding.

'Good riddance,' he mumbled.

Then he thought about sex, and Myers taking his place, and he threw the empty glass across the room where it hit a wall and shattered. He cursed himself for acting like an idiot.

How many people at that moment were looking at the announcement and thinking of Clay? Saying, 'Dumped him in a hurry, didn't she?' 'Boy, that was fast, wasn't it?'

Was Rebecca thinking of him? How much satisfaction did she get in admiring her wedding announcement and thinking of old Clay? Probably a lot. Maybe a little. What difference did it make? Mr. and Mrs. Van Horn had no doubt forgotten about him overnight. Why couldn't he simply return the favor?

She was rushing, that much he knew for certain. Their romance had been too long and too intense and their breakup too recent for her to simply drop him and take up with another. He'd slept with her for four years; Myers for only a month, or less, hopefully not longer.

He walked back to Jackson Square, where the artists and tarot card readers and jugglers and street musicians were already in action. He bought an ice cream and sat on a bench near the statue of Andrew Jackson. He decided that he would call her, and at least pass along his best wishes. Then he decided he would find a blonde bimbo and somehow flaunt her in front of Rebecca. Maybe he would take her to the wedding, of course in a short skirt with legs a mile long. With his money, such a woman should be easy to find. Hell, he'd rent one if he had to.

'It's over ol' boy,' he said to himself, more than once. 'Get a grip.'

Let her go.

Chapter 16

The office dress code had rapidly evolved into an anything-goes style. The tone was set by the boss who leaned toward jeans and expensive T-shirts, with a sports coat nearby in case he went to lunch. He had designer suits for meetings and court appearances, but for the moment both of those were rare events since the firm had no clients and no cases. Everyone had upgraded their wardrobes, much to his satisfaction.

They met late Monday morning in the conference room – Paulette, Rodney, and a rather rough-looking Jonah. Though she had acquired considerable clout in the short history of the firm, Miss Glick was still just a secretary/receptionist.

'Folks, we have work to do,' Clay began the meeting. He introduced them to Dyloft, and relying on Pace's concise summaries, gave a description and history of the drug. From memory, he gave the quick and dirty review of Ackerman Labs – sales, profits, cash, competitors, other legal problems. Then the good stuff –

the disastrous side effects of Dyloft, the bladder tumors, and the company's knowledge of its problems.

'As of today, no lawsuit has been filed. But we're about to change that. On July the second, we start the war by filing a class action here in D.C. on behalf of all patients harmed by the drug. It will create chaos, and we'll be right in the middle of it.'

'Do we have any of these clients?' Paulette asked.

'Not yet. But we have names and addresses. We start signing them up today. We'll develop a plan for gathering clients, then you and Rodney will be in charge of implementing it.' Though he had reservations about television advertising, he had convinced himself flying home from New Orleans that there was no viable alternative. Once he filed suit and exposed the drug, those vultures he'd just met in the Circle of Barristers would swarm to find the clients. The only effective way to quickly reach large numbers of Dyloft patients was by television ads.

He explained this to his firm and said, 'It'll cost at least two million bucks.'

'This firm has two million bucks?' Jonah blurted, saying what everyone else was thinking.

'It does. We start working on the ads today.'

'You're not doing the acting, are you, boss?' Jonah asked, almost pleading. 'Please.' Like all cities, D.C. had been flooded with early-morning and late-night commercials pleading with the injured to call lawyer so-and-so who was ready to kick ass and charged nothing for the initial consultation. Often the lawyers themselves appeared in the ads, usually with embarrassing results.

Paulette also had a frightened look and was slightly shaking her head no.

'Of course not. It'll be done by professionals.'

'How many clients are we looking at?' Rodney asked.

'Thousands. It's hard to say.'

Rodney pointed at each of them, slowly counting to four. 'According to my numbers,' he said, 'there are four of us.'

'We're adding more. Jonah is in charge of expansion. We'll lease some space out in the suburbs and fill it with paralegals. They'll work the phones and organize the files.'

'Where does one find paralegals?' Jonah asked.

'In the employment sections of the bar journals. Start working on the ads. And you've got a meeting this afternoon with a real estate agent out in Manassas. We'll need about five thousand square feet, nothing fancy, but plenty of wiring for phones and a complete computer system, which, as we know, is your speciality. Lease it, wire it, staff it, then organize it. The sooner the better.'

'Yes sir.'

'How much is a Dyloft case worth?' Paulette asked.

'As much as Ackerman Labs will pay. It could range from as little as ten thousand to as much as fifty, depending on several factors, not the least of which is the extent of the damage to the bladder.'

Paulette was working with some numbers on a legal pad. 'And how many cases might we get?'

'It's impossible to say.'

'How about a guess?'

'I don't know. Several thousand.'

'Okay, let's say that's three thousand cases. Three thousand cases times the minimum of ten thousand dollars comes to thirty million, right?' She said this slowly, scribbling the entire time.

'That's right.'

'And how much are the attorneys' fees?' she asked. The other three were watching Clay very closely.

'One third,' he said.

'That's ten million in fees,' she said slowly. 'All to this firm?'

'Yes. And we're going to share the fees.'

The word *share* echoed around the room for a few seconds. Jonah and Rodney glanced at Paulette, as if to say, 'Go ahead, finish it off.'

'Share, in what way?' she asked, very deliberately.

'Ten percent to each of you.'

'So in my hypothetical, my share of the fees would be one million?'

'That's correct.'

'And, uh, same for me?' Rodney asked.

'Same for you. Same for Jonah. And, I must say, I think that's on the low side.'

Low side or not, they absorbed the numbers

in muted silence for what seemed like a very long time, each instinctively spending some of the money. For Rodney, it meant college for the kids. For Paulette, it meant a divorce from the Greek she'd seen once in the past year. For Jonah, it meant life on a sailboat.

'You're serious, aren't you, Clay?' Jonah asked.

'Dead serious. If we work our butts off for the next year, there's a good chance we'll have the option of an early retirement.'

'Who told you about this Dyloft?' Rodney asked.

'I can never answer that question, Rodney. Sorry. Just trust me.' And Clay hoped at that moment that his blind trust in Max Pace was not foolish.

'I almost forgot about Paris,' Paulette said.

'Don't. We'll be there next week.'

Jonah jumped to his feet and grabbed his legal pad. 'What's that Realtor's name?' he asked.

On the third floor of his town house, Clay had put together a small office, not that he planned to do much work there but he needed a place for his papers. The desk was an old butcher block he'd found in an antique store in Fredericksburg, just down the road. It consumed one wall and was long enough for a phone, a fax, and a laptop.

It was there that he made his first tentative entry into the world of mass tort solicitation. He delayed the call until almost 9 P.M., an hour at which some folks went to bed, especially older ones and perhaps those afflicted with arthritis. A stiff drink for courage, and he punched the numbers.

The phone was answered on the other end by a woman, perhaps Mrs. Ted Worley of Upper Marlboro, Maryland. Clay introduced himself pleasantly, identified himself as a lawyer, as if they called all the time and there was nothing to be alarmed about, and asked to speak to Mr. Worley.

'He's watching the Orioles,' she said. Evidently Ted didn't take calls when the Orioles were playing.

'Yes – would it be possible to speak to him for a moment?'

'You say you're a lawyer?'

'Yes ma'am, from right here in D.C.'

'What's he done now?'

'Oh, nothing, nothing at all. I'd like to talk to him about his arthritis.' The first impulse to hang up and run came and went. Clay thanked God no one was watching or listening. Think of the money, he kept telling himself. Think of the fees.

'His arthritis? Thought you were a lawyer, not a doctor.'

'Yes ma'am, I'm a lawyer, and I have reason to believe he's taking a dangerous drug for his arthritis. If you don't mind, I just need him for a second.'

Voices in the background as she yelled something to Ted who yelled something back. Finally, he took the phone. 'Who is this?' he demanded, and Clay quickly introduced himself.

'What's the score?' Clay asked.

'Three–one Red Sox in the fifth. Do I know you?' Mr. Worley was seventy years old.

'No sir. I'm an attorney here in D.C., and I specialize in lawsuits involving defective drugs. I sue drug companies all the time when they put out harmful products.'

'Okay, what do you want?'

'Through our Internet sources we found your name as a potential user of an arthritis drug called Dyloft. Can you tell me if you use this drug?'

'Maybe I don't want to tell you what pre-scriptions I'm taking.'

A perfectly valid point, one Clay thought he was ready for.

'Of course you don't have to, Mr. Worley. But the only way to determine if you're entitled to a settlement is to tell me if you're using the drug.'

'That damned Internet,' Mr. Worley mumbled, then had a quick conversation with his wife who, evidently, was somewhere near the phone.

'What kind of settlement?' he asked.

'Let's talk about that in a minute. I need to know if you're using Dyloft. If not, then you're a lucky man.'

'Well, uh, I guess it's not a secret, is it?'

'No sir.' Of course it was a secret. Why should a person's medical history be anything but con-fidential? The little fibs were necessary, Clay kept telling himself. Look at the big picture. Mr. Worley and thousands like him might never know they're using a bad product unless they were told.

Ackerman Labs certainly hadn't come clean. That was Clay's job.

'Yeah, I take Dyloft.'

'For how long?'

'Maybe a year. It works great.'

'Any side effects?'

'Such as?'

'Blood in your urine. A burning sensation when you urinate.' Clay was resigned to the fact that he would be discussing bladders and urine with many people in the months to come. There was simply no way around it.

The things they don't prepare you for in law school.

'No. Why?'

'We have some preliminary research that Ackerman Labs, the company that makes Dyloft, is trying to cover up. The drug has been found to cause bladder tumors in some of the folks who use it.'

And so Mr. Ted Worley, who just moments earlier had been minding his own business and watching his beloved Orioles, would now spend the rest of that night and most of the next week worrying about tumors growing wild in his bladder. Clay felt rotten and wanted to apologize, but, again, he told himself that it had to be done. How else might Mr. Worley learn the truth? If the poor man indeed had the tumors, wouldn't he want to know about them?

Holding the phone with one hand and rubbing his side with the other, Mr. Worley said, 'You know, come to think of it, I do remember a burning sensation a couple of days ago.'

'What are you talking about?' Clay heard Mrs. Worley say in the background.

'If you don't mind,' Mr. Worley said to Mrs. Worley.

Clay charged in before the bickering got out of hand. 'My firm represents a lot of Dyloft users. I think you should consider getting tested.'

'What kind of test?'

'It's a urinalysis. We have a doctor who can do it tomorrow. Won't cost you a dime.'

'What if he finds something wrong?'

'Then we can discuss your options. When the news of Dyloft comes out, in just a few days, there will be many lawsuits. My firm will be a leader in the attack on Ackerman Labs. I'd like to have you as a client.'

'Maybe I should talk to my doctor.'

'You can certainly do that, Mr. Worley. But he may have some liability too. He prescribed the drug. It might be best if you get an unbiased opinion.'

'Hang on.' Mr. Worley covered the receiver with his hand and had a contentious chat with his wife. When he returned he said, 'I don't believe in suing doctors.'

'Nor do I. I specialize in going after the big corporations that harm people.'

'Should I stop taking the drug?'

'Let's do the test first. Dyloft will likely be pulled off the market sometime this summer.'

'Where do I do the test?'

'The doctor is in Chevy Chase. Can you go tomorrow?'

'Yeah, sure, why not? Seems silly to wait, doesn't it?'

'Yes, it does.' Clay gave him the name and address of a doctor Max Pace had located. The $80 exam would cost Clay $300 a pop, but it was simply the price of doing business.

When the details were finished, Clay apologized for the intrusion, thanked him for his time, and left him to suffer while he watched the rest of the game. Only when he hung up did Clay feel the beads of moisture just above his eyebrows. Soliciting cases by phone? What kind of lawyer had he become?

A rich one, he kept telling himself.

This would require thick skin, something Clay did not possess and was not certain he could develop.

Two days later, Clay pulled into the Worleys' driveway in Upper Marlboro and met them at the front door. The urinalysis, which included a cytological exam, revealed abnormal cells in the urine, a clear sign, according to Max Pace and his extensive and ill-gotten medical research, that there were tumors in the bladder. Mr. Worley had been referred to a urologist whom he would see the following week. The examination and removal of the tumors would be by cystoscopic surgery, running a tiny scope and a knife in a tube through

186

the penis into the bladder, and while this was purported to be fairly routine, Mr. Worley saw nothing ordinary about it. He was worried sick. Mrs. Worley said he hadn't slept the last two nights, nor had she.

As much as he wanted to, Clay could not tell them that the tumors were probably benign. Better to let the doctors do that after the surgery.

Over instant coffee with powdered creamer, Clay explained the contract for his services and answered their questions about the litigation. When Ted Worley signed at the bottom, he became the first Dyloft plaintiff in the country.

And for a while it seemed as if he might be the only one. Working the phones nonstop, Clay succeeded in convincing eleven people to show up for the urinalysis. All eleven tested negative. 'Keep pushing,' Max Pace urged. About a third of the people either hung up or refused to believe Clay was serious about what he was saying.

He, Paulette, and Rodney divided their lists between black-and-white prospective clients. Evidently blacks were not as suspicious as whites because they were easier to persuade to go see the doctor. Or perhaps they enjoyed the medical attention. Or maybe, as Paulette suggested more than once, she had the better gift of gab.

By the end of the week, Clay had signed up three clients who tested positive for abnormal cells. Rodney and Paulette, working as a team, had seven more under contract.

The Dyloft class action was ready for war.

Chapter 17

The Paris adventure cost him $95,300, according to the numbers so carefully kept by Rex Crittle, a man who was becoming more and more familiar with almost all aspects of Clay's life. Crittle was a CPA with a mid-sized accounting firm situated directly under the Carter suite. Not surprisingly, he too had been referred by Max Pace.

At least once a week, Clay walked down the back stairs or Crittle walked up them, and they spent a half an hour or so talking about Clay's money and how to properly handle it. An accounting system for the law firm was basic and easily installed. Miss Glick made all the entries and simply ran them down to Crittle's computers.

In Crittle's opinion, such sudden wealth would almost certainly trigger an audit by the Internal Revenue Service. Notwithstanding Pace's promises to the contrary, Clay agreed and insisted on perfect records with no gray areas when it came to write-offs and deductions. He had just earned more money than he'd ever dreamed of. No sense trying to beat the government out of some taxes. Pay them and sleep well.

'What's this payment to East Media for half a million dollars?' Crittle asked.

'We're doing some television ads for litigation. That's the first installment.'

'Installment? How many more?' He peered over his reading glasses and gave Clay a look he'd seen before. It said, 'Son, have you lost your mind?'

'A total of two million dollars. We're filing a big lawsuit in a few days. The filing will be co-ordinated with an advertising blitz that East Media is handling.'

'Okay,' Crittle said, obviously wary of such large expenditures. 'And I'm assuming there will be some additional fees to cover all this.'

'Hopefully,' Clay said with a laugh.

'What about this new office out in Manassas? A lease deposit of fifteen thousand bucks?'

'Yes, we're expanding. I'm adding six paralegals in an office out there. Rent's cheaper.'

'Nice to see you're worried about expenses. Six paralegals?'

'Yes, four have been hired. I have their contracts and payroll information on my desk.'

Crittle studied a printout for a moment, a dozen questions clicking through the calculator behind his glasses. 'Could I ask why you need six more paralegals when you have so few cases?'

'Now that's an interesting question,' Clay said. He blitzed through the pending class action without mentioning either the drug or its maker, and if his quick summary answered Crittle's questions it wasn't obvious. As an accountant, he was naturally skeptical of any scheme that urged more people to sue.

'I'm sure you know what you're doing,' he said, suspecting Clay had, in fact, lost his mind.

'Trust me, Rex, the money is about to pour in.'

'It's certainly pouring out.'

'You have to spend money to make money.'

'That's what they say.'

The assault began just after sundown on July 1. With everyone but Miss Glick gathered in front of the television in the conference room, they waited until exactly 8:32 P.M., then grew quiet and still. It was a fifteen-second ad that began with a shot of a handsome young actor wearing a white jacket and holding a thick book and looking sincerely at the camera. 'Attention arthritis sufferers. If you are taking the prescription drug Dyloft, you may have a claim against the manufacturer of the drug. Dyloft has been linked to several side effects, including tumors in the bladder.' On the bottom of the screen the bold words: DYLOFT HOT LINE – CALL 1-800-555-DYLO appeared. The doctor continued: 'Call this number immediately. The Dyloft Hot Line can arrange a free medical test for you. Call now!'

No one breathed for fifteen seconds, and no one spoke when it was over. For Clay, it was a particularly harrowing moment because he had just launched a vicious and potentially crippling attack against a mammoth corporation, one that would undoubtedly respond with a vengeance. What if Max Pace was wrong about the drug? What if Pace was using Clay as a pawn in a huge corporate chess match? What if Clay couldn't prove, by expert witnesses, that the drug caused the tumors? He had wrestled with these questions for several weeks, and he had quizzed Pace a thousand times. They had fought twice and exchanged sharp words on several occasions. Max had eventually handed over the stolen, or at least ill-gotten, research on the effects of Dyloft. Clay had had it reviewed by a fraternity brother from Georgetown who was now a physician in Baltimore. The research looked solid and sinister.

Clay had ultimately convinced himself that he was right and Ackerman was wrong. But seeing the ad and flinching at its accusation made him weak in the knees.

'Pretty nasty,' said Rodney, who'd seen the video of the ad a dozen times. Still, it was much harsher on real television. East Media had promised that sixteen percent of each market would see each ad. The ads would run every other day for ten days in ninety markets from coast to coast. The estimated audience was eighty million.

'It'll work,' Clay said, ever the leader.

For the first hour, it ran on stations in thirty markets along the East Coast, then it spread to eighteen markets in the Central Time Zone. Four hours after it began, it finally reached the other coast and hit in forty-two markets. Clay's little firm spent just over $400,000 the first night in wall-to-wall advertising.

The 800 phone number routed callers to the Sweatshop, the new nickname for the shopping center branch of the Law Offices of J. Clay Carter II. There, the six new paralegals took the calls, filled out forms, asked all the scripted questions, referred the callers to the Dyloft Hot Line Web Site, and promised return calls from one of the staff attorneys. Within two hours of the first ads, all phones were busy. A computer recorded the numbers of those callers unable to get through. A computerized message referred them to the Web site.

At nine the next morning, Clay received an urgent phone call from an attorney in a large firm down the street. He represented Ackerman Labs and insisted that the ads be stopped immediately. He was pompous and condescending and threatened all manner of vile legal action if Clay did not buckle immediately. Words grew harsh, then calmed somewhat.

'Are you going to be in your office for a few minutes?' Clay asked.

'Yes, of course. Why?'

'I have something to send over. I'll get my courier. Should take five minutes.'

Rodney, the courier, hustled down the street with a copy of the twenty-page lawsuit. Clay left for the courthouse to file the original. Pursuant to Pace's instructions, copies were also being faxed to the *Washington Post,* the *Wall Street Journal,* and the *New York Times.*

Pace had also hinted that short-selling Ackerman Labs stock would be a shrewd investment move. The stock had closed the Friday before at $42.50. When it opened Monday morning, Clay placed a sell order for a hundred thousand shares. He'd buy it back in a few days, hopefully around $30, and pick up another million bucks. That was the plan, anyway.

His office was hectic when he returned. There were six incoming toll-free lines to the Sweatshop out in Manassas, and during working hours, when all six were busy, the calls were routed to the main office on Connecticut Avenue. Rodney, Paulette, and Jonah were each on the phone talking to Dyloft users scattered around North America.

'You might want to see this,' Miss Glick said. The pink message slip listed the name of a reporter from the *Wall Street Journal.* 'And Mr Pace is in your office.'

Max was holding a coffee cup and standing in front of a window.

'It's filed,' Clay said. 'We've stirred up a hornet's nest.'

'Enjoy the moment.'

'Their lawyers have already called. I sent them a copy of the lawsuit.'

'Good. They're dying already. They've just been ambushed and they know they'll get slaughtered.

This is a lawyer's dream, Clay, make the most of it.'

'Sit down. I have a question.'

Pace, in black as always, fell into a chair and crossed his legs. The cowboy boots appeared to be of rattlesnake.

'If Ackerman Labs hired you right now, what would you do?' Clay asked.

'Spin is crucial. I'd start the press releases, deny everything, blame it on greedy trial lawyers. Defend my drug. The initial goal, after the bomb goes off and the dust is settling, is to protect the stock price. It opened at forty-two and a half, which was very low; it's already at thirty-three. I'd get the CEO on television to say all the right things. I'd get the PR folks cranking out the propaganda. I'd get the lawyers preparing an organized defense. I'd get the sales people to reassure the doctors that the drug is okay.'

'But the drug is not okay.'

'I'd worry about that later. For the first few days, it's all spin, at least on the surface. If investors believe there's something wrong with the drug, they'll jump ship and the stock will keep falling. Once the spin is in place, I would have a serious talk with the big boys. Once I found out that there were problems with the drug, then I'd bring in the number-crunchers and figure out how much the settlements will cost. You never go to trial with a bad drug. Each jury can fill in the blank for a verdict, and there's no way to control the costs. One jury gives the plaintiff a million bucks. The next jury in another state gets mad and awards twenty million in punitive damages. It's a huge crapshoot. So you settle. As you are quickly learning, mass tort lawyers take their percentages off the top, so they're easy to settle with.'

'How much cash can Ackerman afford?'

'They're insured for at least three hundred million. Plus they have about a half billion in cash, most of it generated by Dyloft. They're almost maxed out at the bank, but if I were calling the shots I'd plan on paying a billion. And I would do it fast.'

'Will Ackerman do it fast?'

'They haven't hired me, so they're not too bright. I've watched the company for a long time, and they're not particularly sharp. Like all drugmakers, they're horrified of litigation. Instead of using a fireman like me, they do it the old-fashioned way – they rely on their lawyers, who, of course, have no interest in quick settlements. The principal firm is Walker-Stearns in New York. You'll hear from them very shortly.'

'So no quick settlement?'

'You filed suit less than an hour ago. Relax.'

'I know, but I'm burning up all that money you just gave me.'

'Take it easy. Within a year you'll be even richer.'

'A year, huh?'

'That's my guess. The lawyers have to get fat first. Walker-Stearns will put fifty associates on the case with meters churning at full blast. Mr.

Worley's class action is worth a hundred million bucks to Ackerman's own lawyers. Don't ever forget that.'

'Why don't they just pay me a hundred million bucks to go away?'

'Now you're thinking like a real mass tort boy. They'll pay you even more, but first they have to pay their lawyers. That's just the way it works.'

'But you wouldn't do it that way?'

'Of course not. With Tarvan, the client told me the truth, which seldom happens. I did my homework, found you, and wrapped up everything quietly, quickly, and cheaply. Fifty million, and not a dime to my client's own lawyers.'

Miss Glick appeared in the door and said, 'That reporter from the *Wall Street Journal* is on the phone again.' Clay looked at Pace who said, 'Chat him up. And remember, the other side has an entire PR unit cranking out the spin.'

The *Times* and the *Post* ran brief stories of the Dyloft class action on the front pages of their business sections the following morning. Both mentioned Clay's name, which was a thrill he quietly relished. More ink was given to the defendant's responses. The CEO called the lawsuit 'frivolous' and 'just another example of litigation abuse by the legal profession.' The Vice President for Research said, 'Dyloft had been thoroughly researched with no evidence of adverse side effects.' Both newspapers noted that Ackerman Labs' stock, which had dropped by 50 percent in the three preceding quarters, had taken another blow by the surprise lawsuit.

The *Wall Street Journal* got it right, at least in Clay's opinion. In the preliminaries, the reporter had asked Clay his age. 'Only thirty-one?' he'd said, which led to a series of questions about Clay's experience, his firm, etcetera. David versus Goliath is much more readable than dry financial data or lab reports, and the story took on a life of its own. A photographer was rushed over, and while Clay posed his staff watched with great amusement.

On the front page, far left column, the headline read: THE ROOKIE TAKES ON MIGHTY ACKERMAN LABS. Beside it was a computerized caricature of a smiling Clay Carter. The first paragraph read: 'Less than two months ago, D.C. attorney Clay Carter was laboring through the city's criminal justice system as an unknown and low paid public defender. Yesterday, as the owner of his own law firm, he filed a billion-dollar lawsuit against the third-largest pharmaceutical company in the world, claiming its newest wonder drug, Dyloft, not only relieves acute pain for arthritis sufferers but also causes tumors in their bladders.'

The article was filled with questions about how Clay had made such a radical transformation so quickly. And since he couldn't mention Tarvan or anything related to it, he vaguely referred to the quick settlements of some lawsuits involving people he'd met as a public defender. Ackerman Labs got in a few licks with its typical posturing about lawsuit abuse and ambulance chasers ruining the economy, but the bulk of the story was about Clay and his amazing rise to the forefront of mass tort litigation. Nice things were said about his father, a 'legendary D.C. litigator' who had since 'retired' to the Bahamas.

Glenda at OPD praised Clay as a 'zealous defender of the poor,' a classy remark that would get her lunch in a fancy restaurant. The President of the National Trial Lawyers Academy admitted he had never heard of Clay Carter, but was nonetheless 'very impressed with his work.'

A law professor at Yale lamented 'yet another example of the misuse of class-action litigation,' while one at Harvard said it was 'a perfect example of how class actions should be used to pursue corporate wrongdoers.'

'Make sure this gets on the Web site,' Clay said as he handed the article to Jonah. 'Our clients will love it.'

Chapter 18

Tequila Watson pleaded guilty to the murder of Ramón Pumphrey and was sentenced to life in prison. He would be eligible for parole in twenty years, though the story in the *Post* did not mention that. It did say that his victim had been one of several gunned down in a spate of killings that had seemed unusually random even for a city accustomed to senseless violence. The police had no explanations. Clay made a note to call Adelfa and see how her life was going.

He owed something to Tequila, but he wasn't sure what. Nor was there any way of compensating his ex-client. He rationalized that he had spent most of his life on drugs and would probably spend the rest behind bars anyway, with or without Tarvan, but this did little to make Clay feel honorable. He had sold out, plain and simple. He'd taken the cash and buried the truth.

Two pages over another article caught his attention and made him forget about Tequila Watson. Mr. Bennett Van Horn's pudgy face was in a photo, under his monogrammed hard hat, taken at a job site somewhere. He was intently staring at a set of plans with another man who was identified as the project engineer for BVH Group. The company had become embroiled in a nasty fight over a proposed development near the Chancellorsville battlefield, about an hour south of D.C. Bennett, as always, was proposing one of his hideous collections of houses, condos, apartments, shops, playgrounds, tennis courts, and the obligatory pond, all within a mile of the center of the battlefield and very near the spot where General Stonewall Jackson was shot by Confederate sentries. Preservationists, lawyers, war historians, environmentalists, and the Confederate Society had drawn swords and were in the process of shredding Bennett the Bulldozer. Not surprisingly, the *Post* praised these groups while saying nothing good about Bennett. However, the land in question was privately owned by some aging farmers, and he appeared to have the upper hand, at least for the moment.

The article ran long with accounts of other battlefields throughout Virginia that had been paved by developers. An outfit called the Civil War Trust had taken the lead in fighting back. Its lawyer was portrayed as a radical who was unafraid to use litigation to preserve history. 'But we need money to litigate,' he was quoted as saying.

Two calls later and Clay had him on the phone. They talked for half an hour, and when he hung up he wrote a check for $100,000 to the Civil War Trust, Chancellorsville Litigation Fund.

Miss Glick handed him the phone message as he walked by her desk. He looked at the name twice, and was still skeptical when he sat in the conference room and punched the numbers. 'Mr Patton French,' he said into the phone. The message slip said it was urgent.

'And who's calling, please?'

'Clay Carter, from D.C.'

'Oh yes, he's been expecting you.'

The image of such a powerful and busy lawyer as Patton French waiting for Clay's phone call was difficult to imagine. Within seconds the great man himself was on the phone. 'Hello, Clay, thanks for calling me back,' he said so casually Clay was caught off-guard. 'Nice story in the *Journal*, huh? Not bad for a rookie. Look, sorry I didn't get to say hello when you were down in New Orleans.' It was the same voice he'd heard from behind the microphone, but much more relaxed.

'No problem,' Clay said. There were two hundred lawyers at the Circle of Barristers gathering. There had been no reason for Clay to meet Patton French, and no reason French should know Clay was even there. He had obviously done his research.

'I'd like to meet you, Clay. I think we can do some business together. I was on the Dyloft trail two months ago. You beat me to the punch, but there's a ton of money out there.'

Clay had no desire to crawl into bed with Patton French. On the other hand, his methods of extracting huge settlements from drug companies were legendary. 'We can talk,' Clay said.

'Look, I'm headed to New York right now. What if I pick you up in D.C. and take you with me? I got a new Gulfstream 5 I'd love to show off. We'll stay in Manhattan, have a wonderful dinner tonight. Talk business. Back home late tomorrow. Whatta you say?'

'Well, I'm pretty busy.' Clay vividly remembered his revulsion in New Orleans when French kept mentioning his toys in his speech. The new Gulfstream, the yacht, a castle in Scotland.

'I'll bet you are. Look, I'm busy too. Hell, we're all busy. But this could be the most profitable trip you'll ever make. I'm not taking no for an answer. I'll meet you at Reagan National in three hours. Deal?'

Other than a few phone calls and a game of racquetball that night, Clay had little to do. The office phones were ringing nonstop with frightened Dyloft users, but Clay was not fielding the calls. He hadn't been to New York in several years. 'Sure, why not?' he said, as anxious to see a Gulfstream 5 as he was to eat in a great restaurant.

'Smart move, Clay. Smart move.'

The private terminal at Reagan National was packed with harried executives and bureaucrats hustling through, coming and going. Near the reception counter, a cute brunette in a short skirt held a handmade placard with his name on it. He introduced himself to her. She was Julia, with no last name. 'Follow me,' she said with a perfect smile. They were cleared through an exit door and driven across the ramp in a courtesy van. Dozens of Lears, Falcons, Hawkers, Challengers, and Citations were either parked or were taxiing to and from the terminal. Ramp crews carefully guided the jets past each other, their wings missing by inches. Engines screamed and the entire scene was nerve-racking.

'Where you from?' Clay asked.

'We're based out of Biloxi,' Julia said. 'That's where Mr French has his main office.'

'I heard him speak a couple of weeks ago in New Orleans.'

'Yes, we were there. We're seldom at home.'

'He puts in the hours, doesn't he?'

'About a hundred a week.'

They stopped beside the largest jet on the ramp. 'That's us,' Julia said, and they got out of the van. A pilot grabbed Clay's overnight bag and disappeared with it.

Patton French was, of course, on the phone. He waved Clay aboard while Julia took his jacket and asked him what he wanted to drink. Just water, with lemon. His first view inside a private jet could not have been more breathtaking. The videos he had seen in New Orleans didn't do justice to the real thing.

The aroma was that of leather, very expensive leather. The seats, sofas, headrests, panels, even the tables were done in various shades of blue and tan leather. The light fixtures and knobs and gadget controls were gold-plated. The wood trim was dark and deeply polished, probably mahogany. It was a luxury suite in a five-star hotel, but with wings and engines.

Clay was an even six feet tall, and there was room to spare above his head. The cabin was long with some type of office in the rear. French was way back there, still talking into a telephone. The bar and the kitchen were just behind the cockpit. Julia emerged with his water. 'Better have a seat,' she said. 'We're about to taxi.'

When the plane began moving, French abruptly ended his conversation and charged forward. He attacked Clay with a violent handshake and toothy smile and another apology for not getting together down in New Orleans. He was a bit heavy, graying nicely with thick, wavy hair, probably fifty-five but not yet sixty. Vigor oozed from every pore and breath.

They sat across from each other at one of the tables.

'Nice ride, huh?' French said, waving his left arm at the interior.

'Pretty nice.'

'You got a jet yet?'

'No.' And he actually felt inadequate because he was jetless. What kind of a lawyer was he?

'It won't be long, son. You can't live without one. Julia, get me a vodka. This makes four for me, jets, not vodkas. Takes twelve pilots to keep four jets going. And five Julias. She's cute, huh?'

'She is.'

'Lots of overhead, but then there's lots of fees out there. Did you hear me speak in New Orleans?'

'I did. It was very enjoyable.' Clay lied a little. As obnoxious as French had been from the podium, he'd also been entertaining and informative.

'I hate to dwell on money like that, but I was playing to the crowd. Most of those guys will eventually bring me a big tort case. Gotta keep 'em pumped up, you know. I've built the hottest mass tort firm in America, and all we do is go after the big boys. When you sue companies like Ackerman Labs and any of those Fortune 500 outfits, you gotta have some ammunition, some clout. Their cash is endless. I'm just trying to level the field.'

Julia brought his drink and strapped herself in for takeoff.

'You want some lunch?' French asked. 'She can cook anything.'

'No thanks. I'm fine.'

French took a long swig of the vodka, then suddenly sat back, closed his eyes, and appeared to be praying as the Gulfstream sped down the runway and lifted off. Clay used the break to admire the airplane. It was so luxurious and richly detailed that it was almost obscene. Forty, forty-five million dollars for a private jet! And, according to the gossip among the Circle of

205

Barristers, the Gulfstream company couldn't make them fast enough. There was a two-year backlog!

Minutes passed until they leveled off, then Julia disappeared into the kitchen. French snapped out of his meditation, took another gulp. 'Is all that stuff in the *Journal* true?' he asked, much calmer. Clay had the quick impression that with French the mood swings were rapid and dramatic.

'They got it right.'

'I've been on the front page twice, nothing ever good. No surprise that they don't like us mass tort boys. Nobody does, really, which is something you'll learn. The money takes the sting out of the negative image. You'll get used to it. We all do. I actually met your father once.' His eyes squinted and darted when he talked, as if he was constantly thinking three sentences ahead.

'Really?' Clay wasn't sure he believed him.

'I was with the Justice Department twenty years ago. We were litigating over some Indian lands. The Indians brought in Jarrett Carter from D.C. and the war was over. He was very good.'

'Thank you,' Clay said, with immense pride.

'I gotta tell you, Clay, this Dyloft ambush of yours is a thing of beauty. And very unusual. In most cases, word of a bad drug spreads slowly as more and more patients complain. Doctors are slow as hell in communicating. They're in bed with the drug companies, so they have no incentive to raise the red flag. Plus, in most jurisdictions, the doctors get sued because they prescribed the drug in the first place. Slowly, the lawyers get involved. Uncle Luke has suddenly got blood in his urine for no reason, and after staring at it for a month or so he'll go to his doctor down in Podunk, Louisiana. And the doctor will eventually take him off whatever new miracle drug he had prescribed. Uncle Luke may or may not go see the family lawyer, usually a small-town ham-and-egger who does wills and divorces and in most cases wouldn't know a decent tort if one hit him. It takes time for these bad drugs to get discovered. What you've done is very unique.'

Clay was content to nod and listen. French was content to do the talking. This was leading somewhere.

'Which tells me that you have some inside information.' A pause, a brief gap in which Clay was given the opportunity to confirm that he did indeed have inside information. But he offered no clue.

'I have a vast network of lawyers and contacts from coast to coast. No one, not a single one, had heard of problems with Dyloft until a few weeks ago. I had two lawyers in my firm doing the preliminary workup on the drug, but we were nowhere close to filing suit. Next thing I see is news of your ambush and your smiling face on the front page of the *Wall Street Journal*. I know how the game is played, Clay, and I know you have something from the inside.'

'I do. And I'll never tell anybody.'

'Good. That makes me feel better. I saw your

ads. We monitor such things in every market. Not bad. In fact, the fifteen-second method you're using has been proven as the most effective. Did you know that?'

'No.'

'Hit 'em fast late at night, early in the morning. A quick message to scare them, then a phone number where they can get help. I've done it a thousand times. How many cases have you generated?'

'It's hard to say. They have to do the initial urinalysis. The phones have not stopped ringing.'

'My ads start tomorrow. I have six people in-house who do nothing but work on advertising, can you believe that? Six full-time ad folks. And they're not cheap.'

Julia appeared with two platters of food – a shrimp tray and one covered with cheeses and various meats – prosciutto, salami, and several more Clay could not name. 'A bottle of that Chilean white,' Patton said. 'It should be chilled by now.'

'Do you like wine?' he asked, grabbing a shrimp by its tail.

'Some. I'm no expert.'

'I adore wine. I keep a hundred bottles on this airplane.' Another shrimp. 'Anyway, we figure there are between fifty and a hundred thousand Dyloft cases. That sound close?'

'A hundred might be on the high side,' Clay said cautiously.

'I'm a little worried about Ackerman Labs. I've sued them twice before, you know?'

'I didn't know that.'

'Ten years ago, back when they had plenty of cash. They went through a couple of bad CEOs who made some bad acquisitions. Now they have ten billion in debt. Stupid stuff. Typical of the 1990s. Banks were throwing money at the blue-chips, who took it and tried to buy the world. Anyway, Ackerman is not in danger of bankruptcy or anything like that. And they've got some insurance.' French was fishing here and Clay decided to take the bait.

'They have at least three hundred million in insurance,' he said. 'And perhaps half a billion to spend on Dyloft.'

French smiled and almost drooled over this information. He could not and did not try to hide his admiration. 'Great stuff, son, wonderful stuff. How good is your inside dirt?'

'Excellent. We have insiders who'll spill the beans, and we have lab reports that we're not supposed to have. Ackerman cannot get near a jury with Dyloft.'

'Awesome,' he said as he closed his eyes and absorbed these words. A starving lawyer with his first decent car wreck could not have been happier.

Julia was back with the wine, which she poured into two priceless small goblets. French sniffed it properly and evaluated it slowly and when he was satisfied he took a sip. He smacked his lips and nodded his head, then leaned in for more gossip. 'There is a thrill in catching a big, rich, proud corporation doing something dirty that is better than sex, Clay, better than sex. It's the biggest thrill I know. You catch the greedy bastards putting out bad products that harm innocent people, and you, the lawyer, get to punish them. It's what I live for. Sure, the money is sensational, but the money comes after you've caught them. I'll never stop, regardless of how much money I make. People think I'm greedy because I could quit and go live on a beach for the rest of my life. Boring! I'd rather work a hundred hours a week trying to catch the big crooks. It's my life.'

At that moment, his zeal was contagious. His face glowed with fanaticism. He exhaled heavily, then said, 'You like this wine?'

'No, it tastes like kerosene,' Clay said.

'You're right. Julia! Flush this! Bring us a bottle of that Meursault we picked up yesterday.'

First, though, she brought a phone. 'It's Muriel.' French grabbed it and said, 'Hello.'

Julia leaned down and, almost in a whisper, said, 'Muriel is the head secretary, Mother Superior. She gets through when his wives cannot.'

French slapped the phone shut and said, 'Let me trot out a scenario for you, Clay. And I promise you it is designed to get you more money in a shorter period of time. Much more.'

'I'm listening.'

'I'll end up with as many Dyloft cases as you. Now that you've opened the door, there will be hundreds of lawyers chasing these cases. We, you and I, can control the litigation if we move your

210

lawsuit from D.C. to my backyard in Mississippi. That will terrify Ackerman Labs beyond anything you can imagine. They're worried now because you've nailed them in D.C., but they're also thinking, "Well, he's just a rookie, never been here before, never handled a mass tort case, this is his first class action," and so on. But if we put your cases with mine, combine everything into one class action, and move it to Mississippi, then Ackerman Labs will have one, huge, massive corporate coronary.'

Clay was almost dizzy with doubt and with questions. 'I'm listening,' was all he could manage.

'You keep your cases, I keep mine. We pool them, and as the other cases are signed up and the lawyers come on board, I'll go to the trial judge and ask him to appoint a Plaintiffs' Steering Committee. Do it all the time. I'll be the chairman. You'll be on the committee because you filed first. We'll monitor the Dyloft litigation, try and keep things organized, though with a bunch of arrogant lawyers it's hard as hell. I've done it dozens of times. The committee gives us control. We'll start negotiating with Ackerman pretty soon. I know their lawyers. If your inside dope is as strong as you say, we push hard for an early settlement.'

'How early?'

'Depends on several factors. How many cases are really out there? How quickly can we sign them up? How many other lawyers jump in the fray? And, very important, how severe are the damages to our clients?'

211

'Not very severe. Virtually all the tumors are benign.'

French absorbed this, frowning at first at the bad news, then quickly seeing the good. 'Even better. Treatment is cystoscopic surgery.'

'Correct. An outpatient procedure that can be done for about a thousand dollars.'

'And the long-term prognosis?'

'A clean bill. Stay away from Dyloft and life returns to normal, which for some of these arthritis sufferers is not pleasant.'

French sniffed his wine, swirled it in his goblet, and finally took a sip. 'Much better, don't you think?'

'Yes,' Clay said.

'I did a wine-tasting tour in Burgundy last year. Spent a week sniffing and spitting. Very enjoyable.' Another sip as he pondered and prioritized the next three thoughts, without spitting.

'That's even better,' French said. 'Better for our clients, obviously, because they're not as sick as they could be. Better for us because the settlements will come faster. The key here is getting the cases. The more cases we get, the more control we have over the class action. More cases, more fees.'

'I got it.'

'How much are you spending on advertising?'

'Couple of million.'

'Not bad, not bad at all.' French wanted to ask where, exactly, did a rookie get $2 million for advertising? But he controlled himself and let it pass.

There was a noticeable reduction in power as

the nose dipped slightly. 'How long to New York?' Clay asked.

'From D.C., about forty minutes. This little bird does six hundred miles an hour.'

'Which airport?'

'Teterboro, it's in New Jersey. All the private jets go there.'

'So that's why I haven't heard of it.'

'Your jet's on the way, Clay, get ready for it. You could take away all my toys, just leave me a jet. You gotta have one.'

'I'll just use yours.'

'Start off with a little Lear. You can buy them all day long for a couple of million. You need two pilots, seventy-five grand each. It's just part of the overhead. Gotta have it. You'll see.'

For the first time in his life, Clay was getting jet advice.

Julia removed the trays of food and said they would be landing in five minutes. Clay became entranced by the view of the Manhattan skyline to the east. French fell asleep.

They landed and taxied past a row of private terminals, where dozens of handsome jets were either parked or being serviced. 'You'll see more private jets here than in any other place in the world,' French explained as both looked out the windows. 'All the big boys in Manhattan park their planes here. It's a forty-five-minute drive into the city. If you really have the fuzz, you have your own helicopter to take you from here to the city. That's only ten minutes.'

'Do we have a helicopter?' Clay asked.

'No. But if I lived here, I would have one.'

A limo fetched them on the ramp, just a few feet from where they stepped off the plane. The pilots and Julia stayed behind, tidying up and no doubt making sure the wine was chilled for the next flight.

'The Peninsula,' French said to the driver.

'Yes sir, Mr. French,' he replied. Was this a rented limo or one owned by Patton himself? Surely, the world's greatest mass tort lawyer wouldn't use a car service. Clay decided to let it pass. What difference did it make?

'I'm curious about your ads,' French said, as they moved through the congestion of New Jersey. 'When did you start running them?'

'Sunday night, in ninety markets, coast to coast.'

'How are you processing them?'

'Nine people working the phones – seven paralegals, two lawyers. We took two thousand calls Monday, three thousand yesterday. Our Dyloft Web site is getting eight thousand hits each day. Assuming the usual hit ratio, that's about a thousand clients already.'

'And the pool is how big?'

'Fifty to seventy-five thousand, according to my source, who so far has been pretty accurate.'

'I'd like to meet your source.'

'Forget it.'

French cracked his knuckles and tried to accept this rejection. 'We have to get these cases, Clay.

My ads start tomorrow. What if we divide the country? You take the North and East, give me the South and West. It'll be easier to target smaller markets, and much easier to handle the cases. There's a guy in Miami who'll be on television within days. And there's one in California who, I promise you, is copying your ads right now. We're sharks, okay, nothing but vultures. The race is on for the courthouse, Clay. We have one helluva head start, but the stampede is coming.'

'I'm doing the best I can.'

'Give me your budget,' French said, as if he and Clay had been in business for years.

What the hell, Clay thought. Sitting in the back of the limo together, they certainly seemed like partners. 'Two million for advertising, another two million for the urinalyses.'

'Here's what we'll do,' French said without the slightest gap in the conversation. 'Spend all your money on advertising. Get the damned cases, okay! I'll front the money for the urinalyses, all of it, and we'll make Ackerman Labs reimburse us when we settle. That's a normal part of every settlement, to make the company cover all medicals.'

'The tests are three hundred dollars each.'

'You're getting screwed. I'll put some technicians together and we'll do it much cheaper.' Which reminded French of a story, one about the early days of Skinny Ben litigation. He converted four former Greyhound buses into traveling clinics and raced all over the country screening potential clients. Clay listened with fading interest as they crossed the George Washington Bridge. Another story followed.

Clay's suite at The Peninsula had a view of Fifth Avenue. Once he was safely locked inside, away from Patton French, he grabbed the phone and began searching for Max Pace.

Chapter 19

The third cell phone number found Pace at some undisclosed location. The man with no home had been in D.C. less and less in recent weeks. Of course he was off putting out another fire, nixing another round of nasty litigation for another wayward client, though he didn't admit this. Didn't have to. Clay knew him well enough by now to know that he was a fireman in demand. There was no shortage of bad products out there.

Clay was surprised at how comforting it was to hear Pace's voice. He explained that he was in New York, whom he was with, and why he was there. Pace's first word sealed the deal. 'Brilliant,' he said. 'Just brilliant.'

'You know him?'

'Everybody in this business knows Patton French,' Pace said. 'I've never had to deal with him, but he's a legend.'

Clay gave the terms of the offer from French. Pace quickly caught up and then began thinking ahead. 'If you refile in Biloxi, Mississippi,

Ackerman's stock will take another hit,' he said. 'They're under tremendous pressure right now – pressure from their banks and their shareholders. This is brilliant, Clay. Do it!'

'Okay. Done.'

'And watch the *New York Times* in the morning. Big story about Dyloft. The first medical report is out. It's devastating.'

'Great.'

He got a beer from the mini-bar – $8.00 but who cared – and for a long time sat in front of the window and watched the frenzy on Fifth Avenue. It was not entirely comforting to be forced to rely on Max Pace for advice, but there was simply no one else to turn to. No one, not even his father, had ever been presented with such a choice: 'Let's move your five thousand cases over here and put them together with my five thousand cases, and we'll do not two but one class action, and I'll plunk down a million or so for the medical screenings while you double your advertising plan, and we'll rake forty percent off the top, then expenses, and make us a fortune. Whatta you say, Clay?'

In the past month he'd made more money than he'd ever dreamed of earning. Now, as things spun out of control, he felt as if he was spending it even faster. Be bold, he kept telling himself, this is a rare opportunity. Be bold, strike fast, take chances, roll the dice, and you could get filthy rich. Another voice kept urging him to slow down, don't blow the money, bury it and have it forever.

218

He had moved $1 million to an account off-shore, not to hide but to protect. He would never touch it, not under any circumstances. If he made bad choices and gambled it all away, he'd still have money for the beach. He would sneak out of town like his father and never come back.

The million dollars in the secret account was his compromise.

He tried calling his office but all lines were busy, a good sign. He got Jonah on his cell phone, sitting at his desk. 'It's crazy as hell,' Jonah said, very fatigued. 'Total chaos.'

'Good.'

'Why don't you get back here and help!'

'Tomorrow.'

At seven thirty-two, Clay turned on the television and found his ad on a cable channel. Dyloft sounded even more ominous in New York.

Dinner was at Montrachet, not for the food, which was very good, but for the wine list, which was thicker than any other in New York. French wanted to taste several red burgundies with his veal. Five bottles were brought to the table, with a different glass for each wine. There was little room for the bread and butter.

The sommelier and Patton lapsed into another language when discussing what was in each bottle. Clay was bored with the entire process. A beer and a burger would've been preferable, though he could see his tastes changing dramatically in the near future.

When the wines had been opened and were breathing, French said, 'I called my office. That lawyer in Miami is already on the air with Dyloft ads. He's set up two screening clinics and is running them through like cattle. Name's Carlos Hernández, and he's very, very good.'

'My people can't answer all the calls,' Clay said.

'Are we in this together?' French said.

'Let's go over the deal.'

At which French whipped out a folded document. 'Here's the deal memo,' he said, handing it over while he went for the first bottle. 'It summarizes what we've discussed so far.'

Clay read it carefully and signed at the bottom. French, between sips, signed as well, and the partnership was born.

'Let's file the class action in Biloxi tomorrow,' French said. 'I'll do it when I get home. I've got two lawyers working on it right now. As soon as it's filed, you can dismiss yours in D.C. I know the in-house counsel for Ackerman Labs. I think I can talk to him. If the company will negotiate directly with us, and bypass their outside counsel, then they can save a bloody fortune and give it to us. And it will greatly expedite matters. If their outside lawyers take charge of the negotiations, it could cost us half a year in wasted time.'

'About a hundred million, right?'

'Something like that. That could be our money.' A phone rang somewhere in a pocket and French whipped it out with his left hand while holding a wineglass with his right. 'Excuse me,' he said to Clay.

It was a Dyloft conversation with another lawyer, somebody in Texas, obviously an old friend, one who could talk faster than Patton French. The banter was polite, but French was cautious. When he slapped the phone shut he said, 'Dammit!'

'Some competition?'

'Serious competition. Name's Vic Brennan, big lawyer in Houston, very smart and aggressive. He's onto Dyloft, wants to know the game plan.'

'He got nothing from you.'

'He knows. He's unleashing some ads tomorrow – radio, television, newspaper. He'll pick up several thousand cases.' For a moment, he consoled himself with a sip of wine, one that made him smile. 'The race is on, Clay. We have to get those cases.'

'It's about to get crazier,' Clay said.

French had a mouthful of Pinot Noir and couldn't speak. 'What?' his face said.

'Tomorrow morning, big story in the *New York Times*. The first bad report on Dyloft, according to my sources.'

It was the wrong thing to say, as far as dinner was concerned. French forgot about his veal, which was still in the kitchen. And he forgot about the expensive wines covering his table, though he managed to consume them over the next three hours. But what mass tort lawyer could concentrate on food and wine when the *New York Times* was just hours away from exposing his next defendant and its dangerous drug?

The phone was ringing and it was still dark outside. The clock, when he could finally focus on it, gave the time as five forty-five. 'Get up!' French growled at him. 'And open the door.' By the time he unlocked it, French was pushing it open and marching past with newspapers and a cup of coffee. 'Unbelievable!' he said, flinging a copy of the *Times* on Clay's bed.

'You can't sleep all day, son. Read this!' He was dressed in hotel garb, the complimentary terry-cloth robe and white shower shoes.

'It's not six yet.'

'I haven't slept past five in thirty years. There are too many lawsuits out there.'

Clay wore nothing but his boxer shorts. French gulped coffee and read the story again, peering down his flat nose through reading glasses perched on the tip.

No sign of a hangover. Clay had gotten bored with the wines, which all tasted the same to him anyway, and finished the night with bottled water. French had battled on, determined to declare a winner among the five burgundies, though he was so sidetracked with Dyloft his heart wasn't in it.

The *Atlantic Journal of Medicine* was reporting that dylofedamint, known as Dyloft, had been linked to bladder tumors in about six percent of those who had taken it for a year.

'Up from five percent,' Clay said as he read.

'Isn't that wonderful?' French said.

'Not if you're in the six percent.'

'I'm not.'

Some doctors were already pulling the drug. Ackerman Labs offered a rather weak denial, shifting blame, as always, to greedy trial lawyers, though the company appeared to be hunkering down. No comment from the FDA. A doctor in Chicago ran on for half a column about how great the drug was, how happy his patients were with it. The good news, if it could be called that, was that the tumors did not appear to be malignant, so far anyway. As Clay read the story, he got the feeling that Max Pace had seen it a month ago.

There was only one paragraph about the class action filed in D.C. on Monday, and no mention of the young lawyer who'd filed it.

Ackerman's stock had tumbled from $42.50 Monday morning to $32.50 at the close on Wednesday.

'Should've shorted the damned thing,' French mumbled. Clay bit his tongue and kept a secret, one of the few he'd held on to in the past twenty-four hours.

'We can read it again on the plane,' French said. 'Let's get out of here.'

The stock was at $28 by the time Clay walked into his office and tried to say hello to his weary staff. He went online to a Web site with the latest market movements and checked it every fifteen minutes, counting his gains. Burning money on one front, it was comforting to see some profits on the other.

Jonah was the first to stop by. 'We were here until midnight last night,' he said. 'It's crazy.'

'It's about to get crazier. We're doubling the TV ads.'

'We can't keep up now.'

'Hire some temporary paralegals.'

'We need computer people, at least two. We can't add the data fast enough.'

'Can you find them?'

'Maybe some temps. I know one guy, maybe two, who might be able to come in at night and play catch-up.'

'Get them.'

Jonah started to leave, then turned around and closed the door behind him. 'Clay, look, it's just me and you, right?'

Clay looked around the office and saw no one else. 'What is it?'

'Well, you're a smart guy and all. But do you know what you're doing here? I mean, you're burning money faster than it's ever been burned. What if something goes wrong?'

'You're worried?'

'We're all a little worried, okay? This firm is off to a great start. We want to stay and have fun and make money and all that. But what if you're wrong and you go belly-up? It's a fair question.'

Clay walked around to the edge of his desk and sat on the corner. 'I'll be very honest with you. I think I know what I'm doing, but since I've never done it before, I can't be certain. It's one huge gamble. If I win, then we all make some serious money. If I lose, then we're still in business. We just won't be rich.'

'If you get the chance, tell the others, okay?'

'I will.'

Lunch was a ten-minute sandwich break in the conference room. Jonah had the latest numbers: For the first three days, the hot line had fielded seventy-one hundred calls and the Web site had averaged eight thousand inquiries per day. Information packets and contracts for legal services had been mailed as quickly as possible, though they were falling behind. Clay authorized Jonah to hire two part-time computer assistants. Paulette was given the task of finding three or four additional paralegals to work in the Sweatshop. And Miss Glick was directed to hire as many temporary clerks as necessary to handle the client correspondence.

Clay described his meeting with Patton French and explained their new legal strategy. He showed them copies of the article in the *Times*; they'd been too busy to notice.

'The race is on, folks,' he said, trying his best to motivate a weary bunch. 'The sharks are coming after our clients.'

'We are the sharks,' Paulette said.

Patton French called late in the afternoon and reported that the class action had been amended to add Mississippi plaintiffs and filed in state court in Biloxi. 'We got it right where we want it, pal,' he said.

'I'll dismiss here tomorrow,' Clay said, hoping he was not giving away his lawsuit.

'You gonna tip off the press?'

'I wasn't planning on it,' Clay said. He had no idea how one went about tipping off the press.

'Let me handle it.'

Ackerman Labs closed the day at $26.25, a paper profit of $1,625,000, if Clay bought now and covered his short sale. He decided to wait. The news of the Biloxi filing would hit in the morning, and it would do nothing but hurt the stock.

At midnight, he was sitting at his desk chatting with a gentleman in Seattle who had taken Dyloft for almost a year and was now horrified that he probably had tumors. Clay advised him to get to the doctor as soon as possible for the urinalysis. He gave him the Web site and promised to mail out an information packet first thing tomorrow. When they hung up, the man was on the verge of tears.

Chapter 20

Bad news continued to follow the miracle drug Dyloft. Two more medical studies were published, one of which argued convincingly that Ackerman Labs cut corners on its research and pulled every string it had to get the drug approved. The FDA finally ordered Dyloft off the market.

The bad news was, of course, wonderful news to the lawyers, and the frenzy heated up as more and more latecomers piled on. Patients taking Dyloft received written warnings from Ackerman Labs and from their own doctors, and these dire messages were almost always followed by ominous solicitations from mass tort lawyers. Direct mail was extremely effective. Newspaper ads were used in every big market. And hot lines were all over the television. The threat of tumors growing wild prompted virtually all Dyloft users to contact a lawyer.

Patton French had never seen a mass tort class come together so beautifully. Because he and Clay won the race to the courthouse in Biloxi, their class had been certified first. All other Dyloft plaintiffs wanting in on a class action would be forced to join theirs, with the Plaintiffs' Steering Committee raking off an additional fee. French's friendly judge had already appointed the five-lawyer committee – French, Clay, Carlos Hernández from Miami, and two other cronies from New Orleans. In theory, the committee would handle the large and complicated trial against Ackerman Labs. In reality, the five would shuffle paperwork and cover the administrative chore of keeping fifty thousand or so clients and their lawyers somewhat organized.

A Dyloft plaintiff could always 'opt out' of the class, and take on Ackerman Labs alone in a separate trial. As lawyers around the country collected the cases and put together their coalitions, the inevitable conflicts arose. Some disapproved of the Biloxi class and wanted their own. Some despised Patton French. Some wanted a trial in their jurisdictions, with the chance of a huge verdict.

But French had been through the battles many times before. He lived on his Gulfstream, jetting from coast to coast, meeting the mass tort lawyers who were collecting cases by the hundreds, and somehow holding the fragile coalition together. The settlement would be bigger in Biloxi, he promised.

He talked every day to the in-house counsel at Ackerman Labs, an embattled old warrior who had tried to retire twice but the CEO wouldn't allow it. French's message was clear and simple – let's talk settlement now, without your outside lawyers, because you know you're not going to trial with this drug. Ackerman was beginning to listen.

In mid-August, French convened a summit of the Dyloft lawyers at his sprawling ranch near Ketchum, Idaho. He explained to Clay that his attendance was mandatory, as a member of the Plaintiffs' Steering Committee, and, just as important, the rest of the boys were quite anxious to meet the young upstart who broke the Dyloft case. 'Plus, with these guys you can't miss a single meeting, else they'll stab you in the back.'

'I'll be there,' Clay said.

'I'll send a jet,' French offered.

'No thanks. I'll get there.'

Clay chartered a Lear 35, a handsome little jet about one-third the size of a Gulfstream 5, but since he was traveling alone it was quite adequate. He met the pilots in the private terminal at Reagan National, where he mixed and mingled with the other hotshots, all older than he, and tried desperately to act as if there was nothing special about hopping on board his own jet. Sure it was owned by a charter company, but for the next three days it was his.

Lifting off to the north, he stared down at the Potomac, then the Lincoln Memorial, and, quickly, all the landmarks of downtown. There was his office building, and in the distance, not too far away, was the Office of the Public Defender. What would Glenda and Jermaine and those he'd left behind think if they saw him now?

What would Rebecca think?

If she'd just held on for another month.

He'd had so little time to think about her.

Into the clouds and the view was gone. Washington was soon miles behind. Clay Carter was off to a secret meeting of some of the richest lawyers in America, the mass tort specialists, those who had the brains and brawn to go after the most powerful corporations.

And they wanted to meet him!

His jet was the smallest one at the Ketchum–Sun Valley airport at Friedman, Idaho. As he taxied by Gulfstreams and Challengers he had the ridiculous thought that his jet was inadequate, that he needed a bigger one. Then he laughed at himself – there he was in the leather-lined cabin of a $3 million Lear, and he was debating whether he should get something bigger. At least he could still laugh. What would he be when the laughing stopped?

They parked next to a familiar plane, one with the tail number 000MT. Zero, Zero, Zero, Mass Tort, the home away from home of Patton French himself. It dwarfed Clay's ride, and for a second he looked up in envy at the finest luxury jet in the world.

A van was waiting, with what appeared to be an imitation cowboy behind the wheel. Fortunately, the driver was not much of a talker, and

Clay enjoyed the forty-five-minute ride in silence. They twisted upward on roads that became narrower. Not surprisingly, Patton's spread was postcard perfect and very new. The house was a lodge with enough wings and levels to host a good-sized law firm. Another cowboy took Clay's bag. 'Mr French is waiting on the deck out back,' he said, as if Clay had been there many times.

Switzerland was the topic when Clay found them – which secluded ski resort they preferred. He listened for a second as he approached. The other four members of the Plaintiffs' Steering Committee were lounging in chairs, facing the mountains, smoking dark cigars and working on drinks. When they realized Clay was present, they hopped to attention as if the judge had entered the courtroom. In the first three minutes of excited conversation, he was called 'brilliant,' 'shrewd,' 'gutsy,' and, his favorite, 'a visionary.'

'You gotta tell us how you found Dyloft,' Carlos Hernández said.

'He won't tell,' French said as he mixed some vile concoction for Clay to drink.

'Come on,' said Wes Saulsberry, Clay's newest friend. Within just a few minutes, Clay would learn that Wes had made about half a billion on the tobacco settlement three years earlier.

'I'm sworn to silence,' Clay said.

The other lawyer from New Orleans was Damon Didier, one of the speakers at a session Clay had attended during his Circle of Barristers weekend. Didier was stone-faced and steely-eyed and Clay remembered wondering how this guy could ever connect with a jury. Didier, he found out soon enough, had made a mint when a riverboat packed with fraternity boys sunk into Lake Pontchartrain. Such misery.

They needed patches and medals, like war heroes. This one here they gave me for that tanker explosion that killed twenty. I got this one for those boys who got burned on the off-shore drilling rig. This big one here was for the Skinny Ben campaign. This, the war against Big Tobacco. This, the battle against HMOs.

Since Clay had no war stories, he just listened. Tarvan would blow them away, but he could never tell it.

A butler in a Roy Rogers–style shirt informed Mr French that dinner would be served in an hour. They moved downstairs to a game room with pool tables and big screens. A dozen or so white men were drinking and talking and some were holding pool cues. 'The rest of the conspiracy,' Hernández whispered to Clay.

Patton introduced him to the group. The names, faces, and hometowns quickly blurred. Seattle, Houston, Topeka, Boston, and others he didn't catch. And Effingham, Illinois. They all paid homage to this 'brilliant' young litigator who'd shocked them with his daring assault on Dyloft.

'I saw the ad the first night it was on,' said Bernie somebody from Boston. 'Never heard of Dyloft. So I call your hot line, get a nice guy on the other end. I tell him I've been taking the drug, feed him the line, you know. I go to the Web site. It was brilliant. I said to myself, "I've been ambushed." Three days later I'm on the air with my own damned Dyloft hot line.'

They all laughed, probably because they could each tell similar stories. It had never occurred to Clay that other lawyers would call his hot line and use his Web site in order to steer away cases. But why did this surprise him?

When the admiration was finally over, French said there were a few things to discuss before dinner, which, by the way, would include a fabulous selection of Australian wines. Clay was already dizzy from the fine Cuban cigar and the first double vodka bomb. He was by far the youngest lawyer there, and he felt like a rookie in every way. Especially when it came to drinking. He was in the presence of some professionals.

Youngest lawyer. Smallest jet. No war tales. Weakest liver. Clay decided it was time to grow up.

They crowded around French, who lived for moments like this. He began, 'As you know, I've spent a lot of time with Wicks, the in-house guy at Ackerman Labs. Bottom line is they're going to settle, and do it quickly. They're getting hit from every direction, and they want this to go away as soon as possible. Their stock is so low now they're afraid of a takeover. The vultures, including us, are moving in for the kill. If they know how much Dyloft will cost them, then they can restructure some debt and maybe hang on.

What they don't want is protracted litigation on many fronts, with verdicts landing everywhere. Neither do they want to fork over tens of millions for defense.'

'Poor guys,' someone said.

'*Business Week* mentioned bankruptcy,' someone else said. 'Have they used that threat?'

'Not yet. And I don't expect them to. Ackerman has far too many assets. We've just completed the financial analysis – we'll crunch the numbers in the morning – and our boys think that the company has between two and three billion to settle Dyloft.'

'How much insurance coverage is on the table?'

'Only three hundred million. The company has had its cosmetics division on the market for a year. They want a billion. The real value is about three-fourths of that. They could unload it for half a billion and have enough cash to satisfy our clients.'

Clay had noticed that the clients were rarely mentioned.

The vultures squeezed around French, who continued: 'We need to determine two things. First, how many potential plaintiffs are out there. Second, the value of each case.'

'Let's add 'em up,' drawled someone from Texas. 'I got a thousand.'

'I have eighteen hundred,' French said. 'Carlos.'

'Two thousand,' Hernández said as he began taking notes.

'Wes?'

'Nine hundred.'

The lawyer from Topeka had six hundred, the lowest. Two thousand was the highest until French saved the best for last. 'Clay?' he said, and everyone listened intently.

'Thirty-two hundred,' Clay said, managing a grim poker face. His newly found brethren, however, were quite pleased. Or at least they appeared to be.

'Attaboy,' someone said.

Clay suspected that just under their toothy smiles and 'Attaboys!' were some very envious people.

'That's twenty-four thousand,' Carlos said, doing the quick math.

'We can safely double that, which gets close to fifty, the number Ackerman has pegged. Fifty thousand into two billion is forty thousand bucks per case. Not a bad starting place.'

Clay did some quick math of his own – $40,000 times his 3,200 cases came to something over $120 million. And one third of that, well, his brain froze and his knees went weak.

'Does the company know how many of these cases involve malignant tumors?' asked Bernie from Boston.

'No, they don't. Their best guess is about one percent.'

'That's five hundred cases.'

'At a minimum of a million bucks each.'

'That's another half billion.'

'A million bucks is a joke.'

'Five million a pop in Seattle.'

'We're talking wrongful death, here.'

Not surprisingly, each lawyer had an opinion to offer and they did so simultaneously. When French restored order, he said, 'Gentlemen, let's eat.'

Dinner was a fiasco. The dining room table was a slab of polished wood that came from one tree, one grand and majestic red maple that had stood for centuries until it was needed by wealthy America. At least forty people could eat around it at one time. There were eighteen for dinner, and wisely they had been spread out. Otherwise, someone might have thrown a punch.

In a room full of flamboyant egos, where everyone was the greatest lawyer God created, the most obnoxious windbag was Victor K. Brennan, a loud and twangy Texan from Houston. On the third or fourth wine, about halfway through the thick steaks, Brennan began complaining about such low expectations for each individual case. He had a forty-year-old client who made big bucks and now had malignant tumors, thanks to Dyloft. 'I can get ten million actual and twenty million punitive from any jury in Texas,' he boasted. Most of the others agreed with this. Some even one-upped by claiming that they could get more on their home turf. French held firm with the theory that if a few got millions then the masses would get little. Brennan didn't buy this but had trouble countering the argument. He had a vague notion that Ackerman Labs had much more cash than it was showing.

The group divided on this point, but the lines shifted so fast and the loyalties were so temporary that Clay had trouble determining where most of them stood. French challenged Brennan on his claim that punitive damages would be so easy to prove. 'You got the documents, right?' Brennan asked.

'Clay has provided some documents. Ackerman doesn't know it yet. You boys have not seen them. And maybe you won't if you don't stay in the class.'

The knives and forks stopped as all seventeen (Clay excluded) started yelling at once. The waiters left the room. Clay could almost see them back in the kitchen, hunkering low behind the prep tables. Brennan wanted to fight someone. Wes Saulsberry wasn't backing down. The language deteriorated. And in the midst of the ruckus, Clay looked at the end of the table and saw Patton French sniff a wineglass, take a sip, close his eyes, and evaluate yet another new wine.

How many of these fights had French sat through? Probably a hundred. Clay cut a bite of steak.

When things settled down, Bernie from Boston told a joke about a Catholic priest and the room erupted in laughter. Food and wine were enjoyed for about five minutes until Albert from Topeka suggested the strategy of forcing Ackerman Labs into bankruptcy. He had done it twice, to other companies, with satisfactory results. Both times the target companies had used the bankruptcy laws to screw their banks and other creditors, thus providing more cash for Albert and his thousands of clients. Those opposed voiced their concerns, to which Albert took offense, and soon there was another fight.

They fought over everything – documents again, whether or not to press for a trial while ignoring a quick settlement, turf, false advertising, how to round up the other cases, expenses, fees. Clay's stomach was in knots and he never said a word. The rest seemed to enjoy their food immensely while carrying on two or three arguments simultaneously.

Experience, Clay told himself.

After the longest dinner of Clay's life, French led them downstairs, back to the billiards room where the cognac and more cigars were waiting. Those who had been swearing at each other for three hours were now drinking and laughing like fraternity brothers. At the first opportunity, Clay sneaked away and, after considerable effort, found his room.

The Barry and Harry Show was scheduled for 10 A.M. Saturday morning, time for everyone to sleep off the hangovers and choke down a heavy breakfast. French had made available trout fishing and skeet shooting, neither of which drew a single lawyer.

Barry and Harry had a company in New York

that did nothing but analyze the finances of target companies. They had sources and contacts and spies and a reputation for peeling back the skin and finding the real truth. French had flown them in for a one-hour presentation. 'Costs us two hundred grand,' he whispered proudly to Clay, 'and we'll make Ackerman Labs reimburse us. Imagine that.'

Their routine was a tag team, Barry doing the graphics, Harry with the pointer, two professors at the lectern. Both stood at the front of the small theater, one level below the billiards room. The lawyers, for once, were silent.

Ackerman Labs had insurance coverage of at least $500 million – $300 million from their liability carrier, and another $200 million from a reinsurer. The cash-flow analysis was dense and took both Harry and Barry talking at once to complete. Numbers and percentages spewed forth and soon drowned everyone else in the room.

They talked about Ackerman's cosmetics division, which might fetch $600 million at a fire sale. There was a plastics division in Mexico that the company wanted to unload for $200 million. The company's debt structure took fifteen minutes to explain.

Barry and Harry were also lawyers, and so were quite adept at assessing a company's likely response to a mass tort disaster like Dyloft. It would be wise for Ackerman to settle quickly, in stages. 'A pancake settlement,' Harry said.

Clay was certain that he was the only person

in the room who had no idea what a pancake settlement was.

'Stage one would be two billion for all level-one plaintiffs,' Harry continued, mercifully laying out the elements of such a plan.

'We think they might do this within ninety days,' Barry added.

'Stage two would be half a billion for level-two plaintiffs, those with malignancy who don't die.'

'And stage three would be left open for five years to cover the death cases.'

'We think Ackerman can pay around two-point-five to three billion over the next year, then another half-billion over five years.'

'Anything beyond that, and you could be looking at a chapter eleven.'

'Which is not advisable for this company. Too many banks have too many priority liens.'

'And a bankruptcy would seriously choke off the flow of money. It would take from three to five years to get a decent settlement.'

Of course the lawyers wanted to argue for a while. Vincent from Pittsburgh was especially determined to impress the rest with his financial acumen, but Harry and Barry soon put him back in his place. After an hour, they left to go fishing.

French took their place at the front of the room. All arguments had been completed. The fighting had stopped. It was time to agree on a plan.

Step one was to round up the other cases. Every man for himself. No holds barred. Since they accounted for half of the total, there were still plenty of Dyloft plaintiffs out there. Let's find them. Search out the small-time lawyers with only twenty or thirty cases, bring them into the fold. Do whatever it takes to get the cases.

Step two would be a settlement conference with Ackerman Labs in sixty days. The Plaintiffs' Steering Committee would schedule it and send notices.

Step three would be an all-out effort to keep everyone in the class. Strength in numbers. Those who 'opted out' of the class and wanted to have their own trial would not have access to the deadly documents. It was as simple as that. Hardball, but it was litigation.

Every lawyer in the room objected to some part of the plan, but the alliance held. Dyloft looked as if it would be the quickest settlement in mass tort history, and the lawyers were smelling the money.

Chapter 21

The young firm's next reorganization occurred in the same chaotic fashion as the previous ones, and for the same reasons – too many new clients, too much new paperwork, not enough manpower, an unclear chain of command, and a very uncertain management style because no one at the top had ever managed before, maybe with the exception of Miss Glick. Three days after Clay returned from Ketchum, Paulette and Jonah confronted him in his office with a long list of urgent problems. Mutiny was in the air. Nerves were frayed and the fatigue made bad matters worse.

According to the best estimate, the firm now had 3,320 Dyloft cases, and since the cases were brand-new they all needed immediate attention. Not counting Paulette, who was reluctantly assuming the role of office manager, and not counting Jonah, who was spending ten hours a day on a computer system to keep up with the cases, and, of course, not counting Clay because he was the boss and had to give interviews and travel to

Idaho, the firm had hired two lawyers and now had ten paralegals, none of whom had more than three months' experience, except for Rodney. 'I can't tell a good one from a bad one,' Paulette said. 'It's too early.'

She estimated that each paralegal could handle between one hundred and two hundred cases. 'These clients are scared,' she said. 'They're scared because they have these tumors. They're scared because Dyloft is all over the press. Hell, they're scared because we've scared the hell out of them.'

'They want to be talked to,' Jonah said. 'And they want a lawyer on the other end of the phone, not some frantic paralegal on an assembly line. I'm afraid we'll be losing clients real soon.'

'We're not going to lose clients,' Clay said, thinking of all those nice sharks he'd just met out in Idaho and how happy they'd be to pick up his disgruntled clients.

'We're drowning in paperwork,' Paulette said, taking the tag from Jonah and ignoring Clay. 'Every preliminary medical test has got to be analyzed, then verified with a follow-up. Right now, we think we have about four hundred people who need further testing. These could be the serious cases; these people could be dying, Clay. But somebody has to coordinate their medical care with the doctors. It isn't getting done, Clay, okay?'

'I'm listening,' he said. 'How many lawyers do we need?'

Paulette cast a weary look at Jonah. The two had no answer. 'Ten?' she said.

'At least ten,' Jonah said. 'Ten for now, right now, and maybe more later.'

'We're cranking up the advertising,' Clay said.

There was a long weary pause as Jonah and Paulette absorbed this. He had briefed them on the high points in Ketchum, but not the details. He had assured them that every case they signed up would soon pay big profits, but he had kept settlement strategies to himself. Loose tongues lose lawsuits, French had warned him, and with such an untested staff it was best to keep them in the dark.

A law firm down the street had just given pink slips to thirty-five associates. The economy was soft, billings were down, a merger was in the works; whatever the real reason the story was newsworthy in D.C. because the job market was normally bulletproof. Layoffs! In the legal profession? In D.C.?

Paulette suggested they hire some of those associates – offer them a one-year contract with no promises of any advancement. Clay volunteered to make the calls first thing the next morning. He would also locate office space and furnishings.

Jonah had the rather unusual idea of hiring a doctor for one year, someone to coordinate the tests and medical evidence. 'We can get one fresh out of school for a hundred grand a year,' he said. 'He wouldn't have much experience, but who cares? He's not doing surgery, just paperwork.'

'Get it done,' Clay said.

Next on Jonah's list was the matter of the Web site. The advertising had made it quite popular but they needed full-time people to respond to it. Plus it needed to be upgraded almost weekly with the developments on the class action and the latest bad news about Dyloft. 'All these clients are desperate for information, Clay,' he said.

For those who didn't use the Internet, and Paulette guessed that at least half their clients fell into that group, a Dyloft newsletter was crucial. 'We need one full-time person editing and mailing the newsletter,' she said.

'Can you find someone?' Clay asked.

'I suppose so.'

'Then do it.'

She looked at Jonah, as if whatever needed to be said should come from him. Jonah tossed a legal pad on the desk and cracked his knuckles. 'Clay, we're spending huge amounts of money here,' he said. 'Are you sure you know what you're doing?'

'No, but I think so. Just trust me, okay? We're about to make some serious money. To get there, though, we gotta spend some cash.'

'And you have the cash?' Paulette asked.

'Yep.'

Pace wanted a late drink in a bar in Georgetown, within walking distance of Clay's town house. He was in and out of the city, very vague, as always, about where he'd been and what fire he happened to be fighting. He had lightened up the wardrobe and now preferred brown – brown pointed-toe snakeskin boots, brown suede jacket. Part of his disguise, Clay thought. Halfway through the first beer Pace got around to Dyloft, and it became evident that whatever the current project was it still had something to do with Ackerman Labs.

Clay, with the flair of a fledgling trial lawyer, gave a colorful description of his trip to French's ranch, and the gang of thieves he'd met there, and the contentious three-hour dinner where everybody was drunk and arguing at once, and the Barry and Harry Show. He had no hesitation in giving Pace the details because Pace knew more than anyone.

'I know of Barry and Harry,' Pace said, as if they were characters in the underworld.

'They seemed to know their stuff, and for two hundred grand they should.'

Clay talked about Carlos Hernández and Wes Saulsberry and Damon Didier, his new pals on the Plaintiffs' Steering Committee. Pace said he'd heard of them all.

Into the second beer, Pace asked, 'You sold Ackerman short, right?' He glanced around, but no one was listening. It was a college bar on a slow night.

'A hundred thousand shares at forty-two fifty,' Clay said proudly.

'Ackerman closed today at twenty-three.'

'I know. I do the math every day.'

'It's time to cover the short and buy it back. Like first thing tomorrow morning.'

246

'Something's coming?'

'Yes, and while you're at it, buy all you can at twenty-three, then hang on for the ride.'

'Where might the ride be headed?'

'It'll double.'

Six hours later, Clay was at the office, before sunrise, trying to prepare for another day of pure frenzy. And also anxious for the markets to open. His list of things to do ran for two pages, almost all of it involving the enormous task of immediately hiring ten new lawyers and finding work space to house some of them. It looked hopeless, but he had no choice; he called a Realtor at seven-thirty and yanked him out of the shower. At eight-thirty he had a ten-minute interview with a freshly fired young lawyer named Oscar Mulrooney. The poor guy had been a star student at Yale, then highly recruited, then merged out of a job when a megafirm imploded. He'd also been married for two months and was desperate for work. Clay hired him on the spot for $75,000 a year. Mulrooney had four friends, also from Yale, who were also on the streets looking for work. Go get 'em.

At 10 A.M., Clay called his broker and covered his Ackerman short sale, making a profit of $1.9 million and some change. In the same call, he took the entire profit and bought another two hundred thousand shares at $23, using his margin and some account credit. Online, he watched the market all morning. Nothing changed.

Oscar Mulrooney was back at noon with his friends, all as eager as Boy Scouts. Clay hired the others, then gave them the task of renting their furniture, hooking up their phones, doing everything necessary to begin their new careers as low-level mass tort lawyers. It was up to Oscar to hire five more lawyers who would have to find their own office space, etcetera.

The Yale Branch was born.

At 5 P.M. Eastern Time, Philo Products announced it would buy the outstanding common stock of Ackerman Labs for $50 a share, a merger with a price tag of $14 billion. Clay watched the drama on the big screen in his conference room, alone because everyone else was answering the damned telephones. The nonstop money channels choked on the news. CNN scrambled reporters to White Plains, New York, headquarters of Ackerman Labs, where they loitered by the front gate as if the beleaguered company might step forward and weep for the cameras.

An endless string of experts and market analysts prattled on with all sorts of groundless opinions. Dyloft was mentioned early and often. Though Ackerman Labs had been badly managed for years, there was no doubt Dyloft had succeeded in shoving it off the cliff.

Was Philo the maker of Tarvan? Pace's client? Had Clay been manipulated to bring about a $14 billion takeover? And most troubling, what did it all mean for the future of Ackerman Labs and Dyloft? While it was certainly exciting to calculate his new profits on the Ackerman stock, he had to ask himself if this meant the end of the Dyloft dream.

But the truth was that there was no way to know. He was a small player in a huge deal between two mammoth corporations. Ackerman Labs had assets, he reassured himself. And the company made a very bad product that harmed many. Justice would prevail.

Patton French called from his airplane, somewhere between Florida and Texas, and asked Clay to sit tight for an hour or so. The Plaintiffs' Steering Committee needed an emergency conference call. His secretary was putting one together.

French was back in an hour, on the ground in Beaumont, where he would meet tomorrow with lawyers who had some cholesterol drug cases that they needed his help with, cases worth tons of money, but, anyway, he couldn't find the rest of their steering committee. He'd already talked with Barry and Harry in New York and they were not worried about the Philo takeover. 'Ackerman owns twelve million shares of its own stock, now worth at least fifty bucks a share but maybe more before the dust settles. The company just picked up six hundred million in equity alone. Plus, the government has to approve the merger, and they typically want the litigation cleaned up before saying yes. Also, Philo is notorious for avoiding courtrooms. They settle fast and quiet.'

Sounds like Tarvan, Clay thought.

'Overall, it's good news,' French said, with a fax buzzing in the background. Clay could see him pacing up and down in his Gulfstream as it waited on the ramp in Beaumont. 'I'll keep you posted.' And he was gone.

Chapter 22

Rex Crittle wanted to scold, to be reassured, to lecture, to educate, but his client sitting across the desk seemed completely unshaken by the figures.

'Your firm is six months old,' Crittle said, peering over his reading glasses with a pile of reports in front of him. The evidence! He had the proof that the boutique firm of the Law Offices of J. Clay Carter II was in fact being run by idiots. 'Your overhead began at an impressive seventy-five thousand a month – three lawyers, one paralegal, a secretary, serious rent, nice digs. Now it's a half a million bucks a month, and growing every day.'

'You gotta spend it to make it,' Clay said, sipping coffee and enjoying his accountant's discomfort. That was the sign of a good bean counter – one who lost more sleep over the expenses than the client himself.

'But you're not making it,' Crittle said cautiously. 'No revenue in the past three months.'

'It's been a good year.'

'Oh yes. Fifteen million in fees makes for a splendid year. Problem is, it's evaporating. You spent fourteen thousand bucks last month chartering jets.'

'Now that you mention it, I'm thinking about buying one. I'll need you to crunch the numbers.'

'I'm crunching them right now. You can't justify one.'

'That's not the issue. The issue is whether or not I can afford one.'

'No, you cannot afford one.'

'Hang on, Rex. Relief is in sight.'

'I assume you're talking about the Dyloft cases? Four million dollars for advertising. Three thousand a month for a Dyloft Web site. Now three thousand a month for the Dyloft newsletter. All those paralegals out in Manassas. All these new lawyers.'

'I think the question will be, should I lease one for five years or just buy it outright?'

'What?'

'The Gulfstream.'

'What's a Gulfstream?'

'The finest private jet in the world.'

'What are you going to do with a Gulfstream?'

'Fly.'

'Why, exactly, do you think you need one?'

'It's the preferred jet of all the big mass tort lawyers.'

'Oh, that makes sense.'

'I thought you'd come around.'

252

'Any idea how much one might cost?'

'Forty, forty-five million.'

'I hate to break the news, Clay, but you don't have forty million.'

'You're right. I think I'll just lease one.'

Crittle removed his reading glasses and massaged his long, skinny nose, as if a severe headache was developing there. 'Look, Clay, I'm just your accountant. But I'm not sure if there's anyone else who is telling you to slow down. Take it easy, pal. You've made a fortune, enjoy it. You don't need a big firm with so many lawyers. You don't need jets. What's next? A yacht?'

'Yes.'

'You're serious?'

'Yes.'

'I thought you hated boats.'

'I do. It's for my father. Can I depreciate it?'

'No.'

'Bet I can.'

'How?'

'I'll charter it when I'm not using it.'

When Crittle was finished with his nose, he replaced his glasses and said, 'It's your money, pal.'

They met in New York City, on neutral ground, in the dingy ballroom of an old hotel near Central Park, the last place anyone would expect such an important gathering to take place. On one side of the table sat the Dyloft Plaintiffs' Steering Committee, five of them, including young Clay

253

Carter who felt quite out of place, and behind them were all manner of assistants and associates and gofers employed by Mr. Patton French. Across the table was the Ackerman team, headed by Cal Wicks, a distinguished veteran who was flanked by an equal number of supporters.

One week earlier, the government had approved the merger with Philo Products, at $53 a share, which for Clay meant another profit, somewhere around $6 million. He'd buried half of it off-shore, never to be touched. So the venerable company founded by the Ackerman brothers a century earlier was about to be consumed by Philo, a company with barely half its annual revenues but a lot less debt and a much brighter management.

As Clay took his seat and spread his files and tried to convince himself that, yes, dammit, he did belong there, he thought he noticed some harsh frowns from the other side. Finally, the folks at Ackerman Labs were getting to see in person this young upstart from D.C. who'd started their Dyloft nightmare.

Patton French may have had plenty of backup, but he needed none. He took charge of the first session and soon everyone else shut up, with the exception of Wicks, who spoke only when necessary. They spent the morning nailing down the number of cases out there. The Biloxi class had 36,700 plaintiffs. A renegade group of lawyers in Georgia had 5,200 and were threatening an end run with another class action. French felt confident he could dissuade them. Other lawyers had opted out of the class and were planning solo trials in their backyards, but again, French wasn't worried about them. They did not have the crucial documents, nor were they likely to get them.

Numbers poured forth, and Clay was soon bored with it all. The only number that mattered to him was 5,380 – his Dyloft share. He still had more than any single lawyer, though French himself had closed the gap brilliantly and had just over 5,000.

After three hours of nonstop statistics, they agreed on a one-hour lunch. The plaintiffs' committee went upstairs to a suite, where they ate sandwiches and drank only water. French was soon on the phone, talking and yelling at the same time. Wes Saulsberry wanted some fresh air, and invited Clay for a quick walk around the block. They strolled up Fifth Avenue, across from the park. It was mid-November, the air chilly and light, the leaves blowing across the street. A great time to be in the city.

'I love to come here and I love to leave,' Saulsberry said. 'Right now it's eighty-five in New Orleans, humidity still at ninety.'

Clay just listened. He was too preoccupied with the excitement of the moment; the settlement that was only hours away, the enormous fees, the complete freedom of being young and single and so wealthy.

'How old are you, Clay?' Wes was saying.

'Thirty-one.'

'When I was thirty-three, my partner and I settled a tanker explosion case for a ton of money. A horrible case, a dozen men were burned. We split twenty-eight million in fees, right down the middle. My partner took his fourteen mil and retired. I invested mine in myself. I built a law firm full of dedicated trial lawyers, some really talented people who love what they're doing. I built a building in downtown New Orleans, kept hiring the best folks I could find. Now we're up to ninety lawyers, and in the past ten years we've raked in eight hundred million bucks in fees. My old partner? A sad case. You don't retire when you're thirty-three, it's not normal. Most of the money went up his nose. Three bad marriages. Gambling problems. I hired him two years ago as a paralegal, a sixty-thousand-dollar salary, and he's not worth that.'

'I haven't thought of retiring,' Clay said. A lie.

'Don't. You're about to make a ton of money, and you deserve it. Enjoy it. Get an airplane, buy a nice boat, a condo on the beach, a place in Aspen, all the toys. But plow the real money back into your firm. Take advice from a guy who's been there.'

'Thanks, I guess.'

They turned onto Seventy-third and headed east. Saulsberry wasn't finished. 'You're familiar with the lead paint cases?'

'Not really.'

'They're not as famous as the drug cases, but pretty damned lucrative. I started the rage about ten years ago. Our clients are schools, churches, hospitals, commercial buildings, all with layers of lead paint on the walls. Very dangerous stuff. We've sued the paint manufacturers, settled with a few. Couple of billion so far. Anyway, during discovery against one company I found out about another nice little mass tort that you might want to look at. I can't handle it because of some conflicts.'

'I'm listening.'

'The company is in Reedsburg, Pennsylvania, and it makes the mortar used by bricklayers in new home construction. Pretty low-tech stuff, but a potential gold mine. Seems they're having problems with their mortar. A bad batch. After about three years, it begins to crumble. When the mortar breaks down, the bricks start falling. It's confined to the Baltimore area, probably about two thousand homes. And it's just beginning to get noticed.'

'What are the damages?'

'It costs roughly fifteen thousand to fix each house.'

Fifteen thousand times two thousand houses. A one-third contract and the lawyers' fees equaled $10 million. Clay was getting quick with his figures.

'The proof will be easy,' Saulsberry said. 'The company knows it has exposure. Settlement should not be a problem.'

'I'd like to look at it.'

'I'll send you the file, but you have to protect my confidence.'

257

'You get a piece?'

'No. It's my payback for Dyloft. And, of course, if you get the chance to return the favor someday, then it will be appreciated. That's how some of us work, Clay. The mass tort brotherhood is full of throat-cutters and egomaniacs, but a few of us try to take care of each other.'

Late in the afternoon, Ackerman Labs agreed to a minimum of $62,000 for each of the Group One Dyloft plaintiffs, those with benign tumors that could be removed with a fairly simple surgical procedure, the cost of which would also be borne by the company. Approximately forty thousand plaintiffs were in this class, and the money would be available immediately. Much of the haggling that followed involved the method to be used in qualifying for the settlement. A ferocious fight erupted when the issue of attorneys' fees was thrown on the table. Like most of the other lawyers, Clay had a contingency contract giving him one third of any recovery, but in such settlements that percentage was normally reduced. A very complicated formula was used and argued about, with French being unduly aggressive. It was, after all, his money. Ackerman eventually agreed on the figure of twenty-eight percent for Group One fees.

Group Two plaintiffs were those with malignant tumors, and since their treatments would take months or years, the settlement was left open. No cap was placed on these damages – evidence, according to Barry and Harry, that Philo Products was somewhere in the background, propping up Ackerman with some extra cash. The attorneys would get twenty-five percent in Group Two, though Clay had no idea why. French was crunching numbers too fast for anyone.

Group Three plaintiffs were those from Group Two who would die because of Dyloft. Since there had been no deaths so far, this class was also left open. The fees were capped at twenty-two percent.

They adjourned at seven with the plan to meet the next day to nail down the details for Groups Two and Three. On the elevator down, French handed him a printout. 'Not a bad day's work,' he said with a smile. It was a summary of Clay's cases and anticipated fees, including a seven percent add-on for his role on the Plaintiffs' Steering Committee.

His expected gross fees from Group One alone were $106 million.

When he was finally alone he stood in front of the window in his room and gazed into the dusk settling over Central Park. Clearly, Tarvan had not braced him for the shock of instant riches. He was numb, speechless, frozen in the window forever as random thoughts raced in and out of his severely overloaded brain. He drank two straight whiskeys from the mini-bar with absolutely no effect.

Still at the window, he called Paulette, who snatched the phone after half a ring. 'Talk to me,' she said when she recognized his voice.

'Round one is over,' he said.

'Don't beat around the bush!'

'You just made ten million bucks,' he said, the words coming from his mouth but in a voice that belonged to someone else.

'Don't lie to me, Clay.' Her words trailed off.

'It's true. I'm not lying.'

There was a pause as she began to cry. He backpedaled and sat on the edge of the bed, and for a moment felt like a good cry himself. 'Oh my God,' she managed to say twice.

'I'll call you back in a few minutes,' Clay said.

Jonah was still at the office. He began yelling into the phone, then threw it down to go fetch Rodney. Clay heard them talking in the background. A door slammed. Rodney picked up the phone and said, 'I'm listening.'

'Your share is ten million,' Clay said, for the third time, playing Santa Claus as he would never play it again.

'Mercy, mercy, mercy,' Rodney was saying. Jonah was screaming something in the background.

'Hard to believe,' Clay said. For a moment, he held the image of Rodney sitting at his old desk at OPD, files and papers everywhere, photos of his wife and kids pinned to the wall, a fine man working hard for very low pay.

What would he tell his wife when he called home in a few minutes?

Jonah picked up an extension and they chatted for a while about the settlement conference – who was there, where was it, what was it like? They did not want to let go, but Clay said he had promised to call Paulette again.

When he'd finished delivering the news, he sat on the bed for a long time, sad with the realization that there was no one else to call. He could see Rebecca, and he could suddenly hear her voice and feel her and touch her. They could buy a place in Tuscany or Maui or anywhere she wanted. They could live there quite happily with a dozen kids and no in-laws, with nannies and maids and cooks and maybe even a butler. He'd send her home twice a year on the jet so she could fight with her parents.

Or maybe the Van Horns wouldn't be so awful with a hundred million or so in the family, just out of their reach but close enough to brag about.

He clenched his jaws and dialed her number. It was a Wednesday, a slow night at the country club. Surely she was at her apartment. After three rings she said, 'Hello,' and the sound of her voice made him weak.

'Hey, it's Clay,' he said, trying to sound casual. Not a word in six months, but the ice was immediately broken.

'Hello, stranger,' she said. Cordial.

'How are you?'

'Fine, busy as always. You?'

'About the same. I'm in New York, settling some cases.'

'I hear things are going well for you.'

261

An understatement. 'Not bad. I can't complain. How's your job?'

'I have six more days.'

'You're quitting?'

'Yes. There's a wedding, you know.'

'So I heard. When is it?'

'December twentieth.'

'I haven't received an invitation.'

'Well, I didn't send you one. Didn't think you'd want to come.'

'Probably not. Are you sure you want to get married?'

'Let's talk about something else.'

'There is nothing else, really.'

'Are you dating anyone?'

'Women are chasing me all over town. Where'd you meet this guy?'

'And you've bought a place in Georgetown?'

'That's old news.' But he was delighted that she knew. Perhaps she was curious about his new success. 'This guy's a worm,' he said.

'Come on, Clay. Let's keep it nice.'

'He's a worm and you know it, Rebecca.'

'I'm hanging up now.'

'Don't marry him, Rebecca. There's a rumor he's gay.'

'He's a worm. He's gay. What else? Unload everything, Clay, so you'll feel better.'

'Don't do it, Rebecca. Your parents will eat him alive. Plus your kids will look like him. A bunch of little worms.'

The line went dead.

He stretched out on the bed and stared at the ceiling, still hearing her voice, hit hard with the realization of just how much he missed her. Then the phone erupted and startled him. It was Patton French, in the lobby with a limo waiting. Dinner and wine for the next three hours. Someone had to do it.

Chapter 23

All participants had been sworn to secrecy. Thick documents had been signed by the lawyers promising complete confidentiality concerning the Dyloft negotiations and settlement. Before they left New York, Patton French had told his group, 'It'll be in the papers within forty-eight hours. Philo will leak it, and their stock will go up.'

The following morning, the *Wall Street Journal* ran the story; of course, all blame was laid at the bar. MASS TORT LAWYERS FORCE QUICK DYLOFT SETTLEMENT ran the headline. Unnamed sources had plenty to say. The details were accurate. A pool of $2.5 billion would be set up for the first round of settlements, with another potential $1.5 billion as a reserve for more serious cases.

Philo Products opened at $82 and quickly jumped to $85. One analyst said investors were relieved at news of the settlement. The company would be able to control the costs of litigation. No prolonged lawsuits. No threat of wild verdicts. The trial lawyers had been reined in on this one, and unnamed sources at Philo were calling it a victory. Clay monitored the news on the television in his office.

He also fielded calls from reporters. At eleven, one from the *Journal* arrived, with a photographer. During the preliminaries, Clay learned that he knew as much about the settlement as Clay himself. 'These things are never kept quiet,' he said. 'We knew which hotel you guys were hiding in.'

Off the record, Clay answered all questions. Then on the record, he wouldn't comment on the settlement. He did offer some insights about himself, his rapid rise from the depths of OPD to mass tort zillionaire, all in just a few months, and the impressive firm he was building, etcetera. He could see the story taking shape, and it would be spectacular.

Next morning, he read it online before sunrise. There was his face, in one of those hideous sketches made famous by the *Journal*, and just above it was the headline THE KING OF TORTS: FROM $40,000 TO $100,000,000 IN SIX MONTHS. Under it was a subtitle: 'You gotta love the law!'

It was a very long story, and all about Clay. His background, growing up in D.C., his father, Georgetown Law School, generous quotes from Glenda and Jermaine over at OPD, a comment from a professor he'd forgotten about, a brief recap of the Dyloft litigation. The best part was a lengthy discussion with Patton French, in which the 'notorious mass tort lawyer' described Clay

Carter as our 'brightest young star' and 'fearless' and 'a major new force to be reckoned with.' 'Corporate America should tremble at his name,' continued the bombast. And, finally, 'No doubt, Clay is the newest King of Torts.'

He read it twice then e-mailed it to Rebecca with a note at the top and bottom: 'Rebecca, Please Wait, Clay.' He sent it to her apartment and her office, and, while he was at it, he removed his own message and faxed it to the offices of BVH Group. The wedding was a month away.

When he finally arrived at the office, Miss Glick handed him a stack of messages – about half from law school friends who jokingly asked for loans, about half from journalists of all varieties. The office was even more chaotic than normal. Paulette, Jonah, and Rodney were still floating and completely unfocused. Every client wanted the money that day.

Fortunately, it was the Yale Branch, under the emerging brilliance of Mr Oscar Mulrooney, that stepped up to the task and put together a plan to survive until the settlement. Clay moved Mulrooney into an office down the hall, doubled his salary, and left him in charge of the mess.

Clay needed a break.

Because Jarrett Carter's passport had been quietly confiscated by the U.S. Department of Justice, his movements were somewhat limited. He wasn't even certain he could return to his country, though in six years he had never tried. The wink-and-handshake deal that got him out of town without an indictment had many loose ends. 'We'd better stick to the Bahamas,' he told Clay on the phone.

They left Abaco on a Cessna Citation V, another toy from the fleet Clay had discovered. They were headed for Nassau, thirty minutes away. Jarrett waited until they were airborne before saying, 'Okay, spill your guts.' He was already gulping a beer. And he was wearing frayed denim shorts and sandals and an old fishing cap, very much the expatriate banished to the islands and living the life of a pirate.

Clay opened a beer himself, then began with Tarvan and ended with Dyloft. Jarrett had heard rumors of his son's success, but he never read newspapers and tried his best to ignore any news from home. Another beer as he tried to digest the idea of having five thousand clients at once.

The $100 million closed his eyes, turned him pale, or least a slightly lighter shade of bronze, and it creased his leathery forehead with a wave of thick wrinkles. He shook his head, drank some beer, then began laughing.

Clay pressed on, determined to finish before they landed.

'What are you doing with the money?' Jarrett asked, still in shock.

'Spending it like crazy.'

Outside the Nassau airport they found a cab, a 1974 yellow Cadillac with a driver smoking pot. He got them safely to the Sunset Hotel and

Casino on Paradise Island, facing Nassau Harbor.

Jarrett headed for the blackjack tables with the five thousand in cash his son had given him. Clay headed for the pool and the tanning cream. He wanted sun and bikinis.

The boat was a sixty-three-foot catamaran made by a builder of fine sailboats in Fort Lauderdale. The captain/salesman was a cranky old Brit named Maltbee whose sidekick was a scrawny Bahamian deckhand. Maltbee snarled and fussed until they were out of Nassau Harbor and into the bay. They were headed for the southern edge of channel, for a half day in the brilliant sun and calm water, a lengthy test drive of a boat that Jarrett said could make some real money.

When the engine was turned off and the sails went up, Clay went down to examine the cabin. Supposedly it could sleep eight, plus a crew of two. Tight quarters, but then everything was junior-sized. The shower was too small to turn around in. The master suite would fit in his smallest closet. Life on a sailboat.

According to Jarrett, it was impossible to make money catching fish. Business was sporadic. A charter every day was required to turn a profit, but then the work was too hard for that. Deckhands were impossible to keep. Tips were never enough. Most clients were tolerable but there were plenty of bad ones to sour the job. He'd been a charter captain for five years and it was taking its toll.

The real money was in private sailboat charters for small groups of wealthy people who wanted to work, not be pampered. Semiserious sailors. Take a great boat – your own boat, preferably one without liens on it – and sail around the Caribbean for a month at a time. Jarrett had a friend from Freeport who'd been running two such boats for years and was making serious money. The clients mapped their course, chose their times and routes, selected their menus and booze, and off they went with a captain and a first mate for a month. 'Ten thousand bucks a week,' Jarrett said. 'Plus you're sailing, enjoying the wind and the sun and the sea, going nowhere. Unlike fishing, where you gotta catch a big marlin or everybody's mad.'

When Clay emerged from the cabin Jarrett was at the helm, looking very much at ease, as if he'd been racing fine yachts for years. Clay moved along the deck and stretched out in the sun.

They found some wind and began slicing through the smooth water, to the east along the bay, with Nassau fading in the distance. Clay had stripped down to his shorts and was covered in cream; he was about to doze when Maltbee crept up beside him.

'Your father tells me you're the one with the money.' Maltbee's eyes were hidden behind thick sunshades.

'I guess he's right,' Clay said.

'She's a four-million-dollar boat, practically new, one-of our best. Built for one of those dot-commers who lost his money faster than he made it. A sorry lot of them, if you ask me. Anyway, we're stuck with it. Market's slow. We'll move it for three million, and at that you should be charged with thievery. If you incorporate the boat under Bahamian law as a charter company, there are all sorts of tax tricks. I can't explain them, but we have a lawyer in Nassau who does the paperwork. If you can catch him sober.'

'I'm a lawyer.'

'Then why are you sober?'

Ha, ha, ha; they both managed an awkward laugh.

'What about depreciation?' Clay asked.

'Heavy, quite heavy, but again, that's for you lawyers. I'm just a salesman. I think your old man likes it though. Boats like these are quite the rage from here to Bermuda to South America. It'll make money.'

So says the salesman, and a bad one at that. If Clay bought a boat for his father, his sole dream was that it would break even and not become a black hole. Maltbee disappeared as quickly as he had materialized.

Three days later, Clay signed a contract to pay $2.9 million for the boat. The lawyer, who was in fact not completely sober during either of the two meetings Clay had with him, chartered the Bahamian company in Jarrett's name only. The boat was a gift from son to father, an asset to be hidden away in the islands, much like Jarrett himself.

Over dinner their last night in Nassau, in the back of a seedy saloon packed with drug dealers and tax cheaters and alimony dodgers, virtually all of them American, Clay cracked crab legs and finally asked a question he'd been considering for weeks now. 'Any chance you could ever return to the States?'

'For what?'

'To practice law. To be my partner. To litigate and kick ass again.'

The question made Jarrett smile. The thought of father and son working together. The very idea that Clay wanted him to return; back to an office, back to something respectable. The boy lived under a dark cloud that the old man had left behind. However, given the boy's recent success the cloud was certainly shrinking.

'I doubt it, Clay. I surrendered my license and promised to stay away.'

'Would you want to come back?'

'Maybe to clear my name, but never to practice law again. There's too much baggage, too many old enemies still lurking around. I'm fifty-five years old, and that's a bit late to start over.'

'Where will you be in ten years?'

'I don't think like that. I don't believe in calendars and schedules and lists of things to do. Setting goals is such a stupid American habit. Not for me. I try to get through today, maybe give a thought or two to tomorrow, and that's it. Plotting the future is damned ridiculous.'

'Sorry I asked.'

'Live for the moment, Clay. Tomorrow will take care of itself. You've got your hands full right now, seems to me.'

'The money should keep me occupied.'

'Don't blow it, son. I know that looks impossible, but you'll be surprised. New friends are about to pop up all over the place. Women will drop from the sky.'

'When?'

'Just wait. I read a book once – *Fool's Gold*, or something like that. One story after another about great fortunes that had been lost by the idiots who had them. Fascinating reading. Get a copy.'

'I think I'll pass.'

Jarrett threw a shrimp in his mouth and changed the subject, 'Are you going to help your mother?'

'Probably not. She doesn't need help. Her husband is wealthy, remember?'

'When have you talked to her?'

'It's been eleven years, Dad. Why do you care?'

'Just curious. It's odd. You marry a woman, live with her for twenty-five years, and you sometimes wonder what she's doing.'

'Let's talk about something else.'

'Rebecca?'

'Next.'

'Let's go hit the crap tables. I'm up four thousand bucks.'

When Mr. Ted Worley of Upper Marlboro, Maryland, received a thick envelope from the Law Offices of J. Clay Carter II, he immediately opened it. He'd seen various news reports about the Dyloft settlement. He'd watched the Dyloft Web site religiously, waiting for some sign that it was time to collect his money from Ackerman Labs.

The letter began, 'Dear Mr. Worley: Congratulations. Your class-action claim against Ackerman Labs has been settled in the U.S. District Court for the Southern District of Mississippi. As a Group One Plaintiff, your portion of the settlement is $62,000. Pursuant to the Contract for Legal Services entered into by you and this law firm, a twenty-eight percent contingency for attorneys' fees is now applicable. In addition, a deduction of $1,400 for litigation expenses has been approved by the court. Your net settlement is $43,240. Please sign the enclosed agreement and acknowledgment forms and return them immediately in the enclosed envelope. Sincerely, Oscar Mulrooney, Attorney-at-Law.'

'A different lawyer every damned time,' Mr. Worley said as he kept flipping pages. There was a copy of the court order approving the settlement, and a notice to all class-action plaintiffs, and some other papers that he suddenly had no desire to read.

$43,240! That was the grand sum he would receive from a sleazy pharmaceutical giant that deliberately put into the marketplace a drug that caused four tumors to grow in his bladder? $43,240 for months of fear and stress and uncertainty about living or dying? $43,240 for the ordeal of a microscopic knife and scope in a tube slid up his penis and into his bladder where the four growths were removed one by one and retrieved back through his penis? $43,240 for three days of lumps and blood passed through his urine?

He flinched at the memory.

He called six times and left six hot messages and waited six hours until Mr. Mulrooney called him back. 'Who the hell are you?' Mr. Worley began pleasantly.

Oscar Mulrooney, in the past ten days, had become an expert at handling such calls. He explained that he was the attorney in charge of Mr. Worley's case.

'This settlement is a joke!' Mr. Worley said. 'Forty-three thousand dollars is criminal.'

'Your settlement is sixty-two thousand, Mr. Worley,' Oscar said.

'I'm getting forty-three, son.'

'No, you're getting sixty-two. You agreed to give one-third to your attorney, without whom you would be getting nothing. It's been reduced to twenty-eight percent by the settlement. Most lawyers charge forty-five or fifty percent.'

'Well, aren't I a lucky bastard. I'm not accepting it.'

To which Oscar offered a brief and well-rehearsed narrative about how Ackerman Labs could only pay so much without going bankrupt, an event that would leave Mr. Worley with even less, if anything at all.

'That's nice,' Mr. Worley said. 'But I'm not accepting the settlement.'

'You have no choice.'

'The hell I don't.'

'Look at the Contract for Legal Services, Mr. Worley. It's page eleven in the packet you have there. Paragraph eight is called the Preauthorization. Read the language, sir, and you'll see that you authorized this firm to settle for anything above fifty thousand dollars.'

'I remember that, but it was described to me as a starting point. I was expecting much more.'

'Your settlement has already been approved by the court, sir. That's the way class actions work. If you don't sign the acceptance form, then your portion will stay in the pot and eventually go to someone else.'

'You're a bunch of crooks, you know that? I don't know who's worse – the company that made the drug or my own lawyers who're screwing me out of a fair settlement.'

'Sorry you feel that way.'

'You're not sorry about a damned thing. Paper says you're getting a hundred million bucks. Thieves!'

Mr. Worley slammed the phone down and flung the papers across his kitchen.

Chapter 24

The December cover of *Capitol Magazine* featured Clay Carter, looking tanned and quite handsome in an Armani suit, perched on the corner of his desk in his finely appointed office. It was a frantic last-minute substitution for a story titled 'Christmas on the Potomac,' the usual holiday edition in which a rich old Senator and his newest trophy wife opened their private new Washington mansion for all to see. The couple, and their decorations and cats and favorite recipes, got bumped to the inside because D.C. was first and always a city about money and power. How often would the magazine have the chance at the unbelievable story of a broke young lawyer who got so rich so fast?

There was Clay on his patio with a dog, one he'd borrowed from Rodney, and Clay posing next to the jury box in an empty courtroom as if he'd been extracting huge verdicts from the bad guys, and, of course, Clay washing his new Porsche. He confided that his passion was sailing, and there was a new boat docked down in the Bahamas. No significant romance at the moment, and the story immediately labeled him as one of the most eligible bachelors in town.

Near the back were the pictures of brides, followed by the announcements of upcoming weddings. Every debutante and private school girl and country club socialite in metropolitan D.C. dreamed of the moment when she would arrive in the pages of *Capitol Magazine*. The larger the photo, the more important the family. Ambitious mothers were known to take a ruler and measure the dimensions of their daughters' pictures and those of their rivals, then either gloat or hold secret grudges for years.

There was Rebecca Van Horn, resplendent on a wicker bench in a garden somewhere, a lovely photo ruined by the face of her groom and future mate, the Honorable Jason Shubert Myers IV, cuddling next to her and obviously enjoying the camera. Weddings are for brides, not grooms. Why did they insist on getting their faces in the announcements too?

Bennett and Barbara had pulled the right strings; Rebecca's announcement was the second largest of a dozen or so. Six pages over, Clay saw a full-page ad for BVH Group. The bribe.

Clay reveled in the misery the magazine was causing at that very moment around the Van Horn home. Rebecca's wedding, the big social bash that Bennett and Barbara could throw money at and impress the world, was being upstaged by their old nemesis. How many times would their daughter get her wedding announcement in *Capitol Magazine*? How hard had they worked to make sure she was prominently displayed? And all of it now ruined by Clay's thunder.

And his upstaging was not over.

Jonah had already announced that retirement was a real possibility. He'd spent ten days on Antigua with not one girl but two, and when he returned to D.C., in an early December snowstorm, he confided in Clay that he was mentally and psychologically unfit to practice law any longer. He'd had all he could take. His legal career was over. He was looking at sailboats himself. He'd found a girl who loved to sail and, because she was on the downside of a bad marriage, she too needed some serious time at sea. Jonah was from Annapolis and, unlike Clay, had sailed his entire life.

'I need a bimbo, preferably a blonde,' Clay said as he settled into a chair across from Jonah's desk. His door was locked. It was after six on a Wednesday and Jonah had the first bottle of beer opened. They had compromised on an unwritten rule that there would be no drinking until 6 P.M. Otherwise, Jonah would start just after lunch.

'The hottest bachelor in town is having trouble picking up chicks?'

'I've been out of the loop. I'm going to Rebecca's wedding, and I need a babe who'll steal the show.'

278

'Oh, this is beautiful,' he said as he laughed and reached into a drawer in his desk. Only Jonah would keep files on women. He burrowed through some paperwork and found what he wanted. He tossed a folded newspaper across the desk. It was a lingerie ad for a department store. The gorgeous young goddess was wearing practically nothing below the waist and was barely covering her breasts with her folded arms. Clay vividly remembered seeing the ad the morning it first ran. The date was four months earlier.

'You know her?'

'Of course I know her. You think I keep lingerie ads just for the thrills?'

'Wouldn't surprise me.'

'Her name is Ridley. At least that's what she goes by.'

'She lives here?' Clay was still gawking at the stunning beauty he was holding, in black-and-white.

'She's from Georgia.'

'Oh, a Southern girl.'

'No, a Russian girl. The country of Georgia. She came over as an exchange student and never left.'

'She looks eighteen.'

'Mid-twenties.'

'How tall is she?'

'Five ten or so.'

'Her legs look five feet long.'

'Are you complaining?'

In an effort to appear somewhat nonchalant,

Clay tossed the paper back on the desk. 'Any downside?'

'Yes, she's rumored to be a switch-hitter.'

'A what?'

'She likes boys and girls.'

'Ouch.'

'No confirmation, but a lot of models go both ways. Could be just a rumor for all I know.'

'You've dated her.'

'Nope. A friend of a friend. She's on my list. I was just waiting for a confirmation. Give it a try. You don't like her, we'll find another bimbo.'

'Can you make the call?'

'Sure, no problem. It's an easy call, now that you're Mr. Cover Boy, most eligible bachelor, the King of Torts. Wonder if they know what torts are over in Georgia?'

'Not if they're lucky. Just make the call.'

They met for dinner at the restaurant of the month, a Japanese place frequented by the young and prosperous. Ridley looked even better in person than she did in print. Heads jerked and necks twisted as they were led to the center of the restaurant and placed at a very powerful table. Conversations halted in mid-sentence. Waiters swarmed around them. Her slightly accented English was perfect and just exotic enough to add even more sex to the package, as if she needed it.

Old hand-me-downs from a flea market would look great on Ridley. Her challenge was dressing down, so the clothes wouldn't compete with the blonde hair and aqua eyes and high cheekbones and the rest of the perfect features.

Her real name was Ridal Petashnakol, which she had to spell twice before Clay got it. Fortunately, models, like soccer players, could survive with only one name, so she went just by Ridley. She drank no alcohol, but instead ordered a cranberry juice. Clay hoped she wouldn't order a plate of carrots for dinner.

She had the looks and he had the money, and since they could talk about neither they thrashed about in deep water for a few minutes looking for safe ground. She was Georgian, not Russian, and cared nothing about politics or terrorism or football. Ah, the movies! She saw everything and loved them all. Even dreadful stuff that no one else went to see. Box office disasters were much beloved by Ridley, and Clay was beginning to have doubts.

She's just a bimbo, he said to himself. Dinner now, Rebecca's wedding later, and she's history.

She spoke five languages, but since most were of the Eastern European variety they seemed pretty useless in the fast lane. Much to his relief, she ordered a first course, second course, and dessert. Conversation wasn't easy, but both worked hard at it. Their backgrounds were so different. The lawyer in him wanted a thorough examination of the witness; real name, age, blood type, father's occupation, salary, marital history, sexual history – is it true you're a switch-hitter? But he managed to throttle himself and not pry at all. He nibbled around the edges once or twice, got nothing, and went back to the movies. She knew every twenty-year-old B actor and who he happened to be dating at the moment – painfully boring stuff, but, then, probably not as boring as having a bunch of lawyers talk about their latest trial victories or toxic tort settlements.

Clay knocked back the wine and got himself loosened up. It was a red burgundy. Patton French would've been proud. If only his mass tort buddies could see him now, sitting across from this Barbie Doll.

The only negative was the nasty rumor. Surely she couldn't go for women. She was too perfect, too exquisite, too appealing to the opposite sex. She was destined to be a trophy wife! But there was something about her that kept him suspicious. Once the initial shock of her looks wore off, and that took at least two hours and one bottle of wine, Clay realized he wasn't getting past the surface. Either there wasn't much depth, or it was carefully protected.

Over dessert, a chocolate mousse that she toyed with but did not eat, he invited her to attend a wedding reception. He confessed that the bride was his former fiancée, but lied when he said that they were now on friendly terms. Ridley shrugged as if she preferred to go to the movies. 'Why not?' she said.

As he turned into the drive of the Potomac Country Club, Clay was hit hard by the moment.

His last visit to this wretched place had been more than seven months earlier, a torturous dinner with Rebecca's parents. Then he'd hidden his old Honda behind the tennis courts. Now, he was showing off a freshly detailed Porsche Carrera. Then, he'd avoided the valet parking to save money. Now he'd tip the kid extra. Then, he was alone and dreading the next few hours with the Van Horns. Now he was escorting the priceless Ridley, who held his elbow and crossed her legs in such a way that the slit in her skirt showed all the way to her waist; and wherever her parents happened to be at the moment they damned sure weren't involved in his life. Then, he'd felt like a vagrant on hallowed ground. Now the Potomac Country Club would approve his application tomorrow if he wrote the right check.

'Van Horn wedding reception,' he said to the guard, who waved him through.

They were an hour late, which was perfect timing. The ballroom was packed and a rhythm and blues band played at one end.

'Stay close to me,' Ridley whispered as they entered. 'I won't know anyone here.'

'Don't worry,' Clay said. Staying close would not be a problem. And though he pretended otherwise, he wouldn't know anyone either.

Heads began turning immediately. Jaws dropped. With several drinks under their belts the men did not hesitate to gawk at Ridley as she and her date inched forward. 'Hey, Clay!' someone yelled, and Clay turned to see the smiling face of

Randy Spino, a law school classmate who worked in a megafirm and would never, under normal circumstances, have spoken to Clay in such surroundings. A chance meeting on the street, and maybe Spino would say, 'How's it going?' without breaking stride. But never in a country club crowd, and especially one so dominated by big-firm types.

But there he was, thrusting a hand forward at Clay while showing Ridley every one of his teeth. A small mob followed. Spino took charge, introducing all of his good friends to his good friend Clay Carter and Ridley with no last name. She squeezed Clay's elbow even tighter. All the boys wanted to say hello.

To get close to Ridley they needed to chat with Clay, so it was only a few seconds before someone said, 'Hey, Clay, congratulations on nailing Ackerman Labs.' Clay had never seen the person who congratulated him. He assumed he was a lawyer, probably from a big firm, probably a big firm that represented big corporations like Ackerman Labs, and he knew before the sentence was finished that the false praise was driven by envy. And a desire to stare at Ridley.

'Thanks,' Clay said, as if it was just another day at the office.

'A hundred million. Wow!' This face, too, belonged to a stranger, one who appeared to be drunk.

'Well, half goes for taxes,' Clay said. Who could get by these days on just $50 million?

The mob exploded in laughter, as if Clay had just hit the funniest punch line ever. More people gathered around, all men, all inching toward this striking blonde who looked vaguely familiar. Perhaps they didn't recognize her in full color with her clothes on.

An intense, stuffy type said, 'We got Philo. Boy, were we glad to get that Dyloft mess settled.' It was an affliction suffered by most D.C. lawyers. Every corporation in the world had D.C. counsel, if in name only, and so every dispute or transaction had grave consequences among the city's lawyers. A refinery blows up in Thailand, and a lawyer will say, 'Yeah, we got Exxon.' A blockbuster flops – 'We got Disney.' An SUV flips and kills five – 'We got Ford.' 'We-Gots' was a game Clay had heard until he was sick of it.

I got Ridley, he wanted to say, so keep your hands off.

An announcement was being made onstage and the room became quieter. The bride and groom were about to dance, to be followed by the bride and her father, then the groom and his mother, and so on. The crowd gathered around to watch. The band began playing 'Smoke Gets in Your Eyes.'

'She's very pretty,' Ridley whispered, very close to his right ear. Indeed she was. And she was dancing with Jason Myers who, though he was two inches shorter, appeared to Rebecca to be the only person in the world. She smiled and glowed as they spun slowly around the dance floor, the bride doing most of the work because her groom was as stiff as a board.

Clay wanted to attack, to bolt through the crowd and sucker punch Myers with all the force he could muster. He would rescue his girl and take her away and shoot her mother if she found them.

'You still love her, don't you?' Ridley was whispering.

'No, it's over,' he whispered back.

'You do. I can tell.'

'No.'

The newlyweds would go somewhere tonight and consummate their marriage, though knowing Rebecca as intimately as he did, he knew she had not been doing without sex. She'd probably taken this worm Myers and educated him in the ways of the bed. A lucky man. The things Clay had taught her she was now passing along to someone else. It wasn't fair.

The two were painful to watch, and Clay asked himself why he was there. Closure, whatever that meant. A farewell. But he wanted Rebecca to see him, and Ridley, and to know that he was faring well and not missing her.

Watching Bennett the Bulldozer dance was painful for other reasons. He subscribed to the white man's theory of dancing without moving his feet, and when he tried to shake his butt the band actually laughed. His cheeks were already crimson from too much Chivas.

Jason Myers danced with Barbara Van Horn

who, from a distance, looked as though she'd had another round or two with her discount plastic surgeon. She was poured into a dress that, while pretty, was several sizes too small, so that the extra flab was bulging in the wrong spots and seemed ready to free itself and make everyone sick. She had plastered across her face the phoniest grin she'd ever produced – no wrinkles anywhere, though, due to excessive Botox – and Myers grinned right back as if the two would be close chums forever. She was already knifing him in the back and he was too stupid to know it. Sadly, she probably didn't know it either. Just the nature of the beast.

'Would you like to dance?' someone asked Ridley.

'Bug off,' Clay said, then led her to the dance floor where a mob was gyrating to some pretty good Motown. If Ridley standing still was a work of art, Ridley in full motion was a national treasure. She moved with a natural rhythm and easy grace, with the low-cut dress just barely high enough and the slit in the skirt flying open to reveal all manner of flesh. Groups of men were gathering to watch.

And watching also was Rebecca. Taking a break to chat with her guests, she noticed the commotion and looked into the crowd, where she saw Clay dancing with a knockout. She, too, was stunned by Ridley, but for other reasons. She continued chatting for a moment, then moved back to the dance floor.

Meanwhile, Clay's eyes were working furiously to check on Rebecca without missing a movement from Ridley. The song ended, a slow number began, and Rebecca stepped between them. 'Hello, Clay,' she said, ignoring his date. 'How about a dance?'

'Sure,' he said. Ridley shrugged and moved away, alone for only a second before a stampede surrounded her. She picked the tallest one, threw her arms around him, and began pulsating.

'Don't remember inviting you.' Rebecca said with an arm over his shoulder.

'You want me to leave?' He pulled her slightly closer but the bulky wedding dress prevented the contact he wanted.

'People are watching,' she said, smiling for their benefit. 'Why are you here?'

'To celebrate your wedding. And to get a good look at your new boy.'

'Don't be ugly, Clay. You're just jealous.'

'I'm more than jealous. I'd like to break his neck.'

'Where'd you get the bimbo?'

'Now who's jealous?'

'Me.'

'Don't worry, Rebecca, she can't touch you in bed.' On second thought, perhaps she'd like to. Anyway.

'Jason's not bad.'

'I really don't want to hear about it. Just don't get pregnant, okay?'

'That's hardly any of your business.'

288

'It's very much my business.'

Ridley and her beau swept by them. For the first time Clay got a good look at her back, the full extent of which was on display because her dress didn't exist until just a few tiny inches above her round and perfect cheeks. Rebecca saw it too. 'Is she on the payroll?' she asked.

'Not yet.'

'Is she a minor?'

'Oh no. She's very much the adult. Tell me you still love me.'

'I don't.'

'You're lying.'

'It might be best if you leave now, and take her with you.'

'Sure, it's your party. Didn't mean to crash it.'

'That's the only reason you're here, Clay.' She pulled away slightly but kept dancing.

'Hang in there for a year, okay?' he said. 'By then I'll have two hundred million. We can hop on my jet, blow this joint, spend the rest of our lives on a yacht. Your parents will never find us.'

She stopped moving and said, 'Good-bye, Clay.'

'I'll wait,' he said, then got knocked aside by a stumbling Bennett who said, 'Excuse me.' He grabbed his daughter and rescued her by shuffling to the other side of the floor.

Barbara was next. She took Clay's hand and flashed an artificial smile. 'Let's not make a scene,' she said without moving her lips. They began a rigid movement that no one would mistake for dancing.

'And how are you, Mrs. Van Horn?' Clay said, in the clutches of a pit viper.

'Fine, until I saw you. I'm positive you were not invited to this little party.'

'I was just leaving.'

'Good. I'd hate to call security.'

'That won't be necessary.'

'Don't ruin this moment for her, please.'

'Like I said. I was just leaving.'

The music stopped and Clay jerked away from Mrs. Van Horn. A small mob materialized around Ridley, but Clay whisked her off. They retreated to the back of the room where a bar was attracting more fans than the band. Clay grabbed a beer and was planning an exit when another group of onlookers encircled them. Lawyers in the bunch wanted to talk about the joys of mass torts while pressing close to Ridley.

After a few minutes of idiotic small talk with people he detested, a thick young man in a rented tuxedo appeared next to Clay and whispered, 'I'm security.' He had a friendly face and seemed very professional.

'I'm leaving,' Clay whispered back.

Tossed from the Van Horn wedding reception. Ejected from the great Potomac Country Club. Driving away, with Ridley wrapped around him, he privately declared it to be one of his finest moments.

Chapter 25

The announcement had said the newlyweds would honeymoon in Mexico. Clay decided to take a trip himself. If anyone deserved a month on an island, it was he.

His once formidable team had lost all direction. Perhaps it was the holidays, perhaps it was the money. Whatever the reason, Jonah, Paulette, and Rodney were spending fewer hours at the office.

As was Clay. The place was filled with tension and strife. So many Dyloft clients were unhappy with their meager settlements. The mail was brutal. Dodging the phone had become a sport. Several clients had actually found the place and presented themselves to Miss Glick with demands to see Mr. Carter, who, it happened, was always in a big trial somewhere. Usually, he was hunkering down in his office with the door locked, riding out yet another storm. After one particularly troubling day, he called Patton French for advice.

'Toughen up, ol' boy,' French said. 'It goes with the territory. You're making a fortune in mass torts, this is just the downside. It takes a thick skin.'

The thickest skin in the firm belonged to Oscar Mulrooney, who continued to amaze Clay with his organizational skills and his ambition. Mulrooney was working fifteen hours a day and pushing his Yale Branch to collect the Dyloft money as quickly as possible. He readily assumed any unpleasant task. With Jonah making no secret of his plans to sail around the world, Paulette dropping hints about a year in Africa to study art, and Rodney following along with some vague chatter about just plain quitting, it was obvious that there would soon be room at the top.

It was just as obvious that Oscar was hustling for a partnership, or at least a piece of the action. He was studying the massive litigation still raging over Skinny Bens, the diet pills that had gone awry, and was convinced that at least ten thousand cases were still out there, unclaimed, in spite of four years' worth of nonstop publicity.

The Yale Branch now had eleven lawyers, seven of whom had actually gone to Yale. The Sweatshop had grown to twelve paralegals, all up to their ears in files and paperwork. Clay had no hesitation in leaving both units under the supervision of Mulrooney for a few weeks. He was certain that when he returned, the office would be in better shape than when he left.

*   *   *

Christmas had become a season he tried to ignore, though it was difficult. He had no family to spend time with. Rebecca had always worked hard to include him with whatever the Van Horns happened to be doing, but while he appreciated the effort, he'd found that sitting alone in an empty apartment drinking cheap wine and watching old movies on Christmas Eve was a far better evening than opening gifts with those people. No gift he gave was ever good enough.

Ridley's family was still in Georgia, and likely to stay there. At first, she was certain that she could not rearrange her modeling assignments and leave town for several weeks. But her determination to do so warmed his heart. She really wanted to jet away to the islands and play with him on the beach. She finally told one client to go ahead and fire her; she didn't care.

It was her first trip on a private jet. He found himself wanting to impress her in so many ways. Nonstop from Washington to St Lucia, four hours and a million miles. D.C. was cold and gray when they left, and when they stepped off the plane the sun and the heat hit them hard. They walked through Customs with hardly a glance, at least none directed at Clay. Every male head turned to admire Ridley. Oddly, Clay was getting accustomed to it. She seemed oblivious. It had been a way of life for so long that she simply ignored everyone, which only made matters worse for those gawking. Such an exquisite creature, perfect from head to foot, yet so aloof, so untouchable.

They boarded a commuter for the fifteen-minute flight to Mustique, the exclusive island owned by the rich and famous, an island with everything but a runway long enough for private jets. Rock stars and actresses and billionaires had mansions there. Their house for the next week had once been owned by a prince who sold it to a dot-commer who leased it when he wasn't around.

The island was a mountain surrounded by the still waters of the Caribbean. From three thousand feet up, it looked dark and lush, a picture on a postcard. Ridley clutched and groped as they descended and the tiny airstrip came into the view. The pilot wore a straw cap and could've landed wearing a blindfold.

Marshall, the chauffeur/butler, was waiting with a huge smile and an open Jeep. They threw their rather light bags in the back and started up a winding road. No hotels, no condos, no tourists, no traffic. For ten minutes they did not see another vehicle. The house was on the side of a mountain, as Marshall described it, though it was just a hill. The view was breathtaking – two hundred feet above the water and miles of endless ocean. No other island could be seen; no boats out there, no people.

There were four or five bedrooms, Clay lost count, spread around a main house and connected with tiled walkways. Lunch was ordered; whatever they wanted because there was a full-time chef. And a gardener, two housekeepers, and a butler.

A staff of five – plus Marshall – and they all lived somewhere on the premises. Before they could unpack in the main suite, Ridley had stripped down to virtually nothing and was in the pool. Topless, and if not for a small string that could barely be seen, she would have been completely nude. Just when Clay thought he was accustomed to looking at her, he found himself once more almost dizzy.

She covered up for lunch. Fresh seafood, of course – grilled prawns and oysters. Two beers and Clay was staggering toward a hammock for a long siesta. Tomorrow was Christmas Eve, and he didn't care. Rebecca was away in some tourist trap of a hotel, cuddling with little Jason.

And he didn't care.

Two days after Christmas, Max Pace arrived with a companion. Her name was Valeria, a rugged, crunchy outdoors type with broad shoulders and no makeup and a very reluctant smile. Max was a very handsome fellow, but there was nothing attractive about his friend. Hopefully, Valeria would keep her clothes on around the pool. When Clay shook her hand he felt calluses. Well, at least she wouldn't be a temptation for Ridley.

Pace was quick to change into shorts and head for the pool. Valeria pulled out some hiking boots and asked where the trails were. Marshall had to be consulted, said he was unaware of any trails, which of course displeased Valeria who struck off anyway, in search of rocks to climb. Ridley disappeared into the living room of the main house, where she had a stack of videos to watch.

Because Pace had no background, there was little to talk about. At first, anyway. However, it soon became apparent that he had something important on his mind. 'Let's talk business,' he said after a nap in the sun. They moved to the bar and Marshall brought drinks.

'There's another drug out there,' Pace began, and Clay immediately began seeing money. 'And it's a big one.'

'Here we go again.'

'But the plan is a little different this time. I want a piece of the action.'

'Who are you working for?'

'Me. And you. I get twenty-five percent of the gross attorneys' fees.'

'What's the upside?'

'It could be bigger than Dyloft.'

'Then you get twenty-five percent. More if you want.' The two shared so much dirty laundry, how could Clay say no?

'Twenty-five is fair,' Max said, and reached across for a handshake. The deal was done.

'Let's have it.'

'There's a female hormone drug called Maxatil. Used by at least four million menopausal and post-menopausal women, ages forty-five to seventy-five. It came out five years ago, another wonder drug. It relieves hot flashes and other symptoms of menopause. Very effective. It's also touted to preserve bone strength, reduce hypertension and the risks of heart disease. The company is Goffman.'

'Goffman? Razor blades and mouthwash?'

'You got it. Twenty-one billion in sales last year. The bluest of all blue-chips. Very little debt, sound management. An American tradition. But they got in a hurry with Maxatil, typical story – profits looked huge, drug looked safe, they rammed it through the FDA and for the first few years everybody was happy. Doctors loved it. The women are crazy about it because it works beautifully.'

'But?'

'But there are problems. Huge problems. A government study has been tracking twenty thousand women who've been taking the drug for four years. The study has just been completed, and a report is due in a few weeks. It will be devastating. For a percentage of women, the drug greatly increases the risk of breast cancer, heart attacks, and strokes.'

'What percentage?'

'About eight percent.'

'Who knows about the report?'

'Very few people. I have a copy of it.'

'Why am I not surprised?' Clay took a long pull on the bottle and looked around for Marshall. His pulse was racing. He was suddenly bored with Mustique.

'There are some lawyers on the prowl, but they haven't seen the government report,' Pace continued. 'One lawsuit has been filed, in Arizona, but it's not a class action.'

'What is it?'

'Just an old-fashioned tort case. A one-shot deal.'

'How boring.'

'Not really. The lawyer is a character named Dale Mooneyham, from Tucson. He tries them one at a time, and he never loses. He's on the fast track to get the first shot at Goffman. It could set the tone for the entire settlement. The key is to file the first class action. You learned that from Patton French.'

'We can file first,' Clay said, as if he'd been doing it for years.

'And you can do it alone, without French and those crooks. File it in D.C., then blitz with ads. It'll be huge.'

'Just like Dyloft.'

'Except you're in charge. I'll be in the background, pulling strings, doing the dirty work. I have lots of contacts with all the right shady characters. It'll be our lawsuit, and with your name on it Goffman will run for cover.'

'A quick settlement?'

'Probably not as quick as Dyloft, but then that was remarkably fast. You'll have to do your homework, gather the right evidence, hire the experts, sue the doctors who've been peddling the drug, push hard for the first trial. You'll have to convince Goffman that you are not interested in a settlement, that you want a trial – a huge, public spectacle of a trial, in your own backyard."

'The downside?' Clay asked, trying to appear cautious.

'None that I can see, except that it'll cost you millions in advertising and trial prep.'

'No problem there.'

'You seem to have the knack for spending it.'

'I've barely scratched the surface.'

'I'd like an advance of a million dollars. Against my fee.' Pace took a sip. 'I'm still cleaning up some old business back home.'

The fact that Pace wanted money struck Clay as odd. However, with so much at stake, and with their Tarvan secret, he was in no position to say no. 'Approved,' he said.

They were in the hammocks when Valeria returned, soaked with sweat and appearing somewhat relaxed. She stripped everything off and jumped in the pool. 'A California girl,' Pace said softly.

'Something serious?' Clay asked, tentatively.

'Off and on for many years now.' And he let it go at that.

The California girl requested a dinner that included no meat, fish, chicken, eggs, or cheese. She didn't do alcohol either. Clay arranged grilled swordfish for the rest of them. The meal was over quickly, with Ridley anxious to run and hide in her room and Clay equally as eager to get away from Valeria.

Pace and his friend stayed for two days, which was at least one day too long. The purpose of the trip had been solely business, and since the deal had been struck Pace was ready to leave. Clay watched them speed away with Marshall driving faster than ever.

'Any more guests?' Ridley asked warily.

'Hell no,' Clay said.

'Good.'

Chapter 26

The entire floor above his firm became vacant at the end of the year. Clay leased half of it and consolidated his operations. He brought in the twelve paralegals and five secretaries from the Sweatshop; the Yale Branch lawyers who'd been in other space were likewise transferred to Connecticut Avenue, to the land of higher rents, where they felt more at home. He wanted his entire firm under one roof, and close at hand, because he planned to work them all until they dropped.

He attacked the new year with a ferocious work schedule – in the office by six with breakfast, lunch, and sometimes dinner at his desk. He was usually there until eight or nine at night, and left little doubt that he expected similar hours from those who wanted to stay.

Jonah did not. He was gone by the middle of January, his office cleared and vacated, his farewells quick. The sailboat was waiting. Don't bother to call. Just wire the money to an account in Aruba.

Oscar Mulrooney was measuring Jonah's office

before he got out the door. It was larger and had a better view, which meant nothing to him, but it was closer to Clay's and that was what mattered. Mulrooney smelled money, serious fees. He missed on Dyloft, but he would not miss again. He and the rest of the Yale boys had been shafted by the corporate law they'd been trained to covet, and now they were determined to make a mint in retribution. And what better way than by outright solicitation and ambulance-chasing? Nothing was more offensive to the stuffed shirts in the blue-blood firms. Mass tort litigation was not practicing law. It was a roguish form of entrepreneurship.

The aging Greek playboy who'd married Paulette Tullos and then left her had somehow gotten wind of her new money. He showed up in D.C., called her at the swanky condo he'd given her, and left a message on her answering machine. When Paulette heard his voice, she raced from her home and flew to London, where she'd spent the holidays and was still in hiding. She e-mailed Clay a dozen times while he was on Mustique, telling him of her predicament and instructing him on exactly how to handle her divorce upon his return. Clay filed the necessary papers, but the Greek was nowhere to be found. Nor was Paulette. She might come back in a few months; she might not. 'Sorry, Clay,' she said on the phone. 'But I really don't want to work anymore.'

So Mulrooney became the confidant, the unofficial partner with big ambitions. He and his team had been studying the shifting landscape of class-action litigation. They learned the law and the procedures. They read the scholarly articles by the academics, and they read the down-in-the-trenches war stories from trial lawyers. There were dozens of Web sites – one that purported to list all class actions now pending in the United States, a total of eleven thousand; one that instructed potential plaintiffs on how to join a class and receive compensation; one that specialized in lawsuits involving women's health; one for the men; several for the Skinny Ben diet pill fiasco; several for tobacco litigation. Never had so much brainpower, backed by so much cash, been aimed at the makers of bad products.

Mulrooney had a plan. With so many class actions already filed, the firm could spend its considerable resources in rounding up new clients. Because Clay had the money for advertising and marketing, they could pick the most lucrative class actions and zero in on untapped plaintiffs. As with Dyloft, almost every lawsuit that had been settled was left open for a period of years to allow new participants to collect what they were entitled to. Clay's firm could simply ride the coattails of other mass tort lawyers, sort of pick up the pieces, but for huge fees. He used the example of Skinny Bens. The best estimate of the number of potential plaintiffs was around three hundred thousand, with perhaps as many as a hundred thousand still unidentified and certainly unrepresented. The litigation had been settled; the company was forking over billions. A claimant simply had to register with the class-action administrator, prove her medicals, and collect the money.

Like a general moving his troops, Clay assigned two lawyers and a paralegal to the Skinny Ben front. This was less than what Mulrooney asked for, but Clay had bigger plans. He laid out the war on Maxatil, a lawsuit that he would direct himself. The government report, still unreleased and evidently stolen by Max Pace, was one hundred and forty pages long and filled with damning results. Clay read it twice before he gave it to Mulrooney.

On a snowy night in late January, they worked until after midnight going through it, then made detailed plans for the attack. Clay assigned Mulrooney and two other lawyers, two paralegals, and three secretaries to the Maxatil litigation.

At two in the morning, with a heavy snow hitting the conference room window, Mulrooney said he had something unpleasant to discuss. 'We need more money.'

'How much?' Clay asked.

'There are thirteen of us now, all from big firms where we were doing quite well. Ten of us are married, most have kids, we're feeling the pressure, Clay. You gave us one-year contracts for seventy-five thousand, and, believe me, we're happy to get them. You have no idea what it's like to go to Yale, or a school like it, get wined and dined by the big firms, take a job, get married, then get tossed into the streets with nothing. Does something to the old ego, you know?'

'I understand.'

'You doubled my salary and I appreciate it more than you'll ever know. I'm getting by. But the other guys are struggling. And they're very proud men.'

'How much?'

'I'd hate to lose any of them. They're bright. They work their tails off.'

'Let's do it like this, Oscar. I'm a very generous guy these days. I'll give all of you a new contract for one year, at two hundred grand. What I get in return is a ton of hours. We're on the brink here of something huge, bigger than last year. You guys deliver, and I'll do bonuses. Big fat bonuses. I love bonuses, Oscar, for obvious reasons. Deal?'

'You got it, chief.'

The snow was too heavy to drive in, so they continued the marathon. Clay had preliminary reports on the company in Reedsburg, Pennsylvania, that was making defective brick mortar. Wes Saulsberry had passed along the secret file he'd mentioned in New York. Masonry cement wasn't as exciting as bladder tumors or blood clots or leaky heart valves, but the money was just as green. They assigned two lawyers and a paralegal to prepare the class action and to go find some plaintiffs.

They were together for ten straight hours in the conference room, guzzling coffee, eating stale bagels, watching the snowfall become a blizzard, plotting the year. Though the session began as an exchange of ideas, it grew into something much more important. A new law firm took shape, one with a clear sense of where it was going and what it would become.

The President needed him! Though re-election was two years away his enemies were already raising money by the trainload. He had stood firm with the trial lawyers since his days as a rookie Senator, in fact he'd once been a small-town litigator himself, and was still proud of it, and he now needed Clay's help in fending off the selfish interests of big business. The vehicle he proposed for getting to know Clay personally was something called the Presidential Review, a select group of high-powered trial lawyers and labor types who could write nice checks and spend time talking about the issues.

The enemies were planning another massive assault called Tort Reform Now. They wanted to put heinous caps on both actual and punitive damages in lawsuits. They wanted to dismantle the class-action system that had served them (mass tort boys) so well. They wanted to prevent folks from suing doctors.

The President would stand firm, as always, but he sure needed some help. The handsome, gold-embossed, three-page letter ended with a plea for cash, and lots of it. Clay called Patton French, who, oddly enough, happened to be in his office in Biloxi. French was abrupt, as usual. 'Write the damned check,' he said.

Phone calls went back and forth between Clay

306

and the Director of the Presidential Review. Later, he couldn't remember how much he had initially planned to contribute, but it was nothing close to the $250,000 check he eventually wrote. A courier picked it up and delivered it to the White House. Four hours later, another courier delivered to Clay a small envelope from the White House. The note was handwritten on the President's correspondence card:

Dear Clay: I'm in a Cabinet meeting (trying to stay awake), otherwise I would've called. Thanks for the support. Let's have dinner and say hello.

Signed by the President.

Nice, but for a quarter of a million bucks he expected nothing less. The next day another courier delivered a thick invitation from the White House. URGENT REPLY REQUESTED was stamped on the outside. Clay and guest were asked to attend an official state dinner honoring the President of Argentina. Black tie, of course. RSVP immediately because the event was only four days away. Amazing what $250,000 would buy in Washington.

Ridley, of course, needed the proper dress, and since Clay was paying for it he went shopping with her. And he did so without complaining because he wanted some input into what she wore. Left unsupervised, she might shock the Argentines and everyone else for that matter with see-through fabrics and slits up to her waist. No sir, Clay wanted to see the outfit before she bought it.

But she was surprisingly modest in both taste and expense. Everything looked good on her; she was, after all, a model, though she seemed to be working less and less. She finally chose a stunning but simple red dress that revealed much less flesh than what she normally showed. At $3,000, it was a bargain. Shoes, a string of small pearls, a gold and diamond bracelet, and Clay escaped with just under $15,000 in damages.

Sitting in the limo outside the White House, waiting as the ones in front of them were searched by a swarm of guards, Ridley said, 'I can't believe I'm doing this. Me, a poor girl from Georgia, going to the White House.' She was wrapped around Clay's right arm. His hand was halfway up a thigh. Her accent was more pronounced, something that happened when she was nervous.

'Hard to believe,' he said, quite excited himself.

When they got out of the limo, under an awning on the East Wing, a Marine in parade dress took Ridley's arm and began an escort that took them into the East Room of the White House, where the guests were congregating and having a drink. Clay followed along, watching Ridley's rear, enjoying every second of it. The Marine reluctantly let go, and left to pick up another escort. A photographer took their picture.

They moved to the first cluster of conversation and introduced themselves to people they would never see again. Dinner was announced, and the guests proceeded into the State Dining Room, where fifteen tables of ten were packed together and covered with more china and silver and crystal than had ever been collected in one place. Seating was all prearranged, and no one sat with his or her spouse or guest. Clay escorted Ridley to her table, found her seat, helped her into it, then pecked her on the cheek and said, 'Good luck.' She flashed a model's smile, brilliant and confident, but he knew she was, at that moment, a scared little girl from Georgia. Before he was ten feet away, two men were hovering over her, grasping her hand with the warmest of introductions.

Clay was in for a long night. To his right was a society queen from Manhattan, a shriveled, prune-faced old battle-ax who'd been starving herself for so long she looked like a cadaver. She was deaf and talked at full volume. To his left was the daughter of a Midwestern shopping mall tycoon who'd gone to college with the President. Clay turned his attention to her and labored mightily for five minutes before realizing she had nothing to say.

The clock stopped moving.

His back was to Ridley; he had no idea how she was surviving.

The President spoke, then dinner was served. An opera singer across the table from Clay began to feel his wine and started telling dirty jokes. He was loud and twangy, from somewhere in the mountains, and he was completely uninhibited when it came to using obscenities in mixed company, and in the White House no less.

Three hours after he sat down, Clay stood up and said good-bye to all his wonderful new friends. The dinner was over; a band was tuning up back in the East Room. He grabbed Ridley and they headed for the music. Shortly before midnight, as the crowd dwindled down to a few dozen, the President and First Lady joined the heartier ones for a dance or two. He seemed genuinely pleased to meet Mr. Clay Carter. 'Been reading your press, son, good job,' he said.

'Thank you, Mr. President.'

'Who's the chick?'

'A friend.' What would the feminists do if they knew he used the word *chick*?

'Can I dance with her?'

'Sure, Mr. President.'

And with that, Ms. Ridal Petashnakol, a twenty-four-year-old former exchange student from Georgia, got squeezed and hugged and otherwise networked by the President of the United States.

Chapter 27

Delivery on a new Gulfstream 5 would be a minimum of twenty-two months, probably more, but the delay was not the biggest obstacle. The current price tag was $44 million, fully loaded, of course, with all the latest gadgets and toys. It was simply too much money, though Clay was seriously tempted. The broker explained that most new G-5s were bought by large corporations, billion-dollar outfits who ordered two and three at a time and kept them in the air. The better deal for him, as a sole proprietor, was to lease a slightly older airplane for say, six months, to make sure it was what he wanted. Then he could convert it to a sale, with ninety percent of his rental payments applied to the sales price.

The broker had just the airplane. It was a 1998 model G-4 SP (Special Performance) that a Fortune 500 company had recently traded in for a new G-5. When Clay saw it sitting majestically on the ramp at Reagan National, his heart leaped and his pulse took off. It was snow-white, with a tasteful royal blue striping. Paris in six hours. London in five.

He climbed aboard with the broker. If it was an inch smaller than Patton French's G-5, Clay could not tell. There was leather, mahogany, and brass trim everywhere. A kitchen, bar, and rest room in the rear; the latest avionics up front for the pilots. One sofa folded out into a bed, and for a fleeting instant he thought about Ridley; the two of them under the covers at forty thousand feet. Elaborate stereo, video, and telephone systems. Fax, PC, Internet access.

The plane looked brand-new, and the salesman explained that it was fresh from the shop where the exterior had been repainted and the interior refurbished. When pressed, he finally said, 'It's yours for thirty million.'

They sat at a small table and began the deal. The idea of a lease slowly went out the window. With Clay's income, he would have no trouble obtaining a sweet financing package. His mortgage note, only $300,000 a month, would be slightly more than the lease payments. And if at any time he wanted to trade up, then the broker would take it back at the highest market appraisal, and outfit him with whatever he wanted.

Two pilots would cost $200,000 a year, including benefits, training, everything. Clay might consider putting the plane on the certificate of a corporate air charter company. 'Depending on how much you use it, you could generate up to a million bucks a year in charters,' the broker said, moving in for the kill. 'That'll cover the expenses for pilots, hangar space, and maintenance.'

'Any idea how much I'll use it?' Clay asked, his head spinning with possibilities.

'I've sold lots of planes to lawyers,' the salesman said, reaching for the right research. 'Three hundred hours a year is max. You can charter it for twice that much.'

Wow, Clay thought. This thing might actually generate some income.

A reasonable voice said to be cautious, but why wait? And who, exactly, might he turn to for advice? The only people he knew with experience in such matters were his mass tort buddies, and every one of them would say, 'You don't have your own jet yet? Buy it!'

And so he bought it.

Goffman's fourth-quarter earnings were up from the year before, with record sales. Its stock was at $65, the highest in two years. Beginning the first week in January, the company had launched an unusual ad campaign promoting not one of its many products but the company itself. 'Goffman has always been there,' was the slogan and theme, and each television commercial was a montage of well-known products being used to comfort and protect America: a mother applying a small bandage to her little son's wound; a handsome young man with the obligatory flat stomach, shaving and having a wonderful time doing it; a gray-haired couple on the beach happily free of their hemorrhoids; a jogger in agony, reaching for a painkiller; and so on. Goffman's list of trusted consumer products was lengthy.

Mulrooney was watching the company closer than a stock analyst, and he was convinced that the ad campaign was nothing but a ploy to brace investors and consumers for the shock of Maxatil. His research found no other 'feel-good' messages in the history of Goffman's marketing. The company was one of the top five advertisers in the country, but had always poured its money into one specific product at a time, with outstanding results.

His opinion was shared by Max Pace, who had taken up residence in the Hay-Adams Hotel. Clay stopped by his suite for a late dinner, one delivered by room service. Pace was edgy and anxious to drop the bomb on Goffman. He read the latest revision of the class-action lawsuit to be filed in D.C. As always, he made notes in the margins.

'What's the plan?' he said, ignoring his food and wine.

Clay was not ignoring his. 'The ads start at eight in the morning,' he said with a mouth full of veal. 'A blitz in eighty markets, coast to coast. The hot line is set up. The Web site is ready. My little firm is poised. I'll walk over to the courthouse at ten or so and file it myself.'

'Sounds good.'

'We've done it before. The Law Offices of J. Clay Carter II is a mass tort machine, thank you very much.'

'Your new pals know nothing of it?'

'Of course not. Why would I tell them? We're in bed together with Dyloft, but French and those guys are my competitors too. I shocked them then, I'll shock them now. I can't wait.'

'This ain't Dyloft, remember that. You were lucky there because you caught a weak company at a bad moment. Goffman will be much tougher.'

Pace finally tossed the lawsuit on the dresser and sat down to eat.

'But they made a bad drug,' Clay was saying. 'And you don't go to trial with a bad drug.'

'Not in a class action. My sources tell me that Goffman might want to litigate the case in Flagstaff since it's a single plaintiff.'

'The Mooneyham case?'

'That's it. If they lose, they'll be softer on the issue of settlement. If they win, then this could be a long fight.'

'You said Mooneyham doesn't lose.'

'It's been twenty years or something like that. Juries love him. He wears cowboy hats and suede jackets and red boots and such. A throwback to the days when trial lawyers actually tried their cases. A real piece of work. You should go meet him. It would be worth a trip.'

'I'll put that on my list.' The Gulfstream was just sitting in the hangar, anxious to travel.

A phone rang and Pace spent five minutes in muted conversation on the other side of the suite. 'Valeria,' he said as he returned to the table. Clay had a quick visual of the sexless creature

315

munching on a carrot. Poor Max. He could do so much better.

Clay slept at the office. He had installed a small bedroom and a bath adjacent to the conference room. He was often up until after midnight, then a few hours of sleep before a quick shower, and back to the desk by six. His work habits were becoming legendary not only within his own firm but around the city as well. Much of the gossip in legal circles was about him, at least for the moment, and his sixteen-hour days were often stretched to eighteen and twenty by those at bars and cocktail parties.

And why not work around the clock? He was thirty-two years old, single, with no serious obligations to steal his time. Through luck and a small amount of talent he had been handed a unique opportunity to succeed like few others. Why not pour his guts into his firm for a few years, then chuck it all and go play for the rest of his life?

Mulrooney arrived just after six, already with four cups of coffee under his belt and a hundred ideas on his mind. 'D-Day?' he asked when he barged into Clay's office.

'D-Day!'

'Let's kick some ass!'

By seven, the place was rocking with associates and paralegals watching the clocks, waiting for the invasion. Secretaries hauled coffee and bagels from office to office. At eight, they crammed into the conference room and stared at a wide-screen

TV. The ABC affiliate for metro D.C. ran the first ad:

An attractive woman in her early sixties, short gray hair, smartly cut, designer eyeglasses, sitting at a small kitchen table, staring sadly out a window. Voice-over [rather ominous voice]: 'If you've been taking the female hormone drug Maxatil, you may have an increased risk of breast cancer, heart disease, and stroke.' Close on the lady's hands; on the table, a close-up of a pill bottle with the word **MAXATIL** in bold letters. [A skull and crossbones could not have been more frightening.] Voice-over: 'Please consult your doctor immediately. Maxatil may pose a serious threat to your health.' Close on the woman's face, even sadder now, then her eyes become moist. Voice-over: 'For more information, call the Maxatil Hot Line.' An 800 number flashes across the bottom of the screen. The final image is the woman removing her glasses and wiping a tear from her cheek.

They clapped and cheered as if the money was about to be delivered by overnight courier. Then Clay sent them all to their posts, to sit by the phones and begin collecting clients. Within minutes, the calls started. Promptly at nine, as scheduled, copies of the lawsuit were faxed to newspapers and financial cable channels. Clay called his old pal at the *Wall Street Journal* and leaked the news. He said he might consider an interview in a day or so.

317

Goffman opened at \$65¼ but was soon shot down by the news of the Maxatil lawsuit in D.C. Clay got himself photographed by a stringer as he filed the lawsuit in the courthouse.

By noon, Goffman had fallen to \$61. The company hurriedly released a statement for the press in which it adamantly denied that Maxatil did all the terrible things alleged in the lawsuit. It would defend the case vigorously.

Patton French called during 'lunch.' Clay was eating a sandwich while standing behind his desk and watching the phone messages pile up. 'I hope you know what you're doing,' French said suspiciously.

'Gee, I hope so too, Patton. How are you?'

'Swell. We took a long hard look at Maxatil about six months ago. Decided to pass. Causation could be a real problem.'

Clay dropped his sandwich and tried to breathe. Patton French said no to a mass tort? He passed on a class-action lawsuit against one of the wealthiest corporations in the land? Clay was aware that nothing was being said, a painful gap in the conversation. 'Well, uh, Patton, we see things differently.' He was reaching behind him, groping for his chair. He finally fell into it.

'In fact, everybody passed, until you. Saulsberry, Didier, Carlos down in Miami. Guy up in Chicago has a bunch of cases, but he hasn't filed them yet. I don't know, maybe you're right. We just didn't see it, that's all.'

French was fishing. 'We got the goods on them,'

Clay said. The government report! That's it! Clay had it and French did not. Finally, a deep breath, and the blood started pumping again.

'You'd better have your ducks in a row, Clay. These guys are very good. They make old Wicks and the boys at Ackerman look like Cub Scouts.'

'You sound scared, Patton, I'm surprised at you.'

'Not scared at all. But if you have a hole in your theory of liability, they'll eat you alive. And, don't even think about a quick settlement.'

'Are you in?'

'No. I didn't like it six months ago, don't like it now. Plus, I got too many other irons in the fire. Good luck.'

Clay closed and locked his office door. He walked to his window and stood for at least five minutes before he felt the cool moisture of his shirt sticking to his back. Then he rubbed his forehead and found rows of sweat.

Chapter 28

The headline in the *Daily Profit* screamed: A LOUSY HUNDRED MILLION AIN'T ENOUGH. And things got worse after that. The story began with a quick paragraph about the 'frivolous' lawsuit filed yesterday in D.C. against Goffman, one of America's finest consumer products companies. Its wonderful drug Maxatil had helped countless women through the nightmare of menopause, but now it was under attack by the same sharks that had bankrupted A.H. Robins, Johns Manville, Owens-Illinois, and practically the entire American asbestos industry.

The story hit its stride when it went after the lead shark, a brash young D.C. hotshot named Clay Carter who, according to their sources, had never tried a civil lawsuit before a jury. Nonetheless, he had earned in excess of $100 million last year in the mass tort lottery. Evidently, the reporter had a trusted stable of ready sources. The first was an executive with the U.S. Chamber of Commerce, who railed against lawsuits in general and trial lawyers in particular. 'The Clay Carters of the world will only inspire others to file these contrived suits. There are a million lawyers in this country. If an unknown like Mr. Carter can earn so much so fast, then no decent company is safe.' A law professor at a school Clay had never heard of said, 'These guys are ruthless. Their greed is enormous, and because of it they will eventually choke the golden goose.' A windy Congressman from Connecticut seized the moment to call for immediate passage of a class-action reform bill he'd authored. Committee hearings would take place, and Mr Carter just might be subpoenaed to testify before Congress.

Unnamed sources within Goffman said the company would defend itself vigorously, that it would not yield to class-action blackmail, and that it would, at the appropriate time, demand to be reimbursed for its attorneys' fees and litigation costs due to the outrageous and frivolous nature of the claims.

The company's stock had declined eleven percent, a loss of investors' equity of about $2 billion, all because of the bogus case. 'Why don't the shareholders of Goffman sue guys like Clay Carter?' asked the professor from the unknown law school.

It was difficult material to read, but Clay certainly couldn't ignore it. An editorial in *Investment Times* called upon Congress to take a serious look at litigation reform. It too made much of the fact that young Mr. Carter had made a large fortune in less than a year. He was nothing but a 'bully' whose ill-gotten gains would only inspire other street hustlers to sue everyone in sight.

The nickname 'bully' stuck for a few days around the office, temporarily replacing 'The King.' Clay smiled and acted as if it was an honor. 'A year ago no one was talking about me,' he boasted. 'Now, they can't get enough.' But behind his locked office door he was uneasy and fretted about the haste with which he had sued Goffman. The fact that his mass tort pals were not piling on was distressing. The bad press was gnawing at him. There had not been a single defender so far. Pace had disappeared, which was not unusual, but not exactly what Clay needed at the moment.

Six days after filing the lawsuit, Pace checked in from California. 'Tomorrow is the big day,' he said.

'I need some good news,' Clay said. 'The government report?'

'Can't say,' Pace replied. 'And no more phone calls. Someone might be listening. I'll explain when I'm in town. Later.'

Someone might be listening? On which end – Clay's or Pace's? And who, please? There went another night's sleep.

The study by the American Council on Aging was originally designed to test twenty thousand women between the ages of forty-five and seventy-five over a seven-year period. The group was equally divided, with one getting a daily dose of Maxatil, the other getting a placebo. But after four years, researchers abandoned the project because the results were so bad. They found an increase in the risk of breast cancer, heart disease, and stroke in a disturbing percentage of the participants. For those who took the drug, the risk of breast cancer jumped thirty-three percent, heart attacks twenty-one percent, and strokes twenty percent.

The study predicted that for every hundred thousand women using Maxatil four years or more, four hundred would develop breast cancer, three hundred would suffer some degree of heart disease, and there would be three hundred moderate to severe strokes.

The following morning the report was published. Goffman's stock got hammered again, dropping to $51 a share on the news. Clay and Mulrooney spent the afternoon monitoring Web sites and cable channels, waiting for some response from the company, but there was none. The business reporters who'd scalded Clay when he filed the suit did not call for his reaction to the study. They briefly mentioned the story the following day. The *Post* ran a rather dry summary of the release of the report, but Clay's name was not used. He felt vindicated, but ignored. He had so much to say in response to his critics, but no one wanted to listen.

His anxiety was relieved by the deluge of phone calls from Maxatil patients.

The Gulfstream finally had to escape. Eight days in the hangar, and Clay was itching to travel. He loaded up Ridley and headed west, first to Las

Vegas, though no one around the office knew he was stopping there. It was a business trip, and a very important one. He had an appointment with the great Dale Mooneyham in Tucson to talk about Maxatil.

They spent two nights in Vegas, in a hotel with real cheetahs and panthers on display in a fake game preserve outside the front entrance. Clay lost $30,000 playing blackjack and Ridley spent $25,000 on clothes in the designer boutiques packed around the hotel's atrium. The Gulfstream fled to Tucson.

Mott & Mooneyham had converted an old train station downtown into a pleasantly shabby suite of offices. The lobby was the old waiting area, a long vaulted room where two secretaries were tucked away in corners at opposite ends, as if they had to be separated to keep the peace. On closer inspection, they seemed incapable of fighting; both were in their seventies and lost in their own worlds. It was a museum of sorts, a collection of products that Dale Mooneyham had taken to court and shown to juries. In one tall cabinet was a gas water heater, and the bronze placard above the door gave the name of the case and the amount of the verdict – $4.5 million, October 3, 1988, Stone County, Arkansas. There was a damaged three-wheeler that had cost Honda $3 million in California, and a cheap rifle that had so enraged a Texas jury that it gave the plaintiff $11 million. Dozens of products – a lawn mower, a burned-out frame of a Toyota Celica, a drill press, a defective life vest, a crumpled ladder. And on the walls were the press clippings and large photos of the great man handing over checks to his injured clients. Clay, alone because Ridley was shopping, browsed from display to display, entranced with the conquests and unaware that he had been kept waiting for almost an hour.

As assistant finally fetched him and led him down a wide hall lined with spacious offices. The walls were covered with framed blow-ups of newspaper headlines and stories, all telling of thrilling courtroom victories. Whoever Mott was, he was certainly an insignificant player. The letterhead listed only four other lawyers.

Dale Mooneyham was seated behind his desk and only half-stood when Clay entered, unannounced and feeling very much like a vagrant. The handshake was cold and obligatory. He was not welcome there, and he was confused by his reception. Mooneyham was at least seventy, a big-framed man with a thick chest and large stomach. Blue jeans, gaudy red boots, a wrinkled western shirt, and certainly no necktie. He'd been dying his gray hair black, but was in need of another treatment because the sides were white, the top dark and slicked back with too much grease. Long wide face, the puffy eyes of a drinker.

'Nice office, really unique,' Clay said, trying to thaw things a bit.

'Bought it forty years ago,' Mooneyham said. 'For five thousand bucks.'

'Quite a collection of memorabilia out there.'

'I've done all right, son. I haven't lost a jury trial in twenty-one years. I suppose I'm due for a loss, at least that's what my opponents keep saying.'

Clay glanced around and tried to relax in the low, ancient leather chair. The office was at least five times as big as his, with the heads of stuffed game covering the walls and watching his every move. There were no phones ringing, no faxes clattering in the distance. There was not a computer in Mooneyham's office.

'I guess I'm here to talk about Maxatil,' Clay said, sensing that he might be evicted at any moment.

Hesitation, no movement except for a casual readjusting of the dark little eyes. 'It's a bad drug,' he said simply, as if Clay had no idea. 'I filed suit about five months ago up in Flagstaff. We have a fast-track here in Arizona, known as the rocket-docket, so we should have us a trial by early fall. Unlike you, I don't file suit until my case is thoroughly researched and prepared, and I'm ready to go to trial. Do it that way and the other side never catches up. I've written a book about pre-lawsuit preparation. Still read it all the time. You should too.'

Should I just leave now? Clay wanted to ask. 'What about your client?'

'I just have one. Class actions are a fraud, at least the way you and your pals handle them. Mass torts are a scam, a consumer rip-off, a lottery driven by greed that will one day harm all of us.

326

Unbridled greed will swing the pendulum to the other side. Reforms will take place, and they'll be severe. You boys will be out of business but you won't care because you'll have the money. The people who'll get harmed are all the future plaintiffs out there, all the little people who won't be able to sue for bad products because you boys have screwed up the law.'

'I asked about your client.'

'Sixty-six-year-old white female, nonsmoker, took Maxatil for four years. I met her a year ago. We take our time around here, do our homework before we start shooting.'

Clay had intended to talk about big things, big ideas, like how many potential Maxatil clients were out there, and what did Mooneyham expect from Goffman, and what types of experts was he planning to use at trial. Instead, he was looking for a quick exit. 'You're not expecting a settlement?' he asked, managing to sound somewhat engaged.

'I don't settle, son. My clients know that up front. I take three cases a year, all carefully selected by me. I like different cases, products and theories I've never tried before. Courthouses I've never seen. I get my choice because lawyers call me every day. And I always go to trial. I know when I take a case it will not be settled. That takes away a major distraction. I tell the defendant up front – "Let's not waste our time even thinking about a settlement, okay?"' He finally moved, just a slight shifting of weight to one side, as if he had a bad back or something. 'That's good news for you, son. I'll get first shot at Goffman, and if the jury sees things my way then they'll give my client a nice verdict. All you copy-cats can fall in line, jump on the wagon, advertise for more clients, then settle them cheap and rake yours off the top. I'll make you another fortune.'

'I'd like to go to trial,' Clay said.

'If what I read is correct, you don't know where the courthouse is.'

'I can find it.'

A shrug. 'You probably won't have to. When I get finished with Goffman they'll run from every jury.'

'I don't have to settle.'

'But you will. You'll have thousands of cases. You won't have the guts to go to trial.'

And with that he slowly stood, reached out a limp hand, and said, 'I have work to do.'

Clay hustled from the office, down the hall, through the museum/lobby, and outside into the fierce desert heat.

Bad luck in Vegas and a disaster in Tucson, but the trip was salvaged somewhere over Oklahoma, at 42,000 feet. Ridley was asleep on the sofa, under the covers and dead to the world, when the fax machine began humming. Clay walked to the rear of the dark cabin and retrieved a one-page transmission. It was from Oscar Mulrooney, at the office. He'd pulled a story off the Internet

– the annual rankings of firms and fees from *American Attorney* magazine. Making the list of the twenty highest-paid lawyers in the country was Mr. Clay Carter, coming in at an impressive number eight, estimated earnings of $110 million for the previous year. There was even a small photo of Clay with the caption: 'Rookie of the Year.'

Not a bad guess, Clay thought to himself. Unfortunately, $30 million of his Dyloft settlement had been paid in bonuses to Paulette, Jonah, and Rodney, rewards that at first had seemed generous but in hindsight were downright foolish. Never again. The good folks at *American Attorney* wouldn't know about such bighearted bonuses. Not that Clay was complaining. No other lawyer from the D.C. area was in the top twenty.

Number one was an Amarillo legend named Jock Ramsey who had negotiated a toxic-waste-dump case involving several oil and chemical companies. The case had dragged on for nine years. Ramsey's cut was estimated at $450 million. A tobacco lawyer from Palm Beach was thought to have earned $400 million. Another one from New York was number three at $325 million. Patton French landed at number four, which no doubt irritated him greatly.

Sitting in the privacy of his Gulfstream, staring at the magazine article featuring his photo, Clay told himself again that it was all a dream. There were 76,000 lawyers in D.C., and he was number one. A year earlier he had never heard of Tarvan or Dyloft or Maxatil, nor had he paid much attention to mass tort litigation. A year earlier his biggest dream was fleeing OPD and landing a job with a respectable firm, one that would pay him enough for some new suits and a better car. His name on a letterhead would impress Rebecca and keep her parents at bay. A nicer office with a higher class of clients would allow him to stop dodging his pals from law school. Such modest dreams.

He decided he would not show the article to Ridley. The woman was warming up to the money and becoming more interested in jewelry and travel. She'd never been to Italy, and she'd dropped hints about Rome and Florence.

Everybody in Washington would be talking about Clay's name on the top twenty list. He thought of his friends and his rivals, his law school pals and the old gang at OPD. Mostly, though, he thought of Rebecca.

Chapter 29

The Hanna Portland Cement Company was founded in Reedsburg, Pennsylvania, in 1946, in time to catch the postwar explosion of new home construction. It immediately became the largest employer in the small town. The Hanna brothers ran it with iron fists, but they were fair to their workers, who were their neighbors as well. When business was good, the workers received generous wages. When things were slow, everybody tightened their belts and got by. Layoffs were rare and used only as a last resort. The workers were content and never unionized.

The Hannas plowed their profits back into the plant and equipment, and into the community. They built a civic center, a hospital, a theater, and the nicest high school football field in the area. Over the years, there was a temptation or two to sell out, to take serious cash and go play golf, but the Hanna brothers could never be sure that their factory would remain in Reedsburg. So they kept it.

After fifty years of sound management, the company employed four thousand of the eleven thousand residents of the town. Annual sales were $60 million, though profits had been elusive. Stiff competition from abroad and a slowdown in new housing starts were putting pressure on the income statement. It was a very cyclical business, something the younger Hannas had tried unsuccessfully to remedy by diversifying into related products. The balance sheet currently had more debt than normal.

Marcus Hanna was the current CEO, though he never used that title. He was just the boss, the number-one honcho. His father was one of the founders, and Marcus had spent his life at the plant. No less than eight other Hannas were in management, with several of the next generation out in the factory, sweeping floors and doing the same menial jobs their parents had been expected to do.

On the day the lawsuit arrived, Marcus was in a meeting with his first cousin, Joel Hanna, the unofficial in-house lawyer. A process server bullied his way past the receptionist and secretaries up front and presented himself to Marcus and Joel with a thick envelope.

'Are you Marcus Hanna?' the process server demanded.

'I am. Who are you?'

'A process server. Here's your lawsuit.' He handed it over and left.

It was an action filed in Howard County,

Maryland, seeking unspecified damages for a class of homeowners claiming damages due to defective Portland mortar cement manufactured by Hanna. Joel read it slowly and paraphrased it for Marcus, and when he finished, both men sat for a long time and cursed lawyers in general.

A quick search by a secretary found an impressive collection of recent articles about the plaintiffs' attorney, a certain Clay Carter from D.C.

It was no surprise that there was trouble in Howard County. A bad batch of their Portland cement had found its way there several years earlier. Through the normal channels, it had been used by various contractors to put bricks on new homes. The complaints were fresh; the company was trying to get a handle on the scope of the problem. Evidently, it took about three years for the mortar to weaken and then the bricks began to fall off. Both Marcus and Joel had been to Howard County and met with their suppliers and the contractors. They had inspected several of the homes. Current thinking put the number of potential claims at five hundred, and the cost of repairing each unit at about $12,000. The company had product liability insurance that would cover the first $5 million in claims.

But the lawsuit purported to include a class of 'at least two thousand potential claimants,' each seeking $25,000 in actual damages.

'That's fifty million,' Marcus said.

'And the damned lawyer will rake forty percent off the top,' added Joel.

'He can't do that,' Marcus said.

'They do it every day.'

More generalized cursing of lawyers. Then some specifics aimed at Mr Carter. Joel left with the lawsuit. He would notify their insurance carrier who would assign it to a litigation firm, probably one in Philadelphia. It happened at least once a year, but never one this big. Because the damages sought were much higher than the insurance coverage, Hanna would be forced to hire its own firm to work with the insurance company. None of the lawyers would be cheap.

The full-page ad in the *Larkin Gazette* caused quite a stir in the small town hidden from the world in the mountains of southwest Virginia. Because Larkin had three factories it had slightly more than ten thousand people, a regular population center in the mining country. Ten thousand was the threshold for full-page ads and Skinny Ben screening that Oscar Mulrooney had established. He had studied the advertising and arrived at the opinion that the smaller markets were being overlooked. His research had also revealed that rural women and Appalachian women were heavier than those in cities. Skinny Ben territory!

According to the ad, the screening would take place the following day at a motel north of town and would be conducted by a medical doctor, a real physician. It was free. It was available to any person who had taken benafoxadil, aka Skinny Bens. It was confidential. And it might lead to the recovery of some money from the manufacturer of the drug.

At the bottom of the page, in smaller print, the name, address, and phone number of the D.C. Law Offices of J. Clay Carter II were given, though by the time most readers got that far they had either quit or were too excited about the screening.

Nora Tackett lived in a mobile home a mile outside Larkin. She did not see the ad because she did not read newspapers. She read nothing. She watched television sixteen hours a day, most of the time while eating. Nora lived with the two stepchildren her ex-husband had left behind when he hit the road two years earlier. They were his kids, not hers, and she was still not sure exactly how she'd come to possess them. But he was gone; not a word, not a dime for child support, not a card or a letter or a phone call to check on the two brats he'd forgotten when he fled. And so she ate.

She became a client of J. Clay Carter when her sister saw the *Larkin Gazette* and arranged to come fetch her for the screening. Nora had taken Skinny Bens for a year, until her doctor had stopped prescribing the drug because it was no longer on the market. If she'd lost any weight with the pills, she couldn't tell.

Her sister loaded her into a minivan and thrust the full-page ad in front of her. 'Read this,' MaryBeth demanded. MaryBeth had started down the road to obesity twenty years earlier, but a stroke at the age of twenty-six had been her wake-up call. She was tired of preaching to Nora; they'd fought for years. And they began fighting as they drove through Larkin and headed for the motel.

The Village Inn had been selected by Oscar Mulrooney's secretary because it appeared to be the newest motel in town. It was the only one on the Internet, which hopefully meant something. Oscar had slept there the night before, and as he had an early breakfast in the motel's dirty café he wondered once again how he'd fallen so far so fast.

Third in his class at Yale Law School! Wined and dined by the blue-chip firms on Wall Street and the heavyweights in Washington. His father was a prominent doctor in Buffalo. His uncle was on the Vermont Supreme Court. His brother was a partner in one of the most lucrative entertainment law firms in Manhattan.

His wife was embarrassed that he was off again in the boondocks chasing cases. And so was he!

His tag-team partner was a Bolivian intern who spoke English but did so with an accent so thick even his 'Good Mornings' were hard to understand. He was twenty-five and looked sixteen, even in his green hospital scrubs, which Oscar insisted he wear for credibility. Med school had been on the Caribbean island of Grenada. He'd found Dr Livan in the want-ads and was paying him the stiff sum of $2,000 a day.

Oscar handled the front and Livan took care

of the back. The motel's only meeting room had a flimsy folding partition that the two of them had fought with to unwrinkle and pull across the room, dividing it roughly in half. When Nora entered the front at eight forty-five, Oscar glanced at his watch, then said, as pleasantly as possible, 'Good morning, ma'am.' She was fifteen minutes early, but then they usually showed up before the starting time.

The 'ma'am' was something he caught himself practicing as he drove around D.C. It was not a word he'd been raised with.

Money in the bank, he said to himself as he looked at Nora. At least three hundred pounds and probably pushing four hundred. Sad that he could guess their weight like a huckster at a carnival. Sad that he was actually doing it.

'You the lawyer?' MaryBeth asked, with great suspicion. Oscar had been through it a thousand times already.

'Yes ma'am, the doctor's in the back. I have some paperwork for you.' He handed over a clipboard with questionnaires designed for the simplest of readers. 'If you have any questions, just let me know.'

MaryBeth and Nora backed into folding chairs. Nora fell heavily into hers; she was already sweating. They were soon lost in the forms. All was quiet until the door opened again and another large woman peered in. She immediately locked on to Nora, who was staring back, a deer in headlights. Two fatties caught in their quest for damages.

'Come in,' Oscar said with a warm smile, very much the car salesman now. He coaxed her through the door, shoved the forms into her hands, and led her to the other side of the room. Between two hundred fifty and two hundred seventy-five pounds.

Each test cost $1,000. One out of ten would become a Skinny Ben client. The average case was worth between $150,000 and $200,000. And they were picking up the leftovers because eighty percent of the cases had already found their way into law offices around the country.

But the leftovers were still worth a fortune. Not Dyloft money, but millions anyway.

When the questions were answered, Nora managed to get to her feet. Oscar took the forms, reviewed them, made sure she'd actually taken Skinny Bens, then signed his name somewhere on the bottom. 'Through that door, ma'am, and the doctor is waiting.'

Nora walked through a large slit in the partition; MaryBeth stayed behind where she commenced to chat up the lawyer.

Livan introduced himself to Nora, who understood nothing of what he said. Nor could he understand her either. He took her blood pressure, and shook his head with displeasure – 180 over 140. Her pulse was a deadly 130 per minute. He pointed to a set of industrial meat scales, and she reluctantly stepped on – 388 pounds.

Forty-four years old. In her condition, she would be lucky to see her fiftieth birthday.

He opened a side door and led her outside where a medical van was parked and waiting. 'We do the test in here,' he said. The rear doors of the van were open; two sonographers were waiting, both in white jackets. They helped Nora into the van and arranged her on a bed.

'What's that?' she asked, terrified, pointing at the nearest device.

'It's an echocardiogram,' one said, in English she could understand.

'We scan your chest with this,' said the other, a woman, 'and we take a digital picture of your heart. It'll be over in ten minutes.'

'It's painless,' added the other.

Nora closed her eyes and prayed that she would survive.

The Skinny Ben litigation was so lucrative because the evidence was so easy. Over time, the drug, which ultimately did little to help lose weight, weakened the aorta. And the damage was permanent. Aortic insufficiency, or mitral valve regurgitation, of at least twenty percent was an automatic lawsuit.

Dr Livan read Nora's printout while she was still in prayer, and gave a thumbs-up to the sonographers: twenty-two percent. He took it up front where Oscar was shuffling paperwork for a whole room full of prospects. Oscar returned with him to the back, where Nora was now seated, looking pale and gulping orange juice. He wanted to say, 'Congratulations, Ms. Tackett, your aorta has been sufficiently damaged,' but the congratulations were only for the lawyers. MaryBeth was summoned and Oscar walked them through the litigation scenario, hitting only the high points.

The echocardiogram would be studied by a board-certified cardiologist whose report would be filed with the class-action administrator. The compensation scale had already been approved by the Judge.

'How much?' asked MaryBeth, who seemed more concerned about the money than her sister. Nora appeared to be praying again.

'Based on Nora's age, somewhere in the neighborhood of a hundred thousand dollars,' Oscar said, omitting, for the moment, that thirty percent would go to the Law Offices of J. Clay Carter II.

Nora, wide awake, said, 'A hundred thousand dollars!'

'Yes ma'am.' Like a surgeon before a routine operation, Oscar had learned to lowball his chances of success. Keep their expectations low, that way the shock of the attorneys' fees wouldn't be so great.

Nora was thinking about a new double-wide trailer and a new satellite dish. MaryBeth was thinking about a truckload of Ultra Slim-Fast. The paperwork was completed and Oscar thanked them for coming.

'When do we get the money?' MaryBeth asked.

'We?' asked Nora.

'Within sixty days,' Oscar said, leading them out the side door.

Unfortunately, the next seventeen had insufficient

aortic damage and Oscar was looking for a drink. But he hit paydirt with number nineteen, a young man who jolted the scales at five hundred fifteen pounds. His echocardiogram was beautiful – forty percent insufficiency. He'd taken Skinny Bens for two years. Because he was twenty-six years old, and, statistically at least, he would live for thirty-one more years with a bad heart, his case was worth at least $500,000.

Late in the afternoon there was an ugly incident. A hefty young lady became incensed when Dr Livan informed her that her heart was fine. No damage whatsoever. But she'd heard around town that Nora Tackett was getting $100,000, heard it over at the beauty shop in fact, and, though she weighed less than Nora, she too had taken the pills and was entitled to the same settlement. 'I really need the money,' she insisted.

'Sorry,' Dr Livan kept saying.

Oscar was called for. The young lady became loud and vulgar, and to get her out of the motel he promised to have their cardiologist review her echocardiogram anyway. 'We'll do a second work-up and have the Washington doctors review it,' he said, as if he knew what he was talking about. This settled her enough to move her along.

What am I doing here? Oscar kept asking himself. He doubted if anyone in Larkin had ever attended Yale, but he was frightened nonetheless. He'd be ruined if word got out. The money, just think of the money, he repeated over and over.

They tested forty-one Skinny Ben users in

Larkin. Three made the cut. Oscar signed them up and left town with the bright prospect of about $200,000 in attorneys' fees. Not a bad outing. He raced away in his BMW and drove straight to D.C. His next foray into the heartland would be a similar secret trip into West Virginia. He had a dozen planned for the next month.

Just make the money. It's a racket. It has nothing to do with being a lawyer. Find 'em, sign 'em, settle 'em, take the money and run.

Chapter 30

On May 1, Rex Crittle left the accounting firm where he'd worked for eighteen years and moved upstairs to become the business manager of JCC. With the offer of a huge increase in salary and benefits, he simply couldn't say no. The law firm was wildly successful, but in the chaos it was growing so fast its business seemed out of control. Clay gave him broad authority and parked him in an office across the hall from his.

While Crittle certainly appreciated his own large salary, he was skeptical of everyone's around him. In his opinion, which he kept to himself for the time being, most of the employees were overpaid. The firm now had fourteen lawyers, all making at least $200,000 a year; twenty-one paralegals at $75,000 each; twenty-six secretaries at $50,000 each, with the exception of Miss Glick who earned $60,000; a dozen or so clerks of different varieties, each earning on the average $20,000; and four office gofers at $15,000 each. A total of seventy-seven, not including Crittle and

Clay. Adding in the cost of benefits, the total annual payroll was $8.4 million, and growing almost weekly.

Rent was $72,000 a month. Office expenses – computers, phones, utilities, the list was quite long – were running about $40,000 a month. The Gulfstream, which was the biggest waste of all and the one asset Clay could not live without, was costing the firm $300,000 in monthly mortgage payments and another $30,000 for pilots, maintenance, and hangar fees. The charter revenue Clay was expecting had yet to show up on the books. One reason was that he really didn't want anyone else using his airplane.

According to figures that Crittle monitored daily, the firm was burning around $1.3 million a month in overhead – $15.6 million a year, give or take. Certainly enough to terrify any accountant, but after the shock of the Dyloft settlement and the enormous fees that had flooded in, he was not in a position to complain. Not yet, anyway. He now met with Clay at least three times a week, and any questionable expenditure was met with the usual, 'You gotta spend it to make it.'

And spending they were. If the overhead made Crittle squirm, the advertising and testing gave him ulcers. For Maxatil, the firm had spent $6.2 million in the first four months on newspaper, radio, television, and online advertising. This, he had complained about. 'Full speed ahead,' had been Clay's response. 'I want twenty-five thousand cases!' The tally was somewhere around eighteen thousand, and virtually impossible to monitor because it changed by the hour.

According to one online industry newsletter Crittle peeked at every day, the reason the Carter firm in D.C. was getting so many Maxatil cases was that few other lawyers were aggressively pursuing them. But he kept this gossip to himself.

'Maxatil will be a bigger payday than Dyloft,' Clay said repeatedly around the office, to fire up the troops. And he seemed to truly believe it.

Skinny Ben was costing the firm much less, but the expenses were piling up and the fees were not. As of May 1, they had spent $600,000 on advertising and about that much on medical tests. The firm had 150 clients, and Oscar Mulrooney had floated a memo claiming that each case was worth, on the average, $180,000. At thirty percent, Mulrooney was projecting fees of about $9 million within the next 'few months.'

The fact that a branch of the firm was about to produce such results had everyone excited, but the waiting had become worrisome. Not one dime had been collected from the Skinny Ben class-action settlement, a scheme that was supposed to be automatic. Hundreds of lawyers were involved in it, and, not surprisingly, major disagreements had arisen. Crittle didn't understand the legal intricacies, but he was educating himself. He was fluent in overhead and fee shortages.

The day after Crittle moved in, Rodney moved out, though the two events were not related. Rodney was simply cashing in his chips and moving to the suburbs, to a very nice home on a very safe street, with a church on one end, a school on the other, a park around the corner. He planned to become a full-time coach for his four kids. Employment might come later, and it might not. He'd forgotten about law school. With $10 million in the bank, before taxes, he had no real plans, just a determination to be a father and a husband, and a miser. He and Clay sneaked away to a deli down the street, just hours before he left the office for good, and said their good-byes. They had worked together for six years – five at OPD, the last one at the new firm.

'Don't spend it all, Clay,' he warned his friend.

'I can't. There's too much of it.'

'Don't be foolish.'

The truth was, the firm no longer needed someone like Rodney. The Yale boys and the other lawyers were polite and deferential, mainly because of his friendship with Clay, but he was only a paralegal. And Rodney no longer needed the firm. He wanted to hide his money and protect it. He was secretly appalled at the way Clay was blowing through such a fortune. You pay a price for waste.

With Jonah on a sailboat and Paulette still hiding in London and apparently not coming home, the original gang was now gone. Sad, but Clay was too busy to be nostalgic.

Patton French had ordered a meeting of the steering committee, a logistical impossibility that took a month to put together. Clay asked why they couldn't do things by phone, fax, e-mail, and through secretaries, but French said they needed a day together, the five of them in the same room. Since the lawsuit had been filed in Biloxi, he wanted them there.

Ridley was up for the trip. Her modeling had all but ceased; she spent her time at the gym and put in several hours a day shopping. Clay had no complaints about the gym time, it provided icing for the cake. The shopping concerned him, but she showed remarkable restraint. She could shop for hours and spend a modest amount.

A month earlier, after a long weekend in New York, they had returned to D.C. and driven to his town house. She spent the night, not for the first time and evidently not for the last. Though nothing was said about her moving in, it just happened. Clay could not remember when he realized that her bathrobe and toothbrush and makeup and lingerie were there. He never saw her hauling her stuff into his apartment, it just materialized there. She wasn't pushy; nothing was said. She stayed three consecutive nights, doing all the right things and not getting in the way, then she whispered that she needed a night at home. They didn't talk for two days, then she was back.

Marriage was never mentioned, though he was buying enough jewelry and clothes for a harem. Neither appeared to be looking for anything permanent. They enjoyed each other's company and companionship, but both kept a roving eye. There were mysteries around her that Clay did not want to solve. She was gorgeous and pleasant and okay in the sack, and she did not seem to be a gold digger. But she had secrets.

So did Clay. His biggest secret was that if Rebecca called at the right time, he'd sell everything but the Gulfstream, load her in it, and fly away to Mars.

Instead he was flying to Biloxi with Ridley, who for the trip had chosen a suede mini-skirt that barely covered the essentials, which she had no interest in covering because it was just the two of them on the plane. Somewhere over West Virginia, Clay gave a passing thought to yanking out the sofa and attacking her. The thought lingered, but he managed to put it away, partly out of frustration. Why was he always the one initiating the fun and games? She was a willing player, but she never started things.

Besides, the briefcase was filled with steering committee paperwork.

A Limo met them at the airport in Biloxi. It drove them a few miles to a harbor, where a speedboat was waiting. Patton French spent most of his time on his yacht, ten miles out in the Gulf. He was now between wives. A nasty divorce was raging. The current one wanted half his money and all his hide. Life was much quieter on a boat, as he called the two-hundred-foot luxury yacht.

He greeted them in shorts and bare feet. Wes Saulsberry and Damon Didier were already there, stiff drinks in hand. Carlos Hernández from

Miami was due at any moment. French gave them a quick tour, during which Clay counted at least eight people in perfect white sailor's garb, all standing at the ready in case he needed something. The boat had five levels, six state rooms, cost $20 million, and on and on. Ridley ducked into a bedroom and began shucking clothes.

The boys met for drinks 'on the porch,' as French described it – a small wooden deck on the top level. French was actually going to trial in two weeks, a rarity for him because corporate defendants normally just threw money at him in fear. He claimed to be looking forward to it, and over a round of vodkas bored them all with the details.

He froze in mid-sentence when he saw something below. On a lower deck, Ridley appeared, topless and, at first sight, bottomless as well. But there was a dental-floss bikini in the package, clinging somehow to the right spot. The three older men bolted upright and gasped for breath. 'She's European,' Clay explained as he waited for the first heart attack. 'When she gets near the water, the clothes come off.'

'Then buy her a damned boat,' Saulsberry said.

'Better yet, she can have this one,' French said, trying to collect himself.

Ridley looked up, saw the commotion she was causing, then disappeared. No doubt she was followed by every waiter and staff person on board.

'Where was I?' French said, breathing again.

'You were finished with whatever story you were telling,' Didier said.

Another powerboat was coming near. It was Hernández, with not one but two young ladies in tow. After they unloaded and French got them settled in, Carlos met the boys on the porch.

'Who are the girls?' Wes asked.

'My paralegals,' Carlos said.

'Just don't make them partners,' French said. They talked about women for a few minutes. Evidently, all four had been through several wives. Maybe that was why they kept working so hard. Clay did none of the talking and all of the listening.

'What's up with Maxatil?' Carlos asked. 'I have a thousand cases and I'm not sure what to do with them.'

'You're asking me what to do with your cases?' Clay said.

'How many do you have?' French asked. The mood had changed dramatically; things were serious now.

'Twenty thousand,' Clay said, fudging just a little. Truth was, he didn't know how many cases were in the office. What was a little exaggerating among mass tort boys?

'I haven't filed mine,' Carlos said. 'Proving causation could be a nightmare.' Words that Clay had heard enough and did not want to hear again. For almost four months, he'd been waiting for another big name to dive into the Maxatil pit.

'I still don't like it,' French said. 'I was talking to Scotty Gaines yesterday in Dallas. He has two thousand cases, but isn't sure what to do with them either.'

'It's very difficult to prove causation based solely on a study,' Didier said in Clay's direction, almost lecturing. 'I don't like it either.'

'The problem is that the diseases caused by Maxatil are caused by many other factors as well,' Carlos was saying. 'I've had four experts study this drug. They all say that when a woman is taking Maxatil and gets breast cancer, it's impossible to link the disease to the drug.'

'Anything from Goffman?' French asked. Clay, who was ready to jump overboard, took a long pull on a very strong drink and tried to appear as if he had the corporation dead in the crosshairs.

'Nothing,' he said. 'Discovery is just getting started. I think we're all waiting for Mooneyham.'

'I talked to him yesterday,' Saulsberry said. They might not like Maxatil, but they were certainly monitoring it. Clay had been a mass tort lawyer long enough to know that the greatest fear of all was missing the big one. And Dyloft had taught him that the biggest thrill was launching a surprise attack while everyone else was asleep.

He was not yet sure what Maxatil might teach him. These guys were nibbling around the edges, probing, hoping to learn something from the front lines. But since Goffman had so thoroughly stonewalled the lawsuit since the day he'd filed it, Clay had nothing to give them.

Saulsberry was saying, 'I know Mooneyham very well. We tried some cases together years ago.'

'He's a blowhard,' French said, as if the typical trial lawyer was tight-lipped and one with a big mouth was a disgrace to the profession.

'He is, but he's very good. The old guy hasn't lost in twenty years.'

'Twenty-one,' Clay said. 'At least that's what he told me.'

'Whatever,' Saulsberry said, brushing them aside because he had fresh news. 'You're right, Clay, everybody is watching Mooneyham. Even Goffman. The trial is set for sometime in September. They claim they want a trial. If Mooneyham can connect the dots and prove causation and liability, then there's a good chance the company will set up a national compensation plan. But if the jury goes with Goffman, then the war is on because the company ain't paying a dime to anybody.'

'This is all according to Mooneyham?' French asked.

'Yes.'

'He's a blowhard.'

'No, I've heard it too,' Carlos said. 'I have a source, and he said exactly what Wes is saying.'

'I've never heard of a defendant pushing for a trial,' French said.

'Goffman's a tough bunch,' Didier added. 'I sued them fifteen years ago. If you can prove liability, they'll pay a fair settlement. But if you can't, you're screwed.'

Once again, Clay felt like going for a swim. Fortunately, Maxatil was instantly forgotten when the two Cuban paralegals pranced onto the deck below in very skimpy outfits.

'Paralegals, my ass,' French said, straining for a better view.

'Which one is yours?' Saulsberry asked, leaning out of his chair.

'Take your pick, boys,' Carlos said. 'They're professionals. I brought them as a gift. We'll pass them around.'

And with that the windbags on the top deck were dead silent.

A storm arrived just before dawn and disrupted the quietness of the yacht. French, badly hung over and with a naked paralegal under his sheets, called the captain from his bed and ordered him to head for shore. Breakfast was postponed, not that anyone was hungry. Dinner had been a four-hour marathon, complete with courtroom war stories, dirty jokes, and the obligatory late-night bickering caused by too much alcohol. Clay and Ridley had retired early and double-latched their door.

Moored in Biloxi harbor, riding out the storm, the steering committee managed to review all the documents and memos it was supposed to review. There were directions to the class-action administrator, and dozens of signature blanks to be filled in. Clay was nauseous by the time they finished, and desperate to stand on solid ground.

Not lost in all the paperwork was the latest fee schedule. Clay, or more accurately, his law firm, would soon be receiving another $4 million. Exciting enough, but he wasn't sure if he would realize it when the money arrived. It would make a nice dent in the overhead, but only a temporary one.

It would, however, get Rex Crittle off his back for a few weeks. Rex was pacing the halls like an expectant father, looking for fees.

Never again, he vowed to himself when he stepped off the yacht. Never would he allow himself to be penned up overnight with people he didn't like. A limo took them to the airport. The Gulfstream took them to the Caribbean.

Chapter 31

They had the villa for a week, though Clay doubted he could stay away from the office that long. It was wedged into the side of a hill, overlooking the busy harbor town of Gustavia, a place bustling with traffic and tourists and all kinds of boats coming and going. Ridley had found it in a catalog of exclusive private rentals. It was a fine home – traditional Caribbean architecture, red-tiled roof, long porches and verandas. There were bedrooms and bathrooms too numerous to find, and a chef, two maids, and a gardener. They settled in quickly, and Clay began flipping through real estate guides that someone had been kind enough to leave behind.

Clay's initial encounter with a nude beach was a huge disappointment. The first naked female he saw was a grandmother, a wrinkled old thing who, with proper advice, should've covered much more and exposed much less. Then her husband came strolling by, a large belly hanging low and covering his privates, a rash on his ass, and worse.

Nudity was getting a bad rap. Of course, Ridley was in her element, strutting up and down the beach as heads twisted. After a couple of hours in the sand, they retired from the heat and enjoyed a two-hour lunch at a fabulous French restaurant. All the good restaurants were French, and they were everywhere on the island.

Gustavia was busy. It was hot and not the tourist season, but someone forgot to tell the tourists. They packed the sidewalks as they drifted from store to store, and they crowded the streets in their rented Jeeps and small cars. The harbor was never quiet as small fishing boats jockeyed around the yachts of the rich and famous.

Whereas Mustique was private and secluded, St. Barth was overbuilt and overbooked. But it was still a charming island. Clay loved them both. Ridley, who was showing a keen interest in island real estate, preferred St Barth because of the shopping and the food. She liked busy towns and people. Someone had to gawk at her.

After three days, Clay removed his watch and began sleeping in a hammock on a porch. Ridley read books and watched old movies for long stretches of time. Boredom was creeping in when Jarrett Carter sailed into Gustavia harbor aboard his magnificent catamaran, *The ExLitigator*. Clay was sitting at a bar near the dock, drinking a soda, waiting for his father.

His crew consisted of a fortyish German woman with legs as long as Ridley's, and a roguish old Scotsman named MacKenzie, his sailing instructor. The woman, Irmgard, was at first described as his mate, which in sailing terms meant something very vague. Clay loaded them into his Jeep and drove them to his villa, where they showered forever and had drinks while the sun disappeared into the sea. MacKenzie overdosed on bourbon and was soon snoring in a hammock.

The sailing business had been slow, much like the airplane charter business. *The ExLitigator* had been booked four times in six months. Its longest voyage had been from Nassau to Aruba and back, three weeks that generated $30,000 from a retired British couple. The shortest had been a jaunt to Jamaica, where they'd almost lost the boat in a storm. A sober MacKenzie had saved them. Near Cuba they had a run-in with pirates. The stories rolled forth.

Not surprisingly, Jarrett took a shine to Ridley. He was proud of his son. Irmgard seemed content to drink and smoke and watch the lights down in Gustavia.

Long after dinner, and after the women had retired for the night, Jarrett and Clay moved to another porch for another round. 'Where'd you find her?' Jarrett asked, and Clay gave a quick history. They were practically living together, but neither had mentioned anything more permanent than that. Irmgard was also a temp.

On the legal front, Jarrett had a hundred questions. He was alarmed at the size of Clay's new firm, and felt compelled to offer unsolicited advice on how to run things. Clay listened patiently. The sailboat had a computer with online access, and Jarrett knew about the Maxatil litigation and the bad press that went with it. When Clay reported that he now had twenty thousand cases, his father thought that was too many for any one firm to handle.

'You don't understand mass torts,' Clay said.

'Sounds like mass exposure to me,' Jarrett countered. 'What's your malpractice limit?'

'Ten million.'

'That's not enough.'

'That's all the insurance company would sell me. Relax, Dad, I know what I'm doing.'

And Jarrett couldn't argue with success. The money his son was printing made him long for the glory days in the courtroom. He could hear those faraway, magical words from the jury foreman, 'Your Honor, we, the jurors, find for the plaintiff and award damages in the amount of ten million dollars.' He would hug the plaintiff and say something gracious to the defense counsel, and Jarrett Carter would leave another courtroom with another trophy.

It was quiet for a long time. Both men needed sleep. Jarrett stood and walked to the edge of the porch. 'You ever think about that black kid?' he asked, staring into the night. 'The one who started shooting and had no idea why?'

'Tequila?'

'Yeah, you told me about him in Nassau when we were buying the sailboat.'

'Yeah, I think about him occasionally.'

'Good. Money isn't everything.' And with that, Jarrett went to bed.

The trip around the island took most of the day. The captain seemed to understand the basics of how the boat operated and how the wind affected it, but if not for MacKenzie they might have strayed into the sea and never been found. The captain worked hard at handling his ship, but he was also very distracted by Ridley, who spent most of the day roasting in the nude. Jarrett couldn't take his eyes off her. Nor could MacKenzie, but he could maneuver a sailboat in his sleep.

Lunch was in a secluded cove on the north side of the island. Near St Maarten, Clay took the helm while his father hit the beer. For about eight hours, Clay had been seminauseous, and playing captain did nothing to relieve his discomfort. Life on a boat was not for him. The romance of sailing the world held no appeal; he'd vomit in all the great oceans. He preferred airplanes.

Two nights on land and Jarrett was ready for the sea. They said good-bye early the next morning and his father's catamaran motored out of Gustavia harbor, headed nowhere in particular. Clay could hear his father and MacKenzie bickering as they headed for open water.

He was never certain how the Realtor materialized on the porch of the villa. She was there when he returned, a charming Frenchwoman chatting with Ridley and having a coffee. She said she was in the neighborhood, just stopped by to check on the house, which was owned by one of their clients, a Canadian couple in the midst of a nasty divorce, and how were things?

'Couldn't be better,' Clay said, taking a seat. 'A great house.'

'Isn't it wonderful?' the Realtor gushed. 'One of our finest properties. I was just telling Ridley that it was built only four years ago by these Canadians who've been down twice, I think. His business turned bad. She started seeing her doctor, a real mess up there in Ottawa, and so they've put it on the market at a very reasonable price.'

A conspiratorial glance from Ridley. Clay asked the question left hanging in the air. 'How much?'

'Only three million. Started at five, but, frankly, the market is a bit soft right now.'

After she left, Ridley attacked him in the bed-room. Morning sex was unheard of, but they had an impressive go at it. Same for the afternoon. Dinner in a fine restaurant; she couldn't keep her hands off him. The midnight session began in the pool, went to the Jacuzzi, then to the bedroom and after an all-nighter the Realtor was back before lunch.

Clay was exhausted and really not in the mood for more property. But Ridley wanted the house much more than she had wanted anything, so far, so he bought it. The price was actually on the low end; it was a bargain, the market would tighten up, and he could always sell it for a profit.

During the paperwork, Ridley asked Clay, privately, if it might be wise to put the house in her name, for tax reasons. She knew as much about the French and American tax codes as he did about Georgian inheritance laws, if, in fact they had any. Hell no, he said to himself, but to her he said, firmly, 'No, that won't work, for tax reasons.'

She appeared to be wounded, but the pain passed quickly as he assumed ownership. Clay went to a bank in Gustavia, alone, wired the money from an offshore account. When he met with the property attorney, he did so without Ridley.

'I'd like to stay for a while,' she said as they spent another long afternoon on the porch. He was planning a departure the following morning, and he'd assumed she was leaving too. 'I'd like to get this house in order,' she said. 'Meet with the decorator. And just relax for a week or so.'

Why not? Clay thought. Now that I own the damned place, might as well use it.

He returned to D.C. by himself, and for the first time in several weeks enjoyed the solitude of his Georgetown home.

For several days Joel Hanna had considered a solo act – just him, all alone on one side of the table, facing a small army of lawyers and their assistants on the other side. He would present the company's survival plan; he really needed no help in doing this since it was his brainchild.

But Babcock, the attorney for their insurance

company, insisted on being present. His client was on the front line for $5 million, and if he wanted to be present, then Joel couldn't stop him.

Together they walked into the building on Connecticut Avenue. The elevator stopped on the fourth floor and they entered the lush and impressive suite of the Law Offices of J. Clay Carter II. The logo 'JCC' was broadcast to the world in tall bronze letters hung on a wall that appeared to be cherry or maybe even mahogany. The furniture in the reception room was sleek and Italian. A comely young blonde behind a glass-and-chrome desk greeted them with an efficient smile and pointed to a room just down the hall. A lawyer named Wyatt met them at the door, escorted them in, handled the introductions to and from the gang on the other side, and while Joel and Babcock were unpacking their briefcases another very shapely young lady materialized from nowhere and took their coffee orders. She served them from a silver coffee service with the JCC logo engraved on the pot and also on the fine china cups. When everyone was set and things couldn't be readier, Wyatt barked at an assistant, 'Tell Clay we're all here.'

An awkward minute passed as Mr. JCC kept everyone waiting. Finally, he entered in a rush, jacket off, talking to a secretary over his shoulder, a very busy man. He went straight to Joel Hanna and Babcock and introduced himself as if they were all there voluntarily and about to engage in the common good. Then he hustled around to the other side and assumed the king's throne in the middle of his team, eight feet away.

Joel Hanna couldn't help but think, 'This guy made a hundred million bucks last year.'

Babcock had the same thought, but he added to it the gossip that the kid had never tried a civil lawsuit. He'd spent five years with the crackheads in criminal court, but he'd never asked a jury for a nickel. Through all the posturing, Babcock saw signs of nervousness.

'You said you had a plan,' Mr. JCC began. 'Let's hear it.'

The survival scheme was quite simple. The company was willing to admit, for purposes of this meeting only, that it had manufactured a bad batch of Portland masonry cement, and that because of this, X number of new homes in the Baltimore area would have to be rebricked. A payment fund was needed to compensate the homeowner, while not choking the company to death. As simple as the plan was, it took Joel half an hour to present it.

Babcock spoke on behalf of the insurance company. He admitted there was $5 million in coverage, something he rarely disclosed this early in a lawsuit. His client and the Hanna company would participate in a pool.

Joel Hanna explained that his company was short on cash, but was willing to borrow heavily to compensate the victims. 'This is our mistake, and we intend to correct it,' he said more than once.

'Do you have an accurate count of the number of homes here?' JCC asked, and every one of his minions wrote this down.

'Nine hundred and twenty-two,' Joel said. 'We've gone to the wholesalers, then to the contractors, then to the masonry subs. I think that's an accurate number, but it could be off by five percent.'

JCC was scribbling. When he stopped, he said, 'So if we assume a cost of twenty-five thousand dollars to adequately compensate each client, we're looking at about just over twenty-three million dollars.'

'We are quite certain that it will not cost twenty thousand to fix each house,' Joel said.

JCC was handed a document by an assistant. 'We have statements from four masonry subs in the Howard County area. Each of the four has been on site to see the damage. Each has submitted an estimate. The lowest is eighteen-nine, the highest is twenty-one-five. The average of the four is twenty thousand bucks.'

'I'd like to see those estimates,' Joel said.

'Maybe later. Plus, there are other damages. These homeowners are entitled to compensation for their frustration, embarrassment, loss of enjoyment, and emotional distress. One of our clients is suffering from severe headaches over this. Another lost a profitable sale on his home because the bricks were falling off.'

'We have estimates in the twelve-thousand-dollar range,' Joel said.

'We're not going to settle these cases for twelve thousand dollars,' JCC said, and every head shook on the other side.

Fifteen thousand dollars was a fair compromise and would get new bricks on every house. But such a settlement left only nine thousand dollars for the client after JCC lopped his one-third off the top. Ten thousand dollars would get the old bricks off, the new ones on the premises, but it wouldn't pay the brickmasons to finish the job. Ten thousand dollars would only make matters worse – the home stripped to the Sheetrock, the front yard a muddy mess, flats of new bricks in the driveway but no one to lay them.

Nine hundred twenty-two cases, at $5,000 each – $4.6 million in fees. JCC did the math quickly, amazed at how adept he'd become at stringing together zeroes. Ninety percent would be his; he had to share some with a few lawyers who were latecomers to the action. Not a bad fee. It would cover the cost of the new villa on St Barth, where Ridley was still hiding with no interest in coming home, and after taxes there would be little left.

At $15,000 per claim, Hanna could survive. Taking the $5 million from Babcock's client, the company could add about $2 million in cash currently on hand, funds that were earmarked for plant and equipment. A pool of $15 million was needed to cover every potential claim. The remaining $8 million could be borrowed from banks in Pittsburgh. However, this information was kept between Hanna and Babcock. This was just the first meeting, not the time to play every card.

The issue would boil down to how much Mr. JCC wanted for his efforts. He could broker a fair settlement, perhaps reduce his percentage, still make several million, protect his clients, allow a fine old company to survive, and call it a victory.

Or, he could take the hard line and everybody would suffer.

Chapter 32

Miss Glick sounded a bit rattled over the intercom. 'There are two of them, Clay,' she said, almost in a whisper. 'FBI.'

Those new at the mass tort game look often over their shoulders, as if what they're doing should somehow be illegal. With time, though, their hides grow so thick they think of themselves as Teflon. Clay jumped at the mere mention of the 'FBI,' then chuckled at his own cowardice. He'd certainly done nothing wrong.

They were straight from central casting; two young clean-cut agents whipping out badges and trying to impress anyone who might be watching. The black one was Agent Spooner and the white one was Agent Lohse. Pronounced LOOSH. They unbuttoned their jackets at the same time as they settled into chairs in the power corner of Clay's office.

'Do you know a man by the name of Martin Grace?' Spooner began.

'No.'

'Mike Packer?' asked Lohse.

'No.'

'Nelson Martin?'

'No.'

'Max Pace?'

'Yes.'

'They're all the same person,' Spooner said. 'Any idea where he might be?'

'No.'

'When did you see him last?'

Clay walked to his desk, grabbed a calendar, then returned to his chair. He stalled as he tried to organize his thoughts. He did not, under any circumstances, have to answer their questions. He could ask them to leave at any time and come back when he had a lawyer present. If they mentioned Tarvan, then he would call a halt. 'Not sure,' he said, flipping pages. 'It's been several months. Sometime in mid-February.'

Lohse was the record keeper; Spooner the interrogator. 'Where did you meet him?'

'Dinner, in his hotel.'

'Which hotel?'

'I don't remember. Why are you interested in Max Pace?'

A quick glance between the two. Spooner continued: 'This is part of an SEC investigation. Pace has a history of securities fraud, insider trading. Do you know his background?'

'Not really. He was pretty vague.'

'How and why did you meet him?'

Clay tossed the calendar on the coffee table. 'Let's say it was a business deal.'

'Most of his business partners go to jail. You'd better think of something else.'

'That'll do for now. Why are you here?'

'We're checking out witnesses. We know he spent some time in D.C. We know he visited you on Mustique last Christmas. We know that in January he short sold a chunk of Goffman for sixty-two and a quarter a share the day before you filed your big lawsuit. Bought it back at forty-nine, made himself several million. We think he had access to a confidential government report on a certain Goffman drug called Maxatil, and he used that information to commit securities fraud.'

'Anything else?'

Lohse stopped writing and said, 'Did you short sell Goffman before you filed suit?'

'I did not.'

'Have you ever owned Goffman's stock?'

'No.'

'Any family members, law partners, shell corporations, offshore funds controlled by you?'

'No, no, no.'

Lohse put his pen in his pocket. Good cops keep their first meetings brief. Let the witness/target/subject sweat and maybe do something foolish. The second one would be much longer.

They stood and headed for the door. 'If you hear from Pace, we'd like to know about it,' Spooner said.

'Don't count on it,' Clay said. He could never

betray Pace because they shared so many secrets.

'Oh, we're counting on it, Mr. Carter. Next visit we'll talk about Ackerman Labs.'

After two years and $8 billion in cash settlements, Healthy Living threw in the towel. The company, in its opinion, had made a good-faith effort to remedy the nightmare of its Skinny Ben diet pill. It had tried valiantly to compensate the half million or so injured people who had relied upon its aggressive advertising and lack of full disclosure and taken the drug. It had patiently weathered the frenzied shark attacks by the mass tort lawyers. It had made them rich.

Tattered, shrunken, and hanging on by its fingernails, the company got hammered again and simply couldn't take anymore. The final straw was two wildcat class actions filed by even shadier lawyers who represented several thousand 'patients' who used Skinny Bens but with no adverse effects. They wanted millions in compensation simply because they had consumed the pill, were now worried about it, and might continue to worry about it in the future, thus wrecking their already fragile emotional health.

Healthy Living filed for bankruptcy protection under Chapter 11 and walked away from the mess. Three of its divisions were on the block, and soon the company itself would cease to exist. It flipped the bird to all the lawyers and all their clients and left the building.

The news was a surprise to the financial community, but no group was more shocked than the mass tort bar. They had finally strangled the golden goose. Oscar Mulrooney saw it online at his desk and locked his door. Under his visionary planning, the firm had spent $2.2 million in advertising and medical testing, which had so far yielded 215 legitimate Skinny Ben clients. At an average settlement of $180,000, the cases were worth at least $15 million in attorneys' fees, which would be the basis of his much anticipated year-end bonus.

In the past three months, he'd been unable to get his claims approved by the class-action administrator. There were rumors of dissension among the countless lawyers and consumer groups. Others were having trouble getting the money that was supposedly available.

Sweating, he worked the phone for an hour, calling other lawyers in the class, trying to get through to the administrator, then the Judge. His worst fears were confirmed by a lawyer in Nashville, one with several hundred cases, all filed ahead of Oscar's. 'We're screwed,' the lawyer said. 'HL has liabilities four times that of its assets, and there is no cash. We're screwed.'

Oscar composed himself, straightened his tie, buttoned his sleeves, put on his jacket, and went to tell Clay.

An hour later he prepared a letter to each of his 215 clients. He gave them no false hope. Things indeed looked bleak. The firm would closely monitor the bankruptcy and the company. It would aggressively pursue all possible means of compensation.

But there was little reason to be optimistic.

Two days later, Nora Tackett received her letter. Because the mailman knew her, he knew that she had changed addresses. Nora now lived in a new double-wide trailer closer to town. She was at home, as always, probably watching soap operas on her new wide-screen, eating low-fat cookies, when he placed a letter from a law firm, three bills, and some sales flyers in her box. She had been receiving lots of mail from the lawyers in D.C., and everybody in Larkin knew why. At first her settlement from that diet pill company was rumored to be $100,000, then she told somebody at the bank that it might get closer to $200,000. It jumped again as it got talked about around Larkin.

Earl Jeter, south of town, sold her the new trailer on the news that she was getting close to half a million, and getting it fast. Plus, her sister, MaryBeth, had signed the ninety-day note.

The mailman knew for a fact that the money was causing all sorts of problems for Nora. Every Tackett in the county called her for bail money when there was an arrest. Her kids, or the kids she was raising, were being picked on at school because their mother was so fat and so rich. Their father, a man unseen in those parts for the past two years, was back in town. He told folks at the barbershop that Nora was the sweetest woman he'd ever been married to. Her father had threatened to kill him, and that was another reason she stayed inside with the doors locked.

But most of her bills were past due. As recently as last Friday someone at the bank supposedly said that there had been no sign of any settlement. Where was Nora's money? That was the big question in Larkin, Virginia. Maybe it was in the envelope.

She waddled out an hour later, after making sure no one was nearby. She removed the mail from the box, hustled back into the trailer. Her calls to Mr. Mulrooney were not returned. His secretary said he was out of town.

The meeting occurred late at night, just as Clay was leaving his office. It began with unpleasant business and did not improve.

Crittle walked in with a sour face and announced, 'Our liability insurance carrier is notifying us that they are canceling coverage.'

'What!' Clay yelled.

'You heard me.'

'Why are you telling me now? I'm late for dinner.'

'I've been talking to them all day.'

A brief time-out while Clay flung his jacket on the sofa and walked to the window. 'Why?' he asked.

'They've evaluated your practice and they don't like what they see. Twenty-four thousand Maxatil cases scare them. There's too much exposure if something goes wrong. Their ten million could be a drop in the bucket, so they're jumping ship.'

'Can they do it?'

'Of course they can. An insurance company can terminate coverage anytime it wants. They'll owe us a refund, but it's peanuts. We're naked on this, Clay. No coverage.'

'We won't need coverage.'

'I hear you, but I'm still worried.'

'You were worried about Dyloft too, as I recall.'

'And I was wrong.'

'Well, Rex old boy, you're wrong about Maxatil too. After Mr. Mooneyham gets finished with Goffman in Flagstaff, they'll be anxious to settle. They're already setting aside billions for the class action. Any idea how much those twenty-four thousand cases could be worth? Take a guess.'

'Shock me.'

'Close to a billion dollars, Rex. And Goffman can pay it.'

'I'm still worried. What if something goes wrong?'

'Have a little faith, pal. These things take time. The trial out there is set for September. When it's over, the money will pour in again.'

'We've spent eight million on advertising and testing. Can we at least slow down? Why can't you take the position that twenty-four thousand cases is enough?'

'Because it's not enough.' And with that Clay smiled, picked up his jacket, patted Crittle on the shoulder, and left for dinner.

*   *   *

He was supposed to meet a former college roommate at the Old Ebbitt Grille, on Fifteenth, at eight-thirty. He waited at the bar for almost an hour before his cell phone rang. The roommate was stuck in a meeting that looked as if it would never end. He gave the usual apologies.

As Clay was leaving, he glanced into the restaurant and saw Rebecca having dinner with two other ladies. He stepped back, found his bar stool, and ordered another ale. He was very aware that she had once again stopped him in his tracks. He wanted desperately to talk to her, but he was determined not to interfere. A trip to the rest room would work fine.

As he walked by her table, she looked up and immediately smiled. Rebecca introduced Clay to her two friends, and he explained that he was in the bar waiting for an old college buddy for dinner. The guy was running late, it might be a while, sorry for the interruption. Oh well, gotta run. Nice seeing you.

Fifteen minutes later, Rebecca appeared in the crowded bar and stood close beside him. Very close.

'I just have a minute,' she said. 'They're waiting.' She nodded at the restaurant.

'You look great,' Clay said, anxious to start groping.

'You too.'

'Where's Myers?'

She shrugged as if she didn't care. 'Working. He's always working.'

'How's married life?'

'Very lonely,' she said, looking away.

Clay took a drink. If not in a crowded bar, with friends waiting nearby, she would have spilled her guts. There was so much she wanted to say.

The marriage is not working! Clay fought to suppress a smile. 'I'm still waiting,' he said.

Her eyes were wet when she leaned over and kissed him on the cheek. Then she was gone without another word.

Chapter 33

With the Orioles six runs down to the Devil Rays – of all teams – Mr. Ted Worley awoke from a rare nap and debated whether to sneak to the toilet then or wait until the seventh inning. He'd been asleep for an hour, which was unusual for him because he napped every afternoon at precisely two. The Orioles were dull but they had never put him to sleep.

But after the Dyloft nightmare he didn't push the limits of his bladder. Not too many liquids, no beer at all. And no pressure on the plumbing down there; if he needed to go, then he did not hesitate. And what if he missed a few pitches? He walked to the small guest bathroom down the hall, next to the bedroom where Mrs. Worley was perched in her rocker doing the needlepoint that consumed most of her life. He closed the door behind him, unzipped his pants, and began to urinate. A very slight burning sensation caused him to glance down, and when he did he almost fainted.

His urine was the color of rust – a dark reddish liquid. He gasped and braced himself with one hand against the wall. When he finished, he didn't flush; instead he sat on the toilet seat for a few minutes trying to collect himself.

'What are you doing in there?' his wife yelled.

'None of your damned business,' he snapped back.

'Are you okay, Ted?'

'I'm fine.'

But he wasn't fine. He lifted the lid, took another look at the deadly calling card his body had just discharged, finally flushed, and walked back to the den. The Devil Rays were now up by eight, but the game had lost whatever importance it had in the first inning. Twenty minutes later, after three glasses of water, he sneaked down to the basement and urinated in a small bathroom, as far away as possible from his wife.

It was blood, he decided. The tumors were back, and whatever form they now had they were far more serious than before.

He told his wife the truth the next morning, over toast and jam. He preferred to keep it from her as long as possible, but they were so joined at the hip that secrets, especially any related to health, were difficult to keep. She took charge immediately, calling his urologist, barking at the appointment secretary, lining up a visit just after lunch. It was an emergency and tomorrow just wasn't acceptable.

Four days later, malignant tumors were found

in Mr. Worley's kidneys. During five hours of surgery, the doctors removed all the tumors they could find.

The head of urology was closely monitoring the patient. A colleague at a hospital in Kansas City had reported an identical case a month earlier; a post-Dyloft appearance of kidney tumors. The patient in Kansas City was now undergoing chemotherapy and fading fast.

The same could be expected for Mr. Worley, though the oncologist was much more cautious in his first postop visit. Mrs. Worley was doing her needlepoint while complaining about the quality of the hospital's food, which she did not expect to be delicious but why couldn't it at least be warm? At these prices? Mr. Worley hid under the sheets of his bed and watched the television. He graciously muted the set when the oncologist arrived, though he was too sad and depressed to engage in conversation.

He would be discharged in a week or so, and as soon as he was strong enough they would begin aggressively treating his cancer. Mr. Worley was crying when the meeting was over.

During a follow-up conversation with the colleague in Kansas City, the head of urology learned of yet another case. All three patients had been Group One Dyloft plaintiffs. Now they were dying. A lawyer's name was mentioned. The Kansas City patient was represented by a small firm in New York City.

It was a rare and rewarding experience for a

doctor to be able to pass along the name of one lawyer who would sue another, and the head of urology was determined to enjoy the moment. He entered Mr. Worley's room, introduced himself because they had not met, and explained his role in the treatment. Mr. Worley was sick of doctors and, if not for the tubes crisscrossing his ravaged body, he would have gathered his things and discharged himself. The conversation soon made its way to Dyloft, then the settlement, then to the fertile grounds of the legal profession. This fired up the old man; his face had some color, his eyes were glaring.

The settlement, meager as it was, had been completed against his wishes. A paltry $43,000, with the lawyer taking the rest! He had called and called and finally got some young smart mouth who told him to check the fine print in the pile of documents he'd signed. There was a Pre-authorization clause that allowed the attorney to settle if the money exceeded a very low threshold. Mr. Worley had fired off two poisonous letters to Mr. Clay Carter, neither of which provoked a response.

'I was against the settlement,' Mr. Worley kept saying.

'I guess it's too late now,' Mrs. Worley kept adding.

'Maybe not,' the doctor said. He told them about the Kansas City patient, a man very similar to Ted Worley. 'He's hired a lawyer to go after his lawyer,' the doctor said with great satisfaction.

'I've had a butt full of lawyers,' Mr. Worley said. Doctors too, for that matter, but he held his tongue.

'Do you have his phone number?' Mrs. Worley asked. She was thinking much more clearly than her husband. Sadly, she was also looking down the road a year or two when Ted would be gone.

The urologist just happened to have the number.

The only thing mass tort lawyers feared was one of their own. A predator. A traitor who followed behind fixing their mistakes. A subspecialty had evolved in which a few very good and very nasty trial lawyers pursued their brethren for bad settlements. Helen Warshaw was writing the training manual.

For a breed that professed so much love for the courtroom, tort lawyers fell limp with the visual of themselves sitting at the defense table, looking sheepishly at the jurors as their personal finances were kicked about in open court. It was Helen Warshaw's calling to get them there.

However, it rarely happened. Their cries of Sue the World! and We Love Juries! evidently applied to everyone else. When confronted with proof of liability, no one settled faster than a mass tort lawyer. No one, not even a guilty doctor, dodged the courtroom with as much energy as a TV/billboard lawyer caught scamming a settlement.

Warshaw had four Dyloft cases in her New York office and leads on three more when she received the call from Mrs. Worley. Her small firm had a file on Clay Carter and a much thicker one on Patton French. She monitored the top twenty or so mass tort firms in the country and dozens of the biggest class actions. She had plenty of clients and lots of fees, but nothing had excited her as much as the Dyloft fiasco.

A few minutes on the phone with Mrs. Worley, and Helen knew exactly what had happened. 'I'll be there by five o'clock,' she said.

'Today?'

'Yes. This afternoon.'

She caught the shuttle to Dulles. She did not have her own jet, for two very good reasons. First, she was prudent with her money and didn't believe in such waste. Second, if she ever got sued, she did not want the jury to hear about a jet. The year before, in the only case she'd managed to get to trial, she had shown the jury large color photos of the defendant lawyer's jets, both of them, inside and out. Along with photos of his yacht, Aspen home, etcetera. The jury had been very impressed. Twenty million in punitive damages.

She rented a car – no limo – and found the hospital in Bethesda. Mrs. Worley had collected their papers, which Warshaw spent an hour with while Mr. Worley took a nap. When he woke up, he did not want to talk. He was wary of lawyers, especially the pushy New York female variety. However, his wife had plenty of time and found it easier to confide in a woman. The two went to the lounge for coffee and a long discussion.

The principal culprit was and always would be Ackerman Labs. They made a bad drug, rushed the approval process, advertised it heavily, failed to adequately test it, failed to fully disclose everything they knew about it. Now the world was learning that Dyloft was even more insidious than first thought. Ms. Warshaw had already secured convincing medical proof that recurring tumors were linked to Dyloft.

The second culprit was the doctor who prescribed the drug, though his culpability was slight. He relied on Ackerman Labs. The drug worked wonders. And so on.

Unfortunately, the first two culprits had been fully and completely released from all liability when Mr. Worley settled his claim in the Biloxi class action. Though Mr. Worley's arthritis doctor had not been sued, the global release covered him as well.

'But Ted didn't want to settle,' Mrs. Worley said more than once.

Doesn't matter. He settled. He gave his attorney the power to settle. The attorney did so, and thus became the third culprit. And the last one standing.

A week later, Ms. Warshaw filed a lawsuit against J. Clay Carter, F. Patton French, M. Wesley Saulsberry, and all other known and unknown attorneys who had prematurely settled Dyloft cases. The lead plaintiff was once again Mr. Ted Worley from Upper Marlboro, Maryland, for and on behalf of all injured persons, known and unknown at the time. The lawsuit was filed in United States District Court for the District of Columbia, not too far from the JCC offices.

Borrowing a page from the defendants' own playbook, Ms. Warshaw faxed copies of her lawsuit to a dozen prominent newspapers fifteen minutes after she filed it.

A brusque and burly process server presented himself to the receptionist at Clay's office and demanded to see Mr. Carter. 'It's urgent,' he insisted. He was sent down the hall where he had to deal with Miss Glick. She summoned her boss, who reluctantly came from his office and took possession of the paperwork that would ruin his day. Maybe his year.

The reporters were already calling by the time Clay finished reading the class action. Oscar Mulrooney was with him; the door was locked. 'I've never heard of this,' Clay mumbled, painfully aware that there was so much he didn't know about the mass tort game.

Nothing wrong with a good ambush, but at least the companies he had sued knew they had trouble brewing. Ackerman Labs knew it had a bad drug before Dyloft hit the market. Hanna Portland Cement Company had people on the ground in Howard County assessing the initial claims. Goffman had already been sued by Dale Mooneyham over Maxatil, and other trial lawyers were circling. But this? Clay had had no idea that

Ted Worley was sick again. Not a hint of trouble anywhere in the country. It just wasn't fair.

Mulrooney was too stunned to speak.

Through the intercom Miss Glick announced, 'Clay, there's a reporter here from the *Washington Post*.'

'Shoot the bastard,' Clay growled.

'Is that a "No"?'

'It's a "Hell no!"'

'Tell him Clay's not here,' Oscar managed to say.

'And call security,' Clay added.

The tragic death of a close friend could not have caused a more somber mood. They talked about spin control – how to respond, and when? Should they quickly put together an aggressive denial to the lawsuit and file it that day? Fax copies to the press? Should Clay talk to the reporters?

Nothing was decided because they could not make a decision. The shoe was on the other foot; this was new territory.

Oscar volunteered to spread the news around the firm, spinning everything in a positive light to keep morale up.

'If I'm wrong, I'll pay the claim,' Clay said.

'Let's hope Mr. Worley is the only one from this firm.'

'That's the big question, Oscar. How many Ted Worleys are out there?'

★   ★   ★

Sleep was impossible. Ridley was in St Barth, renovating the villa, and for that Clay was grateful. He was humiliated and embarrassed; at least she didn't know about it.

His thoughts were on Ted Worley. He was not angry, far from it. Allegations in lawsuits are famously off the mark, but these sounded accurate. His former client would not be claiming to have malignant tumors if they did not actually exist. Mr. Worley's cancer was caused by a bad drug, not by a bad lawyer. But to hurriedly settle a case for $62,000 when it was ultimately worth millions smacked of malpractice and greed. Who could blame the man for striking back?

Throughout the long night, Clay drowned in self-pity – his badly bruised ego; the utter humiliation among peers, friends, and employees; the delight of his enemies; the dread of tomorrow and the public flogging he would take in the press, with no one to defend him.

At times he was afraid. Could he really lose everything? Was this the beginning of the end? The trial would have enormous jury appeal – for the other side! And how many potential plaintiffs were out there? Each case was worth millions.

Nonsense. With twenty-five thousand Maxatil cases waiting in the wings he could withstand anything.

But all thoughts eventually came back to Mr. Worley, a client who had not been protected by his lawyer. The sense of guilt was so heavy that he felt like calling the man and apologizing. Maybe he would write him a letter. He vividly remembered reading the two he'd received from his former client. He and Jonah had had a good laugh over them.

Shortly after 4 A.M., Clay made the first pot of coffee. At five, he went online and read the *Post*. No terrorist attacks in the past twenty-four hours. No serial murderers had struck. Congress had gone home. The President was on vacation. A slow news day, so why not put the smiling face of 'The King of Torts' on the front page, bottom half? MASS TORT LAWYER SUED BY THE MASSES was the clever headline. The first paragraph read:

Washington attorney J. Clay Carter, the so-called newest King of Torts, received a taste of his own medicine yesterday when he was sued by some disgruntled clients. The lawsuit alleges that Carter, who earned a reported $110 million in fees last year, prematurely settled cases for small amounts when they were, in fact, worth millions.

The remaining eight paragraphs were no better. A severe case of diarrhea had hit during the night, and Clay raced to the bathroom.

His buddy at the *Wall Street Journal* weighed in with the heavy artillery. Front page, left side, same hideous sketch of Clay's smug face. IS THE KING OF TORTS ABOUT TO BE DETHRONED? was the headline. The tone of the article sounded as if Clay should be indicted and imprisoned rather than simply dethroned. Every business trade group in Washington had ready opinions on the subject. Their delight was thinly concealed. How ironic that they were so happy to see yet another lawsuit. The President of the National Trial Lawyers Academy had no comment.

No comment! From the one and only group that never waivered in its support of trial lawyers. The next paragraph explained why. Helen Warshaw was an active member of the New York Trial Lawyers Academy. In fact, her credentials were impressive. A board-certified trial advocate. Law Review editor at Columbia. She was thirty-eight years old, ran marathons for fun, and was described by a former opponent as 'brilliant and tenacious.'

A lethal combination, Clay thought as he ran back to the bathroom.

Sitting on the toilet he realized that the lawyers would not take sides in this one. It was a family feud. He could expect no sympathy, no defenders.

An unnamed source put the number of plaintiffs at a dozen. Class certification was expected because a much larger group of plaintiffs was anticipated. 'How large?' Clay asked himself as he made more coffee. 'How many Worleys are out there?'

Mr. Carter, age thirty-two, was not available for comment. Patton French called the lawsuit 'frivolous,' a description he borrowed, according to the article, from no less than eight companies he had sued in the past four years. He ventured further by saying the lawsuit '. . . smacked of a conspiracy by the tort reforms proponents and their bene-factors, the insurance industry.' Perhaps the reporter caught Patton after a few stout vodkas.

A decision had to be made. Because he had a legitimate illness he could hunker down at home and ride out the storm from there. Or he could step into the cruel world and face the music. He really wanted to take some pills and go back to bed and wake up in a week with the nightmare behind him. Better yet, hop on the plane and go see Ridley.

He was at the office by seven, with a game face on, high on coffee, bouncing around the halls bantering and laughing with the early shift, making lame but sporting jokes about other process servers on the way and reporters poking around and subpoenas flying here and there. It was a gutsy, splendid performance, one his firm needed and appreciated.

It continued until mid-morning when Miss Glick stopped it cold by stepping into his open office and saying, 'Clay, those two FBI agents are back.'

'Wonderful!' he said, rubbing his hands together as if he might just whip both of them.

Spooner and Lohse appeared with tight smiles and no handshakes. Clay closed the door, gritted his teeth, and told himself to keep performing. But the fatigue hit hard. And the fear.

Lohse would talk this time while Spooner took notes. Evidently, Clay's picture on the front page had reminded them that he was owed a second visit. The price of fame.

'Any sign of your buddy Pace?' Lohse began.

'No, not a peep.' And it was true. How badly he needed Pace's counsel in this time of crisis.

'Are you sure?'

'Are you deaf?' Clay shot back. He was perfectly prepared to ask them to leave when the questions got sticky. They were just investigators, not prosecutors. 'I said no.'

'We think he was in the city last week.'

'Good for you. I haven't seen him.'

'You filed suit against Ackerman Labs on July second of last year, correct?'

'Yes.'

'Did you own any stock in the company before you filed the lawsuit?'

'No.'

'Did you sell the stock short, then buy it back at a lower price?'

Of course he had, at the suggestion of his good friend Pace. They knew the answer to the question. They had the data from the transactions, he was sure of that. Since their first visit, he had thoroughly researched securities fraud and insider trading. He was in a gray area, a very pale one, in his opinion, not a good place to be but far from guilty. In retrospect, he should not have dealt in the stock. He wished a thousand times he had not.

'Am I under investigation for something?' he asked.

Spooner started nodding before Lohse said,
'Yes.'

'Then this meeting is over. My attorney will be
in touch with you.' Clay was on his feet, headed
for the door.

Chapter 34

For the next meeting of the Dyloft Plaintiffs'
Steering Committee, Defendant Patton French
chose a hotel in downtown Atlanta, where he was
participating in one of his many seminars on how
to get rich stalking drug companies. It was an
emergency meeting.

French, of course, had the Presidential Suite,
a gaudy collection of wasted space on the hotel's
top floor, and there they met. It was an unusual
meeting in that there was no comparing notes
about the latest luxury car or ranch, none of that.
Nor did any of the five care to boast about recent
trial victories. Things were tense from the moment
Clay entered the suite, and they never improved.
The rich boys were scared.

And with good reason. Carlos Hernández
from Miami knew of seven of his Dyloft Group
One plaintiffs who were now suffering from
malignant kidney tumors. They had joined the
class action and were now represented by Helen
Warshaw. 'They're popping up everywhere,' he

said, frantically. He looked as if he hadn't slept in days. In fact, all five looked beaten and weary.

'She's a ruthless bitch,' Wes Saulsberry said, and the others nodded in agreement. Evidently, the legend of Ms. Warshaw was widely known. Someone had forgotten to tell Clay. Wes had four former clients now suing him. Damon Didier had three. French had five.

Clay was mightily relieved to have only one, but such relief was temporary. 'Actually, you have seven,' French said, and handed over a printout with Clay's name at the top and a list of ex-clients/ now plaintiffs under it.

'I'm told by Wicks at Ackerman that we can expect the list to grow,' French said.

'What's their mood?' Wes asked.

'Total shock. Their drug is killing people right and left. Philo wishes they'd never heard of Ackerman Labs.'

'I'm with them,' Didier said, shooting a nasty look at Clay, as if to say, 'It's all your fault.'

Clay looked back at the seven names on his list. Other than Ted Worley, he did not recognize any of them. Kansas, South Dakota, Maine, two from Oregon, Georgia, Maryland. How did he come to represent these people? A ridiculous way to practice law – suing and settling for people he'd never met! And now they were suing him!

'Is it safe to assume that the medical evidence is substantial here?' Wes was asking. 'I mean, is there room to fight, to try and prove that this recurring cancer is not related to Dyloft. If so, it gets us off the hook, and Ackerman as well. I don't like being in bed with clowns, but that's where we are.'

'Nope! We're screwed,' French said. At times he could be so blunt it was painful. No sense wasting time. 'Wicks tells me that the drug is more dangerous than a bullet to the head. Their own research people are leaving because of this. Careers are being ruined. The company might not survive.'

'You mean Philo?'

'Yes, when Philo bought Ackerman they thought they had a handle on the Dyloft mess. It now looks as if Groups Two and Three will be much larger and much more expensive. They're scrambling.'

'Aren't we all?' Carlos mumbled, then he too looked at Clay as if a bullet to the head might be in order.

'If we are liable, then there's no way we can defend these cases,' Wes said, stating the obvious.

'We have to negotiate,' Didier said. 'We're talking survival here.'

'How much is a case worth?' Clay asked, his voice still working.

'In front of a jury, two million to ten million, depending on the punitives,' French said.

'That's low,' said Carlos.

'No jury will see my face in court,' Didier said. 'Not with this set of facts.'

'The average plaintiff is sixty-eight and retired,' Wes said. 'So, economically, the damages are not great when the plaintiff dies. Pain and suffering will up the tally. But in a vacuum, you could settle these cases for a million each.'

'This ain't no vacuum,' Didier snapped.

'No kidding,' Wes snapped right back. 'But throw in such beautiful defendants as a bunch of greedy mass tort lawyers, and the value goes through the roof.'

'I'd rather have the plaintiff's side than mine,' Carlos said, rubbing his tired eyes.

Clay noticed that not a single drop of alcohol was being consumed; just coffee and water. He desperately wanted one of French's vodka remedies.

'We're probably going to lose our class action,' French said. 'Everybody who's still in is trying to get out. As you know, very few of the Group Two and Three plaintiffs have settled, and, for obvious reasons, they want no part of this lawsuit. I know of at least five groups of lawyers ready to ask the court to dissolve our class and kick us out. Can't really blame them.'

'We can fight them,' Wes said. 'We got fees out there. And we're gonna need them.'

Nonetheless they were not in the mood to fight, at least not then. Regardless of how much money they claimed to have, each was worried, but at different levels. Clay did most of the listening, and he became intrigued by how the other four were reacting. Patton French probably had more money than anyone there, and he seemed confident he could withstand the financial pressures of the lawsuit. Same for Wes, who had earned $500 million from the tobacco scam. Carlos was cocky at times, but then he couldn't stop fidgeting. It was the hard-faced Didier who was terrified.

They all had more money than Clay, and Clay had more Dyloft cases than any of them. He didn't like the math.

He picked the number of $3 million as a possibility for settlement. If his list stopped with seven names, then he could handle a hit in the $20 million range. But if the list kept growing . . .

Clay brought up the topic of insurance, and was shocked to learn that none of the four had any. They had all been terminated years earlier. Very few carriers of legal malpractice would touch a mass tort lawyer. Dyloft was a perfect example of why not.

'Be thankful you've got the ten million,' Wes said. 'That's money that won't come out of your pocket.'

The meeting was nothing more than a bitch-and-cry session. They wanted the company of each other's misery, but only briefly. They agreed on a very general plan to meet with Ms. Warshaw at some undetermined point in the future and delicately explore the possibility of negotiation. She was making it well known that she did not want to settle. She wanted trials – big, tawdry, sensational spectacles in which the current and past Kings of Torts would be hauled in and stripped naked before the juries.

Clay killed an afternoon and night in Atlanta, where no one knew him.

During his years at OPD, Clay had conducted hundreds of initial interviews, almost all at the jail. They usually started slow, with the defendant, who was almost always black, uncertain about how much he should say to his white lawyer. The background information thawed things somewhat, but the facts and details and truth about the alleged crime were rarely given during the first meeting.

It was ironic that Clay, the white defendant now, was nervously walking into his own initial interview with his black defense lawyer. And at $750 an hour, Zack Battle had better be prepared to listen fast. No ducking and weaving and shadowboxing at that rate. Battle would get the truth, as fast as he could write it down.

But Battle wanted to gossip. He and Jarrett had been drinking buddies years earlier, long before Battle sobered up and became the biggest criminal lawyer in D.C. Oh, the stories he could tell about Jarrett Carter.

Not at $750 an hour, Clay wanted to say. Turn the damned clock off and we'll chat forever.

Battle's office faced Lafayette Park, with the White House in the background. He and Jarrett got drunk one night and decided to drink some beer with the winos and homeless folks out in the park. Cops sneaked up on them, thought they were perverts out looking for action. Both got arrested and it took every favor in the bank to keep it out of the newspapers. Clay laughed because he was supposed to.

Battle gave up booze for pipe tobacco, and his cluttered and dirty office reeked of stale smoke. How is your father? he wanted to know. Clay, quickly, painted a generous and almost romantic picture of Jarrett sailing the world.

When they finally got around to it, Clay told the Dyloft story, beginning with Max Pace and ending with the FBI. He did not talk about Tarvan, but he would if it became necessary. Oddly, Battle took no notes. He just listened, frowning and smoking his pipe, gazing off occasionally in deep reflection, but never betraying what he thought.

'This stolen research that Max Pace had,' he said, then a pause, then a puff. 'Did you have it in your possession when you sold the stock and filed suit?'

'Of course. I had to know that I could prove liability against Ackerman if we went to trial.'

'Then it's insider trading. You're guilty. Five years in the slammer. Tell me, though, how the Feds can prove it.'

When his heart began pumping again, Clay said, 'Max Pace can tell them, I guess.'

'Who else has the research?'

'Patton French, maybe one or two of the other guys.'

'Does Patton French know that you had this information before you filed suit?'

'I don't know. I never told him when I got it.'

'So this Max Pace character is the only person who can nail you.'

The history was pretty clear. Clay had prepared the Dyloft class action but was unwilling to file it unless Pace could produce enough evidence. They had argued several times. Pace walked in one day with two thick briefcases filled with papers and files and said, 'There it is, and you didn't get it from me.' He left immediately. Clay reviewed the materials, then asked a college friend to evaluate their reliability. The friend was a prominent doctor in Baltimore.

'Can this doctor be trusted?' Battle asked.

Before he could say anything, Battle helped him with the answer. 'Here's the bottom line, Clay. If the Feds don't know you had this secret research when you sold the stock short, they can't get you for insider trading. They have the records of the stock transactions, but those alone are not enough. They have to prove you had knowledge.'

'Should I talk to my friend in Baltimore?'

'No. If the Feds know about him, he might be wired. Then you go to prison for seven years instead of five.'

'Would you please stop saying that?'

'And if the Feds don't know about him, then you might inadvertently lead them to him. They're probably watching you. They might tap your phones. I'd ditch the research. Purge my files, just in case they walk in with a subpoena. And I'd also do a lot of praying that Max Pace is either dead or hiding in Europe.'

'Anything else?' Clay asked, ready to start praying.

'Go see Patton French, make sure the research cannot be traced to you. From the looks of things, this Dyloft litigation is just getting started.'

'That's what they tell me.'

The return address was that of a prison. Though he had many former clients behind bars, Clay could not remember one named Paul Watson. He opened it and pulled out a one-page letter, very neat and prepared on a word processor. It read:

Dear Mr Carter: You may remember me as Tequila Watson. I've changed my name because the old one doesn't fit anymore. I read the Bible every day and my favorite guy is the Apostle Paul, so I've borrowed his name. I got a writ-writer here to do it legally for me.

I need a favor. If you could somehow get word to Pumpkin's family and tell them that I'm very sorry for what happened. I've prayed to God and he has forgiven me. I would feel so much better if Pumpkin's family could do the same. I still can't believe I killed him like that. It wasn't me doing the shooting, but the devil, I guess. But I have no excuses.

I'm still clean. Lots of dope in prison, lots of bad stuff, but God gets me through every day.

It would be great if you could write me. I don't get much mail. Sorry you had to stop being my lawyer. I thought you were a cool dude. Best wishes,

Paul Watson

Just hang on, Paul, Clay mumbled to himself. We might be cell mates at the rate I'm going. The phone startled him. It was Ridley, down in St. Barth but wanting to come home. Could Clay please send the jet tomorrow?

No problem, dear. It only costs $3,000 an hour to fly the damned thing. Four hours down, four hours back – $24,000 for the quick round-trip, but that was a drop in the bucket compared to what she was spending on the villa.

Chapter 35

You live by the leak, you die by the leak. Clay had played the game a few times, giving reporters the juicy gossip off the record, then offering smug 'No comments' that were printed a few lines down from the real dirt. It had been fun then; now it was painful. He couldn't imagine who would want to embarrass him even further.

At least he had a little warning. A reporter from the *Post* had called Clay's office, where he'd been directed to the Honorable Zack Battle. He found him and got the standard response. Zack called Clay with a report of the conversation.

It was in the Metro section, third page, and that was a pleasant surprise after months of front-page heroics, then scandals. Because there were so few facts the space had to be filled with something – a photo of Clay. KING OF TORTS UNDER SEC INVESTIGATION. 'According to unnamed sources . . .' Zack had several quotes, all of which made Clay sound even guiltier. As he read the story he remembered how often he'd seen Zack do the same routine – deny and deflect and promise a vigorous defense, always protecting some of the biggest crooks in town. The bigger the crook the faster he ran to the office of Zack Battle, and Clay thought, for the first time, that perhaps he'd hired the wrong lawyer.

He read it at home where he was, thankfully, alone because Ridley was spending a day or two at her new apartment, one Clay had signed the lease for. She wanted the freedom of living in two places, hers and his, and since her old flat was quite cramped Clay had agreed to put her up in nicer digs. Actually, her freedom required a third place – the villa in St. Barth, which she always referred to as 'ours.'

Not that Ridley read newspapers anyway. In fact, she seemed to know little of Clay's problems. Her increasing focus was on the spending of his money, with not much attention to how he made it. If she saw the story on page three, she didn't mention it. Nor did he.

As another bad day wore on, Clay began to realize how few people seemed to acknowledge the story. One pal from law school called and tried to cheer him up, and that was it. He appreciated the call, but it did little to help. Where were his other friends?

Though he tried mightily not to do so, he couldn't help but think of Rebecca and the Van Horns. No doubt they'd been green with envy and sick with regrets when the new King of Torts had been crowned, just weeks earlier, it seemed.

What were they thinking now? He didn't care, he told himself again, and again. But if he didn't care, why couldn't he purge them from his thoughts?

Paulette Tullos dropped in before noon and that raised his spirits. She looked great – the pounds were off, the wardrobe was expensive. She'd been bouncing around Europe for the past few months, waiting for her divorce to become final. The rumors about Clay were everywhere, and she was concerned about him. Over a long lunch, one she paid for, it slowly became apparent that she was also worried about herself. Her cut of the Dyloft loot had been slightly over $10 million, and she wanted to know if she had exposure. Clay assured her she had none. She had not been a partner in the firm during the settlement, just an associate. Clay's name was on all the pleadings and documents.

'You were the smart one,' Clay said. 'You took the money and ran.'

'I feel bad.'

'Don't. The mistakes were made by me, not you.'

Though Dyloft would cost him dearly – at least twenty of his former clients had now joined the Warshaw class action – he was still banking heavily on Maxatil. With twenty-five thousand cases, the payday would be enormous. 'The road's kinda rocky right now, but things will improve greatly. Within a year, I'll be mining gold again.'

'And the Feds?' she asked.

'They can't touch me.'

She seemed to believe this and her relief was obvious. If, in fact, she did believe everything Clay was saying, she was the only one at the table who did so.

The third meeting would be the last, though neither Clay nor anyone on his side of the table realized it. Joel Hanna brought his cousin Marcus, the company's CEO, with him, and left behind Babcock, their insurance counsel. As usual, the two faced a small army on the other side, with Mr. JCC sitting in the middle. The king.

After the customary warm-ups, Joel announced, 'We have located an additional eighteen homes that should be added to the list. That makes a total of nine hundred and forty. We feel very confident that there will not be any more.'

'That's good,' Clay said, somewhat callously. A longer list meant more clients for him, more damages to be paid by the Hanna company. Clay represented almost ninety percent of the class, with a few scattered lawyers hanging around the fringes. His Team Hanna had done a superb job of convincing the homeowners to stick with his firm. They had been assured that they would get more money because Mr. Carter was an expert at mass litigation. Every potential client had received a professionally done packet touting the exploits of the newest King of Torts. It was shameless advertising and solicitation, but those were simply the rules of the game now.

During the last meeting, Clay had reduced his demands from $25,000 per claim to $22,500, a settlement that would net him fees in the neighborhood of $7.5 million. The Hanna company had countered with $17,000, which would stretch its borrowing capacity to the breaking point.

At $17,000 per home, Mr. JCC would earn about $4.8 million in fees, if he clung to his thirty percent contingency. If, however, he cut his share to a more reasonable twenty percent, each of his clients would net $13,600. Such a reduction would reduce his fees by roughly $1.5 million. Marcus Hanna had found a reputable contractor who would agree to repair every home for $13,500.

It had become apparent during the last meeting that the issue of attorneys' fees was at least as important as the issue of compensating the homeowners. However, since the last meeting there had been several stories about Mr. JCC in the press, none of them good. A reduction in fees was not something his firm was prepared to discuss.

'Any movement on your side?' Clay asked, rather bluntly.

Instead of just saying 'No,' Joel went through a short exercise in discussing the steps the company had taken to reevaluate its financial situation, its insurance coverage, and its ability to borrow at least $8 million to add to a compensation pool. But, sadly, nothing had really changed. The business was on the downslope of a nasty cycle. Orders were flat. New home construction was even flatter, at least in their market.

If things looked grim for the Hanna Portland Cement Company, they were certainly no better on the other side of the table. Clay had abruptly stopped all advertising for new Maxatil clients, a move that greatly relieved the rest of his firm. Rex Crittle was working overtime to cut costs, though the culture of JCC had yet to adapt to such radical notions. He had actually broached the subject of layoffs, and in doing so provoked a nasty response from his boss. No significant fees were being generated. The Skinny Ben fiasco had cost them millions, instead of generating another fortune. And with ex-Dyloft clients finding their way to Helen Warshaw, the firm was reeling.

'So there's no movement?' Clay asked when Joel finished.

'No. Seventeen thousand is a stretch for us. Any movement on your side?'

'Twenty-two thousand five hundred is a fair settlement,' Clay said without flinching or blinking. 'If you're not moving, then neither are we.' His voice was hard as steel. His staff was impressed by his toughness, but also anxious for some compromise. But Clay was thinking of Patton French in New York, in the room full of big shots from Ackerman Labs, barking and bullying, very much in control. He was convinced that if he kept pushing, Hanna would buckle under.

The only vocal doubter on Clay's side was a

young lawyer named Ed Wyatt, the head of Team Hanna. Before the meeting, he had explained to Clay that, in his opinion, Hanna would benefit greatly from protection and reorganization under Chapter 11 of the bankruptcy code. Any settlement with the homeowners would be delayed until a trustee could sort out their claims and decide what compensation was reasonable. Wyatt thought the plaintiffs would be lucky to get $10,000 through Chapter 11. The company had not threatened bankruptcy, a normal ploy in these situations. Clay had studied Hanna's books and felt that it had too many assets and too much pride to consider such a drastic move. He rolled the dice. The firm needed all the fees it could squeeze.

Marcus Hanna abruptly said, 'Well, then it's time to go.' He and his first cousin threw their papers together and stormed out of the conference room. Clay tried a dramatic exit too, as if to show his troops that nothing fazed him.

Two hours later, in the U.S. Bankruptcy Court for the Eastern District of Pennsylvania, the Hanna Portland Cement Company filed a Chapter 11 petition, seeking protection from its creditors, the largest of whom were those collected in a class action filed by J. Clay Carter II of Washington, D.C.

Apparently, one of the Hannas understood the importance of leaks as well. The *Baltimore Press* ran a long story about the bankruptcy and the immediate reaction by the homeowners. Its details were deadly accurate and evidence that someone very close to the settlement negotiations was whispering to the reporter. The company had offered $17,000 per plaintiff; a liberal estimate to repair each home was $15,000. The lawsuit could have been fairly settled but for the issue of attorneys' fees. Hanna admitted liability from the very beginning. It had been willing to borrow heavily to correct its mistakes. And so on.

The plaintiffs were extremely unhappy. The reporter ventured out into the suburbs and found an impromptu meeting in a garage. He was given a tour of a few of the homes to survey the damages. He collected numerous comments:

'We should've dealt directly with Hanna.'

'The company was out here before that lawyer got involved.'

'A bricklayer I talked to said he could take off the old and put on the new for eleven thousand dollars. And we turned down seventeen? I just don't understand it.'

'I never met that lawyer.'

'I didn't realize I was in the class action until after it was filed.'

'We didn't want the company to go bankrupt.'

'No, they were nice guys. They were trying to help us.'

'Can we sue the lawyer?'

'I tried calling him, but the lines are busy.'

The reporter was then obliged to provide some background on Clay Carter, and of course he began with the Dyloft fees. Things got worse from there. Three photographs helped tell the story; the first was a homeowner pointing to her crumbling bricks; the second was the group meeting in the garage; and the third was Clay in a tuxedo and Ridley in a beautiful dress as they posed in the White House before the state dinner. She was stunning; he was quite handsome himself, though taken in context, it was difficult to appreciate what an attractive couple they were. A real cheap shot.

'Mr. Carter, seen above at a White House dinner, could not be reached for comment.'

Damned right they're not reaching me, Clay thought.

And so began another day at the offices of JCC. Phones ringing nonstop as irate clients wanted someone to yell at. A security guard in the lobby just in case. Associates gossiping in small groups about the survival of the place. Second-guessing by every employee. The boss locked in his office. No real cases to work on because all the firm had now was a trainload of Maxatil files, and there was little to do with them because Goffman wasn't returning calls either.

Fun and games had been happening all over the District at Clay's expense, though he didn't know it until the story ran in the *Press*. It had started with the Dyloft stories in the *Wall Street Journal*, a few faxes here and there around the city to make sure that those who knew Clay, either from college, law school, his father, or at OPD, got the current news. It picked up steam when *American Attorney* ranked him number eight in earnings – more faxes, more e-mails, a few jokes added in for spice. It became even more popular when Helen Warshaw filed her heinous lawsuit. Some lawyer somewhere in the city, one with too much time on his hands, titled it 'The King of Shorts,' gave it a rough and quick format, and started the faxes. Someone with a slight artistic bent added a crude cartoon of Clay naked with his boxer shorts around his ankles, looking quite perplexed. Any news about him would provoke another edition. The publisher, or publishers, would pick stories off the Internet, print them in a newsletter format, and share them. The criminal investigation was big news. There was the photo from the White House, some gossip about his airplane, one story about his father.

The anonymous editors had been faxing copies to Clay's office from the beginning, but Miss Glick had trashed them. Several of the Yale boys also received faxes, and they too protected their boss. Oscar brought in the latest edition and tossed it on Clay's desk. 'Just so you'll know,' he said. The current edition was a reproduction of the story in the *Press*.

'Any idea who's behind this?' Clay asked.

'No. They're faxed around the city, sort of like a chain letter.'

'Don't these people have better things to do?'

'I guess not. Don't worry about it, Clay. It's always been lonely at the top.'

'So I have my own personal newsletter. My, my, eighteen months ago no one knew my name.'

There was a commotion outside – sharp, angry voices. Clay and Oscar ran from his office into the hallway where the security guard was scuffling with a very disturbed gentleman. Associates and secretaries were entering the picture.

'Where is Clay Carter!' the man yelled.

'Here!' Clay yelled back and walked up to him. 'What do you want?'

The man was suddenly still, though the guard kept his grip. Ed Wyatt and another associate moved close to him. 'I'm one of your clients,' the man said, breathing heavily. 'Let go of me,' he snapped and shook free from the guard.

'Leave him alone,' Clay said.

'I'd like a conference with my attorney,' the man said.

'This is not the way to schedule one,' Clay shot back, very coolly. He was being watched by his employees.

'Yeah, well, I tried the other way, but all the lines are busy. You screwed us out of a good settlement with the cement company. We want to know why. Not enough money for you?'

'I guess you believe everything you read in the newspapers,' Clay said.

'I believe we got screwed by our own lawyer. And we're not taking it without a fight.'

'You folks need to relax and stop reading the papers. We're still working on the settlement.' It was a lie, but one with good intentions. The rebellion needed to be quashed, at least there in the office.

'Cut your fees and get us some money,' the man snarled. 'And that's coming from your clients.'

'I'll get you a settlement,' Clay said with a fake smile. 'Just relax.'

'Otherwise, we're going to the bar association.'

'Keep your cool.'

The man backed away, then turned and left the suite. 'Back to work everybody,' Clay said, clapping his hands together as if everybody had plenty of work to do.

Rebecca arrived an hour later, a random visitor from the street. She stepped into the JCC suite and gave a note to the receptionist. 'Please give that to Mr. Carter,' she said. 'It's very important.'

The receptionist glanced at the security guard, who was on high alert, and it took several seconds to determine that the attractive young lady was probably not a threat. 'I'm an old friend,' Rebecca said.

Whatever she was, she managed to fetch Mr. Carter out of the back faster than anyone in the short history of the firm. They sat in the corner of his office; Rebecca on the sofa, Clay in a chair pulled as close as possible. For a long time nothing was said. Clay was too excited to utter a coherent sentence. Her presence could mean a hundred different things, none of them bad.

He wanted to lunge at her, to feel her body

again, to smell the perfume on her neck, to run his hands along her legs. Nothing had changed – same hair style, same makeup, same lipstick, same bracelet.

'You're staring at my legs,' she finally said.

'Yes I am.'

'Clay, are you okay? There's so much bad press right now.'

'And that's why you're here?'

'Yes. I'm concerned.'

'To be concerned means you still care about me.'

'I do.'

'So you haven't forgotten about me?'

'No, I have not. I'm sort of sidetracked right now, with the marriage and all, but I still think about you.'

'All the time?'

'Yes, more and more.'

Clay closed his eyes and placed a hand on her knee, one that she immediately removed and flung away. 'I am married, Clay.'

'Then let's commit adultery.'

'No.'

'Sidetracked? Sounds like it's temporary. What's going on, Rebecca?'

'I'm not here to talk about my marriage. I was in the neighborhood, thought about you, and just sort of popped in.'

'Like a lost dog? I don't believe that.'

'You shouldn't. How's your bimbo?'

'She's here and there. It's just an arrangement.'

Rebecca mulled this over, obviously unhappy with the arrangement. Okay for her to marry someone else, but she didn't like the idea of Clay hooking up with anyone.

'How's the worm?' Clay asked.

'He's okay.'

'That's a ringing endorsement from the new wife. Just okay?'

'We get along.'

'Married less than a year and that's the best you can do? You get along?'

'Yes.'

'You're not giving him sex, are you?'

'We're married.'

'But he's such a little twerp. I saw you dancing at your reception and I wanted to vomit. Tell me he's lousy in bed.'

'He's lousy in bed. What about the bimbo?'

'She likes girls.' They both laughed, and for a long time. And then they were silent again, because there was so much to say. She recrossed her legs while Clay watched closely. He could almost touch them.

'Are you going to survive?' she asked.

'Let's not talk about me. Let's talk about us.'

'I'm not going to have an affair,' she said.

'But you're thinking about one, aren't you?'

'No, but I know you are.'

'But it would be fun, wouldn't it?'

'It would, and it wouldn't. I'm not going to live like that.'

'I'm not either, Rebecca. I'm not sharing. I

once had all of you, and I let you get away. I'll wait until you're single again. But would you hurry, dammit?'

'That might not happen, Clay.'

'Yes it will.'

Chapter 36

With Ridley in bed beside him, Clay spent the night dreaming of Rebecca. He slept off and on, always waking up with a goofy smile on his face. All smiles vanished, though, when the phone rang just after 5 A.M. He answered it in the bedroom, then switched to a phone in his study.

It was Mel Snelling, a college roommate, now a physician in Baltimore. 'We gotta talk, pal,' he said. 'It's urgent.'

'All right,' Clay said, his knees buckling.

'Ten A.M., in front of the Lincoln Memorial.'

'I can do that.'

'And there's a good chance someone will be following me,' he said, then his line went dead. Dr. Snelling had reviewed the stolen Dyloft research for Clay, as a favor. Now the Feds had found him.

For the first time, Clay had the wild thought of just simply running. Wire what was left of the money to some banana republic, skip town, grow a beard, disappear. And, of course, take Rebecca with him.

Her mother would find them before the Feds.

He made coffee and took a long shower. He dressed in jeans, and would have said good-bye to Ridley but she hadn't moved.

There was a very good chance Mel would be wired. Since the FBI had found him, they would try their customary bag of dirty tricks. They would threaten to indict him too if he refused to snitch on his friend. They would harass him with visits, phone calls, surveillance. They would pressure him to put on a wire and lay the trap for Clay.

Zack Battle was out of town, so Clay was on his own. He arrived at the Lincoln Memorial at nine-twenty and mixed with the few tourists who were there. A few minutes later, Mel appeared, which immediately struck Clay as odd. Why would he get there half an hour before their meeting? Was the ambush being organized? Were Agents Spooner and Lohse close by with mikes and cameras and guns? One look at Mel's face and Clay knew that the news was bad.

They shook hands, said their hellos, tried to be cordial. Clay suspected that every word was being recorded. It was early September, the air chilly but not cold; Mel, however, was bundled up as if snow was expected. There could be cameras under all that garb. 'Let's go for a walk,' Clay said, sort of pointing down The Mall toward the Washington Monument.

'Sure,' Mel said, shrugging. He didn't care. Obviously, no trap had been planned near Mr. Lincoln.

'Did they follow you?' Clay asked.

'I don't think so. I flew from Baltimore to Pittsburgh, Pittsburgh to Reagan National, grabbed a cab. I don't think anybody's behind me.'

'Is it Spooner and Lohse?'

'Yes, you know them?'

'They've stopped by a few times.' They were walking beside the Reflecting Pool, on the sidewalk on the south side. Clay was not going to say anything that he didn't want to hear again. 'Mel, I know how the Fibbies operate. They like to pressure witnesses. They like to wire people and collect their evidence with gadgets and high-tech toys. Did they ask you to wear a wire?'

'Yes.'

'And?'

'I told them, "Hell no."'

'Thank you.'

'I have a great lawyer, Clay. I've spent some time with him, told him everything. I did nothing wrong because I didn't trade the stock. I understand you did, which I'm sure you would handle differently now if given the chance. Maybe I had some inside information, but I did nothing with it. I'm clean. But the pinch comes when I'm subpoenaed by the grand jury.'

The case had not yet been presented to the grand jury. Mel was indeed listening to a good lawyer. For the first time in four hours, Clay's breathing relaxed a little.

'Go on,' he said cautiously. His hands were stuck deep in the pockets of his jeans. Behind his sunglasses, his eyes were watching every person around them. If Mel had told the Feds everything, why would they need wires and mikes?

'The big question is how did they find me? I told no one I was reviewing the stuff. Who did you tell?'

'Absolutely no one, Mel.'

'That's hard to believe.'

'I swear. Why would I tell anyone?'

They stopped for a moment to let the traffic pass on Seventeenth Street. When they were walking again, they drifted to the right, away from a crowd. Mel said, almost under his breath, 'If I lie to the grand jury about the research, they'll have a hard time indicting you. But if I get caught lying, then I go to jail myself. Who else knows I reviewed the research?' he asked again.

And with that, Clay realized there were no wires, no mikes, no one was listening. Mel wasn't after evidence – he just wanted to be reassured. 'Your name is nowhere, Mel,'' Clay said. 'I shipped the stuff to you. You copied nothing, right?'

'Right.'

'You shipped it back to me. I reviewed it again. There was no sign of you anywhere. We talked by phone a half a dozen times. All of your thoughts and opinions about the research were verbal.'

'What about the other lawyers in the case?'

'A few of them have seen the research. They know I had it before we filed suit. They know a doctor reviewed it for me, but they don't have a clue who he is.'

'Can the FBI pressure them to testify that you had the research before you filed suit?'

'No way. They can try, but these guys are lawyers, big lawyers, Mel. They don't scare easily. They've done nothing wrong – they didn't trade in the stock – and they'll give the Feds nothing. I'm protected there.'

'Are you certain?' Mel asked, anything but certain.

'I'm positive.'

'So what do I do?'

'Keep listening to your lawyer. There's a good chance this thing won't get to a grand jury,' Clay said, more of a prayer than a fact. 'If you hold firm, it'll probably go away.'

They walked a hundred yards without a word. The Washington Monument was getting closer. 'If I get a subpoena,' Mel said, slowly, 'we'd better talk again.'

'Of course.'

'I'm not going to jail over this, Clay.'

'Neither am I.'

They stopped in a crowd on a sidewalk near the monument. Mel said, 'I'm going to disappear. Good-bye. From me, no news is good news.' And with that, he darted through a group of high school students and vanished.

The Coconino Country Courthouse in Flagstaff was relatively quiet the day before the trial. Business was routine; no hint of the historic and far-reaching conflict soon to be raging there. It was the second week in September, the temperature already pushing 105. Clay and Oscar walked around the downtown area, then quickly entered the courthouse in search of air-conditioning.

Inside the courtroom, though, pretrial motions were being argued and things were tense. No jury sat in the box; that selection process would begin promptly at nine the following morning. Dale Mooneyham and his team covered one side of the arena. The Goffman horde, led by a fancy litigator from L.A. named Roger Redding, occupied the other half. Roger the Rocket, because he struck fast and hard. Roger the Dodger, because he went all over the country, fighting the biggest trial lawyers he could find, dodging big verdicts.

Clay and Oscar took seats with the other spectators, of which there was an impressive number just for motion arguments. Wall Street would watch the trial very closely. It would be a continuing story in the financial press. And, of course, the vultures like Clay were quite curious. In the front two rows were a dozen or so corporate clones, no doubt the very nervous folks from Goffman.

Mooneyham lumbered around the courtroom like a barroom bully, bellowing at the Judge, then at Roger. His voice was rich and deep and his words were always contentious. He was an old warrior, with a limp that appeared to come and go. Occasionally, he picked up a cane to move around with, then at times seemed to forget it.

Roger was Hollywood cool – meticulously tailored, a head full of salt-and-pepper hair, strong chin, perfect profile. Probably wanted to be an actor at some point. He spoke in eloquent prose, beautiful sentences that rolled out with no hesitation. Never an 'Uh' or an 'Ah' or a 'Well . . .' No false starts. When he began arguing a point, he used a splendid vocabulary that anyone could understand, and he had the talent of keeping three or four arguments alive at one time before tying them all beautifully together into one superbly logical point. He had no fear of Dale Mooneyham, no fear of the Judge, no fear of the facts of the case.

When Redding argued even the smallest of issues, Clay found himself mesmerized. A frightening thought hit: If Clay was forced to trial in D.C., Goffman would not hesitate to send Roger the Rocket into battle there.

While he was being entertained by the two great lawyers on the stage before him, Clay was recognized. One of the lawyers at a table behind Redding glanced around the courtroom and thought he saw a familiar face. He nudged another one, and together they made the positive ID. Notes were scribbled and handed to the suits in the front rows.

The Judge called a fifteen-minute recess so he could visit the toilet. Clay left the courtroom and went to find a soda. He was followed by two men who finally cornered him at the end of the hallway. 'Mr. Carter,' the first said pleasantly. 'I'm Bob

Mitchell, vice president and in-house counsel for Goffman.' He shoved a hand forward and squeezed Clay's tightly.

'A pleasure,' Clay said.

'And this is Sterling Gibb, one of our attorneys from New York.' Clay was obliged to shake hands with Gibb as well.

'Just wanted to say hello,' Mitchell said. 'No surprise to see you here.'

'I have a slight interest in this trial,' Clay said.

'That's an understatement. How many cases do you have now?'

'Oh, I don't know. Quite a few.' Gibb was content to just smirk and stare.

'We watch your Web site every day,' Mitchell was saying. 'Twenty-six thousand at last count.' Gibb changed his smirks; it was obvious he detested the mass tort game.

'Something like that,' Clay said.

'Looks like you've pulled the advertising. Finally got enough cases, I guess.'

'Oh, you never have enough, Mr. Mitchell.'

'What are you going to do with all those cases if we win this trial?' Gibb asked, finally speaking.

'What are you going to do if you lose this trial?' Clay fired back.

Mitchell took a step closer. 'If we win here, Mr. Carter, you'll have a helluva time finding some poor lawyer who wants your twenty-six thousand cases. They won't be worth much.'

'And if you lose?' Clay asked.

Gibb took a step closer. 'If we lose here, we're

coming straight to D.C. to defend your bogus class action. That is, if you're not in jail.'

'Oh, I'll be ready,' Clay said, laboring under the assault.

'Can you find the courthouse?' Gibb asked.

'I've already played golf with the Judge,' Clay said. 'And I'm dating the court reporter.' Lies! But they stalled them for a second.

Mitchell caught himself, thrust out his right hand again, and said, 'Oh well, just wanted to say hello.'

Clay shook it and said, 'So nice to hear from Goffman. You've hardly acknowledged my lawsuit.' Gibb turned his back and walked away.

'Let's finish this one,' Mitchell said. 'Then we'll talk.'

Clay was about to reenter the courtroom when a pushy reporter stepped in front of him. He was Derek somebody with *Financial Weekly* and wanted a quick word or two. His newspaper was a right-wing, trial lawyer–hating, tort-bashing, corporate mouthpiece, and Clay knew better than to give him even a 'No comment' or a 'Kiss off.' Derek's name was vaguely familiar. Was he the reporter who'd written so many unkind things about Clay?

'Can I ask what you're doing here?' Derek said.

'I guess you can.'

'What are you doing here?'

'Same thing you're doing here.'

'And that is?'

'Enjoying the heat.'

'Is it true that you have twenty-five thousand Maxatil cases?'

'No.'

'How many?'

'Twenty-six thousand.'

'How much are they worth?'

'Somewhere between zero and a couple of billion.'

Unknown to Clay, the Judge had gagged the lawyers for both sides from then until the end of the trial. Since he was willing to talk, he attracted a crowd. He was surprised to see himself surrounded by reporters. He answered a few more questions without saying much at all.

The *Arizona Ledger* quoted him as claiming his cases could be worth $2 billion. It ran a photo of Clay outside the courtroom, microphones in his face, with the caption 'King of Torts in Town.' A brief summary of Clay's visit followed, along with a few paragraphs about the big trial itself. The reporter did not directly call him a greedy, opportunistic trial lawyer, but the implication was that he was a vulture, circling, hungry, waiting to attack Goffman's carcass.

The courtroom was packed with potential jurors and spectators. Nine A.M. came and went with no sign of the lawyers or the Judge. They were in chambers, no doubt still arguing pretrial issues. Bailiffs and clerks busied themselves around the bench. A young man in a suit emerged from the back, passed through the bar, and headed down the center aisle. He abruptly stopped, looked directly at Clay, then leaned down and whispered, 'Are you Mr. Carter?'

Taken aback, Clay nodded.

'The Judge would like to see you.'

The newspaper was in the middle of the Judge's desk. Dale Mooneyham was in one corner of the large office. Roger Redding was leaning on a table by the window. The Judge was rocking in his swivel chair. None of the three were happy. Very awkward introductions were made. Mooneyham refused to step forward and shake Clay's hand, preferring instead to offer a slight nod and a look that conveyed hatred.

'Are you aware of the gag order I've put in place, Mr. Carter?' asked the Judge.

'No sir.'

'Well, there is one.'

'I'm not one of the attorneys in this case,' Clay said.

'We work hard at having fair trials in Arizona, Mr. Carter. Both sides want a jury as uninformed and as impartial as possible. Now, thanks to you, the potential jurors know that there are at least twenty-six thousand similar cases out there.'

Clay was not about to appear weak or apologetic, not with Roger Redding watching every move.

'Maybe it was unavoidable,' Clay said. He would never try a case in front of this judge. No sense being intimidated.

'Why don't you just leave the state of Arizona?' Mooneyham boomed from the corner.

'I really don't have to,' Clay shot back.

'You want me to lose?'

And with that, Clay had heard enough. He wasn't sure how his presence might harm Mooneyham's case, but why run the risk?

'Very well, Your Honor, I guess I'll be seeing you.'

'An excellent idea,' the Judge said.

Clay looked at Roger Redding and said, 'See you in D.C.'

Roger smiled politely, but slowly shook his head no.

Oscar agreed to remain in Flagstaff and monitor the trial. Clay hopped on the Gulfstream for a very somber ride home. Banished from Arizona.

Chapter 37

In Reedsburg, the news that Hanna was laying off twelve hundred workers brought the town to a halt. The announcement came in a letter written by Marcus Hanna and given to all employees.

In fifty years, the company had been through only four layoffs. It had weathered cycles and slowdowns and had always worked hard to keep everyone on the payroll. Now that it was in bankruptcy, the rules were different. The company was under pressure to prove to the court and to its creditors that it had a viable financial future.

Events beyond the control of management were to blame. Flat sales were a factor, but nothing the company hadn't seen many times before. The crushing blow was the failure to reach a settlement in the class-action lawsuit. The company had bargained in good faith, but an overzealous and greedy law firm in D.C. had made unreasonable demands.

Survival was at stake, and Marcus assured his people that the company was not going under.

Drastic cost cutting would be required. A painful reduction in expenses for the next year would guarantee a profitable future.

To the twelve hundred getting pink slips, Marcus promised all the help the company could provide. Unemployment benefits would last for a year. Obviously, Hanna would hire them back as soon as possible, but no promises were made. The layoffs might become permanent.

In the cafés and barbershops, in the hallways of the schools and the pews of the churches, in the bleachers at soccer and peewee football games, on the sidewalks around the town square, in the beer joints and pool halls, the town talked of nothing else. Every one of the eleven thousand residents knew someone who'd just lost his or her job at Hanna. The layoffs were the biggest disaster in the quiet history of Reedsburg. Though the town was tucked away in the Alleghenies, word got out.

The reporter for the *Baltimore Press* who had written three articles about the Howard County class action was still watching. He was monitoring the bankruptcy filing. He was still chatting with the homeowners as their bricks fell off. News of the layoffs prompted him to go to Reedsburg. He went to the cafés and pool halls and soccer games.

The first of his two stories was as long as a short novel. An author bent on deliberate slander could not have been crueller. All of Reedsburg's misery could have easily been avoided if the class-action lawyer, J. Clay Carter II of D.C., had not been strident in his quest for large fees.

Since Clay did not read the *Baltimore Press*, and in fact he was dodging most papers and magazines, he might have avoided the news from Reedsburg, at least for a while. But the still-unknown editor(s) of the unauthorized and unwelcome newsletter faxed it over. The latest copy of 'The King of Shorts,' obviously thrown together in a hurry, ran the *Press* story.

Clay read it and wanted to sue the newspaper. However, he would soon forget about the *Baltimore Press* because a larger nightmare was looming. A week earlier, a reporter from *Newsweek* had called and, as usual, been stiff-armed by Miss Glick. Every lawyer dreams of national exposure, but only if it's the high-profile case or billion-dollar verdict. Clay suspected this was neither, and he was right. *Newsweek* was not really interested in Clay Carter, but rather, his nemesis.

It was a puff piece for Helen Warshaw, two pages of glory that any lawyer would kill for. A striking photo had Ms. Warshaw in a courtroom somewhere, standing in front of an empty jury box, looking quite tenacious and brilliant, but also very believable. Clay had never seen her before, and he'd hoped she would somehow resemble a 'ruthless bitch,' as Saulsberry had called her. She did not. She was very attractive – short, dark hair and sad brown eyes that would hold the attention of any jury. Clay stared at her and wished he had her case rather than his. Hopefully, they would never meet. And if so, never in a courtroom.

Ms. Warshaw was one of three partners in a New York firm that specialized in attorney malpractice, a rare but growing niche. Now she was going after some of the biggest and richest lawyers in the country, and she was not going to settle. 'I've never seen a case with as much jury appeal,' she said, and Clay wanted to slit his wrists.

She had fifty Dyloft clients, all dying, all suing. The story gave the quick and dirty history of the class-action litigation.

Of the fifty, for some reason the reporter focused on Mr. Ted Worley, of Upper Marlboro, Maryland, and ran a photo of the poor guy sitting in his backyard with his wife behind him, their arms crossed, both faces sad and frowning. Mr. Worley, weak and trembling and angry, recounted his first contact with Clay Carter, a phone call from nowhere while he was trying to enjoy an Orioles game, the frightening news about Dyloft, the urinalysis, the visit from the young lawyer, the filing of the lawsuit. Everything. 'I didn't want to settle,' he said more than once.

For *Newsweek* Mr. Worley produced all of his paperwork – the medical records, the court filings, the insidious contract with Carter that gave the lawyer the authority to settle for any amount over $50,000. Everything, including copies of the two letters Mr. Worley had written to Mr. Carter in protest of the 'sell-out.' The lawyer did not answer the letters.

According to his doctors, Mr. Worley had less than six months to live. Slowly reading each awful word of the story, Clay felt as if he was responsible for the cancer.

Helen explained that the jury would hear from many of her clients by video, since they would not last until the trial. A rather cruel thing to say, Clay thought, but then everything in the story was wicked.

Mr. Carter declined to comment. For good measure, they threw in the White House photo of Clay and Ridley, and they couldn't resist the tidbit that he had donated $250,000 to the Presidential Review.

'He's gonna need friends like the President,' Helen Warshaw said, and Clay could almost feel the bullet between his eyes. He flung the magazine across his office. He wished he'd never been to the White House, never met the President, never written that damned check, never met Ted Worley, never met Max Pace, never thought about going to law school.

He called his pilots and told them to hustle to the airport. 'Going where, sir?'

'I don't know. Where do you want to go?'

'Beg your pardon?'

'Biloxi, Mississippi.'

'One person or two?'

'Just me.' He hadn't seen Ridley in twenty-four hours and had no desire to take her with him. He needed time away from the city and anything that reminded him of it.

But two days on French's yacht did little to help. Clay needed the company of another conspirator, but Patton was too preoccupied with other class actions. They ate and drank too much.

French had two associates in the courtroom in Phoenix and they were sending e-mails by the hour. He continued to discount Maxatil as a potential target, but he was still watching every move. It was his job, he said, since he was the biggest tort lawyer of them all. He had the experience, the money, the reputation. All mass tort, should, sooner or later, land on his desk.

Clay read the e-mails, and he talked to Mulrooney. Jury selection had taken one full day. Dale Mooneyham was now slowly laying out the plaintiff's case against the drug. The government study was powerful evidence. The jury was keenly interested in it. 'So far, so good,' Oscar said. 'Mooneyham is quite the actor, but Roger has better courtroom skills.'

While French juggled three calls at once, with a crushing hangover, Clay sunned on the upper deck and tried to forget his problems. Late on the second afternoon, after a couple of vodkas on the deck, French asked, 'How much cash you got left?'

'I don't know. I'm afraid to crunch the numbers.'

'Take a guess.'

'Twenty million, maybe.'

'And how much insurance?'

'Ten million. They canceled me, but they're still on the line for Dyloft.'

French sucked on a lemon and said, 'I'm not sure thirty million is enough for you.'

'Doesn't appear to be sufficient, does it?'

'No. You have twenty-one claims now, and the number can only go up. We'll be lucky if we can settle these damned things for three mil each.'

'How many do you have?'

'Nineteen, as of yesterday.'

'And how much cash do you have?'

'Two hundred million. I'll be all right.'

Then why don't you just loan me, say, fifty million? Clay managed to be amused at the way they threw around the numbers. A steward brought more alcohol, which they needed.

'And the other guys?' Clay asked.

'Wes is fine. Carlos can survive if his number stays below thirty. Didier's last two wives cleaned him out. He's dead. He'll be the first one to go bankrupt, which he's done before.'

The first one? And who might be the second one?

After a long silence, Clay asked, 'What happens if Goffman wins in Flagstaff? I have all these cases.'

'You're gonna be one sick puppy, that's for damned sure. Happened to me ten years ago with a bunch of bad baby cases. I hustled around, signed 'em up, sued too fast, then the wheels came off and there was no way to recover anything. My clients were expecting millions because they had these little deformed babies, you know, and so they were emotional as hell and impossible to deal with. Bunch of 'em sued me, but I never paid. The lawyer can't promise a result. Cost me a bunch of dough, though.'

'That's not what I want to hear.'

'How much have you spent on Maxatil?'

'Eight million just in advertising.'

'I'd just sit on them for a while, see what Goffman does. I doubt they'll offer anything. They're a bunch of hardasses. With time, your clients will revolt and you can tell them to get lost.' A big drink of vodka. 'But think positive. Mooneyham hasn't lost in ages. A big verdict, and the whole world is different. You're sitting on a gold mine, again.'

'Goffman told me they were coming straight to D.C. next.'

'They could be bluffing, depends on what happens in Flagstaff. If they lose big, then they have to think about settling. A split-decision – liability but small damages – and they might want to try another one. If they choose yours, then you can bring in a trial stud and whip their asses.'

'You wouldn't advise me to try it myself?'

'No. You don't have the experience. It takes years in the courtroom before you're ready for the big leagues, Clay. Years and years.'

As fiery as he was about big lawsuits, it was obvious to Clay that Patton had no enthusiasm for the scenario he had just laid out. He was not volunteering to be the trial stud in the D.C. case. He was just going through the motions in an effort to comfort his young colleague.

Clay left late the next morning and flew to Pittsburgh, anywhere but D.C. En route, he talked to Oscar, and he read the e-mails and news reports of the trial in Flagstaff. The plaintiff, a sixty-six-year-old woman with breast cancer, had testified and presented her case beautifully. She was very sympathetic, and Mooneyham played her like a fiddle. Go get 'em, ol' boy, Clay kept mumbling to himself.

He rented a car and drove northeast for two hours, into the heart of the Allegheny Mountains. Finding Reedsburg on the map was almost as difficult as finding it on a highway. As he crested a hill on the edge of town, he saw a mammoth plant in the distance. WELCOME TO REEDSBURG, PENNSYLVANIA, a large sign said. HOME OF THE HANNA PORTLAND CEMENT COMPANY. FOUNDED IN 1946. Two large smokestacks emitted a chalky dust that drifted slowly away with the wind. At least it's still operating, Clay thought.

He followed a sign to downtown and found a parking place on Main Street. Wearing jeans and a baseball cap, with three days' worth of dark stubble, he was not worried about being recognized. He walked into Ethel's Coffee Shop and took a seat on a wobbly stool at the counter. Ethel herself greeted him and took his order. Coffee and a grilled cheese sandwich.

At a table behind him two old-timers were talking football. The Reedsburg High Cougars had lost three straight, and both of them could do a better job calling plays than the head coach. There was a home game that night, according to the schedule on the wall near the cash register.

When Ethel brought the coffee she said, 'You just passing through?'

'Yes,' Clay said, realizing that she knew every one of Reedsburg's eleven thousand souls.

'Where you from?'

'Pittsburgh.'

He couldn't tell if that was good or bad, but she left with no further questions. At another table, two younger men were talking about jobs. It was soon clear that neither was employed. One wore a denim cap with a Hanna Cement logo on the front. As Clay ate his grilled cheese, he listened as they fretted over unemployment benefits, mortgages, credit-card bills, part-time work. One was planning to surrender his Ford pickup to the local dealer who had promised to resell it for him.

Against the wall by the front door was a folding table with a large plastic water bottle on it. A handmade poster urged everyone to contribute to the 'Hanna Fund.' A collection of coins and bills half-filled the bottle.

'What's that for?' Clay asked Ethel when she refilled his cup.

'Oh, that. It's a drive to collect money for the families laid off out at the plant.'

'Which plant?' Clay asked, trying to appear ignorant.

'Hanna Cement, biggest employer in town. Twelve hundred folks got laid off last week. We stick together around here. Got those things all over town – stores, cafés, churches, even the schools. Raised over six thousand so far. Money'll go for light bills and groceries if things get bad. Otherwise, it'll go to the hospital.'

'Did business turn bad?' Clay said, chewing. Putting the sandwich in his mouth was easy; swallowing was becoming more difficult.

'No, the plant's always been well run. The Hannas know what they're doing. Got this crazy lawsuit down around Baltimore somewhere. Lawyers got greedy, wanted too much money, forced Hanna into bankruptcy.'

'It's a damned shame,' said one of the oldtimers. Coffee shop conversations were shared by all present. 'Didn't have to happen. The Hannas tried to settle the damned thing, made a good-faith effort, but these slimebags in D.C. had 'em at gunpoint. Hannas said, "Screw you," and walked away.'

In a flash, Clay thought: Not a bad summary of events.

'I worked there forty years, never missed a paycheck. A damned shame.'

Because Clay was expected to say something to move along the conversation, he said, 'Layoffs are rare, huh?'

'The Hannas don't believe in laying folks off.'

'Will they hire them back?'

'They'll try. But the bankruptcy court is in charge now.'

Clay nodded and quickly turned back to his sandwich. The two younger men were on their feet, heading for the cash register. Ethel shooed them away. 'No charge, fellas. It's on the house.'

They nodded politely, and as they left both dropped some coins into the Hanna Fund. A few minutes later, Clay said good-bye to the old-timers, paid his bill, thanked Ethel, and dropped a $100 bill into the water bottle.

After dark, he sat alone on the visitors side and watched the Reedsburg Cougars do battle with the Enid Elk. The home stands were filled almost to capacity. The band was loud, the crowd rowdy and eager for a win. But the football failed to hold his attention. He looked at the roster and wondered how many players listed there were from families hit by the layoffs. He gazed across the field to the rows and rows of Reedsburg fans and wondered who had jobs and who did not.

Before the kickoff, and just after the national anthem, a local minister had prayed for the safety of the players, and for the renewed economic strength of the community. He had ended his prayer with, 'Help us through these hard times, O God. Amen.'

If Clay Carter had ever felt worse, he could not remember when.

Chapter 38

Ridley called early Saturday evening, quite upset. She had been unable to locate Clay for four days! No one at the office knew where he was, or if they knew they wouldn't tell her. He, on the other hand, had made no effort to call her. Both had more than one phone. Was this any way to advance a relationship? After listening to the whining for a few minutes, Clay heard something buzz in the line and asked, 'Where are you?'

'St. Barth. In our villa.'

'How'd you get down there?' Clay, of course, had been using the Gulfstream.

'I chartered a smaller jet. Too small, actually, we had to stop in San Juan for fuel. It wouldn't make it here nonstop.'

Poor girl. Clay wasn't sure how she knew the number of the air charter service. 'Why are you down there?' he asked, a stupid question.

'I was so stressed out because I couldn't find you. You can't do that again, Clay.'

He tried to link the two – his disappearance

and her escape to St. Barth, but quickly gave it up.

'I'm sorry,' he said. 'I left town in a hurry. Patton French needed me in Biloxi. I was too busy to call.'

A long pause as she debated whether she should forgive him right then or wait a day or two. 'Promise me you won't do it again,' she whimpered.

Clay wasn't in the mood for either whining or promising, and he found himself relieved that she was out of the country. 'It won't happen again. Relax, enjoy yourself down there.'

'Can you come down?' she asked, but without any feeling. Sort of a perfunctory request.

'Not with the trial in Flagstaff getting close.' He doubted seriously if she had an inkling about the trial in Flagstaff.

'Will you call me tomorrow?' she asked.

'Of course.'

Jonah was back in town, with many adventures to report from the sailing life. They were to meet at nine at a bistro on Wisconsin Avenue for a late and long dinner. Around eight-thirty, the phone rang, but the caller hung up without a word. Then it rang again, and Clay grabbed it as he was buttoning his shirt.

'Is this Clay Carter?' a male voice asked.

'Yes, who is this?' Because of the sheer number of disgruntled clients out there – Dyloft and Skinny Ben and, now, especially, those irate home-owners up in Howard County – Clay had changed numbers twice in the past two months. He could handle the abuse at the office, but he preferred to live in peace.

'I'm from Reedsburg, Pennsylvania, and I have some valuable information about the Hanna company.'

The words were chilling, and Clay sat on the edge of his bed. Keep him on the phone, he said as he tried to think clearly. 'Okay, I'm listening.' Someone from Reedsburg had somehow acquired his new, unlisted phone number.

'We can't talk over the phone,' the voice said. Thirty years old, white male, high school education.

'Why not?'

'It's a long story. There are some papers.'

'Where are you?'

'I'm in the city. I'll meet you in the lobby of the Four Seasons Hotel on M Street. We can talk there.'

Not a bad plan. There would be plenty of foot traffic in the lobby, just in case someone wanted to pull out a gun and start shooting lawyers. 'When?' Clay asked.

'Real soon. I'll be there in five minutes. How long will it take you?'

Clay was not going to mention the fact that he lived six blocks away, though his address was no secret. 'I'll be there in ten minutes.'

'Good. I'm wearing jeans and a black Steelers cap.'

'I'll find you,' Clay said, then hung up. He

finished dressing and hustled out of his town house. Walking rapidly along Dumbarton, he tried to imagine what information he could need or even want on the Hanna company. He'd just spent eighteen hours in Reedsburg, and was trying, quite unsuccessfully, to forget about the place. He turned south on Thirty-first Street, mumbling to himself, lost in a world of conspiracies and payoffs and spy scenarios. A lady passed with a small dog in search of a suitable spot on the sidewalk to relieve itself. A young man in a black biker's jacket with a cigarette hanging from his mouth approached, though Clay barely saw him. As the two passed, in front of a poorly lit town house and under the limbs of an old red maple, the man suddenly, with perfect timing and precision, unloaded a short right cross that caught Clay directly on the chin.

Clay never saw it. He remembered a loud pop in his face, and his head crashing into a wrought-iron fence. There was a stick of some sort, and another man, two of them up there throwing punches and flailing away. Clay rolled to his side and managed to get a knee under himself, then the stick landed like a gunshot on the back of his skull.

He heard a woman's voice in the distance, then he passed out.

The lady had been walking her dog when she heard a commotion behind her. There was a fight of some sort, two against one, with the man on the ground getting the worst of it. She ran closer and was horrified to see two men in black jackets hammering away with large black sticks. She screamed, they ran. She whipped out her cell phone and dialed 911.

The two men ran down the block and disappeared around the corner of a church on N Street. She tried to assist the young man on the ground, who was unconscious and bleeding badly.

Clay was taken to George Washington University Hospital where a trauma team stabilized him. The initial exam revealed two large head wounds caused by something blunt, a cut on his right cheekbone, a cut in his left ear, and numerous contusions. His right fibula was cracked neatly in two. His left kneecap was in pieces and the left ankle was broken. His head was shaved and eighty-one stitches were required to close the two large cuts. His skull was badly bruised but not fractured. Six stitches in his cheekbone, eleven in his ear, and they rolled him into surgery to put his legs back together.

Jonah began calling after waiting impatiently for thirty minutes. He left the restaurant after an hour and headed on foot to Clay's town house. He knocked on the door, rang the bell, cursed just under his breath, and was ready to throw rocks at the windows when he saw Clay's car parked between two others down the street. He thought it was Clay's car, anyway.

He walked slowly toward it. Something was wrong there, he just wasn't sure what. It was a black Porsche Carrera all right, but it was covered with a white dust. He called the police.

A torn and empty Hanna Portland Cement bag was found under the Porsche. Someone had evidently covered the car with cement, then thrown water at it. In spots, especially on the roof and the hood, large patches of the cement had dried and stuck to the car. As the police inspected it, Jonah told them that its owner was unaccounted for. After a long computer search, Clay's name popped up, and Jonah took off for the hospital. He called Paulette, and she was there before he arrived. Clay was in surgery, but it was only broken bones and probably a concussion. His injuries did not appear life-threatening.

The lady with the dog told police the assailants were both white males. Three college boys entering a bar on Wisconsin Avenue reported seeing two white males in black jackets hurry around the corner from N Street. They hopped into a metallic green van, where a driver was waiting for them. It was too dark to see the license plates.

The call Clay had received at 8:39 P.M. was traced to a pay phone on M Street, about five minutes from his town house.

The trail grew cold quickly. It was, after all, only a beating. And a Saturday night beating at that. The same night would see two rapes in the city, two drive-by shootings that injured five, and two murders, both of which appeared to be completely at random.

* * *

Since Clay had no family in the city, Jonah and Paulette assumed the roles of spokesmen and decision makers. At 1:30 A.M., a doctor reported to them that the surgery had gone smoothly, all the bones were set and ready to heal, some pins and screws had been installed, things couldn't be better. They would closely monitor brain activity. They were sure there was a concussion but didn't know how serious it was. 'He looks awful,' she warned them.

Two hours went by, as Clay was slowly moved upstairs. Jonah had insisted on a private room. They finally saw him just after 4 A.M. A mummy would have had less wrapping.

Both legs were in thick, full-length casts suspended a few inches off the bed by a complex series of cables and pulleys. A sheet hid his chest and arms. Heavy gauze covered his skull and half his face. His eyes were swollen and shut; mercifully he was still unconscious. His chin was swollen, his lips puffy and blue. Blood had dried on his neck.

They stood in muted silence, taking in the full extent of his wounds, listening to the monitors click and beep, watching his chest move up and down, very slowly. Then Jonah started laughing. 'Look at that son of a bitch,' he said.

'Hush, Jonah,' Paulette hissed, ready to slap him.

'There lies the King of Torts,' Jonah said, shaking with suppressed laughter.

Then, she too saw the humor. She managed to

laugh without opening her mouth, and for a long moment they both stood at the foot of Clay's bed, working hard to contain their amusement.

When the humor passed, she said, 'You should be ashamed.'

'I am. I'm sorry.'

An orderly rolled in a bed. Paulette would take the first night, Jonah would get the second.

Fortunately, the assault was too late to make the Sunday *Post*. Miss Glick called each member of the firm and asked them not to visit the hospital and not to send flowers. They might be needed later in the week, but for now just say prayers.

Clay finally came back from the dead around noon Sunday. Paulette was tossing on the foldaway when he said, 'Who's there?'

She jumped up and ran to his side. 'It's me, Clay.'

Through his swollen and blurry eyes he could see a black face. It certainly wasn't Ridley. He reached out with a hand and said, 'Who?'

'Paulette, Clay. Can't you see?'

'No. Paulette? What are you doing here?' His words were thick, slow, and painful.

'Just taking care of you, boss.'

'Where am I?'

'George Washington University Hospital.'

'Why, what happened?'

'It's what they call an old-fashioned ass-kicking.'

'What?'

'You got jumped. Two guys with sticks. You need some pain pills?'

'Please.'

She raced from the room and found a nurse. A doctor showed up a few minutes later and, in excruciating detail, explained to Clay just how badly he'd been beaten. Another pill, and Clay drifted away again. Most of Sunday was spent in a pleasant fog, with Paulette and Jonah baby-sitting as they read the newspapers and watched pro football.

The stories hit with a fury on Monday, and they were all the same. Paulette muted the television and Jonah hid the newspapers. Miss Glick and the rest of the firm circled the wagons and had 'No comment' for everyone. She received an e-mail from a sailboat captain claiming to be Clay's father. He was near the Yucatán Peninsula in the Gulf of Mexico and could someone please update him on Clay's condition? She did so – stable condition, broken bones, concussion. He thanked her and promised to check back the following day.

Ridley arrived Monday afternoon. Paulette and Jonah cleared out, happy to leave the hospital for a while. Evidently, Georgians did not understand proper hospital waiting rituals. Whereas Americans move in with their beloved sick and wounded, those from other cultures deem it more practical to stop by for an hour, then let the hospital take care of its patients. Ridley showed great affection for a few minutes and tried to interest Clay in the latest renovations to their villa. His head pounded worse and he called for a pill. She relaxed on the foldaway and tried to nap, exhausted, she said, from the flight home. Nonstop. On the Gulfstream. He fell asleep too, and when he awoke she was gone.

A detective stopped by for a follow-up. All suspicion pointed to some thugs from Reedsburg, but there was scant proof. Clay was unable to describe the man who threw the first punch. 'I never saw it,' he said, rubbing his chin. To make Clay feel better, the cop had four large, color photos of the black Porsche, heavily spotted with white cement, and Clay needed another pill.

Flowers poured in. Adelfa Pumphrey, Glenda at OPD, Mr. and Mrs. Rex Crittle, Rodney, Patton French, Wes Saulsberry, a judge Clay knew from Superior Court. Jonah brought a laptop, and Clay had a lengthy chat with his father.

'The King of Shorts' newsletter published three editions on Monday, each filled with the latest newspaper stories and gossip about Clay's beating. He saw none of it. Hidden away in his hospital room, he was sheltered by his friends.

Early Tuesday morning, Zack Battle stopped by on his way to the office and delivered some welcome news. The SEC was suspending its investigation of Clay. He had talked to Mel Snelling's lawyer in Baltimore. Mel wasn't budging, wasn't caving in to FBI pressure. And without Mel, they could not put together the necessary evidence.

'I guess the Feds saw you in the papers and figured you've been punished enough,' Zack said.

'I'm in the paper?' Clay asked.

'A couple of stories.'

'Do I want to read them?'

'I advise you not to.'

The boredom of the hospital was hitting hard – the traction, the bedpans, the relentless visits by the nurses at all hours, the grave little chats with the doctors, the four walls, the dreadful food, the endless rebandaging of his injuries, the taking of blood for yet more tests, the sheer tedium of lying there, unable to move. The casts would be his for weeks, and he could not envision surviving life in the city with a wheelchair and crutches. At least two additional operations were planned, minor ones, they promised him.

The aftershocks of the actual beating came to haunt him, and he remembered more of the sounds and physical sensations of being pummeled. He saw the face of the man who threw the first punch, but couldn't be sure if it was real or just a dream. So he didn't tell the detective. He heard screams from the darkness, but they too could easily be part of the nightmare. He remembered seeing a black stick the size of a baseball bat rising into the air. Mercifully, he had been knocked out and could not recall most of the blows.

The swelling began to subside; his head was clearing. He quit the pain pills so he could think and try to run the office by phone and e-mail.

Things were quite hectic there, according to everyone he talked to. But he suspected otherwise.

Ridley was good for an hour late in the morning and another late in the afternoon. She stood by his bed and was very affectionate, especially when the nurses were around. Paulette detested her and was quick to disappear when she entered the room.

'She's after your money,' she said to Clay.

'And I'm after her body,' Clay said.

'Well, right now she's getting the better end of the deal.'

Chapter 39

To read, he was forced to raise half of the bed, and since his legs were already pointed upward, he sort of folded himself into a V. A painful one. He could hold that position for no more than ten minutes before lowering the bed and relieving the pressure. With Jonah's laptop resting on both casts, he was browsing through the newspaper articles from Arizona when Paulette answered the phone. 'It's Oscar,' she said.

They had talked briefly on Sunday night, but Clay had been drugged and incoherent. Now he was wide awake and ready for details. 'Let's hear it,' he said, lowering the bed and trying to stretch out.

'Mooneyham rested Saturday morning. His case could not have been more perfect. The guy is brilliant, and he has the jury eating out of his hands. The Goffman boys were strutting when the trial started, now I think they're running for the bunkers. Roger Redding put on their star expert yesterday afternoon, a researcher who testified that there is no direct link between the drug and the plaintiff's breast cancer. I thought the guy was very good, very believable, hell he has three doctorates. The jury paid attention. Then Mooneyham ripped him to shreds. He pulled out some bad research the guy did twenty years ago. He attacked his credentials. The witness was completely slain when it was over. I'm thinking, "Somebody call nine-one-one, get this poor guy outta here." I've never seen a witness so thoroughly humiliated. Roger was pale. The Goffman boys were sitting there like a bunch of thugs in a police lineup.'

'Beautiful, beautiful,' Clay kept saying, the phone stuck to the gauze on the left side of his face, opposite the slashed ear.

'Here's the good part. I found out where the Goffman folks are staying, so I switched hotels. I see them at breakfast. I see them in the bar late at night. They know who I am, so we're like two rabid dogs circling each other. They have an in-house lawyer named Fleet who caught me in the hotel lobby yesterday after adjournment, about an hour after the slaughter of their expert. He said he wanted to have a drink. He had one, I had three. The reason he had only one is because he had to go back to the Goffman suite on the top floor where they spent the night pacing the floors, kicking around the possibilities of a settlement.'

'Say it again,' Clay said softly.

'You heard me. Goffman, at this very moment,

is thinking about settling with Mooneyham. They are terrified. They're convinced, like everybody else in the courtroom, that this jury is about to nuke their company. Any settlement will cost a fortune because the old stud doesn't want to settle. Clay, he is eating their lunch! Roger is excellent, but he can't carry Mooneyham's briefcase.'

'Back to the settlement.'

'Back to the settlement. Fleet wanted to know how many of our cases are legitimate. I said, "All twenty-six thousand." He beats around the bush for a while, then asks if I think you would consider settling them for something in the neighborhood of a hundred thousand each. That's two point six bil, Clay. Are you doing the math?'

'It's done.'

'And the fees?'

'Done.' And with that the pain immediately vanished. The throbbing skull was still. The heavy casts were featherlike. The delicate bruises ceased to exist. Clay felt like crying.

'Anyway, it definitely was not an offer to settle, just the first feeler. A real tense one. You hear a lot of rumors around the courthouse, especially from the lawyers and stock analysts. According to the gossip, Goffman could afford a compensation pool of up to seven billion. If the company settled now, its stock price might hold steady because the Maxatil nightmare would be over. That's one theory, but after the bloodletting yesterday, it makes a lot of sense. Fleet came to me because we have the biggest class. The courthouse gossip puts the number of potential claims at somewhere around sixty thousand, so we have about forty percent of the market. If we're willing to settle for around a hundred grand each, then they can predict their costs.'

'When do you see him again?'

'It's almost eight here, the trial resumes in an hour. We agreed to meet outside the courtroom.'

'Call me as soon as you can.'

'Don't worry, chief. How are the broken bones?'

'Much better now.'

Paulette took the phone. Seconds later, it rang again. She answered, handed it back to Clay, and said, 'It's for you, and I'm getting out of here.'

It was Rebecca, in the hospital's lobby, on her cell phone, wondering if a quick visit would be appropriate. Minutes later, she walked into his room and was shocked at the sight of him. She kissed him on the cheek, between bruises.

'They had sticks,' Clay said. 'To even things out. Otherwise, I would've had an unfair advantage.' He punched the controls to the bed and began raising himself into the V.

'You look awful,' she said. Her eyes were moist.

'Thank you. You, on the other hand, look spectacular.'

She kissed him again, same place, and began rubbing his left arm. A moment of silence passed between them.

'Can I ask you a question?' Clay said.

'Sure.'

'Where is your husband right now?'

'He's in either São Paulo or Hong Kong. I can't keep track.'

'Does he know you're here?'

'Of course not.'

'What would he do if he knew you were here?'

'He would be upset. I'm sure we'd fight.'

'Would that be unusual?'

'Happens all the time, I'm afraid. It's not working, Clay. I want out.'

In spite of his wounds, Clay was having an awesome day. A fortune was within his grasp, as was Rebecca. The door to his room opened quietly and Ridley entered. She was at the foot of his bed, unnoticed, when she said, 'Sorry to interrupt.'

'Hi, Ridley,' Clay said weakly.

The women gave each other looks that would terrify cobras. Ridley moved to the other side of the bed, directly opposite Rebecca, who kept her hand on Clay's bruised arm. 'Ridley, this is Rebecca, Rebecca, this is Ridley,' Clay said, then gave serious consideration to pulling the sheets over his head and pretending to be dead.

Neither smiled. Ridley reached over just a few inches and began gently rubbing Clay's right arm. Though he was being pampered by two beautiful women, he felt more like fresh roadkill seconds before the wolves arrived.

Since there was absolutely nothing anybody could say for a few seconds, Clay nodded to his left and said, 'She's an old friend,' then to his right, and said, 'She's a new friend.' Both women, at least at that moment, felt much closer to Clay than just a mere friend. Both were irritated. Neither flinched nor moved an inch. Their positions had been staked out.

'I believe we were at your wedding reception,' Ridley said, finally. A not too subtle reminder to Rebecca that she happened to be married.

'Uninvited as I recall,' Rebecca said.

'Oh, darn, time for my enema,' Clay said, and nobody laughed but him. If a catfight broke out across his bed, he'd be mauled even worse. Five minutes earlier he'd been on the phone to Oscar, dreaming of record fees. Now, two women were drawing swords.

Two very beautiful women. Things could be worse, he told himself. Where were the nurses? They barged in at all hours of the day, with no regard for privacy or sleep patterns. Sometimes they came in pairs. And if a visitor happened to be in Clay's room, a needless drop-in by a nurse was guaranteed. 'Anything we can get for you, Mr. Carter?' 'Adjust your bed?' 'Want the TV on?' 'Or off?'

The halls were silent. Both women pawed at him.

Rebecca blinked first. She had no choice. She did, after all, have a husband. 'I guess I'll be going.' She left the room slowly, as if she didn't want to leave, didn't want to concede territory. Clay was thrilled by that.

As soon as the door closed, Ridley withdrew to the window, where she stood for a long time and looked at nothing. Clay scanned a newspaper, completely unconcerned with her and whatever her moods might be. The cold shoulder she was working diligently to deliver happened to be welcome.

'You love her, don't you?' Ridley said, still looking out the window, trying to appear wounded.

'Who?'

'Rebecca.'

'Oh, her. Naw, she's just an old friend.'

With that she wheeled around and walked to the side of his bed. 'I'm not stupid, Clay!'

'Didn't say you were.' He was still reading the newspaper, quite unmoved by this attempt at high drama. She grabbed her purse and stomped out of his room, heels clicking as loudly as possible. A nurse entered shortly thereafter, to inspect him for damages.

Oscar called a few minutes later, on his cell phone outside the courtroom. A quick recess had been ordered. 'Rumor has it Mooneyham turned down ten million this morning,' he said.

'Fleet tell you this?'

'No, we didn't meet. He was tied up with some motions. I'll try and catch him during lunch.'

'Who's on the stand?'

'Another Goffman expert, a female professor from Duke who's discrediting the government study on Maxatil. Mooneyham is sharpening his knives. Should be ugly.'

'Do you believe the rumor?'

'I'm not sure what to believe. The Wall Street boys seem excited about it. They want a settlement because they figure that's the best way to predict costs. I'll call you back during lunch.'

There were three possible outcomes in Flagstaff; two would be delightful. A verdict against Goffman would put enormous pressure on the company to settle and avoid years of litigation and the constant barrage of big verdicts. A midtrial settlement there would likely mean a national compensation plan for all plaintiffs.

A verdict in favor of Goffman would force Clay to scurry around and prepare for his own trial in D.C. That prospect brought back the sharp pains in his skull and legs.

Lying motionless for hours in a hospital bed was sufficient torture in itself. Now, the silent phone made matters much worse. At any moment, Goffman could offer Mooneyham enough money to make him settle. His ego would push him all the way to a verdict, but could he ignore the interests of his client?

A nurse closed the blinds, turned off the lights and the TV. When she was gone, Clay rested the phone on his stomach, pulled the sheets over his head, and waited.

Chapter 40

The next morning, Clay was taken back to surgery for some minor adjustments to the pins and screws in his legs. 'A bit of tweaking,' his doctor had called it. Whatever it was required a full dose of anesthesia, which wiped out most of the day. He returned to his room just after noon, and slept for three hours before the drugs wore off. Paulette, not Ridley and not Rebecca, was waiting when he finally came around. 'Any word from Oscar?' he said, with a thick tongue.

'He called, said the trial was going well. That's about it,' Paulette reported. She adjusted his bed and his pillow and gave him water, and when he was awake for good, she left to run errands. On the way out, she handed him an overnight envelope, unopened.

From Patton French. A handwritten note passed along his best wishes for a speedy recovery, and something else that Clay could not decipher. The attached memo was to the Dyloft Plaintiffs' Steering Committee (now Defendants). The

Honorable Helen Warshaw had submitted her weekly additions to her class action. The list was growing. Residual Dyloft damage was popping up all over the nation, and the Defendants were sinking deeper into the quicksand. There were now 381 members of the class, with 24 of them ex-JCC clients who'd signed up with Ms. Warshaw, up three from the week before. As always, Clay slowly read the names, and again wondered how their paths had ever crossed.

Wouldn't his former clients love to see him laid up in the hospital – cut, broken, and bruised? Perhaps one was down the hall, having tumors and organs removed, huddling with loved ones as the clock ticked loudly. He knew he didn't cause their diseases, but for some reason he felt responsible for their suffering.

Ridley finally stopped by on her way home from the gym. She hauled in some books and magazines and tried to appear concerned. After a few minutes she said, 'Clay, the decorator called. I need to return to the villa.'

Was the decorator male or female? He pondered the question but did not ask.

What an excellent idea!

'When?' he asked.

'Tomorrow, maybe. If the plane is available.' Why wouldn't it be available? Clay certainly wasn't going anywhere.

'Sure. I'll call the pilots.' Getting her out of town would make his life easier. She was of no benefit around the hospital.

'Thanks,' she said, then sat in the chair and began flipping through a magazine. After thirty minutes her time was up. She kissed him on the forehead and disappeared.

The detective was next. Three men from Reedsburg had been arrested early Sunday morning outside a bar in Hagerstown, Maryland. There had been a fight of some sort. They tried to leave the scene, in a dark green minivan, but the driver misjudged something and drove them into a drainage ditch. The detective produced three color photos of the suspects – all rough-looking characters. Clay could not identify any of them.

They worked at the Hanna plant, according to the Chief of Police in Reedsburg. Two had recently been laid off, but that was the only information the detective had managed to extract from the authorities up there. 'They're not very cooperative,' he said. Having been to Reedsburg, Clay could understand why.

'If you can't identify these guys, then I have no choice but to close the file,' the detective said.

'I've never seen them before,' Clay said.

The detective placed the photos back in his file and left forever. A parade of nurses and doctors followed with much probing and groping, and after an hour Clay fell asleep.

Oscar called around 9:30 P.M. The trial had just adjourned for the day. Everyone was exhausted, primarily because Dale Mooneyham had caused such massive carnage in the courtroom. Goffman had reluctantly hauled out its third expert, a spineless horn-rimmed in-house lab rat who'd been in charge of the clinical trials for Maxatil, and after a wonderful and creative direct examination by Roger the Dodger, Mooneyham had proceeded to butcher the poor boy on cross.

'It's an old-fashioned rump-humping.' Oscar laughed. 'Goffman should be afraid to call any more witnesses.'

'Settlement?' Clay asked, drugged and sluggish and sleepy, but trying desperately to catch the details.

'No, but it should be a long night. Rumor is that Goffman might try one more expert tomorrow, then plug the dike and hunker down for the verdict. Mooneyham refuses to talk to them. He looks and acts as if he expects a record verdict.'

Clay passed out with the phone wedged against the side of his head. A nurse removed it an hour later.

Goffman's CEO arrived in Flagstaff late Wednesday night and was rushed downtown to a tall building where the lawyers were conspiring. He was briefed by Roger Redding and the rest of the defense team and shown the latest numbers by the boys in finance. Every discussion was centered around a doomsday scenario.

Because Redding's rear-end had been so thoroughly whipped, he was adamant that the defense stick to its game plan and call its remaining witnesses. Surely, the tide would turn. Surely, he would find his stride and score some points with his jury. But Bob Mitchell, the chief in-house counsel and a vice president, and Sterling Gibb, the company's longtime lawyer and golfing buddy of the CEO, had seen enough. One more witness assassination by Mooneyham and the jurors might jump from their seats and attack the nearest Goffman executive. Redding's ego was badly bruised. He wanted to push on, hoping for a miracle. To follow him was bad advice.

Mitchell and Gibb met with the CEO alone, around 3 A.M., over doughnuts. Just the three of them. As bad as things were for the company, there remained some secrets about Maxatil that could never be revealed. If Mooneyham had this information, or if he could beat it out of a witness, then the sky would indeed fall on Goffman. At that point in the trial, they put nothing past Mooneyham. The CEO finally made the decision to stop the bloodletting.

When court was called to order at 9 A.M., Roger Redding announced that the defense would rest.

'No further witnesses?' the Judge asked. A fifteen-day trial had just been cut in half. He had a week of golf coming up!

'That's correct, Your Honor,' Redding said with a smile at the jurors, as if all was well.

'Any rebuttal, Mr Mooneyham?'

The plaintiff's lawyer slowly got to his feet. He scratched his head, scowled at Redding, and said, 'If they're done, then so are we.'

The Judge explained to the jurors that they

465

would be in recess for an hour while he took up some matters with the lawyers. When they returned, they would hear the closing arguments, and by lunchtime they would have the case.

With everyone else, Oscar ran into the hallway, clutching a cell phone. There was no answer in Clay's hospital room.

He spent three hours waiting in X Ray, three hours on a gurney in a busy hall where nurses and orderlies rushed by chatting about nothing. He'd left his cell phone behind and so for three hours he was isolated from the world while he waited in the depths of George Washington University Hospital.

The X rays took almost an hour, but could've taken less if the patient had not been so uncooperative and aggressive and, at times, downright profane. The orderly wheeled him back to his room and happily left him there.

Clay was napping when Oscar called. It was five-twenty his time, three-twenty in Phoenix.

'Where have you been?' Oscar demanded.

'Don't ask.'

'Goffman threw in the towel first thing this morning, tried to settle, but Mooneyham wouldn't talk. Everything happened real fast after that. Closing arguments began around ten, I guess. The jury got the case at exactly noon.'

'The jury has the case?' Clay asked, practically yelling at the phone.

'Had.'

'What?'

'Had the case. It's over. They deliberated for three hours and found in favor of Goffman. I'm sorry, Clay. Everybody here is in shock.'

'No.'

'Afraid so.'

'Tell me you're lying, Oscar.'

'I wish. I don't know what happened. Nobody does. Redding gave a spectacular closing argument, but I watched the jurors. I thought Mooneyham had them.'

'Dale Mooneyham lost a case?'

'Not just any case, Clay. He lost our case.'

'But how?'

'I don't know. I would've bet the farm against Goffman.'

'We just did.'

'I'm sorry.'

'Look, Oscar, I'm lying here in bed, all alone. I'm closing my eyes now, and I want you to just talk to me, okay. Don't leave me. There's no one else around. Just talk to me. Tell me something.'

'After the verdict, I got cornered by Fleet, and two other guys – Bob Mitchell and Sterling Gibb. Real sweet boys. They were so happy they were about to pop. They began by asking if you're still alive – how do you like that? Then they sent their regards, real sincere like. They told me that they're bringing their show on the road – Roger the Dodger and Company – and the next trial will be in D.C., against Mr. Clay Carter, the King of Torts, who, as we all know, has never tried a tort case. What could I say? They had just beaten a great lawyer in his own backyard.'

'Our cases are worthless, Oscar.'

'They certainly think so. Mitchell said they would not offer one cent for any Maxatil case anywhere in the country. They want trials. They want vindication. A clear name. All that crap.'

He kept Oscar on the phone for over an hour, as his unlit room grew dark. Oscar replayed the closing arguments and the high tension of waiting for the verdict. He described the shock on the plaintiff's face, a dying woman whose lawyer wouldn't take whatever Goffman was offering, supposedly $10 million. And Mooneyham, who hadn't lost in so long he had forgotten how to lose, demanding that the jury be required to fill out questionnaires and explain themselves. After Mooneyham caught his breath and managed to get to his feet, with his cane of course, he made a total ass of himself. And there was shock on the Goffman side, where the crowd of dark suits sat with lowered heads in what appeared to be a mass prayer until the jury foreman uttered his majestic words. There had been a stampede from the court-room as the Wall Street analysts rushed to make their calls.

Oscar ended his narrative with, 'I'm going to a bar now.'

Clay called a nurse and asked for a sleeping pill.

Chapter 41

After eleven days of confinement, Clay was finally set free. A lighter cast was placed on his left leg, and, though he couldn't walk, he could at least maneuver a little. Paulette pushed his wheelchair out of the hospital to a rented van driven by Oscar. Fifteen minutes later, they rolled him into his town house and locked the door. Paulette and Miss Glick had turned the downstairs den into a temporary bedroom. His phones, fax, and computer had been moved to a folding table near his bed. His clothes were stacked neatly on plastic shelves by the fireplace.

For the first two hours he was home, he read mail and financial reports and clippings, but only what Paulette had screened. Most of what had been printed about Clay was kept away from him.

Later, after a nap, he sat at the kitchen table with Paulette and Oscar announced that it was time to start.

The unraveling began.

★ ★ ★

The first issue was his law firm. Crittle had managed to trim a few costs, but the overhead was still galloping along at a million bucks a month. With no current revenues, and none expected, immediate layoffs were unavoidable. They went down a list of the employees – lawyers, paralegals, secretaries, clerks, gofers – and made the painful cuts. Though they considered the Maxatil cases worthless, it would still take work to close the files. Clay kept four lawyers and four paralegals for the job. He was determined to honor every contract he'd signed with his employees, but to do so would eat up some badly needed cash.

Clay looked at the names of the employees who had to go, and it made him ill. 'I want to sleep on this,' he said, unable to make the final decision.

'Most of them are expecting it, Clay,' Paulette said.

He stared at the names and tried to imagine the gossip that had been raging about him in the halls of his own firm.

Two days earlier, Oscar had reluctantly agreed to go to New York and meet with Helen Warshaw. He had presented a broad picture of Clay Carter's assets and potential liabilities, and basically begged for mercy. His boss did not want to file for bankruptcy, but if pushed too hard by Ms. Warshaw he would have no choice. She had been unimpressed. Clay was a member of a group of lawyers, her defendants, with a combined net worth that she estimated at $1.5 billion. She could not allow Clay to settle his cases for, say, a meager $1 million each, when the same cases against Patton French might fetch three times that much. Plus, she was not in a settling mood. The trial would be an important one – a bold effort at reforming abuses in the system, a media-hyped spectacle. She planned to savor every moment of it.

Oscar returned to D.C. with his tail between his legs, certain that Helen Warshaw, as the lawyer for Clay's biggest group of creditors, wanted blood!

The dreaded word *bankruptcy* had first been uttered by Rex Crittle in Clay's hospital room. It had cut through the air like a bullet and landed like a mortar. Then it was used again. Clay began saying it, but only to himself. Paulette said it once. Oscar had used it in New York. It didn't fit and they didn't like it, but over the past week it had become part of their vocabulary.

The office lease could be terminated, through bankruptcy.

The employment contracts could be compromised, through bankruptcy.

The Gulfstream could be sent back on better terms, through bankruptcy.

The disgruntled Maxatil clients could be stiff-armed, through bankruptcy.

The disgruntled Hanna plaintiffs could be convinced to settle, through bankruptcy.

And, most important, Helen Warshaw could be reined in, through bankruptcy.

Oscar was almost as depressed as Clay, and after a few hours of misery he left for the office.

Paulette rolled Clay outside and onto the small patio where they had a cup of green tea with honey. 'I got two things to say,' she said, sitting very close and staring at him. 'First, I'm going to give you some of my money.'

'No you're not.'

'Yes I am. You made me rich when you didn't have to. I can't help it that you're a stupid white boy who's lost his ass, but I still love you. I'm going to help you, Clay.'

'Can you believe this, Paulette?'

'No. It's beyond belief, but it's true. It's happened. And things'll get much worse before they get better. Don't read the papers, Clay. Please. Promise me that.'

'Don't worry.'

'I'm going to help you. If you lose everything, I'll be around to make sure you're okay.'

'I don't know what to say.'

'Say nothing.'

They held hands and Clay fought back tears. A moment passed. 'Number two,' she said. 'I've been talking to Rebecca. She's afraid to see you because she might get caught. She's got a new cell phone, one her husband knows nothing about. She gave me the number. She wants you to call her.'

'Female advice please?'

'Not from me. You know how I feel about that Russian hussy. Rebecca's a sweet girl, but she's got some baggage, to put it mildly. You're on your own.'

'Thanks for nothing.'

'You're welcome. She wanted you to call her this afternoon. Husband's out of town or something. I'll leave in a few minutes.'

Rebecca parked around the corner and hustled down Dumbarton Street to Clay's door. She was not good at sneaking around; neither was he. The first thing they decided was that they would not continue it.

She and Jason Myers had decided to dissolve their marriage amicably. He had initially wanted to seek counseling and delay a divorce, but he also preferred to work eighteen hours a day, whether in D.C., New York, Palo Alto, or Hong Kong. His massive firm had offices in thirty-two cities, and he had clients around the world. Work was more important than anything else. He'd simply left her, with no apologies and with no plans to change his ways. The papers would be filed in two days. She was already packing her bags. Jason would keep the condo; she had been vague on where she would go. In less than a year of marriage, they had accumulated little. He was a partner who made $800,000 a year, but she wanted none of his money.

According to Rebecca, her parents had not interfered. They had not had the opportunity. Myers didn't like them, which was no surprise, and Clay suspected that one reason he preferred the firm's branch office in Hong Kong was because it was so far away from the Van Horns.

Both had a reason to run. Clay would not, under any circumstances, remain in D.C. in the years to come. His humiliation was too raw and deep, and there was a big world out there where people didn't know him. He craved anonymity. For the first time in her life, Rebecca just wanted to get away – away from a bad marriage, away from her family, away from the country club and the insufferable people who went there, away from the pressures of making money and accumulating stuff, away from McLean and the only friends she'd ever known.

It took an hour for Clay to get her in the bed, but sex was impossible, with the casts and all. He just wanted to hold her and kiss her and make up for lost time.

She spent the night and decided not to leave. Over coffee the next morning, Clay began with Tequila Watson and Tarvan and told her everything.

Paulette and Oscar returned with more unpleasantries from the office. Some instigator up in Howard County was encouraging the homeowners to file ethics complaints against Clay for the botched Hanna settlement. Several dozen had been received by the D.C. Bar. Six lawsuits had been filed against Clay, all by the same attorney who was actively soliciting more. Clay's office was finalizing a settlement plan to be put before the judge in the Hanna bankruptcy. Oddly enough, the firm might be awarded a fee, though one far less than what Clay had turned down.

There was an urgent Warshaw motion to take the depositions of several of the Dyloft plaintiffs. Urgency was required because they were dying, and their video depositions would be crucial to the trial, which was expected in about a year. To employ the usual defense tactics of stall, delay, postponement, and outright procrastination would have been enormously unfair to these plaintiffs. Clay agreed to the schedule of depositions suggested by Ms. Warshaw, though he had no plans to attend them.

Under pressure from Oscar, Clay finally agreed to lay off ten lawyers and most of the paralegals, secretaries, and clerks. He signed letters to every one of them – brief and very apologetic. He took full responsibility for the demise of his firm.

Frankly, there was no one else to blame.

A letter to the Maxatil clients was hammered out. In it, Clay recapped the Mooneyham trial in Phoenix. He held to the belief that the drug was dangerous, but proving causation would now be 'very difficult, if not impossible.' The company was not willing to consider an out-of-court settlement, and, given Clay's current medical problems, he was not in a position to prepare for an extended trial.

He hated to use his beating as an excuse, but Oscar prevailed. It sounded believable in the letter. At this low point in his career, he had to grab whatever advantage he could find.

He was therefore releasing each client, and doing so in sufficient time for each to hire another lawyer and pursue Goffman. He even wished them luck.

The letters would cause a storm of controversy. 'We'll handle it,' Oscar kept saying. 'At least we'll be rid of these people.'

Clay couldn't help but think of Max Pace, his old pal who'd gotten him into the Maxatil business. Pace, one of at least five aliases, had been indicted for securities fraud, but had not been found. His indictment claimed that he used insider information to sell almost a million shares of Goffman before Clay filed suit. Later, he covered his sale and slipped out of the country with around $15 million. Run, Max, run. If he was caught and hauled back for a trial he might spill all their dirty secrets.

There were a hundred other details on Oscar's checklist, but Clay grew weary.

'Am I playing nurse tonight?' Paulette whispered in the kitchen.

'No, Rebecca's here.'

'You love trouble, don't you?'

'She's filing for divorce tomorrow. An uncontested divorce.'

'What about the bimbo?'

'She's history if she ever comes back from St. Barth.'

For the next week, Clay never left his town house. Rebecca packed all of Ridley's things into 30-gallon trash bags and stuffed them in the basement. She moved in some of her own stuff, though Clay warned her that he was about to lose the

476

house. She cooked wonderful meals and nursed him whenever he needed it. They watched old movies until midnight, then slept late every morning. She drove him to see his doctor.

Ridley called every other day from the island. Clay did not tell her she'd lost her place; he preferred to do that in person, when and if she returned. The renovation was coming along nicely, though Clay had seriously curtailed the budget. She seemed oblivious to his financial problems.

The last lawyer to enter Clay's life was Mark Munson, a bankruptcy expert who specialized in large, messy, individual crashes. Crittle had found him. After Clay retained him, Crittle showed him the books, the leases, the contracts, the lawsuits, the assets, and the liabilities. Everything. When Munson and Crittle came to the town house, Clay asked Rebecca to leave. He wanted to spare her the gruesome details.

In the seventeen months since he'd left OPD, Clay had earned $121 million in fees – $30 million had been paid to Rodney, Paulette, and Jonah as bonuses; $20 million had gone for office expenses and the Gulfstream; $16 million down the drain for advertising and testing for Dyloft, Maxatil, and Skinny Bens; $34 million for taxes, either paid or accrued; $4 million for the villa; $3 million for the sailboat. A million here and there – the town house, the 'loan' to Max Pace, and the usual and expected extravagances of the newly rich.

Jarrett's fancy new catamaran was an interesting issue. Clay had paid for it, but the Bahamian company that held its title was owned completely by his father. Munson thought the bankruptcy court might take one of two positions – either it was a gift, which would require Clay to pay gift taxes, or it was simply owned by someone else and thus not part of Clay's estate. Either way, the boat remained the property of Jarrett Carter.

Clay had also earned $7.1 million trading in Ackerman stock, and though some of this was buried offshore it was about to be hauled back. 'If you hide assets you go to jail,' Munson lectured, leaving little doubt that he did not tolerate such thinking.

The balance sheet showed a net worth of approximately $19 million, with few creditors. However, the contingent liabilities were catastrophic. Twenty-six former clients were now suing for the Dyloft fiasco. That number was expected to rise, and though it was impossible to throw darts at the value of each case, Clay's legitimate exposure was significantly more than his net worth. The Hanna class-action plaintiffs were festering and getting organized. The Maxatil backlash would be nasty and prolonged. None of those expenses could be predicted either.

'Let the bankruptcy trustee deal with it,' Munson said. 'You'll walk away with the shirt on your back, but at least you won't owe anything.'

'Gee thanks,' Clay said, still thinking about the

sailboat. If they were successful in keeping it away from the bankruptcy, then Jarrett could sell it, buy something smaller, and Clay could have some cash to live on.

After two hours with Munson and Crittle, the kitchen table was covered with spreadsheets and printouts and discarded notes, a debris-strewn testament to the past seventeen months of his life. He was ashamed of his greed and embarrassed by his stupidity. It was sickening what the money had done to him.

The thought of leaving helped him survive each day.

Ridley called from St. Barth with the alarming news that a FOR SALE sign had appeared in front of 'their' villa.

'That's because it's now for sale,' Clay said.

'I don't understand.'

'Come home and I'll explain it to you.'

'Is there trouble?'

'You might say that.'

After a long pause, she said, 'I prefer to stay here.'

'I can't make you come home, Ridley.'

'No, you can't.'

'Fine. Stay in the villa until it sells. I don't care.'

'How long will that be?'

He could see her doing everything imaginable to sabotage a potential sale. At the moment, Clay just didn't care. 'Maybe a month, maybe a year. I don't know.'

'I'm staying,' she said.

'Fine.'

Rodney found his old friend sitting on the front steps of his picturesque town house, crutches by his side, a shawl over his shoulders to knock off the autumn chill. The wind was spinning leaves in circles along Dumbarton Street.

'Need some fresh air,' Clay said. 'I've been locked in there for three weeks.'

'How are the bones?' Rodney asked, as he sat beside him and looked at the street.

'Healing nicely.'

Rodney had left the city and become a real suburbanite. Khakis and sneakers, a fancy SUV to haul kids around. 'How's your head?'

'No additional brain damage.'

'How's your soul?'

'Tortured, to say the least. But I'll survive.'

'Paulette says you're leaving.'

'For a while, anyway. I'll file for bankruptcy next week, and I will not be around here when it happens. Paulette has a flat in London that I can use for a few months. We'll hide there.'

'You can't avoid a bankruptcy?'

'No way. There are too many claims, and good ones. Remember our first Dyloft plaintiff, Ted Worley?'

'Sure.'

'He died yesterday. I didn't pull the trigger, but I sure didn't protect him either. His case in front of a jury is worth five million bucks. There are twenty-six of those. I'm going to London.'

'Clay, I want to help.'

'I'm not taking your money. That's why you're here, and I know it. I've had this conversation twice with Paulette and once with Jonah. You made your money and you were smart enough to cash out. I wasn't.'

'But we're not going to let you die, man. You didn't have to give us ten million bucks. But you did. We're giving some back.'

'No.'

'Yes. The three of us have talked about it. We'll wait until the bankruptcy is over, then each of us will do a transfer. A gift.'

'You earned that money, Rodney. Keep it.'

'Nobody earns ten million dollars in six months, Clay. You might win it, steal it, or have it drop out of the sky, but nobody earns money like that. It's ridiculous and obscene. I'm giving some back. So is Paulette. Not sure about Jonah, but he'll come around.'

'How are the kids?'

'You're changing the subject.'

'Yes, I'm changing the subject.'

So they talked about kids, and old friends at OPD, and old clients and cases there. They sat on the front steps until after dark, when Rebecca arrived and it was time for dinner.

Chapter 42

The *Post* reporter was Art Mariani, a young man who knew Clay Carter well because he'd documented his astounding rise and his equally amazing crash with careful attention to detail and a reasonable dose of fairness. When Mariani arrived at Clay's town house, he was greeted by Paulette and led down the narrow hall to the kitchen where folks were waiting. Clay hobbled to his feet and introduced himself, then went around the table – Zack Battle, his attorney; Rebecca Van Horn, his friend; and Oscar Mulrooney, his partner. Tape recorders were plugged in. Rebecca made the rounds with the coffeepot.

'It's a long story,' Clay said, 'but we have plenty of time.'

'I have no deadline,' Mariani said.

Clay took a swig of coffee, a deep breath, and jumped into the story. He began with the shooting of Ramón 'Pumpkin' Pumphrey by his client, Tequila Watson. Dates, times, places, Clay had notes of everything and all the files. Then Washad Porter and his two murders. Then the other four. Camp Deliverance, Clean Streets, the amazing results of a drug called Tarvan. Though he would never mention the name of Max Pace, he described in detail Pace's history of Tarvan – the secret clinical trials in Mexico City, Belgrade, and Singapore, the manufacturer's desire to test it on those of African descent, preferably in the United States. The drug's arrival in D.C.

'Who made the drug?' Mariani asked, visibly shaken.

After a long pause in which he seemed unable to speak, Clay answered, 'I'm not completely sure. But I think it's Philo.'

'Philo Products?'

'Yes.' Clay reached for a thick document and slid it over to Mariani. 'This is one of the settlement agreements. As you will see, there are two offshore companies mentioned. If you can penetrate them, pick up the trail, it will probably lead you to a shell company in Luxembourg, then to Philo.'

'Okay, but why do you suspect Philo?'

'I have a source. That's all I can tell you.'

This mysterious source selected Clay from all the attorneys in D.C. and convinced him to sell his soul for $15 million. He quickly quit OPD and opened his own firm. Mariani already knew much of this. Clay signed up the families of six of the victims, easily convinced them to take $5 million and keep quiet, and within thirty days had the matter wrapped up. The details poured forth, as did the documents and settlement agreements.

'When I publish this story, what happens to your clients, the families of the victims?' Mariani asked.

'I've lost sleep worrying about that, but I think they'll be fine,' Clay said. 'First, they've had the money for a year now, so it's safe to assume a lot of it has been spent. Second, the drugmaker would be insane to try and set aside these settlements.'

'The families could then sue the manufacturer directly,' Zack added helpfully. 'And those verdicts could destroy any big corporation. I've never seen a more volatile set of facts.'

'The company won't touch the settlement agreements,' Clay said. 'It's lucky to get out with a fifty-million settlement.'

'Can the families set the agreements aside when they learn the truth?' Mariani asked.

'It would be difficult.'

'What about you? You signed confidentiality agreements?'

'I'm not a factor anymore. I'm about to be bankrupt. I'm about to surrender my license to practice law. They can't touch me.' It was a sad admission, one that hurt Clay's friends as much as it hurt him.

Mariani scribbled some notes and shifted gears. 'What happens to Tequila Watson, Washad Porter, and the other men who were convicted of these murders?'

'First, they can probably sue the drugmaker,

which won't help them much in prison. Second, there's a chance their cases could be reopened, at least the sentencing aspect.'

Zack Battle cleared his throat and everyone waited. 'Off the record. After you publish whatever you decide to publish, and after the storm dies down, I plan to take these cases and have them reviewed. I'll sue on behalf of the seven defendants, that is, if we can identify the pharmaceutical company. I might petition the criminal courts to reopen their convictions.'

'This is very explosive,' Mariani said, stating the obvious. He studied his notes for a long time. 'What led to the Dyloft litigation?'

'That's another chapter for another day,' Clay said. 'You've documented most of it anyway. I'm not talking about it.'

'Fair enough. Is this story over?'

'For me it is,' Clay said.

Paulette and Zack drove them to the airport, to Reagan National where Clay's once-beloved Gulfstream sat very close to the spot where he'd first seen it. Since they were leaving for at least six months, there was a lot of luggage, especially Rebecca's. Clay, having shed so much in the past month, was traveling light. He got about fine with his crutches, but he couldn't carry anything. Zack acted as his porter.

He gamely showed them his airplane, though they all knew this was its final voyage. Clay hugged Paulette and embraced Zack, thanked them both and promised to call within days. When the co-pilot locked the door, Clay pulled the shades over the windows so he would see none of Washington when they lifted off.

To Rebecca, the jet was a ghastly symbol of the destructive power of greed. She longed for the tiny flat in London, where no one knew them, and no one cared what they wore, drove, bought, ate, or where they worked, shopped, or vacationed. She wasn't coming home. She had fought with her parents for the last time.

Clay longed for two good legs and a clean slate. He was surviving one of the more infamous melt-downs in the history of American law, and it was further and further behind him. He had Rebecca all to himself, and nothing else mattered.

Somewhere over Newfoundland, they unfolded the sofa and fell asleep under the covers.

Author's Note

It is here that authors often submit massive disclaimers in an effort to cover their rears and, hopefully, avoid liability. There is always the temptation to simply create a fictional place or entity rather than research the real ones, and I confess I would rather do almost anything than verify details. Fiction is a marvelous shield. It's very easy to hide behind. But when it ventures near the truth, it needs to be accurate. Otherwise, the author needs a few lines in this space.

The Public Defender Service in Washington, D.C., is a proud and vibrant organisation that has zealously protected the indigent for many years. Its lawyers are bright, committed, and very tight-lipped. Downright secretive. Its inner workings remain a mystery, so I simply created my own Office of the Public Defender. Any resemblance between the two is purely coincidental.

Mark Twain said he often moved cities, counties, and even entire states when necessary to help a story along. Nothing gets in my way either. If I can't find a building, then I'll construct one on the spot. If a street does not fit on my map, then I won't hesitate to either move it or draw a new map. I would guess that about half the places in this book are described somewhat correctly. The other half either don't exist or have been modified or relocated to such an extent that no one would recognize them. Anyone looking for accuracy is wasting time.

That's not to say I don't try. My idea of research is frantically working the telephone as the deadline draws near. I leaned on the following people for advice, and it's here that I thank them: Fritz Chockley, Bruce Brown, Gaines Talbott, Bobby Moak, Penny Pynkala and Jerome Davis.

Renee read the rough draft and didn't fling it at me – always a good sign. David Gernert picked it to pieces, then helped me put it together again. Will Denton and Pamela Creel Jenner read it and offered salient advice. When I had written it for the fourth time and everything was correct, Estelle Laurence read it and found a thousand mistakes.

All of the above were eager to help. The mistakes, as always, are mine.